*A rugged tyc...*
*a v...*
*Extraordina...*

# To Wear His Ring

Three dangerously attractive heroes from
three favourite authors!

a rugged tycoon, a formidable single dad and and
a world-weary bachelor...

Extraordinary men deserve special women...

# To Wear His Ring

## IN OR LIES

### PENNY JORDAN

Three dangerously attractive heroes from
the Crighton aristocracy

# To Wear His Ring

International bestselling author

DIANA PALMER

JAN COLLEY

WENDY WARREN

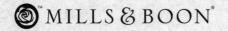

First published in Great Britain 2010
Harlequin Mills & Boon Limited,
Eton House, 18-24 Paradise Road, Richmond, Surrey TW9 1SR

TO WEAR HIS RING © by Harlequin Enterprises II B.V./S.à.r.l 2010

*Circle of Gold, Trophy Wives* and *Dakota Bride* were first published in Great
Britain by Harlequin Mills & Boon Limited in separate, single volumes.

*Circle of Gold* © Diana Palmer 2000
*Trophy Wives* © Janet Colley 2005
*Dakota Bride* © Wendy Warren 2002

ISBN: 978 0 263 88044 1

05-0910

Printed and bound in Spain
by Litografia Rosés S.A., Barcelona

# CIRCLE OF GOLD

## BY
## DIANA PALMER

**Diana Palmer** has a gift for telling the most sensual tales with charm and humour. With over forty million copies of her books in print, she is one of North America's most loved authors and considered one of the top ten romance authors in America.

Diana's hobbies include gardening, archaeology, anthropology, iguanas, astronomy and music. She has been married to James Kyle for over twenty-five years and they have one son.

**Look for a new novel from Diana Palmer, *The Maverick*, in December 2010 in Desire™.**

# Chapter 1

Kasie Mayfield was excited. Her gray eyes were brimming with delight as she sat in the sprawling living room at the Double C Ranch in Medicine Ridge, Montana. There was a secretarial position available on the mammoth Double C, and she had the necessary qualifications. She was only twenty-two, but she had a certificate from secretarial school and plenty of initiative. Besides all that, the position was secretary to John Callister, the second son of the well-known family that headed not only a publishing empire in New York City, but a cattle empire out West.

There was a very interesting story about the ranch in a magazine that Kasie was reading while she waited her turn to be interviewed. The elder Callisters lived in New York, where they published, among others, a famous sports magazine. When they weren't in the city, they lived in Jamaica on an ancestral estate. The Callister who had founded the American branch of the family had been a British duke. He bought an obscure little magazine in New York City in 1897 and turned it into a publishing conglomerate. One of his sons had emigrated to Montana and founded the ranch. It eventually passed to Douglas Callister, who had raised the boys, Gilbert and John. Nobody talked about why the uncle had been given custody of both boys and left them the ranch when he died. Presumably it was some dark family secret. Apparently there wasn't a lot of contact between the boys and their parents.

Gilbert, the eldest at thirty-two, had been widowed three years ago. He had two young daughters, Bess, who was five, and Jenny, who was four. John had never married. He was a rodeo champion and did most of the traveling that accompanied showing the ranch's prizewinning pedigree black Angus bulls. Gil was the power in the empire. He was something of a marketing genius, and he dealt with the export business and sat on the boards of two multinational corporations. But mostly he ran the ranch, all thirty thousand acres of it.

There was a photograph of him in the magazine, but she didn't need it to know what he looked like. Kasie had gotten a glimpse of him on her way into the house to wait for her turn to be interviewed. One glimpse had been enough. It shocked her that a man who didn't even know her should glare at her so intently.

A more conceited woman might have taken it for masculine interest. But Kasie had no ego. No, that tall, lanky blond man hadn't liked her, and made no secret of it. His pale blue eyes under that heavy brow had pierced her skin. She wouldn't get the job. He'd make sure of it.

She glanced at the woman next to her, a glorious blonde with big brown eyes and beautiful legs crossed under a thigh-high skirt. Then she looked at her own ankle-length blue jumper with a simple gray blouse that matched her big eyes. Her chestnut hair was in a long braid down her back. She wore only a little lipstick on her full, soft mouth, and no rouge at all on her cheeks. She had a rather ordinary oval face and a small, rounded chin, and she wore contact lenses. She wasn't at all pretty. She had a nice figure, but she was shy and didn't make the most of it. It was just as well that she had good office skills, she supposed, because it was highly unlikely that anybody would ever want to actually marry her. She thought of her parents and her brother and had to fight down tears. It was so soon. Too soon, probably. But the job might keep her from thinking of what had happened....

"Miss Mayfield!"

She jumped as her name was called in a deep, authoritative tone. "Yes?"

"Come in, please."

She put a smile on her face as she clutched her small purse in her hands and walked into the paneled office, where plaques and photos of bulls lined the walls and burgundy leather furniture surrounded the big mahogany desk. A man was sitting there, with his pale eyes piercing and intent. A blond man with broad shoulders and a hard, lean face that seemed to be all rocky edges. It was not John Callister.

She stopped in front of the desk with her heart pounding and didn't bother to sit down. Gil Callister was obviously doing the interviews, and now she was sure she wouldn't get the job. She knew John Callister from the drugstore where she'd worked briefly as a stock clerk putting herself through secretarial courses. John had talked to her, teased her and even told her about the secretarial job. He'd have given her a chance. Gil would just shoot her out the door. It was obvious that he didn't like anything about her.

He tossed a pen onto the desk and nodded toward the chair facing it. "Sit down."

She felt vulnerable. The door was closed. Here she was with a hungry tiger, and no way out. But she sat anyway. Never let it be said that she lacked courage. They could throw her into the arena and she would die like a true Roman... She shook herself. She really had to stop reading the Plinys and Tacitus. This was the new millennium, not the first century A.D.

"Why do you want this job?" Gil asked bluntly.

Her thin eyebrows lifted. She hadn't expected the question. "Because John is a dish?" she ventured dryly.

The answer seemed to surprise him. "Is he?"

"When I worked at the drugstore, he was always kind to me," she said evasively. "He told me about the job, because he knew I was just finishing my secretarial certificate at the vocational-technical school. I got high grades, too."

Gil pursed his lips. He still didn't smile. He looked down at the résumé she'd handed him and read it carefully, as if he was looking for a deficiency he could use to deny her the job. His mouth made a thin line. "Very high grades," he conceded with obvious reluctance. "This is accurate? You really can type 110 words a minute?"

She nodded. "I can type faster than I can take dictation, actually."

He pushed the résumé aside and leaned back. "Boyfriends?"

She was nonplussed. Her fingers tightened on her purse. "Sir?"

"I want to know if you have any entanglements that might cause you to give up the job in the near future," he persisted, and seemed oddly intent on the reply.

She shifted restlessly. "I've only ever had one real boyfriend, although he was more like a brother. He married my best friend two months ago. That was just before I moved to Billings," she added, mentioning the nearby city, "to live with my aunt. So, I don't date much."

She was so uncomfortable that she almost squirmed. He didn't know about her background, of course, or he wouldn't need to ask such questions. Modern women were a lot more worldly than Kasie. But she'd said that John was a dish. She flushed. Good grief, did he think she went around seducing men or something? Was that why he didn't want her in his house? Her expression was mortified.

He averted his eyes. "You have some odd character references," he said after a minute, frowning at them. "A Catholic priest, a nun, a Texas Ranger and a self-made millionaire with alleged mob ties."

She only smiled demurely. "I have unique friendships."

"You could put it that way," he said, diverted. "Is the millionaire your lover?"

She went scarlet and her jaw dropped.

"Oh, hell, never mind," he said, apparently disturbed that he'd asked the question and uncomfortable at the reaction it drew. "That's none of my business. All right, Kasie…" He hesitated. "Kasie. What's it short for?"

"I don't know," she blurted out. "It's my actual name."

One eye narrowed. "The millionaire's name is K.C.," he pointed out. "And he's at least forty."

"Thirty-seven. He saved my mother's life, while she was carrying me," she said finally. "He wasn't always a millionaire."

"Yes, I know, he was a professional soldier, a mercenary." His eyes narrowed even more. "Want to tell me about it?"

"Not really, no," she confided.

He shook his head. "Well, if nothing else, you'll be efficient. You're also less of a distraction than the rest of them. There's nothing I hate more than a woman who wears a skirt up to her briefs to work and then complains when men stare at her if she bends over. We have dress codes at our businesses and they're enforced—for both sexes."

"I don't have any skirts that come up to my…well, I don't wear short ones," she blurted out.

"So I noticed," he said with a deliberate glance at her long dress.

She fumbled with her purse while he went over the résumé one last time. "All right, Kasie, you can start Monday at eight-thirty. Did John tell you that the job requires you to live here?"

"No!"

His eyebrows arched. "Not in his room, of course," he added just to irritate her, and then looked satisfied when she blushed. "Miss Parsons, who has charge of my daughters, lives in. So does Mrs. Charters who does the cooking and housekeeping. We have other part-time help that comes infrequently. Board and meals are provided by us, in addition to your salary.'' He named a figure that made Kasie want to hold on to something. It was astronomical compared to what she'd made working at the drugstore part-time. ''You'll be a private secretary,'' he added. ''That means you may have to travel with us from time to time.''

''Travel?'' Her face softened.

''Do you like to travel?'' he asked.

''Oh, yes. I loved it when I was little.''

She wondered by the look he gave her if he assumed that her parents had been wealthy. He could not know, of course, that they were both deceased.

''Do you want the job?'' he asked.

''Yes,'' she said.

''All right. I'll tell the others they can leave.'' He got to his feet, elegant and lithe, moving with a grace that was unequaled in Kasie's circle of acquaintances. He opened the office door, thanked the other young women for coming and told them that the position had been filled. There was a shuffle of feet, some murmuring, and the front door closed.

''Come on, Kasie,'' Gil said. ''I'll introduce you to...''

''Daddy!'' came a wail from the end of the hall. A little girl with disheveled long blond hair came running and threw herself at Gil, sobbing.

He picked her up, and his whole demeanor changed. ''What is it, baby?'' he asked in the most tender tone Kasie had ever heard. ''What's wrong?''

''Me and Jenny was playing with our dollies on the

deck and that bad dog came up on the porch and he tried to bite us!''

''Where's Jenny?'' he demanded, immediately threatening.

A sobbing little voice answered him as the younger girl came toddling down the hall rubbing her eyes with dirty little fists. She reached up to Gil, and he picked her up, too, oblivious to her soiled dress and hands.

''Nothing's going to hurt my babies. Did the dog bite either of you?'' Gil demanded.

''No, Daddy,'' Bess said.

''Bad doggie!'' Jenny sobbed. ''Make him go away!''

''Of course I will!'' Gil said roughly, kissing little cheeks with a tenderness that made Kasie's heart ache.

A door opened and John Callister came down the hall, looking very unlike the friendly man Kasie knew from the drugstore. His pale eyes were glittering in his lean, dark face, and he looked murderous.

''Are they all right?'' he asked Gil, pausing to touch the girls' hair. ''It was that mangy cur that Fred Sims insisted on bringing with him when he hired on. I got between it and the girls and it tried to bite me, too. I called Sims up to the house and told him to get rid of it and he won't, so he's fired.''

''Here.'' Gil handed his girls to his brother and started down the hall with quick, measured steps.

John stared after him. ''Maybe Sims will make it to his truck before Gil gets him,'' he murmured. ''But I wouldn't bet on it. Are my babies all right?'' he asked, kissing their little damp cheeks as the girls clung to either shoulder.

"Bad old doggie," Bess sobbed. "Our Missie never bites people!"

"Missie's a toy collie," John explained to a silent Kasie with a smile. "She lives indoors. Nothing like that vicious dog Sims keeps. We've had trouble from it before, but Sims was so good with horses that we put up with it. Not any more. We can't let it endanger the girls."

"If it would come right up on the porch and try to bite them, it doesn't need to be around children," Kasie agreed.

The girls looked at her curiously.

"Who are you?" Bess asked.

"I'm Kasie," she replied with a smile. "Who are you?"

"I'm Bess," the child replied. "That's Jenny. She's just four," she added, indicating the smaller child, whose hair was medium-length and more light brown than blond.

"I'm very glad to meet you both," Kasie said, smiling warmly. "I'm going to be Mr. Callister's secretary," she added with an apologetic glance at John. "Sorry."

"Why are you sorry?" John asked amusedly. "I only flog secretaries during full moons."

Her eyes crinkled with merriment and she grinned.

"Gil won't let me hire secretaries because I have such a bad track record," John confessed. "The last one turned out to be a jewel thief. You, uh, don't like jewels?" he added deliberately.

She chuckled. "Only costume jewelry. And unless you wear it, we shouldn't have a problem."

There was a commotion outside and John grimaced. "He'll come back in bleeding, as usual," he

muttered. "I just glare at people. Gil hits." He gave
Kasie a wicked grin. "Sometimes he hits me, too."

The girls giggled. "Oh, Uncle Johnny," Bess
teased, "Daddy never hits you! He won't even hit us.
He says little children shouldn't be hitted."

"Hit," Kasie corrected absently.

"Hit," Bess parroted, and grinned. "You're nice."

"You're nice, too, precious," Kasie said, reaching
out to smooth back the disheveled hair. "You've got
tangles."

"Can you make my hair like yours?" Bess asked,
eyeing Kasie's braid. "And tie it with a pink ribbon?"

The opening of the back door stopped the conversation dead. Gil came back in with his shirt and jeans
dusty and a cut at the corner of his mouth. As he
came closer, wiping away the blood, his bruised and
lacerated knuckles became visible.

"So much for that little problem," he said with
cold satisfaction. His eyes were still glittery with temper until he looked at the little girls. The anger
drained out of him and he smiled. "Dirty chicks," he
chided. "Go get Miss Parsons to clean you up."

John put them down and Bess looked up at her
father accusingly. "Miss Parsons don't like little
kids."

"Go on. If she gives you any trouble, come tell
me," Gil told the girls.

"Okay, Daddy!"

Bess took Jenny's hand and, with a shy grin at
Kasie, she drew the other child with her up the winding staircase.

"They like Kasie already," John commented.
"Bess said…"

"Miss Parsons takes care of the kids," Gil said shortly. "Show Kasie the way we keep records. She's a computer whiz in addition to her dictation skills. She should be able to get all those herd records onto diskettes for you. Then we can get rid of the paper clutter before we end up buried in it."

"Okay," John said. He hesitated. "Sims get off okay?"

"Sure," Gil said easily. "No problem." He wiped the blood away from his mouth with a wicked look at his brother before he turned and went up the staircase after the children.

John just shook his head. "Never mind. Come on, Kasie. Let's get you started."

Kasie moved into the house that weekend. Most of her parents' things, and her own, were at Mama Luke's, about ten miles away in Billings, Montana, to whom she'd come for refuge after losing her family. She had only the bare necessities of clothing and personal items; it barely filled one small suitcase. When she walked into the ranch house with it, Gil was on the porch with one of his men. He gave her a curious appraisal, dismissing the man.

"Where's the rest of your stuff?" he asked, glancing past her at the small, white used car she drove, which she'd parked beside the big garage. "In the trunk?"

"This is all the stuff I have," she said.

He looked stunned. "Surely you have furniture…?"

"My other things are at my aunt's house. But I don't have much stuff of my own."

He stepped aside to let her go inside, his face curious and his eyes intent on her. He didn't say a word, but he watched her even more closely from then on.

The first week on the job, she lost a file that Gil needed for a meeting he was flying to in the family Piper plane. It was an elegant aircraft, twin-engine and comfortable. Gil and John could both fly it and did, frequently, trucking the livestock they were showing from one state to the next with employees. Kasie wished she could go with the livestock, right now. Gil was eloquent about the missing file, his deep voice soft and filled with impatience.

"If you'll just be quiet for a minute, Mr. Callister, I'll find it!" she exclaimed finally, driven to insubordination.

He gave her a glare, but he shut up. She rustled through the folders on her desk with cold, nervous hands. But she did find the file. She extended it, sheepishly, grimacing at the look in his eyes.

"Sorry," she added hopefully.

It didn't do any good. His expression was somber and half-angry. His eyes glittered down at her. She thought absently that he looked very nice in a gray vested suit. It suited his fair hair and light eyes and his nice tan. It also emphasized the excellent fitness of his tall, muscular body. Kasie thought idly that he must have women practically stalking him when he went to dinner meetings. He was striking just to look at, in addition to that very masculine aura that clung to him like his expensive cologne.

"Where's John?" he asked.

"He had a date," she said. "I'm trying to cope with the new tax format."

His eyes narrowed. "Surely they taught tax compilation at your school?"

She grimaced. "Well, actually, they didn't. It's a rather specialized skill."

"Buy what you need from the bookstore or the computer store and have them send me the bill," he said shortly. "If you can't cope, tell me that, too."

She didn't dare. She wouldn't have a job, and she had to support herself. She couldn't expect Mama Luke to do it. "I can cope, sir," she assured him.

His eyes narrowed as he stared down at her. "One thing more," he added curtly. "My girls are Miss Parsons' responsibility, not yours."

"I only read them a story," she began, blushing guiltily.

His eyebrows arched. "I was referring to the way you braided Bess's hair," he said. "I thought it was an isolated incident."

She swallowed. Hardly isolated. The girls were always somewhere close by when Kasie stopped for lunch or her breaks. She shared her desserts with the children and frequently read to them or took them on walks to point out the various sorts of flowers and trees around the ranch house. Gil didn't know that and she'd hoped the girls hadn't said anything. Miss Parsons was curt and bullying with the children, whom she obviously disliked. It was inevitable that they'd turn to Kasie, who adored them.

"Only one story," she lied.

He seethed. "In case you didn't get the message the first time, Kasie, I am not in the market for a wife or a mother for my daughters."

The insult made her furious. She glared up at him, forgetting all her early teachings about turning cheeks and humility. "I came to work here because I need a job," she said icily. "I'm only twenty-two, Mr. Callister," she added. "And I don't have any interest in a man almost old enough to be my father, with a ready-made family to boot!"

His reaction was unexpected. He didn't fire back. He grew very quiet. He turned and went out of the room without another word. A minute later, she heard the front door close and, soon, an engine fire up.

"So there," she added to herself.

Gil came home from his trip even quieter than when he'd left. There was tension between him and Kasie, because she hadn't forgotten the insulting remark he'd made to her before he left. As if she'd come to work here just so she could chase him. Really! But there was another complication now, as well. Kasie was a nervous wreck trying to keep him from seeing how much time she actually spent with his little girls. She didn't need to worry when he was off on his frequent business trips, but they suddenly stopped. He started sending Brad Dalton, his manager, to seminars and conferences. He stayed home on the pretext of overseeing massive improvements on the property.

It was just after roundup, when the cattle business was taking up a little less of his time. But there were new bunkhouses being built, as well as new wells being dug in the pastures and new equipment brought in for tagging and vaccinations of new calves. The trucks were being overhauled, along with the other farm machinery such as tractors and combines that harvested the grain crops. The barns were repaired, a new silo erected. It was a busy time.

Kasie found herself involved unexpectedly with Gil when John went out of state to show two new bulls at a pedigree competition and Gil's secretary, Pauline Raines, conveniently sprained her thumb and couldn't type.

"I need these yesterday," he said without preamble, laying a thick sheaf of papers beside Kasie's neat little hand on the desk. "Pauline can't do them. She missed the tennis ball and hit her thumb with the tennis racket."

She managed not to make a disparaging comment—barely. She didn't like Pauline any more than Gil's daughters did. The woman was lazy and seductive, and always hanging on Gil like a tie. What little work she actually did was of poor quality and she was pitifully slow as well. She worked at the ranch office near the front of the house three days a week, and Kasie had already inherited a good deal of her work. Pauline spent her time by the pool when Gil wasn't watching. Now, Kasie thought miserably, she was going to end up doing not only John's paperwork, including the unbelievably complex taxes that she was still struggling to understand, but Gil's as well.

"I don't guess she could type with her toes?" she murmured absently.

There was an odd sound, but when she looked up, Gil's hard face was impassive. "How long will it take?" he persisted.

She looked at the pages. They weren't data, as she'd first thought, but letters to various stock producers. They all had different headings, but the same basic body. "Is this all?" she asked with cool politeness.

He glowered at her. "There are fifty of them.
They'll have to be done individually..."

"No, they won't," she said gently. "All you have
to do—" she opened a new file, selected the option
she needed and began typing "—is type the body of
the letter once and then just type the various addresses
and combine them. An hour's work."

He looked as if he'd been slapped. "Excuse me?"

"This word processor does all that for you," she
explained. "It's very simple, really."

He looked angry. "I thought you had to type all
fifty individually."

"Only if you're using a prehistoric typewriter and
carbon system," she pointed out.

He was really angry now. "An hour?" he repeated.

She nodded. "Maybe less. I'll get right on it," she
added quickly, hoping to appease him. Heaven only
knew what had set him off, but she recognized that
glitter in his eyes.

He left her and went to make some phone calls.
When he came back, Kasie was printing the letters
out, having just finished the mailing labels. There was
a folding machine that made short work of folding
the letters. Then all she had to do was stuff, lick,
stamp and mail the envelopes.

Gil put on the stamps for her. He watched her curiously. Once, when she looked up into his eyes, it
was like an electric shock. Surprised, she dropped her
gaze and blushed. Really, she thought, he had a
strange effect on her.

"How do you like your job so far?" he asked.

"Very much," she said. "Except for the taxes."

"You'll get used to doing them," he assured her.

"I suppose so."

"Can you manage John's load and mine as well, or do you want me to get a temporary to help you?"

"There isn't a lot," she pointed out. "If I get overwhelmed, I'll say so."

He finished stamping the envelopes and stacked them neatly to one side. "You're very honest. It's unusual in most people." He touched a stamp with a floral motif. "My wife was like that." He smiled. "She said that lies were a waste of time, since they got found out anyway." His eyes were far away. "We were in grammar school together. We always knew that we'd marry one day." The smile faded into misery. "She was a wonderful rider. She rode in the rodeo when she was younger. But a gentle horse ran away with her and a low-lying limb ended her life. Jenny was only a year old when Darlene died. Bess was two. I thought my life was over, too."

Kasie didn't know what to say. It shocked her that a man like Gil would even discuss something so personal with a stranger. Of course, a lot of people discussed even more personal things with Kasie. Maybe she had that sort of face that attracted confidences.

"Do the girls look like her?" she asked daringly.

"Bess does. She was blond and blue-eyed. She wasn't beautiful, but her smile was." His eyes narrowed in painful memory. "They had to sedate me to make me let go of her. I wouldn't believe them, even when they swore to me that no means on earth could save her…" His fingers clenched on top of the envelope and he moved his hand away at once and stood up. "Thanks, Kasie," he said curtly, turning away, as if it embarrassed him to have spoken of his wife at all.

"Mr. Callister," she said softly, waiting until he

turned to continue. "I lost…some people three
months ago. I understand grief."

He hesitated. "How did they die?"

Her face closed up. "It was…an accident. They
were only in their twenties. I thought they had years
left."

"Life is unpredictable," he told her. "Sometimes
unbearable. But everything passes. Even bad times."

"Yes, that's what everyone says," she agreed.

They shared a long, quiet, puzzling exchange of
sorrow before he shrugged and turned away, leaving
her to her work.

# *Chapter 2*

Kasie was almost tearing her hair out by the next afternoon. John's mail was straightforward, mostly about show dates and cancellations, transportation for the animals and personal correspondence. Gil's was something else.

Gil not only ran the ranch, but he dealt with the majority of the support companies that were its satellites. He knew all the managers by first names, he often spoke with state and federal officials, including well-known senators, on legislation affecting beef production. Besides that, he was involved in the scientific study of new grasses and earth-friendly pesticides and fertilizers. He worked with resource and conservation groups, even an animal rights group; since he didn't run slaughter cattle and was rabidly proconservation, at least one group was happy to have his name on its board of directors. He was a powerhouse of energy, working from dawn until well after

dark. The problem was, every single task he under-
took was accompanied by a ton of paperwork. And
his part-time secretary, Pauline Raines, was the most
disorganized human being Kasie had ever encoun-
tered.

John came home late on Friday evening, and was
surprised to find Kasie still at work in the study.

He scowled as he tossed his Stetson onto a rack.
"What are you doing in here? It's almost ten o'clock!
Does Gil know you're working this much overtime?"

She glanced up from the second page of ten that
she was trying to type into the computer. None of
Pauline's paperwork had ever been keyed in.

She held up the sheaf of paperwork in six files with
a sigh. "I think of it as job security," she offered.

He moved around beside the desk and looked over
what she was doing. "Good God, he's not sane!" he
muttered. "No one secretary could handle this load
in a week! Is he trying to kill you?"

"Pauline hurt her thumb," she said miserably. "I
get to do her work, too, except that she never put any
of the records into the computer. It's got to be done.
I don't see how your brother ever found anything in
here!"

"He didn't," John said dryly, his pale eyes twinkling. "Pauline made sure of it. She's indispensable,
I hear."

Kasie's eyes narrowed. "She won't be for long,
when I get this stuff keyed in," she assured him.

"Don't tell her that unless you pay up your life
insurance first. Pauline is a girl who carries grudges,
and she's stuck on Gil."

"I noticed."

"Not that he cares," John added slowly. "He

never got over losing his wife. I'm not sure that he'll ever remarry.''

''He told me.''

He glanced down at her. ''Excuse me?''

''He told me specifically that he didn't want a mother for the girls or a new wife, and not to get my hopes up.'' She chuckled. ''Good Lord, he must be all of thirty-two. I'm barely twenty-two. I don't want a man I'll have to push around in a wheelchair one day!''

''And I don't rob cradles,'' came a harsh, angry voice from the doorway.

They both jumped as they looked up to see Gil just coming in from the barn. He was still in work clothes, chaps and boots and a sweaty shirt, with a disreputable old black Stetson cocked over one eye.

''Are you trying to make Kasie quit, by any chance?'' John challenged. ''Good God, man, it'll take her a week just to get a fraction of the information in these spreadsheets into the computer!''

Gil frowned. He pulled off his hat and ran a hand through his sweaty blond hair. ''I didn't actually look at it,'' he confessed. ''I've been too busy with the new bulls.''

''Well, you'd better look,'' John said curtly.

Gil moved to the desk, aware of Kasie's hostile glare. He peered over her shoulder and cursed sharply. ''Where did all this come from?'' he asked.

''Pauline brought it to me and said you wanted it converted to disk,'' she replied flatly.

His eyes began to glitter. ''I never told her to land you with all this!''

''It needs doing,'' she confessed. ''There's no way you can do an accurate spreadsheet without the comparisons you could use in a computer program. I've reworked this spreadsheet program,'' she said, indicating the screen, ''and made an application that will work for cattle weight gain ratios and daily weighing, as well as diet and health and so forth.''

''I'm impressed,'' Gil said honestly.

''It's what I'm used to doing. Taxes aren't,'' she added sheepishly.

''Don't look at me,'' John said. ''I hate taxes. I'm not learning them, either,'' he added belligerently. ''Half this ranch is mine, and on my half, we don't do tax work.'' He nodded curtly and walked out.

''Come back here, you coward!'' Gil muttered. ''How the hell am I supposed to cope with taxes and all the other routine headaches that you don't have, because you're off somewhere showing cattle!''

John just waved his hand and kept walking.

''Miss Parsons knows taxes inside out,'' Kasie ventured. ''She told me she used to be an accountant.''

He glared at her. ''Miss Parsons was hired to take care of my daughters.'' He kept looking at Kasie, and not in any friendly way. It was almost as if he knew…

She flushed. ''They couldn't get the little paper ship to float on the fish pond,'' she murmured uneasily, not looking at him. ''I only helped.''

''And fell in the pond.''

She grimaced. ''I tripped. Anybody can trip!'' she added in a challenging tone, her gray eyes flashing at him.

''Over their own feet?'' he mused.

Actually it had been over Bess's stuffed gorilla. The thing was almost her size and Kasie hadn't realized it was there. The girls had laughed and then wailed, thinking she'd be angry at them. Miss Parsons had fussed for hours when Bess got dirt on her pretty yellow dress. But Kasie didn't scold. She laughed, and the girls were so relieved, she could have cried. They really didn't like Miss Parsons.

He put both hands on his lean hips and studied her with reluctant interest. "The girls tell me everything, Kasie," he said finally. He didn't add that the girls worshiped this quiet, studious young woman who didn't even flirt with John, much less the cowboys who worked for the family. "I thought I'd made it perfectly clear that I didn't want you around them."

She took her hands off the keyboard and looked up at him with wounded eyes. "Why?"

The question surprised him. He scowled, trying to think up a fair answer. Nothing came to mind, which made him even madder.

"I don't have any ulterior motives," she said simply. "I like the girls very much, and they like me. I don't understand why you don't want me to associate with them. I don't have a bad character. I've never been in trouble in my life."

"I didn't think you had," he said angrily.

"Then why can't I play with them?" she persisted. "Miss Parsons is turning them into little robots. She won't let them play because they get dirty, and she won't play with them because it isn't dignified. They're miserable."

"Discipline is a necessary part of childhood," he said curtly. "You spoil them."

"For heaven's sake, somebody needs to! You're never here," she added shortly.

"Stop right there, while you still have a job," he interrupted, and his eyes made threats. "Nobody tells me how to raise my kids. Especially not some frumpy little backwoods secretary!''

Frumpy? Backwoods? Her eyes widened. She stood up. She was probably already fired, so he could just get it from the hip. ''I may be frumpy,'' she admitted, ''and I may be from the backwoods, but I know a lot about little kids! You don't stick them in a closet until they're legal age. They need to be challenged, made curious about the world around them. They need nurturing. Miss Parsons isn't going to nurture them, and Mrs. Charters doesn't have time to. And you aren't ever here at bedtime, even if you're not away on business,'' she repeated bluntly. ''Whole weeks go by when you barely have time to tell them good-night. They need to be read to, so they will learn to love books. They need constructive supervision. What they've got is barbed wire and silence.''

His fists clenched by his side, and his expression darkened. She lifted her chin, daring him to do anything.

''You're an expert on children, I guess?'' he chided.

''I took care of one,'' she said, her eyes darkening. ''For several months.''

''Why did you quit?''

He was assuming that she'd meant a job. She didn't. The answer to his question was a nightmare. She couldn't bear to remember it. ''I wasn't suited to the task,'' she said primly. ''But I won't corrupt your little girls by speaking to them.''

He was still glowering. He didn't want Kasie to grow close to the girls. He didn't want her any closer to him than a desk and a computer was. His eyes went involuntarily to the desk piled high with Pauline's undone work. The files were supposed to have been converted to computer months earlier, when he'd hired the woman. He'd assumed that it had been done, because she was always ready with the information he needed. He felt suddenly uneasy.

"Check out Black Ribbon's growth information for me," he said suddenly.

She hesitated, but apparently she was still working for him. She sat down and pulled the information up on the computer. He went to his desk and pulled a spreadsheet from a drawer. He brought it to Kasie and had her compare it with the figures she'd just put into the computer. There was a huge difference, to his favor.

He said a word that caused Kasie's face to grow bright red. That disturbed him, but he didn't allude to it. "I've made modifications to improve what seemed like a deficiency in diet. Now it looks as if it wasn't even necessary. How long will it take you to get the breeding herd information transcribed?"

"Well, I've done about a third of it," she said. "But John has letters and information to be compiled for this new show…"

"You're mine until we get this information on the computer. I'll make it all right with John."

"What about Pauline?" she asked worriedly.

"Pauline is my concern, not yours," he told her.

"Okay, boss. Whatever you say."

He made an odd gesture with one shoulder and gave her a long scrutiny. "I told you to let me know if there was too much work. Why didn't you?"

"I thought I could keep up," she said simply. "I wouldn't have complained as long as I could do it within a couple of weeks, and I can."

"Working fourteen-hour shifts," he chided.

"Well, work is work," she said. "I don't mind. It's not as if I have an active social life or an earth-shaking novel to write or anything. And I get paid a duke's ransom as it is."

He frowned. "Why don't you have a social life?"

"Because cowboys stink," she shot right back.

He started to speak, burst out laughing and walked to the door. "Stop that and go to bed. I'll have you some help by morning. Good night, Kasie."

"Good night, Mr. Callister."

He hesitated, turned, studied her, but he didn't speak. He left her tidying up and went upstairs to change out of his work clothes and have a shower.

The next morning, when she went into the office, Pauline was there and so was Gil. They stopped talking when Kasie walked in, so she assumed that they'd been talking about her. Apparently it hadn't been in a friendly way. Pauline's delicate features were drawn in anger and Gil's eyes were narrow and glittery.

"It's about time you got down here!" Pauline said icily.

"It's eight twenty-five," Kasie said, taken aback. "I'm not supposed to be in here until eight-thirty."

"Well, let's get started, then," Pauline said, flopping down at the computer.

"Doing what, exactly?" Kasie asked, disconcerted.

"Teach her how to put information on the computer," Gil said in a voice that didn't invite argument. "And while she's doing that, you can tackle John's work."

Kasie grimaced. Her pupil didn't look eager or willing. It was going to be a long morning.

\* \* \*

It was, too. Pauline made the job twice as tedious, questioning every keystroke twice and grumbling—when Gil was out of the office—about having to work with Kasie.

"Look, this wasn't my idea," Kasie assured her. "I could do it myself if Mr. Callister would just let me."

Pauline didn't soften an inch. "You're trying to get his attention, playing up to those kids," she accused. "You want him."

Kasie just looked at her. "I love children," she said quietly. "But I don't want to get married."

"Who said anything about marriage?" Pauline chided.

Kasie averted her eyes. "I needed a job and John needed a secretary," she murmured as she turned a spreadsheet page.

"Funny. You call him John, but Gil is 'Mr. Callister.' Why?"

The younger woman blinked. "John is just a few years older than I am," she replied.

Pauline frowned. "How old are you?"

"Twenty-two."

There was a long pause. "Well!" she said finally. She pursed her lips and entered a number into the computer. "You think Gil is old, do you?"

"Yes." She didn't, really, but it seemed safer to say so. She did, after all, have to work with this perfumed barracuda for the immediate future.

Pauline actually smiled. But only for a minute. "What do I do now?" she asked when she finished entering the last number.

Kasie showed her, faintly disturbed by that smile. Oh, well, she'd figure it out later, maybe.

*   *   *

Pauline went home at five o'clock. By now, she had a good idea of how to use the computer. Practice would hone her skills. Kasie wondered why Gil, who had the lion's share of the work, only had a part-time secretary.

When he came back in, late Saturday night, dressed in evening clothes with a black tie and white ruffled shirt, Kasie was still in the office finalizing the spreadsheets. She looked up, surprised at how handsome he was dressed like that. Even if he wasn't really good-looking, he had a natural authority and grace of carriage that made him stand out. Not to mention a physique that many a Hollywood actor would have coveted.

"I thought I told you to give up this night work," he said curtly.

She spared him a glance while she saved the information onto a diskette. "You won't let me play with the girls. I don't have anything else to do."

"Watch television. We have all the latest movies on pay-per-view. You can watch any you like. Read a book. Take up knitting. Learn Dutch. But," he added with unnatural resentment, "stay out of the office after supper."

"Is that an order?" she asked.

"It damned well is!"

He was absolutely bristling, she thought, frowning as she searched his pale blue eyes. She closed the files and shut down the program, uneasy because he was glowering at her.

She got up, neat and businesslike in her beige pantsuit, with her chestnut hair nicely braided and hanging down her back.

But when she went around the desk to go to the door, he blocked her path. She wasn't used to men this close and she backed up a step, which only made things worse. He was so tall that she wished she were wearing high heels. The top of her head barely came up to his nose.

His pale eyes glittered even more. "Old age isn't contagious," he said with pure venom in his deep voice.

"Sir?"

"And don't call me sir!"

She swallowed. He was spoiling for a fight. She couldn't bear the thought of one. Her early life had been in the middle of a violent battleground, and loud noises and voices still upset her. "Okay," she agreed immediately.

He slammed his hands into his pockets and glared more. "I'm thirty-two. Ten years isn't a generation and I'm not a candidate for Social Security."

"Okay," she repeated uneasily.

"For God's sake, stop agreeing with me!" he snapped.

She started to say "Okay" again, and bit her tongue. She was as rigid as a ruler, waiting for more explosions with her breath trapped in her throat.

He took his hands out of his pockets and they clenched at his sides as he looked down at her with more conflicting emotions than he'd ever felt. She wasn't beautiful, but there was a tenderness in her that he craved. He hadn't had tenderness in his life since Darlene's untimely death. This young woman made him hungry for things he couldn't grasp. He didn't understand it, and it angered him.

Kasie was wavering between a dash for the door

or backing up again. "Do you want me to quit?" she blurted out.

His teeth ground together. "Yes."

She swallowed. "All right. I'll leave in the morning." She moved around him to the door, trying not to take it personally. Sometimes people just didn't like other people.

"No!"

His voice stopped her with her hand on the doorknob.

There was a long pause. Kasie turned, surprised by his indecision. From what she already knew of Gil Callister, he wasn't a man who had trouble making decisions. But he seemed divided about Kasie.

She went toward him, noticing the odd expression on his face when she stopped within arm's length and folded her hands at her waist.

"I know you don't like me," she said gently. "It's all right. I'll really try hard to stay away from the girls. Once Pauline learns how to input the computer files, you won't even have to see me."

He seemed troubled now. Genuinely troubled. He sighed as if he were carrying the weight of the world on his shoulders. At that moment, he looked as if he needed comforting.

"Bess would love it if you took her and Jenny to one of those cartoon movies," she said out of the blue. "There's a Sunday matinee at the Twin Oaks Cinema."

He still didn't speak.

She searched his cold eyes. "I'm sorry that I've gone behind your back to spend time with them. It's not what you think. I mean, I'm not trying to worm my way into your family, even if Pauline does think so. The girls...remind me...of my own little niece.'' Her voice almost broke but she controlled it quickly.

''Does she live far away?'' he asked abruptly.

Her eyes darkened. ''Very...far away...now,'' she managed. She forced a smile. ''I miss her.''

She had to turn away then, or lose control of her wild emotions.

''You can stay for the time being,'' he said finally, reluctantly. ''It will work out.''

''That's what my aunt always says,'' she murmured as she opened the door.

''I didn't know you had family. Your parents are dead, aren't they?''

''They died years ago, when I was little. My aunt was in charge of us until we started school.''

''Us?''

She couldn't say it, she couldn't, she couldn't. ''I ha...have a twin brother,'' she corrected quickly.

She lifted her head, praying for strength. ''Good night, Mr. Callister.''

She heard the silence of his disapproval, but she was too upset to care. She went up the staircase with no hesitation at all, straight to her room. She locked the door and lay down on the covers, crying silently so that no one would hear.

There was a violent storm that night. The lightning lit up the whole sky. Kasie heard engines starting up and men's voices yelling. The animals must be unsettled. She'd read that cattle didn't like lightning.

She got up to look out the window, and then she heard the urgent knocking at her door.

She went to it, still in her neat thick white cotton gown that concealed the soft lines of her body. Her hair was loose down her back, disheveled, and she was barely awake.

She opened the door, and looked down. There were Bess and Jenny with tears streaming down their faces. Bess was clutching a small teddy bear, and Jenny had her blanket.

"Oh, my babies, what's wrong?" she asked softly, going down on her knees to pull them close and cuddle them.

"The sky's making an awful noise, Kasie, and we're scared," Bess said.

She threw caution to the winds. She was already in so much trouble, surely a little more wouldn't matter.

"Do you want to climb in with me?" she asked softly.

"Can we?" Bess asked.

"Of course. Come on."

They climbed into bed with her and under the covers, Jenny on one side and Bess on the other.

"Want a story," Jenny murmured.

"Me, too," Bess seconded.

"Okay. How about the three bears?"

"No, Kasie, that's scary," Bess said. "How about the mouse and the lion?"

"Aren't you scared of lions?" she asked the girls.

"We like lions," Bess told her contentedly, cuddling closer. "Daddy took us to the zoo and we saw lions and tigers and polar bears!"

"The lion it is, then."

And she proceeded to tell them drowsily about the mouse who took out the thorn in the lion's paw and made a friend for life. By the time she finished, they were both asleep. She kissed their pretty little sleeping faces and folded them close to her as the lightning

flashed and the thunder rolled. She wondered just before she fell asleep how much trouble she'd be in if
their father came home and found them with her, after
she'd just promised not to play with them. If only,
she thought, Gilbert Callister would get a thorn in his
paw and she could pull it out and make friends with
him....

It was almost two in the morning when Gil and
John got back from the holding pens. There had been
a stampede, and two hundred head of cattle broke
through their fences and spilled out into the pasture
that fronted on a highway. The brothers and every
hand on the place were occupied for three hours
working in the violent storm to round them up and
get them back into the right pasture and fix the fence.
It helped that the lightning finally stopped, and in its
wake came a nice steady rain. But everyone was
soaked by the time they finished, and eager for a
warm, dry bed.

Gil stripped off his wet clothes and took a shower,
wrapping a long burgundy silk robe around his tall
body before he went to check on the girls. He opened
the door to the big room they shared and his heart
skipped a beat when he realized they were missing.

Where in hell was Miss Parsons and where were
his children? He went along to her room and almost
knocked at the door, when he realized suddenly where
the girls were most likely to be.

With his lips making a thin line, he went along the
corridor barefoot to Kasie's room. Without knocking,
he opened the door and walked in. Sure enough,
curled up as close as they could get to her, were Bess
and Jenny.

He started to wake them up and insist that they go back to bed, when he saw the way they looked.

It had been a long time since he'd seen their little faces so content. Without a mother—despite the housekeeper and Miss Parsons—they were sad so much of the time. But when they were around Kasie, they changed. They smiled. They laughed. They played. He couldn't remember the last time he'd seen them so happy. Was it fair to deny them Kasie's company just because he didn't like her? On the other hand, was it wise to let them get so attached to her when she might quit or he might fire her?

The question worried him. As he pondered the situation, Kasie moved and the cover fell away from her sleeping form. He moved closer to the bed in the dim light from the security lights outside, and abruptly he realized that she was wearing the sort of gown a dowager might. It was strictly for utility, plain and white, with no ruffles or lace or even a fancy border. He scowled. Kasie was twenty-two. Was it normal for a woman her age to be so repressed that she covered herself from head to toe even in sleep?

She moved again, restlessly, and a single word broke from her lips as the nightmare came again.

"Kantor," she whispered. "Kantor!"

# Chapter 3

Without thinking, Gil reached down and shook Kasie's shoulder. "Wake up, Kasie!" he said firmly.

Her eyes opened on a rush of breath. There was horror in them for a few seconds until she came awake and realized that her boss was standing over her. She blinked away the sleepiness and pulled herself up on an elbow. Her beautiful thick chestnut hair swirled around her shoulders below the high neck of the gown as she stared at him.

"You were having a nightmare," he said curtly. "Who's Kantor?"

She hesitated for a few seconds. "My brother," she said finally. "My twin." She noticed that he was wearing a long robe and apparently nothing under it. Thick dark blond hair was visible in the deep vee of the neckline. She averted her eyes almost in panic. It embarrassed her to have him see her in her nightgown; almost as much as to see him in a robe.

"Why do you have nightmares about him?" he asked gently.

"We had an argument," she said. She pushed back her hair. "I don't want to talk about it."

His eyes narrowed. Apparently it was a painful subject. He let it drop. His eyes went to the girls and not without misgiving. "Why are they in here with you?"

"The storm woke them up. They got scared and came to me," she said defensively. "I didn't go get them."

He was studying them quietly. His expression was hard, grave, wounded.

"I'm sure they went to look for you first," she began defensively.

His eyes glittered down into hers. "We've had this conversation before. Miss Parsons is supposed to be their governness," he emphasized.

"Miss Parsons is probably snoring her head off," she said curtly. "She sleeps like the dead. Bess had a fever week before last, and she didn't even get up when I woke her and told her about it. She said that a fever never hurt anybody!"

"That was when she had strep and I took her to the doctor," he recalled. "Miss Parsons said she was sick. I assumed that she'd been up in the night with her."

"Dream on."

He glared at her. "I'll excuse it this time," he said, ignoring the reference he didn't like to Miss Parsons and her treatment of Bess. He'd have something to say to the woman about that. "Next time, come and find me if you can't wake Miss Parsons."

She just stared back, silent.

"Did you hear me, Kasie?" he demanded softly.

"All right." She glanced from one side of her to the other. "Do you want to wake them up and carry them back to their own beds?"

He looked furious. "If I do, we'll all be awake the rest of the night. We had cattle get out, and we got soaked trying to get them back in. I'm worn-out. I want to go to sleep."

"Nobody here is stopping you," she murmured.

His pale eyes narrowed. "I should have let you go when you offered to resign," he said caustically.

"There's still time," she pointed out, growing more angry by the minute.

He cursed under his breath, glared at her again and walked out.

The next morning, Kasie woke to soft pummeling little hands and laughing voices.

"Get up, Kasie, get up! Daddy's taking us to the movies today!"

She yawned and curled up. "Not me," she murmured sleepily. "Go get breakfast, babies. Mrs. Charters will feed you."

"You got to come, too!" Bess said.

"I want to sleep," she murmured.

"Daddy, she won't get up!" Bess wailed.

"Oh, yes, she will."

Kasie barely had time to register the deep voice before the covers were torn away and she was lifted bodily out of the bed in a pair of very strong arms.

Shocked, she stared straight into pale blue eyes and felt as if she'd been electrified.

"I'll wake her up," Gil told the girls. "Go down and eat your breakfast."

"Okay, Daddy!"

The girls left gleefully, laughing as they went to the staircase.

"You look like a nun in that gown," Gil remarked as he studied his light burden, aware of her sudden stillness. Her face was very close. He searched it quietly. "And you've got freckles, Kasie, just across the bridge of your nose."

"Put...put me down," she said, unnerved by the proximity. She didn't like the sensations it caused to feel his chest right against her bare breasts.

"Why?" he asked. He gazed into her eyes. "You hardly weigh anything." His eyes narrowed as he studied her face thoroughly. "You have big eyes," he murmured. "With little flecks of blue in them. Your face looks more round than oval, especially with your hair down. Your mouth is—" he searched for a word, more touched than he wanted to be by its vulnerability "—full and soft. Half-asleep you don't come across as a fighter. But you are, aren't you?"

Her hands were resting lightly around his neck and she stared at him disconcertedly while she wondered what John or Miss Parsons would say if they walked in unexpectedly to find them in this position.

"You should put me down," she said huskily.

"Don't you like being carried?" he murmured absently.

She shivered as she remembered the last time she'd been carried, by an orderly in the hospital...

She pushed at him. "Please."

He set her back down, scowling curiously at the odd pastiness of her complexion. "You're mysterious, Kasie."

"Not really. I'm just sleepy." She folded her arms

over her breasts and flushed. "Could you leave, please, and let me get dressed?"

He watched her curiously. "Why don't you date? And don't hand me any bull about stinking cowboys."

She was reluctant to tell him anything about herself. She was a private person. Her aunt, Mama Luke, always said that people shouldn't worry others with their personal problems. She didn't.

"I don't want to get married, ever."

He really scowled then. "Why?"

She thought of her parents and then of Kantor, and her eyes closed on the pain. "Love hurts too much."

He didn't speak. For an instant, he felt the pain that seemed to rack her delicate features, and he understood it, all too well.

"You loved someone who died," he recalled.

She nodded and her eyes met his. "And so did you."

For an instant, his hard face was completely unguarded. He was vulnerable, mortal, wounded. "Yes."

"It doesn't pass away, like they say, does it?" she asked softly.

"Not for a long time."

He moved a step closer, and this time she didn't back up. Her eyes lifted to his. He slid his big, lean hand into the thick waves of her chestnut hair and enjoyed its silkiness. "Why don't you wear your hair down, like this?"

"It's sinful," she whispered.

"What?"

"When you dress and wear your hair in a way

that's meant to tempt men, to try to seduce them, it's sinful,'' she repeated.

His lips fell open. He didn't know how to answer that. He'd never had a woman, especially a modern woman, say such a thing to him.

''Do you think sex is a sin?'' he asked.

''Outside of marriage, it is,'' she replied simply.

''You don't move with the times, do you?'' he asked on an expulsion of breath.

''No,'' she replied.

He started smiling and couldn't stop. ''Oh, boy.''

''The girls will be waiting. Are you really taking them to a movie?'' she asked.

''Yes.'' One eye narrowed. ''I need to take you to one, too. Something X-rated.''

She flushed. ''Get out of here and stop trying to corrupt me.''

''You're overdue.''

''Stop or I'll have Mama Luke come over and lecture you.''

He frowned. ''Mama Luke?''

''My aunt.''

''What an odd name.''

She shrugged. ''Our whole family runs to odd names.''

''I noticed.''

She made a face. ''I work for you. My private life is my own business.''

''You don't have a private life,'' he said, and smiled tenderly.

''I'm a great reader. I love Plutarch and Tacitus and Arrian.''

''Good God!''

''There's nothing wrong with ancient history.

Things were just as bad then as they are now. All the
ancient writers said that the younger generation was
headed straight to purgatory and the world was corrupt.''

"Arrian didn't."

"Arrian wrote about Alexander the Great," she reminded him. "Alexander's world was in fairly good
shape, apparently."

"Arrian wrote about Alexander in the distant past,
not his own present." His eyes became soft with affection as he looked at her. "Why don't I like you?
There isn't a person in my circle of acquaintances
who would even know who Arrian was, much less
what he wrote about."

"I don't like you much, either," she shot right
back. "But I guess I can stand it if you can."

"I'll have to," he mused. "If I let you walk out,
the girls will push me down the staircase and call you
back to support them at my funeral."

She shivered abruptly and wrapped her arms
around herself. Funeral. Funeral…

"Kasie!"

Her somber eyes came up. She was barely
breathing. "Don't…joke about things like that."

"Kasie, I didn't mean it that way," he began.

She forced a smile. "Of course not. I have to get
dressed."

He lifted an eyebrow. "You might as well come
as you are. I haven't seen a gown like that since I
stayed with my grandmother as a child." He shook
his head. "You'd set a lingerie shop back decades if
that style caught on."

"It's a perfectly functional gown."

"Functional. Yes. It's definitely functional. And about as seductive as chain mail," he added.

"Good!"

He burst out laughing. "All right, I'm leaving."

He went out, sparing her a last, amused glance before he closed the door.

Kasie dressed in jeans and a dark T-shirt. She put her long hair in a braid and pulled on sneakers. She felt a twinge of guilt because she'd missed so many Sunday sermons in past months. But she couldn't reconcile her pain. It needed more time.

The whole family was at the table when she joined them for breakfast. John gave her a warm smile.

"I hear you had visitors last night," he told Kasie with a mischievous glance at the two little girls, who were wolfing down cereal.

"Yes, I did," Kasie replied with a worried glance that encompassed both Gil and Miss Parsons.

"You should have called me, Miss Mayfield," Miss Penny Parsons said curtly and glanced at Kasie with cold dark eyes. "I take care of the children."

Kasie could have argued that point, but she didn't dare. "Yes, Miss Parsons," she said demurely.

Gil finished his scrambled eggs and lifted his coffee cup to his firm lips. He was wearing slacks and a neat yellow sports shirt that emphasized his muscular arms. He looked elegant even in casual wear, Kasie thought, and remembered suddenly the feel of those strong arms around her. She flushed.

He noticed her sudden color and caught her gaze. She couldn't seem to look away, and he didn't even try to. For a space of seconds, they were fused in some sort of bond, prisoners of a sensual connection that made Kasie's full lips part abruptly. His gaze fell to them and lingered with unexpected hunger.

Kasie dropped her fork onto her plate and jumped at the noise. "Sorry!" she said huskily as she fumbled with the fork.

"Didn't get much sleep last night, did you?" John asked with a smile. "Neither did any of us. About midnight, I thought seriously about giving up cattle ranching and becoming a door-to-door vacuum cleaner salesman."

"I felt the same way," Gil confessed. "We're going to have to put a small line cabin out at the holding pens and keep a man there on stormy nights."

"As long as I'm not on your list of candidates," John told his brother.

"I'll keep that in mind. Bess, don't play with your food, please," he added to the little girl, who was finished with her cereal and was now smearing eggs around the rim of her plate.

"I don't like eggs, Daddy," she muttered. "Do I gotta eat 'em?"

"Of course you do, young lady!" Miss Parsons said curtly. "Every last morsel."

Bess looked tortured.

"Miss Parsons, could you ask Mrs. Charters to see me before she plans the supper menu, please?" Gil asked.

Miss Parsons got up. "I will. Eat those eggs, Bess."

She left. Gil gave his oldest daughter a sign by placing his forefinger across his mouth. He lifted Bess's plate, scraped the eggs onto his, and finished them off before Miss Parsons returned.

"Very good," she said, nodding approvingly at

Bess's plate. "I told you that you'd grow accustomed
to a balanced breakfast. We must keep our bodies
healthy. Come on, now, girls. We'll have a nice nap
until your father's ready to go to the movies."

Bess grimaced, but she didn't protest. She got up
with Jenny and was shepherded out by the governess.

"Marshmallow," John chided the older man, pok-
ing the air with his fork. "You should have made her
eat them herself."

"When you start eating liver and onions voluntar-
ily, I'll make Bess eat eggs," Gil promised. "Want
to come with us to the movies?" He named the picture they were going to see.

"Not me," John said pleasantly. "I'm going to
Billings to see a man about some more acreage." He
glanced at Kasie speculatively. "Want to tag along,
Kasie?"

The question surprised her. While she was trying
to think of a polite way to say she didn't, Gil answered for her.

"Kasie's going with us to the movies," he replied,
and his pale eyes dared her to argue. "The girls will
have conniptions if we leave her behind. Besides, she
likes cartoons. Don't you, Kasie?"

"I'm just crazy about them, Mr. Callister," she
agreed with a tight smile, angry because he'd more
or less forced her into agreeing to go.

"Mr. Callister was our father," Gil said firmly.
"Don't use it with us."

She grimaced. "I work for you. It doesn't seem
right."

John was gaping at her. "You're kidding."

"No, she isn't," Gil assured him. "When you have

a free minute, get her to tell you why she braids her hair. It's a hoot.''

She glared at Gil. ''You cut that out.''

He wiped his mouth with a white linen napkin and got to his feet. ''I've got some phone calls to make before we go. We'll leave at one, Kasie.''

''Phone calls on Sunday?'' she asked John when his brother had left them alone.

''It's yesterday in some parts of the world, and tomorrow in some other parts,'' he reminded her. ''You know how he is about business.''

''Yes,'' she agreed.

''What amazes me,'' he mused, watching her, ''is how much he grumbles about you. He loves women, as a rule. He's always doing little things to make the job easier for Mrs. Charters. He lets Pauline get away with only working three days of the week, when he needs a full-time secretary worse than I do. But he's hard on you.''

''He doesn't like me,'' she said quietly. ''He can't help it.''

''You don't like him, either.''

She smiled sheepishly. ''I can't help it, either.'' She picked up on something he'd said earlier. ''How can Pauline make ends meet with only a part-time job?'' she asked curiously.

''She's independently wealthy,'' John told her. ''She doesn't need a job at all, but she caught Gil at a weak moment. He doesn't have many of them, believe me. I think she attracted him at first. Now things have cooled and he's stuck with her. She's tenacious.''

''Why would she need to work?'' she wondered aloud.

"Because Gil needed a secretary, of course. She hasn't had any business training, and I don't doubt that the files are in a hellacious mess."

"Couldn't he get somebody else?"

"He tried to. Pauline cried all over him and he gave up."

"He doesn't look like a man who'd even notice tears," she said absently.

"Appearances are deceptive. You saw how he was when the dog threatened the girls," he reminded her. "He's not immune to tears."

"I'd need convincing," she said and grinned wickedly.

He leaned back in his chair with his coffee cup in his hand and studied her. "You're good with the kids," he said. "You must have spent a lot of time around children."

She lowered her eyes to her empty plate. "I did. I'm not formally taught or anything, but I do know a few things."

"It shows. I've never seen Bess respond to any of her various governesses. She liked you on sight."

"How many governesses has she had?" she asked curiously.

"Four. This year," he amended.

Her eyebrows arched. "Why so many?"

"Are you afraid of spiders, garter snakes, or frogs?" he asked.

She shook her head. "Why?"

"Well, the others were. They got downright twitchy about opening drawers or pulling down bedcovers," he recalled with a chuckle. "Bess likes garter snakes. She shared them with the governesses."

"Oh, dear," Kasie said.

"You see the point. That's why Miss Parsons was hired. She's the next best thing to a Marine DI, as you may have noticed."

Her face lightened. "So that's why he hired her. I did wonder."

John sighed. "I wish he'd hired her to do the tax work on the payroll instead. She's a natural, and since she's a retired accountant that experience would make her an asset. We have a firm of C.P.A.'s to do yearly stuff, but our bookkeeper who did payroll got married and moved to L.A. just before we hired you."

"And Miss Parsons got hired to look after the girls. She really dislikes children," she added.

"I know. But Gil refuses to believe it. He's been lax about work at the ranch for a while. He stayed on the road more and more, avoiding the memories after Darlene died. I felt bad for him, but things were going to pot here. I have to travel to show the bulls," he added, "because the more competitions we win, the higher the prices we can charge for stud fees or young bulls. The ranch can't run without anybody oversee-ing it." He pursed his lips as he studied her. "I gather that you said something to him about neglecting the girls. I thought so," he mused when she shifted un-comfortably. "I've told him, too, but he didn't listen to me. Apparently he listens to you."

"He's already tried to fire me once," she pointed out.

"You're still here," he replied.

"Yes. But I can't help but wonder for how much longer," she murmured, voicing her one real fear. "I could go back and live with my aunt, but it isn't fair to her. I have to work and support myself. This was the only full-time job that I was qualified for. Jobs

are thin on the ground, regardless of the reports coming out about how great the economy is.''

"How did you end up in Medicine Ridge in the
first place?'' he wondered.

"I was living with my aunt in Billings when I saw
the ad for this job in the local paper. I'd already been
all over Billings hoping for a full-time job and
couldn't find one. This one seemed tailor-made for
me.''

"I'm glad you applied for it,'' he said. "There
were a lot of candidates, but we ruled out most of
them in less than five minutes each. You were the
only woman out there who could even type.''

"You're kidding.''

"No. They thought I wanted beauty instead of
brains. I didn't.'' He smiled. "Not that you're bad on
the eyes, Kasie. But I wasn't running a pageant.''

"I was surprised that your brother hired me,'' she
confessed. "He seemed to dislike me on sight. But
when he found out how fast I could type, he was a
lot less antagonistic.''

He wasn't going to mention what Gil had said to
him after he hired Kasie. It had been against Gil's
better judgment, and he'd picked her appearance and
her pert manner to pieces. It was interesting that Gil
was antagonistic toward her. Very interesting.

"You're a whiz at the computer,'' John said. "A
real asset. I didn't realize what you could do with a
spreadsheet program until you modified ours. You're
gifted.''

"I love computers,'' she said with a smile. "Pauline is going to enjoy them, too, when she learns just
a little more. Once she discovers the Internet, she'll
be even more efficient. There are all sorts of Web

sites dedicated to the cattle industry. It would be great for comparisons—even for buying and selling bulls. You could have your own Web site.''

John let out a low whistle. "Funny, I hadn't even considered that. Kasie, it might revolutionize the way we do business, not to mention cutting down on the amount of travel we have to do every year.''

"That's what I thought, too," she said, smiling at him.

"Mention it to Gil when you go to the movies," he coaxed. "Let's see what he thinks.''

"He might like the idea better if it came from you," she said.

"I think he'll like it, period. I already do. Can you make a Web site?''

She grimaced. "No, I can't. But I know a woman who can," she added. "She works out of Billings. I met her when we were going to secretarial school. She's really good, and she doesn't charge an arm and a leg. I can get in touch with her, if you like.''

"Go ahead. We do a lot of communication by e-mail, but neither of us even thought about putting cattle on our own site. It's a terrific idea!''

"You sound like Bess," Gil said from the doorway. "What's terrific?''

"We're going on the Internet," John said.

His big brother frowned. "The Internet?''

"Kasie can tell you what she's proposed. It could open new doors for us in marketing. It's international.''

Gil was quick. He caught on almost at once. "You mean, get a Web site and use it to buy and sell cattle," he said.

"It will save you as much time as sending e-mail

back and forth between potential buyers and sellers already does,'' she added.

''Good idea.'' Gil studied her with a curious smile. ''Full of surprises aren't you, Miss Mayfield?''

''She's gifted,'' John said, grinning at his brother. ''I told you so. Now maybe you can stop talking about firing her, hmm?''

Gil pressed his lips together and refused to rise to the bait. ''It's almost one o'clock. If we're going to the movies, let's go. Kasie, fetch the girls.''

She almost saluted, but he looked vaguely irritated. It looked as though nothing she suggested was ever going to please him. She wondered why she didn't just walk out and leave him to it. The thought was painful. She went up to get the little girls, more confused than ever.

## Chapter 4

The girls chattered like birds all the way to town in Gil's black Jaguar. Kasie sat in front and listened patiently, smiling, while they told her all about the movie they were going to see. They'd seen the previews on television when they watched their Saturday morning cartoons.

It was a warm, pretty day, and trees and shrubs were blooming profusely. It should have been perfect, but Kasie was uneasy. Maybe she shouldn't have mentioned anything about Web sites, but it seemed an efficient way for Gil and John to move into Web-based commerce.

"You're brooding," Gil remarked. "Why?"

"I was wondering if I should have suggested anything about Internet business," she said.

"Why not? It's a good idea," he said, surprising her. "John told me about the Web site designer. Tomorrow, I want you to get in touch with her and get the process started.''

''She'll need you to tell her what you want on the site.''

''Okay.''

She glanced in the back seat where the girls were sharing a book and enthusing over the pop-up sections.

''I brought it home for them yesterday,'' he commented, ''and forgot to give it to them. They love books.''

''That's the first step to getting them to love reading,'' she said, smiling at the little heads bowed over the books. ''Reading to them at night keeps it going.''

''Did your mother read to you?'' he asked curiously.

''She probably did,'' she mused, smiling sadly. ''But Kantor and I were very young when she and our father...died. Mama Luke read to us, when we were older.''

''I suppose you liked science fiction,'' he murmured.

''How did you know?'' she asked.

''You love computers,'' he said with a hint of a smile.

''I guess they do fit in with science fiction,'' she had to admit. She eyed him curiously. ''What sort of books did you like to read?''

''Pirate stories, cowboy stories. Stuff like that. Now, it's genetics textbooks and management theory,'' he added wryly. ''I hardly ever have time to read just for fun.''

''Do your parents help you with the ranch?''

He seemed to turn to ice. "We don't talk about our parents," he said stiffly.

That sounded odd. But she was already in his bad book, so she didn't pursue it. "It's nice of you to take the girls to the movies."

He slowed for a turn, his expression taut. "I don't spend enough time with them," he said. "You were right about that. It isn't a lack of love. It's a lack of delegation. You'd be amazed how hard it is to find good managers who want to live on a cattle ranch."

"Maybe you don't advertise in a wide enough range," she suggested gently.

"What?"

She plunged ahead. "There are all sorts of trade magazines that carry ads with blind mailboxes," she said. "You can have replies sent to the newspaper and nobody has to know who you are."

"How do you know about the trade magazines?" he asked.

She grinned sheepishly. "I read them. Well, I ought to know something about cattle, since I work for a ranch, shouldn't I?"

He shook his head. "You really are full of surprises, Kasie."

"Kasie, what's this big word?" Bess asked, thrusting the book at her. Kasie took it and sounded the word out phonetically, coaching the little girl in its pronunciation. She took the book back and began to teach the word to Jenny.

"You're patient," Gil remarked. "I notice that Miss Parsons doesn't like taking time to teach them words."

"Miss Parsons likes numbers."

"Yes. She does." He pulled into the theater parking lot, which was full of parents and children. He got everyone out and locked the door, grimacing as they walked past several minivans.

"They're handy for little kids," Kasie said wickedly. "Mothers love them, I'm told."

"I love my kids, but I'm not driving a damned minivan," he muttered.

She grinned at his expression. The little girls ran to get in line, and struck up a conversation with a child they knew, whose bored mother perked up when she saw Gil approaching.

"Hi, Gil!" she called cheerily. "We're going to see the dinosaur movie! Is that why you're here?"

"That's the one," he replied, pulling bills out of his wallet. He gave one to each of the little girls, and they bought their own tickets. Gil bought his and Kasie's as they came to the window. "Hi, Amie," he called to the little girl with Bess and Jenny, and he smiled. She smiled back. She was as dark as his children were fair, with black eyes and hair like her mother's.

"We're going to sit with Amie, Daddy!" Bess said excitedly, waving her ticket and Jenny's.

"I guess that leaves me with you and...?" the other woman paused deliberately.

"This is Kasie," Gil said, and took her unexpectedly by the arm, with a bland smile at Amie's mom. "You're welcome to join us, of course, Connie."

The other woman sighed. "No, I guess I'll sit with the girls. Nice to have seen you," she added, and moved ahead with the girls, looking bored all over again.

Gil slid his hand down into Kasie's. She reacted nervously to the unexpected touch, but his fingers clung, warm and strong against her own. He drew her along to the line already forming alongside the velvet ropes as the ticket takers prepared to let people through to the various theaters.

"Humor me," he said, and it looked as though he were whispering sweet nothings into her ear. "I'm the entrée, in case you haven't noticed."

Kasie glanced around and saw a number of women with little children and no man along, and two of them gave him deliberate, wistful glances and smiled.

"Single moms?" she whispered back, having to go on tiptoe.

He caught her around the waist and held her against his hip. "No. Get the picture?"

Her breath caught. "Oh, dear," she said heavily.

He looked down into her wide eyes. "You're such a child sometimes," he said softly. "You don't see ugliness, do you? You go through life looking for rainbows instead of rain."

"Habit," she murmured, fascinated by the pale blue lights in his eyes.

"It's a rather nice habit," he replied. The look lasted just a few seconds too long to be polite, and Kasie felt her heart begin to race. But then, the line shifted and diverted him. He moved closer to the ticket-taker, keeping the girls ahead carefully in sight while his arm drew Kasie along with him.

She liked the protectiveness of that muscular arm. He didn't look like a body-builder, all his movements were lithe and graceful. But he worked at physical labor from dawn until dusk most days. She'd seen him throw calves that had to be doctored. She'd seen him throw bulls, too. He was strong. Involuntarily she relaxed against him. It was delicious, the feeling of security it gave her to be close to him, to the warm strength of him.

The soft movement caught him off guard and sent a jolt of sensation through him that he hadn't felt in a long time. He looked down at her with curious, turbulent eyes that she didn't see. She was smiling and waving at the girls, who were darting off down into the theater with the little girl and her mother.

"They like you," he said.

"I like them."

He handed their tickets to the uniformed girl, who smiled as she handed back the stubs and pointed the way to the theater that was showing the cartoon movie.

Gil caught Kasie's hand in his and drew her lazily along with him through the crowd of children and parents until they reached the theater. But instead of going down to the front, he drew Kasie to an isolated double-seat in the very back row and sat down beside her. His arm went over the back of the chair as the theater darkened and the previews began showing.

Kasie was electrified by the shift in their relationship. She felt his lean fingers on her shoulder, bringing her closer, and his cheek rested against her temple. She hadn't ever been to a movie with a man. There had been a blind double date once, and the boy sat on his own side of the seat and looked nervous until they got home again. This was worlds away from that experience.

"Comfortable?" he asked at her ear, and his voice was like velvet.

"Yes," she said unsteadily.

His chest rose and fell and he found himself paying a lot more attention to the feel of Kasie's soft hair against his skin than the movie. She smelled of spring roses. Her hair was soft, and had a faint herbal scent of its own. Twenty-two. She was twenty-two. He was thirty-two, and she'd already said that he was too old for her.

He scowled as he thought about that difference. She needed someone as young as she was, with that same vulnerable, kind, generous spirit. He had two little girls and a high-pressure business that gave him little free time. He was still grieving, in a way, for Darlene, whom he'd loved since grammar school. But there was something about Kasie that made him hungry. It wasn't desire, although he was aware of heady sensations when she was close to him. No, it was the sort of hunger a man got when he was standing outside in the snow with a wet coat and soaked jeans, looking through the window at a warm, glowing fireplace. He couldn't really explain the feelings. They made him uneasy.

He noticed that she was still a little stiff. He touched a curl at her ear. "Hey," he whispered.

She turned her head and looked up at him in the semidarkness.

"I'm not hitting on you," he whispered into her ear. "Okay?"

She relaxed. "Okay."

The obvious relief in her voice made him feel guilty and offended. He moved his arm back to the chair and forced himself to watch the movie. He had to remember that Kasie worked for him. It wasn't fair to use her to ward off other women. But…was it really that?

The dinosaur movie was really well-done, Kasie thought as she became involved in the storyline and the wonder of creatures that looked really alive up there on the screen. It was a bittersweet sort of cartoon, though, and she was sorry for the little girls. Because when it was over, Bess and Jenny came to them crying about the dinosaurs that had died in the film.

"Oh, sweetheart, it was only a movie," Kasie said at once, and bent to pick up Bess, hugging her close. "Just a movie. Okay?"

"But it was so sad, Kasie," cried the little girl. "Why do things have to die?"

"I don't know, baby," she said softly, and her eyes closed for an instant on a wave of remembered pain. She'd lost so many people she loved.

Gil had Jenny up in his arms, and they walked out of the theater carrying the children. Behind them, other mothers were trying to explain about extinction.

"There, there, baby," he cooed at Jenny and kissed her wet eyes. "It was only make-believe. Dinosaurs don't really talk, you know, and they had brains the size of peas." He shifted her and smiled. "Hey, remember what I told you about chickens, about how they'll walk right up to a rattlesnake and let it strike them? Well, dinosaurs didn't even have brains that big."

"They didn't?" Bess asked from her secure hold on Kasie.

"They didn't," Gil said. "If a meteor had struck them, they'd be standing right in its path waiting for it. And they wouldn't be discussing it, either."

Kasie laughed as she looked at Gil, delighted at the way he handled the sticky situation. He was, she thought, a marvelous parent.

"Can we get some ice cream on the way home?" Bess asked then, wiping her tears.

"You bet. We'll stop by the yogurt place."

"Thanks, Daddy!" Bess cried.

"You're the nicest daddy," Jenny murmured against his throat.

"You really are, you know," Kasie agreed as they strapped the little girls into the back seat.

His eyes met hers across the children. "I'm a veteran daddy," he told her dryly.

"Is that what it is?" Kasie chuckled.

"You get better with practice, or so they tell me. Do you like frozen yogurt? I get them that instead of ice cream. It's healthy stuff."

"I like it, too," Kasie said as she got into the front seat beside him.

"We'll get some to take home for Mrs. Charters and Miss Parsons," he added, "so that we don't get blamed for ruining their appetites for supper."

"Now that's superior thinking," Kasie had to admit.

He started the engine and eased them out of the crowded parking lot.

The yogurt shop was a few miles from home. They stopped and got the treat in carryout cups, because Gil was expecting a phone call from a buyer out of state.

"I don't like to work on Sundays," he remarked as they drove home. "But sometimes it's unavoidable."

"Do you ever take the girls to church?"

He hesitated. "Well…no."

She was watching him with those big, soft gray

eyes, in which there wasn't condemnation or censure. It was almost as if she knew that his faith had suffered since the death of his wife. No, for longer than that. It had suffered since childhood, when his parents had…

"I haven't gone for several months, myself," Kasie remarked quietly. She twisted her purse slowly in her hands. "If I…start back, I could take them with me, if you didn't mind."

"I don't mind," he replied.

Her eyes softened and she smiled at him.

He tore his gaze away from that warm affection and forced it back to the road. His hand tightened on the steering wheel. She really was getting to him. He wished he knew some way to head off trouble. He found her far too attractive, and she continued to make her lack of receptiveness known. He didn't want to do something stupid and send her looking for another job.

"I enjoyed today," he said after a minute. "But you remember that Miss Parsons is supposed to be responsible for the girls," he added with a stern glance. "You have enough to do keeping John's paperwork current. Understand?"

"Yes, I do. I'll try very hard to stop interfering," she promised.

"Good. Pauline is out of town for the next week, but she'll be home in time for the pool party we're giving next Saturday. She'll be in the office the following Monday morning. You can give her another computer lesson."

She grimaced. "She doesn't like me."

"I know. Don't let it worry you. She's efficient."

She wasn't, but apparently she'd managed to con-

ceal it from Gil. Kasie wondered how he'd managed
not to notice the work Pauline didn't do.

"Did John have a secretary before me?" she asked
suddenly.

"He did, and she was a terrific one, too. But she
quit with only a week's notice."

"Did she say why?" she fished with apparent un-
concern.

"Something about being worked to death. John
didn't buy it. She didn't have that much to do."

She did, if she was doing John's work and having
Gil's pawned off on her as well. Kasie's eyes narrowed. Well, she wasn't going to get away with it
now. If Pauline started expecting Kasie to do her job
for her, she was in for a surprise.

"Funny," Gil murmured as he turned onto the
black shale ranch road that led to the Double C.
"Pauline said she couldn't use the computer, but she
always had my herd records printed out. Even if they
weren't updated properly."

Kasie didn't say a word. Surely he'd work it out
by himself one day. She glanced back at the girls,
who were still contentedly eating frozen yogurt out
of little cups. They were so pretty and sweet. Her
heart ached just looking at them. Sandy had been just
Bess's age...

She bit down hard on her lip. She mustn't cry.
Tears were no help at all. She had to look ahead, not
backward.

Gil pulled up in front of the house and helped Kasie
get the girls out.

"Thanks for the movie," Kasie told him, feeling
shy now.

"My pleasure," he said carelessly. "Come on,

girls, let's get you settled with Miss Parsons. Daddy's got to play rancher for a while."

"Can't we play, too?" Bess asked, clinging to his hand.

"Sure," he said. "Just as soon as you can compare birth weight ratios and compute projected weaning weight."

Bess made a face. "Oh, Daddy!"

"I'll make a rancher out of you one day, young lady," he said with a grin.

"Billy's dad said he was sure glad he had a son instead of girls. Daddy, do you ever wish me and Jenny was boys?" she asked.

He stopped, dropped to one knee and hugged the child close. "Daddy loves little girls," he said softly. "And he wouldn't trade you and Jenny for all the boys in the world. You tell Billy I said that."

Bess chuckled. "I will!" She kissed his cheek with a big smack. "I love you, Daddy!"

"I love you, too, little chick."

Jenny, jealous, had to have a hug, too, and they ended up each clinging to a strong, lean hand as they went into the house.

Kasie watched them, feeling more lost and alone than she had in months. She ached to be part of a family again. Watching Gil with the girls only emphasized what she'd lost.

She went up onto the porch and up the staircase slowly, her hand smoothing over the silky wood of the banister as she tried once again to come to grips with her loss.

She was curled up in her easy chair watching an old movie on television when there was a soft knock at the door just before it opened. Bess and Jenny sneaked in wearing their gowns and bathrobes and slippers, peering cautiously down the hall before they closed the door.

"Hello," Kasie said with a smile, opening her arms as they clambered up into the big chair with her and cuddled close. "You smell nice."

"We had baths," Bess said. "Miss Parsons said we was covered with chocolate sauce." She giggled. "We splashed her."

"You bad babies," she chided softly and kissed little cheeks.

"Could you tell us a story?" they asked.

"Sure. What would you like to hear?"

"The one with the bears."

"Okay." She started the story, speaking in all the different parts, while they snuggled close and listened with attention.

Just to see if they were really listening, she added, "And then the wolf huffed and puffed…"

"No, Kasie!" Bess interrupted. "That's the pig story!"

"Is it?" she exclaimed. "All right, then. Well, the bears came home…"

"Huffing and puffing?" came a deep, amused query from the doorway. The little girls glanced at him, looking guilty and worried. "Miss Parsons is looking for you two fugitives," he drawled. "If I were you, I'd get into my beds real fast. She's glowering."

"Goodness! We got to go, Kasie!" Bess said, and she and Jenny scrambled to their feet and ran past their father down the hall, calling good-nights as they went.

Gil studied Kasie from the doorway. She was wearing her own white gown, with a matching cotton robe this time, and her long hair waved around her shoulders. She looked very young.

"You weren't reading from a book. What did you do, memorize the story?" he asked curiously.

"I guess so," she confided, smiling. "I've told it so many times, I suppose I do have it down pretty well."

"Who did you tell it to?" he asked reasonably.

The smile never faded, but she withdrew behind it. "A little girl who stayed with us sometimes," she replied.

"I see."

"They came in and asked for a story," she explained. "I hated telling them to go away…"

"I haven't said a word."

"You did," she reminded him worriedly. "I know that Miss Parsons looks after them. I'm not trying to interfere."

"I know that. But it's making things hard for her when they come to you instead," he said firmly.

She grimaced. "I can't hurt their feelings."

"I'll speak to them." He held up a hand when she started to protest. "I'll speak to them nicely," he added. "I won't make an issue of it."

She hesitated. "Okay."

"You have your own duties," he continued. "It isn't fair to let you take on two jobs, no matter how you feel about it. I don't pay Miss Parsons to sit and read tax manuals."

Her eyes widened. "You're kidding," she said, sitting up straight. "She reads tax manuals? What for? Did you ask her?"

"I did. She says she reads them for pleasure," he said. "Apparently she didn't really want to retire from the accounting business, but she was faced with a clerical position or retirement," he added with a droll smile.

"Oh, dear."

He pushed away from the door facing. "Don't stay up too late. John needs to get an early start. He'll be away for a week showing Ebony King on the road."

"He's the new young bull," Kasie recalled. "He eats corn out of my hand," she added with a smile. "I never thought of bulls as being gentle."

"They're a real liability if they're not," he pointed out. "A bull that size could trample a man with very little difficulty."

"I guess he could." She stood up, with her hands in the pockets of the cotton robe. "I'm sorry about the girls coming in here."

"Oh, hell, I don't mind," he said on a rough breath. "But it isn't wise to let them get too attached to you, Kasie. You know it, and you know why."

"They think you're going to marry Pauline," she blurted out, and then flushed at having been so personal with him.

"I haven't thought a lot about remarrying," he replied quietly. His eyes went over her with a suddenly intent appraisal. "But maybe I should. They're getting to the age where they're going to need a woman's hand in their lives. I love them, but I can't see things from a female point of view."

"You've done marvelously with them so far," she told him. "They're polite and generous and loving."

"So was their mother," he remarked and for a few

seconds, his face was lined with grief before he got it under control. "She loved them."

"You said Bess was like her," she reminded him.

"Yes," he said at once. "She had long, wavy blond hair, just that same color. Jenny looks more like me. But Bess is more like me."

She smiled. "I've noticed. She has a very hard head when she doesn't want to do something."

He shrugged. "Being stubborn isn't always a bad thing. Persistence is the key to most successes in life."

"Yes." She searched his hard face, seeing the years of work and worry. It was a good, strong face, but it wasn't handsome.

He was looking at her, too, and something stirred inside him, a need that he had to work to put down. He moved out the door. "Sleep well, Kasie," he said curtly.

"You, too."

He closed the door behind him, without looking at her again. She went back to her movie, but with much less enthusiasm.

# Chapter 5

The week went by slowly, and the girls, to Kasie's dismay, became her shadows. She worried herself sick trying to keep Gil from noticing, especially after the harsh comments he'd made about her job responsibilities. It didn't help that she kept remembering the feel of his arm around her at the movie theater, and the warm clasp of his big lean hand in her own. She was afraid to even look at him, because she was afraid her attraction to him might show.

Saturday came and the house was full of strangers. Kasie found it hard to mix with high society people, so she stuck to Miss Parsons and the girls. Miss Parsons took the opportunity to sneak back inside the house while Kasie watched the girls. Everything went well at first, because Gil was too busy with guests to notice that Miss Parsons was missing. But not for long. Kasie had given the girls a beach ball to play with, which was her one big mistake of the morning.

It wouldn't have been so bad if she'd just let the children's beach ball fly into the swimming pool in the first place. The problem was that, if she didn't stop it, Pauline was going to get it in the mouth, which wouldn't improve the already-bad situation between her and Kasie. Bess and Jenny didn't like Gil Callister's secretary. Neither did Kasie, but she loved the little girls and didn't want them to get into trouble. So she gave in to an impulse, and tried valiantly to divert the ball from its unexpecting target.

Predictably, she overreached, lost her footing and made an enormous splash as she landed, fully clothed, in the deep end. And, of course, she couldn't swim...

Gil looked up from the prospectus he'd been reading when he heard the splash. He connected Kasie's fall, the beach ball, and his two little blond giggling daughters at once. He shook his head and grimaced. He put aside the prospectus and dived in to save Kasie, Bermuda shorts, Hawaiian shirt and all.

Her late parents had lived long enough to see the irony of the second name they'd given her. Her middle name was Grace, but she wasn't graceful. She was all long legs and arms. She wasn't pretty, but she had a lovely body, and the thin white dress she was wearing became transparent in the water. It was easily noticed that she was wearing only the flimsiest of briefs and a bra that barely covered her pert breasts. Just the thing, she thought miserably, to wear in front of the Callisters' business partners who were here for a pool party on the big ranch. Feline blond Pauline Raines was laughing her head off at Kasie's desperate treading of water. Just you wait, lady, she fumed. Next time I'll give Bess a soccer ball to bean you with and I won't step in the way...!

Her head went under as her arms gave out. She took a huge breath as powerful arms encircled and lifted her clear of the deep water. It would have to be Gil who rescued her, she thought miserably. John wasn't even looking their way. He'd have dived in after her in a minute, she knew, if he'd seen her fall. But while he was nice, and kind, he wasn't Gil, who was beginning to have a frightening effect on Kasie's heart. She glanced at Pauline as she spluttered. Kasie wished that she was beautiful like Pauline. She looked the very image of an efficient secretary. Kasie had great typing speed, dictation skills and organizational expertise, but she was only ordinary-looking. Besides, she was a social disaster, and she'd just proved it to Gil and all the guests.

Gil had been unexpectedly kind to her at the theater when he'd taken her with the girls to see the movie. She still tingled, remembering his hand holding hers. This, however, was much worse. Her breasts were almost bare in the thin blouse, and she felt the hard muscular wall of his chest with wonder and pleasure and a little fear, because she'd never felt such heady sensations in her body before. She wondered if he'd fire her for making a scene at this pool party, to which a lot of very wealthy and prominent cattlemen and their wives had been invited.

To give him credit, she hadn't exactly inspired confidence on the job in the past few weeks. Two weeks earlier, she tripped on the front steps and landed in a rosebush at the very feet of a visiting cattleman from Texas who'd almost turned purple trying not to laugh. Then there had been the ice-cream incident last week, which still embarrassed her. Bess had threatened Kasie with a big glop of chocolate ice cream. While

Kasie was backing away, laughing helplessly, Gil had come into the house in dirty chaps and boots and shirt with his hat jerked low over one blue eye and his mouth a thin line, with blood streaming from a cut on his forehead. Bess had thrown the ice cream at Kasie, who ducked, just in time for it to hit Gil right in the forehead. While he was wiping it off, Kasie grabbed the spoon from Bess and waited for the explosion as her boss wiped the ice cream away and looked at her. Those blue eyes could cut like diamonds. They actually glittered. But he hadn't said a word. He'd just looked at her, before he turned and continued down the hall to the staircase that led up to his room.

Now, here she was half-drowned from a swimming pool accident, having made a spectacle of herself yet again.

"I wonder if I could get work in Hollywood?" she sputtered as she hung on for dear life. "There must be a market for terminal clumsiness somewhere!"

Gil raised an eyebrow and gave her a slow, speaking glance before he pulled her close against his chest and turned toward the concrete steps at the far end. He walked up out of the pool, streaming water, and started toward the house. "Don't struggle, Kasie," he said at her temple, and his voice sounded odd.

"Sorry," she coughed. "You can put me down, now. I'm okay. I can walk."

"If I put you down, you're going to become the entertainment," he said enigmatically at her ear. He looked over his shoulder. "John, look after the girls until I get back!" he called.

"Oh, I'll watch them, Gil!" Pauline interrupted lazily. "Come over here, girls!" she called, without even looking in their direction.

"John will watch them," Gil said emphatically and didn't move until his lean, lanky brother jumped up and went toward his nieces, grinning.

Gil went up the staircase with Kasie held close to his chest. "Why can't you swim?" he asked.

His deep, slow voice made her feel funny. So did the close, almost intimate contact with him. She nibbled on her lower lip, feeling soggy and disheveled and embarrassed. "I'm afraid of the water."

"Why?" he persisted.

She wouldn't answer him. It would do no good, and she didn't want to remember. Probably he'd never seen anyone drown. "Sorry I messed up the pool party," she murmured.

He shook her gently as they passed the landing and paused at her bedroom door. "Stop apologizing every second word," he said curtly as he put her down. He held her there with two big, lean hands on her upper arms and studied her intently in the dim light of the wall sconces.

The feel of all that warm strength against her made her giddy. She'd never been so close to him before. He was ten years older than Kasie, and he had an authority and maturity that must have been apparent even when he'd been her age. She had tried to think of him as Bess and Jenny's daddy, but after their closeness at the movie theater, it was almost impossible to think of him as anything but a mature, sexy man.

"I can't seem to make you understand that the girls are Miss Parsons' responsibility, not yours!" He saw her faint flush and scowled down at her. "Speaking of Miss Parsons, where in hell is she?"

She cleared her throat and pushed back a soggy strand of dark hair. "She's in the office."

"Doing what?"

She shifted, but he didn't let go of her arms. That unblinking, ferocious blue stare robbed her of a smart retort. "All right," she said heavily. "She's doing the withholding on John's tax readout." He didn't speak. She looked up and grimaced. "Well, I'm not up on tax law, and she is."

"So you traded duties without permission, is that it?"

She hesitated. "Yes. I'm sorry. But it's just for today! You already know that she doesn't...well, she doesn't like children very much, really, and I hate taxes..."

"I know."

"I shouldn't have given them the beach ball. I thought they were going into the shallow part of the pool with it. And then Bess threw it..."

"Right at Pauline's expensive new coiffure," Gil finished for her. He pursed his sensuous lips and searched her face. "You won't tell on them, of course. You took the blame for the ice cream, too. And when one of Jenny's toys tripped you on the front steps and you went into the rosebush, you blamed that on clumsiness."

"You knew?" she asked, surprised.

"I've been a father for five years," he mused. "I know all sorts of things." His pale blue eyes slid very slowly down Kasie's wet dress and narrowed on what was showing. She had the most delicious body. Every line and curve of it was on view where the thin dress was plastered to her body. Her breasts were perfectly shaped and the nipples were dusky. The feel of her against his chest, even through her wet blouse and his cotton shirt, had almost knocked the breath out of him. It upset him that he was noticing these things about her. He was beginning to react to them, too. He had to get out of here. She was so young…

He cursed under his breath. "You'd better change," he said curtly. He turned on his heel and went toward the staircase.

"About Miss Parsons…!" she called after him, in one last attempt to ward off retribution.

"You might as well consider the girls your job from now on," he said angrily. "I can see that it's a losing battle to keep you away from them. I'll give Miss Parsons to John. He won't enjoy the view as much, but keeping out of prison because we can't figure out tax forms might sweeten the deal," he said, without breaking stride. "When you have some spare time, you can continue giving Pauline computer lessons. That includes Monday morning. Mrs. Charters can watch the girls while you work with Pauline."

"But I'm not a trained governess. I'm a secretary!" she insisted.

"Great. You can let Bess dictate letters to you for her dolls."

"But…!"

It was too late. He never argued. He just kept walking. She threw up her hands and went back into her room. She started toward the bathroom to change out of her wet things when she got a look at herself in the mirror. The whole outfit was transparent. She remembered Gil's intent stare and blushed all the way to her toes. No wonder he'd been looking at her. Everything she had was on view! She wondered how she'd ever be able to look him in the eye again.

She changed and went back to the pool party, dejected and miserable. It was hard to believe that she'd not even had a mild crush on John when she first went to work for the Callisters. He was handsome, and very sexy, but she just didn't feel that way about him. Fortunately he'd never felt that way about her, either. John had some secret woman in his past, and now he didn't get serious about anyone. Kasie had heard that from Mrs. Charters, who was a veritable storehouse of information about it. John didn't look to Kasie like a man with a broken heart. But maybe he played the field to camouflage it.

Kasie had never really been in love. She'd had crushes on TV celebrities and movie stars, and on boys at school—and one summer she'd had a real case on a boy who lived near Mama Luke, her aunt, in Billings. But those had all been very innocent, limited to kisses and light caresses and not much desire.

All that had changed when Gil Callister held her hand at the movies. And when Gil had carried her up the staircase this morning, she was on fire with pleasure. She was still shivery with new sensations, which she didn't understand at all. Gil was her boss and he disliked her. She'd been spending more time with the girls than the grown-ups because John didn't like to do paperwork and he was always dodging dictation. He could usually be found out with the men on the ranch, helping with whatever routine task was going on at the time. Gil did that, too, of course, but not because he didn't like paperwork. Gil rarely ever sat still.

Mrs. Charters said it was because he'd loved his wife and had never gotten over her unexpected death from a freak horseback-riding accident. She was only twenty-six years old.

That had been only three years ago. Since then, Gil had hired a succession of nurses, at first, and then motherly governesses to watch over the girls. Old Mrs. Harris had retired and then Gil had hired Miss Parsons in desperation, over a virtual flood of young marriageable women who had their eye on either Gil or John. Kasie remembered Gil saying that he had no interest in marriage ever again. At that time, she couldn't have imagined feeling attracted to a widowed man with two children who had the personality of a spitting cobra.

For her first few weeks on the job, he'd watched Kasie. He hadn't wanted his children around Kasie, and made it plain. Amazing, how much that had hurt.

They were such darling little girls.

At least, she thought, now she could spend time with them and not have to sneak around doing it. Gil might not like her, but he couldn't deny that his daughters did. Probably he felt that he didn't have a choice.

Kasie was going to miss the secretarial work, and she wondered how Gil would manage with Pauline, who absolutely hated clerical duties. The woman only did it to be near Gil, but he didn't seem to realize it. Or if he did, he didn't care.

She tried to picture Gil married to Pauline and it wounded her. Pauline was shallow and selfish. She didn't really like the girls, and she'd probably find some way to get them out of her hair when she and Gil married, if they did. Kasie hated the very idea of such a marriage, but she was a little nobody in the world and Gil Callister was a millionaire. She couldn't even tease him or flirt with him, because he might think she was after him for his wealth. It made her self-conscious, so she became uneasy around him and tongue-tied to boot.

That made him even more irritable. Sunday afternoon there was another storm and he and the men had to go out and work the cattle. He came in just after dark, drenched, unfastening his shirt on the way into the office. His hair was plastered to his scalp and his spurs jingled as he walked, his leather bat-wing chaps making flapping noises with every stride of his long, powerful jean-clad legs. His boots were soaked, too, and caked with mud.

"Mrs. Charters will be after you," Kasie remarked as she lifted her eyes from the badly scribbled notes John had left, which Miss Parsons had asked her to help decipher. Miss Parsons had already gone up to bed, anticipating a very early start on work the next morning.

"It's my damned house," he shot at her irritably, running a hand through his drenched hair to get it off his forehead. "I can drip wherever I please!"

"Suit yourself," Kasie replied. "But red mud won't come out of Persian wool carpets."

He gave her a hard glare, but he sat down in a chair and pulled off the mud-caked boots, tossing them onto the wide brick hearth of the fireplace, where they wouldn't soil anything delicate. His white socks were soaked as well, but he didn't take them off. He sat down behind his desk, picked up the telephone and made a call.

"Where are the girls?" he asked while he waited for the call to be answered.

"Watching the new *Pokémon* movie up in their room," Kasie said. "Miss Parsons can't read John's handwriting, so I'm deciphering this for her so she can start early tomorrow morning on the payroll and the quarterly estimated taxes that are due in June. If that's all right," she added politely.

He just glared at her. "Hello, Lonnie?" he said suddenly into the telephone receiver he was holding. "Can you give me the name of that mechanic who worked on Harris's truck last month? Yes, the one who doesn't need a damned computer to tell him what's wrong with the engine. Got his number? Just a minute." He fished in the drawer for a pen, grabbed an envelope and wrote a number on it. "Sure thing. Thanks." He hung up and dialed again.

While he spoke to the mechanic, Kasie finished transcribing John's terrible handwriting neatly for Miss Parsons.

Gil hung up and got to his feet, retrieving his boots. "If you've got a few minutes free, I need you to take some dictation for me," he told Kasie.

"I'll be glad to."

He gave her a narrow appraisal. "I've got a man coming over to look at my cattle truck," he added. "If he gets here while I'm in the shower, show him into the living room and don't let him leave. He can listen to an engine and tell you what's wrong with it."

"But it's Sunday," she began.

"I need the truck to haul cattle tomorrow. I'm sure he went to church this morning, so it's all right," he assured her dryly. "Besides…"

The ringing of the phone interrupted him. He jerked up the receiver. "Callister," he said.

There was a pause, during which his face became harder than Kasie had ever seen it. "Yes," he replied to a question. "I'll talk to John when he gets back in, but I can tell you what the answer will be." He smiled coldly. "I'm sure that if you use your imagination, you can figure that out without too much difficulty. No, I don't. I don't give a damn. Do what you please with them." There was a longer pause and Kasie thought she'd never seen such coldness in a man's eyes. "I don't need a thing, thanks. Yes. You do that."

He hung up. "My parents," he said harshly. "With an invitation to come and bring the girls to their estate on Long Island next week."

"Are you going?"

He looked briefly sardonic. "They're hosting a party for some people who are interested in seeing what a real cattleman looks like," he said surprisingly. "They're trying to sell them on an advertising contract for their sports magazine and they think John and I might be useful." He sounded bitter and angry. "They try this occasionally, but John and I don't go. They can make money on their own. I'll be upstairs if the mechanic comes. Tell him the truck's in the barn with one of my men. He can go right on out."

"Okay."

He walked out and Kasie stared after him. The conversation with his parents hadn't been pleasant for him. He seemed to dislike them intensely. She knew that they were never mentioned around the girls, and John never spoke of them, either. She wondered what they'd done to make their sons so hostile. Then she remembered what Gil had said, about their being used by their parents only to make money, and it all began to make sense. Perhaps they didn't really want children at all. What a pity, that their sons were nothing more than sales incentives to them.

The mechanic did come while Gil was upstairs. Kasie went with him onto the long porch and showed him where the barn was, so that he could drive on down there and park his truck. The rain had stopped, though, so he didn't have to worry about getting wet. There was a pleasant dripping sound off the eaves of the house, and the delicious smell of wet flowers in the darkness.

Kasie sat down in the porch swing and rocked it into motion. It was a perfect night, now that the storm had abated. She could hear crickets, or maybe frogs, chirping all around the flowering shrubs that surrounded the front porch. It reminded her, for some reason, of Africa. She vaguely remembered sitting in a porch swing with her mother and Kantor when their father was away working. There were the delicious smells of cooking from the house, and the spicy smells drifting from the harbor nearby, as well as the familiar sound of African workers singing and humming as they worked around the settlement. It was a long time ago, when she still had a family. Now, except for Mama Luke, she was completely alone. It was a cold, empty feeling.

The screen door suddenly opened and Gil came out onto the porch. His blond hair was still damp, faintly unruly at the edges and tending to curl. He was wearing a blue checked Western shirt with clean jeans and nice boots. He looked just the way a working cowboy should when he was cleaned up, she thought, trying to imagine him a century earlier.

"Is the mechanic here?" he asked abruptly when he spotted Kasie in the swing.

"Yes, I sent him on down to the barn."

He went down the steps gracefully and stalked to the barn. He was gone about five minutes and when he came out of the barn, so did the mechanic. They shook hands and the mechanic drove off.

"A fuse," he murmured, shaking his head as he came up the steps and dropped into the swing at Kasie's side. "A damned fuse, and the whole panel went down. Imagine that."

"Sometimes it's the little things that give the most trouble," she murmured, shy with him.

He put an arm behind her and rocked the swing into motion. "I like the way you smell, Kasie," he said lazily. "You always remind me of roses."

"I'm allergic to perfume," she confided. "The florals are the only ones I can wear without sneezing my head off."

"Where are my babies?" he asked.

"Mrs. Charters is baking cookies with them in the kitchen," she said, smiling. "They love to cook. So do I. We've all learned a lot from Mrs. Charters."

He looked down at her in the darkness. One lean hand went to the braid at the back of her head, and he tugged on it gently. "You're mysterious," he murmured. "I don't really know anything about you."

"There's not much to tell," she told him. "I'm just ordinary."

He shifted, and she felt his powerful thigh against her leg. Her body came alive with fleeting little stabs of pleasure. She could feel her breath catching in her throat as she breathed. He was too close.

She started to move, but it was too late. His arm curled her into his body, and the warm, hard pressure of his mouth pushed her head back against the swing while he fed hungrily on her lips.

Part of her wanted to resist, but a stronger part was completely powerless. She reached up and put her arms around his neck and opened her lips for him. She felt him stiffen, hesitate, catch his breath. Then his mouth became rough and demanding, and he dragged her across his legs, folding her close while he kissed her until her mouth was swollen and tender.

He nibbled her upper lip, fighting to breathe normally. "Don't let me do this," he warned.

"You're bigger than I am," she murmured breathlessly.

"That's no excuse at all."

Her fingers trailed over his hard mouth and down to his chest where they rested. She stared at the wide curve of his mouth with a kind of wonder that a man like this, good-looking and charming and wealthy, would look twice at a chestnut mouse like Kasie. Perhaps he needed glasses.

He touched her oval face, tracing its soft lines in a warm, damp darkness that was suddenly like an exotic, faraway place. Kasie felt as if she'd come home. Impulsively, she let her head slide down his arm until it rested in the crook of his elbow. She watched his expression harden, heard his breathing change. His lean fingers moved down her chin and throat until they were at the top button of her shirtwaist dress. They hesitated there.

She lay looking up at him patiently, curiously, ablaze with unfamiliar longings and delight.

"Kasie," he whispered, and his long fingers began to sensually move the top button out of its buttonhole. As it came free, he heard her soft gasp, felt the jerk of her body, and knew that this was new territory for her.

His hand started to slide gently into the opening he'd made. He watched Kasie, lying so sweetly in his embrace, giving him free license with her innocence, and he shivered with desire.

But even as he felt the soft warmth of the skin at her collarbone, laughing young voices came drifting out onto the porch as the front door opened.

Gil moved Kasie back into her own seat abruptly and stood up.

"Daddy's home!" Bess cried, and she and Jenny ran to him, to be scooped up and kissed heartily.

"I'll, uh, just go and get my pad so that you can dictate that letter you mentioned," Kasie said as she got up, too.

"You will not," Gil said, his voice still a little husky. "Go to bed, Kasie. It can wait. In the morning, you can tutor Pauline on the computer, so that she can take over inputting the cattle records. John won't be in until late tonight, and he leaves early tomorrow for the cattle show in San Antonio. There's nothing in the office that can't wait."

She was both disappointed and relieved. It was getting harder to deny Gil anything he wanted. She couldn't have imagined that she was such a wanton person only a few weeks ago. She didn't know what to do.

"Okay, I'll call it a night," she said, trying to disguise her nervousness. "Good night, babies," she told Bess and Jenny with a smile. "Sleep tight."

"Will you tell us a story, Kasie?" Bess began.

"I'll tell you a story tonight. Kasie needs her rest. All right?" he asked the girls.

"All right, Daddy," Jenny murmured, laying her sleepy head on his shoulder.

They all went upstairs together. Kasie didn't quite meet his eyes as she went down the hall to her own room. She didn't sleep very much, either.

# Chapter 6

Pauline Raines was half an hour late Monday morning. Gil had already gone out to check on some cattle that was being shipped off. John had left before daylight to fly to San Antonio, where the cattle trailer was taking his champion bull, Ebony King, for the cattle show. While the girls took their nap, Kasie helped Miss Parsons with John's correspondence and fielded the telephone. Now that it was just past roundup, things weren't quite as hectic, but sales reports were coming in on the culled cattle being shipped, and they weren't even all on the computer yet. Neither were most of the new calf crop.

Miss Parsons had gone to the post office when Pauline arrived wearing a neat black suit with a fetching blue scarf. She glared at Kasie as she threw her purse down on the chair.

"Here I am," she said irritably. "I don't usually come in before ten, but Gil said I had to be early, to work on this stupid computer. I don't see why I need to learn it.''

''Because you'll have to put in all the information we're getting about the new calves and replacement heifers,'' Kasie explained patiently. ''It's backing up.''

''You can do that,'' Pauline said haughtily. ''You're John's secretary.''

''Not anymore,'' she replied calmly. ''I'm going to take care of the girls while Miss Parsons takes my place in John's office. She's going to handle all the tax work.''

That piece of information didn't please Pauline. ''You're a secretary,'' she pointed out.

''That's what I told Mr. Callister, but it didn't change his mind,'' Kasie replied tersely.

''So now I'll have to do all your work while Miss Parsons does taxes? I won't! Surely you'll have enough free time to put these records on the computer! Two little girls don't require much watching. Just put them in front of the television!''

Kasie almost bit her tongue right through keeping back a hot reply. ''It isn't going to be hard to use the computer. It will save you hours of paperwork.''

Pauline gave her a glare. ''Debbie always put these things on the computer.''

''Debbie quit because she couldn't do two jobs at once,'' Kasie said, and was vindicated for the jibe when she saw Pauline's discomfort. ''You really will enjoy the time the computer saves you, once you understand how it works.''

''I don't need this job, didn't anyone tell you?'' the older woman asked. ''I'm wealthy. I only do it to be near Gil. It gives us more time together, while we're seeing how compatible we are. Which reminds me, don't think you're onto a cushy job looking after those children," she added haughtily. "Gil and I are going to be looking for a boarding school very soon."

"Boarding school?" Kasie exclaimed, horrified.

"I've already checked out several," Pauline said. "It isn't good for little girls to become too attached to their fathers. It interferes with Gil's social life."

"I hadn't noticed."

Pauline frowned. "What do you mean, you hadn't noticed?"

"Well, Mr. Callister is almost a generation older than I am," she said deliberately.

"Oh." Pauline smiled secretively. "I see."

"He's a very kind man," Kasie emphasized, "but I don't think of him in that way," she added, lying through her teeth.

Pauline for once seemed speechless.

"Here, let's get started," Kasie said as she turned on the computer, trying to head off trouble. She hoped that comment would keep her out of trouble with Pauline, who obviously considered Gil Callister her personal property. Kasie had enough problems without adding a jealous secretary to them. Even if she did privately think Gil was the sexiest man she'd ever known.

Pauline seemed determined to make every second of work as hard as humanly possible for Kasie. She insisted on three coffee breaks before noon, and the pressing nature of the information coming in by fax kept Kasie working long after Pauline called it a day at three in the afternoon and went home. If Mrs. Charters hadn't helped out by letting Bess and Jenny make cookies, Kasie wouldn't have been able to do as much as she did.

She'd only just finished the new computer entries when Gil came in, dusty and sweaty and half out of humor. He didn't say a word. He went to the liquor cabinet and poured himself a scotch and water, and he drank half of it before he even looked at Kasie.

It took her a minute to realize that he was openly glaring at her.

"Is something wrong?" she asked uneasily.

"Pauline called me on the cell phone a few minutes ago. She said you're making it impossible for her to do her job," he replied finally.

Her heart skipped. So that was how the other woman was going to make points—telling lies.

"I've been showing her how to key in this data, and that's all I've done," Kasie told him quietly. "She hates the computer."

"Odd that she's done so well with it up until now," he said suspiciously.

"Debbie did well with it," Kasie replied bluntly, flushing a little at his angry tenseness. "She was apparently having to put her own work as well as Pauline's into the computer."

He took another sip of the drink. He didn't look convinced. "That isn't what Pauline says," he told her. "And I want to know why you suddenly want my girls in a boarding school, after you've spent weeks behind my back and against instructions winning them over, so they're attached to you." He added angrily, "I meant it when I said I have no plans to marry. So if that changes your mind about wanting to take care of them, say so and I'll give you a reference and two weeks severance pay!"

He really did look ferocious. Kasie's head was spinning from the accusations. "Excuse me?"

He finished the drink and put the glass down firmly on the counter below the liquor cabinet. His pale eyes were glittery. "John and I spent six of the worst years of our lives at boarding school," he added unexpectedly. "I'm not putting my babies in any boarding school."

Kasie felt as if she were being attacked by invisible hands. She stood up, her mind reeling from the charges. Pauline had been busy!

"I haven't said anything about boarding school," she defended herself. "Pauline said…"

He held up a hand. "I know Pauline," he told her. "I've known her most of my life. She doesn't tell lies."

Boy, was he in for a shock a little further on down the road, she thought, but she didn't say anything else. She was already in too much trouble, and none of it of her own making.

She didn't say a word. She just looked at him with big, gray, wounded eyes.

He moved closer, his mind reeling from Pauline's comments about Kasie. He didn't want to believe that Kasie was so two-faced that she'd play up to the girls to get in Gil's good graces and then want to see them sent off to boarding school. But what did he really know about her, after all? She had no family except an aunt in Billings, or so she said, and except for the information on her application that mentioned secretarial school, nothing about her early education was apparent. She was mysterious. He didn't like mysteries.

He stopped just in front of her, his face hard and threatening as he glared down at her.

"Where were you born?" he asked abruptly.

The question surprised her. She became flustered. "I, well, I was born in...in Africa."

He hadn't expected that answer, and it showed. *"Africa?"*

"Yes. In Sierra Leone," she added.

He frowned. "What were your parents doing in Africa?"

"They worked there."

"I see." He didn't, but she looked as if she hated talking about it. The mystery only deepened.

"Maybe you're right," she said, unnerved by his unexpected anger and the attack by Pauline, which made her look like a gold digger. "Maybe I'm not the best person to look after the girls. If you like, I'll hand in my notice...!"

He had her by both shoulders with a firm grip and the expression on his face made her want to back away.

"And just for the record, ten years isn't a generation!" he said through his teeth as he glared down at her. His gaze dropped to her soft, generous mouth and it was like lightning striking. He couldn't help himself. The memory of her body in his arms on the porch swing took away the last wisp of his willpower. He bent quickly and took that beautiful softness under his hard lips in a fever of hunger, probing insistently at her tight mouth with his tongue.

Kasie, who'd never been kissed in any intimate way, even by Gil, froze like ice at the skillful, invasive intimacy of his mouth. She couldn't believe what was happening. Her hands against his chest clenched and she closed her eyes tightly as she strained against his hold.

Slowly it seemed to get through to him that she was shocked at the insistence. He lifted his demanding mouth and looked at her. This was familiar territory for him. But, it wasn't for her, and it was apparent. After the way she'd responded to him the night before, he was surprised that she balked at a deep kiss. But, then, he remembered her chaste gowns and her strange attitude about wearing her beautiful hair loose. She wasn't fighting him. She looked... strange.

His lean hands loosened, became caressing on her upper arms under the short sleeve of her dress. "I'm sorry. It's all right," he breathed as he bent again. "I won't be rough with you. It's all right, Kasie..."

His lips barely brushed hers, tender now instead of demanding. A few seconds of tenderness brought a sigh from her lips. He smiled against her soft mouth as he coaxed it to part. He nibbled the full upper lip, tasting its velvety underside with his tongue, enjoying her reactions to him. He felt her young body begin to relax into his. She worked for him. She was an employee. He'd just been giving her hell about trying to trap him into marriage. So why was he doing this...? She made a soft sound under her breath and her hands tightened on the hard muscles of his upper arms. His brows began to knit as sensation pulsed through him at her shy response. What did it matter *why* he was doing it, he asked himself, and threw caution to the winds.

His arms went around her, gently smoothing her against the muscular length of him, while his mouth dragged a response under its tender pressure. He felt her gasp, felt her shiver, then felt her arms sliding around his waist as she gave in to the explosion of warm sensation that his hungry kiss provoked in her.

It was like flying, he thought dizzily. He lifted her against him, feeding on the softness of her mouth, the clinging wonder of her arms around him. It had been years since a kiss had been this sweet, this fulfilling. Not since Darlene had he been so hungry for a woman's mouth. Darlene. Darlene. Kasie was so much like her…

Only the need to breathe forced him to put her down and lift his head. His turbulent eyes met her dazed ones and he had to fight to catch his breath.

"Why did you do that?" she asked unsteadily.

He was scowling. He touched her mouth with a lean forefinger. "I don't know," he said honestly. "Do you want me to apologize?" he added quietly.

"Are you sorry?" she returned.

"I am not," he said, every word deliberate as he stared into her eyes.

That husky statement made her tingle all over with delicious sensations, but he still looked formidable. His lean fingers caught her shoulders and gently moved her away. She looked as devastated as he felt.

Her eyes searched his quietly. She was shaking inside from the delicious crush of his mouth, so unexpected. "What did you mean, about ten years not being a generation?" she asked suddenly.

"You harp on my age," he murmured coolly, but he was still looking at her soft, swollen mouth. "You shouldn't tell Pauline things you don't want me to hear. She can't keep a secret."

"I wouldn't tell her my middle name," she muttered. "She hates me, haven't you noticed?"

"No, I hadn't."

"It would never have been my idea to send the girls to boarding school," she insisted. "I love them."

His eyebrows lifted. Kasie didn't appear to be lying. But Pauline had been so convincing. And Kasie was mysterious. He wanted to know why she was so secretive about her past. He wanted to know everything about her. Her mouth was sweet and soft and innocent, and he had to fight not to bend and take it again. She was nervous with him now, as she hadn't been before. That meant that the attraction was mutual. It made him feel a foot taller.

"Pauline wants to go down to Nassau for a few days with the girls. I want you to come with us," he said abruptly.

She gaped at him. "She won't want me along," she said with conviction.

"She will when she has to start looking out for Bess and Jenny. Her idea of watching them is to let them do what they please. That could be disastrous even around a swimming pool."

She grimaced. It would be a horrible trip. "We'd have to fly," she said, hating the very thought of getting on an airplane. She'd lost everyone she'd ever loved in the air, and he didn't know.

"The girls like you," he persisted gently.

"I'd really rather not," she said worriedly.

"Then I'll make it an order," he said shortly. "You're coming. Have you got a current passport?"

"Yes," she said without thinking.

He was surprised. "I was going to say that if you didn't have one, a birth certificate or even a voter's registration slip would be adequate.'' He was suspicious. "Why do you keep a passport?''

"In case I get kidnapped by terrorists,'' she said, tongue in cheek, trying to put aside the fear of the upcoming trip.

He rolled his eyes, let her go and walked to the door. "We'll go Friday,'' he said. "Don't take much with you,'' he added. "We'll fly commercial and I don't like baggage claim.''

"Okay.''

"And stop letting me kiss you,'' he added with faint arrogance. "I've already made it clear that there's no future in it. I won't marry again, not even to provide the girls with a grown-up playmate.''

"I do know that,'' she said, wounded by the words. "But I'm not the one doing the grabbing,'' she pointed out.

He gave her an odd look before he left.

She could have told him that she didn't have much to take anywhere, and she almost blurted out why she was afraid of airplanes. But he was already out the door. She touched her mouth. She tasted scotch whiskey on her lips and she was amazed that she hadn't noticed while he was kissing her. Why had he kissed her again? she wondered dazedly. The other question was why had she kissed him back? Her head was reeling with the sudden shift in their relationship since the night before. Kissing seemed to be addictive. Perhaps she should cut her losses and quit right away. But that thought was very unpleasant indeed. She decided that meeting trouble head-on was so much better than running from it. She had to conquer her fear and try to put the past behind her once and for all. Yes, she would go to Nassau with him and the girls—

and Pauline. It might very well put things into perspective if she saw Pauline and Gil as a family, while there was still time to stop her rebellious heart from falling in love.

Kasie's seat was separated from Gil's, Pauline's and the girls' by ten rows. Gil didn't appear pleased and he tried to change seat assignments, but it wasn't possible. Kasie was rather relieved. She was uncomfortable with Gil since he'd kissed her so passionately.

Pauline was furious that Kasie had been included in the trip. She was doing everything in her power to get Kasie out of Gil's life, but nothing was going the way she planned. She'd envisioned just the four of them in the exquisite islands, where she could convince Gil that they should get married. He agreed to her suggestion about the trip more easily than she'd hoped, and then he said Kasie would have to come along to take care of the girls. He didn't even mention boarding school, as if he didn't believe Kasie had suggested it. Pauline was losing ground with him by the day. She could cheerfully have pushed Kasie out of the terminal window. Well, she was going to get rid of Miss Prim over there, whatever it took. One way or another, she was going to get Kasie out of Gil's house!

They boarded the plane, and Kasie smiled with false bravado as she passed the girls with a wave and found her window seat. There was only one seat next to hers. She was watching the people file in while she fought her own fear. Seconds later, a tall blond man wearing khakis swung into the seat beside hers and gave her an appreciative smile.

"And I thought this was going to be a boring flight," he chuckled as he stuffed his one carry-on bag under the seat in front of him and fastened his seat belt. "I'm Zeke Mulligan," he introduced himself with a smile. "I write freelance travel articles for magazines."

"I'm Kasie Mayfield," she replied, offering her small hand with a wan smile. "I'm a governess to two sweet little girls."

"Where are the sweet little girls?" he asked with a grin.

"Ten rows that way," she pointed. "With their dad and his venomous secretary."

"Ouch, the jealousy monster strikes, hmm?" he asked. "Does she see you as competition?"

"That would be one for the books," she chuckled. "She's blond and beautiful."

"What are you, chestnut-haired and repulsive?" he chided. "Looks aren't everything, fellow adventurer."

"Adventuress," she corrected. She glanced out the window and noticed the movement of the motorized carts away from the plane. It was going to take off soon. Sure enough, she heard the rev of the engines and saw the flight attendants take up their positions to demonstrate the life vests even as the plane started to taxi out of its concourse space. "Oh, gosh," she groaned, tightening her hands on the arms of her seat.

"Afraid of flying?" he asked gently.

"I lost my family in a plane crash," she said in a rough whisper. "This is the first time I've flown, since I lost them. I don't know if I can…!"

She'd started to pull at her seat belt. He caught her hand and stilled it. "Listen to me," he said gently, "air travel is the safest kind. I've been knocking around on airplanes for ten years, I've been around the world three times. It's all right," he stressed, his voice low and deep and comforting. His fingers contracted around hers. "You just hold on to me. I'll get you through takeoff and landing. Once you've conquered the fear, you'll be fine."

"Are you sure?" she asked on a choked laugh.

"I walked away from a crash once," he told her quietly. "A week later I had to get on a plane for Paris. Yes," he added. "I'm sure. If I could do it, I know you can."

Her lips parted as she let out the breath she'd been holding. He was nice. He was very nice. He made her feel utterly safe. She clung to his hand as the airplane taxied to the runway and the pilot announced that they were next in line to take off.

"Here we go," her seat companion said in her ear. "Think of *Star Trek* when the ship goes into light speed," he added on a chuckle. "Think of it as being flung up into the stars. It's exciting. It's great!"

She held on tighter as the plane taxied onto the runway, revved up its engines and began to pick up speed.

"We can even sing the Air Force song as we go," he said. "I spent four years in it, so I can coach you if you can't remember the words. Come on, Kasie. Sing!"

Kasie started to hum the words of the well-known song.

The passengers around them noticed Kasie's terror and her companion's protective attitude, and suddenly they all started singing the Air Force song. It diverted Kasie with uproarious laughter as the big airplane shot up into the blue sky, leaving her stomach and her fears far behind.

"I'm very grateful," she told him when they were comfortably leveled off and the flight attendants were getting the refreshment cart ready to take down the aisle. "You can't imagine how terrified I was to get on this plane."

"Yes, I can. I'm glad I was here. Where are you staying in Nassau?" he added.

She laughed. "I'm sorry. I don't know! I didn't realize that until just now. My boss will have all the details in hand, and a driver to meet us when we land. I didn't ask."

"New Providence is a small island," he told her. "We'll see each other again. I'm at the Crystal Palace on Cable Beach. You can phone me if you get a few free minutes and we'll have lunch."

"Do you go overseas to do stories?" she asked.

He nodded. "All over the world. It's a great job, and I actually get paid to do it." He leaned close to her ear. "And once, I worked for the CIA."

"You didn't!" she exclaimed, impressed.

"Just for a year, while I was in South America," he assured her. "I might have kept it up, but I was married then and she didn't want me taking chances, especially while she was carrying our son."

"She doesn't travel with you?" she asked curiously.

"She died, of a particularly virulent tropical fever," he said with a sad smile. "My son is six, and I leave him with my parents when I have to go away during his school year. During the summer, he goes places with me. He loves it, too."

He pulled out his wallet and showed her several

photographs of a child who was his mirror image. "His name's Daniel, but I call him Dano."

"He really is cute."

"Thanks."

The flight attendant was two rows away, with snack meals and drinks. Kasie settled down to lunch with no more reservations. She'd landed on her feet. She wondered what Gil would think if he saw her with this nice young man. Nothing, probably, she thought bitterly, not when he was so wrapped up in Pauline. Well, she wasn't going to let that spoil her trip.

Nassau was unexpected. Kasie fell in love with it on first sight. She'd seen postcards of the Bahamas, and she'd always assumed that the vivid turquoise and sapphire color of the waters was exaggerated. But it wasn't. Those vivid, surreal colors were exactly what the water looked like, and the beaches were as white as sugar. She stared out the window of the hired car with her breath catching in her chest. She'd gone overseas with her parents as a child, but to distant and primitive places. She remembered the terror of those places far better than she remembered the scenery, even at so young an age. Even now, it was hard to think about how she'd lost the parents who'd loved her and Kantor so much. It was harder to think of Kantor…

"Do stop pressing your nose against the glass, Kasie. You look about Jenny's age!" Pauline chided from her seat beside Gil.

"That's funny," Bess said with a giggle, not understanding the words were meant to hurt.

"I've never seen anything so beautiful," Kasie

murmured a little shyly. "It really does look like paradise."

Pauline yawned. Gil ignored her and watched Kasie a little irritably as she and the girls enthused over the beach.

"When can we go swimming in the ocean, Daddy?" Bess asked excitedly.

"We have to check into the hotel first, baby," Gil told her. "And even then, the beach is dangerous. Kasie doesn't swim."

"Oh, we can take them with us," Pauline said lazily. "I'll watch them."

It occurred to Gil that he never trusted Pauline with his children. She wasn't malicious, she just didn't pay attention to what they were doing. She'd be involved in putting on sunscreen and lying in the sun, not watching children who could become reckless. Bess was especially good at getting into trouble.

"That's Kasie's job," Gil said, and put a long arm around Pauline just to see the reaction it got from Kasie. It was a constant source of anger that he couldn't keep his hands off Kasie when he was within five feet of her, and he still didn't trust her.

Kasie averted her eyes. Odd, how much it hurt to see Pauline snuggle close to Gil as if she were part of him. Remembering the hungry, masterful way he'd kissed her in the study, Kasie flushed. She knew things about Gil Callister that she shouldn't know. He made her hungry. But he was showing her that he didn't feel the same way. It was painfully obvious what his relationship was with Pauline. Even though she'd guessed, it hurt to have it pointed out to her like this.

She knew then that she was going to have to resign

her job when they got back to the States. If he married Pauline, there was no way she could live under the same roof with them.

Gil saw the reaction that Kasie was too young to hide, and it touched him. She felt something. She was jealous. He could have cheered out loud. It didn't occur to him then why he was so happy that Kasie was attracted to him.

"Who was the man you were talking to on the concourse, Kasie?" Gil asked unexpectedly.

"His name was Zeke," she replied with a smile. "He had the seat next to mine."

"I noticed him. He's good-looking," Pauline said. "What does he do?"

"He's a freelance writer for several travel magazines," Kasie told her. "He's down here doing a story on a new hotel complex."

Gil didn't look pleased. "Apparently you made friends quickly."

"Well, yes," she confessed. "I was a little nervous about flying. He talked to me while we got airborne." She grinned. "Didn't you hear us all singing the Air Force song?"

"So that's what it was," Pauline scoffed. "Good Lord, I thought the plane was full of drunks."

"Why were you afraid of flying?" Gil persisted.

Kasie averted her eyes to the girls. "My family died in an airplane crash," she said, without mentioning under what circumstances.

He shifted uncomfortably and looked at his daughters, who were watching for exciting little glimpses of people playing in the surf on the white beaches as they passed them.

"I'm all right now," she said. "the flight wasn't so bad."

"Not with a handsome man to hold your hand," Pauline teased deliberately.

"He *was* handsome," Kasie agreed, but without enthusiasm, and without noticing that Gil's eyes were beginning to glint with anger. He leaned back, glaring at Kasie.

She wondered what she'd done to provoke that anger. It made her uneasy. Pauline obviously didn't like it, either, and the woman was giving Kasie looks that promised retribution in the near future. Kasie had a feeling that Miss Raines would make a very bad enemy, and deep in her stomach, she felt icy cold.

# Chapter 7

It took an hour to get checked into the luxury hotel. The girls played quietly in the marble-floored lobby with a puzzle book Kasie had brought along for them, while Pauline complained loudly and nonstop about the inconvenience of having to wait for a room to be made ready. By the time the clerk motioned them to the desk, Gil was completely out of humor. He hadn't smiled since they got off the plane, in fact. When they were given keys to a two-bedroom suite and a single adjoining room, Pauline's expression lightened.

"Oh, that's nice of you, darling, letting Miss Mayfield have a room of her own."

Gil gave her a look that combined exasperation with impatience. "The girls can't be alone at night in a strange hotel," he said curtly. "Kasie's staying in the room with them, and the other bedroom in the suite is mine. You get the single."

"Why can't I just share with you, darling?" Pauline purred, enjoying Kasie's sudden flush.

Gil looked furious. He glared down at her from his superior height. "Maybe you've forgotten that I don't move with the times," he said quietly.

Pauline laughed a little nervously. "You're kidding. What's so bad about two...friends sharing a room?"

"I'm not kidding," Gil said flatly. He handed Pauline her key and motioned for Kasie and the girls to follow him.

Pauline stomped into the elevator, fuming. She gave Kasie a ferocious glare before she folded her arms over her chest and leaned back against the wall. The bellboy signaled that he'd wait for the next elevator to bring their luggage up, because six other people had jumped into the elevator right behind Pauline.

Gil and Pauline led the way down the hall, with Kasie and the girls following suit.

"At least, you can take me out tonight," Pauline told Gil, "since Kasie's along to baby-sit. Come on, darling, please? They have the most beautiful casino over on Paradise Island, and floor shows, too."

"All right," he said. "Let me get the girls and Kasie settled first, and find out about room service. You will want to have supper up here, won't you?" he asked Kasie stiffly.

"Of course," she said, not wanting to make things worse than they were—if that was possible.

"Good. Kasie can take the girls out to the beach while I check with the concierge about reservations," he added, watching Pauline's face beam. "I'll pick you up at your room at five-thirty."

"But that only gives me an hour to dress," she moaned.

"You'd look beautiful in a pillowcase, and you know it," he chided. "Go on."

"Okay." Pauline walked off to her own room without a word to the girls or Kasie.

Gil opened the door, noting that the bellboy was coming down the hall toward them with the luggage on a rolling carrier. He motioned Kasie and the girls inside.

"The bedrooms both have two double beds," he told Kasie stiffly. "And there's a balcony off the sitting room, if you want to sit outside and watch the surf after the girls get to sleep," he added, indicating the French doors that led onto a small balcony with two padded chairs.

"We'll be fine," she told him.

"Don't let them stay up past eight, no matter what they say," he told her. "And don't you stay up too late, either."

"I won't."

He hesitated at the door to his own room and looked at Kasie for a long moment, until her heart began to race. "You didn't tell me that you lost your family in an air crash. Why?"

"The subject didn't come up," she said gruffly.

"If it had," he replied curtly, "you wouldn't have been sitting alone, despite Pauline's little machinations with the seat assignments."

She was taken aback by the anger in his tone. "Oh."

"You make me feel like a gold-plated heel from time to time, Kasie," he said irritably. "I don't like it."

"I was all right," she assured him nervously. "Zeke took care of me."

That set him off again. "You're getting paid to take care of my children, not to holiday with some refugee from a press room," he pointed out, his voice arctic.

She stiffened. "I hadn't forgotten that, *Mr.* Callister," she added deliberately, aware that the girls had stopped playing and were staring up at the adults with growing disquiet. She turned away. "Come on, babies," she said with a forced smile. "Let's go change into our bathing suits, then we can go play on the beach!"

"All of you stay out of the water," Gil said shortly. "And I want you back up here before I leave with Pauline."

"Yes, sir," Kasie said, just because she knew it made him angry.

He said something under his breath and slammed the door to his own room behind him. Kasie had a premonition that it wasn't going to be much of a holiday.

She and the girls played in the sand near the ocean. On the way outside, Kasie had bought them small plastic buckets and shovels from one of the stores in the arcade. They were happily dumping sand on each other while, around them, other sun-worshipers lay on towel-covered beach chaise lounges or splashed in the water. The hotel was near the harbor, as well, and they watched a huge white ocean liner dock. It was an exciting place to visit.

Kasie, who'd only ever seen the worst part of foreign countries, was like a child herself as she gazed with fascination at rows of other luxury hotels on the beach, as well as sailboats and cruise ships in port. Nassau was the brightest, most beautiful place she'd ever been. The sand was like sugar under her feet, although hot enough to scorch them, and the color of the water was almost too vivid to believe. Smiling, she drank in the warmth of the sun with her eyes closed.

But it was already time to go back up to the room. She hated telling the girls, who begged to stay on the beach.

"We can't, babies," she said gently. "Your dad said we have to be in the room when he leaves. There's a television," she added. "They might have cartoons."

They still looked disappointed. "You could read us stories," Bess said.

Kasie smiled and hugged her. "Yes, I could. And I will. Come on, now, clean out your pails and shovels, and let's go."

"Oh, all right, Kasie, but it's very sad we have to leave," Bess replied.

"Don't want to go." Jenny pouted.

Kasie picked her up and kissed her sandy cheek. "We'll come out early in the morning, and look for shells on the beach!"

Jenny's eyes lit up. She loved seashells. "Truly, Kasie?"

"Honest and truly."

"Whoopee!" Bess yelled. "I'll get Jenny's pail, too. Can we have fish for supper?"

"Anything you like," Kasie told her as she put Jenny down and refastened her swimsuit strap that had come loose.

Above them, at the window of his room, Gil

watched the byplay, unseen. He sighed with irritation as he watched the girls respond so wholeheartedly to Kasie. They loved her. How were they going to react if she decided to quit? She was very young; too young to think of making a lifelong baby-sitter. Pauline said she'd been very adamant about sending the girls away to school, but that was hard to believe, watching her with them. She was tender with them, as Darlene had been.

He rammed his hands hard into the pockets of his dress slacks. It hurt remembering how happy the two of them had been, especially after the birth of their second little girl. In the Callister family, girls were special, because there hadn't been a girl in the lineage for over a hundred years. Gil loved having daughters. A son would have been nice, he supposed, but he wouldn't have traded either of his little jewels down there for anything else.

It wounded him to remember how cold he'd been to Kasie before and after the plane trip. He hadn't known about her family dying in a plane crash. He could only imagine how difficult it had been for her to get aboard with those memories. And he'd been sitting with Pauline, talking about Broadway shows. Pauline had said that Kasie wanted to sit by herself, so he hadn't protested.

Then, of course, there was this handsome stranger who'd comforted her on the flight to keep her from being afraid. He could have done that. He could have held her hand tight in his and kissed her eyes shut while he whispered to her...

He groaned out loud and turned away from the window. She was worming her way not only into his life and his girls' lives, but into his heart as well. He hadn't been able to even think about Pauline in any romantic way since Kasie had walked into his living room for the job interview. Up until then, he'd found the gorgeous blonde wonderful company. Now, she was almost an afterthought. He couldn't imagine why. Kasie wasn't really pretty. Although, she had a nice figure and a very kisseable mouth and those exquisitely tender eyes...

He jerked up the phone and dialed Pauline's extension. "Are you ready to go?" he asked.

"Darling, I haven't finished my makeup. You did say five-thirty," she reminded him.

"It is five-thirty," he muttered.

"Give me ten more minutes," she said. "I'm going to make you notice me tonight, lover," she teased. "I'm wearing something very risqué!"

"Fine," he replied, unimpressed. "I'll see you in ten minutes."

He hung up on her faint gasp of irritation. He didn't care if she wore postage stamps, it wasn't going to cure him of the hunger for Kasie that was tormenting him.

He heard the suite door open and the sound of his children laughing. Strange how often they laughed these days, when they'd been so somber and quiet before. She brought out the best in people. Well, not in himself, he had to admit. She brought out the worst in him, God knew why.

He went out into the big sitting room, still brooding.

"Daddy, you look nice!" Bess said, running to him to be picked up and kissed heartily. "Doesn't he look nice, Kasie?" she asked.

"Yes," Kasie said, glancing at him. He was dishy

in a tuxedo, she thought miserably, and Pauline probably looked like uptown New York City in whatever she was wearing. Pauline was like a French pastry, while Kasie was more like a stale doughnut. The thought amused her and she smiled.

"Bess, get the menu off the desk and take it in your room. You and Jenny decide what you want to eat," Gil told them.

"Yes, Daddy," Bess said at once, scooping up the menu and her sister's hand as they left the room.

"Don't let them fill up on sweets," he cautioned Kasie. His pale eyes narrowed on her body in the discreet, one-piece blue bathing suit she was wearing with sandals and a sheer cover-up in shades of blue. Her hair was down around her shoulders. She looked good enough to eat.

"I won't," she promised, moving awkwardly toward the bathroom with the towel she'd been sunbathing on.

"Next time, get a towel from the caretaker down on the beach," he said after she'd put the towel in the bathroom. "They keep them there for beach use."

She flushed. "Sorry. I didn't know."

He moved toward her. In flats, she was even shorter than usual. He looked down at her with narrow, stormy eyes. The curves of her pretty breasts were revealed in the suit and he thought for one insane instant of bending and putting his mouth right down on that soft pink skin.

"Mr. Callister," she began, the name almost choking her as his nearness began to have the usual effect on her shaking knees.

His lean hand moved to her throat and touched it lightly, stroking down to her bare shoulder and then back to her collarbone. "You've got sand on your skin," he observed.

"We had a little trouble making a sand castle, so the girls covered me up instead," she said with an unsteady laugh.

His hand flattened on the warm flesh and he looked into her huge, soft eyes, waiting for a reaction. Her pulse became visible in her throat. His blood began to surge, hot and turbulent, in his veins. His fingers spread out deliberately, so that the touch became intimate.

She wasn't protesting. She hadn't moved an inch. She didn't even seem to be breathing as she looked up into his pale, glittery eyes and waited, spellbound, for whatever came next.

Without saying a word, his fingers slid under the strap that held up her bodice. They inched into the suit and traced exquisite patterns on the soft, bare flesh that had never been exposed to the sun, or to a man's eyes. He watched her lips part, her eyes dilate with fascination and curiosity.

His hand stilled as he realized what he was doing. The girls were right in the next room, for God's sake. Was he losing his mind?

He jerked his hand back as if he'd scalded it and his expression became icy. "You'd better change," he said through his teeth.

She didn't move. Her eyes were wide, curious, apprehensive. She didn't understand his actions or his obvious anger.

But he was suspicious of her. He didn't trust her, and he didn't like his unchecked response to her. She could be anybody, with any motive in mind. She dressed like a repressed woman, but she never resisted anything physical that he did to her. He began to wonder if she was playing up to him with marriage in mind—or at least some financially beneficial liaison. He knew that she wasn't wealthy. He was. It put him at a disadvantage when he tried to puzzle out her motives. He knew how treacherous some women could be, and he'd been fooled once in recent months by a woman out for what she could get from him. She'd been kind to the girls, too, and she'd played the innocent with Gil, leading him on until they ended up in her bedroom. Of course, she'd said then, they'd have to get married once they'd been intimate…

He'd left her before the relationship was consummated, and he hadn't called her again. Not that she'd given up easily. She'd stalked him until he produced an attorney and a warrant, at which point she'd given up the chase.

Now, he was remembering that bad experience and superimposing her image over Kasie's innocent-looking face. He knew nothing about her. He couldn't take the risk of believing what he thought he saw in her personality. She could be playing him for a sucker, very easily.

"You don't hold anything back, do you?" he asked conversationally, and it didn't show that he'd been affected by her. "Are you like that all the way into the bedroom?" he added softly, so that the girls wouldn't hear.

Kasie drew in a long breath. "I wouldn't know," she said huskily, painfully aware that she'd just made an utter fool of herself. "I'll get dressed."

"You might as well, where I'm concerned," he said pleasantly. "You're easy on the eyes, Kasie, but in the dark, looks don't matter much."

She stared at him with confusion, as if she couldn't believe she was hearing such a blatant remark from him.

He slid his hands into his pockets and studied her arrogantly from head to toe. "You'd need to be prettier," he continued, "and with larger...assets," he said with a deliberate study of her pert breasts. "I'm particular about my lovers these days. It takes a special woman."

"Which, thank God, I'm not," she choked, flushing. "I don't sleep around."

"Of course not," he agreed.

She turned away from him with a sick feeling in her stomach. She'd loved his touch. It had been her first experience of passion, and it had been exquisite because it was Gil touching her. But he thought she was offering herself, and he didn't want her. She should be glad. She wasn't a loose woman. But it was a deliberate insult, and she wondered what she'd done to make him want to hurt her.

Her reaction made him even angrier, but he didn't let it show. "Giving up so easily?" he taunted.

She kept her back to him so that he wouldn't see her face. "We've had this conversation once," she pointed out. "I know that you don't want to remarry, and I've told you that I don't sleep around. Okay?"

"If I catch you in bed with that hack writer, I'll fire you on the spot," he added, viciously.

She turned then and glared at him from wet eyes. "What's the matter with you?" she asked.

"A sudden awakening of reason," he said enigmatically. "You look after the girls. That's your job."

"I never thought it involved anything else," she said.

"And it doesn't," he agreed. "The fringe benefits don't include the boss."

"Some fringe benefit," she scoffed, regaining her composure. "A conceited, overbearing, arrogant rancher who thinks he's on every woman's Christmas list!"

He lifted an eyebrow over eyes with cynical sophistication gleaming in them. "Don't look for me under your Christmas tree," he chided.

"Don't worry, I won't." She turned and kept walking before he could say anything worse. Of all the conceited men on earth!

He watched her go with mixed emotions, the strongest of which was desire. She made him ache all over. He checked his watch. Pauline's ten minutes were up, and he wanted out of this apartment. He called a good-night to the girls and went out without another word to Kasie.

When he got back in, at two in the morning, he paused long enough to open Kasie's door and look in.

She was wearing another of those concealing cotton gowns, with the covers thrown off. Jenny was curled up against one shoulder and Bess was curled into the other. They were all three asleep.

Gil ground his teeth together just looking at the picture they made together. His girls and Kasie. They looked more like mother and daughters. The thought hurt him. He closed the door with a little jerk and went back into his own room. Despite Pauline's alluring gown and her spirited conversation, he had been morose all evening.

Pauline had noticed, and knew the reason. She was,

she told herself, going to get rid of the competition.
It only needed the right set of circumstances.

Fate provided them only two days later. Kasie and
Gil were barely speaking now. She avoided him, and
he did the same to her. If the girls noticed, they kept
their thoughts to themselves. Impulsively Kasie
phoned Zeke at his hotel and asked if he'd like to
come over and have lunch with her at the hotel, since
she couldn't leave the girls.

He agreed with flattering immediacy, and showed
up just as Kasie was drying off the girls.

"Surely you aren't going to take them to lunch with
you?" Pauline asked, laughing up at Zeke, who attracted her at once. "I'll watch them while you eat."

"Please can't we stay and play in the pool?" Bess
asked Kasie. "Miss Raines will watch us, she said so."

"Please," Jenny added with a forlorn look.

"You'll be right inside, won't you?" Pauline asked
cunningly. "Go ahead and enjoy your lunch. I'm not
going anywhere."

For an instant, Kasie recalled that Gil didn't trust
Pauline with the girls. But it was only for a few
minutes and, as Pauline had said, they were going to
be just inside the nearby restaurant that overlooked
the pool.

"Well, all right then, if you really don't mind,"
she told Pauline. "Thank you."

"It's my pleasure. Have fun now," Pauline told
her. "And don't worry. Gil's not going to be back
for at least a half hour. He's at the bank."

Kasie brooded over it even while she and Zeke ate
a delicious seafood salad. They were seated at a win-

dow overlooking the swimming pool, but a row of hedges and hibiscus obscured the view so that only the deep end of the pool could be seen from their table.

"Stop worrying," Zeke told her with a grin. "Honestly, you act as if they were your own kids. You're just the governess."

"They're my responsibility," she pointed out. "If anything happened to them…"

"Your friend is going to watch them. Now stop arguing and let me tell you about this new hotel and casino they're opening over on Paradise Island."

"Okay," she relented, smiling. "I'll stop brooding."

Outside by the pool, Pauline had noticed that Kasie and her companion couldn't see beyond the hedges. She smiled coldly as she looked at the little girls. Jenny was sitting on the steps of the wading pool, playing with one of her dolls in the water.

Closer to Pauline, Bess was staring down at the swimming pool where the water was about six feet deep—far too deep for her to swim in.

"I wish I could dive," she told Pauline.

"But it's easy," Pauline told her, making instant plans. "Just put your arms out in front of you like this," she demonstrated, "and jump in. Really, it's simple."

"Are you sure?" Bess asked, thrilled that an adult might actually teach her how to dive!

"Of course! I'm right here. How dangerous can it be? Go ahead. You can do it."

Of course she could, Bess thought, laughing with delight. She put her arms in the position Pauline had demonstrated and shifted her position to dive in.

There wasn't anybody else around the pool to notice
if she did it wrong. She'd show her daddy when he
came back. Wouldn't he be surprised?

She moved again, just as Pauline suddenly turned
around. Her leg accidentally caught one of Bess's.
Pauline fell and so did Bess, but Bess's head hit the
pavement as she went down. The momentum kept her
going, and she rolled into the pool, unconscious.

"Oh, damn!" Pauline groaned. She got to her feet
and looked into the pool, aware that Jenny was
screaming. "Do shut up!" she told the child. "I'll
have to get someone..."

But even as she spoke, Gil came around the corner
of the hotel, oblivious to what had just happened.

"Daddy!" Jenny screamed. "Bess falled in the
swimmy pool!"

Gil didn't even break stride. He broke into a run
and dived in the second he was close enough. He
went to the bottom, scooped up his little girl and
swam back up with all the speed he could muster.
Out of breath, he coughed as he lifted Bess onto the
tiles by the pool and climbed out himself. He turned
the child over and rubbed her back, aware that she
was still breathing by some miracle. She coughed and
water began to dribble out of her mouth, and then to
gush out of it as she regained consciousness.

"Call an ambulance," he shot at Pauline.

"Oh, dear, oh, dear," she murmured, biting her
nails.

"Call a damned ambulance!" he raged.

One of the pool boys saw what was going on and
told Gil he'd phone from inside the hotel.

"Where's Kasie?" Gil asked Pauline with hateful

eyes as Jenny threw herself against him to be comforted. Bess was still coughing up water.

There it was. The opportunity. Pauline drew in a quick breath. "That man came by to take her to lunch. You know, the man she met on the plane. She begged me to watch the girls so they'd have time to talk."

Gil didn't say anything, but his eyes were very expressive. "Where is she?"

"I really don't know," Pauline lied, wide-eyed. "She didn't say where they were going. She was clinging to him like ivy and obviously very anxious to be alone with him," she added. "I can't say I blame her, he's very handsome."

"Bess could have died."

"But I was right here. I never left them," she assured him. "The girls mean everything to me. Here, let me have Jenny. I'll take care of her while you get Bess seen to."

"Want Kasie," Jenny whimpered.

"There, there, darling," Pauline said sweetly, kissing the plump little cheek. "Pauline's here."

"Damn Kasie!" Gil bit off, horrified at what might have happened. Kasie knew he didn't trust Pauline to watch the girls. Why had Kasie been so irresponsible? Was it to get back at him for what he'd said the night they arrived in Nassau?

When the ambulance arrived, Kasie and Zeke left their dessert half-eaten and rushed out the door. Zeke had to stop to pay the check, but Kasie, apprehensive and uneasy without knowing exactly why, rounded the corner of the building just in time to see little Bess being loaded onto the ambulance.

"Bess! What happened?!" Kasie asked, sobbing.

"She hit her head on the pool, apparently, and almost drowned, while you were away having a good time with your boyfriend,'' Gil said furiously. The expression on his face could have backed down a mob. ''You've got a ticket home. Use it today. Go back to the ranch and start packing. I want you out of my house when I get back. I'll send your severance pay along, and you can thank your lucky stars that I'm not pressing charges!''

''But, but, Pauline was watching them—'' Kasie began, horrified at Bess's white face and big, tragic eyes staring at her from the ambulance.

''It was your job to watch them,'' Gil shot at her. ''That's what you were paid to do. She could have died, damn you!''

Kasie went stark white. ''I'm sorry,'' she choked, horrified.

''Too late,'' he returned, heading to the ambulance. ''You heard me, Kasie,'' he added coldly. ''Get out. Pauline, take care of Jenny until I get back.''

''Of course, darling,'' she cooed.

''And get her away from the swimming pool!''

''I'll take her up to my room and read to her. I hope you'll be fine, Bess, darling,'' she added.

Kasie stood like a little statue, sick and alone and frightened as the ambulance closed up and rushed away, its lights flashing ominously.

Pauline turned and gave Kasie a superior appraisal. ''It seems you're out of a job, Miss Mayfield.''

Kasie was too sick at heart to react. She didn't have it in her for a fight. Seeing Bess lying there, so white and fragile was acutely painful. Even Jenny seemed not to like her anymore. She buried her face against Pauline and clung.

Pauline turned and carried the child back to her

chaise lounge to get her room key. Not bad, she thought, for a morning's work. One serious rival accounted for and out of the way.

Zeke caught up with Kasie at the pool. "What happened?" he asked, brushing a stray tear from Kasie's cheek.

"Bess almost drowned," she said huskily. "Pauline promised to watch her. How did she hit her head?"

"I wouldn't put much past that woman," he told Kasie somberly. "Some people won't tolerate rivals."

"I'm no rival," she replied. "I never was."

Having noted the expression on her boss's face at the airport when he'd said goodbye to Kasie, he could have disputed that. He knew jealousy when he saw it. The man had been looking at him as if he'd like to put a stake through his heart.

"He fired me," Kasie continued dazedly. "He fired me, without even letting me explain."

"Trust me, after whatever she told him, it wouldn't have done any good. Go home and let things cool down," he added. "Most men regain their reason when the initial upset passes."

"You know a lot about people," Kasie remarked as they started up to her room.

"I'm a reporter. It goes with the territory. I'll go with you to the airport and help you change the ticket," he added grimly. "Not that I want to. I was looking forward to getting to know you. Now we'll be ships that passed in the night."

"So we will. Do you believe in fate?" she asked numbly.

"I do. Most things happen for a reason. Just go with the flow." He grinned. "And don't forget to give me your home address! I won't be out of the country forever."

# Chapter 8

It didn't take long for Kasie to pack. She wouldn't let herself think of what was ahead, because she'd cry, and she didn't have time for tears. She changed into a neat gray pantsuit to travel in, and picked up her suitcase and purse to put them by the door. But she stopped long enough to find the phone number of the hospital and check on Bess. The head nurse on the floor, once Kasie's relationship to the girls was made clear, told her that the child was sitting up in bed asking for ice cream. Kasie thanked her and hung up. She wondered if the news would have been quite as forthcoming if she'd mentioned that she'd just been fired.

She moved out into the sitting room with her heart like a heavy weight in her chest. She looked around to make sure she hadn't forgotten anything and went into the hall with her small piece of carry-on luggage on wheels and her pocketbook. It was the most painful moment of her recent life. She thought of never seeing the girls and Gil again, of having Gil hate her. Tears stung her eyes, and she dashed at them impatiently with a tissue.

As she passed Pauline's room, she hesitated. She wanted to say goodbye to little Jenny. But on second thought, she went ahead to the elevator, deciding that it would only make matters worse. Besides, Pauline was probably still at the hospital with Gil. She wished she knew what had really happened by the pool. She should never have left the girls with Pauline, despite the other woman's assurances that she'd look after them. Gil had said often enough that she was responsible for them, not Pauline. She should have listened.

Downstairs, Zeke was waiting for her. He put her small bag into the little car he'd rented at the airport and drove her to the airport to catch her flight.

At the hospital, Bess was demanding ice cream. Gil hugged her close, more frightened than he wanted to admit about how easily he could have lost her forever.

"I'm okay, Daddy," she assured him with a grin.

"Does your head hurt?" he asked, touching the bandage the doctor had placed over the cut, which had been stitched.

"Only a little. But ice cream would make it feel better," she added hopefully.

"I'll see what I can do," he promised with a strained smile.

The nurse came in, motioning Pauline and Jenny in behind her. "I thought it might help to let her sister see her," she told Gil confidentially.

"Hi, Bess," Jenny said, sidling up to the bed. "Are you okay?"

"I'm fine," Bess assured her. "But it was real scary." She glared at Pauline. "It was your fault. You tripped me."

"Bess!" Gil warned his daughter while wondering at Pauline's odd expression.

"I did not trip you!" Pauline shot back.

"You did so," Bess argued. "I wouldn't dive in, and you tripped me so I'd fall in."

"She's obviously delirious," Pauline said tautly.

"You told Kasie you'd stay right with us," she continued angrily. "And she told us not to go swimming, but you showed me how to dive and you told me to dive into the pool. And when I didn't, you tripped me!"

Pauline was flushed. Gil was looking vaguely murderous. "She did hit her head, you know," she stammered. "I was telling her how to dive, I didn't tell her to actually do it!"

"You tripped me and I hurt myself!" Bess kept on.

Pauline backed away from Gil. "What do I know about kids?" she asked impatiently. "She said she wanted to learn how to swim. I showed her a diving position. Then I slipped on the wet tiles and fell against her. It was an accident. I never meant to hurt her. You must know that I wouldn't deliberately hurt a child!" she added fiercely.

He was still silent, as the fear for Bess began to fade and his reason came back to him.

Pauline grabbed up her purse. "I was just trying to do Kasie a favor," she muttered. "That reporter wanted to take her to lunch and I told her to go ahead, that I'd watch the kids. Besides, she was just in the restaurant next to the pool!"

Gil felt his stomach do a nosedive. So Kasie hadn't deserted the kids. Pauline had told her to go, and she'd been right inside. He'd fired Kasie, thinking she was at fault!

"I imagine that reporter went home with her," Pauline continued deliberately. "They were all over each other when he came to pick her up. Besides, governesses are thick on the ground. It won't be hard to replace her."

"Or you," he said coldly.

She looked shocked. "You can't mean you're firing me?"

"I'm firing you, Pauline," he said, feeling like a prize idiot. Kasie was gone, and it was as much Pauline's fault as it was his own. He knew she didn't like Kasie. "I need a full-time secretary. We've discussed this before."

She started to argue, but it was obvious that there was no use in it. She might still be able to salvage something of their relationship, just the same, if she didn't make a scene. "All right," she said heavily. "But we might as well enjoy the vacation, since we're here."

His face became hard. He thought of Kasie going back to Montana, packing, leaving. For an instant he panicked, thinking that she might go so far away that he'd never find her.

Then he remembered her aunt in Billings. Surely she wouldn't be that hard to locate. He'd give it a few days, let Kasie get over the anger she must be feeling right now. Maybe she'd miss the girls and he could persuade her to come back. God knew, she wouldn't miss him, he thought bitterly. He'd probably done more damage than he could ever make up to

her. But when they got back, he was going to try.
Misjudging Kasie seemed to be his favorite hobby
these days, he thought miserably.

"Yes," he told Pauline slowly. "I suppose we
might as well stay."

Pauline had hardly dared hope for so much time
with him. She was going to try, really try, to take care
of the girls and make them like her.

"Bess, shall I go and ask if they have chocolate
ice cream?" she asked, trying to make friends. "I'm
really sorry about accidentally knocking you into the
pool."

"I want Kasie," Bess muttered.

"Kasie's gone home," Gil said abruptly, not adding that he'd fired her.

"Gone home?" Bess's face crumpled. "But
why?"

"Because I told her to," he said shortly. "And
that's enough about Kasie. We're going to have a
good time... Oh, for God's sake, don't start bawl-
ing!"

Now it wasn't just Bess crying, it was Jenny, too.
Pauline sighed heavily. "Well, we're going to have a
very good time, aren't we?" she said to nobody in
particular.

Mama Luke never pried or asked awkward questions. She held Kasie while she cried, sent her to unpack and made hot chocolate and chicken soup. That
had always been Kasie's favorite meal when she was
upset.

Kasie sat down across from her at the small kitchen
table that had a gaily patterned tablecloth decorated
with pink roses and sipped her soup with a spoon.

"You don't have to say a word," Mama Luke told her gently, and smiled. She had eyes like her sister, Kasie's mother, dark brown and soft. She had dark hair, too, which she kept short. Her hands, around the mug, were thin and wrinkled now, and twisted with arthritis, but they were loving, helping hands. Kasie had always envied her aunt her ability to give love unconditionally.

"I've been a real idiot," Kasie remarked as she worked through her soup. "I should never have let Pauline look after the girls. She isn't really malicious, but she's hopelessly irresponsible."

"You haven't had a man friend in my recent memory," Mama Luke remarked. "I'm sure you were flattered to have a handsome young man want to take you out to lunch."

"I was. But that doesn't mean that I should have let Pauline talk me into leaving the girls with her. Bess could very easily have drowned, and it would have been my fault," she added miserably.

"Give it time," the older woman said gently. "First, let's get you settled in. Then you can help me with the garden," she added with a grin.

Despite her misery, Kasie laughed. "I see. You're happy to have me back because I'm free labor."

Mama Luke laughed, too. It was a standing joke, the way she press-ganged even casual visitors into taking a turn at weeding the garden. She prescribed it as the best cure for depression, misery and anxiety. She was right. It did a lot to restore a good mood.

In the days that followed, Kasie worked in the garden a lot. She thought about Gil, and the hungry way he'd kissed her. She thought about the girls and missed them terribly. She'd really expected Gil to phone her. He knew she had an aunt in Billings, and it wouldn't have taken much effort for him to track her down. In fact, she'd put Mama Luke's telephone number down on her job application in case of emergency.

The thought depressed her even more. He knew where she'd be, but apparently he was still angry at her. God knew what Pauline had said at the hospital about how the accident happened. She'd probably blamed the whole thing on Kasie. Maybe the girls blamed her, too, for leaving them with Pauline, whom they disliked. She'd never felt quite so alone. She thought of Kantor and grew even sadder.

Mama Luke came out into the garden and caught her brooding. "Stop that," she chided softly. "This is God's heart," she pointed out. "It's creation itself, planting seed and watching little things grow. It should cheer you up."

"I miss Bess and Jenny," she said quietly, leaning on her hoe. She was dirty from head to toe, having gotten down in the soil to pull out stubborn weeds. There was a streak of it across her chin, which Mama Luke wiped off with one of the tissues she always carried in her pocket.

"I'm sure they miss you, too," the older woman assured her. "Don't worry so. It will all come right. Sometimes we just have to think of ourselves as leaves going down a river. It's easy to forget that God's driving."

"Maybe He doesn't mind back seat drivers," Kasie said with a grin.

Mama Luke chuckled. "You're incorrigible. Almost through? I made hot chocolate and chicken with rice soup."

"Comfort food." Kasie smiled.

"Absolutely. Stop and eat something."

Kasie looked at the weeding that still had to be done with a long sigh. "Oh, well, maybe the mailman has some frustrations to work off. He's bigger than I am. I'll bet he hoes well."

"I'll try to find out," she was assured. "Come on in and wash up."

It was good soup and Kasie had worked up an appetite. She felt better. But she still hated the way she'd left the Callister ranch. Probably everybody blamed her for Bess's accident. Especially the one person from whom she dreaded it. "I guess Gil hates me."

The pain in those words made Mama Luke reach out a gentle hand to cover her niece's on the table. "I'm sure he doesn't," she contradicted. "He was upset and frightened for Bess. We all say things we shouldn't when our emotions are out of control. He'll apologize. I imagine he'll offer you your job back as well."

Kasie shifted in the chair. "It's been a week," she said. "If he were going to hire me back, he'd have been in touch. I suppose he still believes Pauline and thinks he's done the best thing by firing me."

"Do you really?" Her aunt pursed her lips as her keen ears caught the sound of a car pulling up in the driveway. "Finish your hot cocoa, dear. I'll go and see who that is driving up out front."

For just a few seconds, Kasie hoped it would be Gil, come to give her back her job. But that would take a miracle. Her life had changed all over again. She was just going to have to accept it and get a new job. Something would turn up somewhere, surely.

She heard voices in the living room. One of them was deep and slow, and she shivered with emotion as she realized that she wasn't dreaming. She got up and went into the living room. And there he was.

Gil stopped talking midsentence and just looked at Kasie. She was wearing old jeans and a faded T-shirt, with her hair around her shoulders. He'd missed her more than he thought he could miss anyone. His heart filled with just the sight of her.

"I believe you, uh, know each other," Mama Luke said mischievously.

"Yes, we do," Kasie said. She recalled the fury in his pale eyes as he accused her of causing Bess's accident, the fury as he fired her. It was too painful to go through again, and he didn't look as if he'd come to make any apologies. She turned away miserably. "If you'll excuse me, I have to clean up," she called over her shoulder.

"Kasie…!" Gil called angrily.

She kept walking down the hall to her room, and she closed and locked the door. The pain was just too much. She couldn't bear the condemnation in his eyes.

Gil muttered under his breath. "Well, so much for wishful thinking," he said almost to himself.

"Come along and have some hot cocoa, Mr. Callister," Mama Luke said with a gentle smile. "I think you and I have a lot to talk about."

He followed her into the small, bright kitchen with its white and yellow accents. She motioned him into a chair at the table while she poured the still-hot cocoa into a mug and offered it to him.

"I'm Sister Luke," she introduced herself, noting his sudden start. "Yes, that's right, I'm a nun. My order doesn't wear the habit. I work with a health outreach program in this community.''

He sipped cocoa, feeling as if more revelations were in store, and that he wasn't going to like them.

She sipped her own cocoa. He was obviously waiting for her to speak again. He studied her quietly, his blue eyes troubled and faintly disappointed at Kasie's reception.

''She's still grieving,'' she told Gil. ''She didn't give it enough time before she started back to work. I tried to tell her, but young people are so determined these days.''

He latched on to the word. ''Grieving?''

''Yes.'' Her dark eyes were quiet and soft as they met his. ''Her twin, Kantor, and his wife and little girl died three months ago.''

His breath caught. ''In an airplane crash,'' he said, recalling what Kasie had said.

''Airplane crash?'' Her eyes widened. ''Well, I suppose you could call it that, in a manner of speaking. Their light aircraft was shot down—''

''What?'' he exploded.

She frowned. ''Don't you know anything about Kasie?''

''No. I don't. Not one thing!''

She let out a whistle. ''I suppose that explains some of the problem. Perhaps if you knew about her background...'' She leaned back in her chair. ''Her parents were lay missionaries to Africa. While they were working there, a rebel uprising occurred and they were killed.'' She nodded at his look of horror. ''I had already taken my vows by then, and I was the only family that Kasie and Kantor had left. I arranged to have them come to me, and I enrolled them in the school where I was teaching, and living, at the time. In Arizona,'' she added. ''Kantor wanted nothing more than to fly airplanes. He studied flying while he was in school and later went into partnership with a friend from college. They started a small charter service. There was an opportunity in Africa for a courier service, so he decided to go there and set up a second headquarters for the company. While he was there, he married and had a little girl, Sandy. She and Lise, Kantor's wife, came and stayed with Kasie and me while Kasie was going through secretarial school. Kantor didn't want them with him just then, because there was some political trouble. It calmed down and he came and rejoined his family. He wanted to bring everyone home to Africa.''

She grimaced. ''Kasie didn't want him to go back. She said it was too risky, especially for Lise and Sandy. She adored Sandy…'' She hesitated, and took a steadying breath, because the memory was painful. ''Kantor told her to mind her own business, and they all left. That same week, a band of guerrillas attacked the town where he had his business. He got Lise and Sandy in the plane and was flying them to a nearby town when someone fired a rocket at them. They all died instantly.''

''My God,'' he said huskily.

''Kasie took it even harder because they'd argued. It took weeks for her to be able to discuss it without breaking down. She'd graduated from secretarial college and I insisted that she go to work, not because of money, but because it was killing her to sit and brood about Kantor.''

He wrapped both hands around the cocoa mug and stared into the frothy liquid. ''I knew there was something," he said quietly. "But she never talked about anything personal."

"She rarely does, except with me." She studied him. "She said that your wife died in a riding accident and that you have two beautiful little girls."

"They hate me," he said matter-of-factly. "I fired Kasie." He shrugged and smiled faintly. "John, my brother, isn't even speaking to me."

"They'll get over it."

"They may. I won't." He wouldn't meet her eyes. "I thought I might persuade her to come back. I suppose that's a hopeless cause?"

"She's hurt that you misjudged her," she explained. "Kasie loves children. It would never occur to her to leave them in any danger."

"I know that. I knew it then, too, but I was out of my mind with fear. I suppose I lashed out. I don't know much about families," he added, feeling safe with this stranger. He looked up at her. "My brother and I were never part of one. Our parents had a governess for us until we were old enough to be sent off to school. I can remember months going by when we wouldn't see them or hear from them. Even now," he added stiffly, "they only contact us when they think of some new way we can help them make money."

She slid a wrinkled hand over his. "I'm sorry," she said gently. She removed her hand and pushed a plate of cookies toward him. "Comfort food," she said with a gleeful smile. "Indulge yourself."

"Thanks." He bit into a delicious lemon cookie.

"Kasie says you love your girls very much, and that you never leave them with people you don't trust. She's hating herself because she did leave them against her better judgment. She blames herself for the accident.''

He sighed. ''It wasn't her fault. Not really.'' His eyes glittered. ''She wanted to have lunch with a man she met on the plane. A good-looking, young man,'' he added bitterly. ''Pauline admitted causing the accident, but I was hot because Kasie was upset about flying and I didn't know it until it was too late. She was sitting all by herself.'' His face hardened. ''If I'd known what you just told me, we'd have gone by boat. I'd never have subjected her to an airplane ride. But Kasie keeps secrets. She doesn't talk about herself.''

''Neither do you, I think,'' she replied.

He shrugged and picked up another cookie. ''She looks worn,'' he remarked.

''I've had her working in my garden,'' she explained. ''It's good therapy.''

He smiled. ''I work cattle for therapy. My brother and I have a big ranch here in Montana. We wouldn't trade it for anything.''

''I like animals.'' She sipped cocoa.

So did he. He looked at her over the mug.

''Kasie mentioned she was named for the mercenary K.C. Kanton.'' She raised an eyebrow amusedly. ''That's right. I'm not sure how much she told you, but when Jackie, her mother, was carrying her, there was a guerrilla attack on the mission. Bob, my brother-in-law, was away with a band of workers building a barn for a neighboring family. They'd helped a wounded mercenary soldier hide from the same guerrillas, part of an insurgent group that wanted to overthrow the government. He was well enough to get around by then, and he got Jackie out of the mission and through the jungle to where Bob was. Kasie and Kantor were born only a day later. And that's why she was named for K.C. Kantor.''

''They both were named for him,'' he realized. ''Amazing. What I've heard about Kantor over the years doesn't include a generous spirit or unselfishness.''

''That may be true. But he pays his debts. He'd still like to take care of Kasie,'' she added with a soft chuckle. ''She won't let him. She's as independent as my sister used to be.''

It disturbed him somehow that Kasie was cherished by another man who could give her anything she wanted. ''He must be a great deal older than she is,'' he murmured absently.

''He doesn't have those kind of feelings for her,'' she said quietly, and there was pain in her soft eyes. ''He missed out on family life and children. I think he's sorry about that now. He tried to get her to come and stay with him in Mexico until she got over losing her twin, but she wouldn't go.''

''One of her other character references was a Catholic priest.''

She nodded. ''Father Vincent, in Tucson, Arizona. He was the priest for our small parish.'' She sighed. ''Kasie hasn't been to mass since her brother died. I've been so worried about her.''

''She mentioned taking the girls with her to church,'' Gil said after a minute. ''If I can get her to come back to work for me, it might be the catalyst to help her heal.''

''It might at that,'' she agreed.

Gil took another cookie and nibbled it. ''These are good.''

"My one kitchen talent," she said. "I can make cookies. Otherwise, I live on TV dinners and the kindness of friends who can cook."

He sipped cocoa and thought. "How can I get her to go back with me?" he asked after a minute.

"Tell her the girls are crying themselves to sleep at night," she suggested gently. "She misses Sandy even more than her twin. She and the little girl were very close."

"She's close to my girls," he remarked with a reminiscent smile. "If there's a storm or they get frightened in the night, I can always find them curled up in Kasie's arms." His voice seemed to catch on the words. He averted his eyes toward the hallway. "The light went out of the house when she left it."

She wondered if he even realized what he was saying. Probably not. Men seemed to miss things that women noticed at once.

"I'll go and get her," she said, pushing back her chair. "You can sit by my fishpond and talk with the goldfish."

"My uncle used to have one," he recalled, standing. "I haven't had one built because of the girls. When they're older, I'd like to put in another one."

"I had to dig it myself, and I'm not the woman I used to be. It's only a little over a foot deep. One of my neighbors gave me his used pond heater when he bought a new one. It keeps my four goldfish alive all winter long." She moved to the door. "It's just outside the back door, near the birdbath. I'll send Kasie out to you."

He went out, his hands in his pockets, thinking how little he'd known about Kasie. It might be impossible for them to regain the ground they'd lost, but he wanted to try. His life was utterly empty without her in it.

Mama Luke knocked gently at Kasie's door and waited until it opened. Kasie looked at her guiltily.

"I was rude. I'm sorry," she told the older woman.

"I didn't come to fuss," Mama Luke said. She touched Kasie's disheveled hair gently. "I want you to go out and talk to Mr. Callister. He feels bad about the things he said to you. He wants you to go back to work for him."

Kasie gave her aunt a belligerent look. "In his dreams," she muttered.

"The little girls miss you very much," she said.

Kasie grimaced. "I miss them, too."

"Go on out there and face your problem squarely," Mama Luke coaxed. "He's a reasonable man, and he's had a few shocks today. Give him a chance to make it up to you. He's nice," she added. "I like him."

"You like everybody, Mama Luke," Kasie said softly.

"He's out by the goldfish pond. And don't push him in," she added with a wicked little smile.

Kasie chuckled. "Okay."

She took a deep breath and went down the hall. But her hands trembled when she opened the back door and walked outside. She hadn't realized how much she was going to miss Gil Callister until she was out of his life. Now she had to decide whether or not to risk going back. It wasn't going to be an easy decision.

# Chapter 9

Gil was sitting on the small wooden bench overlooking the rock-bordered oval fishpond, his elbows
resting on his knees as he peered down thoughtfully
into the clear water where water lilies bloomed in
pink and yellow profusion. He looked tired, Kasie
thought, watching him covertly. Maybe he'd been
away on business and not on holiday with Pauline
after all.

He looked up when he heard her footsteps. He got
to his feet. He looked elegant even in that yellow polo
shirt and beige slacks, she thought. He wasn't at all
handsome, but his face was masculine and he had a
mouth that she loved kissing. She averted her eyes
until she was able to control the sudden impulse to
run to him. Wouldn't that shock him, she thought
sadly.

He looked wary, and he wasn't smiling. He studied

her for a long time, as if he'd forgotten what she looked like and wanted to absorb every detail of her.

"How are the girls?" she asked quietly. "Is Bess going to be all right?"

"Bess is fine," he replied. "She told me everything." He grimaced. "Even Pauline admitted that she'd told you to go and have lunch with what's-his-name, and she'd watch the girls. She said she slipped and tripped Bess. I imagine it's the truth. She's never been much of a liar, regardless of her faults," he returned, his voice flat, without expression. "They told me you phoned the hospital to make sure Bess was all right."

"I was worried," she said, uneasy.

He toyed with the change in his pocket, making it jingle. "Bess wanted you, in the hospital. When I told her you'd gone home, she and Jenny both started crying." The memory tautened his face. "For what it's worth, I'm sorry that I blamed you."

She'd never wanted to believe anything as much as that apology. But it was still disturbing that he'd accused her without proof, that he'd assumed Bess's accident was her fault. She wanted to go back in the house. But that wouldn't solve the problem. She had to try and forget. He was here and he'd apologized. They had to go from there. "It's all right," she said after a minute, her eyes on the fish instead of him. "I understand. You can't help it that you don't like me."

"Don't…like you?" he asked. The statement surprised him.

She toyed with the hem of her shirt. "You never wanted to hire me in the first place, really," she continued. "You looked at me as if you hated me the minute you saw me."

His eyes were thoughtful. "Did I?" He didn't want to pursue that line of conversation. It was too new, too disturbing, after having realized how he felt about her. "Why do you call your aunt Mama Luke?" he asked to divert her.

"Because when I was five, I couldn't manage Sister Mary Luke Bernadette," she replied. "She was Mama Luke from then on."

He winced. "That's a young age to lose both parents."

That's why I know how Bess and Jenny feel," she told him.

His expelled breath was audible. "I've made a hell of a mess of it, haven't I, Kasie?" he asked somberly. "I jumped to the worst sort of conclusions."

She moved awkwardly to the other side of the fishpond and wrapped her arms around her body. "I wasn't thinking straight. I knew you didn't trust Pauline to take care of the girls, but I let myself be talked into leaving them with her. You were right. Bess could have drowned and it would have been my fault."

"Stick the knife right in, don't be shy," he said through his teeth. His blue eyes glittered. "God knows, I deserve it."

Her eyes met his, wide with curiosity. "I don't understand."

She probably didn't. "Never mind." He stuck his hands into his pockets. "I fired Pauline."

"But…!"

"It wasn't completely because of what happened in Nassau. I need someone full-time," he interrupted. "She only wanted the job in the first place so that she could be near me."

The breeze blew her hair across her mouth. She pushed it back behind her ear. "That must have been flattering."

"It was, at first," he agreed, "I've known Pauline for a long time, and her attention was flattering. However, regardless of how Bess fell into the water, Pauline didn't make a move to rescue her. I can't get over that."

Kasie understood. She'd have been in the pool seconds after Bess fell in, despite the fact that she couldn't swim.

His piercing blue eyes caught hers. "Yes, I know. You'd have been right in after her," he said softly, as if he'd read the thought in her mind. "Even if you'd had to be rescued as well," he added gently.

"People react differently to desperate situations," she said.

"Indeed they do." His eyes narrowed. "I want you to come back. So do the girls. I'll do whatever it takes. An apology, a raise in salary, a paid vacation to Tahiti…"

She shrugged. "I wouldn't mind coming back," she said. "I do miss the girls, terribly. But…"

"But, what?"

She met his level gaze. "You don't trust me," she said simply, and her eyes were sad. "At first you thought I was trying to get to you through the girls, and then you thought I wanted them out of the way. In Nassau, you thought I left them alone for selfish reasons, so that I could go on a lunch date." She smiled sadly. "You have a bad opinion of me as a governess. What if I mess up again? Maybe it would be better if we just left things the way they are."

The remark went through him like hot lead. He

hadn't trusted Kasie because she was so mysterious about her past. Now that he knew the truth about her, knew of the tragedies she'd suffered in her young life, lack of trust was no longer going to be a problem. But how did he tell her that? And, worse, how did he make up for the accusations he'd made? Perhaps he could tell her the truth.

"The girls' last governess was almost too good to be true," he began. "She charmed the girls, and me, until we'd have believed anything she told us. It was all an act. She had marriage in mind, and she actually threatened me with my own children. She said they were so attached to her that if I didn't marry her, she'd leave and they'd hate me."

She blinked. "That sounds as if she was a little unbalanced."

He nodded, his eyes cold with remembered bitterness. "Yes, she was. She left in the middle of the night, and the next morning the girls were delighted to find her gone."

He shook his head. "She was unstable, and I'd left the kids in her hands. It was such a blot on my judgment that I didn't trust it anymore. Especially when you came along, with your mysterious past and your secrets. I thought you were playing up to me because I was rich."

It hurt that he'd thought so little of her. "I see."

"Do you? I hope so," he replied heavily, and with a smile. "Because if I go back to Medicine Ridge without you, I wouldn't give two cents for my neck. John's furious with me. He's got company. Miss Parsons glares at me constantly. Mrs. Charters won't serve me anything that isn't burned. The girls are the worst, though," he mused. "They ignore me completely. I feel like the ogre in that story you read them at bedtime.''

"Poor ogre," she said quietly.

He began to smile. He loved the softness of her voice when she spoke. For the first time since his arrival, he was beginning to think he had a chance. "Feeling sorry for me?" he asked gently. "Good. If I wear on your conscience, maybe you'll feel sorry enough to come home with me.''

She frowned. "What did Mama Luke tell you?" she asked suddenly.

"Things you should have told me," he replied, his tone faintly acidic. "She told me everything, in fact, except why you don't like the water.''

She stared down into the fishpond, idly watching the small goldfish swim in and out of the vegetation. "When I was five, just before my parents were… killed," she said, sickened by the memory, "one of my friends at the mission in Africa got swept into the river. I saw her drown.''

"You've had a lot of tragedy in your young life," he said softly. He moved a step closer to her, and another, stopping when he was close enough to lift a lean hand and smooth his fingers down her soft cheek. "I've had my own share of it. Suppose we forget the past few weeks, and start over. Can you?''

Her eyes were troubled. "I don't know if it's wise," she said after a minute. "Letting the girls get attached to me again, I mean.''

His fingers traced her wide, soft mouth. "It's too late to stop that from happening. They miss you terribly. So do I," he added surprisingly. He tilted her chin up and bent, brushing his lips tenderly over her mouth. His heavy eyebrows drew together at the delight that shafted through him from the contact. "When I think of you, I think of butterflies and rainbows," he whispered against her mouth. "I hated the world until you came to work for John. You brought the light in with you. You made me laugh. You made me believe in miracles. Don't leave me, Kasie."

He was saying something, more than words. She drew back and searched his narrow, glittery eyes. "Leave…you?" she questioned the wording.

"You don't have an ego at all, do you?" he asked somberly. "Is it inconceivable that I want you back as much as my girls do?"

Her heart jumped. She'd missed him beyond bearing. But if she went back, could she ever be just an employee again? She remembered the hard warmth of his mouth in passion, the feel of his arms holding her like a warm treasure. She hesitated.

"I don't seduce virgins," he whispered wickedly. "If that wins me points."

She flushed. "I wasn't thinking about that!"

He smiled. "Yes, you were and that's the main reason I won't seduce you."

"Thanks a lot."

He cocked an eyebrow. "You might sound a little more grateful," he told her. "Keeping my hands off you lately has been a world-class study in restraint."

Her eyes widened. "Really?"

She was unworldly. He loved that about her. He loved the way she blushed when he teased her, the way she made his heart swell when she smiled. He'd been lonely without her.

"But I'll promise to keep my distance," he added gently. "If you'll just come back."

She bit her lower lip worriedly. She did need the

job. She loved the girls. She was crazy about Gil. But there were so many complications…

"Stop weighing the risks," he murmured. "Say yes."

"I still think…"

"Don't think," he whispered, placing a long forefinger over her lips. "Don't argue. Don't look ahead. We're going to go home and you're going to read the girls to sleep every night. They miss their stories."

"Don't you read to them?" she asked, made curious by a certain note in his voice.

"Sure, but they're getting tired of *Green Eggs and Ham.*"

"They have loads of other books besides Dr. Seuss," she began.

He glowered at her. "They hid all the other books, including *Green Eggs and Ham,* but at least I remember most of that story. So they get told it every night. Two weeks of that and I can't even look at ham in the grocery story anymore without gagging…"

She was laughing uproariously.

"This is not funny," he pointed out.

"Oh, yes, it is," she said, and laughed some more.

He loved the sound. It reminded him of wind chimes. His heart ached for her. "Come home before I get sick of eggs, too."

"All right," she said. "I guess I might as well. I can't live here with Mama Luke forever."

"She's a character," he remarked with a smile. "A blunt and honest lady with a big heart. I like her."

"She must like you, too, or she wouldn't have threatened to have you break down my bedroom door."

He pursed his lips. "Nice to have an ally with divine connections."

"She does, never doubt it," she told him, laughing. "I'll just go throw a few things into my suitcase."

He watched her go with joy shooting through his veins like fireworks. She was coming back. He'd convinced her.

Now all he had to do was make her see him as something more than an intolerant, judgmental boss. That was not going to be the easiest job he'd ever tackled.

Kasie kissed Mama Luke goodbye and waited while she hugged Gil impulsively.

"Take care of Kasie," her aunt told him.

He nodded slowly. "This time, I'll do better at that."

Mama Luke smiled.

They got into his black Jaguar and drove away, with Kasie leaning out the window and waving until her aunt was out of sight.

Gil watched her eyes close as she leaned back against the leather headrest. "Sleepy?"

"Yes," she murmured. "I haven't slept well since I came back from Nassau."

"Neither have I, Kasie," he said.

Her head turned and she looked at him quietly. It made her tingle all over. He was really a striking man, all lean strength and authority. She'd never felt as safe with anyone as she did with him.

He felt her eyes on him; warm, soft gray eyes that gave him pleasure when he met them. Kasie was unlike anyone he'd every known.

"Did Pauline finish keying in the herd records to

the computer before she left?'' she asked, suddenly remembering the chore that had been left when they went to Nassau.

"She hasn't been around since we came home," he said evasively. "I think she's visiting an aunt in Vermont."

She traced a line down the seat belt that stretched across her torso. "I thought you were going to marry her."

He had a good idea where she'd heard that unfounded lie. "Never in this lifetime," he murmured. "Pauline isn't domestic."

"She's crazy about you."

"The girls don't like her."

She pursed her lips. "I see."

He chuckled, glancing at her while they stopped for a red light. "Besides, after they found out that I'd fired you, they made Pauline's life hell. Their latest escapade was to leave her a nice present in her pocketbook."

"Oh, dear."

"It was a nonpoisonous snake," he said reassuringly. "But she decided that she'd be better off not visiting when the girls were around. And since they were always around..."

She shook her head. "Little terrors," she said, but in a tone soft with affection.

"Look who's talking," he said with a pointed glare.

"I've never put snakes in anybody's purse," she pointed out. "Well, not yet, anyway."

He gave her an amused glance. "Don't let the girls corrupt you."

She smiled, remembering how much fun she'd had

with the little girls. It made her happy that they wanted her back. Except for her aunt, she was alone in the world. She missed being part of a whole family, especially on holidays like Christmas.

The light changed and he pulled back out into traffic. Conversation was scanty the rest of the way home, because Kasie fell asleep. The lack of rest had finally caught up with her.

She was jolted awake by a firm hand on her shoulder.

"Wake up. We're home," Gil said with a smile.

She searched his blue eyes absently for a moment before the words registered. "Oh." She unfastened her seat belt and got out as he did.

The girls were sitting on the bottom step of the staircase when the door opened and Kasie walked in with Gil.

"Kasie!" Bess cried, and got up to run and throw herself into Kasie's outstretched arms.

"Bess!" Kasie hugged her close, feeling tears sting her eyes. She was so much like Sandy.

Jenny followed suit, and Kasie ended up with two arms full of crying little girls. She carried them to the staircase and sat down, cuddling them both close. Her face was wet, but she didn't care. She loved these babies, far more than she'd realized. She held them and rocked them and kissed wet little cheeks until the sobs eased.

"You mustn't *ever* leave us again, Kasie," Bess hiccuped. "Me and Jenny was ever so sad."

"Yes, we was," Jenny murmured.

"Oh, I missed you!" Kasie said fervently as she dug into her pocket for a tissue and wiped wet eyes all around.

"We missed you, too," Bess said, burying her face in Kasie's shoulder while Jenny clung to her neck.

Gil watched them with his heart in his throat. They looked as if they belonged together. They looked like a family. He wanted to scoop all three of them up in his arms and hold them so tight they'd never get away.

While he was debating that, John came down the hall and spotted Kasie. He grinned from ear to ear. "You're back! Great! Now maybe Mrs. Charters will cook something we can eat again!"

"That's not a nice way to say hello," Kasie chided with a smile.

"Sure it is! What good is a man without his stomach?" John asked. He moved closer to Kasie and the girls and bent to kiss Kasie's wet cheek. "Welcome back! It's been like a ballpark in January. Nobody smiled."

"I'm happy to be back," Kasie said. "But what about all those herd records that need putting into the computer?" she asked, realizing that Gil never had answered her when she'd questioned him about them.

"Oh, those. It turns out that Miss Parsons is a computer whiz herself," he said to Kasie's amusement. "She's got everything listed, including the foundation bloodlines. And remember that Internet site you suggested? It's up and running. We're already getting three hundred hits a day, along with plenty of queries from cattlemen around the country!"

"I'm so glad," Kasie said sincerely.

"So are we. Business is booming. But the babies have been sad." He glanced at his older brother meaningfully. "We missed you."

"It's nice to be back," Kasie said.

"Are we ever going to have lunch?" John asked then. "I'm fairly starved. Burned eggs and bacon this morning didn't do a lot for my taste buds."

"Mine, either," Gil agreed. "Go tell Mrs. Charters Kasie's back and is having lunch with us," he suggested. "That might get us something edible, even if it's only cold cuts."

"Good thinking," John said, smiling as he went out to the kitchen.

"Our eggs wasn't burned," Bess pointed out.

"Mrs. Charters wasn't mad at you, sweetheart," Gil told her. "You two need to run upstairs and wash your hands and faces before we eat."

"Okay, if Kasie comes, too," Bess agreed.

Kasie chuckled as both girls grabbed a hand and coaxed her to her feet. "I gather that I'm to be carefully observed from now on, so I don't make a run for the border," she murmured to Gil.

"That's right. Good girls," Gil said, grinning. "Keep her with you so she doesn't have a chance to escape."

"We won't let her go, Daddy," Bess promised.

They tugged her up the staircase, and she went without an argument, waiting in their rooms while they washed their hands and faces.

"Daddy was real mad when we came home," Bess told Kasie. "So was Uncle Johnny. He said Daddy should go and get you and bring you home, but Daddy said you might not want to, because he'd been bad to you. Did he take away your toys, Kasie and put you into time-out?"

"Heavens, no," she said at once.

"Then why did you go away?" the child insisted. "Was it on account of Pauline said you left us alone?

We told Daddy the truth, and Pauline went away. We don't like her. She's bad to us when Daddy isn't looking. He won't marry Pauline, will he, Kasie?''

"I don't think so," she said carefully.

"Me and Jenny wish he'd marry you," Bess said wistfully. "You're so much fun to play with, Kasie."

Kasie didn't dare say anything about marriage. "You can't decide things like that, sweetheart," she told Bess. "People don't usually marry unless they fall in love."

"Oh."

The child looked heartbroken. Kasie went down on her knees and caught Bess gently by the waist. "What do you want to do after we have lunch?" she asked, changing the subject.

"Could we swim in the pool?"

She'd forgotten that the family had a swimming pool. "I suppose so," she said, frowning. "But it's pretty soon after your accident, Bess. Are you sure you want to?"

"Daddy and me went swimming the day after we came home," Bess said matter-of-factly. "Daddy said I mustn't be afraid of the water, after I fell in, so he's giving me swimming lessons. I love to swim, now!"

So some good had come out of the accident. That was reassuring. "Let's go down and eat something. Then we have to wait a little while."

"I know. We can pick flowers while we wait, can't we? There's some pretty yellow roses in a hedge behind the swimming pool," Bess told her.

"I love roses," Kasie said, smiling. "But perhaps we'd better not pick any until someone tells us it's all right."

"Okay, Kasie."

They went downstairs and Kasie helped Mrs. Charters set the table. She was welcoming and cheerful about having Kasie back again. John talked easily to Kasie and the children. Gil didn't. He picked at his food and brooded. He watched Kasie, but covertly. She wondered what was going on in his mind to make him so unhappy.

He looked up and met Kasie's searching eyes, and she felt her stomach fall as if she was on a roller coaster. Her hands trembled. She put them in her lap to hide them, but her heartbeat pounded wildly and her nervousness was noticeable. Especially to the man with the arrogant smile, who suddenly seemed to develop an appetite.

# Chapter 10

For the next few days, Gil seemed to watch every move Kasie made. He was cordial with her, but there was a noticeable difference in the way he treated her since her return. He was remote and quiet, even when the family came together at mealtimes, and he seemed uncomfortable around Kasie. She noticed his reticence and understood it to mean that he was sorry for the way he'd treated her before. He didn't touch her at all these days, nor did he seem inclined to include her when he took the girls to movies and the playground, even though he asked her along. But she always refused, to the dismay of the children. She excused it as giving them some time alone with their father. Gil knew that wasn't the truth. It made matters worse.

John left Thursday for a conference that Gil had been slated to attend, and Gil stayed home. Kasie noticed that he seemed unusually watchful and he was always around the ranch even when he wasn't around the house. He didn't explain why. Kasie would have loved thinking that it was because he was interested in her, but she knew that wasn't the reason. There was more distance between them now than there had ever been before.

Mrs. Charters mentioned that there was some uneasiness among the cowboys because of a threat that had been made. Kasie tried to ask Gil about it. He simply ignored the question and walked away.

He was missing at breakfast early one Monday morning. The girls were sleeping late, so Kasie walked into the dining room and found only John at the table.

"Pull up a chair and have breakfast," he invited with a grin. "I have to move bulls today, so I'm having seconds and thirds. I have to keep up my strength."

"If you keep eating like that, you could carry the bulls and save gas," she said wickedly. "I thought you had to go to Phoenix to show a bull this week?"

He averted his eyes. "I thought I'd put it off for another couple of weeks." He sipped coffee and studied Kasie quietly. "There's a new Western showing at the theater downtown. How would you like to pack up the girls and go with me to see it?"

Her eyes lit up. "I'd love to," she said at once.

He grinned. "Okay. We'll go tomorrow night. I, uh, noticed that you don't like going to movies with my brother, even if the girls go along."

"I just thought he'd like some time alone with them," she hedged. "After all, I'm just the governess."

He poured himself more coffee before he replied. "That's a bunch of hogwash, Kasie."

She drew in a long breath. "He makes me uncomfortable," she said. "I always feel like he's biding his time, waiting for me to make another mistake or do something stupid."

He chuckled. "He doesn't lie in wait to ambush you," he said softly. "He meant it when he apologized, you know. He was sorry he misjudged you. Believe me, it's a rare thing for him to make a mistake like that. But he's had some hard blows from women in recent years."

"I felt really bad about what happened," she said with a wistful sadness in her eyes. "I should have remembered that he never trusted Pauline to look after the girls. I'd met this man on the plane, and he invited me to lunch. I liked him. He kept me from being afraid on the way to Nassau."

John's face sobered, and she realized that Gil must have told him about her past. "I'm sorry about your brother and his family," he said, confirming her suspicions. "Gil and I haven't really been part of a family since our uncle died."

"Don't you ever go to see your parents?" she asked curiously.

"There was a time when they offered an olive branch, but you know Gil," he said soberly. "He's slow to get over things, and he refused to talk to them. Maybe they did neglect us, but I never thought it was malicious. They had kids before they were ready to have them. Lots of people are irresponsible parents. But you can't hold grudges forever." He frowned. "On second thought, maybe Gil can."

She smiled and reached across the table to lay her

hand over his. "Maybe one day you can try again. It would be nice for the girls to have grandparents."

"The only ones they have left are our parents. Darlene's died years ago." He caught her hand in his and held it tight. "You make the hardest things sound simple. I like myself when you're around, Kasie."

She laughed gently. "I like you, too," she said.

"I never believed you had anything to do with Bess getting hurt," he said somberly. "Anyone could see how much you care about the girls."

"Thanks. It's nice to know that at least one grown-up person in your family believed I was innocent," she said, oblivious to the white-faced, angry man standing in the hall with an armload of pale pink roses. "It hurt terribly that Gil thought I'd ever put the girls at risk in any way, least of all by neglecting them. But it wasn't the first time he's accused me of ulterior motives. I should be used to it by now. I think he's sorry he rehired me, you know," she added sadly, clinging to his hand. "He looks through me when he isn't glaring at me."

"Gil's had some hard knocks with women," John repeated, letting go of her hand. "Just give him time to adjust to being wrong. He rarely is." He picked up a forkful of eggs. "If it's any consolation, he roared around here for two weeks like every man's nightmare before he went after you. He wanted you to have enough time to get over the anger and let him explain his behavior. He would have gone sooner, he said, but he wasn't sure he could get in the front door."

She remembered her lacerated feelings when she'd arrived at her aunt's house. "It would have been tricky, at that," she agreed. "He was the last person on earth I wanted to see when I first came back from Nassau.''

Footsteps echoed out in the hall and a door slammed. Kasie frowned.

''Sounds like Gil's going to bypass breakfast again this morning,'' John remarked as he finished his eggs. ''He doesn't have much of an appetite these days.''

''I'll just check and make sure it isn't the girls,'' Kasie said.

''Suit yourself, but I know those footsteps. He only walks that way when he's upset. God help whatever cowboy he runs into on his way.''

Kasie didn't reply. She walked into the hall and there, on the hall table, was an armload of pink roses with the dew still clinging to the silky, fragrant petals. It took a few seconds for her to realize that Gil must have heard every word she'd said. She groaned inwardly as she gathered up the roses. Well, that was probably the end of any truce, she thought. He'd think she couldn't forgive him, and that would make him even angrier. Unless she missed her guess, he was going to be hell to live with from now on.

She took the roses to the kitchen and found a vase for them, which she filled with water before she arranged the flowers in it. With a sigh, she took them upstairs to her room and placed them on the dresser. They were beautiful. She couldn't imagine what had possessed Gil Callister to go out and cut her a bouquet. But the gesture touched her poignantly.

Sure enough, when Gil came in early for supper, he was dusty and out of humor. He needed a shave. He glared at everybody, especially Kasie.

''Aren't you going to clean up first?'' John asked, aghast, when he sat down to the table in his chaps.

"What for?" he muttered. "I've got to go right back out again." He reached for his coffee cup, which Mrs. Charters had just filled, and put cream in it.

"Is something wrong?" John asked then, concerned.

"We've got a fence down." His eyes met his brothers. "It wasn't broken through. It was cut."

John stared at the older man. "Another one? That makes two in less than ten days."

"I know. I can't prove it, but I know it was Fred Sims."

John nodded slowly. "That makes sense. One of the cowboys who was friendly with him said Sims hasn't been able to find another job since we fired him."

Gil's pale blue eyes glittered. "That damned dog could have bitten my babies," he said. "No way was he going to keep it here after it chased them onto the porch."

"Bad doggie," Jenny agreed.

Bess nodded. "We was scared, Daddy."

"Sims is going to be scared, if I catch him within a mile of my property," Gil added.

"Don't become a vigilante," John cautioned his older brother. "Call the sheriff. Let him handle it. That's what he gets paid to do."

"He can't be everywhere," Gil replied, eyes narrowed. "I want all the cowboys armed, at least with rifles. I'm not taking any chances. If he's brazen enough to cut fences and shoot livestock, he's capable of worse."

Kasie felt her heart stop. So that was why he'd been around the ranch so much lately. The man, Sims, had threatened vengeance. Apparently he was killing cattle as well as cutting fences to let them escape. She pictured Gil at the end of a gun and she felt sick all over.

"I'll make sure everyone's been alerted and prepared for danger," John agreed. "But you stay out of it. You're the one person around here that Sims would enjoy shooting."

"He'd be lucky to get off a shot," Gil replied imperturbably. He finished his meal and wiped his mouth. "I've got to get back out there. We haven't finished stringing wire, and it's not long until dark."

"Okay. I'll phone the vet about those carcasses we found. I want him to look for bullet wounds."

"Good idea."

Gil finished the last sip of his coffee in a grim silence that seemed to spread to the rest of the family. The girls, sensing hidden anger in the adults around them, excused themselves and went upstairs to play in their room while Mrs. Charters cleaned away the dishes. John went to make a phone call.

Gil got to his feet without looking at Kasie and started toward the front door. Kasie caught up with him on the porch. It was almost dark. The sky was fiery red and pink and yellow where the sun was setting.

"Thank you," she blurted out.

He stopped and turned. "For what?"

His hat was pulled low over his eyes, and she couldn't see the expression in them, but she was pretty sure that he was scowling.

She went closer to him, stopping half an arm's length away. "For the roses," she said hesitantly. "They're beautiful."

He didn't move. He just stood there, somber, quiet.

"How do you know they were meant for you?" he drawled. "And how do you know I brought them?"

She flushed scarlet. She didn't know for sure, but she'd assumed.

He averted his eyes, muttering under his breath. "You're welcome," he said tersely.

"That man, Sims," she continued, worried. "The day you fired him, John said that he had a mean temper and that he carried a loaded rifle everywhere with him. You…you be careful, okay?"

She heard the soft expulsion of breath. He moved a step closer, his lean hands lifting her oval face to his. She could see the soft glitter of his blue eyes in the faint light from the windows.

"What do you care if I get myself shot?" he asked huskily. "I'm the one who sent you packing without even giving you the chance to explain what happened in Nassau."

"Pauline didn't like me," she said. "And you trusted her. I was just a stranger."

"Not anymore, Kasie," he said gruffly.

"I mean, you didn't know anything about me," she persisted. She searched his eyes, feeling jolts of electricity flow into her at the exquisite contact. "I was upset and I behaved badly when you came to Mama Luke's. But deep inside, I didn't blame you for not trusting me."

His lean hands tightened on her face. "I've done nothing but torment you since the first day you came here," he bit off. "I didn't want you in my life, Kasie," he whispered as he bent toward her. "I still don't. But a man can only stand so much…!"

His mouth caught hers hungrily. His arms swallowed her up against him, so that not an inch of space separated them. For long, achingly sweet seconds, they clung to each other in the soft darkness.

He drew away from her finally and stood just looking at her in a tense, hot silence. His hands were firm around her arms, and she swayed toward him helplessly.

She felt her knees go shaky, as if they had jelly in them instead of bone and cartilage. "Look, I'm very old-fashioned," she began in a choked tone.

"I almost never make love to women on the floor of the front porch."

She stared at him dimly, only slowly becoming aware that he was smiling and the words were both affectionate and teasing.

A tiny laugh burst from her swollen lips, although the kiss had rattled her.

"That's better," he said. His eyes narrowed. "How do you feel about my brother?"

Her mind refused to function. "How do I what?"

"Feel about John," he persisted coolly. "When I asked you why you wanted this job, you said it was because John was a dish. I know you had a crush on him. How do you feel now?"

She was at a loss to know what to say. "I like…him," she blurted out. "He's been kind to me."

"Kinder than I have, for damned sure," he agreed at once. "And he believed you were innocent when I didn't."

She frowned. "You explained why."

His hands tightened on her arms and his lips flattened. "He's younger than I am, single and rich and easygoing," he said harshly. "Maybe he'd be the best thing that ever happened to you."

Her eyes widened. "Thank you. I've always wanted a big, strong man to plan my future for me."

He let her go abruptly, angry. "You said it yourself. I'm a generation older than you with a ready-made family."

She couldn't make heads or tails of what he was saying. Her mind was spinning as she looked up at him.

"Maybe you're what he needs, too," he added coldly. "Someone young and optimistic and intelligent."

"Are you going to buy the ring, too?"

He turned away. "That wasn't funny."

"I don't want to marry your brother. Thanks, anyway."

He kept walking.

She ran after him. "That man Sims has got a gun," she called. "Don't you dare go out there and get shot!"

He paused on the top step and looked back at her as if he had doubts about her sanity. "John's going out with me as soon as he finishes his phone calls."

"Great!" she exclaimed angrily. "I can worry about both of you all night!"

"Worry about my daughters," he told her bluntly. "That's your only responsibility here. You work for me, remember?"

"I remember," she replied irritably. "Do you?"

"Stay in the house with the girls until I tell you otherwise. I don't want any of you on the porch or in the yard until we settle this, one way or another."

He did think there was danger. She heard it in every word. "I won't let anything happen to Bess and Jenny. I promise."

He glared at her. "Can you shoot?"

She shook her head. "But I know how to dial 911."

"Okay. Keep one of the wireless phones handy, just in case."

She moved toward him another step, wrapping her arms tight around her body. "Have you got a cell phone?"

He indicated the case on his belt. That was when she noticed an old Colt .45 strapped to his other hip, under the denim shirt he was wearing open over his black T-shirt.

Her breath caught. Until that minute, when she saw the gun, it was a possibility. But guns were violent, chaotic, frightening. She bit her lower lip worriedly.

"I'll be late. Make sure you lock the doors before you go upstairs. John and I have keys."

"I will," she promised. "You be careful."

He ignored the quiet command. He took one long, last look at her and went on down the steps to his pickup truck, which was parked nearby.

She stood at the top of the steps until he drove away, staring after him worriedly. She wanted to call him back, to beg him to stay inside where he'd be safe from any retribution by that man Sims. But she couldn't. He wasn't the sort of man to run from trouble. It wouldn't do any good to nag him. He was going to do what he needed to do, whether or not it pleased her.

She got the girls ready for bed and tucked them in. She read them a Dr. Seuss book they hadn't heard yet. When they grew drowsy, she pulled the covers over them and tiptoed to the door, pausing to flick off the light switch as she went out into the hall.

She left the door cracked and went on down the hall to her own room. She got ready for bed and curled up on her pillows with a worn copy of Tacitus' *The Histories.* ''I wonder if you ever imagined that people in the future would still be reading words you wrote almost two thousand years ago,'' she murmured as she thumbed through the well-read work. ''And nothing really changes, does it, except the clothes and the everyday things. People are the same.''

Her heart wasn't in the book. She laid it aside and turned off the lights, thinking how it would have been two thousand years ago to watch her husband put on his armor and march off to a war in some foreign country behind one of the Roman generals. That made her think of Gil and she gnawed her lip as she lay in the darkness, waiting for some sound that would tell her he was still all right.

It was two o'clock in the morning before she heard a pickup truck pull up at the bottom of the steps out front. She threw off the covers and ran to the window, peering out through the lacy curtain just in time to see Gil and John climb wearily out of the truck. John had a rifle with the breech open under one arm. He led the way into the house, with Gil following behind.

At least, thank God, they were both still alive, she thought. She went back to bed and pulled the covers up to her chin. Relieved, she slept.


She'd forgotten John's invitation to the movies, but he hadn't. And he looked odd, as if he was pondering something wicked, when he waited for her to come down the stairs with the girls.

Kasie was wearing a pretty dark green silk pantsuit with strappy sandals and her hair around her shoulders. She smiled at the little girls in their skirt sets. They looked like a family, and John was touched. He went forward to greet them, pausing to kiss Kasie's cheek warmly.

Gil, who was working in the office, came into the hall just in time to see his brother kissing Kasie. His eyes splintered with unexpected helpless rage. His fists clenched at his side. She wouldn't leave the house with him, but here she was dressed to the nines and all eager to jump into a car with his brother.

John glanced at him warily and hid a smile. "We're off to the movies! Want to come?"

"No," Gil said abruptly. He avoided looking at Kasie. "I've got two more hours of work to finish in the den."

"Let Miss Parsons do it and come with us," John persisted.

"I gave Miss Parsons the day off. She's visiting a friend."

"Let it wait until tomorrow, then."

"No chance. Go ahead and enjoy yourselves, but don't get too comfortable. Watch your back," he said tersely, and returned into the study. He closed the door firmly behind him.

John, for some ungodly reason, was rubbing his hands together with absolute glee. Kasie gave him a speaking glance, which he ignored as he herded them out into the night.

The movie was one for general audiences, about a famous singer. John didn't really enjoy it, but Kasie and the girls did. They ate popcorn and giggled at the funny scenes, and moaned when the heroine was mis-judged by the hero and thrown out on her ear.

"That looks familiar, doesn't it?" John murmured outrageously.

"She should hit him with a brickbat," Kasie muttered.

"With a head that hard, I don't know if it would do any good," he said, and Kasie thought for a minute that it didn't sound as if he were referring to the movie. "But I have a much better idea, anyway. Wait and see."

She pondered that enigmatic remark all through the movie. They went home, had dinner and watched TV, but it wasn't until the girls went up to bed and the study door opened that Kasie began to realize what John was up to. Because he waited until his brother had an unobstructed view of the two of them at the foot of the staircase. And then he bent and kissed Kasie. Passionately.

Kasie was shocked. Gil was infuriated. John winked at Kasie before he turned to face his brother. "Oh, there you are," he told Gil with a grin. "The movie was great. I'll tell you all about it tomorrow. Sleep well, Kasie," he added, ruffling the hair at her temple.

"You, too," she choked. She could barely manage words. John had never touched her before, and she knew that it hadn't been out of misplaced passion or raging desire that he'd kissed her. He'd obviously done it to irritate his big brother. And it was working! Gil looked as if he wanted to bite somebody.

He moved close to Kasie when John was out of sight up the steps, whipping out a snow-white handkerchief. He caught her by the nape and wiped off her smeared lipstick.

"You aren't marrying my brother," he said through his teeth.

"Excuse me?"

"I said, you aren't marrying John," he repeated harshly. "You're an employee here, and that's all. I am not going to let my brother become your meal ticket!"

She actually gasped. "Of all the unfounded, unreasonable, outrageous things in the world to say to a woman, that really takes the cake!" she raged.

"I haven't started yet," he bit off. He threw the handkerchief down on the hall table and pulled her roughly into his arms. "I've never wanted to hit a man so badly in all my life," he ground out as his mouth went down over hers.

She couldn't breathe. He didn't seem to notice, or care. His mouth was warm, hard, insistent. She clung to his shirtfront and let the sensations wash over her like fire. He was insulting her. She shouldn't let him. She should make him stop. It was just that his mouth was so sweet, so masterful, so ardent. She moaned as the sensations piled up on themselves and left her knees wobbling out from under her.

He caught her closer and lifted her against him, devouring her mouth with his own. She felt her whole body begin to shiver with the strength of the desire he was teaching her to feel. Never in her life had she known such pleasure, but even the hungry force of the kiss still wasn't enough to ease the ache in her.

Her arms went up and around his neck and she held on as if she might die by letting go. He groaned huskily as his body began to harden. He wanted her. He wanted to lay her down on the Persian carpet, make passionate love to her. He wanted…

He dragged his mouth from hers and looked down at her with accusation and raging anger.

"I'm mad," he growled off. "You aren't supposed to enjoy it."

"Okay," she murmured, trying to coax his mouth back down onto hers. She had no will, no pride, no reason left. She only wanted the pleasure to continue. "Come back here. I'll pretend to hate it."

"Kasie…"

She found his mouth and groaned hoarsely as he gave in to his own hunger and crushed her against the length of his tall, fit body. It was the most glorious kiss of her entire life. If only it would never end…

But it did, all too soon, and he shot away from her as if he'd tasted poison. His eyes glittered. "If you ever let him kiss you again, I'll throw both of you out a window!"

She opened her mouth to speak, but before she could manage words, the front doorbell rang.

It was one of the cowboys. Two more head of cattle had been shot, and the gunman was still out near the line cabin. One of the cowboys had him pinned down with rifle fire and needed reinforcements. It took Gil precisely five minutes to call John, load his Winchester and get out the door. He barely took time to caution Kasie about venturing outside until the situation was under control. She didn't even get a chance to beg him to be careful. She went upstairs, so that she'd be near the girls, but she knew that this was one night she wouldn't sleep a wink.

# Chapter 11

Kasie lay awake for the rest of the night. When dawn broke, she still hadn't heard Gil come into the house. And once she'd thought she heard a shot being fired. Remembering how dangerous the man Sims was supposed to be made her even more uneasy. What if Gil had been shot? How would she live? She couldn't bear the thought of a world without Gil in it.

She got up and dressed just as Mrs. Charters went into the kitchen to start breakfast. John and Gil were nowhere in sight.

"Have they come in at all?" she asked Mrs. Charters.

"Not yet," the older woman said, and looked worried. "There were police cars and sheriff's cars all over the place about two hours ago," she added. "I saw them from my house."

"I thought I heard a shot, but I didn't see anything," Kasie said, and then she really worried.

"You couldn't have seen them, it was three miles and more down the road. But I'm sure we'd have heard if anything had happened to Gil or John."

"Oh, I hope so," Kasie said fervently.

"I'll make coffee," she said. "You can have some in a minute."

"Thanks, Mrs. Charters. I'm going to go sit on the front porch."

"You do that, dear."

The ranch was most beautiful early in the morning, Kasie thought, when dawn broke on the horizon and the cattle and horses started moving around in the pastures. She loved this part of the day, but now it was torment to sit and wonder and not be able to do anything. Had they found Sims? Was he in custody or still at large? And, most frightening of all, was the memory of that single gunshot. Had Gil been hurt?

She nibbled at her fingernails in her nervousness, a habit left over from childhood. There didn't seem to be a vehicle in the world. The highway was close enough that the sound of moving vehicles could be heard very faintly, but at this hour there was very little traffic. In fact, there was none.

She got up from the porch swing and paced restlessly. What if Gil had been shot? Surely someone would have phoned. John would, she was certain. But what if the wound was serious, so serious that he couldn't leave his brother's side even long enough to make a phone call? What if…!

The sound of a truck coming down the long ranch road caught her attention. She ran to the top of the steps and stood there with her heart pounding like mad. It was one of the ranch's pickup trucks. She recognized it. Two men were in the cab. They were in a flaming rush. Was it John and one of the hands, come to tell her that Gil was hurt, wounded, dying?

Dust flew as the driver pulled up sharply at the front steps. Both doors flew open. Kasie thought she might faint. John got out of the passenger side, whole and undamaged and grinning. Gil got out on the other side, dusty and worn, with a cut bleeding beside his mouth. But he was all in one piece, not injured, not shot, not...

"Gil!" She screamed his name, blind and deaf and dumb to the rest of the world as she came out of her frozen trance and dashed down the steps, missing the bottom one entirely, to rush right into his arms.

"Kasie..." He couldn't talk at all, because she was kissing him, blindly, fervently, as if he'd just come back from the dead.

He stopped trying to talk. He kissed her back, his arms enfolding her so closely that her feet dangled while he answered the aching hunger of her mouth.

She was shaking when he lifted his head. His eyes were glittery with feeling as he searched her eyes and saw every single emotion in her. She loved him. She couldn't have told him any plainer if she'd shouted it.

John just chuckled. "I'll go drink coffee while you two...talk," he murmured dryly, bypassing them without a backward glance.

Neither of them heard him or saw him go. They stared at each other with aching tenderness, touching faces, lips, fingertips.

"I'm all right," he whispered, kissing her again.

"Sims took a shot at us, but he missed. It took two sheriff's deputies, the bloodhounds and a few ranch hands, but we tracked him down. He's in jail, nursing his bruises."

She traced the dried blood on his cheek. "He hit you."

He shrugged. "I hit him, too." He smiled outrageously. "So much for pretending that you only work for me, Kasie," he said with deliberate mischief in his tone.

She touched his dusty hair. "I love you," she said huskily. Her eyes searched his. "Is it all right?"

"That depends," he mused, bending to kiss her gently. "We discussed being old-fashioned, remember?"

She flushed. "I wasn't suggesting…"

He took her soft upper lip in both of his and nibbled it. "This is the last place in the world that you and I could carry on a torrid affair," he pointed out. "The girls can take off doorknobs if they have the right tools, and Mrs. Charters probably has microphones and hidden cameras in every room. She always knows whatever's going on around here." He lifted his head and searched her eyes. "I'm glad you love children, Kasie. I really don't plan to stop at Bess and Jenny."

She flushed softly. "Really?"

"We should have one or two of our own," he added quietly. "Boys run in my family, even if Darlene and I were never able to have one. If we had a son or two, it would give Bess and Jenny a chance to be part of a big family."

Her eyes grew dreamy. "We could teach all of them how to use the computer and love cattle."

He smiled tenderly. "But first, I think we might get married," he whispered at her lips. "So that your aunt doesn't have to be embarrassed when she tells people what you're doing."

"We wouldn't want to embarrass Mama Luke," she agreed, bubbling over with joy.

"God forbid," he murmured. He kissed her again, with muted passion. "She can come to the wedding." He hesitated and his eyes darkened. "I'm not sure about my brother. I could have decked him for kissing you!"

"I still don't know why he did," she began.

He chuckled. "He told me. He wanted to see if I was jealous of you. I gave him hell all night until Sims showed up. He laughed all the way back to the ranch. So much for lighting fires under people," he added with a faint grin. "I'll let him be best man, I guess, but he's going to be the only man in church who doesn't get to kiss the bride!"

She laughed. "What a wicked family I'm marrying into," she said as she reached up to kiss him. "And speaking of wicked, we have to invite K.C.," she added shyly.

He froze, lifting his head. "I don't know about that, Kasie…"

"You'll like him. Really you will," she promised, smiling widely.

He grimaced. "I suppose we each have to have at least one handicap," he muttered. "I have a lunatic brother and you're best friends with a hit man."

"He's not. You'll like him," she repeated, and drew his head down to hers again. She kissed him with enthusiasm, enjoying the warm, wise tutoring of his hard mouth. "We should go and tell the babies," she whispered against his mouth.

"No need," he murmured.

"Uncle John, look! Daddy's kissing Kasie!"

"See?" he added with a grin as he lifted his head and indicated the front door. Standing there, grinning also, were John, Bess, Jenny, Mrs. Charters, and Miss Parsons.

The wedding was the social event of Medicine Ridge for the summer. Kasie wore a beautiful white gown with lace and a keyhole necklace, with a Juliet cap and a long veil. She looked, Gil whispered as she joined him at the altar, like an angel.

Her excited eyes approved his neat gray vested suit, which made his hair look even more blond. At either side of them were Bess and Jenny in matching blue dresses, carrying baskets of white roses. Next to them was John, his brother's best man, fumbling in his pocket for the wedding rings he was responsible for.

As the ceremony progressed, a tall, blond man in the front pew watched with narrowed, wistful eyes as his godchild married the eldest of the Callister heirs. Not bad, K.C. Kantor thought, for a girl who'd barely survived a military uprising even before she was born. He glanced at the woman seated next to him, his eyes sad and quiet, as he contemplated what might have been if he'd met Kasie's aunt before her heart led her to a life of service in a religious order. They were the best of friends and they corresponded. She would always be family to him. She was the only family he had, or would ever have, except for that sweet young woman at the altar.

"Isn't she beautiful?" Mama Luke whispered to him.

"A real vision," he agreed.

She smiled at him with warm affection and turned her attention back to the ceremony.

As the priest pronounced them man and wife, Gil lifted the veil and bent to kiss Kasie. There were sighs all around, until a small hand tugged hard at Kasie's skirt and a little voice was heard asking plaintively, "Is it over yet, Daddy? I have to go to the bathroom!"

Later, laughing about the small interruption as they gathered in the fellowship hall of the church, Kasie and Gil each cuddled a little girl and fed them cake.

"It was nice of Pauline to apologize for what she did in the Bahamas," Kasie murmured, recalling the telephone call that had both surprised and pleased her the day before the ceremony.

"She's really not that bad," Gil mused. "Just irresponsible and possessive. But I still didn't want her at the wedding," he added with a grin. "Just in case."

"I still wish you'd invited your parents," Kasie told Gil gently.

"I did," he replied. "They were on their way to the Bahamas and couldn't spare the time." He smiled at her. "Don't worry the subject, Kasie. Some things can't be changed. We're a family, you and me and the girls and John."

"Yes, we are," she agreed, and she reached up to kiss him. She glanced around them curiously. Mama Luke intercepted the glance and joined them.

"He left as we were coming in here," she told

Kasie. "K.C. never was one for socializing. I expect he's headed for the airport by now."

"It was nice of him to come."

"It was," she agreed. She handed a small box to Kasie. "He asked me to give this to you."

She frowned, pausing to open the box. She drew out a gold necklace with a tiny crystal ball dangling from it. Inside the ball was a tiny seed.

"It's a mustard seed," Mama Luke explained. "It's from a Biblical quote—if you have even that amount of faith, as a mustard seed, nothing is impossible. It's to remind you that miracles happen."

Kasie cradled it in her hand and looked up at Gil with her heart in her eyes. "Indeed they do," she whispered, and all the love she had for her new husband was in her face.

The next night, Kasie and Gil lay tangled in a king-size bed at a rented villa in Nassau, exhausted and deliciously relaxed from their first intimacy.

Kasie moved shyly against him, her face flushed in the aftermath of more physical sensation than she'd ever experienced.

"Stop that," he murmured drowsily. "I'm useless now. Go to sleep."

She laughed with pure delight and curled closer. "All right. But don't forget where we left off."

He drew her closer. "As if I could!" He bent and kissed her eyes shut. "Kasie, I never dreamed that I could be this happy again." His eyes opened and looked into hers with fervent possession. "I loved Darlene. A part of me will always love her. But I would die for you," he added roughly, his eyes blazing with emotion.

Overwhelmed, she buried her face in his throat and shivered. "I would die for you," she choked. She clung harder. "I love you!"

His mouth found hers, hungry for contact, for the sharing of fierce, exquisite need. He drew her over his relaxed body and held her until the trembling stopped. His breath sighed out heavily at her ear. "Forever, Kasie," he whispered unsteadily.

She smiled. "Forever."

They slept, eventually, and as dawn filtered in through the venetian blinds and the sound of the surf grew louder, there was a knock on the door.

Gil opened his eyes, still drowsy. He looked down at Kasie, fast asleep on her stomach, smiling even so. He smiled, too, and tossed the sheet over her before he stepped into his Bermuda shorts and went to answer the door.

The shock when he opened it was blatant. On the doorstep were a silver-haired man in casual slacks and designer shirt, and a silver-haired woman in a neat but casual sundress and overblouse. They were carrying the biggest bouquet of orchids Gil had ever seen in his life.

The man pushed the bouquet toward Gil hesitantly and with a smile that seemed both hesitant and uncertain. "Congratulations," he said.

"From both of us," the woman added.

They both stood there, waiting.

As Gil searched for words, there was movement behind him and Kasie came to the door in the flowered cotton muu-muu she'd bought for the trip, her long chestnut hair disheveled, smiling broadly.

"Hello!" she exclaimed, going past Gil to hug the

woman and then the man, who both flushed. "I'm so glad you could come!"

Gil stared at her. "What?"

"I phoned them," she told him, clasping his big hand in hers. "They said they'd like to come over and have lunch with us, and I told them to come today. But I overslept," she added, and flushed.

"It's your honeymoon, you should oversleep," Gil's mother, Magdalene, said gently. She looked at her son nervously. "We wanted to come to the wedding," she said. "But we didn't want to, well, ruin the day for you."

"That's right," Jack Callister agreed gruffly. "We haven't been good parents. At first we were too irresponsible, and then we were too ashamed. Especially when Douglas took you in and we lost touch." He shrugged. "It's too late to start over, of course, but we'd sort of like to, well, to get to know you and John. And the girls, of course. That is, if you, uh, if you…" He shrugged.

Kasie squeezed Gil's hand, hard.

"I'd like that," he said obligingly.

Their faces changed. They beamed. For several seconds, they looked like silver-haired children on Christmas morning. And Gil realized with stark shock that they were just that—grown-up children without the first idea of how to be parents. Douglas Callister had kept the boys, and he hadn't approved of his brother Jack, so he hadn't encouraged contact. Since the elder Callisters didn't know how to approach their children directly, they lost touch and then couldn't find a way to reach them at all.

He looked down at Kasie, and it all made sense.

She'd tied the loose ends up. She'd gathered a family back together.

She squeezed Gil's hand again, looking up at him with radiant delight. "We could get dressed and meet them in the restaurant. After we put these in water," she added, hugging the bouquet to her heart and sniffing them. "I've never had orchids in my life," she said with a smile. "Thank you!"

Magdalena laughed nervously. "No, Kasie. Thank *you*."

"We'll get dressed and meet you in about fifteen minutes, in the restaurant," Gil managed to say.

"Great!" Jack said. He took his wife's hand, and they both smiled, looking ten years younger. "We'll see you there!"

The door closed and Gil looked down at Kasie with wonder.

"I thought they might like to visit us at the ranch next month, too," Kasie said, "so they can get to know the babies."

"You're amazing," he said. "Absolutely amazing!"

She fingered the necklace K.C. had given her at the wedding. "I like miracles, don't you?"

He burst out laughing. He picked her up and swung her around in an arc while she squealed and held on to her bouquet tightly. He put her down gently and kissed her roughly.

"I love you," he said huskily.

She grinned. "Yes, and see what it gets you when you love people? You get all sorts of nice surprises. In fact," she added with a mischievous grin, "I have all sorts of surprises in store for you."

He took a deep breath and looked at her with warm affection. "I can hardly wait."

She kissed him gently and went to dress. She gave a thought to Gil's Darlene, and to her own parents, and her lost twin and his family, and hoped that they all knew, somehow, that she and Gil were happy and that they had a bright future with the two little girls and the children they would have together. As she went to the closet to get her dress, her eyes were full of dreams. And so were Gil's.

\* \* \* \* \*

# TROPHY WIVES

## BY
## JAN COLLEY

Thanks for the support of romance writing
organisations everywhere, and all the multi-published
authors who give up their time to help the newbies.

**Jan Colley** lives in Christchurch, New Zealand, with her
long-suffering fireman and two cats who don't appear
to suffer much at all. She started writing after selling
a business because, at tender middle age, she is a firm
believer in spending her time doing something she loves.
A member of the Romance Writers of New Zealand and
Romance Writers of Australia, she is determined that
this book will be the first of many. She enjoys reading,
travelling and watching rugby, and would be tickled pink
to hear from readers. E-mail her at vagabond23@yahoo.
com.

# One

**H**er heels clicked across the big expanse of floor, quick and sharp. Head swiveling, she dismissed the individuals milling this way and that. Where *was* he?

Who could blame him for not waiting? She was nearly an hour late, after all. Could she never get anything right?

There. Sitting alone by the domestic arrivals gate. Exactly where he was supposed to be.

Lucy replaced her impatient expression with a determined smile. Ethan Rae. Mr. Ethan Rae. She started quickly toward him across the concourse of the small airport, mentally chanting an apology. Mr. Rae. I am so sorry.

Her heels made a cheerful ditty on the polished linoleum. The sound kept up with her, and, as she drew level with the slumped figure in the chair, she was astonished to see no movement.

He was asleep!

Hot guilt washed over her and she nervously chewed her bottom lip. She was in *so* much trouble. Tom had already scalped her for the mix-up over ordering the luxury van that they used to escort clients from the airport to the lodge. By the time she had worked it out, it was too late to do anything else but collect him herself.

"Wha-a-a-t?" her half brother had practically yelled down the phone. "You can't pick him up in the Beast. Couldn't you have ordered him a car—limo, rental—anything?"

"Everything is booked. There's an APEC conference on in town, remember?"

"What about your car?"

She grimaced. "I'm having it cleaned. Why didn't you check his arrival time, Tom? We had a deal."

"Well, yes," he conceded, and Lucy was gratified to hear some guilt in his voice. "I've got rather a lot on my plate at the moment." His heavy sigh down the line was timed for maximum sympathy.

"You're not the only one. Besides you know how I am. You're supposed to check these things." Lucy tried to recall the fax containing details of the man's booking. "Who ever uses the twenty-four-hour clock, anyway?"

Tom sighed again. "Well, get here as soon as you can. And apologize like hell. Drinks start at seven-thirty. I need you here."

The current object of her agitation snoozed on, oblivious. She felt a headache twinge behind her eyes. She stood, clutching her wallet with both hands in front of her, wondering how to proceed.

Good suit, she noted, being rather an expert at clothes. Conservative, but expensive. The jacket was unfastened, revealing a stone-colored shirt wrapped around a long, lean torso with impressively broad shoulders. Long legs, crossed at the ankles, thrust into soft leather shoes. Well-tended hands lay on the armrests of the narrow chair, fingers splayed, giving the impression that he was ready to spring into action in an instant.

The thick hair on his bowed head was the color of bitter chocolate, with a fine tracing of silver at the neatly trimmed sideburns. It would grow wavy, she decided, if it were allowed. His skin was tan and smooth with a dark bluish shadow around his relaxed jaw.

She guessed he was little more than thirty, younger than she'd expected. Only the very rich could afford to stay at Summerhill, her family homestead, and enjoy the exclusive hunting, trekking and charters they offered. Usually the very rich were older—and accompanied.

A warm shiver of interest stirred, deep inside. Maybe her day was about to get better, after all.

The man's eyelids stirred. Lucy drew herself up to her full five-foot-five, inhaling apprehensively. Apology time. Her mind clicked into her best customer-service mode, her face into a smile she hoped conveyed apology and courtesy. She cleared her throat gently. "Mr. Rae? Ethan Rae?"

She watched his eyes squeeze tight. His mouth twisted in a grimace, then softened. The fingers of his left hand flexed then curled around the arm of his chair. When she looked back at his face, his eyelids had risen, but, because of his slumped position, he was looking down at her feet. Lucy waited.

And waited. He appeared to be conducting a fairly thorough examination of her painted toenails, her feet encased in strappy turquoise sandals, then her legs and finally the hem of the sea-green tunic that floated below the waist of her silk pants. He was actually studying her—minutely. Not even bothering to grant her the courtesy and respect of looking at her face.

Lucy shifted slightly, and the breath that escaped from her lips had no taint of apology now.

But still he dawdled, his shuttered eyes resting now on her hips, a tiny line creasing his forehead. And then they traveled on, up over the swell of her breasts. Instinctively, she tugged the edge of her blue-green silk shawl a little higher as his eyes lingered over pale skin exposed by the spaghetti straps of her tunic.

By the time his gaze reached her face, she felt as flushed as a schoolgirl. But it wasn't schoolgirl indignation she was feeling. Discomfort jostled with appreciation of his dark good looks, and a little thrill of awareness that she wasn't the only one pleasantly surprised by the meeting. A knowing and rather pleased smile quirked her brows as she met his gaze.

Not that she cared, but no sign of apology crossed his unwavering look. Pale blue eyes, in shocking contrast to his deeply tanned face, met hers and continued to scrutinize bluntly, curiously, in a haze of drowsy appreciation.

Lucy lifted her chin. "Mr. Ethan Rae?" She was thankful that there was no hint in her voice of the butterflies that leapt to life in her midriff.

Still regarding her intently, his head inclined an inch. Lucy exhaled. "Lucy McKinlay." She offered her hand. "I've come to drive you out to Summerhill."

He blinked, ignoring her outstretched hand, and slowly raised himself to his feet. She stepped back involuntarily. His long lean frame unwound itself to loom above her, with only inches between them.

Her heart gave a lazy, rolling thump, just once.

Ethan Rae stretched and ran one hand through his hair. An interesting little cowlick flicked up at the front, incongruous when matched with his stern and conservative air. She rather liked it.

His eyes narrowed, crinkling at the corners and pierced her with a glittering lance. "Evening." His voice was deep, lazy.

Lucy pursed her lips to stop the teasing smile that threatened to erupt. This man was a client. Flirting would be unprofessional and inappropriate.

But tempting. Very tempting… "I'm sorry I'm late, Mr. Rae."

He glanced at the silver timepiece on his wrist. "One hour late."

Three short words, but Lucy lost herself in the deep, flowing timbre of his voice. "Sorry," she said again, too distracted to look contrite. "Do you have luggage?"

His pale orbs flicked to an expensive-looking bag under the chair beside his.

Lucy reached for the bag. "You travel light."

Ethan Rae intercepted her with his shoulder, all signs of drowsiness gone, and hoisted the bag. "I've got it."

Lucy turned and led him through the terminal toward the exit, totally aware of his presence behind her, of his eyes on her. She consciously tightened every inch of her spine, lifted her head and walked as if she were on a catwalk. The shawl dipped down at the back and she did nothing to halt the slide. She didn't mind at all showing off the almost backless tunic top, loving how the silk swished and rustled with the movement of her thighs. If he wanted to look, he could look. It might take his mind off her tardiness.

He was the most attractive man her eyes had been treated to in a long while. She obviously spent too much time with older men.

"Did you have a hard night?" she asked brightly, determined to charm him. It was a seventy-minute drive to their destination. Lust was uncomfortable enough. Disapproving silence would be worse.

Ethan blinked as the crisp night air touched his face. He drew level with her in long gliding strides. His brows rose at her question but he did not speak.

A man of few words, she deduced. "You were sleeping."

"Long flight," was his eventual response, matched with a lengthy gaze.

A man who considers every word uttered to him and by him. The commentary hummed in her brain. "From Sydney?"

He nodded briefly. "Started a couple of days ago. From Saudi."

Lucy nodded and turned to the pay-to-go station, feeding her ticket and some coins into the slot to pay for parking. Then she faced him and took a deep breath. "About the transportation…" She reluctantly gestured toward the filthiest and most ancient four-wheel-drive in the park. "I have to apologize. Again."

Ethan stopped and stared disbelievingly. She swung herself up into the driver's seat of the Land Rover and leaned over to unlock and push open his door. After a few seconds of hesitation, his hand snaked around the passenger door to pull up the lock on the back. Lucy heard the slide of his bag in the back while she gave the passenger seat a quick and ineffectual swipe. Grimacing, nose twitching, he eased himself in beside her and settled back.

She put the key in the ignition and then turned to face him. "You see, I was supposed to order you a car. But I got the times mixed up."

"Yours?" he asked, staring at the dust-covered dash, the mud and plant matter under his expensive shoes, the barely transparent windscreen. Preparing to rest his arm along the doorframe, he thought better of it and leaned forward to stare at a dubious dark stain running along the bottom of the window.

"No. Mine is—indisposed at the moment," Lucy told him, backing out of the parking space. "Mrs. Seymour's horrible little bichon frise indisposed it this afternoon." Her mouth turned down as she recalled the whining woman from Auckland and her grotty little dog, whom she had gratefully delivered to the airport just a few hours ago. When she glanced at him his brows were raised in query. "Put it this way," she told him with a wry smile. "You think this smells bad…"

The Land Rover shuddered to a halt before the arm of the exit station. "By the time I found out about the car mix-up, it was too late to find any other vehicle. Normally, I wouldn't dream of picking up a client in the Beast."

Lucy laboriously wound the window down, then entered the ticket into the slot and watched the barrier arm rock and bounce up. The vehicle lurched forward unsteadily while she rewound the stubborn window. She could feel his gaze on her but kept her eyes on the road ahead.

"You pick up all your guests looking like that?" His tone had lost the sleepy, lazy quality of before.

"We're having cocktails tonight in honor of a VIP. The other guests are welcome to attend. It's sort of a meet-and-greet thing." She shot him a welcoming look. "If you're not too tired."

His eyes flashed over her. "Wide awake, suddenly," he told her enigmatically.

Lucy felt her face flame in a burst of pleasure and focused on the road. It was nice to be noticed, especially after the day she'd had. A million errands, the loathsome dog and her error over Ethan's ETA meant she'd only had time for the quickest of showers and a lick of makeup to go with the cocktail outfit that was supposed to impress tonight.

"McKinlay," he said, dragging his seatbelt over his shoulder. "You're part of the Summerhill family."

Lucy nodded.

"What's your role in the operation?"

"I run errands. Pick-ups, drop-offs. And I look after the wives and partners of the guests."

Ethan squinted at her, nodding slowly. "You look after the trophy wives of the trophy hunters." It wasn't a question.

Lucy was surprised at the disdain in his voice. "We don't put it quite like that," she said carefully.

"No? What would you call a woman who is married—or not—to someone thirty years older and loaded?"

"Lucky?" Lucy quipped, but judging from the compression of his mouth, he didn't appreciate her joke.

She'd have to tread carefully during the next few days and restrain her occasionally irreverent perspective. The VIP they were wining tonight was Magnus Anderson, the founder of the exclusive club that Summerhill was part of. There were fewer than twenty-five lodges worldwide recommended by the club's bi-annual publication, the revered Global List.

Magnus and his wife had landed yesterday. They were supposedly here for a week's delayed honeymoon, but their guest had indicated his displeasure at certain rumors regarding the quality and financial stability of the Summerhill operation. Lucy would do or say nothing to jeopardize their place in the organization.

If Summerhill were ousted from the club, there was nowhere to go but down.

"What does entertaining the wives involve?"

Again, Lucy pondered. "Whatever they want to do to stop them from getting bored and lonely and intruding on their husbands' hunting. I can provide information, or an itinerary. Transport." She saw his eyes flick around the filthy cab. "Make bookings. Or I can escort them places."

One of his dark brows arched curiously.

Lucy shrugged. "Shopping. Bungee-jumping. Lunch. Whatever…"

Ethan frowned out the windscreen. She got the distinct impression that she and her clients had just gone down a notch in his estimation. But an instant later she felt his raking gaze again. "Like a professional companion."

"I suppose I am." She smiled brightly and nodded. "Some like company, but sometimes they just want bookings made or suggestions."

"Enjoy it?" he asked, rather tersely.

Lucy nodded. "Most of the time."

He was silent as the big motor swept a roundabout and eased into the light flow of traffic. Several minutes passed until she hit the city limits and headed toward the west coast. Dusk had done its worst and the city lights behind cast a softly mauve glow.

Ethan stretched back in his seat and yawned widely.

"Sleep if you want," she offered. "It's over an hour's drive."

He rubbed his hands together and leaned forward to

peer at the instrument panel. "Colder than I expected. I left forty degrees."

"What were you doing in the Middle East?"

"Developing a tourist resort." He fiddled with the heating dial. "Winter in New Zealand should be a refreshing change."

Suddenly a cloud of chaff puffed out from the vents. Her breath caught in her throat as she watched the millions of particles rise up to the cab's ceiling and then settle, painfully slowly, onto his expensively clad knees.

Lucy bit her bottom lip and forbade herself to smile. When she dared glance at him again, he was shaking his head.

"Dare you to laugh," he murmured, but his mouth had pursed into a reluctant grin.

Now that was worth waiting for. She allowed her own smile to form. The glint in his pale eyes and a flash of white teeth lit up his face, revealing the leanness of his cheeks and no-nonsense jawline, the straight length of his nose, and his lips—not full but not ungenerous either.

At least there was a semblance of humor there. The situation wasn't hopeless. "I wouldn't dream of it," she told him, rolling her eyes. "Sorry."

His wry grunt reassured her. "I know little about Summerhill," he commented. "It used to be a high-country station, didn't it?"

Lucy automatically recited a brief history of her heritage. "The house was built in the late 1860s by a wealthy Scotsman who farmed, at that time, about one hundred thousand acres. Over the years, parts of the land were sold off—to other farmers, to the conservation department. The original family sold the remaining forty thousand acres to my grandfather."

She paused as the familiar ache settled over her heart. Her own father had continued to farm in the very toughest high-country conditions to provide for his young family. Until her mother had left when Lucy was eight.

"Only about half of it is arable. The rest is…" she broke off, a lump in her throat. How to describe it? Unbearably beautiful? Savage and remote? Her own special kingdom? "Mountains, forest, a gorge…" Pride and regret swelled the lump in her throat, rendering her voice uncharacteristically thready. Her heritage had long suffered her indifference. And now, when its importance to her transcended everything else, it might be dangerously late and dependent on others.

She felt Ethan's interested gaze and shook her head, knowing whatever words she chose would be inadequate. "Well, it's something. Wild and remote."

She ventured a glance. He nodded as if he understood.

"My half brother, Tom, changed the dynamics of the farm about five years ago to incorporate luxury accommodation and a restaurant, and he set up mountain hunting safaris, trekking and adventure tours."

What she didn't say was that Tom had set up the lodge against their father's wishes. But her father had no fight left in him and Lucy was off overseas, enjoying herself.

"Who are your main clients?"

"Americans. Germans. Indonesians. And you Australians."

"What sort of adventure tours?"

"Jet-boating. White-water rafting is popular. Heli-skiing. Fishing—the Rakaia River that flows through the farm is famous for salmon. Have you been to the South Island before?"

He shook his head. "My mother owns a small kiwifruit holding in North Island. I try to get over once or twice a year."

"It's quite different," Lucy explained. "North Island farms seem so…civilized in comparison."

"What do you farm?"

"Beef." She'd do well to change the subject. The farm wasn't high on Tom's list of priorities at the moment. And Tom's priorities were a mystery to all. "Are you warm enough?"

As if she'd reminded him, he grunted and absently brushed at the debris on his trousers.

"How long is your holiday?" she ventured.

He stifled a yawn and shrugged. "Undecided. Few days, maybe a week." He faced her and she felt his gaze move over her like a slow burn. "Problem?"

"No. We're not too busy at the moment." If we get kicked out of the club, she thought, business will slow permanently.

"Perhaps I'll make use of your escort service."

"Pardon?"

"Just think of me as a trophy wife."

She laughed. "I think that might be a bit difficult."

"Why's that, Ms. McKinlay?" he asked in that wonderful baritone that washed over her skin like a caress.

Lucy kept her eyes on the road, but her lips tightened at the effect his deep gravelly voice, slow and so masculine, had on her nerve endings. Calm down, Flirty Luce; he's out of bounds… "Why don't you call me Lucy?" Ethan only nodded and she felt a girlish kick of pleasure at the knowledge that he would be staying and might be needing company.

"Who lives at Summerhill?"

"My half brother, Tom. And Ellie, the housekeeper. She's been with us forever." Lucy's voice softened fondly. "She was Dad's primary caregiver when he had the stroke." She glanced at Ethan. "My father died three months ago."

"Sorry to hear that," he murmured.

You wouldn't be if you had seen him, Lucy thought. Dying was preferable to living the way Thomas McKinlay Senior had lived those last few months after the stroke. He'd been totally incapacitated: unable to walk, talk, feed or bathe himself. She couldn't bear it....

"And you?"

Ethan's question startled her. "What?"

"Do you live at Summerhill?"

"A lot of the time. I have an apartment in town. It's handy if I have late pick-ups or drop-offs."

"You look like a city girl."

Lucy laughed. "I can't decide if that's a compliment or not. What does a city girl look like?"

He took his time answering. "Too delicate to be a farm girl, I suppose."

"Delicate? Looks can be deceiving. I delivered my fair share of lambs and calves as a kid. And I like to ride. Do you? We have horses."

Ethan nodded and, undeterred by his earlier experience, he reached his hand out to the instrument panel again. "Haven't ridden in years. I'd like that."

Techno music blared out from the ancient radio. The alacrity with which the volume was turned down prompted a smile from Lucy. "I bet you're a jazz man."

Another flash of white teeth. "Now, how would that be obvious?"

Oh, I dunno. The slow stroke of your fingers over your jaw. The black-velvet voice. And eyes that should, by rights, freeze hell over, but instead crackle with heat. Aloud, she told him she had once caught the New Orleans Mardi Gras, and they discovered they had actually been there the same year.

The conversation progressed onto a range of artists. Ethan was obviously an aficionado, whereas Lucy had a wide range of tastes and wouldn't be pinned down to specifics.

She smiled into the night. It was fun to pass the miles in good-natured banter. The next few days promised to be interesting.

But Ethan took issue when Lucy lamented that she could not dance to jazz. "There's dancing, and there's dancing," he told her, and the warmth inside the car seemed to wind up a notch. "Jazz is sultry. Music for hot nights." He paused, then took a soft hissing breath. "Or cold nights and a big fire."

His voice sizzled along the back of her neck. Lucy imagined that voice spilling into her ear millimeters away, pressed up close in the light of a leaping fire.

Her throat went dry. "Are you warm enough?" she asked, forgetting she had already inquired.

"Plenty."

They passed the last half hour in silence. He hunkered back in his seat with his head on the rest and appeared to drift off to sleep. There was little traffic and the silence wasn't at all awkward. Lucy had learned these last six months to read people well and act accordingly. There were times to fill every second with conversation, and times to sit and let the other person take the lead. She could be quiet, if that's what the client wanted. Funny, when she remembered always being in trouble at school for excessive chatter. Always being in trouble at school for everything….

She glanced often at the man at her side. He was as delicious as a Chocolate Thin biscuit, she decided, then changed her mind with a grin. Lean, not thin, shoulders *that* broad, or legs—as far as she could decently tell—that looked long, strong and robust could never be termed thin. No way, no how.

So far, she liked everything about him. He had an honest, appreciative way of looking at her. He digested every word spoken to him and considered every word he spoke back. It showed in the long pauses punctuating his conversation, as if he were listening intently for the truth in your voice.

His voice: lazy, deep and gritty. Slow, almost a drawl. John Wayne! Lucy almost gasped when she realized he sounded just like the cowboy in the movies. "A man's gotta *do* what a man's gotta do…."

Altogether an intriguing package. She wondered what his marital status was. He wore no ring, but that meant little.

She turned off at the sign to the nearby ski village and began the gentle incline, flashing through the tiny settlements that nestled beside the Rakaia River in the shadow of the Southern Alps. With nothing but the drone of the engine in her ears, it seemed she was the only person awake in the world.

Finally they turned into a long driveway. Lucy checked her watch. Seven-twenty. The cattle stop at the start of the gravel drive caused Ethan to stir and rub his face briskly.

The house made a picture. Against a black canvas, the rambling two-story structure glittered impressively from every room. Summerhill was a kilometer from the road and flanked by the Rakaia River, about three hundred metres away, with sturdy foothills to the back. Slender poplars lined the driveway and marched on to meet the willows Lucy's grandfather had planted alongside the river.

Lucy pulled to one side, turned the ignition off, and they stepped out into the cool night air. Ethan stretched and retrieved his bag from the back.

"I'll show you to your room."

He followed her up the steps to the entrance. She stopped at the top and gestured for him to precede her into the house.

They stepped into the wide entrance, a massive area itself, yet dominated by a huge stairway. An imposing wapiti stag head with fourteen-point antlers stared balefully at an early twenties portrait of the house on the opposite wall. The old Oriental rug under their feet was faded now, but with enough color to give the kauri wood of the paneling and floorboards a lift.

The hallway was deserted.

"Follow me, Mr. Rae."

"Ethan," he murmured, looking around, seemingly in no hurry. He followed her up the staircase, head swiveling as she pointed out where to find the dining room and bar, the covered swimming pool and other outside amenities.

She stopped by a closed door with a key in the lock and pushed her way into a large and sumptuously decorated room. She noted with satisfaction that the rich velvet drapes were closed and the gas fire, housed in the best of all the antique fireplaces in the lodge, glowed cozily. Moving to the huge bed, she flicked the bedside lamps on.

It was a handsome room with great views through the floor-to-ceiling double doors out to the balcony. A little masculine for her taste—but comfortable, with two sofas to relax on, a good sized desk, table and chairs and an adjoining bathroom with shower and spa-bath.

Ethan tossed his bag onto the bed and made a quick

inspection of the facilities then came to stand right in front of her. "Looks comfortable." He nodded approvingly.

She offered him the key and began to turn away, but then hesitated. "Please do join us for drinks, if you're not too tired. The trophy room is left at the bottom of the stairs. If not, call room service and they can send up anything you wish."

He inclined his head. "Thanks. I'll freshen up, see how I feel."

Lucy stared up into eyes that could melt the coldest heart. How could ice-blue eyes be so warm? A buzz of sensual awareness lifted the hairs on the back of her neck.

Cause and effect. Bemused, she felt her belly clench and the skin of her exposed cleavage prickle. Knowing full well what that signaled, she took a quick step back, drawing the folds of cool silk closer. A raging red flush clawing up her chest and throat would look fetching in the glow of the fire. Not.

She nodded and turned on her heel. A small smile curved her lips as she sashayed down the hallway. Of course he would come down for drinks. He *had* to.

He made her feel reckless. He made her want to flirt. But then, she had always been flighty. Everyone said so.

# Two

**E**than expelled a lengthy breath as the door closed behind her. Her fresh scent still clung to his nostrils, but the rustle of the fabric of that stunning outfit was gone.

Blindsided, he thought, stroking his chin and staring at the closed door. Like a skier in an avalanche, right from that first long look.

He was horny, that was all. It had been way too long since his last break, and the Middle East wasn't the easiest place to spend a year.

Shrugging out of his jacket, he scooped up his toilet bag, walked into the bathroom and turned the shower on. He scrubbed away his traveling grime and jet lag, but couldn't quite get the sight of her from his mind's eye or the zing of berries and roses from his nostrils.

*Ethereal* was the word that sprang to mind. All that milky skin from her face, down her throat and over the top of her shoulders. Even her beautifully shaped lips were pale. Only her eyes, a warm Mediterranean blue, made her real. Otherwise, he could well believe her to be a fairy princess in a story somewhere, dappled sunlight on her gossamer threads.

Ethan turned the shower off, chuckling at his cheesy notions.

But her eyes held secrets and laughter and womanly desires. She was not indifferent to him, and she was too young to be subtle about it. Not that he minded forward women. She wanted him, all right. He bet she was even now thinking about him, his dark hands on her white skin, his mouth crushed to hers… Get a grip!

Too young, too innocent and light years away from the women he generally dated. He tied a towel around his midriff and padded back into the bedroom. Not to mention probably a gold digger. Women who worked in an environment of money usually wanted it for themselves.

Women and money. As he dressed, a tiny part of him admired the single-minded way young and beautiful women went after money. They smelled it. They coveted it. They would do anything to get it. Which reminded him. That was part of the reason he was here.

He retrieved his phone from the suit jacket he'd tossed on the bed and stabbed numbers into it.

Magnus was more of a father to him than his own. An honorable man. A sensible man. A widower for many years, it didn't surprise Ethan he wanted company again, someone to contemplate retirement with.

But to marry a woman thirty years his junior having known her barely two months was totally out of character. When Ethan, just days ago, had received an anonymously sent packet of newspaper clippings regarding the death of a multimillionaire Texan, he could not ignore it.

The phone was answered on the third ring. He recognized the casual voice of the man he'd met briefly the day before in Sydney. As they spoke, Ethan sat on the bed, phone cradled between his ear and shoulder, and reached for his briefcase. He tipped the clippings out onto the bed. The top one showed Magnus and the new Mrs. Anderson on their wedding day.

"I've started with her background," the private investigator told him. "Julie May Stratton. Born in West Virginia, in the mountains. Father was a trapper. Six kids."

While the man spoke, Ethan sifted through some of the other clippings. They were the worst kind of scandal sheets. Grainy and dated photos, outrageous headlines. Hillbilly Makes Good, one screamed. The Millionaire and the Trapper's Daughter! said another.

He listened to her early history, up until she was working as an air hostess. Ethan bent down and shoved his feet into shoes.

"She finished up in Dallas. And that's where she met her husband. Twenty years older son from his first marriage, and from good ranching stock. His family wasn't happy. Hell, the whole city wasn't happy. Linc Sherman the Third was one of the most eligible divorced men in Dallas."

Ethan listened to the sound of papers being rustled.

"When he died, the city's press and broadcasters really did a number on Julie. For months, she was practically under house arrest, with the family ranting and raving."

Ethan smiled. "You sound almost sympathetic."

"Call me old-fashioned, Mr. Rae, but I like a bit of evidence. They were alone on the yacht. No firearms on board that had been fired. No residue on her. She claims to have had one too many glasses of champagne and didn't even hear him get up. It was all very convenient, but also very circumstantial."

No Charges Brought! headed one of the most vitriolic of the clippings. The article went on to lament the intelligence of the entire Dallas police force. Ethan's mouth tightened in distaste. The press was all for implementing the death penalty in this particular case.

The investigator told him of the political pressure the police were under because of Linc Sherman's standing in the city. But forensics, medical experts, lie detectors—she came through them all. And a witness had seen a yacht close to where the Shermans were moored. It was identical to one Julie had told police she'd seen earlier that evening, one her husband had waved to but gotten no response. Despite massive publicity all over the States, no one had come forward to be eliminated from the inquiry as a suspect and the yacht was never found.

After the Dallas police had wound up their investigation, Julie Stratton Sherman had moved to Australia, changed her name to Juliette and shaved four years off her age. Hardly incriminating, but still…

"What was he worth?" He whistled at the answer. "Big step up for a hillbilly."

Even after paying off a hit man, Ethan reasoned, it would be a huge inheritance. But then, she hadn't gotten anything yet. Why would she be in a hurry to kill off another husband? Forty million dollars wouldn't be much good to her if she were in jail serving time for murder.

His tension eased a little. His shoelaces tied, he sat back and retrieved the phone from his shoulder. "Keep digging. I want to know every move she's made since she's been in Australia. Every place she's lived, every party she's been to, every boyfriend she's had."

Ethan broke the connection, stood and moved to his open briefcase on the desk. Until the private investigator reported back to him with something more concrete than innuendo, he planned to keep a very close eye on the new Mrs. Anderson.

He checked his watch. Barely twenty minutes had passed since Lucy had shown him to his room. He lifted out the report he had compiled on the Middle Eastern project. He wanted everything relevant at his fingertips in the morning. Preparation was key and his boss demanded the best.

Juliette Anderson and the completed development were not the only pressing matters on his agenda. His hand rested briefly on another file and he felt the familiar zip of excitement tickle his shoulder blades. Turtle Island. Possibly his greatest triumph. If he could pull this sale off, it would be the deal of the century.

It would also have just that small whiff of revenge about it....

He checked his appearance in the mirror and pocketed the key Lucy had given him. You made a plan and you stuck to it, he thought as he left the room. That was the only way to get ahead. Nothing left to chance. Not like his father.

The remembered taste of poverty slicked over his tongue like diesel. It was a taste you never forgot. That taste had spurred Ethan to put his own goals in motion at an early age to ensure his comfort and security. He had spent fifteen years working his way up in Magnus's corporation. Now he was at the very top, on the verge of the biggest and most satisfying deal of his career. Then he would have the freedom to decide what the next fifteen years would bring.

Not too bad for trailer trash.

He found his way to the trophy room bar. Plaque-mounted stags' heads and plump fish, not surprisingly, adorned the walls. There was a hunters' gallery in an alcove, and upholstered window seats all around, jazzed up with bright cushions. One wall was entirely glass and he'd bet there was a great view in the daytime.

A heavily jowled man behind the bar was handing an Asian couple some well-dressed glasses. Ethan glanced around and spotted Lucy over by a huge stone fireplace. She and Magnus looked up as he approached.

"Ethan, my boy," his boss boomed, with a broad smile and a hefty clap on the back.

Ethan answered his smile with one of his own. In the six months since he'd last seen Magnus, he appeared to have lost weight and shed a few wrinkles. Ethan thought he'd never looked better. They shook hands warmly, then Magnus tugged him forward and turned to bring his wife into the fray.

Juliette Anderson was a stunner. Statuesque, golden, gracious. She looked like a beauty queen, vibrantly apart from and above other mere mortals. Glossier hair, brighter eyes, skin that glowed. Surely that flawless complexion, swept-up hair and perfectly buffed fingernails could only be achieved with a large team of stylists on hand around the clock.

"Ethan, it gives me great pleasure to introduce my wife. Juliette, meet Ethan Rae, a man I consider as close as a son."

Magnus stepped back, releasing Ethan's hand.

"Pleasure, Ms. Anderson," Ethan murmured.

"Please, Juliette."

He saw Lucy offer Magnus something off the heavy platter of hors d'oeuvres she carried. Narrowing his gaze, he murmured "Julie," in a lowered voice.

Her golden eyes opened wide, then a definite arctic blast seemed to wash across her face. She took his hand. "Ju. Lee. Ette." Her voice also lowered and there was a peculiarly intense diction to the syllables.

"Juliette," Ethan repeated smoothly.

The woman nodded tightly. Lucy intervened with her platter of nibbles. When he glanced back at Juliette, her face had reverted to serene loveliness.

Ethan believed in laying his cards on the table. As soon as he could get her on her own, he would find out just what her game was. At least now, she knew he was watching her.

"Good evening," came a voice from behind him. "Can I get you something from the bar?"

"My brother Tom," Lucy told him.

"Half brother," Tom corrected, extending his hand.

Ethan took an immediate and unexpected dislike to the man. Was it the heavy, untoned look of him? The moist softness of his hand? Or the almost imperceptible glance of disdain that he shot at Lucy while correcting her? Ethan wasn't usually so quick to judge, but he trusted his instincts. "Wine. White and dry, thanks."

The man turned away. Ethan watched him walk up to the bar, thinking there was little familial resemblance. Lucy was delicate, with a purity of proportion in her facial features. Tom looked as if neither his clothes nor his skin fit properly. Perhaps he'd recently put on weight, but he didn't look as though he'd give a damn.

Lucy held up her platter. "Care for something?"

Ethan smiled at her, selecting a couple of delicious morsels and the napkins she offered.

"It's been too long," Magnus rumbled, taking another savory. He rolled his eyes at Lucy. "Like a son to me, yet too busy to make it home for my wedding. And now he invites himself on my honeymoon."

Juliette took her husband's arm. "The wedding was two months ago. And if this *was* our honeymoon, do you think I would agree to you going hunting for a week and leaving me all alone?"

"It's four days, my sweet. Three nights and four days. And you will have Lucy to keep you company."

Lucky Juliette, Ethan wanted to say. Instead he followed Magnus and Juliette over to a large sofa by the window, and answered his boss's questions about his flight and accommodations. That did not stop his eyes tracking Lucy as she served the other couples in the room. Her easy charm and bright smile drew a favorable response from men and women alike. Her pretty outfit floated around her body in a swirl of sea-greens and blues. She was light and grace, and impossible not to watch.

Juliette excused herself to freshen up before dinner. There was a moment's silence, then Magnus leaned forward. "She's something, isn't she?"

"Stunning," Ethan replied woodenly.

"I'm talking about our hostess," Magnus chuckled. "You haven't taken your eyes off her since you came in."

A jet of guilty pleasure whooshed up Ethan's breastbone, but he kept his voice casual. "A little young for me."

Magnus cleared his throat.

"Oh, Christ, Magnus. Sorry. I didn't mean…"

Magnus didn't appear to take offense. "That's all right, boy. I know I'm being tarred with your father's brush, and I can't blame you for it."

Ethan's hand curled into a fist in his lap. The way his mother had been discarded like yesterday's news after the old man had struck it lucky still burned. After ten years—more—of slave labor and biting poverty. Just tossed aside for a younger model. He could forgive his father some things. Not that.

He took a deep breath and rested his hands on his thighs. "What do you really know about her, Magnus?"

"All I need to know. She makes me happy. I know some folk think I'm a silly old fool. I didn't expect to find this sort of thing again. I've been on my own more than a dozen years, Ethan."

"I know," Ethan murmured, remembering the day of Theresa Anderson's funeral. "I wish you all the best, you know that."

"Thank you, Ethan."

He wouldn't push it tonight. He had little to go on anyway. Now wasn't the time.

"Actually I'm here on business, Magnus. I have a proposal and I didn't want to wait."

Magnus watched his wife re-enter the room. "Tomorrow, I think. No business tonight."

Juliette sat and began whispering into her husband's ear. "Are you coming in to dinner?" Magnus asked.

Ethan stretched. "Do you mind if I don't? I'm beat."

Tom seemed to have disappeared, along with all but one of the other couples. Lucy wiped glasses behind the bar. He excused himself and approached.

"You've lasted well for someone with jet lag. More wine?"

He nodded when she held up a bottle of chardonnay. "Half a glass. Think I'll call it a night."

She looked surprised. "Aren't you going in to dinner with the others?"

"No. These were delicious." He indicated the depleted platter of food. "Are you the chef?"

She shook her head. "If you get hungry in the night, just call room service."

He raised an eyebrow. "If I get hungry at three in the morning, you'll bring me a sandwich?"

A slight flush tinged her cheeks, telling him she wasn't slow on the uptake.

"Chef leaves around midnight, I'm afraid. Anyway, it's bad for the digestion to eat at that time of the day."

There was no mistaking the voluptuous lilt of her voice or the sparkle in her eyes. Ethan was enjoying himself. He must have tipped over into holiday mode earlier than the usual couple of days it took for him to unwind.

"I'll remember that," he said somberly, "and confine my appetite to chef's hours." He leaned back a little, and saw Tom re-enter the room. "Come show me the hunting gallery."

She put her tea towel down and accompanied him to the alcove. Hunting did not interest him in the slightest, but it was no hardship to be in close proximity to Lucy as she explained that wapiti were what North Americans call elk, and that thar and sika were different varieties of deer found here. He learned they were in the roar, or mating season. This was the preferable time to hunt because the animals were endowed with impressive antlers which dropped off after the season. Why else would Magnus, a keen trophy hunter, be here now?

There were ample photos in the alcove of successful hunters astride their kills, which included mountain goats and wild pigs. But what he enjoyed most was Lucy's evident pride in the magnificent landscape as she pointed to locations she had ridden to or picnicked at.

They were alone in the bar now, except for Tom.

Everyone else had retired to bed or gone through to the restaurant.

"You didn't say you knew the Andersons," she commented.

"You didn't ask." He shrugged. "First time I've met his wife. His wedding was—unexpected."

Tom approached, having cleared the tables. "I must apologize for the welcome you received today."

Ethan cocked a brow at him, noting that Lucy took a step back.

"It was not up to our usual high standard, I assure you."

Lucy half turned away, pursing her lips. Darn Tom. Why did he have to make a song and dance about everything? No doubt Ethan would have forgotten the whole thing if Tom hadn't brought it up.

She felt herself flush deeply at Tom's next missive. "A series of unfortunate incidents regarding vehicles—and my sister's poor timekeeping, I'm afraid."

Her heart sank.

"Was she late?" Ethan's quick response jolted her in mid cringe. "I'm afraid I was so charmed by your sister, I barely noticed the time or the transportation."

"Oh. Well, that's very generous of you." Tom sounded a little strained.

Lucy glowed with delight from the top of her head to her toes. What a nice thing to say—and how smooth. Tom was not going to like being put in his place like that one little bit, and she would no doubt have to pay for it. But for now, she reveled in the pleasure of approbation. She charmed him. Of course she did.

She could barely contain herself from skipping as all three walked to the bar, but she did manage a grateful grin at her champion.

"If there is anything we can do," Tom continued, "to make your stay with us more comfortable…"

Ethan glanced at Tom briefly, then returned his gaze to her. "Any chance of organizing a fax in my room?"

Lucy nodded. "I'll get on it first thing in the morning." She gave him a warm smile that she hoped conveyed the gratitude she felt. It was not often someone stuck up for her. She wanted him to know she was aware of it, and thankful.

Not just thankful. Absurdly pleased.

He smiled back. After a minute, Tom took a step back, huffing about clearing up.

"Goodnight, Lucy." Ethan threw a nod at Tom. "Tom."

"Sleep well."

She reluctantly turned back to Tom as he wiped the top of the stone bar. It had been a shock to discover earlier that Ethan was the vice-president of Magnus Anderson's company. Tom was fit to be tied, frantic in case she'd said anything inappropriate. The slight undertone of flirting on the way here did not worry her—to her mind it was mutual and harmless. But she could possibly have been more—deferential or something. Tom had a real bee in his bonnet about Magnus and his precious club.

"I told you he was cool about it."

"It's not the point. I need you to pick your socks up. No more fiascos like today. This is a five-star operation, and our guests don't want excuses. They want professional courtesy. Excellent facilities. Punctual service."

Exasperation, something she rarely gave in to, bubbled to the surface. "You should have confirmed the time. That's our deal. And do you think I can just conjure up vehicles out of nowhere?"

He scowled. He was a big man, like their father, but lately he had appeared more beefy than powerful.

"We need the club, Lucy. We cannot afford *not* to be on the Global List."

She rolled her eyes. "Seems to me we'd be a lot busier if we were allowed to advertise in the normal places, instead of just the stupid list."

"The Global List is regarded as one of the top three accommodation publications in the world. I don't think you appreciate the honor it is to be included."

Lucy privately thought it was a bit high-handed of the club to demand exclusive advertising rights. "Honor is all very nice, Tom, but it won't pay the bills, and you do seem worried about money all of a sudden."

"Which is something you have never given the slightest thought to," Tom retorted. "Swanning off all over the world for years with your hand out."

That stung, even as she recognized the truth in it. She loved traveling, and goodness knows she hadn't been wanted around here since her mother had left. But the moment she'd heard of her father's stroke, she had come home.

Never mind that it served as a timely escape from a tricky entanglement.

And when Tom had asked, she was only too pleased to help him with the business. But the truth was, she didn't really care about the lodge. Of course she would hate to see it fail, but her love was the forty thousand acres of countryside. Her birthright—and Tom's.

"I'm sorry for that, and I'll do anything I can to help."

Trouble was, with the life she had led so far, she didn't know how much help she would be.

"Anything?"

She touched his hand, feeling sorry he'd had to carry this burden alone. "Anything. You're really worried, aren't you?"

"I am. If you want to help, I'd like you to think about selling the land. Part of it, anyway."

Lucy jerked her hand back. "The land? Our land?"

"Lucy, since the farm manager quit a year ago, I've let the farm run right down. Half the stock that's left is wild. And the rest I pay next door to drench and move. We either need the farm to pay its own way or get the money for it. Otherwise how will we keep this place up to scratch?"

She could hardly believe her ears. Foreboding, deep and menacing, hollowed out her stomach. "What's going on, Tom? Why are things so bad?"

He turned away from her, his shoulders slumped. "It's a downturn in the market, that's all. We have to be prepared to explore other options."

"I'd sell the lodge before the land any day," she declared. "This is farming country. It's McKinlay farming country."

"It's a last resort, Lucy. Let's hope it doesn't come to that. We have to make sure Magnus has a great hunt and his wife has an equally good time." He turned off the lights to the bar and stood at the door, impatiently waving her through.

"You wouldn't… You can't be serious." How could he drop a bombshell like that and then just expect her to go to bed? She stalked past him, fingers of agitation squeezing her throat.

"And try to organize a tour or something for Rae," Tom ordered, his imperious voice riling her further. "I don't like the idea of him sniffing around while I'm on the hunt."

"Perhaps I should give him a tour of me," she told him snippily. "I could seduce him. Get him on our side that way."

She almost laughed at her half brother's shock.

"You will not! You'll keep your distance and be totally professional with that guy. I know his type—all business. He'd eat you for breakfast."

Lucy turned her back on him. "Man, I wish I knew what was bugging you lately." She shot him a scowl as she stomped off down the hall. "I was joking."

"I mean it, Lucy," Tom called after her. "Keep away from Rae. He's dangerous."

# Three

Lucy rose in the half light, too restless to sleep. As was her custom when she stayed at Summerhill, she put her swimsuit on under a warm track suit, tossed a towel around her shoulders and skipped downstairs and out to the pool. It was just past six-thirty and she expected to have the pool to herself, but, to her dismay, she had been superseded.

A dark-haired figure made short work of the thirty-three-meter pool, long powerful arms scything effortlessly through the water.

Yes. She had wondered if he might be a swimmer or long-distance runner. Ethan would not lift weights or play a stop-start team sport. His body had the long clean lines that epitomised endurance, power with leashed—as opposed to explosive—energy.

She watched from the door as he executed a perfect turn: sleek, smooth, long-reaching. Lucy could not tear her eyes away and just as she was about to step fully into the room, Tom's comment of the night before came back to her. *Keep away.... He's dangerous.*

The whole upsetting conversation returned and she backed away.

It was necessary to release some tension, get moving. If swimming was out, an early-morning ride was the next best thing. Ten minutes later she exited the house and walked quickly to the stables. Monty, her horse, nickered in greeting. She lifted the pail of water to his gray nose and dug a couple of sugar cubes, filched from the breakfast tables, from her pocket.

"Monty the Monster," she chanted as she saddled him. He tossed his head and nudged her, looking for more sugar. "Frisky today." Lucy raised the pail again. He'd need a drink. She intended to use him hard.

They set off into the cool, dim morning, the struggling sun unable to pierce the clouds. The first part of the trail was tricky, especially in the dawn light. But about half an hour up, the trail planed out into a fast ride along the top of the huge gorge that ringed the valley. And when Monty took that final step up out of the scree and thistle and onto the plateau she pulled him up, patting and talking for a minute, and then gave him his head.

"Go boy, go!"

Lucy hunched forward, every muscle in her body screaming. Cold tears stung her cheeks. Her mouth twisted in concentration and velocity and her eyes squeezed into thin slits. Her Polar Fleece cap protected her ears, and sheepskin-lined gloves ensured her fingers were not stiffened with the cold.

"Ha! Good fella!" she yelled, her legs jammed hard into the horse's flanks.

They raced just a few feet from the lip of the gorge

that sliced the land down sixty or seventy meters to the river below. This gorge ringed Thunderstrike Valley for as far as the eye could see, across to the great Southern Alps.

When it was over, they slumped, heads hanging, breathing in great gulps of freezing air. Her cheek rested on the steaming neck of the animal for a minute or more until the horse moved restlessly. Then she roused herself and slid shakily down.

She loosened Monty's saddle and drew a grubby scrap of towelling from the saddlebag, rubbing the horse's chest and sides briskly. He seemed intent on backing away from her toward a patch of greenery. She tugged him over to a big overhang of rock. It crouched like a frog, ten meters from the edge of the gorge. Boulders and shrubs of prickly, yellow-flowered gorse clustered at its base. There was an opening that you could not see unless you stood directly in front of it.

Her special place.

She pulled off her hat and looped the reins over Monty's neck, leaving him to fossick through the tussock for food.

Stiff-arming a clump of gorse, she bent slightly and moved fully into the aperture. There was a large flat rock, fully three square meters and slightly elevated, so the view was unhindered above the foliage at the entrance. And the view was spectacular.

Her mother had sometimes brought her here as a child, placing her in front of her on the saddle. Lucy remembered the smell of her, her mother's long hair tickling Lucy's face, the thrill of clinging to the horse, as it climbed almost vertically up the steep cliff.

"I spy, with my little eye—" her childish voice would ring out in the semicave "—something beginning with…"

She'd help unwrap the sandwiches they had brought.
They would play for hours. Once they'd been caught in
a storm. Her mother pulled her well back into the cave
and held her close, pressing her head into her bosom. But
Lucy wasn't having it. "I want to see!" She squirmed and
managed to ease her head around to watch the tongues
of electricity lashing the valley. She exulted at the show,
but her mother had trembled.

Now, a watery sun eased out of the dawn, and the
early winter snowcaps of the mountains were hidden in
thick pearl clouds. It was so quiet, the silence surged at
her. She strained to see the snaking river below. Her
eyes prickled and blurred, like the mist that snagged on
the tops of the trees on the foothills.

She could not lose this. Her whole aimless existence
came down to this, the panorama laid out in front of her.
She had carried it all over the world inside her, and it
far surpassed any landscape she had seen. Somehow,
this view intermingled with her need to belong. Her last
resort.

In truth, she knew that the times up here with her
mother were the last times she had felt truly cherished.
Had felt lovable.

Monty nickered and blew and was answered in kind.
Alarmed, Lucy craned her neck around the gorse in
time to see Ethan Rae dismount from Tilly, one of
Summerhill's mares. A jolt of pleased agitation surged
through her. Would this man not leave her in peace?

Ethan walked straight up to Monty and placed a confident hand on the gelding's neck.

Fighting a wild urge to stay hidden, Lucy slid along
on her bottom to the entrance, then stood, using her arm
to brush back the gorse. She didn't want him to worry.
"How did you find your way up here?" she called.

His dark head snapped up and swiveled to find her. Was it pleasure causing her blood to race in her veins, or irritation at being disturbed while in an emotional mood?

"Followed you when you left the pool." He turned his back momentarily to loop his mare's reins around her neck and give Monty another pat.

As he approached, he made a thorough perusal of her warm sheepskin jacket and riding boots over black denims. "Beautiful place."

Lucy nodded. "My special place."

"Can see why."

She noticed he was still looking at her rather than the view. "I used to come up here with my mother."

Lucy tugged off her gloves, tossed them down and dug her bare hands deep into her pockets. Without invitation, he sat himself down on her rock. It was a big rock with more than enough room for two, but she remained on her feet. Somehow sharing her rock in this place, her special place, seemed too…intimate. Especially with someone who tickled her hormones the way he did.

If he had even an inkling of the thoughts racing through her mind, he seemed at ease with it. He made himself comfortable and peered up at her. "Are you like your mother?"

She kicked her toe into a tussock. "Physically." Too much, she thought. She nearly smiled, remembering Ellie's screams, as if there'd been a murder, when she'd found Lucy in the kitchen, scissors in hand and a pile of silvery locks slithering around her feet.

"Are you close?"

Lucy felt her mother's hands in her hair, braiding it. Remembered the smell of the rose-scented lotion she liked to wear. "I thought so."

There were many happy memories. All the neighboring farms got together and helped each other at busy
times. The big old table in the dining room was often
crammed to over-capacity, and elbows cracked and
nudged. Loud and raucous laughter rang out, exciting
the array of dogs banished to the step. And Thomas
would be at the head of the table, louder and happier
than everyone.

"I haven't seen her since she left."

He raised his dark brows.

"I was eight," she told him. "She ran off with one of
the cowhands." She folded her arms around herself.
"She was twenty years younger than Dad," she told
him, as if to qualify it.

In the pause that followed, Lucy felt a confusing disquiet that she had just divulged her mother's true behavior to a virtual stranger. It had long been her way to
make up the most extravagant fairy tales to her foreign
friends. Her loving indulgent parents. Wonderful home-
life. Mother-daughter shopping excursions to London
and Paris.

Somehow it seemed wrong to lie here, in this place.
Maybe it was because it was not only the last place she
had felt lovable, but also honest.

Ethan nodded. "He never remarried?"

"No. It knocked the stuffing out of him."

Belle's defection had stunned the small community
where the McKinlays were practically royalty. Thomas
McKinlay was a big man in the district. Many had
warned him about taking such a young bride.

"You were close to your father?" he asked.

Lucy considered. Close? After his stroke, he could
hardly tell her he didn't want her around. When her
mother had left, so had he in a sense. His withdrawal from

her was nearly complete, as if she wasn't worthy of his regard. "Not really. Not since I was little." She shrugged and turned away. "I looked too much like Mum."

Cutting her hair short hadn't changed anything. Not in her father's embittered eyes. "It wasn't his fault. He was heartbroken. Humiliated. Before he had the stroke six months ago, I hadn't really been home, except for the odd weekend, since I was sent away to boarding school."

She liked it that he didn't mutter trite platitudes. Why should he care that her parents hadn't loved her?

"Were you good at school?"

Distracted by his interest, she eased down onto the rock, careful to keep plenty of distance between them. "Terrible." She grinned. "I mean, really."

"Academically or behaviorally?"

"Both. I'm dyslexic."

Ethan blew out a long breath. "Not a hanging offence."

She pointed her pert nose in the air and put on an aristocratic tone. "Not allowed at *my* school. It didn't happen to high-class, privately educated 'gels' like me. And we dyslexics became expert at covering it up."

"How?"

"By being naughty, of course," Lucy replied promptly.

Like most dyslexics, she had mastered any number of ways to cover up her disability so as not to be singled out as different. Usually, this involved getting into trouble or charming people. She laughed a lot, chattered a lot and found that teachers and schoolmates overlooked homework not done, exams failed or not attended.

"Not one teacher tried…?"

"Listen, I was rich. I suppose they thought I'd be all right. We high-class 'gels' are only biding our time till our posh wedding to some rich guy anyway, right?" She laughed. "Who needs education?"

Ethan drew his knees up and wrapped his arms around them. "Yesterday—you said you'd mixed up the times."

Lucy rolled her eyes. Because of his reaction last night, she didn't feel embarrassed. "See, it seems perfectly logical to someone like me to take the seven out of seventeen hundred hours and translate that to 7:00 p.m."

He nodded, a smile tugging the corner of his mouth. "Of course. My fault."

She liked him for saying that, even though it wasn't true. Then she remembered who he worked for. "You don't have to worry, Ethan. Tom takes care of all the office stuff, the bookings and so on. Yesterday was just a misunderstanding. It was me that goofed."

He held up his hands. "Not worried."

A faint pole of yellow light slanted between them from the entrance, distracting her. She pushed herself to her feet. "The sun's arrived."

Ethan watched her walk away to stand at the edge of the gorge. "Poor little rich girl" went through his mind. Beauty, money, prestige. But it wasn't all roses in this garden of Eden. Dyslexic. Cut off from the love she craved, the love of her parents. Maybe, he thought, the two of them were not so different after all.

Except that she still found it within herself to be loyal toward her jerk of a brother and compassionate in the face of her parents' indifference. Could he?

His own proud and aloof attitude toward his father

had never softened over the years. He had long ignored the resignation in his father's voice when Ethan once again cancelled a family dinner or rushed off ten minutes after arriving.

He knew he didn't have it in him, like Lucy, to be compassionate toward a man he had no respect for, purely because that man was his father.

"Look!" Her voice, girlishly excited, roused him. He rose from the rock and walked to her.

"A rainbow." She pointed out over the valley, squinting a little in the silvery haze.

Ethan exhaled, coming level with her. "You can see forever."

Lucy nodded and let her head loll back a little.

"Where does your place end?"

Her arm, still outstretched, made a long sweep. They stood at the head of the valley with the Alps at the far end. It was not a picture-perfect postcard; it was too rugged. The mountains jutted from the milky water of the winding river. Gouges, crude and immense, were hewn into closer, dun-coloured foothills that had their own kind of magnificence. Great swatches of dark, dull green denoted forest that halted and then started up again without any sort of order.

He could barely take it all in. The vision seemed magnified, too big for a country the size of New Zealand. A long-buried scrap of wonder rose up from his jaded mind and soared from the bottom of the far-off rainbow, which curved down to kiss the silvery rock, to the hazy tips of the mountains.

It was another world from the one he knew. He was used to taming land. It was his profession. But the lands that attracted tourists were calm and tranquil places. There was no calmness here, it was savage in parts.

He was reminded of his childish pledge, at the age of twelve, that one day he would farm. The land he had grown up on was cruel, endless and dry, spirit-sapping. He and his father had not been good enough to save it. Somehow he had always wanted to put that right.

And his time was coming, he knew. Once Turtle Island was done and dusted, he would have the rest of his life to search for the perfect piece of land, the perfect wife and set about proving he could be a better farmer, husband and father than his own father had been.

The vista soared and roared. He turned to look at Lucy. The wind, stronger here at the edge, lifted her pale hair toward the weak sun. It sparkled and he could not help himself—he who maintained control in every situation, who never lost sight of his goals. He reached out and touched her hair and she turned to face him with a soft cry of surprise that was stolen by the fitful breeze.

It almost burned him, the look on her face of pride and ownership and fierce love for this land of hers. She was part of it. She was nature, but not in a robust way—more childlike. The blue haze of the mountains shone in her eyes. The silver of scree and rock were mirrored in her hair. She moved with the graceful sway of the trees. She would change with the seasons and the ebb of the atmosphere, and he admired that—wanted that—because he and his father had failed so abysmally.

Entranced, he moved toward her, wondering if she realized that he was going to kiss her. His fingers laced through her hair. His other hand pulled on the side of her open jacket, his eyes on hers, clearly signaling his intention.

She did not step back, although her arms seemed to clamp to her sides.

Oh yes, I am going to kiss you, Lucy McKinlay,

right or wrong. It was a rare moment in Ethan's life. He knew he'd spend a lifetime wondering if he did not go with the instinct driving him right now.

His mouth descended onto hers and the first touch of her slowed him down. There was no hurry. If he had to do this, he would do it properly.

With his tongue he traced the shape of her small mouth, lingering in the bow in the center of her top lip. Cool in the morning chill, and incredibly soft. He coaxed her lips apart and thought of nature—cold morning air, snow on your tongue, fresh-cut grass. The swirling sea-colors of her outfit last night as she moved around the bar, bending and straightening, smiling and chatting. That vision had kept him awake for most of the night, so restless that he was compelled to take an early-morning swim. And to knock himself out trying to impress her when he saw her at the door to the pool.

Lucy's mouth kissed back, warming and accepting. Her tongue did not shy from his, her breath shuddered into his mouth. Her hair was as soft and fine as he had ever felt. His fingers threaded through it, discovering the shape of her skull, making her gasp when he massaged the base of it. He wanted more, but it wasn't so much carnal or wanting to go farther, as it was just to continue. The taste of her, the feel of her skin, it all combined into a whole delicious addictive feast.

But her arms were rigid at her sides. It was that fact that pricked his comprehension, brought him back through the clouds. His hands moved to her shoulders and ran lightly down her arms, as if to thaw their stiffness. He leaned back slightly, a little breathless but wanting to see her response.

Her eyes remained closed. She captured her bottom lip with small white teeth and drew it into her mouth, inhaling. Then her eyes opened and slowly focused on him.

Heavy-lidded and fringed by light-brown lashes that seemed longer at the outer corners, there was real depth in those lovely blue eyes. Surprise. Embers of heat going up in a little shower of sparks. He'd thought her unresponsive. Afraid, even, when he'd felt the tension in her arms. She wasn't. A strong tremor rolled through her slender body, still pressed up against his. She was holding back, but she was as affected as he was. Her hands fisted and she pulled them back behind her, as if that might stop the trembling.

Lucy McKinlay might be innocent. She might even be a common gold digger. But he had never wanted to claim and tame someone so much.

"I—we—we'll be late for breakfast," she whispered and pulled dazedly from his embrace, took a couple of unfirm steps back.

As if waking from a dream, he squinted at her, wondering what on earth had just possessed him.

"I must get back." Distance had made her stronger, firmer.

She turned her back on him. He watched her walk to her horse, take some time inspecting the saddle, crooning to the animal. Her hat and gloves were next for a fastidious inspection before being tugged on—and all without looking at him once. Finally she mounted and nudged her horse with the slightest pressure of her legs and moved to Ethan's mare, leaning down to collect the reins. "Are you coming down now?"

He took the reins she held out and nodded curtly, telling himself he was relieved she did not want to talk about what had just occurred. He needed time to sort it out in his head. Not given to uncontrollable urges, he had to wonder if the magic of the landscape had some-how drugged him.

# Four

**E**than had scheduled a meeting with Magnus after lunch. On the way to the conference facility, he paused by the front door to look out onto the veranda. Juliette lounged on a hammock-chair that rocked gently as she moved her crossed ankles in a lazy circular motion. She read aloud from a glossy brochure or magazine. Lucy listened from the bench seat, her bare feet tucked up under her.

From twenty feet away, she looked like anyone else. You had to get close to appreciate the silky radiance of her skin, the warmth and sparkle of her eyes.

Correction. You had to get close enough to touch her on a hilltop with a magical view to get really carried away. He was still shaking his head over his impetuous actions that morning. Perhaps it was the contrast between her and the type of women he usually came into contact with.

Women like Juliette.

His eyes narrowed as he studied the new Mrs. Magnus Anderson. Growing up in Australia, he was used to tanned and toned athletic girls. As he got older and traveled all corners of the world, he was confronted with more tanned and toned women, but with a subtle difference. They got their tan and their tone from the beauty parlor and the personal trainer.

Sleek and bronzed. Stylishly dressed. Immaculately made-up and coiffed. The perfect companion. He stared hard at her. What was she hiding? And what were her intentions toward Magnus?

With a start, he realised that Lucy was looking right at him. He met her eyes and all thoughts of Juliette were whisked away.

He did not smile in greeting. So they had a secret to share, a bit of a kiss when they'd only just met. Good sense told him to step back. It wasn't his style to deliberately hurt, confuse or treat women carelessly. With little time to socialize, he made sure his partners knew the score. No romance. No promise of anything more. The few women he dated were of similar disposition to him: ambitious, busy, on the way up with no time to spare.

There was something vulnerable about that doll-like mouth, something that both drew him to her and warned him off. She had not smiled and from where he stood, he could not read her expression. Then she nodded and turned back to Juliette.

Magnus was in an exuberant mood. Ethan tossed his briefcase on the table and poured himself a coffee, and for the next hour or so, they went through every detail of the successful completion of the Middle Eastern resort.

At the conclusion, Ethan stretched and stood to re-fill his cup. Magnus sorted the sheaf of papers in front of him and fussed in his top pocket for a cigar, which he clamped down on enthusiastically. It was in defer-ence to his doctor, Ethan knew, that he only actually smoked one cigar a day, but he chomped through four or five others.

"Looking pleased with yourself," Ethan commented, resuming his seat.

Magnus removed the cigar and pointed it at him, his eyes twinkling. "It's marriage, my boy. You should try it."

Ethan considered again raising the subject of the newspaper clippings, but he hated to blight his boss's relaxed good humor. It could wait till they were back in Sydney. Or until he had something concrete from the P.I. "Just like a newlywed," he sighed. "You must try and fix up all your poor, miserable, single friends."

"Uh-huh." Magnus leaned back in his chair and squinted at him. "Got a bit of a light in your own eye today."

Ethan pushed the unbidden thought of Lucy firmly away. "There is something else." He pulled his open briefcase toward him, his mouth tightening into a cau-tious grin. The Turtle Island file was on top and he lifted it and placed it on the table. Magnus's big hand landed on the plain manila folder and he slid it closer, flipping back the cover.

While he studied the file, Ethan paced, savoring the anticipation of his boss's reaction. Turtle Island had historical significance to MagnaCorp. He counted on Magnus jumping at the chance to recoup a substantial loss suffered.

He sat down again, his hand threatening to drum up a tattoo of impatience on the table.

Finally Magnus cleared his throat, his head still bent but the last page of the slim file inching closed. He picked up his cigar, tapped the end of it on the table and brought it slowly to his mouth. The chair creaked as he shifted to face Ethan.

The older man's eyes were lit up with guarded pleasure. "When did you start on this?"

"Got the tip-off a month ago."

"You've been busy."

Ethan nodded. "I'm the only player. Clark knows."

Magnus eyed him, nodding slowly. "Clark's a good man."

Ethan leaned back in his own seat, folding his arms. "Is it a go?"

Magnus roused himself. "Your father—" He tapped the file. "He did all the work on this, twenty years ago. Would have clinched it, too, but for the coup."

Ethan sighed. The old man read him like a book. "Before my time."

He was well aware of the history. Nearly twenty years ago, before this priceless piece of land had been nationalized, there were only two companies in the Pacific large enough to buy the rights to develop the bay into the world's most exclusive resort. "You also spent millions," he reminded him. "Lawyers, surveyors, architects…"

"And we both lost."

"Here it is. You don't want it?"

"Hell, yes. It would be the jewel in my crown. I'd be thrilled for you if it wasn't *your* father and *this* island."

"It's business," Ethan told him stubbornly.

"You know, Ethan, you only took the job I offered you to rub his nose in it. Else you'd be running his corporation now, instead of mine. He'd welcome you, and it wouldn't be like working for someone else. You're his only son. His rightful heir."

"I've earned my money—sufficient, I think—my way."

"You've done well." Magnus pursed his mouth thoughtfully. "If you ever decide to call in ownership of all your units at the same time, you'd damn near break me."

They smiled at the joke. Magnus had been among the top five Australasians on the rich list for the last decade.

From the time Ethan had completed his first project for MagnaCorp, he'd deferred the generous bonuses his boss offered in lieu of a down payment on a small portion of land on every project since. Sometimes this took the shape of a unit to be let out, a small piece of beachfront. In one case, he'd purchased the resort golf course.

"I want you to think about this, long and hard. Jackson's done well these last few years, even if he didn't do right by you and your mother."

"My father doesn't even feature in my thoughts most of the time. Some families just aren't that close."

"Yes but his failures made you what you are today," Magnus insisted. "Forgive him, Ethan. Don't allow him to leave this world with regrets. You do, and you'll do the same."

Ethan blew out a long breath and leaned toward the table. He picked up the Turtle Island file and saluted his boss with it. "Duly noted. And appreciated. Now, can we get down to business?"

Magnus grinned. "I swear, I've never met anyone as single-minded as you. Loosen up, son. Quit ticking things off that interminable list in your head. Come hunting with us."

Ethan shook his head. "Not my idea of fun, old man. I'll stick around here, enjoy the scenery."

A smile nagged the corners of Magnus's mouth. "Little Miss Lucy does kind of light up a room, even in the middle of nowhere, doesn't she?" The smile broadened when he saw Ethan's guarded expression.

"Let me have a go at Turtle Island, Magnus," he hedged.

Magnus shook his head ruefully. "All right, son. If you think you can swing Turtle Island without causing an irretrievable break between you and your father, then go for it. I have every faith in you."

Ethan slapped the file on the table in elation. "I'll call Clark now, get the ball rolling."

Magnus waved his hand. "Since you'll be hanging around here, how about doing something for me? I've been hearing some disturbing things about Summerhill. It's why I chose this as a belated honeymoon."

"What sort of things?" Ethan's interest piqued.

"Cutbacks. Maintenance issues. The word is, they're close to the wall. The integrity of the club is paramount. There can be no hint of impropriety."

The reference to the club made Ethan smile. Now that Ethan managed most of the affairs of MagnaCorp, Magnus had slowed down some, but the club was his pet. "Sure. I'll ask a few questions. Looks okay, so far." Better than okay, he thought, almost giving a wolfish grin. Lucy's tantalizing presence could help him overlook just about anything. "The accommodation is spot-on, if a bit faded. Incredible location."

"Mmm. Keep your ear to the ground. And have a bit of a rest. I'll be back Wednesday, and we fly out on Friday." He stood slowly. "Keep tomorrow night free. Tom has offered us some tickets for New Zealand versus Argentina. One of his friends has a corporate box. Whaddya say? It's compulsory to see a rugby game when in New Zealand."

Ethan closed his briefcase and picked up his jacket. "Who's coming?" he asked casually.

Magnus turned to the door, but not before Ethan caught a definite gleam in his eye. "My wife and I. You and Lucy. Sadly, Tom will be busy with arrangements for our safari. We'll have dinner afterwards and Lucy was going to see about booking a hotel in town for the night, save driving back."

Lucy allowed herself a small smile of satisfaction. Nothing had gone wrong for once. She had checked the Andersons and Ethan into their hotel and had had time to call in to the apartment and pick up her beloved New Zealand jersey. The real stroke of luck was finding a rare parking spot on the street not three blocks from the stadium. They would be seated in good time.

The atmosphere was festive as thirty-seven thousand people poured in through the gates. A fireworks display sent big puffs of smoke rolling across the field and into the stands. Lucy paused a minute—she loved fireworks—then noticed Ethan had stopped to turn and look at her.

She had planned to avoid him as much as politely possible for the duration of his stay and had managed that nicely since yesterday's incident on the gorge. But today they had all ganged up on her, even Tom. "Take my SUV," he'd insisted, when she'd protested that four would be a bit of a squeeze in the Alfa.

Ethan had turned back to say something to Magnus. A body bumped into her and she stepped aside, her eyes intermittently on the fireworks and Ethan's tall figure a few feet ahead. "Sorry," she murmured auto-matically, then felt someone grip her arm.

A face, clean-shaven and loose-looking, peered at her closely. Because of the crush behind, she strove to keep walking but his grip tightened.

"Ms. McKinlay."

A waft of strong alcohol preceded his words and she stiffened. The face looked vaguely familiar, but distaste muddled her memory. "I'm sorry, I…"

"Joseph Dunn. Friend of your brother's."

A small spurt of relief was wiped out by the realiza-tion that he still hung on to her arm. "Oh. Okay."

While she stammered, her eyes lifted over the man's shoulder and she saw Ethan frowning back at her.

"We met at the casino one night, not long after you came home."

Lucy did not remember but she did know his face. She tried to think of something to say to politely extricate herself from his grasp. "Nice to see you," she murmured, lifting her arm pointedly. To her confusion, he seemed to grip her harder. Giving up the pretence of politeness, she pulled against him. "Excuse me," she began icily.

"Where's your brother?" The fleshy lips were no longer smiling. It was as if he too had given up on diplo-macy.

"Tom?" A little scared now, she registered that Ethan was pushing toward her, only a few feet away.

"Yes, Tom." The tone was now openly belligerent. "I know he's here. I saw his car."

Perhaps emboldened by rescue at hand, she tugged sharply to free herself.

"Hey!" She heard Ethan's voice crack through the din of the crowd. The man checked.

"What do you want?" she hissed.

He glanced quickly over his shoulder then his fingers dug deep into her arm, so hard that tears of pain and outrage sprang into her eyes. He shoved his face very close. "Tell him I'm looking for him." With that, he gave her a small but quite rough push.

A little dazed and off balance, she heard a louder "Hey!" close now, right in front of her, and then the tang of Ethan's aftershave blitzed the smell of alcohol and malice away. Her head cleared. He came level with her, moving determinedly in the direction of the departing man. Without thinking, Lucy raised her hand quickly. "Leave it!" She slapped her hand quite forcefully on his chest.

His wide chest.

His hard chest.

His heart beat strongly under her flat palm. He looked down at it, possibly surprised at the force she'd used or perhaps it was the commanding tone of voice. Then he looked at her face.

She stared back, trying to think of something to say. Her train of thought was completely attuned to the rhythm of his heart under her hand. And the warmth of his skin under the shirt invited each of her fingers to flex and flatten out, pressing fractionally closer.

"You okay? What did he...?"

Lucy gingerly took control of herself, lifting her hand off his chest. "He was just being vulgar." She started to walk in the direction he'd come from. "Come on, they'll be wondering."

Ethan's hand landed on her arm, the same arm. His grip was gentle, but his voice was not. "Lucy."

She tensed, inhaling deeply. This had to be handled with a light touch. She had no idea what that man had wanted with Tom, but her gut feeling was it had something to do with money.

Turning slowly to face him, she looked pointedly at his hand on her arm. "Gosh, it's my week for being manhandled." With satisfaction, she saw his eyes narrow at the coolness she'd imparted.

There were people everywhere, pushing impatiently to get to their seats. Ethan guided her determinedly to the side of the thoroughfare. When her back was against the wall, he leaned in close. His hands were on the wall on either side of her, cutting off her escape, but he did not touch her.

"What was that about?" His voice was low and tense.

Lucy quailed when she saw how tightly reined he was; his jaw was clamped, his eyes flashing. Why he was angry with her? "It was nothing."

His breath puffed over her face. "Ex-boyfriend?"

She shuddered. "No."

"His hands were on you."

She saw then it was not her he was angry with. God help Joseph Dunn if Ethan stumbled across him tonight. "As were yours, yesterday morning," she said carefully.

As a distraction, it worked. He shifted slightly, leaning on his arms, and his eyes slid down to her lips. A breathless shiver of excitement fizzed through her. Her fingers curled in remembrance of his heartbeat.

He was thinking of their morning kiss, as she was.

"Did I bully you yesterday morning?" he asked softly, and brought his eyes back to hers.

Smouldering voice. Smouldering eyes. Desire, not just excitement or anticipation but hot, flowing, knee-trembling desire rolled through every cell of her. And he saw it, recognized it. She saw his pupils dilate, his lips part slightly, and Lucy had to fight not to sag against him, helpless with longing.

And then the stadium erupted. Loudspeakers, applause, music rushed into the vacuum between them and sanity returned. Lucy shook her head and ducked quickly under his arm. "Forget it. Let's go." She made a timely escape, breathing deeply.

Ethan straightened. Following, he glared at the sea of people, as if to pick out the obnoxious man. "What did he want with your brother?"

She could not escape him; his long legs ate up the ground. "My brother? I told you, he was just trying it on. We'll miss kick-off."

She flicked him a nervous look and knew he saw right through her lie. He must have heard the man.

He moved to her side and put his arm through hers decisively. "You'll tell me later."

It sounded like a threat but she was somehow soothed by the touch of his arm running the length of hers.

This was a revelation. He was being protective, even territorial, of her. A champion. That was a first, ever since she'd been a kid, anyway. It was hard to know how to feel about it. No doubt she'd be called to account at some stage. By then, she hoped she'd have thought up something to distract him.

Several distractions went through her mind over the course of the game. The corporate box catered for about twenty but seemed to be well over-subscribed tonight. Magnus and Juliette had managed to snare a leaner and some stools right in front of the big glass doors, but it was a crush. Stuck in between Magnus and Ethan, she wrapped her arms around her torso and tried to diminish her size.

It was no good. The whole of her right leg was pressed up against his left. She felt on fire all down that side. If she moved to sip her drink, her elbow touched him. If he half turned to exchange a word with Magnus, his breath lifted strands of her hair. If she leaned forward to talk to Juliette, he seemed to fill the space behind so she could not lean back without touching him.

This attraction was fast becoming overwhelming, especially since her skin—her very nerve endings—were already sensitized by their altercation earlier. She was totally aware of every breath he took. Of every muscle in his long, taut thigh pressed against hers. He had rolled his shirt sleeves up a little and her eyes strayed, time and again, to the coffee-colored skin of his forearm with its sprinkling of springy-looking dark hair, and to his hands—long-fingered and spread wide on his thighs.

Worst of all was his reaction to the accidental touches. A stillness which told her more than the many three-second meetings of their eyes. A stillness that seemed to pass from him into her. An awareness of each other breathing, moving, just being. They spoke hardly at all, and the silences were fraught with a constant hum of excitement and perplexity.

What a relief to finally leave the small area and lose herself in other people again, although Ethan stuck quite close to her this time.

The crowd was in high spirits as they swept onto the streets. The plan was that Lucy would drop the Australians at their central hotel, go back to the apartment and change and meet them at the new jazz restaurant she'd booked, by ten or ten-thirty.

But when they came to the spot where Tom's SUV should have been, it was nowhere to be seen. Lucy knew she'd left it right here; she recalled seeing the black balloons fastened to the lamppost right beside where she'd parked.

Where a green Toyota now sat. She shook her head. "Good grief, it must be the next street over."

"Look." Juliette was looking at the ground, moving the toe of her expensive boot over the road. "Glass."

Ethan crouched. "Broken car-window glass." He picked up a fragment. "Someone broke into it and drove it away."

"I don't believe it." Lucy squatted beside him, rummaging in her bag for her phone. She was hot with embarrassment. What a great impression of her city this would leave on the visitors. "I'll call a cab."

It was handy having a few connections in the tourist business and five minutes or so later, a corporate cab pulled up alongside.

When they reached the hotel, Ethan got out to let Magnus and Juliette out and then insisted, despite her objections, on accompanying her to the police station.

Half an hour later, they were still in the queue and she was still objecting. It was a busy Saturday night with an assortment of drunks, assaults and reports of thefts to entertain them. Finally they stood in front of a young policeman and Lucy outlined why they were there.

"Fill this in." A form was placed on the counter. Her heart sank. Filling in forms on the spot with people watching—him watching—was as much fun as being in the dentist's chair. Both men's eyes on her, she picked up the pen and frowned down at the paper. Her face felt hot. The text in front of her danced behind her eyes.

"Registration number?" the officer inquired, tapping his keyboard.

Lucy wished the ground would open up and swallow her. In times of stress, her dyslexia was exacerbated.

She knew there was nothing wrong with her intellect, just the way her brain processed words and figures.

Right. And it didn't matter how often she heard those words, or read the literature from well-meaning disability learning centers. She felt so dumb, having to punch her PIN number in three times at the front of a queue, putting numbers back to front. Names, too—if she was given a written message to call someone she didn't know called Joe Brown, Lucy was likely to say, "Is that Brown Joe?" when the called person answered.

Then she felt Ethan's fingers cover hers, easing the pen from her iron grip.

"Call Tom," he murmured, his lips brushing her ear and making her shiver.

Vastly relieved, she pressed the speed dial on her phone. Tom answered on the third ring. Quickly she explained the situation and requested the car registration number.

Tom didn't respond. Someone in the queue behind muttered loudly about the time they were taking.

"Tom?" The growing worry must not show in her voice. Not with *him* standing there.

"I forgot to register it."

"What? When?" Her voice was low, her face turned away to hide her confusion.

Tom sighed heavily. "Last year."

"Last year?" She swallowed a very unladylike oath, snapped the phone off and slowly turned back to the cop, unwilling to face Ethan. "It appears he forgot to register it."

The cop looked disgusted.

"But you can still look for it, can't you?"

From the corner of her eye she saw Ethan lay the pen carefully on the counter and lift the form. His hand landed lightly on her shoulder. "I'd say your credibility's shot," he told her quietly. Turning, he coaxed her toward the exit, crumpling the form into a ball. They moved outside, Lucy glad of the cool night air on her burning face. Sighing miserably, she sank down on the bottom step leading into the station. Ethan remained standing, leaning against the wall of the building.

Lucy stared at his feet. "I can read and write, you know. It's just when I'm not prepared or people are watching, I get flustered."

He did not answer and she shot a look at his face. His expression was serious and concerned.

Then he moved, startling her. "Shove up." He sat down. "What was the name of the guy at the stadium?"

"I—don't know," she lied and then put her head in her hands. What was going on with Tom? They'd never been close, but they were family. His recent moods and the problems he kept alluding to were beginning to really worry her.

"Why are you covering up for him?"

"Who?"

"Your brother."

"I'm not."

"Lucy, he sent clients out in an unregistered vehicle, which was subsequently stolen, probably by a disgruntled associate."

"We don't know that."

"I heard the guy. He'd seen the car and you're to tell Tom he's looking for him."

Could this night get any worse? Lucy searched the streets, trying desperately to think of a way to deflect him. "My, Grandma. What big ears you have."

They were interrupted by a couple trying to pass. Ethan rose and Lucy pressed close to the railing to let them through. He put his hands in his pockets and stared down at her. "What sort of trouble is Tom in?"

She pushed herself to her feet. "He's not. Let's get to the restaurant. You've wasted enough time on me to-night."

He just stood there, looking at her. "I have time to waste."

Silence, and that peculiar stillness, rolled between them. After the evening spent pressed up against him, being so aware of him, and being in no doubt that he felt the same, it was tempting, *so* tempting, to give in, twine her arms around his neck and forget her problems for the rest of this night.

She was experiencing this way too much today. It was hard to recall they had met only a couple of days earlier. There was a familiarity and intensity that was usually reserved for more…intimate acquaintances.

Breaking eye contact, she took the last step down. "Ethan, I'm sure that person had nothing to do with the car. But I'll tell Tom, and then it's his decision if he wants to involve the police. Satisfied?"

Her pulse leapt when he sought her eyes and swept her with a rare, reluctant smile, his dark brows arched.

Lucy shook her head and began to walk away from temptation.

His voice behind her made her check. "One condition."

She looked back over her shoulder at him.

"Magnus and Juliette are on their honeymoon." He drew level with her. "So let's you and I leave them to it and have a drink."

# Five

"**U**nless," he continued, "you'd rather go home."

Lucy blinked at him, swallowing hard. Images of being alone together, enclosed within four walls, with a bed not too far away, leapt between them.

"Uh—I think there's a bar around here somewhere." Her eyes slid away and he smiled. A drink would do, for now.

They jostled their way to the bar at a noisy pub a couple of blocks away. The only perch was outside, leaning on a forty-four-gallon barrel with the smokers, nursing their beers. Ethan pulled his jacket closer around his neck.

"Shouldn't you call Magnus and tell them not to wait for us?"

Ethan shook his head. He'd already told Magnus that when they'd dropped them off. Reporting a crime on a Saturday night when there was a big game on in town would have been a long job.

Lucy was quiet, and, although he badly wanted to know what was going on with her brother, he thought he'd let her loosen up with some friendly chitchat first.

He sipped from his bottle and followed her gaze to a young couple leaning on their own drum a few feet away. There was some pretty heavy kissing going on there. It amused him when Lucy turned back and shifted so she was facing away from them.

"Why aren't you hunting with the others tomorrow?" She took the slice of lemon from the neck of the beer bottle and raised it to her nose, inhaling deeply.

He shook his head distastefully. "Not into blood sports."

"Why not?"

He sighed. "As a kid, my job was to shoot or cut the throats of the animals on our farm."

"Why?"

"They were starving."

"Why?" she repeated.

"Drought." Ethan bared his teeth mirthlessly. "My father and I were piss-poor farmers."

A movement caught his eye and they both glanced over at the couple again. The guy had put his fingers in the girl's waistband and pulled her lower body flush against his. Their kisses were deep. They kept breaking off to talk, but all the time he was tugging her gently into the front of him.

"Where was this?" Lucy asked, bringing him back.

"Western Australia."

"How old were you?"

"Moved to the farm when I was six. Walked off it at twelve."

"Are you an only child?"

He nodded.

"When did the drought end?"

Ethan shrugged. "We left when the bank foreclosed. Moved into a trailer park in Perth." He narrowed his eyes at her. "Nosy, aren't you?"

She nodded, not in the least self-conscious. "Are your parents still together?"

"He kicked my mother out when I was thirteen."

Lucy's eyes widened. He could almost hear her mind ticking over. Maybe they had something in common. Lonely children, dysfunctional families…

"Kicked her out for a girl five years older than me. She was only interested after he won the state lottery. Trailer trash no more." He raised his bottle and clinked hers in a salute.

She stared at him, fiddling with the stud in her ear. Women, he thought wryly. Nothing fascinated them more than someone's troubles.

"What happened to your mum?"

"Came back to New Zealand. She's from Kaikohe."

"Why?"

His brows rose.

"I mean, why did she leave *you*?" She had said exactly what was in her mind, judging by the hand she clamped to her mouth. Ethan nearly laughed out loud. A blush streaked her cheeks. She was embarrassed, but she wanted to know. That was the sort of thing women liked to know.

He looked at her seriously for a moment. "Farming the outback's tough for a woman. After the farm, he drank and she worked. Couldn't afford a school uniform, so she home-schooled me in between cleaning jobs. Then one day, my father spent his last dollar on the lottery and it came in. I was sent to a private school. They bought a big house. Mum stopped work, got her hair done." He took a long pull on his bottle, enjoying the total concentration on Lucy's face. It was no hardship being the object of her avid attention.

Where was he? "Might have been a lousy farmer, the old man, but turned out he was lucky as sin on the share market. Doubled his money in little more than a year." He set his bottle down very carefully. "And that's when the fortune hunters started sniffing around."

It was the longest speech he had made. Lucy looked riveted. He decided to give her a bit of a jolt, so he hit her with the full intensity of his eyes. "Young, beautiful women who'd do anything for money." His voice was low and loaded. "You know the type."

He watched her blink, as if surprised, then her head nodded once, slowly, as if something had suddenly clicked in her mind.

Was she a gold digger, he wondered? He swore he could see no guile in her eyes, though it was dark out here. But a couple of her lighthearted quips had stuck under his collar like grit.

And yet, there was a freshness about her that did not equate with any of the parade of girls his father traded in at the rate of one every couple of years. Or the women who schmoozed in the corporate world he moved in. He couldn't imagine anyone more different.

"I was settled in a good school. I guess she didn't want to disrupt my schooling any more than it had been. I spent every holiday with her."

"What happened to you after she left?" Lucy asked.

He considered. "Did well at school. Made the national swim team."

"I knew it," she smiled. "I thought you looked like a swimmer."

"Could have made the Olympics."

"But?"

Another long pause while he assessed how much more to divulge. He wasn't one for baring his soul but he felt easy, comfortable. Burning up for her, sure, but enjoying himself and quite prepared to continue. "Wasn't part of the plan."

"The plan?" Lucy shifted against the barrel.

"To—succeed. No luck involved."

"To succeed where your father failed," she told him triumphantly.

He grinned at the sparkle in her eyes. "Dammit, you're right, Freud!"

"You haven't forgiven him, have you?" Her head was cocked to one side, the grin fading.

"Have you forgiven your parents?"

Lucy's mouth twisted, just for a moment. Her thumb knuckle pressed on her chin. "I don't suppose it's easy being a parent." She smiled sadly. "If I ever get the chance, I'll know what *not* to do."

"I'll drink to that," Ethan said, raising his bottle and toasting her. "Here's to making a better job of it."

They clinked bottles.

"Would you like to see your mother again?"

Lucy picked at the label of her bottle. "No." She shook her head. "She made her choice and obviously I didn't figure."

"She was walking from your father, not you."

Her smile held a gentle rebuke. "Oh, Ethan. If that were the case she would have kept in touch, like your mother."

She inhaled deeply then looked up at him seriously. "But I do regret that I let Dad get away with ignoring me all those years. If I'd tried a bit harder…"

"Maybe if *he'd* tried a bit harder," he told her and

there was an edge to his voice. Why should she feel bad about it? It was she who had been treated shabbily.

Where was this coming from, this protective thing he had going on here? He'd always been a loner, proud of it. Had no problem with the strongest-of-the-pack-survive rule.

"You have to forgive them, don't you?" she was saying. "They're family, and you only get one."

He frowned. "I think that's—generous, considering what your parents did."

She lifted her shoulders in a shrug. "What's the point in being bitter?"

Ethan found that interesting. He would not have described himself as bitter. But it had never occurred to him that his father deserved forgiveness. Hell, if that were the case, what did his poor mother deserve?

And then the thought popped into his mind that his mother had been perfectly happy, these last ten years. His father had been generous with the settlement and she had a nice spread and seemed happy with Drako, her boy-toy up north.

"Actually—" she broke into his thoughts, and her tone was much lighter "—if you want to think about it, we've got quite a lot in common. My mum married a much older man, then took off with a younger one. Your dad likes younger women. Just think what our combined gene pool would produce."

Ethan had already started laughing at her words. But when Lucy realized what she'd said, the look of shock that crossed her face really did him in. That's when he threw back his head and let rip.

Her hand was clamped over her mouth again but as he laughed she relaxed. Her elbows rested on the barrel and she leaned on them, shading her eyes.

"Don't worry about me," Ethan chuckled. "Just say exactly what's on your mind."

She shook her head, still hiding her eyes, but she was smiling ruefully. "I can't believe I said that." She sighed. "Strike that from the record."

He cleared his throat, still grinning. It felt good—great. He couldn't remember the last time he'd shared a good laugh with a woman. Man, she was cute.

"I'm sorry. Tom's always saying I need to engage brain before mouth."

Their smiles faded. Tom seemed to have that effect. "You're very loyal," Ethan said quietly, and watched a mini slide-show of expression on her face. From humor to caution in one second. She would be hopeless at poker. "Your brother doesn't know how lucky he is."

Lucy pursed her lips. "And have you succeeded? With your success plan?"

He decided to let her get away with changing the subject. He was having a good time. Why waste it on Tom McKinlay? "Nearly," he answered. "A couple of things on the list still to be ticked off."

"Don't stop now," she encouraged him.

"Kissing you again is right at the top," he murmured, holding her gaze.

He heard the little catch in her throat. She glanced at him then away. And he was amused to see she focused on the couple swallowing tongues for quite awhile this time. Only that's not all they were doing. The boy's knee was right between the girl's legs now and there was some pretty suggestive rubbing going on. Lucy was blushing prettily when she eventually turned back to him.

"But I think you know that," he continued in the same teasing tone.

"Oh," was all she had to say, and she wouldn't meet his gaze.

The air seemed to crackle in his ears. He could not recall ever being so aware of a woman. This whole night had been one long exercise in self-restraint. Not just his sexual self-restraint, although that was compelling after being pressed up against her for the duration of a rugby game. But keeping it loose had not been easy when he knew she was lying about the slob who'd shoved her. And it would take some time to forget the shame burning in her eyes when faced with completing a simple form. Lucy McKinlay touched him in ways he had not expected.

She had stopped ravaging the bottle label. It blew in long strips around the rim of their barrel. Instead, the bottle's neck was being strangled in a white-knuckled fist. Finally she put it down between them with a sharp rap and frowned.

"Ethan, you're a client. I have to keep things on a professional level."

Ethan snorted. "Hardly a doctor-patient relationship."

She looked heavenward but did raise a smile. "I'm not saying I'm not tempted, but…I'm trying really hard…."

He waited.

She sighed heavily, obviously uncomfortable. "Just—nothing's going to happen between us. Not while you're a guest at Summerhill."

He squinted at her. "I move out of Summerhill and into a hotel, you'll go out with me?"

A resigned laugh bubbled up in her throat. "No! Not while Magnus and Juliette are here. Maybe not ever."

He shook his head. "Not ever's a long time, Lucy."

"I've known you two days," she pointed out reasonably.

"Yeah." Ethan nodded. "Surprised me, too." He stroked his chin and saw that her eyes followed the movement. "I don't take enough holidays."

"All business?" Her tone was gentle but it sounded like a taunt.

"You're the one trying to be professional."

She broke eye contact and rubbed her forehead. He swore any professional thoughts were blasted away when she copped an eyeful of the young lovers. The girl was practically riding the guy's leg—her feet were all but off the ground. They both watched shamelessly. When Lucy finally dragged her eyes back to his, he met and held her gaze for long seconds. Brazen images— bare skin, mouths seeking, frantic touching—danced behind his eyes and were mirrored in hers.

She swept up the fallen strips of label distractedly and stuffed them down the throat of her empty bottle. "Will you be here when Juliette and I get back?"

He raised his brows.

"From Queenstown," she explained. "We'll probably be back Wednesday."

"I'm trying to set up a meeting in Sydney for the end of the week."

Ethan fancied she looked a little downcast. Something compelled him to start negotiating. "Even if I do have to go before you get back, they're only meetings. And meetings don't take forever."

"And the flight's only a few hours," she encouraged him.

"Exactly." Ethan leaned forward and rested his elbow on the barrel. "You might think," he said slowly, "that takes the pressure off."

Lucy nodded, looking relieved.

Until he reached for her hand and sandwiched it between both of his. Her eyes flew wide and he stroked firmly over the base of her thumb to confirm the scramble of her pulse.

The girl with her boyfriend's knee wedged between her thighs gave a low breathless moan. It hung between them, and they stared at each other, connected by the lingering memory of the moan and the thumping of her pulse under his thumb.

"However," he murmured, "I don't think you should be too complacent."

Tom picked her up early the next day in one of the lodge's vehicles, anxious to be on the road. It was safari day for the hunters, and the day Lucy and Juliette were to leave for Queenstown. On the way to the Australians' hotel, she advised Tom to report the stolen car, regardless of the registration issue. He seemed vague about Joseph Dunn, which perplexed her. "Whatever." She shrugged. "Probably just kids. It just seemed strange he actually mentioned seeing your car."

They arrived back at Summerhill and organized their day. The four hunters, Tom, Stacey the tracker, Magnus and an Indonesian guest, departed. Lucy and Juliette packed and she arranged for Ellie to drop them at the airstrip. Summerhill had its own airstrip. A good proportion of the guests chartered light aircraft for hunting or excursions. The women would first be flown to Aorangi, Australasia's highest mountain, and then to Queenstown, a popular tourist mecca in the south.

Lucy had put her luggage in the car boot and was walking down the hallway when a hand snaked out of the alcove going into Tom's office. Suddenly she was hauled up against a wall of warm skin, taut muscle and bone.

"Not thinking of leaving without saying goodbye?"

"Ethan!" Her heart thumped against her ribs. For one awful moment, Joseph Dunn's face had flashed through her mind. "What are you…?"

"Told you not to be complacent."

She relaxed slightly, her eyes adjusting to the gloom with the aid of the gleam of his teeth.

One slick maneuver and she found herself turned, her back against the wall—or at least the wall-mounted firearms cabinet. His teeth flashed again. "Wow. Nice suit. But I'd love to see you in red."

Lucy felt herself flush. As was her way, she was taking her client's lead. Juliette favored short skirts, in vibrant reds and pinks. Lucy's choice was a dusky-pink color with a barely-there skirt and high black pumps. The lacy black cami under the jacket touched it off nicely even though she would be no match for the beauty and wealth of Mrs. Anderson.

"The guys in Queenstown won't know what hit them when you two roll into town."

His hands snaked around her waist, inside the jacket. "Ethan, I thought we agreed last night…"

"…that we had a mutual attraction." He leaned back, smiling and swaying her gently.

"That nothing was going to…" She couldn't help it, she was smiling back.

"…happen last night," he finished.

She shook her head. "Ha, ha. I have to go. The plane's waiting."

"She can afford a few more minutes." He leaned in close, eyes slanted down to her mouth. His thighs brushed hers. Lucy's breath hissed through her lips as warmth flooded her agitated body. When she felt herself about to sag against him, she put a restraining hand on his chest and leaned her head back.

An unexpected jerk and a sharp click behind her head claimed Ethan's attention.

He frowned. "Bit lax isn't it? The firearms cabinet left unlocked?"

Lucy was still concentrating on his mouth, centimeters away. "Tom must have forgotten," she said dreamily.

The stern, all-business look he gave her snapped her out of her fog.

"Tom forget often?"

"No, I don't think so."

This was bad. This was a serious issue, one that could have their firearms license revoked. New Zealand's firearms laws were strictly enforced. This could impinge on staying in the club. "I'll get the key."

Ethan fingered the cabinet's latch. "It's not good enough, Lucy. Anyone could have access."

Lucy did the only possible thing she could think of. She reached up to tangle her fingers in his thick hair and pulled his head down to hers.

His hair was soft, inviting her to twist and tug gently. She felt his hand, still around her waist, spread and lift and next thing she was on tiptoe, planted against the length of him like ivy. He held back slightly, his brow still furrowed in a frown. His free hand moved up to the back of her head and his fingers mirrored what hers were doing.

She tugged him closer and he sank into her mouth. Hot and humid, his satiny-slick tongue danced with hers. Lucy wound her hands around his neck and pressed her tingling nipples into him. She fought to breathe; he took all her air and gave it back in miserly doses and she heard his breath rasping through his nostrils.

His strength surprised her. The tension in his neck, each and every finger spread wide on her back, the muscles in his thighs pressed up against hers—it was all leashed power.

Her mind shut down. She didn't care about the key or the cabinet. She didn't worry that someone would walk down the hallway and see them. Professionalism was as far from her mind as Africa. Her blood was roaring. She wanted him unleashed.

Lucy moaned, a sound of impatience that sounded like "more." She caged his face with both hands and kissed as she'd dreamed of doing the last few days, since that first long look. His body was firm all over. In one place, cast iron. But all that flashed in her agitated mind. It was his mouth she wanted, his earthy, erotic flavor that went straight to her head like champagne, sweeping all obstacles aside.

Ethan pulled away first. That embarrassed her, though it took a moment or two to understand. She looked at his throat, gulping in some much-needed air. When she dredged up the nerve to look at his face, his pale-blue eyes simmered. He carefully exhaled.

"Oh, boy," he said softly. "You have my undivided attention."

"I'd better go," she whispered back.

Ethan took a reluctant step back and she weaved around him and started to walk, hoping her knees would hold her until she got out of his sight. She made it ten feet before her name clipped her to a halt. Turning reluctantly back because she just *knew* she'd be the color of mortified beetroot, she focused again on the golden skin of his throat.

"The key?" He jabbed his thumb toward the cabinet. Lucy nodded at him stupidly. "Silly me."

She walked unsteadily toward him, veered left into Tom's office and found the key in the top drawer. All the while, his eyes burned into her. He took the key, locked the cabinet then dropped it back into her palm.

"Key should be locked away also," he told her gently.

"Okay." She proceeded to replace the key right where she'd found it and walked out past him, still with the stupid half smile on her face. "See ya," she murmured dazedly, and escaped up the stairs.

# Six

Lucy happily escaped the crowds at the gondola and chose a much quieter observation point, only a couple of hundred meters from the township. The view might not be as spectacular but pretty landscapes were not lacking in her life. Summerhill was her magic place.

She fished in her purse for coins to operate the shiny telescope, new since her last visit.

Bored, bored, bored. Poor Juliette had barely been out of her room since they had arrived, having succumbed to some sort of tummy bug. They'd had such a nice time the first day, flying over Aorangi, then jet-boating on the lake when they got to Queenstown, and a nice dinner last night. Then Juliette canceled breakfast and it all went downhill from there. Her illness set in and Lucy was left to amuse herself.

A noisy family group ascended the lookout platform and two or three young children scampered about. Lucy panned the township and easily picked out her hotel, the largest in Queenstown and right on the waterfront. Her room on the fourth floor boasted views over the supermarket parking lot. Juliette had the ninth floor Presidential Suite, and a presidential balcony to go with it.

And there she was! Lucy grinned in childish elation. Juliette stood on her balcony, wearing *that* robe. The filmy deep purple number Lucy had admired last night. The robe that would look average on anyone else but Juliette with her statuesque figure.

She was distracted by the determined gaze of the youngest of the family group who fixed her with a come-on-lady! look. When she beaded in on Juliette again, she realized her friend wasn't alone. It was difficult to discern expression—she fiddled with the focus dial—but Juliette appeared to be shaking her head and her mouth was open.

Then a cocoa-dark head moved into view and Lucy's stomach lurched. His back was turned, but she would know that haughty bearing, those broad shoulders anywhere. He was jacketless and his shirtsleeves were rolled up midway to his elbows.

Lucy stepped back, her lips moving soundlessly as questions reared up like hands in a classroom.

"Mum, I want a go!" the small boy yelled. Lucy ignored him and moved forward again.

Ethan and Juliette. In her suite. Midday in Queenstown, hundreds of kilometers from where he was meant to be. When Juliette was supposed to be ill and had insisted Lucy follow the schedule they had planned.

With Juliette in *that* robe.

Suddenly Juliette swirled around and made for the

balcony door. Ethan grabbed her arm, holding her just above the elbow. They stood for some moments like that and again Lucy could not focus quite well enough to say for sure what the woman's emotions were.

But one thing was as obvious as a train wreck. These two people had a lot more going on than they had disclosed.

The little boy sighed loudly. Lucy glanced at him and pulled a scowling face. His eyes widened, but he didn't say anything.

Over on the balcony, Juliette had tugged her arm away and disappeared into the suite. Lucy watched Ethan hesitate for a second or two and run his hands through his hair. Then he moved inside with a determined stride, closing the glass door behind him. Lucy squinted but the reflection off the glass prevented her seeing inside the suite.

Her head lifted above the telescope. She stared out into space, a million questions pelting her, until a polite cough behind her made her turn. "Oh." She looked at the entire family line-up in a daze. "Sorry."

"That's all right, dear," the woman said kindly. "Is it a nice view?"

Lucy stepped off the platform. The impatient child scampered up and took her place, and Lucy just nodded and walked away.

"Foreigner, I think," she heard the woman comment.

As she began the walk down, she attempted to find a plausible explanation. They wouldn't. They were not cheats. She refused to believe she could be so wrong about people.

He'd come with a message from Magnus. He was bored and looking for Lucy. It wasn't him. She could not be one hundred percent sure...

Disappointment turned her mouth down. Of course that was Ethan. No one could emulate those endless legs, that eat-up-the-miles gait as he'd followed Juliette inside.

That made a lie of his assertion that he'd never met Magnus's wife before his arrival at Summerhill. She had been right beside them at their odd, tension-filled introduction. Then there were the loaded looks he shot Juliette when he thought no one was watching. Lucy thought it was because of his disdain for wealthy women, especially after hearing the story of his childhood. It would be strange if he weren't carrying around some residual prejudice.

A couple of anguished hours later, she knocked on Juliette's door. That took a lot of courage. If he'd been there, Lucy had no idea what she would have said. But he wasn't—unless he was hiding in the shower. And Juliette was still pale and subdued.

"Have you been out?" Lucy's voice caught in her throat as she walked into the suite and saw through to the rumpled bed. *Stop.*

"No," Juliette said.

"Did you get the doctor?"

"No. I'm feeling a little better."

"Poor you," Lucy mumbled. "You must have been bored silly today." Her eyes searched Juliette's face.

"I just read." The woman shrugged.

Lucy left to arrange the charter flight that would leave half a day earlier than they had planned. Her feet dragged. It was true. If it had been an innocent visit, Juliette would have mentioned it.

They were lovers. Liars. Betraying Magnus.

Oh, they made a handsome couple. Juliette was exactly the sort of woman she would expect Ethan to have on his arm—lovely, sophisticated, worldly. He wouldn't seriously be interested in an undersized airhead like her. No brains to save her. No qualifications. Poverty grinning over her threshold.

Oh, he didn't know that. That was the whole point...

But he seemed to like her. His eyes told her he liked her very much. His mouth told her he was hungry for hers. He didn't even seem to mind that she walked around with her big, fat foot in her mouth all day.

Lucy's chest tightened. How could someone you barely knew have the power to hurt you this much?

He wouldn't take her in again. She did not mind being thought of as an easy touch, but she was damned if she would let that man kindle hope in her again. She was nothing but a diversion. A subterfuge. It was Juliette he wanted.

The morning flight back to Summerhill was a quiet affair. Juliette still claimed to feel awful. Lucy's suspicions and hurt had ballooned overnight but she did not broach the subject. She was torn. She wanted to know— *how* she wanted to know. But one word from Juliette could make or break Summerhill in Magnus's eyes. Lucy could not afford to alienate her.

They arrived back at Summerhill in the early afternoon, much more restrained than before. Lucy jumped out and hefted Juliette's classy luggage and vanity from the boot.

Ellie welcomed them back. "Let me," she ordered.

Lucy normally wouldn't dream of letting the older woman carry luggage upstairs, but Summerhill wasn't her comforting refuge today. She had no wish to run into Ethan while she felt so raw.

Citing an appointment, she bade them a brisk goodbye and roared off into town.

\* \* \*

It was the morning from hell.

At ten-thirty, Summerhill's former meat supplier from the village turned up at her apartment, saying he had already been to the lodge looking for Tom. It transpired that he had instigated proceedings against Summerhill for unpaid accounts. Tom was to have responded to the civil court claim to pay the arrears within thirty days or dispute the claim. Time was up. The civil court, in the absence of any action by the lodge to respond, had made judgment in favor of Hogan's Meats.

Lucy was stunned. It was the first she had heard of it. She and Tom had known the Hogans all their lives. Mr. Hogan told her that Summerhill owed several thousand to the family-owned business, which had been chasing them up for over a year.

Mr. Hogan warned her that if full payment was not received within a month, he would make application to put Summerhill Lodge Holdings into liquidation. In that event, he said, he would be at the front of a very long queue.

She sat at her desk with the official documents in her hand and Mr. Hogan sitting across from her. Staring blindly at the papers, she apologized again and again and promised to make Tom write the check the moment he returned from the hunt.

Then Mr. Hogan passed a comment that stopped her in her tracks.

"I'm talking now as an old friend of your father's. Well, used to be. There are a lot of people getting pretty tired of dealing with Summerhill. You'd better shape up. Someone's sniffing around. People don't know if it's the Inland Revenue Department or a liquidator. Hell, could be a private investigator. I personally wish you no harm, at least I won't once I get my money. But there are others who would gladly blab. Missed payments, wages held back, bad debts. Watch your back is what I'm saying."

After he'd gone, Lucy succumbed to a teeth-clenching tension headache, accompanied by a fit of self-indulgent crying. God, she was so stupid, so naive to think she could help run this business. Everyone would be so much better off without her.

Foreboding prickled at the back of her neck. There was something going on here that she had no comprehension of, and Tom obviously found her too lacking in business sense to share his problems.

Why had she come back? She had never been wanted here. What was different? So much easier to run away, as she always had when their indifference rankled.

The doorbell rang again. Now what? She hurriedly blew her nose and wiped her face on the way to the door. Ethan Rae, looking dangerously alert for the hour, strolled into the hallway. "Morning."

Too surprised to protest, she took a step back and he walked past her. Closing her eyes, her body sank back against the wall for a few fortifying seconds. This was just what she needed. She pushed herself away from the wall. "What can I…" Hurrying after him, she almost ran into the solid wall of his back, finding he'd stopped to let her catch up. She dug her toes into the floor and suppressed a sigh of frustration. "Do for you?"

Ethan stepped back against the wall and motioned her past. "*This* is where you live."

She led the way into her little office. He followed at his own pace, giving her living room an interested study.

"Is that a McCahon?" He gestured to a painting in the dining area by a well-known New Zealand artist whose works spanned the fifties through to the eighties. "That must be quite valuable."

"A twenty-first-birthday present from my father," she told him. Her father had used money as a way to keep distance. Like this apartment he'd bought for her when she was barely out of school—it had kept her away from Summerhill and out of his hair.

Lucy sat at her desk, turning the legal documents facedown. It was so unfair. After the morning she'd just endured and before she could compose herself, Ethan was the very last person she wanted to see.

He did not budge when she indicated the chair behind him, just stood looking down at her intently. Could he see how upset and tense she was? It was her curse to have a damn face that showed everything. She dragged on all her reserves in a massive effort to relax.

He looked so good, still in snappy black pants but a more casual butter-colored shirt that did wonderful things for his eyes. It was hard to recall what she was angry with him for.

"Can I help you with something?" She focused on a spot over his shoulder.

"Spend the day with me." No hesitation. Just like that.

Her eyes skidded to his and astonishment pushed her voice up high. "What?"

"It's what you do, isn't it? Entertain clients?"

"Um—today?" Her voice sounded thready.

His eyes narrowed with something like concern. "Yes, today. What's wrong, Lucy?"

If he starts being nice to me, I'll burst into tears, she thought frenziedly. Forget this morning, and *be careful*. She must not let on about the morning's events. She cleared her throat, seeking a firmer tone. "I can't today. You should have given me some warning."

He perched on the edge of her desk and she tried not to be riveted by the pull of expensive black fabric stretched across long thighs.

"What are you doing?"

"What?" she squeaked, dragging her eyes back to his face.

"Today. Meetings? Clients to keep waiting at the airport? Lovely trophy wives to entertain?"

That comment jabbed her right in the heart. He had been the one entertaining a lovely trophy wife. Should she casually ask, "By the way, how long have you and Juliette been lovers?"

Lucy took a deep breath, wishing him away. Wishing her brain would unscramble enough for her to give him a professional and firm negative. Above all else, she couldn't afford to show her distress. If he knew of the financial problems besetting Summerhill, Magnus would hear of it and Tom would go ape.

She kept her eyes down, ineffectually moving things around on her desk and mangling the tissue in her hands into a mess of tufts.

But her heart leapt into her throat when his index finger landed under her chin, tilting it up.

"You've been crying." His voice was gentle. It nearly did her in completely when he pulled another tissue from the box and handed it to her.

Ethan sensed the moment he walked in that she was upset, shaken even. Why that should concern him, he had no idea, yet it did. He wasn't even sure why he was here, except that he'd utilized his time well in the last couple of days and felt he deserved a break. He'd spent hours preparing for the Turtle Island meetings. Made a few inquiries around the region regarding Summerhill.

Today he had come straight from the Seabrook MacKenzie Dyslexia Center in town and had a pocketful of leaflets, but stayed his hand from reaching for them.

He was looking forward to some more of the easy, flirting banter they seemed to draw from each other. Maybe looking forward to another delicious kiss.

Okay, maybe hoping for a lot more than that.

But something was badly wrong. She looked beaten. Forgetting the brochures, he pulled a tissue from the box on her desk and handed it to her.

She took the tissue he offered and disposed of the remains of the one in her hand. "No I haven't."

She was lying. Her eyelashes were wet. He marveled at the surge of testosterone that rolled through him. Ever since he'd met Lucy McKinlay, he'd been walking around baring his teeth and beating his chest. Trying to impress her in the pool. Wanting to rip that guy's face off at the game.

"Who's upset you? Is it Tom?" The harshness of his voice grated. Now he was ready to take on her brother. What was the matter with him?

Lucy shook her head, moving pads and pens, a stapler from one place to another on her desk. Anything to avoid looking right at him. "Tom's away, remember?"

She sniffed loudly. There was a slightly sullen plumpness to her lips and her back was ramrod straight.

Ethan got up off the desk, pulled the chair up and sat with his elbows on her desk. "I'm not leaving until you tell me what's wrong." He leaned forward and down so their faces were on the same level.

Lucy shook her head stubbornly. For a brief second, he considered leaving her to her mood. He had work to do. He needed to stay focused, not run around mopping up tears.

But right now, she wasn't talking.

He sighed. "Okay, Lucy, show me how upset you're *not* by coming out with me."

Then her features changed subtly, as if she had made a decision. She stood and moved around the desk. By the time she got to him and looked down on him, the sullenness had fallen away. Her eyes lit up the room with sunshine. A saucy little smile whispered of an intimacy he could only dream of.

"You're right. It's a beautiful winter's day. Let's not waste it indoors."

She hadn't put out her hand but he felt a sweet glow of warmth as if she had touched him. Something worrisome nagged at him.

But he pushed it away. He was happy to be here. He could tell himself all day that he was doing his job, checking out Summerhill for Magnus. But in truth, he couldn't stay away.

Lucy chattered on brightly, grabbing her coat, telling him she would drive, gathering up a handful of brochures to look at. The chattering continued as she dashed confidently around the streets in her little car. She allowed him the odd grunt or nod to the questions she asked, but for the most part, he sat quietly, wondering what she was hiding.

His inquiries in the village had turned up quite a bit to be concerned about. Tom was in it right up to his neck and Ethan bet that Lucy had little idea of what was going on. From what he'd heard, things were accelerating and it was only a matter of time until the other shoe dropped.

And this burst of bright activity and energy—he realized Lucy was trying to distract him. Just like the other day at the firearms cabinet when she had kissed him to distract him, to conceal something, to cover up for her brother.

What had she said? She was naughty at school to cover up her dyslexia. The more he thought about it, the more he was sure she used her charm to cover up a deep sense of powerlessness at what was happening in her life.

# Seven

"Talk a lot, don't you?" he injected in a rare pause.

She compressed her lips in a rueful grin. "Have you only just noticed?"

Ethan chuckled and stretched, glad to be here with her. He was too big for this tiny sports car, which only served to remind him of her proximity and the scent he missed when she wasn't around.

He could be distracted. Lust rippled over his nerve endings and he sighed in pleasure. Lust he could handle.

"I'm glad you invited me out," he told her.

"Really?" The word turned down at the end, telling him dyslexic she may be, but she recognized tongue-in-cheek when she heard it. "What did you have in mind?"

"You're the tour guide. Make a plan."

Whatever was worrying her, she'd obviously decided to put it behind her. "That's right. There has to be a plan."

"Uh-huh."

"Do you ever do anything just for the hell of it?"

Ethan thought for a few seconds. "Once, on a mountain, I kissed a girl after knowing her only a few hours."

Lucy glanced at him briefly. He caught a flash of that flirty look she got sometimes, right before she remembered she was trying to keep it professional.

Then she grinned. "Truly heroic."

They drove through a long tunnel and into a small harbor town about twenty minutes from the city center. A visiting cruise ship dominated the berthed container ships and fishing vessels.

"I heard this ship was in town. How about a cruise tour?"

The *Princess Athena* was one of the largest liners in the world. Three hundred meters long, sixteen stories high, and solid-gold luxury.

The passengers were off sightseeing or shopping in Christchurch. Parts of the ship were on display to interested sightseers, though the security guards nearly outnumbered the visitors.

Lucy dragged him from bars to ballrooms to casinos to beauty salons and boutique shops. Afterwards they tossed a coin for choice of food and ended up eating fish and chips out of paper on a low wall along one of the lesser wharfs. They watched kids fishing off the wharf, bundled up in brightly colored anoraks. The sea chopped up into agitated whitecaps and seagulls screeched and strutted around them.

"I am seriously going to have to find myself a rich husband, and fast," Lucy commented, her eyes on the *Princess Athena*.

Ethan had been munching on a satisfyingly salty

piece of fish which suddenly turned to paste in his mouth. He wished she hadn't said that.

"I defy you to find me one woman," she continued, "barring the criminally insane, who would turn down a cruise on a baby like that."

An excited cry from the clutch of children distracted her. "Oh look, they've caught something."

Ethan flung the piece of food into the air. Seagulls rose up and then down to scramble for their prize.

But when she turned back to him, her face was so open and animated, no trace of the shadows of the morning. He told himself it was a throwaway remark.

Anyway, at this point, they were sharing a friendly day out. Nothing more complicated than that.

"Tell me about your job," Lucy demanded, choosing a fat chip, bending her head back to lower it into her mouth.

Ethan explained his role in Magnus's corporation. Scouting tourist resort locations, negotiating the deal, organizing architects and surveyors and necessary permits. "Everything from bribery to schmoozing with local councils, religious leaders and politicians."

Once the consents were secured, he would hire and supervise building crews, interior designers and tradespeople for the finishing. The management and staff came last. "I generally stay around for the first month or so of operation," he explained. "One project can take up to two years."

He told her about Turtle Island, his father and Magnus's history with the island, and how once it was completed—provided he got the deal—it would be his last.

"What then?"

"I don't know. Some piece of farm land somewhere."

"You want to farm?" she asked curiously. "I'd have

thought you would shy away from that, after your childhood."

"Part of me wants to prove I can do it, I suppose," he said thoughtfully. "Prove I can make a better job of it this time round."

"Prove you are a better farmer than your father, you mean."

Ethan chuckled. "That wouldn't be hard." He lifted his bottled water and took a swig. "Enough about me. Did you always want to look after trophy wives?"

Lucy laughed and wiped her fingers on a tissue. "Being dyslexic kind of stifles any great ambition. I've never really thought in terms of a long-lasting career. But there are a few things I'd like to do to improve Summerhill."

"Such as?" he asked, interested.

Lucy shrugged. "They'll never come to anything. Tom doesn't think I have a lot to offer."

Remembering the brochures, he wiped his hands and drew them from his jacket pocket. "I went to the Seabrook MacKenzie Dyslexia center this morning."

She took the brochures, a little line between her brows as she perused them quickly.

"Have you ever had an assessment, Lucy?"

She shook her head. "They once arranged an appointment for me at school." She shrugged carelessly. "Must've been busy that day."

"People with learning disabilities have different strengths and weaknesses. They learn to enhance their strengths to compensate." He tapped the brochures she still held. "Without an assessment, you won't know what your strengths are. It wouldn't take long, Lucy. Half a day."

Another rise of her shoulders. "Tom does the office stuff. I spent ages memorizing all the brochures and tourist stuff so I don't really need to be able to read. I mean, I *can* read, just not quickly and it's hard with other people about."

"I think you're selling yourself short."

"Just be glad you're not my boss," she quipped. "How come you know so much about it?"

"Dyslexia is something Magnus cares a lot about—he's dyslexic himself. He's made sure his workforce is well-supported. Do you know, one in ten people have a learning difficulty?"

Lucy grinned. "We're sneaking around all over the place."

Ethan guessed she was so accustomed to sweeping her problems under the carpet, she probably did not even notice she was being flippant. He pushed the brochures toward her. He was a patient man.

"Tell me about your plans for Summerhill."

"Ideas, not plans," she corrected him. "Plans have to be written down."

"Okay." He took a small notebook and pen from his jacket's inside pocket. "You tell me the ideas, I write them down and get my secretary to type them up." He looked at her, his pen poised over the notebook.

Lucy gulped. "That's nice of you, but they're not ready to be drawn up into a business plan. They're just some thoughts…"

"What thoughts, Lucy?"

She wiped her mouth and hands and picked up the remnants of the cooling food, dumping it onto the ground a few feet away. With enough racket to wake the dead, the seagulls closed in and Lucy dropped the empty paper into a bin close by.

She sat back down hesitantly, obviously afraid he would laugh at her ideas. He convinced her otherwise.

She had some great ideas, and he told her so. Courtesy vans for the village restaurants. Targeted advertising to golf clubs because of the world class Terrace Downs golf course that had been completed nearby recently. A health and beauty spa for the guests, including massage, hair salon, facials and a gym. Using Summerhill as a conference and function center. Tom could still have his hunting safaris but they could also offer weddings, whodunit nights, workshops…the list was endless.

Ethan was impressed. He wrote everything down, cautioning against one or two things, just from a financial perspective. But most of her ideas were very viable, relevant to her market, and wouldn't cost too much in initial outlay.

"And then I could spend some time on the farm. Tom doesn't have time these days—he's more interested in the lodge. Since the farm manager quit, things have gotten out of hand. I'd love to see it back to full production."

Ethan had noticed the farm's neglect on his rides. It was very understocked, the pastures in poor condition.

They talked till the wind rose and chased the sun and the children away. Lucy lapped up his praise of her ideas as if she had never received a compliment in all her life.

"You are as sharp as a tack, Lucy," he told her, "and don't you let anyone tell you any different."

She glowed, a stranger to approbation. A late bloomer, and it occurred to him he'd like to nurture that and watch it grow. Without her brother pushing her down all the time, there were no limits to what she could achieve with a little encouragement.

And then he remembered Turtle Island. If Magna-

Corp successfully negotiated the deal, there would be no way he could spare the time to enjoy watching her grow.

How far was New Zealand from the islands, anyway?

Lucy uncapped a bottle of water and drank deeply, bending her head back and exposing the milky skin of her throat. A substantial urge to kiss her steamrolled him so completely, he held his breath for an age, worried there wouldn't be another. She was so fresh, with a natural, almost childlike beauty. Her eyes showed every emotion.

She brought the bottle away and licked her lips, then raised her eyes to his. Ethan was a second or two behind, his eyes still devouring the sight of the tip of her pink tongue slipping between her lips and trapping a bead of moisture at one corner. He mimicked her, an involuntary action, his own tongue darting out and touching his mouth. This close, he could see traces of the beige-pink-tinted lip gloss she applied regularly.

He saw his thoughts, his desire leap in her eyes. Some magnetic force seemed to drag them toward each other, eyes locked, oblivious to their surroundings. The pull was palpable in the diminishing distance.

She broke the impasse when he lifted his hand, intending to cup her face and draw her to him. The desire on her face was extinguished in one blink. Then it was all motion and half sentences: "Well, we'd better…" She scooped up their water bottles. "Look at the time." Slapping pockets for keys. "Got everything?" Hustling him toward the car.

When they reached the car, Ethan grabbed her hand and tugged gently until they leaned on the passenger door, side by side. He absently twisted the chunky white-gold channel ring that emphasized her delicate bones, and tried to absorb, to understand the all-con-suming desire he had for her.

Never had he let his desires rule him. Always, he played the seduction game without losing sight of who he was, why he was there, where this was going—or not, usually. Right at this moment, the *Titanic* could be sinking and he wouldn't budge an inch if she were in his arms. Damn fool. He was so consumed by want, it didn't even frighten him.

He laced his fingers through hers, studied her small white hand, short neat nails painted with a clear gloss. He traced the visible bluish veins under the skin, wanted to be that life force for her.

There was no telling where this preoccupation would lead, but he was fast coming to the conclusion it was a necessary journey.

But then Lucy trembled and tugged to free her hand, accompanied by a small huff of agitation. He watched her chin rise in defiance and her small tense body brace.

"What?"

"Why bother flirting with me when we both know it's Juliette you want?" Her eyes were dark with disap-pointment, her voice cool.

He hadn't seen that coming and was jolted right out of desire and swimming in confusion. "Where the hell did that come from?"

"I saw you in Queenstown. On her balcony."

Realization dawned. He raised his hands to his head, rested them there. There was no easy way out of this. "Did you ask her about it?"

Lucy hesitated. "Let's say I gave her the opportunity to tell me you were there." Her mouth turned down miserably. "She didn't take it."

Ethan considered his options. He hadn't gained a

thing in the trip to Queenstown. Juliette was so incensed, she had virtually thrown him out of her hotel suite. But last night at Summerhill after he'd shown her the newspaper clippings he'd been sent, she calmed enough to talk to him.

"Lucy, I have no romantic interest in Juliette." He said it quietly and tried to convey sincerity, for it was the truth.

She raised her chin, one brow arched high, her eyes direct and challenging.

He sighed. "I had some concerns about her reasons for marrying Magnus."

He'd spent an hour on the phone to the investigator yesterday. Forensics had concluded a silencer had been used, which explained Juliette's claim she had not heard the shot and had slept the night, discovering her husband's body on deck the next morning. There were actually several witnesses, not just the one reported by the papers, who had seen a strange yacht in the vicinity. Yet, that vessel had disappeared off the face of the earth.

Ethan rubbed a hand over his face. She had made a new life for herself after two years of hateful media intrusion and innuendo. If the Australian press got wind of the story, her nightmare would begin all over again. And that would be devastating, for her and for a well-respected and successful businessman.

Juliette had sworn him to secrecy until she could talk to Magnus about it. He inhaled deeply, looking into Lucy's eyes. "I'm going to have to ask you to trust me on this. For now."

Lucy slumped a little. The defiance seemed to tick slowly over into acceptance as he watched, but it was a bitter sort of acceptance. The shadows from this morning had returned.

"Trust you, hey?" Her mouth curved in a small smile that did not reach her eyes. And then she shrugged and turned away.

While he battled with his conscience, Lucy walked around to the driver's door, yanking it open. Before she got in, she looked haughtily across the roof of the car. "Doesn't matter to me. I'm just a professional companion, remember? And—" she raised her arm and checked her watch "—I'll be on overtime if I don't get you back to your car soon."

Ethan flinched as the door slammed shut.

She got behind the wheel, fuming with indignation. For a few minutes today, she'd been on the trip of a lifetime. She had basked in the glow of his praise. For a few minutes, she'd felt that he liked her for herself. Found her funny and charming, saw past the dyslexia. He had listened, encouraged, offered to help.

And man, he was the sexiest thing on legs. Every single feature, every aspect of him seemed to pull her toward him, draw her in until she wanted to be absorbed by him. One smoldering look—and with his deeply tanned skin, dark hair and those glorious pale eyes, he smoldered like embers ever threatening to ignite into a bush fire.

But she needed to clear up the Juliette thing.

When he balked at telling her the full story, she was plunged back into cold familiar waters. Silly little Lucy. Gullible, aching for affection and attention. She'd believe anything.

Oh, she knew he wanted her. Even the most sophisticated and experienced seducer could not fake the desire she'd glimpsed. But he did not think enough of her to tell the truth. He'd expected mindless response to his praise and pretence at caring. God help her, he'd very nearly gotten it!

He wanted her to trust him? He would have to work harder than that.

Ethan opened the passenger door and climbed in. His movements were slow and deliberate, and although she did her level best not to look at him, the waves of frustration sloughed off him and settled over her.

Her indignation cooled a little. Remember what's at stake here. She may already have endangered Summerhill by accusing him of having an affair with his boss's wife. Having him sulk for the rest of the day was not a good idea. She was supposed to be helping him enjoy his stay.

Tension sizzled. She breathed it in. "I'm sorry," she said, not intending it to sound so tight.

"What do you have to be sorry about?"

"I've upset you."

His lips pursed. "Hmm. Upset?" His legs stretched out in a taut line and he rested his hands on his thighs. "Well now. Horny? Very. Confused? Worried that your brother is taking advantage of you?"

He paused and flexed his fingers.

Lucy's mind skittered away from all but the safest word. "Confused?"

He grunted. "I don't need this, Lucy. I've got stuff to do."

"Don't let me stop you," she responded tartly.

"But you do, and that's the rub. Even when I'm not with you, I'm thinking about you and worrying about you, and dreaming of that damn mouth of yours."

Said mouth dropped open, but all she could manage was "Oh." There wasn't really a lot you could say to that.

With his deep slow drawl still echoing in her ears,

she felt herself blush. There was nothing she could do about that either. She kept her eyes firmly on the road ahead and that was the last they spoke.

But her body and mind spoke—plenty. She was so aware of every movement, every breath he took. For the most part he stared straight ahead. But now and again she felt a wave of heat as he glanced over at her. Lucy did not return his glances but steamed away in her own humid shell.

She felt she was clinging to a cloud and any minute her weight would drag her through it. The longer and more tense the silence, the more heavy-limbed and languorous she felt. His breathing sounded loud in her ears—but maybe it was her own. She changed gears, navigated, all on autopilot, while struggling with equal measures of worry and desire and self-righteousness. If she couldn't tamp it down, she thought she might explode.

All of a sudden they were in the underground garage at her building and she was turning off the ignition. Before she had time to wonder why she hadn't dropped him at his rental car across the road, he made his move. She heard the click of his seatbelt release almost just before she felt her own released. Without a word, his hands gripped her shoulders, turning her quickly, then moving down to clamp around her waist and lift her right up out of her seat. Her hands flailed for balance and a surprised shriek raced out of her throat. "What—?"

Next moment, she was hoisted over the handbrake and plonked ungraciously and haphazardly onto his lap, bumping her head on the ceiling of the car. Quick as a flash, one hand clasped the back of her neck and her head was pulled down, close to his face.

Lucy suddenly remembered to breathe and exhaled

raggedly. Ethan's eyes were open and they flashed bright with anger. He held her head fast, millimeters away. His hot breath huffed across her face and his fingers laced through her hair. "It's *you* I want, not Juliette," he growled. "And to hell with your professionalism!"

Then his mouth claimed hers and Lucy was lost. His lips forced hers open. Teeth scraped and ground together. His tongue burst into her mouth, demanding her response, not her permission. This was no magical fairy-tale kiss on a mountain, with Mother Nature smiling benevolently down. Nor a stolen smooch in an alcove that she had initiated. This was hard, carnal. As if he was staking a claim.

And after the tensions of the day, it mirrored her feelings exactly.

As her initial shock subsided, Lucy was taken over by the heat of his body, the pressure of his mouth. Her taut muscles relaxed, sank into him as he deepened the kiss. Her hands were trapped between them and she struggled vaguely to free them but his chest was unyielding, his arms like iron. One hand moved, uncurled so the palm was flat against his chest. The other remained fisted with his shirt locked into it, only now she pulled him closer.

Perhaps realizing Lucy was past struggling, Ethan's hand at the back of her head gentled. Straightening his fingers, he stroked and tugged at her hair. She shivered, every nerve ending rising to the surface.

His tongue also gentled. Instead of insistence, there was now an erotic rhythm that had her squirming even closer. Their tongues met, slid over each other and back again, and she felt the different textures of his, and his gentle but insistent probing. Her breath started to labor in serious excitement.

He made her feel things she'd never experienced. How could she resist the pull of her body when it responded to him so frenetically? When this ended, when he was gone, would she ever feel desire again?

Her head fell back slightly and she gasped as he moved his mouth down her throat then along her jawline to end with a hot lick and suck at the base of her ear. She arched her back, surging against him. His hand left her head and joined the other in a firm caress down the length of her sides, and soon she felt them inside her knit top.

As they strained against each other, she heard a moan of impatience—hers. They writhed and pressed. She rubbed her bottom down into his lap, seeking, finding the hard ridge that strained up to meet her, and heard his grunt, desperate and loud in the confined space. Lucy squirmed in his lap, trying to crawl in as close as she could get.

His hands spanned her waist and were then inching up toward her breasts. A slave to sensation at this point, Lucy shamelessly dipped her body down, craving the exquisite torment when his thumbs grazed over her aching nipples. The blood roared in her ears. So far, so fast, she couldn't believe she was this close. One more thrust of his tongue, one more squeeze of her nipples to send a flame of pure lust licking downward, one more mighty flex of his thighs to push and grind him into the most sensitive part of her. She was seconds away, the scream already tearing up toward her throat.

And then he tore his mouth from hers, his chest rising against her. His hands stilled their torture. She opened her eyes, moaning with impatience. Their breath mingled, hot and humid. He looked up into her eyes and said, "Your call."

"Upstairs, now!" Lucy gasped.

She scrambled back over to her side of the car, haphazardly pulling down her top. Grabbing the keys from the ignition, she opened the door, fumbled for her bag, and rounded the car, intent only on getting upstairs.

Ethan was alighting from the passenger side. She hesitated impatiently, her pulse hammering in her throat. Hurry, hurry, she chanted mentally, the fingers of one hand pressing on the spot in her chest where the blood pounded and rushed. When she knew Ethan was right behind her, she turned toward the stairs and ran—smack!—into a stranger.

# Eight

**T**he man put out a steadying hand from where he leaned against the wall of the underground garage. Lucy backed away as if he held a whip.

She could only imagine her dishevelled appearance, but his eyes were on Ethan, who drew alongside her. Then he looked back at her shame-burned face. "Lucy McKinlay, I presume?"

"How—how do you know?"

He indicated the number of her parking spot. The number of her apartment.

His eyes slid back to her. With a smug little look on his face, he introduced himself as a detective.

Ethan moved closer, tidying his shirt. His arms dropped to his sides. One of them brushed against hers and he deliberately stepped slightly in front, shielding her.

The only thought Lucy could put together was that

she was as bad as her mother. She didn't suppose he was there to arrest them for lewd public behavior, but still, to know he'd seen them in the car, practically like animals... Shame, shame, so hot, she could die of it.

Ethan exhaled. "What's the problem, detective?"

"And you are, sir?"

"Ethan Rae. I'm a friend."

The detective gave another smug little smile then got down to business. He had already been to the lodge looking for Tom, and wanted to know where he had been on Saturday night.

Lucy felt completely senseless. She struggled to keep up. It took a few seconds for her to recall that Saturday had been the night of the rugby game and the stolen car. The foreboding that had lodged in her gut for the last day bubbled up again.

Tom was at home that night, she told him cautiously. She had called him there around 10:00 p.m. He asked if Tom had mentioned the car being stolen. She was about to go into details when Ethan put a restraining hand on her back.

"We had the car. It was gone when we came out of the game. We didn't know the registration number and phoned Tom to get it and he said not to bother reporting it right then. He would do it the next morning."

Lucy nodded. "He *must* have reported it."

The detective shook his head, staring at her accusingly.

"He didn't report it. Were you aware the vehicle was unregistered?"

The pressure of Ethan's hand on her back increased. "No. Detective, when we got to the station, there was a queue a mile long and we had restaurant reservations. Tom assured us he would take care of it."

"That car was found at the scene of a suspicious fire."

The rest of the conversation was a blur. The detective asked if anyone could corroborate their story and when Tom would be back. He handed her his card. Lucy closed her eyes in embarrassment when he apologized for interrupting them. When he'd gone, she sagged against the car.

"What's going on, Lucy? Just what's Tom into?"

"I—I don't know," she managed.

"What was that scumbag's name at the rugby?"

"Joseph Dunn. I told Tom. He had to have reported it, for the insurance, right?" With relief, she thought he couldn't file an insurance claim without reporting the car stolen, so no one could accuse him of insurance fraud.

Ethan looked thoughtful. "Maybe this Dunn is trying to set him up."

"But why?"

"Money's my guess. I knew he was in trouble. Didn't realize how deep."

Lucy looked at him sharply. "What do you mean, you knew?"

There was quite a pause. "I've heard some things."

The meat supplier's words that morning flitted around her mind. *Inland Revenue, a private investigator...* "You've heard what? From who?"

"People in the village."

*Watch your back...* "You've been asking questions about us in the village?"

Ethan rubbed his neck self-consciously. "Magnus asked me to make a few inquiries. He's heard rumors of financial difficulties."

Lucy reeled in the face of his discomfort. He wouldn't—

she'd trusted him. Her lips moved, but she had nothing to say. All she wanted to hear was his denial.

Finally he looked at her and she saw his conscience laid bare. He exhaled. "Magnus takes his club very seriously. He won't tolerate any hint of scandal."

For Lucy, Magnus's expectations were nothing as important as Ethan's role in all this. "Who have you been asking?"

Guilt deepened his tan. "I didn't have to look far."

"Who?" she demanded.

"It's amazing what the locals come up with when you mention where you're staying."

Something in her chest cramped up. There was another long silence while she tried to contain the welling of betrayal. He had spent hours today building her up, showing her he cared and offering his help. Today she had truly felt that anything seemed attainable.

Please, please deny it, she prayed. Deny it, or explain. Give me something…

"It's not to hurt you," he told her softly, reaching out to touch her arm. "That's the last thing—"

She flinched, clamping her arm to her side. "Get out."

Shock and shame and sadness engulfed her. And then the fear. He had the power to destroy them; she had been warned. *Keep your distance, he's all business.*

"Lucy, I want to help."

She shook her head and stepped back. "I want you to go."

"Come upstairs, we'll talk."

Her face flamed with self-disgust when she remembered her impassioned plea of just minutes ago. *Upstairs, now!* "Just go."

Ethan sighed heavily and rubbed his face. After a

long moment when she refused to look at him, he leaned close. "Will you come back to the lodge tonight?"

At the thought of Summerhill, she felt an incredible yearning to be there. To take Monty up to the gorge, to her special place. She wanted peace.

But she carefully erased any sign of interest on her face and instead, faced him with scorn. "Why? Did you think I would sleep with you now?"

It was his turn to flinch. Again he raised his hand toward her. She thrust her chin out defiantly. "Go away." Her voice rang out loud and hard.

Ethan's eyes narrowed but he stepped back. "Cool off for a bit. I'll be back."

Barely able to see where she was going, she walked slowly for the stairs. Her throat closed with anguish. Why would he want to harm her? And why lead her on, fuel her passion, make her feel special and wanted if he were trying to finish off her business?

Because he worked for Magnus. Tom was right. Magnus was intent on getting them off the list. And Ethan was the destroyer.

She leaned on the balustrade, closing her eyes against a painful pounding in her head. This was how her day had started. Confusion and hurt about Ethan and Juliette, fear at the court papers. She had wanted to cry at his thoughtfulness when he'd shown her the brochures from the dyslexia center. Then layer upon layer of approval and admiration, of encouragement and offers of help. An intensity of desire that rocked her—and shocked him also, she was sure.

She shook her bag irritably when she could not locate her key. Muttering mutinously, she tipped the entire contents onto the landing.

In truth, the anger was directed more at herself than

Ethan. It was too late to firewall it. She cared—desperately—about him. She grasped the elusive key in her hand and squeezed it as hard as she could, wincing as it dug into her palm.

And that gave him the power to wound her more deeply than anything had in years. If only she'd kept it professional, but she couldn't even get that right. Why did everything she touched end up in such an unholy mess?

His fingers tapped restlessly on the steering wheel of his rental car. He checked his watch again. Half an hour. She had been in there for half an hour.

His clamorous body had finally subsided after being pushed up to exploding point. The look and feel and smell of her seeped into every corner of his being. Colored everything to the point where he was high when he could see her, and in the depths of depression when he could not.

Only once had he ever felt a fraction of this turmoil for a woman and he'd been barely a man then. She'd been on the swim team at university. But she could not understand his decision to quit swimming when he was a certainty for the Olympics. She could not understand his need to stick to his goals, to exorcise the mess his father had made of everything, and show him that he—Ethan—could do better.

He rubbed his face and checked his watch again. Come on, come on. His hands slapped a drumroll on his thighs. He was so wired. If that detective had not burst in on the scene, he would be deep inside her sweet body now, where he'd wanted to be since the second he first saw her. There would be one more expression to add to his catalog of "Lucy" expressions. He wanted to be an inch away from her face, to watch that sweet mouth curve into a smile of pure satisfaction.

His body signalled its approval of the direction of his thoughts just as his cell phone beeped. It was Clark Seller in the Sydney office.

Clark could barely contain his excitement. The Minister for the Interior for the islands had unexpectedly decided to attend a Pacific Tourism Council in Sydney. He could meet with Ethan tomorrow.

Tomorrow! Damn, damn. Ethan groaned. How could he leave tomorrow without straightening this mess out?

Lucy's face swam in front of his eyes as he'd last seen it. Let down. Scared. He would never have believed himself capable of putting that look on anyone's face. Especially not on her face.

And then his world tipped a little on its axis. It was an indistinct slide of his insides—distant, like a dream in which you're falling over a cliff. A beautiful soundless freefall, without fear—after all, it's just a dream. Right?

Clark's insistent voice intruded and Ethan did something unprecedented. "You handle it."

"What?" Clark was incredulous, but Ethan reassured him that he was more than equipped to handle this preliminary meeting. There would be no negotiations. It was more or less just a feeler.

He hung up and opened the car door. He'd had it with cooling his heels out here.

Lucy's apartment building was beside a busy intersection and the traffic lights had just turned green so he had to wait half a minute to cross the road. The wind was blustery and turned to the south. Bitterly cold, he rubbed his arms as he dodged through the line of stationary vehicles.

He opened the gate and passed through just in time to see the underground garage door closing behind a red sports car. Lucy's red Alfa Romeo.

Cursing, he turned back to fumble at the gate latch just as her car drove right past him.

"Red. Red!" he shouted at the traffic lights and broke into a trot. The lights were not on his side. They went amber and she barrelled through and turned right. Ethan had a near miss with a white utility van as he raced across the road and jumped in his car.

And went nowhere fast. The driver of the van was blocking his way to the far-right lane and the lights stayed red. By the time he finally got going, she must have had nearly five minutes on him. Not being familiar with the one-way-street system in this town cost him precious time and he swore viciously when he ended up going full circle and arrived back outside her apartment building. But at least from here he knew the way to Summerhill.

Where else would she go? Fuming, he raced through the streets and got onto the ring road that led out of the city and toward the West Coast.

Annoyance drilled his temples. Lucy McKinlay had cut him off at the knees. What was he thinking? Turtle Island was his ultimate deal. His biggest, his last, his final revenge. Where was his infamous focus? He was *not* handing over control. No way. This was still his baby.

Come on, Rae. Think! He held engineering and business degrees. Solving problems was his forte. Political, legal, employment—how could one small personal dilemma slip under his grid and turn his lights out?

It was an utterly wretched ninety-minute drive with no sign of her car ahead, but there was more than one route to the mountains. Finally the turn-off to the ski village flashed by and he decelerated. The weather was closing in fast. Ethan thought fleetingly of the hunting party and hoped they were home safe.

Soon, on the long driveway up to the lodge, he caught sight of a flash of red by the stables and swung the steering wheel that way. Surely she would not be fool enough to go riding when dusk was on them and a storm was brewing.

It must have been zero degrees with a windchill factor of formidable proportions when he alighted. The rain was just starting in earnest—big, fat skin-shrinking drops with the promise of more. He ducked his head and raced for the stable entrance.

Lucy sat huddled with her knees drawn up to her chin in a corner of Monty's stall. Her face was a mixture of sullen surprise and resignation.

"No." Ethan shook his head.

Petulantly she jerked to her feet. "I know that. Leave me alone." She froze him with a look of such disdain, he hardly registered that she'd pushed past him.

Her turning her back on him, walking away, sharpened his temper. Frustration gnawed at him, born of the simmering sexual tension he had kept reined in all this long day. He made a grab for her arm, but she easily shook him off and walked out into the night. It took him a few seconds to register she had just walked out on him—again—and then he followed, almost disbelieving.

Icy rain slashed at his face the moment he was out the door. The wind howled, buffeting him. Such was the deluge, it took him a while to make her out because he, naturally, was looking toward their vehicles.

Lucy, unpredictably, had stomped off in the direction of the house with her arms wrapped around herself.

She still wore a light knit top and a leather jacket that was more stylish than protective against the elements.

His temper surged, warming him. He ducked his head and set off after her, snagging her arm in a vice-like grip. It was hard to make out her face in the gathering darkness and driving rain, but her eyes flashed dangerously.

"Leave me alone!"

He pulled her to a standstill. "Get in the car."

She attempted to release her arm, to no avail. "Just what is your agenda, Ethan?" Her voice surged and faded as the wind whipped parts of the question away.

"Right now, it's to get out of this blasted storm. Get in the car."

She pulled away, successfully this time, swearing colorfully.

"Spoiled brat!" he yelled after her in complete exasperation.

With a resigned glance at the two cars parked outside the stables, he caught up to her and fell into step beside her. It was slow going into the teeth of the driving southerly and both of them hunched over grimly, not looking at each other.

"Stop running away from me," he demanded through clenched teeth.

"You stop running after me," she retorted. "Why are you trying to hurt Summerhill?" She pulled up smartly and faced him.

"I'm not." He took his hand from his pocket and turned her toward the house, urging her on. "It's my job, Lucy. Do you really think Magnus doesn't suspect what's going on here? That's why he asked me to look into it."

"So you admit it." She shook her dripping head in

disgust. "You're running around digging up dirt so you can kick us out of the club."

"It's not like that. I can help you."

"We don't need *your* help," she snapped, but her voice sounded decidedly shaky now.

Ethan swiped at the water streaming down his face, and peered at her. Her pale hair was plastered to her head. In the glow of the house lights, ten meters away, her eyes were dark smudges, the color of the storm.

His heart lurched and squeezed. Ah, Lucy, what are you doing to me? He planted his feet stubbornly.

"You being nice to me today." Her voice shook. "Giving me the rope to hang myself. Making me trust you so I'll tell you what Magnus needs to get us off the list."

He rocked back on his heels. "Wrong."

"You're using me to cover up your affair with Juliette."

The sour taste of injustice flooded his throat. "Wrong again. But there are problems here."

"If you take us off the Global List, we're finished."

"The situation isn't irretrievable. I can make Magnus see that."

She turned away from him again. "Maybe you won't be Magnus's golden-haired boy when he knows that you're his wife's lover."

Her foot was on the bottom step of the veranda before he hauled on her arm. "For the last time, I am *not* Juliette's lover."

"Oh, bugger off!" She poured all her strength into freeing her arm, but he held fast and turned her.

"Listen to me. Someone sent me some newspaper clippings a few days ago. Juliette was investigated for the death of her first husband. No charges in the end, but I had to make sure."

Lucy's mouth dropped open.

Ethan took advantage of her momentary immobilization to move a step closer. "I had to check it out but I couldn't get her on her own here. So I followed you down south."

She swallowed, her eyes as big as saucers. "You thought she…?"

He nodded. "She threw me out. But I talked to her here last night. She went through hell as tabloid fodder for two years. Even though there was no evidence, everyone in the States thought she was guilty. That's why she moved to Australia. New name, new age, new husband."

"Why didn't you tell me? Does Magnus know?"

Ethan put his hands on her shoulders. "That's why I didn't tell you. He's bound to find out at some stage. She made me swear not to say anything until she's had a chance to talk to him."

"Do you believe her?"

He nodded. "Yeah, I do. She's a nice lady who's had a rough time. Do you believe me?"

Lucy wrapped her arms about herself. "So you're not having an affair with your boss's wife?"

He shook his head.

She held his gaze, her chin raised. There was a mighty struggle in her face. The desire to believe him warring with distrust. The hunger for his words to be true. Had she never trusted, never felt supported?

He grabbed her hands in his. "Let's get it all out in the open. All of it." He turned her and pushed her up the remaining steps, out of the deluge. At the door, he put his hands in her hair, combing it back with his fingers, squeezing the moisture out. "Lucy, I *don't* want Juliette, but I *do* want you. I *have* been asking questions, but I'll do everything I can to help." He touched her face gently. "I'm worried, Lucy. I'm worried that your brother is in over his head and dragging you down with him."

She nodded. "I'm a little scared, too. I had a visitor this morning, the lodge's former meat supplier, before you arrived. He's already got a judgment from the civil court for unpaid accounts. Now he's threatening to put us into liquidation."

Ethan swore under his breath. He knew from his inquiries that the rot had spread a lot farther than the local butcher. "No wonder you were upset this morning."

She looked up at him, dripping and shaking with cold. "Tom just runs rings around me lately. He won't tell me what's wrong."

He pulled her close. "We'll sort it out." He felt her head bump against his chest and heard her muffled "Okay."

Fierce with relief, he crushed her to him. She shivered, and it went bone-deep as his arms pressed her saturated clothes to her body. Then he lifted her off the ground and against him. "You're driving me mad," he muttered. "It's all wrong, but God help me, Lucy, I want you. Only you."

And then he was kissing her deeply with a hunger that was more to do with feeding a soul than assuaging a need.

They made puddles on the step. "We need to get you warm," he told her when he noticed she was practically shivering out of the circle of his arms. "Inside."

He followed her up the stairs, holding her hand, knowing he was walking headlong into repercussions. They passed his room, her boots squelching in time with his thumping heart. Once he entered her room, there would be no going back.

She stopped at a door on the other side of the second floor from the guest accommodation. Lucy could hardly open the door, she was shaking so much.

"Shower." She pointed to the bathroom as he closed her door.

Ethan put his hands on her hips and walked her ahead of him into the bathroom. The decision was made. He wouldn't shy from it—he would face it with his usual consummate efficiency. There had to be a way to fit this vital and growing need for her in with achieving his goals.

Reaching into the stall, he turned the shower on. Lucy flipped the fan heater on and shed her soaked-through jacket and boots while he lifted two big towels from the top of the vanity and threw them on the floor. And when steam began fogging up the glass shower door, he pushed her gently inside the stall, kicked off his shoes and followed himself.

Lucy's eyes closed in bliss as the strong jet of hot water rained over her, seeping through her clothes. A sigh, deep and tremulous, rose from her lips and eased his tension somewhat. She let the spray run on her back for a minute then pulled him close so he could enjoy it, too. Together they faced the spray. His hands began rubbing, in short, hard strokes down her back and sides.

Minutes passed and finally her shaking subsided. She looked around in wonder, as if she wasn't sure how she came to be in this place. In her shower, fully clothed and with him. And then her eyes warmed as she focused on him.

Ethan's blood began to hum. Fear, distrust, betrayal, all extinguished now. He'd seen this in her eyes today also, on the wall by the sea and later in the car. Heavy-lidded, pupils dilated with sultry awareness. His body took that last leap into an adrenaline-drenched response.

His hands felt as useless as frozen legs of lamb as he peeled her top over her head. Rose-pink lace with pale green ribbon; the sight of her bra erased any thought of Turtle Island or repercussions. Suddenly the only relevant detail he craved was whether her underwear matched.

For about one second, until Lucy reached behind her and flicked her bra free with one hand. Now he was just impatient to see the rest of her. He helped push the bra up and off her shoulders.

He wanted his hands on her, but his focus did seem to be skew-whiff at the present. He was momentarily halted by her fingers at his shirt, and he would have to say she won in the dexterity stakes. All buttons undone in the time it took for him to undo the snap at the waist-band of her jeans.

Ethan slid the heavy denim down her legs and took her panties with them. Did they match? He couldn't remember because by then, he was running his hands up the back of her legs, amazed at how long and lithe they were for someone so small. He really must slow and pay attention, but he did not want to miss a single second, or bypass a single inch of her. He wanted to see and taste and feel everything.

As he stood to full height, his hands stopped on her behind. Smooth, curved, a delicious handful. Lucy meanwhile, busied herself with his slacks and Ethan let out a careful breath as he was freed completely from the shackles of wet clothing.

Finally naked—and for a little while, it seemed enough just to look. With his hands cupping her bottom and hers resting on his chest, his mind was at peace with the confessions and decisions of the last hour.

Her skin had the soft luster of pearl. Her arms and shoulders were delicate, her body slim but not angular. Sweetly rounded curves next to his long slashing lines of lean muscle. So many contrasts, not only to him but to anyone he'd been with before. Mostly, he felt so big next to her small frame.

Water cascaded down her face and body and she shimmered like the fairy he had thought of when he first saw her. Her small hands rested flat on his chest, providing yet another shocking contrast to his own coloring.

Need for her rolled through him, burst out in a ragged exhalation. He placed his hands on hers—they were warm now—and felt his own heart pumping through them. Ethan shut the water off and backed out of the shower, pulling her with him. He swathed them both in one large soft towel.

They maneuvered into the bedroom still bound in the towel. Lucy's cheeks were rosy, her breathing quick. He pulled the towel closer around them, warm, damp bodies bumping against each other as they jostled.

Light drifted in from the living room and combined with the open bathroom door to cast an eerie glow. Ethan looked around the big room, his gaze halting at an armchair by the window with a stuffed toy holding a balloon. His heart stopped. Raising his hands to his head he pulled the towel down over his face, swearing succinctly.

"What is it?"

He looked down into her face, shook his head wryly. "We have to go to my room."

"Your room?"

"Condoms." His face screwed up into a grimace. "I had a couple in my wallet, which is still in the car. But I have some in my case."

Lucy smiled easily and opened her mouth to speak. Then a muted flash of orange lit the room, snagging her attention. Next thing he knew, she had twisted away, leaving him clutching an armful of damp towel and nothing else.

She ran over to the window, dragging aside heavy drapes. "Look!"

## Nine

# Nine

Lucy waited for another stab of lightning. There was a young magnolia to the left of her window, its branches reaching just below her sill. Right now, it whipped about gracefully. The storm had worsened while they were in the shower.

The music of it enthralled her. The wind howled menacingly and she felt the eaves of the old house vibrate under the force of it. The rain was heavy and hard on the old iron roof. And something deeper—a long roll of thunder, not too far away. She closed down a quick, skimming thought that it rumbled a warning.

The tree thrashed in a flamboyant dance. Its branches reached up in an entreaty. Will I? Do I trust him enough? She sensed Ethan come up behind her and she began to sway with the wind. Then a great flash of sheet lightning lit the room up again. Lucy laughed in pure delight.

He moved in close and put his hands around her

waist. They looked almost black against her paleness. She put her hands on top of his and leaned back into his warmth, still swaying. The thunder rolled on, making the house shudder—or maybe it was just her. The lightning continued to strike, moving around the valley in an arc.

Their reflection in the window danced, faded, surged, like her thoughts, her fears, the need piercing her. Thousands of raindrops raced each other down the glass. He was hard to see in the window because he was so dark. As she swayed, they moved in time to the rhythm she created. Their hands were light on her body and her movement meant they slid over her, branding her with the touch she directed.

The storm noise intensified to a crescendo any orchestra would have been proud of. It seemed the lightning, having belted every valley and hill and mountain and gorge around Summerhill, was now coming for the house itself. Confrontation. She glimpsed the stables and outbuildings as they lit up, a beacon of courage. But then their reflections shifted.

Nestling her head into his throat, her arms slid behind her to pull him closer. His hands firmed on their teasing exploration of her abdomen and rib cage. At the very moment his fingers brushed over the tingling tips of her breasts, she felt the unmistakable thickness of him push between her thighs. Trance-like, she watched their reflections melting into the rain trailing down the windowpane. Lightning seemed to strike and flow from his eyes.

"Are you the devil?" she breathed.

His teeth flashed in a brief smile, then he was kissing her neck while his fingers pinched and stroked her nipples. Lucy's insides melted and started to flow and she squeezed her thighs, trapping him. His groan puffed hot into her ear.

Then the shock of him gliding hot and hard against her blurred the blasts of lightning. A ragged sob washed from her throat as the heavens poured down outside. A distant rolling tension started deep down, relentless as the thunder. Gone were all thoughts of consequences or the future—she surrendered to the storm within.

Ethan nipped into her neck and she rocked back against him, her breasts filling his palms. Man, this was heaven, and he never wanted to stop.

She swayed and undulated against his shaft and then loosened her grip. Hot as lava. He groaned. This was hell, and he needed more.

Keeping one hand on her breast, he moved the other down to stroke the smooth skin of her bottom, gently tugging then pushing back to create a delicious rhythmic friction for both of them. Her ragged gasp, his heavy one, added to the turbulence outside.

Another clout of lightning lit the room and she leaned forward, with only his hand at her breast to stop her toppling. And he knew what she wanted. Him. Inside her now, like this. From behind.

He wanted that, too. But her face…it was a promise he'd made to himself. To watch her come apart.

And storm or no storm, he did not do unprotected sex; it wasn't part of the plan.

Sensing his impending withdrawal, she clamped her legs together, whimpering a denial. He persisted—sweet agony—and turned her. She gulped air. There was nothing sleepy about her eyes now. Demanding, fierce with need. Their bodies surged together, mouths seeking, sucking, sampling. Her arms were around his neck. Rock-hard nipples chafed his rib cage, which dragged another groan of impatience from his throat. If she didn't stop, he'd lose it.

She didn't stop. She pushed against him and, unprepared, he stepped back. And again. She had a plan but his mouth was too busy, too full of her to ask. She kept pushing till they reached her bedside table and she yanked open the drawer and pressed something into his hand. Then she hauled herself up against him, pressing and swaying and rubbing.

He fumbled with the packet, the blood roaring in his ears. She moved one hand down between them to help. He pressed her hand into his side with his arm. Not helping!

In the few seconds it took to sheath himself, he dragged in a lungful of air and tried to slow things. Ethan was at ease with the act of love, if not the emotion. If ever he could be generous, make it special, it should be now. Because he cared now as he'd never done before.

He forced himself to block out the lithe body gyrating against him, those impatient little breaths deep in her throat and her busy hands roaming and stroking. His arms slid around her waist and he drew her close, smiling tightly at the impatience in her eyes.

"Easy," he murmured.

Then his mouth took hers so deeply, so possessively, he swallowed her protest and she sagged against him.

She hadn't reckoned on being gentled, he guessed. He molded her body against him, inhaled the clean warmth of her, swayed with her and felt the hum deep in her throat. As his tongue teased over and under hers, she stilled and accepted.

But only for a few seconds. What she then did to his tongue should have been a felony. In a shock of disintegrating control, he imagined that part of her, the mouth that he dreamed about, on another part of his body, mimicking that motion. That other part of his body that was now straining between them, demanding critical attention.

His hands moved down to the back of her thighs and he braced and lifted her against him. Her legs instantly locked around his waist.

And then she did it. Reached down and cupped him while sliding up and down against him. Before his knees buckled, he turned and they fell on the bed with a *whump!*

He buried his mouth into the fragrant hollow at the base of her throat, inhaling deeply. When her arms tightened around his back, he raised his head. The eerie flashing of the lightning clouded her eyes. He touched his lips to hers, a soft whisper of a kiss, at the instant he slid into her body. Both of them exhaled, stilled.

So hot. The pleasure of being deep inside her was all concentrated there in a burst of tingling vibrations. For moments he lay, holding his breath, letting his body breathe for him. He felt a single thread of steel form and run the length of his insides, pulling tighter and tighter.

Their eyes were locked on each other's, building an immeasurable, searing passion. His surprise at the intensity of it glowed in her eyes. It robbed them of breath, girding them for something a little dangerous, but vital and inevitable.

Then Lucy hissed in a quick breath through her nose and licked the corner of his mouth. "Not easy," she pleaded.

Lifting slightly, he took some weight on his knees and slipped his hands under her buttocks. Then she lifted her hips jerkily and his descent into the storm began.

She met him eagerly, triumph glowing in her eyes. He pulled her body up against him with every stroke. Within the confines of her body, there were no limits, only rising layers of euphoria. In one deep stroke, he could feel her boundaries.With the next, he floundered as she stretched and flowed and tightened around him. He forgot everything else. This was all that mattered. Lucy, here, under him.

Their hips whipped like well-oiled pistons, smooth, deep, in complete tandem. A dizzying surge of vibrations plucked at the steel thread inside, quivering to every extremity. In a mind that was rapidly being obliterated by raw sensation, Ethan sensed a sultry, subtle change. From warm inside to drenchingly blazing hot.

She was close. She surged against him and he arched his back as her nails dug deeply into his flesh, urging him on. She was close and he needed to see, but her head had rolled to the side. He would not let her hide. He breathed her name, once, then again, louder. She turned her face and her eyes snapped open.

Lightning slashed through the window again and Ethan got what he wanted. Lucy, helplessly crying out against his mouth, unable to contain the flow of ecstasy.

Ethan pitched headlong into the storm and soared out over the valley. He felt the thread snap and blow the back of his head out, then streak through him to blast out of the soles of his feet.

She ripped his guts, his heart out.

They stretched on their sides in her bed, sighing in pleasure, freed from the shackles of a shrieking tension built up over days—decades—of need.

Several long minutes passed and their breathing returned to normal. Moving her head to the side, she peered at him drowsily. "You are the devil," she whispered, licking her parched lips.

His eyes fixed on her face, brightening with humor. "You're not quite the angel I thought you were."

"What makes you say that?"

"Could have something to do with a big box of…" He turned his head to squint at a box lying on its side in the open drawer of her bedside table. His arm rose and he twisted it around. "*Sixty* condoms…"

"It was a joke," she protested mildly. "A farewell present from a silly friend in New York."

His head sank back onto the pillow and the bed shook with his lazy laughter.

Lucy giggled. "It was fun coming through customs. I haven't used any of them, till now."

He crooked an eyebrow.

"Six months."

"Honored." His head inclined in a salute.

He turned her palm. "Who was your last?" Then he pressed his lips to it. "Was he special?"

That one little act brought a rush of emotion to her throat. Way to make a girl feel special, she thought.

They sat up, arranged pillows behind their heads and pulled the duvet over them.

"He was my tutor. I'd started a film-making course in New York, paid for, as usual by my poor father."

She stretched and put her arms behind her head.

Lucy had had one or two promising relationships before Jerry, but she'd learned at an early age that to expect love just because you gave it was setting yourself up for a fall. Sure enough, one day she discovered she was far from the first of his students to have gone down that road.

From there, she ceased to see herself as a love interest, realizing she was one in a long line of gullible girls. The thrill was gone. She ended the relationship and abandoned the course.

"What made you come home?" Ethan asked, stroking her hair.

"The break-up with Jerry sort of coincided with Dad's stroke." She turned into him and snuggled under his chin. "I suddenly realized how aimless and self-serving my life was. And failing on the course. That was the third course Dad had shelled out for over the years."

"Poor little rich girl." He dropped a kiss on her head.

"I never did get the chance to tell him I was sorry. I mean, I did, but after the stroke. Who knows whether he understood."

Those first few days after the stroke still haunted her. Her father was so confused about what was happening to him. He would stare at his useless hand, his uncooperative leg. He had stared at her, too, as if he could not place her.

"Maybe *he* should have told *you* he was sorry."

It was his tone that lifted her head. "What did he have to be sorry about?"

"For neglecting you all those years, blaming you for what your mother did to him." His voice was quiet. "Sounds to me like he didn't deserve your compassion."

She laid her head down again and snuggled in closer. They listened to the rain beat loudly on the roof and the wind keen. Lucy felt she never wanted to move from here.

"You do realize—" Ethan put his hand under her chin and tilted her face up to him "—being naughty, charming your way through life—it's all just a cry for attention."

She blinked at him. How did he see that so quickly? It had taken her some years to figure that out.

A tiny spurt of something broke inside her. It was so unexpected, so unfamiliar, it almost hurt. She'd have called it hope if she hadn't crushed it down ruthlessly, as was her habit.

She'd long since given up hope of a kind word from her father, a kiss or cuddle like she'd had when she was small, before Belle had left. Long since given up hope of a fairy-tale love. It was best that way. She was living proof. The *love* word made people run—her faster than most.

She leaned close and kissed his chest. She would enjoy tonight. Tomorrow would come. For now, keep things nice and easy.

He lifted her chin toward him again. "Let's make a plan."

She grinned, shaking her head. "You and your plans."

His index finger traced the shape of her lips. "You are very beautiful," he murmured. "And you were not part of the plan."

No, Lucy thought sadly. I never am. But her smile didn't slip.

"Told you about Turtle Island, didn't I? It's going to be huge. It's going to be the premier luxury resort in the world. It's also going to take up most of my time over the next couple of years."

Her heart sank even as hope burgeoned inside. And again, she quelled it. Don't get your hopes up. He's already talking about leaving, and that will be that.

"But the islands are only three or four hours away. You can come visit. We'll drink kava in the sun."

"That's a nice idea," Lucy told him brightly and, as was her way, pushed the maudlin thoughts aside.

"Get an assessment done, Lucy. Soon. I'll get those

business plans drawn up, we will sort out this mess with Tom, and you can start putting some of those ideas into effect. You do own fifty per cent of this operation."

She sighed. "He won't listen."

"He damned well will. There's more to you than he thinks. Let's show him."

*Let's.* What a small, inconsequential word. She tried to picture it in her mind, the shape of it, the number of letters. From his mouth, it meant *two*. Two of them. Together. Us.

Hope and longing flared again. Get it out of your mind. She rubbed her cheek up under his chin. He could use a shave. She could use some sense.

She looked down his relaxed body. So long, so strong. Her hand smoothed the light sprinkling of hair on his broad chest. What a view.

A muscle in his upper thigh twitched. Lucy turned her head to lick at his nipple, see it respond. Her finger glided slowly lower, over his tawny belly. She raised her face again, and nibbled on the bristles along his jawline. They kissed, deep and lingering. His arms tightened and she felt his hands spread wide. Her heart stuttered.

Much later, the sounds of his ecstasy trickled from his lips after a torturously slow and gentle seduction. He smoothed her hair, still looking intently into her eyes. Something flowed between them—a sensation as lush and complex as a fine wine. He'd filled her with a million pinpricks of light and sweetness that swelled and burst and streamed through her with agonizing slowness.

It was the best—and the worst—she had ever felt. She tore her gaze away and pushed him and curled up hard into him. Whimpering with gratification, she hoped he did not notice the couple of baffling tears she shed.

*  *  *

They dressed haphazardly and wandered downstairs in search of food, barefoot and holding hands. The electrical storm had long passed but heavy rain and high winds still lashed the house. Lucy's quiet and sultry chatter checked at the sound of distress in the kitchen. They opened the door to find Ellie, Summerhill's housekeeper, calling into the radiotelephone, looking and sounding agitated.

Lucy moved to her side immediately. "What is it?"

Ellie stared at her. "What are you doing here?" She broke off to look at Ethan, a puzzled line appearing between her brows as she took in their disheveled appearance. "I thought you were in town. Your car…"

"It's down at the stables. Ellie, what's wrong?"

"Oh, Lucy, it's a terrible mess. There's been an accident."

Ellie spoke into the RT in her hand. "Summerhill to Tom, can you hear me, Tom?"

Another faint crackle, nothing intelligible. The older woman looked at Lucy's worried face. "I got the first call about ten. His radio was wet and running out of power. There was a landslide. The hut they were in—Craiglea—was nearly wiped out. They decided to try to make it to the ford. Tom said it wasn't too bad at that stage. But he was wrong. From what I can make out, one or both Jeeps were washed into the river in a flash flood."

"Oh no," Lucy whispered.

"Anyone hurt?" Ethan demanded.

"The signal was weak, but I don't think so. I think he said they all ended up in the water and have lost everything, rifles, food, wet-weather gear, the lot. He saved just the one radio."

Lucy and Ethan stared at each other. Guilt radiated between them. While they'd been enjoying themselves, they hadn't given a thought to the hunting party. And now those people, people close to them, were in danger.

"Search and Rescue, Ellie, have you called them?"

Ellie nodded. "The local police are tied up. There's flooding right along the river. They have sent for police from town to assess the situation."

"Are there other huts?" Ethan asked tersely.

"Which side of the river, Ellie?"

"Mountain side. Fernlea would be the closest."

Lucy looked at Ellie in consternation. "That's miles. They'll never make it in this weather on foot."

Even as she said that, something niggled in her brain, some long-distant memory. She pushed it aside to listen to Ellie.

"Not easy to find either. It's straight up into the hills. Stupid, stupid." She tsked. "Why didn't they stay put at Craiglea? Made the best of it? I talked to Tom at three, soon as I knew the storm was on the way. He wanted to show Mr. Anderson one more spot."

"Any ideas, Ellie?"

The older woman inhaled, looking at each of them in turn. "We stay put and wait. It's up to the police to decide if Search and Rescue can attempt a river crossing in the dark while the storm is still going on. We'll just have to hope Tom and the others can find some shelter and keep warm."

"How many of them?" Ethan asked, looking at Lucy.

"Tom, Stacey, Magnus and Mr. Endo, one of the other guests."

"Oh, my," Ellie suddenly exclaimed. "I suppose we should tell Mrs. Anderson and Mrs. Endo. I've talked to Marie, Stacey's wife."

"I'll go to Juliette, you take Mrs. Endo. Ethan, put some coffee on. And keep an ear out for the radio."

"Shouldn't we go after them?" Ethan asked.

Ellie shook her head adamantly. "There's enough fool folk in the bush for one night. The police should be here soon. Just pray this storm lets up."

# Ten

**E**than made a big pot of coffee and fiddled with the radio, to no avail. Soon Juliette and the Indonesian woman joined him and Lucy and Ellie in the kitchen. Juliette confessed to lying awake worrying about the storm. Ethan felt sorry for the Indonesian woman. Her English was poor and there was no way of knowing how much she understood.

While they waited for the police he and Lucy braved the rain to check on the horses. To their horror, the river, two hundred meters away, was now within a meter of the stables. It took them nearly an hour to lead the half dozen animals back up to the barn where the Jeeps were kept, and to move their cars out of reach of the water.

A two-man team of police experienced in mountain search and rescue arrived, reporting widespread flooding for miles around. The weather was still atrocious. They spread maps all over the big kitchen table. Lucy stepped back, admitting that maps were beyond her, and Ellie showed them Tom's last known location. The area was steep and densely forested. After an hour's deliberation and calls to local search and rescue personnel, it was decided to wait until daybreak to attempt to send a team across the river.

Hour after hour they waited. At about four in the morning, Ethan left the cops in the kitchen and stretched out on one of the couches in the lounge. He scraped his hand along his jaw and thought he must look like hell.

Lucy sat across from him, talking to Juliette. Lucy looked utterly adorable. Her hair had been saturated and dried so many times today—not to mention enduring a sexathon—that it spiked out in all directions. She looked like a trendy hairdresser with a sticky-product fetish. Except that she wore a blue check shirt and jeans and woolly socks—the perfect farm girl.

The women talked quietly and his eyelids drifted shut. Nothing to be done till the morning. He might as well sleep.

He heard Juliette tell Lucy she couldn't bear having to bury another husband. She talked of her first husband and the night that had changed her life, pitching her into a living hell for two years. Lucy did not let on that she already knew about it.

"I've paid my dues. I just want to be with Magnus for as long as we have and be pampered and pamper him back. Is that so wrong?"

"No, of course not. Doesn't he know…?"

"I'll tell him, as soon as he…" Juliette's voice hitched. "I was foolish to think I could hide it.

"I know people think I'm a gold digger." The sadness in her voice was evident.

Ethan would not have done anything differently. The

newspaper clippings needed to be checked out. But he was glad things had turned out both for Juliette and his friend.

She continued sadly. "Truth is, I love him to bits and I'm proud to be his wife. I would never cheat on him. Growing up dirt-poor, I know I have a lot to be grateful for, and I am."

"It's obvious how close you are," Lucy murmured.

"It's not a one-way street. He gets his masculinity fed. He's proud to have me on his arm. And he was so lonely when I met him. Now he laughs all the time. I make him laugh."

Ethan had to agree with that.

"He also loves giving things. He's generous. And he has someone to fuss over him now, make sure he takes his pills.

"But all some people see is he'll be dead in a few short years, and I will still be young, and rich."

"Not the ones that know you both, surely," Lucy protested.

Ethan heard a mirthless chuckle. "People get jealous, I'm living a dream life."

There was a pause, and drowsiness pressed down on his mind.

"You must see a lot of rich old men through here, honey. Tell me you never thought about it—snagging one and being obscenely rich."

Ethan inhaled sharply through his nostrils, held it. Time stood still for a moment, or seemed to in his mind. He opened his eyes, somewhat reluctantly.

Lucy was grinning. "Oh, yeah. All the time."

She's joking, he told himself.

"Sadly, most of them bring their wives."

She must be…

"Their trophy wives," Juliette sighed.

"Ethan said that," Lucy said cheerily. She turned her head and looked at him. On seeing his eyes open, she smiled an intimate little smile. "Oh. You're awake."

Ethan relaxed. She had a hell of a smile. He drank it in and smiled back.

Juliette stood and stretched. "I need some aspirin."

Lucy rose also. "I'll get you some."

Juliette said she had plenty in her room and excused herself. Lucy came over to Ethan's couch and perched on the edge. She expressed grave fears for the farm animals on the grazing land close to the river. They agreed that as soon as the search and rescue team was dispatched, they would go check on the stock. From what they had seen by the stables, the river had burst its banks in a big way. There could be substantial losses.

At five-thirty, the rest of the search and rescue team arrived. It was dark and still raining heavily, but the wind had dropped.

The team discussed their options over coffee and Ellie's warm date scones. Lucy stood behind the seated men, chewing on her bottom lip worriedly, but she suddenly snapped her fingers. "Ellie, did you say Tom tried to cross at the ford?"

She had remembered something: an old Department of Conservation hut. "Tom would know of it. It's not used anymore. They might have headed there for shelter."

"Are you sure it's in this area?" the team leader asked.

"I stayed there once, camping out, when I was a kid. All I know is, it's only about half an hour's ride on the other side of the ford, in a big stand of pine."

"May not even be still standing," Ellie said dubiously.

"It's worth a shot," one of the men said. "How deep is the ford usually?"

"Usually only one, one and a half feet, but…" Lucy shrugged again.

Ethan guessed the whole landscape would have changed in this storm. The radio news said it was the worst flood in the area for fifty years.

A rescue helicopter from town was already on alert. As soon as it was light, it would be flown to the top of the gorge. One team would climb from there down into the stand of pine it was hoped the hunters were holed up in. Another team would drive to the ford—if that were possible—and attempt a river crossing, then up through the bush to the vicinity of the hut.

The condition of the hunters and the safety of the river crossing or the climb would determine how the party would be brought out.

As soon as it was light, the team set off, promising to keep in touch by radiotelephone. Ethan and Lucy stood on the veranda and stared in shock at the unfamiliar look of the terrain in front of the house. The normally benign Rakaia had spread into a huge lake that encroached up past the stables. It wasn't so deep, but the area it covered was impressive.

"Lucky you thought to move the horses," Ethan murmured.

"We'd better feed them. Then I'll call the neighbor. Apparently he looks after a lot of our stock, and I hope he'll know where they are."

According to the news, many of the lower-lying farms in the district had been flooded, and not just pasture. Summerhill was lucky because the house was on a rise. There were several properties with a couple of feet of water flowing through. They also still had phone access and power, unlike some of the more remote properties.

Lucy called their nearest neighbor and discovered he had been up for hours and had already seen to most of the animals on his and Summerhill's land. "There's just one group of ours he's a bit worried about—down in the south pasture. He thinks there's around fifty head there. But the land does rise at one end. He hopes the animals have made their way to the top.

"He offered to go check," she continued. "But I'm tired of sitting around the house worrying. I'll go."

Ellie fixed them a big breakfast and shortly after eight, Lucy saddled up Monty and the mare Tilley for Ethan. They were well wrapped up in oilskins, boots and gloves and Lucy made Ellie promise to call her on her cell phone the moment any news came in from the rescue team.

"Lead on, cowgirl." Ethan grinned, saluting her.

They set off into the dim morning, heavy rain making conversation difficult. Lucy was in awe at the massive lake the river had made of her land. It was sluggish and not deep but they had to take care in the dips and valleys. Luckily she had a good memory and guided them confidently to the pasture they were seeking, about an hour's ride from the house.

Three hours later, they had nearly all of the cattle herded into the gardens around the lodge, to Ellie's dismay. They saw only two dead cattle in the floodwaters, and one trembling beast had to be roped and hauled up out of a water-filled hole. Then they rode over to check on the neighbor.

Ellie rang while they were still there to say the hunting party were all alive and well and had made it safely across the river. Tom was the only one with an injury—a suspected broken wrist. They had indeed sheltered in the old DOC hut. Lucy's recollection had saved hours of searching.

"Hell of a memory you got there." Ethan gave her a high five and she pushed her hood back and grinned with relief.

They set off for home midafternoon. Weary as he was, his muscles protesting at the unaccustomed hours in the saddle, Ethan looked around in wonder at the damage Mother Nature could inflict. He had previously experienced the other end of the spectrum, where she refused to provide *any* water, the greatest necessity of life.

Lucy seemed to be ambling along at half his pace. He reined in and waited, struck by her desolate expression. She was looking around, not at the flooding but the gorge and the mountains. She looked at it as if she'd never see it again.

"Great country, Lucy."

"Even like this," she agreed. "You know, I loved traveling, but wherever in the world I was, however hard I looked, Summerhill has always been the most exotic place for me." She looked at him curiously. "Do you have an exotic place? Somewhere you keep locked away inside?"

Wherever you are, he thought promptly, and clamped his mouth shut before he made a complete ass of himself. He shook his head.

They moved off.

"I guess I'm dreading seeing Magnus."

Ethan tried to suppress a smile. "His bark's worse than his bite."

They continued on in silence for a minute, the horses stirring up squelching mud in the waterlogged pasture.

"If he takes us off the Global List, Tom wants to sell," she told him suddenly.

He pulled to a stop. "Sell the lodge?" he asked in surprise.

She shook her head. "The land, not the lodge. He's never cared about the land." The desolate expression was back.

"How do you feel about that?"

Lucy gave a barely-there rise of her shoulders. "I've always found the house a bit depressing since Mum left. Every minute I could, I'd be out here, riding, camping, just walking. I couldn't bear it if he sold even an inch of it."

Ethan scratched his head. What a load on her shoulders at the moment. "You must have a say."

"I can't tell him what to do with his fifty per cent."

He nodded and thought for a few moments. He had nothing to do with Magnus's club or the Global List, but he knew that Magnus took it very seriously indeed. "I'll talk to him, but I can't promise anything. Magnus would probably overlook some things. It's the hint of financial embarrassment that could be the sticking point. I know he's heard rumors. The sort of people that belong to the club don't like rumors."

Lucy nodded, sighing heavily. Ethan stared at her mouth, wanting to kiss her troubles away. "Lucy, if you're out of the club, it's not the end of the world. With the right marketing, you can still run a good business."

"The prestige of it is a big thing with Tom. But the main reason is the exclusive advertising rights. We won't have time to build a new market and be able to trade our way out of debt before—before it's too late."

He didn't want to tell her that as far as creditors went, the meat supplier she already knew about was in the basket named peanuts. There was a whole lot worse to come.

"Cheer up. We'll talk to him tonight and then I can work on Magnus. But if I can't swing it, I'll set up something with my marketing team. We can't get you into all the printed accommodation publications overnight, but there are lots of ways to target your market that get results in months rather than years."

"Really?" She looked up at him hopefully and his heart squeezed. Tom and her father had kept her down for so long. No wonder her confidence was shot. She needed to know that anything was possible.

She needed to know he would help.

She was already perking up. "Hey, you're not too bad on that horse, for a city slicker," she told him with a big grin.

"Kid, I was riding when you were still a twinkle in your daddy's eye."

"You reckon?" She laughed and leaned over to give him a playful push. And somehow lost her balance, ending up flat on her back in a pool of mud.

Ethan grabbed Monty's bridle to bring him to a standstill so he didn't step on Lucy. "Jesus! You okay?"

She lay there for a couple of seconds, a surprised look on her face. When she started to gurgle with laughter, he relaxed.

"I dare you to laugh." She gasped.

His mouth tightened with the effort of not smiling. He couldn't do anything about the sparkle in his eyes. "Wouldn't dream of it," he told her solemnly.

Leaning down, he put out his hand. She grabbed it, but before she hauled herself up out of the mud, she squinted up at him. "You know," she said, matter-of-factly, "just for a moment, you sitting up there tall enough to touch the sky, you reminded me of my father when I was little."

He gestured at his hand, indicating she get up. "There's a worrying thought."

Lucy giggled as she was hauled up to her feet and

stood, swaying slightly with one hand on Monty's back. She took off one glove and wiped her hair, grimacing at the sludge that appeared on her hand.

"Even with you looking like something the cat dragged in," Ethan continued as she heaved herself up into the saddle, "I am definitely not harboring any fatherly feelings toward you."

They arrived back at Summerhill to find the hunters were home, except for Tom who was at the local medical center having his wrist X-rayed. Magnus and Juliette had retired to their suite, both of them exhausted and emotional. The Indonesians seemed to be treating the whole thing as part of their scheduled activity. They sat in front of the fire, poring over the menu for dinner.

Ethan excused himself and went to his room to take a call from his Sydney office.

Clark in Sydney had bad tidings. The minister for the Interior had gone back on his word to consider MagnaCorp's offer before going public. Turtle Island was now officially on the market.

He sat down in the armchair and stared into the gas fire. Okay, this was the worst-case scenario, but MagnaCorp had the inside running. Ethan had already spent a month on the tender. He was way ahead of the competition. And he had access to all the information and reports Magnus had compiled twenty years ago.

Information that his father would also have on file.

Ethan leaned back in his chair and put his hands behind his head. He couldn't let Magnus and the team down. He would leave soon. After showering he'd go see if Magnus had emerged. He had only a short time to try to persuade his boss to give Summerhill another chance. To help Lucy find out what the hell was going on with Tom.

A short time to spend every waking minute with her, reassuring her, making love to her.

It was cozy by the fire. His last thoughts before he drifted off to sleep were of Lucy looking around at her embattled heritage with such heartache on her face, and then grinning like a naughty child as she wrung the mud from her hair.

Lucy woke him an hour later. She had filled her bath with bubbles, too many bubbles, and wanted to share....

An hour or two later, her stomach gurgled with hunger—or motion sickness. "I'll make us a sandwich."

She tidied the rumpled bed around his drowsy form, doubting he would be awake by the time she got back with the food.

On the way downstairs, her smile faded with each step. She wondered at how torn she felt. On the one hand, she was infused with the well-being that making love with Ethan brought. On the other, she had a heavy heart. Even after a fun-filled hour of giggling and making an unholy mess of her bathroom and then her bed, she felt a weird sense of loss.

His office had called. He hadn't said anything about it, but it was a reminder that he had a whole other life out there, one she wasn't part of. She had to get used to the idea that this little sojourn would soon be over and life would get back to normal.

Lucy wondered if she could ever feel normal again.

Somehow in the last week, her whole perception of herself had undergone radical surgery. She did have something to offer. Instead of letting Tom make all the decisions and ride roughshod over her, she had to persuade him that his half sister had half a brain and wasn't entirely the ditz he thought she was. Ethan built her up, made her feel smart and sexy, not clumsy and stupid. She felt as if she mattered, even knowing he would not be around for much longer.

And that was killing her. She wanted him around, for a long time. Maybe forever. She was falling hopelessly in love.

"And we all know what that means," she murmured to the stag's head at the bottom of the stairs. She had to tell someone, but wasn't quite masochistic enough to tell the man himself. "That means the next thing I hear will be the sound of his running feet."

Well, hell! Nothing was forever. He was here now. He'd promised to help. No point getting down about things she couldn't change.

Forcing a lighter step, she heaped bread and bags of salad vegetables and cheese onto the kitchen counter. She had barely begun when Tom walked in, looking dirty and pale.

Lucy smiled and offered to make him a sandwich. "How's the wrist?"

He held up his plastered limb. "Hellish sore. How was Magnus?"

She shrugged. "By the time Ethan and I got back, they'd gone up to their room." She explained they'd been riding, checking out the stock.

"God," Tom groaned, sitting at the big kauri-wood table, "I have royally screwed up, haven't I?"

"Could have been worse," Lucy told him lightly. He looked so beaten.

"I think we have to face the fact that there will be some changes around here." He examined the plaster cast morosely.

"That's not necessarily a bad thing, is it?" Lucy was thinking of the badly maintained Jeeps, the chef who kept calling in sick, the hunting guide who disregarded a weather report and put lives in danger. The firearms cabinet…

"Tom. I need to talk to you about a couple of things."

He sighed heavily. "Can't it wait? I'm beat."

She ignored that and placed his sandwich beside him. "John Hogan came to see me yesterday. He got his judgment and we have a month to pay or he's starting proceedings for real."

Tom closed his eyes.

"How can things be so bad, we can't even pay an old family friend what we owe him?"

"Everything's gone to hell. Everything I touch."

Lucy, with her back to him, raised her eyes heavenwards. Self-pity was not going to solve anything. "That's not all. I had a visit from a detective. You didn't report the car stolen, or what I told you about Joseph Dunn. Just what's that about?"

Tom slumped. His cast hit the table with a thump. Alarmed, she forgot her sandwich and sat beside him, her hand on his shoulder. "Please talk to me, Tom."

He took a deep breath. "I owe Dunn some money."

Ethan was right. "How much?"

He slumped even farther. It would not have surprised Lucy if he shed tears, he was so down. "How much, Tom?"

He swallowed. "Thousands." It was almost a whisper.

Lucy stared at him, her stomach churning with nerves. There was a long and tense pause. "Your car was found at the scene of an arson. The police want to know whether you had anything to do with it. Did you?"

"I swear. No way, Lucy."

"Ethan thinks Joseph Dunn might be setting you up. Making it look like you were there."

"I wouldn't put it past him. He's a nasty piece of work."

"You have to go see the police. First thing. Tell them about him."

"I will."

He stared down at his untouched sandwich for a long time. "I've let you down. Let everyone down."

She rubbed his shoulder. She might be angry and bewildered but he was family, her only family, and that mattered.

"I never meant for any of this to happen," he was saying.

And then, the dam broke and words just flowed out of him. She stared at his face, disbelieving, and listened while he told a tale so harrowing, she could never have imagined it. How he'd gambled his way into debt. Owed money all over town. How it had been the reason for his marriage break-up shortly before their father had had his stroke.

How he had remortgaged part of their property.

Lucy struggled to take it all in. She reeled with each revelation as if they were blows. He had single-handedly gambled them into debt. To think that he could remortgage a family business and farm that had been theirs for generations.

Fear crawled around her neck. She jumped to her feet and moved quickly to the huge chest against the wall, rummaging through the drawers.

"What are you doing?"

She returned to the table, empty-handed and agitated. "I remember Mum used to stash a pack of cigarettes in there somewhere. I've never wanted to start, but I do right now."

Tom's eyes slid away, but not before she noticed the disparaging look he got whenever her mother was mentioned.

"You never liked my mother, did you?"

He shrugged. "No staying power," he drawled, encompassing her in a sweep of a glance that seemed to imply she was of similar ilk.

"And that's the killer, isn't it?" She leaned forward, her face close to his. "You feel you're the rightful heir to Summerhill because you were born first, to Dad's first wife. You hate that he left half to me."

His eyes met hers and he nodded. "That, and the fact that you've hardly been here. Had nothing to do with building up the lodge…"

"Dad never wanted the lodge in the first place," she countered hotly. "You took advantage of his depression to bully him into it. He was a farmer."

Tom wouldn't meet her eyes and she spent the next moments trying to swallow the anger churning inside. Anger wasn't a normal emotion for her. Usually she met the world with a smile, no matter how anguished she felt. If the world didn't smile back, it was time to move on.

Several big breaths later, she felt composed enough to look at him. "You have to get help. Gambling is an addiction. There are people, organizations who can help you."

After a long time, he raised his head. His eyes were tormented. "On the way back from the police station, I'll go see a business broker. I can't see any other way to make the mortgage payments, or stall the liquidators."

Lucy bridled. "There has to be another way. I won't sell."

"If you're going to be stubborn about it, then we'll have to cut it down the middle. Lucy, I've blown it with Magnus."

She shook her head impatiently. She knew the club

was important, but in the last forty-eight hours, it had assumed less importance for her than her other problems. Especially the one tearing her heart up. "Not necessarily. Ethan is going to bat for us with Magnus."

He stared at her and she saw a nasty little slide of understanding in his eyes. "Ethan this, Ethan that. You two seem cozy."

"He wants to help."

Her hackles rose as he scorched her with a look of such contempt. "He knows, doesn't he? You've been shooting your mouth off."

"He found out on his own. And he was with me when the police came. There wasn't much point in denying anything."

A sneer twisted the corner of his mouth. "You just wait, little sister. We'll be off the list, there will be forty thousand acres of Summerhill land on the market, and your champion will be nowhere to be seen." He shook his head in disgust. "I told you to keep away. You're not equipped to deal with business matters."

There it was again, that disdain for her ability. Lack of respect, even though none of this was her fault. The closeness she'd earlier felt toward him drained away like dirty bathwater.

"Maybe you're not equipped to handle maintenance and safety issues."

"I'm not letting the lodge go down," Tom said belligerently. "I've worked too hard, lost too much, to lose it too."

Lucy stood abruptly and loomed over him. "Then you'll have a fight on your hands," she told him grimly. "I'm sure there is a law about a person who defrauds his business partner to pay gambling debts. And like it or not, Tom, I am your business partner."

His eyes widened. Lucy had never spoken to him like
that before. She'd always deferred to him. He was so
much smarter than her, and she'd felt so guilty over her
past indifference.

Not anymore.

# Eleven

Lucy tossed and turned all night and woke at dawn. Creeping out of bed so as not to wake Ethan, she made instant coffee and curled up on the armchair beside the big window, opening the drapes just a sliver.

How she wished to be able to enjoy their first morning waking together. Who knew how many more they'd have?

He'd been asleep when she'd returned from the kitchen last night. She'd snuggled up close, taking comfort from his inert warmth. Pretending he'd be there forever. Trying to erase Tom's contempt and the horror of her financial situation.

What was she worth? What was her value? Not in monetary terms, but in purpose. Tom had been stupid, but she had to accept some responsibility. How different things might have been if she had given instead of always taking. As if taking were her right and there was no effort required on her part to sustain this land of hers.

She sat there in a fearful misery for an hour before Ethan woke. Tousled, naked, a sleepy smile on his wicked lips, he brought a little burst of hope to her heart.

He was starving, so Lucy phoned the kitchen and cajoled a light breakfast. She crawled back into bed and told him the whole story of her conversation with Tom last night.

"How could he remortgage without your consent?" he demanded.

"He had power of attorney for Dad. After the stroke, Dad was deemed to be incapable."

"You have to find out how much and how immediate the debt is," he told her brusquely.

Lucy didn't miss the inflection on *you*. It was an unwelcome reminder that their short interlude was drawing to a close.

"Trouble is," he continued, "there are unlikely to be any records of gambling debts. I'll go see Magnus first thing and try to stall his decision for a bit. You don't want Tom flying off the handle and making rash decisions."

Room service arrived with their breakfast and Ethan disappeared into the bathroom to dress. Lucy poured coffee for herself. Ethan liked tea in the mornings. A piece of useless information she would hold in her heart.

How little she knew of him. How was it possible to feel so much so quickly, with as much room for growth as a root-bound potted plant? She wondered if in ten years, she would recall that little detail: I once fell in love with a man who liked to drink tea in the mornings.

He returned from the bathroom in pants and with his shirt unbuttoned, and sat down opposite her. She offered the teapot, waiting for him to raise his cup. He seemed subdued. "I have to get back to Sydney." His eyes glided to her face. "Tomorrow."

Lucy's heart sank. The teapot stilled in midair. So soon....

He pushed his cup toward her. "There's a problem." He looked straight at her then. "I had hoped for a few more days."

She began to pour, feeling a tremble threaten her fingers. "Work's important," she said inanely.

"Will you be all right?"

"'Course." Said lightly, as in "Don't be silly." She set the pot down carefully.

Ethan leaned back, still looking at her. "I have to go. But..."

Lucy blinked. Was that guilt in his eyes? "Can't be helped." The last thing she wanted was to make him feel guilty. None of this was his problem.

"I'll be back—soon as I can—if you want, that is..."

And then you'll go again. And soon, you'll be immersed in your project. And I'll be here, and the calls will come less often. "I hope you get the deal. It's important to you."

"Paramount," Ethan told her. "After this one, a change of direction."

Lucy tried to look interested, but it was hard when she was saying goodbye inside.

"I was thinking of buying some land somewhere. Do you think you could live anywhere else but Summerhill?"

Lucy looked up sharply. He had asked the question in the same breath as he finished the statement, she noted. If she had done that, it would suggest she was breathless, nervous. She tried and failed to imagine Ethan nervous—although she had seen breathless….

She repeated the question in her head. Could she live anywhere else? With you? she wanted to ask. Maybe with you, she answered herself. Her fingers made a mess of toast crumbs on her plate. Was he asking her to go with him?

Her overactive brain then slipped in a worrying new thought. Was he just trying to prepare her for the worst? They hadn't discussed what he had found out in the village. Maybe he was trying to tell her she didn't have a hope in hell of keeping Summerhill anyway. "If I did that, Tom would just carve it up."

Ethan nodded slowly. She could see the sky blue of her robe in his eyes, but beyond that were shadows of regret. The two things she would hate most for him to take away from here were regret and guilt.

"Lucy, I'll be at the end of the phone."

Shame put an edge on her voice. "Don't worry," she insisted. "I told him I'd fight him about selling the land."

"I know you will."

Yes, she thought. You gave me that. A week ago, I wouldn't have fought.

An awful uncomfortable silence ensued as they both pretended to be busy with their breakfast. She darted furtive looks at him across the small table. Can I live with this? With his body every few months and his deep, slow voice on the phone. He will go. And I will visit occasionally. And it won't be more than we are able to give.

Lucy inhaled, making a conscious effort not to clench her jaw. She couldn't take pity from him. She did not want sacrifices and ultimatums. She looked up to see him watching her, concern darkening his eyes.

He exhaled noisily. "Dammit! I'll stay…"

Her whole body tensed. She would not be a liability. His liability. Making a snap decision, she rose abruptly. There was one way she knew of to shut a man up before he said something that could not be reversed.

Her body would succor them both. A fist of desire tightened in her stomach. It was desperate and consuming, and she saw that he recognised it. Perhaps awash with his unwanted guilt, he approved of it.

*This* is what I can give, and it *is* heartfelt, and it doesn't need words.

He rose, too, as she reached for him. They came together at the edge of the table and her hands were at his belt, tugging him toward the bed. As they lurched together, he cupped her face and kissed her deeply.

Lucy sighed into his mouth, overcome by a mindless lust. She pushed the shirt off his shoulders. Biceps bunched and rippled under her eager strokes. She dug her nails into his flat belly, then scraped gently down. Impatient to tear those pants off, loving the feel of taut and supple skin and his earthy, morning-male scent.

She strove to shrink his focus to nothing but sensation. When he was far away, she wanted him to remember this—how she made him feel. No guilt to taint his memory. She wanted a physical, tangible memory of her to stay inside him. She wanted to *be* inside him.

Long, taut and muscular, his skin taunted her fingertips. Her nerve endings hummed with the anticipation of having everything she wanted right here in front of her, drowning in need.

The lower she went, the more still he became, but she heard the blood rushing through his veins. Down, she pushed at his trousers and briefs, bending her knees. Up, her hands smoothed around his buttocks, kneading the clenched muscles. His thighs strained like tree trunks, but he quivered when she took him in her hands. She made one long firm stroke from his heated curved underside up the length of him, loving the tensile resistance and the way he strained toward her. Her fingertips swept over the thick tip of him. His groan swept from his fingers into her mind as his hands landed lightly on her head.

She felt the heat flooding into him, the satiny skin tight and hot, scorching a trail to her heart.

Ethan couldn't watch when he saw her perfect lips part and close around him. Too erotic. With the unmanageable hang-up he had about her mouth, he wouldn't last ten seconds if he watched.

The need to thrust screamed through him. He braced his thighs, confident in his strength, and was shocked to find himself trembling.

He knew what she was doing. Once again, deflecting attention away from her problems, her desolation by using her impressive arsenal. Charm, kissing, sex. He'd learned that about her.

He groaned as she took him deeper. Hell of a way to cope.

But she was tough enough to cope with Tom, even if she didn't know that yet, and Ethan fully intended to back her up all the way.

Just not in person right now. And he felt bad about that.

He felt terrible about that.

More—too much! He wanted her beautiful mouth on his. Whispering her name, he stroked through her hair down to her face and coaxed her up. She met his lips with her own when he dipped his head. Something brimmed in her eyes, abstract and sad, but before he could wonder, worry, he was taken over by her kiss, distracted by the feel of her body against his. He molded her body close and felt the cool slide of his wet erection against her robe-covered belly. The blue of her eyes now smoked up into something more immediate.

She pressed forward into him, her spine arched. He slipped the loose knot of her robe so that it hung down, still covering her breasts. Mesmerized by the luster of her skin against the cool blue of the fabric, he reached out and touched her through the robe. She took a deep breath in, so her chest rose and rose. The silky fabric slid under his fingers and over her skin with a liquid sensuality that nevertheless dried his throat like chalk.

Around and around in little circles, under and over, slipping and sliding like an ice cube melting. Her breath stopped when the material sighed over the hard tips of her breasts. His throat closed when she let her head loll back, his whispered name trickling out through her parted lips.

It was an age before she reached for another breath. As he took his silken touch lower, he drew the robe slowly down her arms. Where the fabric touched, his mouth followed. Her marble skin quivered and tightened. He rubbed and licked and kissed his way right down to her toes, then discarded the robe and started up again. Her sweet musky smell broke over him, making him sweat with greed. With one arm wrapped around her to support her trembling legs, his mouth and fingers took what he needed and gave her the release she craved.

As if he'd turned a switch, her every muscle seized. On and on, it screeched and ripped through her, that fine edge between pleasure and pain not just blurred but shattered like a windscreen. Holding her together by the tips of her fingernails, by the edge of her teeth. When his hands began to soothe the cramped muscles in the backs of her legs, she flopped back onto the bed, quaking. She had kissed the sky with his name on her lips. But now—in a minute when she got her breath—she was filled with another burn. Aggravated by aftershocks of such sweetness, she needed his abrasive invading presence inside her. Needed to be stretched, filled, grounded.

With arms that felt like jelly, she gripped his shoulders and hauled him up over her. With a mouth that wanted to sob with the ecstasy that streamed through every cell, every particle that made her whole, she crooned her wish into his ear, then kissed him. Felt his smile against her lips and tasted herself and his need.

There was nothing more ragingly erotic than a woman who talked dirty, especially when it filtered out through the lips of an angel.

He wanted to immerse himself, to feel her moving, flowing under and around him. Their kiss promised pleasure to come, and an exchange of tenderness that bewildered him. Too much emotion. He broke off the kiss and nuzzled her throat. Dangerous, maybe life-altering emotion.

He reached toward the depleted box of condoms on her bedside table where they had been since last night. Quickly sheathing himself, he lay back over her, sinking into her kiss again. His hands moved, inch by inch up her forearms, entwining her fingers in his.

Face-to-face, bodies pressed together, his hips hunched into the cradle of hers. He eased into her and in the brightening morning light, watched her eyes fill with warmth, spiced with danger.

Slow and deep. Sweat broke out on his forehead and he nipped and nuzzled her mouth, swallowing her labored little breaths. Her hips rocked and rolled, and he felt himself so deep, so lushly gloved. The humming in his ears sounded like an old refrigerator, surging and retreating and vibrating.

She rocked and squeezed and her inner thighs gripped him in velvet welcome. The blood screamed through his every vein, every artery. He felt again the change in her body temperature and an intimate swelling. Heard the desperate sighs that signaled her focus. Her fingers were locked onto his and she seemed to gather for a last great push. Ethan tensed and thrust deep.

Lucy shattered. Incoherent baby words rushed out of her mouth as her head thrashed from side to side. He heard his name, felt her contractions dissolve him into a heavy, drenching mist of pure pleasure.

Afterward she lay on her side but cuddled in close. Her drawn-up knees were jammed into his gut and she held him tightly.

"I really love that thing you do," he murmured into her hair.

"What thing?"

"After you come. All elbows and knees and head, like you're trying to climb right inside my rib cage."

He felt her mouth move against his throat. "Do I? Sorry."

Ethan increased the pressure of his arms, holding her closer. "I love it. It's what it's all about, isn't it?"

He listened to her breathing pan out and deepen. He bet she'd gotten little sleep last night after Tom's bombshell.

He pressed his lips to the top of her head, feeling little peace himself. Or eagerness to get back to work. Or even self-satisfaction after the best sex of his life.

She was warm and smelled sexy. For a moment, his chest expanded so completely, his arms were compelled to cuddle her closer. Then a hollow feeling deflated him.

First things first. Get Turtle Island started. Land the deal.

Lousy timing, when everything was crashing around her ears. Could he stall, just for a couple of days? On the other hand, he had read the economy reports. Could the islanders afford to alienate MagnaCorp?

Ethan craned his neck to look at the curve of Lucy's cheek, the shadows her lashes made on her pale skin.

Be patient, stick to the plan and in a couple of short years—less—he could relax, kick back, contemplate the future. Maybe with Lucy in it—if she still wanted him.

Contemplate Lucy.

Her knees scraped down his body slowly and now there was no impediment between them. She nestled in closer with a contented sigh. His heart swelled again, perplexing him. So much more intimacy than ever before.

Contemplate love. Loving Lucy.

Ethan squeezed his eyes shut, then snapped them open again.

Lucy donned raincoat and gum boots and walked down to clean out the stables. Their stablehand had been cut off by the flood yesterday and she couldn't return the horses to the stable until the stalls had been cleared.

She found the smell of sodden slimy straw and mud quite suited her mood. Rank and festering.

Lucy was tired of people she cared about being indifferent toward her. She must deserve it, because that was all she had ever inspired in people—at least the people she wanted love from. Basically, she wasn't lovable. Had never been, starting from the day her mother had left.

Sweep, sweep. She was working up a sweat here.

There was something about her that meant she would never be number one. She would always be part-time, long-distance, ditzy, nice little Lucy.

Her pique was unreasonable. She could no more expect him to give up his job, his life than he could expect her to walk away from her birthright. She leaned on her broom, panting with exertion and frustration. *If* that is what he had been referring to.

Although if Tom had his way, her birthright would be chopped up and flushed away. And what would she be left with then?

What she'd always had. Nothing. Nobody. And nowhere to run. She bent her back to her work and was vigorous about it.

What were the options? The most logical and probable: stay here and battle Tom's obstinacy, possibly his enemies and definitely his demons, while trying somehow to turn Summerhill from a debt-ridden, badly-run lodge and neglected farm, into—what? Did she even have any idea?

Or she could jump on the nearest plane and fly off to—Paris? Prague?—though the language would be a problem and languages were *so* not her forte. Didn't matter where. It had always worked for her in the past. Until her father had gotten sick and the vein of money had become plugged.

But—she pulled her hat off, overheating. Maybe

Ethan loved her, or could grow to love her. He gave her something. Hope. With him, anything seemed possible. She felt smart, not dumb. She had good ideas. And perhaps now a little belief in herself.

Her mind darted about like a blind moth.

What would he do if she told him, right now, she loved him? Would he run just as everyone she had ever cared for had? Could she ever be happy with only a part of him?

A familiar figure slopped across the yard outside the stables. The stablehand had arrived. She watched him approach but was so deep in thought, she didn't really register she was no longer alone.

He stopped and they looked at each other, then he reached out for the broom. "Jeez," he said, wheezing a little. "We've been in drought for three years and now this. It's all or nothing, eh?"

He tugged the broom from her grasp and began sweeping. Lucy looked after him, his words seeping through the fetid smell of the stable.

All or nothing. Why did it have to be? She could eat two pieces of the pie, couldn't she? Instead of the whole thing or none at all.

She started for the house before she lost her nerve. Maybe the fermenting straw had addled her brain, but she was going to walk into the house and tell him she was in love with him. She was going to face the issue instead of running. This was life. There was no fairy-tale family life, no loving, indulgent parents. Just Lucy and her equal love for Summerhill land and for Ethan Rae.

Ethan took the stairs two at a time, fuelled by anger, shame—and relief. In his room, he tossed his bag onto the bed and began to fill it. Relief? Because there was no choice to be made now. Everything was back to normal.

Acid rose in his throat like the burn of Tom's words.

Ethan and Magnus had been in the conference facility for half an hour before Tom burst in. Magnus's overriding concern was safety—his wife had let slip about the afternoon weather report Tom had chosen to ignore.

"Can't control the weather," Tom had snapped, shooting a venomous look at Ethan. He obviously thought Lucy had blabbed.

Poor sap. His back was against the wall. Unwittingly, Magnus built the fire, stoked it, till Tom felt he had no option but to blame Lucy for everything.

"Lady Luck turns her back sometimes, Magnus," Tom had wheedled. "It's cyclical. You're a businessman. You know that."

"Not good enough, son. A big part of your business is safety." Magnus paused, and hammered home the second nail in Lucy's coffin. "If Lucy hadn't remembered that hut, we'd still be out there now."

Now Ethan yanked savagely on the zip of the suit compartment of his bag and heard the door open. He threw Lucy an icy look when she entered his room but forced himself to continue with his mental checklist. Shirt, underwear, toiletries—he was nearly done. His movements were quick and efficient but tension wired his jaw and stretched his spine into a hostile rod.

From the corner of his eye, he saw her hover in the doorway, her black jeans stained and tucked into long woolly socks that dropped bits of plant matter onto the floor. She looked flushed and rumpled.

"What are you doing?" she asked quietly, twisting her hands together in front of her.

His hands crushed the clothing down, then he hauled on the zip. Lucy flinched at the scraping thud of the bag hitting the floor. He continued to pretend to ignore her, moving to the table to organize his laptop and briefcase.

"You really had me going," he muttered after an age.

"Wh-what do you mean?"

"Should have chosen your accomplice with more care." Bitterness scoured his throat. Tom's sneering face flashed past his eyes. "Your brother loused it up for you."

Without looking at her, Ethan sensed her cringe with foreboding. Not his problem. Laptop snapped shut, papers stacked, briefcase closed. "If he'd just been patient...but Tom couldn't leave it alone. He burst in, ranting and raving about how he knew we were cutting him loose. How, because of *our* pillow talk, Magnus knew about the court case, the gambling, the debt, the shady associates." He smiled grimly at his watch, slapped his pockets. "Funny thing was, I hadn't told Magnus any of that."

Before Tom's intrusion, Ethan had secured a stay in the decision about Summerhill's place on the Global List. He'd also mentioned that Lucy had some good ideas that deserved to be given a chance. In an effort to calm Tom, Magnus suggested he take a leaf out of his sister's book.

A red rag to a bull...

The elderly, respected businessman was unprepared for Tom's insults, the final one: that his precious club was a highfalutin bag of hot air that Summerhill could manage without. Magnus had stormed out, calling loudly to his wife to get her things.

Ethan laid the briefcase and laptop on top of his bag and scooped up his jacket. Lucy stood silent. Not wanting to, knowing he shouldn't, he raked his eyes over her face. Not just milky-pale now, a much more deathly hue. Her eyes were anguished; those perfect lips parted slightly.

Ethan blinked and looked away, pushing his arms into the sleeves of his jacket. Maybe he wasn't quite as cold, as pitiless as his sense of justice demanded. Seeing her lips tremble would only haunt him later.

"And then he told me about your carefully orchestrated plan. How you agreed to do *anything* for Summerhill, even prostitute yourself to snag a rich husband."

"What?" Her voice was faint. "No."

He turned his back and walked to the window. The lush green of freshly saturated pasture was soothing, but he'd need a whole universe of it to forget Tom's fleshy lips spitting out the truth. According to him, his sister might not have much in the brain department, but she was as skilled as her worthless mother when it came to playing men—and Ethan had been played like a flute.

*Did you think you were the first?* Tom had taunted. *You were just rich and single and about thirty years younger than her usual smorgasbord. Ask her why she came home.*

"You told him you would seduce me," Ethan muttered, "get me—and therefore Magnus—on side. I was your ticket to saving your land."

"No."

Ethan turned to her, glowering. "Can you deny it?"

Her lips moved soundlessly. Something awful—a realization—limped across her face. Then guilt. Somehow, without moving a muscle she seemed to shrink. His heart lurched even lower, his jaw clamped even tighter.

"It was a joke," she whispered. "The first night we met. I was fooling around."

"Very funny." He walked to his luggage, took the briefcase and laptop in one hand and shouldered the big bag.

Damn those trembling lips. He had to get out of here. There was a deal to clinch. He should have known better than to mess with emotions while there was work to do.

An image of his father, smiling benevolently at a twenty-something busty blonde danced in his mind. That one had lasted two or three years but the result was the same. When it ended, she still took his father to the cleaners.

*Ask her why she came home…*

She was frozen to the spot.

He glared down at her. "Why *did* you come home, Lucy?"

Her shoulders jerked. If she was surprised about anything, it was the way he sounded. She had come to love his voice. Deep and smooth as caramel.

She wanted to cover her ears. He was so harsh, so bitingly cold. This was the man she was about to confess her love for?

"The stroke." Her voice wavered. She made an effort. "Dad's stroke." Firmer.

He stared at her face for a long moment. "Wasn't it because Tom stopped the party fund?"

Lucy exhaled noisily, opened her mouth, but he cut her off. Disdain twisted his mouth and he clucked his tongue. "Such low expectations, Lucy. I'm wealthy but hardly in the league of some of the men you entice here. And you'd have to wait a while to inherit."

She just shook her head miserably. She knew she should defend herself. But her words would bounce off that rigid form, the pitiless glitter in his eyes. What had she ever done or said that made a difference to anyone before?

"I had wondered if you were a common gold digger from the first. In your position, it wouldn't be surprising and you were quite open with your charming little quips about wanting a rich husband."

She shook her head miserably. "Ethan, if you can believe that…" Her voice sounded about a hundred years old to her ears.

"I thought you were different. Thought I was a good judge of character—something I will have to reevaluate."

His hands gripped his luggage tightly. He straightened. "Your big miscalculation was, I despise women like you. You must have seen that from the get-go."

Lucy exhaled, a long ragged breath. "Walk away then." Her shoulders jerked in another pitiful excuse for a shrug. "It's easiest."

He jerked his chin toward the table. "My check for the accommodation."

Lucy's eyes followed the movement and stayed there. She heard but didn't watch, knew well enough the sight of a door close in her face. She stared blindly at the table, amazed that there was no pain. Just a constriction in her chest, like the old, familiar iron lung had taken up residency. Without making a conscious decision, her legs took her over to the table. The check lay there, flat, unfeeling.

That was something else she knew well. A check, if not to make you feel better, then to keep you quiet until the next time something rose up and lodged in your throat so you made a fuss about it. Till someone noticed and looked at you, sighed a long-suffering sigh and wrote out another check.

Outside, the van moved off down the driveway, crunching on the gravel. She hadn't even said goodbye to Juliette.

# Twelve

**E**than walked out of the elevator on the ninth floor to the sharp sound of applause. Dog-tired, bemused, he was surrounded by smiling colleagues shaking his hand, slapping his back. The small throng dispersed when Clark approached with a grin as wide as the Grand Canyon. "We got the fax half an hour ago. You did it!"

Clark led him to the anteroom of Magnus's office, still pumping his hand heartily. Even the very proper Beryce, Magnus's PA for twenty years, was rising, smiling, ushering them through the door into the office.

Where was the relief, he wondered as he was enveloped in a bear hug? The triumph? The satisfaction that accompanied revenge?

His boss sloshed overgenerous slugs of cognac into glasses, serving the three of them, lighting their cigars. The excited flow of words between the other two men never faltered. They toasted each other and sat.

"Holy cow, boy! It's the deal of the century, even though it cost me both arms and both legs."

Ethan listened, drank, smoked and chastised himself for his lack of enthusiasm.

"When can you get started?"

He swallowed the burning liquid and squinted through a heavy haze of smoke. "You like the islands, Clark?" he asked finally. "Pack enough for a couple of years."

He drained his glass and watched the delight fade on his mentor's face.

Hours later, fuzzy-headed from unaccustomed afternoon drinking, he walked into his harbor-side apartment, tossed his jacket over a chair and called his father in Perth. "How you doing?"

"What?"

Ethan was ashamed at the astonishment in Jackson Rae's voice. His usual inquiries were about work, or the latest squeeze. They exchanged stilted pleasantries then Ethan took a deep breath. "You're out of the picture for Turtle Island."

There was a long pause. "How did you know I bid?"

"Didn't. I guessed you would."

"Should have known you wouldn't call just to say gidday."

Ethan knew he deserved that. In the silence that followed, he racked his brain to come up with something to soften the blow. He had a lot to learn about building bridges. But you had to start somewhere. "I'm—sorry."

"Must have been a hell of a deal," his father growled.

"It was. I've resigned," he added.

There was another lengthy pause. "You and that old reprobate fallen out?"

"Parted on excellent terms." A throb in his temple reminded him of the depleted level of liquid left in the brandy bottle. They had parted close. Maudlin close.

"What will you do? There is a place for you here."

Ethan smiled at the lightning-quick offer. "Thanks but no, Dad." He heard his father's breath catch. He probably hadn't called him Dad since he'd been a young boy. At school, he was "sir." On his rare home visits, he used "Father," and on his few-and-far-between phone calls he usually just announced, "It's Ethan," to preclude having to use a title. "I'm going to farm."

"Farm? But don't you remember…? You can't rewrite history, son."

Ethan smiled into the phone. "I'm going to try."

The smooth hum of the Nissan wasn't a bit like the Alfa's deeper, frothy growl. She supposed she would miss her status symbol but she'd only had it a few months. Tom had grumbled, but Lucy insisted it would add class to the operation. She wasn't aware back then of how much financial trouble they were in.

A sign flashed by indicating the turn-off for the inland route to the mountains. Why was she not driving to the airport? The smart black briefcase on the passenger seat positively groaned with ready money. Enough to live on for a good while, she considered.

Lucy checked the rearview mirror and indicated a lane change. She noticed the same line by her mouth she had seen that morning, making up. The iron band around her torso seemed to tighten.

Damn him. Wrinkles. A pain around the heart. A ruby-red suit. *I'd love to see you in red.*

But up ahead the morning sun glistened off a jagged jawline of fresh-coated mountains. She forced the sad-

ness away. If she gave in to it, she had better be prepared
to spend the rest of her life running. And if thinking of
a way to save her land kept her from giving in to the
heartbreak that would shatter her, that was as good an
excuse as any in a life full of excuses.

By the time she parked outside the lodge and
marched up to the door of Tom's office, she was resolute. Not nice, malleable little Lucy now. She knew she
was strong. Ethan had given her that, if nothing else.

For the last two weeks, Tom had been subdued and
surprisingly receptive to her suggestions. He felt guilty
about the debts and his part in Ethan's departure, for
which he had confessed all and apologized repeatedly.
She understood better why Ethan had run.

That didn't make it any easier to bear.

Tom had better appreciate her efforts today. She'd
raised enough to cover their creditors and Tom's personal gambling debt—assuming he had disclosed everything. But they would have to generate a lot more
income to cover the payments for the part-mortgage he
had taken out against the property.

Resolute maybe, but she still crossed the fingers of
her free hand.

Her heels clicked across the wooden floor, quick and
sharp. And stopped dead.

Ethan Rae sat across from Tom, the big kauri-wood
desk between them. Her heart seemed to squeeze and
crumple. A kaleidoscope of frantic thoughts whirled
through her brain.

Her eyes drank him in. God, he looked good. Lucy
had tried to forget his features, his commanding presence. Powerful. Alert and primed for success. Without
doubts.

She would not be moved by the warm approval that

leapt into his eyes as they roved over her body. The suit wasn't for him.

She deliberately turned her head without acknowledging him. "I thought we had an appointment."

"Ethan surprised me. Want some coffee?"

Lucy walked toward them on legs that felt like glass. A fierce compulsion to run far and fast tangled up the words in her throat. Before her nerve fled, she placed the briefcase on the corner of the desk and drew out a sheaf of papers.

"There is enough there to clear all our debt, except for the mortgage."

Tom took the papers she offered. "You sold the apartment?" His voice was incredulous. He held up the valuation on the apartment.

"The auction's next week." She didn't divulge the estate agent's warning that an urgent auction rarely reached the reserve. "I sold the car and the painting."

Had Ethan jerked in surprise then? She recalled his interest in the valuable gift from her father. So what? She forced her attention back to her brother.

She had never seen Tom really surprised. His fleshy mouth opened and closed spasmodically.

"God, Luce, this is—stunning."

"There's more." She indicated the large white envelope under the checks. Tom drew out the information on Gamblers Anonymous, flushing deeply. The appointment card was stapled to the front. Ten o'clock next Thursday morning. She would be accompanying him. "And I went to see the police. They're looking into Joseph Dunn. They know him well."

Her hands were empty now. She raised her chin and walked to the window. Minutes ticked by and she knew, by the tightening of her pores, that Ethan's eyes bored into her back. This was her biggest test. Get the business out of the way and escape.

But why was he here? More accusations? Maybe an apology…but that was silly. Why, then, would he be meeting with Tom?

She did not turn around until she heard Tom's exhalation. Wound as tight as a spring, she knew to look at Ethan would unravel her. Lucy acknowledged she would have to go through the pain of losing him one day, but not here, not now and certainly not with him present.

Her brother's eyes shone as he looked up at her. "I don't know what to say. This is amazing." Tom shifted in his chair and Lucy didn't miss the quick conspiratorial look that passed between the two men.

She walked back over to his desk and sat. "We'd be debt-free, Tom, except for the mortgage. So you see, we don't need the club." Of their own accord, her eyes flicked disdainfully to the man at her left. "And we don't need to sell the land."

Tom fidgeted with his pen and shuffled papers. "Ah. Well, that's why Ethan is here. He's come up with a very interesting business proposition."

A shard of ice slipped through the band of steel around her chest. A business proposition? Was he trying to buy their land? He knew their backs were against the wall. He also knew that if he threw money at Tom…

"It's a lease, Lucy," Tom went on. "If Ethan were to lease the arable land from us, it would mean he pays us a lump sum up front and a yearly rent for whatever term we decide on."

"But—we don't need to sell…"

"Not sell. Lease. He'd be like a tenant."

The shard of ice hurtled around in a flyaway panic

that even the tight band around her chest could not contain. It would be impossible to conduct a business relationship with Ethan Rae. Not when she felt the way she did about him. Not when he'd made it brutally clear what his opinion of her was.

She glanced at him briefly, fearfully. "I don't understand."

"Ethan wants to farm. He would set up the farm at his own expense."

Lucy felt stupid and covered it up with a scowl. "No. It's McKinlay land."

Ethan cleared his throat, startling her. "Tom, would you mind?"

Panic gripped her. Don't leave me alone with him, she implored Tom with her eyes. But he was rising, nodding, closing the door behind him.

Silence engulfed the room like a cloud. Lucy tried to hold all that she was feeling in her hands, clasped in a death grip in her lap.

Ethan lounged three feet away, long legs stretched out in front of him. Finally, he spoke. "A lease means that the land is still yours and Tom's, Lucy. You are the legal owners. I would just be borrowing it for whatever period you decide. Two years, ten, twenty…"

She inhaled—as much as possible with her ribs in an iron corset. Since talking was beyond her, she might as well listen.

"The initial lump sum could get rid of your debt."

She flicked a hand at the papers on the desk and felt his eyes on her.

"You are incredible." His voice had altered, from businesslike to soft. "Your family doesn't deserve you."

A hard little knot of hurt made her want to cut. "What

would you know of family? You won't even forgive
your father."

The guilt she felt at that remark irked her even more.
He'd hurt her, dammit. She was sick of sheathing her
claws. Turning in her seat, she faced him. "In fact,
you're not a very forgiving man, are you Ethan? I don't
think I'd like you as a business partner or tenant or
whatever it is you're talking about."

He had been looking at the desk in front of him, but
now he faced her. He was hunched back in his seat with
his hands in his pockets. After a lengthy pause, he spoke.
"Unlike your father, you now have a mortgage to fur-
nish. This way, you will get an income from the land."

Lucy sighed. Confusion—and curiosity—retracted
her claws. "So what do you get out of it?"

"The profits from what I produce. I pay for everything—stock, feed, fertilizer. And I keep the profits."

"What about the lodge?"

"Not affected in any way. The lease would only cover
the productive farming land. You and Tom would continue to run the lodge as you are now."

She was not looking at him but heard the smile in his
voice. "Well, maybe not quite as you are now, I hope."

Lucy didn't smile in return.

"You could implement some of your very good ideas
for the lodge. Once the financial pressure is off, Lucy,
anything is possible."

"Who would look after the farm?" Her voice was
faint. It was inconceivable to her that she would be
sharing this part of the world with this man. She really
would have to run.

"Me."

Panic sharpened her tone. "From Sydney? Or Turtle…Tortoise Island or whatever it is?"

He shook his head.

She was tired of guessing. "You're a businessman, not a farmer," she informed him impatiently.

"Told you I wanted to farm one day."

"One day!" She jumped to her feet. "What about your job? Your big important deal?" She only allowed him a heartbeat or two before continuing. "Thanks for the offer, but don't worry about us. We'll manage."

"I resigned," he told her quietly, looking up at her.

Her heart gave a jolt. Flooded her with something— hope? It slopped against the iron band around her chest.

She pushed it down.

His eyes caressed her face. His expression rocked her—all regret and apology. Another wave of confusion swept her. How different he looked and sounded from the icy stranger of a week ago. How could he hate her, hurt her like that and yet expect to work alongside her? Was it to humiliate her? Her eyes and throat ached with unshed tears. Please go and let me cry in peace, she begged silently, looking down at her shoes.

"Lucy, I'm sorry."

She pursed her lips to quell that damn hope that seemed to swell inside again. His voice was dangerous, reminded her of what they'd shared—and lost.

"Truly sorry." He rose, took two steps until he stood in front of her. His aftershave, tangy and fresh, wafted to her and she breathed it in on a slow careful inhalation.

"I should never have believed Tom and gone off half-cocked."

Her fingers curled into fists by her sides.

"You weren't in the plan, and you know me. I never deviate from the plan." He paused again, but she still couldn't trust herself to speak.

Undaunted by her silence, he continued. "That last day, making love to you, I was *this* close to saying to hell with the job. *This* close to saying I'm not leaving you while everything is crashing around your ears. That scared the daylights out of me."

Lucy heard the snap of his fingers and then her heart beating. Strong, steady, resonant.

"When Tom said what he did, it was a lifeline. I grabbed it and ran."

She could not bring herself to look at him yet, but she had to know. "Wh-what changed your mind?"

He paused. "I was doing the same thing I'd done all my working life. Trying to prove I was better at it than Dad. And this deal—Turtle Island—it was the biggie. The one that would really kick him in the guts because of his history with it."

Lucy did look up at him then. His eyes glowed with regret. "All through this last week, I've thought only of you. Your loyalty and compassion, and how you've learned to cope. Your strength and your wonderful bond with this land. Made my goals seem petty and mean." His voice softened. "And I was missing you bad and feeling like a heel because I'd run out on you, accusing you of something I knew you weren't and could never be."

He flexed and curled his hands. "I was a coward, Lucy. Easier to walk away, close a deal, blame you for something you didn't do, than face the fact that I'm in love with you."

Lucy's heart stopped. She dug her nails into her palms to feel the scrape of something real. Forced her scurrying mind to slow, to comprehend. He loved her? Hope reared up again.

"Make me a better man, Lucy." His smooth, dark voice curled around her, at once soothing and agitating.

"Give me some of that compassion and loyalty of yours. I don't want my son not to talk to me for twenty years."

Her heart jerked again. How was it possible to still be standing while racked with so many different emotions?

So she sat down with a plop. "You are a good man, Ethan," she whispered. "You're kind. You know how to get the best out of people. You understand how I feel about Summerhill, and you've helped me to stand and fight and actually believe I can do it."

"You can do it. You have done it." He pointed at the papers on Tom's desk. "But you don't have to do it on your own." He squatted down in front of her and took her hand. "I'm not doing anything for the next fifty years. Let me help you. Let's make this our business, Lucy. Do it with me."

"I—I don't know what to say." She stared down at him, searched his face and found honesty and sincerity.

"Say you accept my apology. Say you love me, too. Say you'll marry me."

Her eyes blurred. When was the killer blow going to come? Things like this didn't happen in real life.

"I was coming to tell you," she blurted, "the other day, before you left, that I love you. That we'd work it out somehow."

He pressed her hand to his lips. "I'm sorry I ruined it. Say it now. And say yes."

She shook her head in wonder. "You would live here with me, without owning a bit of it?"

"You and Summerhill come as a package deal, evidently." They smiled at each other. "Don't care where we live. We could build up on the gorge, if you like."

"No electricity. No water. No access."

"It's what I do, Lucy."

She nodded, eyes shining.

"Anyway," he continued, "I have property all over the world."

"You do?" Her face fell when he nodded. "But then I'd be like a trophy wife."

Ethan threaded his fingers through hers, kissed her hand again. "You own this incredible land. And if you say yes to the lease, soon you will own the best, most productive high-country station in New Zealand."

She looked down into his eyes. There it was: a warmth and reassurance she could bathe in. A respect and admiration hope could flourish in.

He stood, taking her hands and pulling her up. "Say yes, Lucy."

"What am I saying yes to again?" She could almost hear the iron chains around her torso shattering. Hope, love streaked through the ruins, making her giddy.

"Yes, you accept my apology?"

"Yes."

"Yes, you love me, too?"

"Oh, yes!"

"Yes, you'll marry me?"

She hesitated. "*If* you invite your father to the wedding."

He nodded, smiling. "And yes to the lease. I need something to occupy my time while you're off with your trophy wives."

"I suppose I could put my X to that." She sighed.

Ethan moved back a step. "Almost forgot." He took something from his jacket pocket and handed it to her. "For you."

They were tickets of some kind.

"He is a world-renowned expert on learning disabilities. The seminar is in Sydney next month, which gives you time to organize an assessment beforehand."

Really, she was touched, but old habits die hard. She gave a mock sigh. "Oh, Ethan. But there are lots more exciting things to do in Sydney than some boring old—"

He held up his index finger. "We'll make it a brief stopover on the way to our honeymoon." He slid his arms around her waist. "It's time to front up, Lucy. Stop pretending it doesn't exist and doesn't matter."

She rolled her eyes. "Okay then. If you insist."

She put her arms around him, too, laying her head on his chest. She felt oddly quiet, full—cherished. For the first time in a long time.

Through the window, she saw the line of trees, a guard of honor leading to the river. And beyond, the lofty ridges and steep spurs of the far off Alps, wreathed in snow.

She might not have the best business head in the world, but Lucy McKinlay knew a good deal when she saw one.

# DAKOTA BRIDE

BY
WENDY WARREN

For Gail Springer, dear friend,
who never let me give her a book, but rather bought
every one I wrote and then mailed them to me to
autograph – SAE enclosed! Your humour, support and
encouragement was unfailing and will cheer me always.
And for Brandi, Shawn and Jeremy Springer,
Gail's true loves.

**Wendy Warren** lives with her husband, Tim, and their dog, Chauncie, near the Pacific Northwest's beautiful Willamette River, in an area surrounded by giant elms, bookstores with cushy chairs and great theatre. Their house was previously owned by a woman named Cinderella, who bequeathed them a gardenful of flowers they try desperately (and occasionally successfully) not to kill, and a pink General Electric oven, circa 1948, that makes the kitchen look like an *I Love Lucy* rerun.

A two-time recipient of Romance Writers of America's RITA® Award for Best Traditional Romance, Wendy loves to read and write the kind of books that remind her of the old movies she grew up watching with her mum – stories about decent people looking for the love that can make an ordinary life heroic. When not writing, she likes to take long walks with her dog, settle in for cosy chats with good friends and sneak tofu into her husband's dinner. She always enjoys hearing from readers and may be reached at PO Box 82131, Portland, OR 97282-0131, USA.

# Chapter One

Clouds hovered above the North Dakota prairie like a hand-me-down quilt—cozy and welcome at first, oppressively weighty if you'd been under them awhile.

Annette Owens lifted her face to the gunmetal sky and dared it to *do* something. Almost immediately, a brash wind rose in reply, whipping the dark curls back from her face.

Unclipping the barrette at the nape of her neck, Nettie shook her hair free and laughed. "Touché," she commended, filling her lungs with the crisp, rushing air.

So often lately she felt just like this sky—heavy and stuck. There were times when the desire to change, to…*burst free* became almost unbearable.

Gazing across farmland as achingly endless as the unpatterned sky, Nettie frowned. What would happen, she wondered, if she mentioned the keen restlessness she'd been feeling to anyone she knew—to a friend in town, perhaps, or to one of her sisters?

A smile—wry, self-effacing and just a bit naughty—curved her lips.

"They'd call up Doc Brody, and he'd prescribe enough tranquilizers to sedate the World Wrestling Federation."

A woman with her recent history could not go wild and crazy, after all, without the neighbors starting a phone tree. Not in Kalamoose, North Dakota, anyhow.

And that was, she supposed, understandable. For the past two years, she hadn't stepped foot outside the city limits of her small town, and the city limits of Kalamoose were, to say the least, cramped. For a year before that, she had barely stepped foot outside the clapboard house that stood as a stalwart haven behind her.

Agoraphobia—secondary to post-traumatic stress—that was the official diagnosis of her "condition." In layman's terms, that meant she was afraid. Of everything.

Taking several steps forward, Nettie watched her feet make imprints in the tall grass and pondered the facts.

*Everything.* Yeah, that about covered it.

She was afraid of what had already happened and might happen again and of things that had never happened and probably never would. She worried about her sisters and herself. She worried about her friends and their farms and about what would happen if the price of wheat fell. She worried about hurricanes in the east and earthquakes on the west coast.

And lately, she'd been worrying that she worried *too damn much.*

She hadn't always been this way. Once, she had been more like her sisters, with Sara's courage and Lilah's daring. There had been a time when the world beyond Kalamoose had seemed as tempting as an ice cream in the middle of summer, and Nettie had been ravenous for every delicious bite.

The wind stirred around her, its boldness invigorating. Nettie stood still, spreading her arms to the gathering gusts. When the first drops of rain pelted the ready earth, she began to run.

Her feet were bare, the grass was cool and tender and her summer skirt swirled around her legs as they pumped. She jogged the first steps, then picked up speed until all she could hear was the wind rushing against her ears and the echo-y pounding of her feet against the hard ground.

The rain began falling in slashes, mingling with her perspiration, and Nettie felt her skin cool even as her body continued to heat. She ran like a wild thing, like one of the antelope that roamed the Dakota prairie, refusing to stop even when the toll on her body became uncomfortable, slowing only as she approached the rutted dirt road that marked the end of her property.

Bending forward, she put her hands on her knees. Her shoulders heaved; her breath came in staccato gasps that burned the back of her throat. Her heart pounded the way it did when she had one of those episodes her doctors in Chicago had told her were panic attacks.

For three years, if anyone had asked her what she wanted, Nettie would have answered, "to stop being afraid."

But life, she had learned since, refused to be purchased so cheaply—with the absence of something. And that's what she wanted again: Life. The rain on her face and the wind all around, and her body on fire.

She had no idea, anymore, how to make it happen, or if she even could. It had been so long....

As the rain softened to a drizzle, Nettie straightened and looked up. A pocket of sky was beginning to clear. Shimmying through the clouds were twin arcs of translucent color, as if someone had taken a paintbrush and slashed watercolor across the sky.

A wondering smile curved Nettie's lips. Well, what do you know?

She laughed. A double rainbow. Now, who could ignore a sign like that?

Coffee and grease. Those were the first two aromas Chase Reynolds noticed when he entered the small country diner at quarter past eight Thursday evening...or was it Friday?

Having been on the road, driving, for most of the last three days, Chase was beginning to lose track of time and distance. At the moment all he knew was that he was in North Dakota, and he was starving.

The half-lit neon sign he'd spied from the road said Good Eats. If he'd learned one thing on his impromptu flight across the back roads of America, it was never to eat anyplace with "Grandma's" or "Good" in its name. "Grandma" inevitably turned out to be an ex-mess-hall cook in a love affair with white gravy. Unfortunately, five cups of coffee and a stale chocolate muffin from a gas station mini-mart outside Fargo had carried Chase as far as they were going to.

"Hi, honey. You want the counter or a booth?" A middle-aged blond waitress, whose breast pocket read Gloria in three-inch-tall embroidered white letters, approached him with a menu in one hand and a glass coffee pot in the other.

Falling into habit, Chase took quick note of all entrances and exits off the dining area, pinpointing where he could sit to maintain a view of the door without being immediately noticeable himself. When he realized what he was doing, a wry quirk curled his lips. The art of defensive dining. It came automatically these days—a swift, clever assessment of his surroundings. It hardly seemed necessary in a backwater burg like this, however, which was, after all, why he had chosen to drive through backwater burgs: the blessed anonymity. Most of the tiny towns through which he'd passed hadn't seen a major newspaper since Reagan beat Mondale.

Turning his smile on the waitress, he requested a booth, then followed her to a spot by the window. There was only one other party present, a pair of men who were, at the moment, studying the Porsche Chase had parked out front. Harmless. They could look at the car all they wanted as long as they didn't recognize him. Choosing the side of the booth that faced the door, he sat with his back to the other men.

Accepting the laminated pink menu Gloria handed him, he ordered the first thing he saw, requested a cup of coffee and hunkered over it as the waitress moved off to place his order.

What he needed, aside from a hot meal, was about a week's worth of uninterrupted sleep.

With the desire for sanctuary uppermost in his mind, he had decided to take an old friend up on a long-standing offer to visit a two-hundred-acre barley farm in the "wilds" of central North Dakota.

A wry smile quirked Chase's lips. As hideouts went, the farm ought to do; so far even *he* couldn't find it.

Selecting a package of soda crackers from a wicker basket on the table, he opened it neatly and ate. Once he fueled up—body and vehicle—he'd get back on the road. When he arrived at his destination, he'd sleep as long as his racing mind allowed, and then, God willing, he'd be able to figure out the next step in a game plan he was, after all, making up as he went along.

"Hello!" Stepping over the threshold of the Kalamoose County Jail, Nettie attempted to close the heavy door while she balanced a china dessert dish, a steaming mug with The Fuzz written across it in gold lettering, and a bundle of newly laundered sheets that were folded and tucked under her arm. She glanced around. It was after suppertime on Friday evening, but the sheriff, who'd been at work since early that morning, was nowhere in sight.

"Anybody home?" Nettie called as she stepped farther into the room.

After a few seconds, a figure emerged from the storeroom. Arms full of files, the sheriff greeted Nettie with a pleased smile and a bald, "What did you bring me?"

Nettie shook her head. "No one will ever be able to accuse you of standing on ceremony."

"Ain't it the truth?" The files hit the desk with a thunk and slid atop other papers already obscuring the wood surface. "Everyone knows you got all the manners in the family."

Clearing a space atop the desk, Nettie deposited the hot coffee and a healthy serving of peach pie. She grinned as Sara grabbed the dessert and took an unabashedly hearty bite, leaning against the edge of the desk to eat.

"Yum."

Annette Owens's eldest sister, Sara, had been the sheriff of Kalamoose, North Dakota, since their uncle Harmon Owens had passed away two years ago. Being Uncle Harm's deputy had given their neighbors plenty of time to get used to Sara wearing a badge, and though she was only thirty—and a woman—no one in the otherwise conservative town seemed to have any complaints.

"Heaven," Sara murmured, savoring the dessert. "Net, your baking is getting as good as Mama's ever was."

"Thanks." Nettie accepted the compliment with a smile and a rueful shrug. She baked when she felt tense or blue. Since moving back to Kalamoose, she'd spent so much time with her hands in flour, she felt like the Pillsbury Doughboy.

Nettie was five years younger than Sara, but eons different from her sister in both appearance and manner. While Nettie had inherited her grandmother O'Malley's fall of black curls, fair skin and round curves, Sara took after the Owens side of the family. She was tall and reed-thin, with an approach toward life and people that was as bold and unabashed as her fiery-red hair.

Watching Sara purr over the dessert like a cat lapping cream, Nettie shook her head. "How is it you never gain weight?"

Sara's slim shoulders lifted inside her khaki uniform. "Pact with the devil. Hey!" She stabbed the air with her fork as Nettie idly began stacking the lose pages scattered across the desk. "Don't mess up those papers."

Nettie raised the thin sheaf she'd collected. "These were in order?"

"Well, I know what's there. I'm looking for something."

"What?"

Sara reached for her coffee, blew and took a big swallow. "An all-points bulletin I got last week about— Wait a sec." She cut her explanation short as a police radio crackled to life.

"Watchdog One to Red Sheriff. Come in, Red Sheriff. Over."

The reedy voice of Ernie Karpoun, owner of Good Eats, the local diner, sputtered over the radio.

Nettie arched a brow. "Watchdog One?" Ernie was five-feet-four inches when he wore his lifts, and in all his seventy-two years he'd never weighed more than a hundred and fifteen pounds. Gazing pointedly at the copper hair Sara usually slicked into a low bun, she said, "And what did he call you? Red Sheriff?" She grinned. "Catchy."

"Oh, knock it off! I told him a dozen times not to do that," Sara grumbled. Taking her plate with her, she sat down in front of the radio and pressed a button. "What is it, Ernie?" No response. She rolled her eyes and hit the button again. "Ten-four, Watchdog, what have you got?"

Nettie laughed. She'd been back in town three years now, but there were still times when she forgot how small this place really was.

"What I've got is a pack of trouble ready to happen. I think you'd better warm up the squad car, Sheriff. Over."

"Oh, yeah?" Meeting her sister's eyes, Sara shook her head.

Trouble at the Good Eats generally meant someone had discovered the french fries came frozen. ''What's up?''

''You know that fella who's been robbing banks out toward Fargo? Over.''

Nettie sat on the edge of the desk, glad she'd decided to venture over to the jail tonight. It beat hanging around an empty house. With Lilah in California and Sara at work most nights since her deputy moved to Minot, evenings gave Nettie too much time to think.

Sara leaned over to scoop up another bite of pie. ''Yeah?''

''Our bank could be hit next. Over.''

''Really?'' A tiny smile curved Sara's lips.

Nettie swung her legs as she listened to the exchange. This was far more interesting than a rerun of ''Law and Order.''

For the past several weeks, the evening news had been peppered with stories about a man the media had dubbed the ''Gentleman Caller,'' a tall, well-spoken male between thirty and forty who had robbed no fewer than twelve branches of the Bank of North Dakota, relieving them of hefty five-figure sums each time. According to eyewitnesses, the Gentleman Caller was polite, worked alone and never resorted to violence, at least not yet.

''What makes you think he's interested in us, Ernie?'' Sara asked, lining up another big spoonful of pie. ''Far as I know, the Gentleman Caller prefers savings and loans in bigger cities. We've got a tiny branch of the Bank of North Dakota. I doubt he's interested in us.''

''Yeah? Then what's he doing in Kalamoose? Over.''

Sara nearly choked. ''Explain that,'' she ordered when she stopped coughing.

''That fella is sitting here in my diner right now!'' Ernie's excitement came through loud and clear. ''He come in about thirty minutes ago. I wasn't sure it was him at first, but... Uh-oh. Gloria just waved to me. That's our signal for when he's gettin' ready to leave. He ordered the chicken fried steak platter. It comes with mashed potatoes and corn—it's a lot of food, you know—but he's a quick eater, I noticed that right off the bat. Probably got used to eatin' fast because he's always on the run and lookin' over his shoulder. Bet he swallows a lot of air—''

''Ernie!'' Sara snapped. Nettie had one hand over her mouth, trying to contain her laughter. "Tell me exactly why you think your customer could be the Gentleman Caller. What does he look like?"

"He looks like that drawing they had in the paper a couple weeks back. Kinda normally-like, you know. Gloria says he's good lookin'. Got a few days' growth on his face, probably for a disguise."

Nettie was surprised to see Sara actually taking notes. "You're not seriously considering this?" She shook her head. "Sara, that composite in the paper was so generic it could have been you."

Sara waved at her to hush. Nettie rolled her eyes. None of the eyewitness accounts about the Gentleman Caller jived. Several frightened bank employees swore he'd flashed a gun; others said he'd merely claimed to have one. He'd been described variously as suave, dangerous, unflappable and, by one particularly whimsical teller, sweet.

"And," Ernie's voice crackled across the Kalamoose airwaves again, this time with ominous portent. "He's wearing a Ducks' cap."

"Ducks' cap?" Sara repeated, scribbling again.

"Anaheim Ducks."

"I don't remember that from the bulletin."

"It weren't in the bulletin. But tell me this—what kinda fella roots for a hockey team in a city that wouldn't recognize snow if they stepped on it? Anaheim. Shee-oot!"

Nettie rocked with laughter. Sara shot her a dirty look, then growled tightly into the radio, "Ernie, I can't question somebody because you don't like the Ducks."

"I don't like Anaheim."

Flinging herself against the back of the chair, Sara hurled her pencil at the CB. "Aw, for crying out loud!"

"Okay, Sheriff, how 'bout this: You know how when Gloria puts the food down, she sets the check down, too? Well, this fella paid right away, and when he reached into his pocket, he took out a wad of cash big enough to choke a horse. Smallest bill he had was a C-note. I gotta go into the safe to make change. And he started askin' Gloria about the layout of the town, too. Where's the market and how late does it stay open? And he's been real polite like they say, but he talks quiet, unnatural soft, like he's disguisin' his voice. And he don't make eye contact if he can help it.'' There was a slight pause. ''Over.''

The sudden tensing of Sara's shoulders telegraphed her alertness. Nettie's grin faded. She sat motionless, watching her sister's reaction.

''Oh, boy! Gloria just signaled me again. He finished the potatoes. You better get here, Sheriff, and I mean quick-like. Over.''

Leaning forward, Sara spoke calmly but firmly. ''I'll be at the diner in a few minutes. Keep him there if you can, Ernie.''

''Well, sure we can!'' There was a brief pause. ''How? Over.''

Sara was already on her feet. ''Give him free pie, coffee… Have Gloria spill lemonade on his trousers… You'll think of something. But don't try to detain him against his will or do anything to make him suspicious, you hear?''

''Roger, Sheriff, you can count on us.'' Ernie sounded like a radio spot for the United States Marine Corps. ''Over and out.''

As Sara prepared to leave, her hands moved automatically to her gun belt, checking to make sure everything was in place.

Nettie's eyes widened as an eerie chill skittered up her spine. ''You're serious about this?''

Sara was too preoccupied to reply. She reached for her hat.

Hopping off the desk, Nettie moved swiftly toward her sister. ''Sara, do you honestly think this man is the bank robber?''

Sara answered vaguely, her mind on the business ahead. ''I don't know. Could be.''

Despite her initial disbelief, Nettie's heart began to pound. ''You're not going to go over there alone then?''

''What?'' Sara plucked her jacket off a wooden rack by the door. ''''Course I am. What are you talking about?''

Nettie began chewing on a thumbnail, realized what she was doing and whipped her hand down and behind her back. Scarcely two hours earlier she'd promised herself she would stop worrying and start living.

She'd always had rotten timing when it came to resolutions.

''If this man is the Gentleman Caller,'' she began, knowing she would not win a battle against fear when the safety of someone she loved was at stake, ''then he's a hunted felon. When

hunted felons feel cornered, they strike out. You could be walking into a potentially explosive situation. Call for backup.''

Sara looked at her sister. ''Have you been watching 'Dragnet'
again?'' She headed for the door.

''That's not funny.'' Nettie followed after her. ''Why can't
you wait until—''

''Fifty thousand dollars in reward money if this is the guy,
Nettie.'' It was all Sara had to say. Opening the door, she strode
to a squad car parked by the curb out front.

Nettie rushed outside, alarm bells ringing in her head like a
Sunday call to church. She knew exactly what her sister was
thinking. Kalamoose was in financial distress, nearly bankrupt,
a state of affairs that had become a fact of life for the struggling
farming community. Years ago, Sara had gotten it into her head
that she was going to do more than protect and serve; she was
hell-bent on saving the town she loved. Fifty thousand dollars
in reward money would be a good start.

When Sara wanted something badly enough, she could be
single-minded, unafraid and, too often, downright reckless.

''Don't go!'' Nettie blurted as Sara got in the squad car. ''You
know how Ernie likes to exaggerate. This man probably isn't a
thief at all.'' She endeavored to sound reasonable. ''He's probably a tourist who forgot to buy traveler's checks. You'll be
wasting your time.''

Sara made a face. ''A tourist in Kalamoose?'' She started the
car.

Good point. Kalamoose wasn't even on the way to anyplace.
''A lost tourist.'' Nettie groped for a logical argument, but time
was an issue so she settled for a highly emotional plea. ''Sara,
please don't go there alone. I'll be worried sick.''

The headlights came on, but out of respect for her sister, Sara
took a moment to lean out the window. ''I'm the sheriff, Net,
this is my job. Go home, will you, please? And try to relax.
Play one of those California mood music tapes Lilah sent you.
I'll be home soon.'' She backed away from the curb while she
was still speaking, turned the car and sped down the block.

Nettie stood at the curb, feeling chastened, damned ridiculous—and scared.

She walked back to the jail and opened the door, but changed her mind about going inside. It was cooler on the street, easier to breathe.

All right, so she was a coward. But she'd learned some things about life that Sara hadn't yet…Lilah, either. Like about how even when you were absolutely certain there were no more low cards in the deck, Fate could pull another one out of her sleeve. If she was overly cautious, it was only because she had learned the hard way to grab whatever control she could in life; there wasn't much.

Still, as she stood on the deserted street the bitter taste of shame filled her mouth. Her sister was willing to march into the lion's den, and her own grand contribution to the situation was to stay home and fret.

Leaning back against the cold brick of the building, she gritted her teeth in sheer frustration. Oh, how she had come to loathe feeling alone and afraid.

It was pitch black with a multitude of visible stars in the sky when Chase walked into the Kalamoose jail with his hands cuffed behind his back and his eyes narrowed into two angry slits.

If anyone had told him that his first arrest would come at the hands of a skinny girl sheriff in a town so small you could spit and overshoot the city limits, he never would have believed it. Over the past years, he'd gotten himself into some pretty close calls—pelted by gunfire, detained by officials in three foreign countries and interrogated by the best agents the FBI had to offer. He'd managed to emerge every time without a scratch.

Less than an hour after arriving in Kalamoose, North Dakota, however, he was handcuffed; and that was only after he'd been force-fed pie and soaked to the skin by a flying pitcher of lemonade. He just didn't get it.

"Keep moving!" Snapping the order, the foul-tempered sheriff gave him another in a series of small shoves. Chase clenched his jaw. If she did that just one more time, he would not be responsible for his actions.

As his eyes adjusted to the dim light of the jail, he glanced around, amazed by what he saw. Curtains, cute curtains with ruffled edges, framed every window. The building was old, a squat brick-and-wood structure that looked like it hadn't seen many updates through the years, but there was a vase with flowers perched on a small wood table, and pictures, mostly pastoral scenes of grazing sheep, dotted the walls.

Aw, hell, he thought, stopping dead in his tracks, I've been arrested by the sheriff of Mayberry, RFD.

Irritated by his abrupt halt, the sheriff jabbed him again, "I said—" she began, but Chase spun around before she could finish.

"Do not," he growled, enunciating each word clearly through gritted teeth, "do that again."

To her credit, the gangly sheriff glared back at him, hesitating only a fraction despite the fact that she was a good four inches shorter than his six-foot one.

"Don't tell me what to do, smart mouth," she shot back, "you're the one wearing the bracelets." With a decided lack of subtlety, her right hand moved to rest on her gun. "Your room's on the left." She hitched her chin. "Head over. Continental breakfast is at eight."

Giving her a long, malevolent glare, Chase ultimately complied with the order, largely because he was too damned tired to argue anymore tonight. For some reason, the yokels in this misbegotten haystack had it in for him, and he'd sealed his own fate for the night by failing to provide identification for the good sheriff. He complied with her command s-l-o-w-l-y, though, strolling to the cell as if he was on a nature walk and couldn't be troubled to rush.

If his right to a phone call was granted, he'd ring his lawyer, who was probably tired of hearing from him this month, and then Nick, who expected him to arrive at the ranch, wherever it was, sometime tomorrow. In the meantime all he could do was get some sleep and try not to imagine the publicity this arrest would generate if the AP picked up on it. And that really irritated him, because publicity, good or bad, could only interfere with what he needed to do right now.

His approach came to a halt several feet in front of the cell. Chased blinked, wondering if his tired eyes deceived him: It appeared that the cell on his left was already occupied.

Lying on her side on the narrow cot, eyes closed, hands tucked beneath her cheek, was a woman whose lush beauty seemed almost cherubic. Chase's brows rose. Her ebony curls were glossy and thick; escaping from a loosely gathered ponytail, they tumbled across the blue pillow and against her silky cheek. She wore a round-necked white T-shirt; a thin, waist-length sweater; and a skirt that skimmed a pair of wondrously round hips and long legs. There was nothing intentionally provocative about the way she was dressed; she possessed an inherent sensuality, and Chase felt his body react immediately. The response surprised him. Women had been the furthest thing from his mind of late…though he'd always considered himself a man with an open mind.

"Nettie!"

Behind him, the sheriff's exclamation held surprise and agitation. As Chase took a step closer to the cell, the sleeping beauty stirred. Long lashes fluttered, the cupid's lips twitched. When she opened her eyes, she looked directly at him.

"Well, well," he murmured, a slow smile curving his mouth as if he were flirting at a nightclub bar, not standing in a tiny town jail with his hands cuffed behind his back. "Tell me again, sheriff…what time is the continental breakfast?"

# Chapter Two

Nettie popped up on the cot as if her spine were a spring. Hands braced on either side of her, fingers curled over the edge of the mattress, she gazed at the man standing outside the cell.

From beneath the bill of his cap, his shadowed eyes seemed to gleam, like animal eyes staring out from a cave. Nettie caught a flash of white teeth when he smiled, and her heart skittered with a shot of adrenaline. Frantically, she struggled to shake off the lingering effects of sleep. She had decided there was no way she was going to go home and stew while the action happened someplace else. Unfortunately, exhaustion had overtaken her while she was tidying the jail and she'd dozed off waiting for the action to begin. When the man spoke again, his voice came to her like a slow rolling tide.

"Hello, Sleeping Beauty. Are you always here to greet the inmates or did I get lucky tonight?"

The last syllable had barely rolled off his tongue before he was lurching forward—shoved from behind.

"You keep your nasty thoughts to yourself!"

Sara's ringing growl cut through the fog in Nettie's brain. As the man stumbled and caught himself, Nettie saw the flash of silver binding his wrists. Her breath stopped. Sara had returned with the Gentleman Caller!

Tall, imposing and angry, the bank robber took a deep breath and turned with deliberate slowness to face Sara. He spoke through clenched teeth. "I asked you not to push me again." His tone shifted with such subtlety from the silky drawl he'd used with Nettie that one could almost miss the threat—almost. "Didn't I?"

"Yeah." One corner of Sara's mouth curled derisively. "But you forgot to say please."

Sara! Nettie wanted to wave her arms, stop her sister from saying or doing anything more.

Nettie realized already that this "Gentleman Caller" was not the benign anti-hero the press made him out to be. Tension enlivened his every muscle. There was a final-straw grimness to the line of his lips. Also, he was unpredictable, smiling one moment, growling the next. Moreover, he was large. Even with his hands cuffed behind his back, he would be stronger than Sara. And Sara hadn't yet learned fear.

When he took a step in Sara's direction, Nettie's response was swift and unpremeditated. She jumped from the cot and rushed to the open cell door.

"Leave her alone!" Her throat clutched at the words.

Chase turned at the choked order. His eyes widened when he saw the beautiful woman—Nettie—standing at the cell door like an avenging angel, her lips parted, blue eyes blazing, escaped black curls wild about her face. She grasped the bars of the cell door in such a white-knuckled grip, he was sure the steel longed to cry out for mercy.

His brows swooped into a frown. Why was she afraid? Other than telling Olive Oyl not to shove him, he'd been pretty damn nice so far. What did she think he was going to do? Chase held her gaze, questioning her. It was strange, but everything else faded away in that moment—the jail, the sheriff, his predicament—until he saw only the brave, frightened beauty before him and felt only the tightness in his own chest as he realized that for her, fear was nothing new.

*Don't be afraid, angel, not of me.*

Lost in the silent communication, he took a step toward her, intending to reach up, forgetting the handcuffs on his wrists. He felt the slice of the steel rings at the same time that he saw her jerk back. A second later, he heard the sheriff's gun being whisked from its leather holster.

"Hold it! Take one more step, and you'll walk bowlegged the rest of your days." The sheriff's voice was low and deadly serious. "My gun's aimed behind your knee."

Chase froze. He sucked in a breath, then spoke with forced control. "Really. Which one?"

"That's your guess, smart mouth. Nettie, come out of there." Obviously surprised by the sheriff's threat to shoot, Nettie complied, moving carefully.

It may have been his anger over having a loaded pistol pointed his way, or the stress that had been mounting inside him for weeks... It could have been his frustration over frightening the fragile beauty or all three factors combined, but something inside Chase started to feel like a geyser held too long in check.

He released a startlingly rude word and then bit it off with hard-won control. Turning slowly in the hope she wouldn't shoot him before he could insult her some more, he said, "Let me spell it out for you— I've had all the country hospitality I'm going to take for one night. If there is anyone in this town who isn't one can short of a six-pack, get him over here and tell him to call my lawyer."

"Get in that cell right now, mister! You're making me lose my patience."

Chase responded to her order with a bark of laughter. "That's priceless! I'm being held at gunpoint—probably illegally—and you're losing your patience? Let me guess: That's a toy gun and Barney Fife is your favorite action-adventure hero."

*"Get...in...the...cell."* Raising the gun, Sara spat the words through gritted teeth, her expression suggesting she'd just as soon put a hole in him and toss his carcass in the alley as lock him safely behind bars.

Standing to the side of the cell, Nettie shook her head. If they kept baiting each other, someone was sure to snap. Sara looked like steam might shoot out of her ears at any moment, and the stranger seemed poised to pounce.

When Sara issued another order, to which the man growled, "Make me," Nettie's heart began to palpitate. The desire to flee was almost overpowering. This time, however, she shut her mind against the fear. She could not, would not, allow her anxiety to paralyze her, not when a member of her family was in danger.

Raised voices buzzed in her ears as she used the adrenaline shooting through her veins to move with a purpose. Praying her rubbery legs would continue to hold her, she fled to the storeroom where Sara kept the guns.

It didn't take long to grab the rifle she knew Sara kept loaded. Raising it, Nettie checked and then released the safety lock the way her father and Uncle Harm had taught all three of the Owens girls years ago. Taking a deep, determined breath, she turned and raced back to the cell.

When she arrived, the Gentleman Caller was in mid threat, leaning forward as if he no longer cared a bit about the gun pointed his way. He smiled evilly. "I sincerely hope you know of a good paper route, because when I'm through suing you for false arrest you can kiss your current job good-bye."

Nettie winced. Unbeknownst to him, he'd just hit Sara where it hurt the most. "Is that so?" Sara snarled back. "Let me tell you something. Not only will I have a job after your trial, I'll send you a thank-you note. I wouldn't be surprised if someone named a city—or maybe a bank—after me."

He scowled. "You're delusional."

"No, just happy. In case you haven't been reading the papers lately, there's a fifty-thousand-dollar reward for your arrogant hide—"

"What?"

"—and I'm going to collect it!"

"The only thing you're going to collect is dust while your sanity hearing is pending, you nutcase. Now take these damn handcuffs off me!" His roar shook the rafters.

"Stop it, both of you!" Punctuating the order, Nettie cocked the Winchester. A bullet slid loudly into the chamber.

Chase and the sheriff each gave a jolt and then froze.

Chase turned his head slowly. The other woman, Nettie, stood ten feet away, a wood-stocked rifle hoisted in her thin arms. Her face was flushed and her arms shook so badly it looked like she was dancing a jig with the rifle, but the expression in her eyes was fierce and determined.

"Stop it, I said," she repeated, though no one had moved a pinky since she'd cocked the gun. "You ought to be ashamed, acting like this," she admonished in a voice that telegraphed her strain. "Why can't you behave like a normal sheriff and bank robber?"

"Bank rob—" Chase's stunned protest was abbreviated by the rifle being raised a notch. Figuring he'd tempted fate enough for the time being, he nodded in what he hoped was a conciliatory manner. "Okay. You're absolutely right. We should all calm down." He smiled. "I'm sure we can work out whatever misunderstanding has brought us all here."

"Oh, gag me," Sara muttered.

"I'd love to," Chase growled back.

"That's enough! *I want quiet!*" Nettie shouted the command with more force than anyone including her, thought she possessed.

"Okay!" Chase and Sara answered in unison and each backed up a step.

"I have a problem with tension," Nettie shared with them.

"Okay," they answered again.

"So no more arguing."

They nodded, and she released a long, slow breath. "All right. Now you—" Indicating Chase, she directed him with the gun barrel. "Please step into the cell as my sister asked."

Sister? Chase glanced between the two women. This whole situation was starting to seem more and more surreal, like a Robert Altman movie. Or *Nightmare on Elm Street*. Maybe if he fell asleep on the cot, he'd awaken to find this was all a bizarre dream, induced by stress and a very greasy chicken-fried steak.

He studied Nettie, her eyes wide and glowing blue, like a sea on fire. Wielding a rifle and fighting to be brave only made her seem more vulnerable. Illogically, he had the impulse to comply with her request—for now, at least.

"All right." Slowly, he moved, demonstrating how cooperative he intended to be. "I'll step into the cell." He flicked a quick, sour glance at the sheriff. "But only because you said please."

He was halfway across the cell's threshold when he felt a boot pressed firmly to the seat of his jeans. Caught off guard and unbalanced by his bound hands, he stumbled headlong onto the cot as the boot shoved him forward. Angry as a bull, he let loose a string of oaths as he fell onto the narrow cot and his shoulder smacked into the brick wall.

"Sara! What's the matter with you? I told you to behave."

"I don't have to behave. I'm the sheriff." She pointed to Chase. "And I don't like his attitude."

Chase had never before hit a woman. Fortunately, he thought he could make a pretty good case that this sheriff was no woman.

Lowering the rifle, Nettie took a few steps toward a wood chair. "I can't take anymore. I have to sit down," she muttered. As she collapsed onto the hard seat, her exhausted muscles shook and the rifle slipped from her grasp. The butt of the gun thunked onto the hardwood floor.

KA-BLAM!

The blast that echoed through the jail jolted them all. Nettie heard a shriek, which turned out to be her own, a loud curse—Sara's—and a series of sharp pings as the discharged bullet ricocheted first off the iron cell bars, then the light fixture above the cot, imbedding itself finally in the brick wall behind Chase.

There was a moment of stunned silence from the dazed trio, punctuated only by a tinny creak as the light fixture swayed.

Heart pounding, Nettie looked at Sara, who for once seemed incapable of immediate speech. With his hands still bound behind his back, the Gentleman Caller lowered his head, shaking it. It took Nettie only a moment to realize the man was laughing. The low chuckle was rich with irony and seemed to blend perfectly with the creak-creak of the light fixture.

Nettie looked up. She tilted her head, realizing that the short chain suspending the fixture from the ceiling had been sliced through. The severed link struggled to hang on, but with each rusty creak the connection grew more and more tenuous, and then—

"Oh! Look—" Nettie started a warning she had no time to finish before the hanging light cracked loose, plummeting. It might have landed harmlessly on the cot—if the Gentleman Caller's head hadn't gotten in the way. "—out," she finished.

With his arms behind his back, he had no way to protect himself, even if there had been time. Unfortunately his thin canvas cap offered no protection against the thunk of steel against skull.

A moment's surprise crossed his whiskered face. He blinked and wagged his head as if to clear it.

Nettie and Sara watched open-mouthed as he teetered, looked curiously at the light, then back at them.

"When," he asked, working hard to make his lips and tongue form letters, "do I get my free phone call?"

With that, their Gentleman Caller fell soundly, face-first onto the cot.

"Do you see any blood?"

"A little." Gingerly, Nettie parted the man's dark hair to examine his scalp. "His hair is so thick."

"To cover his thick skull, I suppose."

"Sara, stop it! You're making everything worse. Haven't we got enough trouble?"

"What trouble?" Sara waved a hand at the figure lying on the cot. "He hit his head and got a boo-boo." But she didn't look altogether confident right now, and Nettie was glad to see it.

"He's out cold, and we're responsible," she countered firmly. "If we haven't already killed him, we'd better hope he wakes up with amnesia."

Reaching into her sweater pocket, Nettie withdrew a clean tissue and pressed it gently but firmly against the wound, wincing in sympathy. Though she could never figure out why, the fears that had governed her life the past few years would sometimes abate at the oddest times—when she was in the midst of an actual crisis, for instance. Efficiently, she placed two fingers beneath the man's unshaven jaw to check for a pulse. His skin was warm, alive. He didn't feel unconscious at all.

"Is he still kickin'?"

It took Nettie a moment to register Sara's question. She pulled her hand away quickly. "Yes—" Her mouth felt dry and her tongue thick. She swallowed and tried again. "Yes, his…his pulse is steady. Strong." Like the rest of him.

"Good. So he'll come to and— What do you mean 'we're responsible'?" Sara jumped back to Nettie's previous comment. "This was an accident."

Nettie spared her sister a look that said *puh-lease*. "Is it standard practice to boot your prisoners into the cell?'' She shook her head. ''And I had no business handling that rifle.''

Sara frowned. ''Yeah. I almost had a heart attack. I haven't seen you pick up a gun in years. What got into you?''

''I was afraid the two of you were going to kill each other. And I do know how to handle a gun,'' she reminded her sister for the record. Of herself, Lilah and Sara, she'd always been the best shot, but popping soda cans at fifty paces was different from pointing a rifle at another human being. Still, she refused to take all the responsibility for the trouble they were currently in. And she did sense trouble. Studying the man's features, peaceful and handsome in repose, she said, ''Sara, are you sure he's the Gentleman Caller?''

''What? Of course!'' Sara put both hands on her gun belt. ''Although, I don't have to be positive, you know. I had a reasonable suspicion. And he wasn't carrying ID.''

''Did he say why?''

Sara snorted. ''Yeah. He said he thinks he lost his wallet at a taco place somewhere in Nebraska. I should have arrested him just for being a lousy liar. Plus he's got that wad of cash in his pocket.''

''But if he really did lose his wallet—''

''Oh, come on! He resisted arrest. Why are you defending him?''

''I'm not defending him. I'm concerned. He said he was going to sue you for false arrest.''

''He was bluffing.''

''You shouldn't have bickered and sniped at him.''

''Me?'' Sara gestured angrily. ''He—''

''There's something familiar about him. Without his cap, I mean. He reminds me of someone. Who does he look like?''

Sara crossed her arms. ''He looks like the composite sketch of the Gentleman Caller.''

''Do you have the composite sketch? I haven't seen it since it was in the paper. Where is it?''

Sara hesitated a bit too long. ''I was looking for it when you came in tonight.''

Nettie thought it prudent, for the time being at least, not to comment on her sister's organizational skills. She folded the tissue. ''He stopped bleeding.'' She checked her watch, biting her bottom lip. "He's been out for four minutes now. Maybe we ought to call Doc Brody."

Mere mention of the elderly physician evoked an expression of sheer horror from Sara. "What for?" She gestured to the man lying unconscious on the cot. "You said his pulse is strong." Leaning forward, she gave him a shake. "Come on, buddy. Get up." She jiggled him again. "Come on."

Nettie wagged her head. Doc Brody had mended every broken limb Sara had ever had, and there had been plenty of them. He thought she was an unladylike hooligan. He was also one of only two men who could make Sara feel like she was ten years old again, and she generally went to any length to avoid him.

"Hey, look," Sara said. "He moved!"

"Of course he moved, Sara, you're shaking him." Taking her sister's arm, Nettie directed her out of the cell. "You go get the first-aid kit. It has smelling salts. We'll try that, but if it doesn't work, we've got to get some help."

"All right," Sara said, but she hung back, reluctant to leave Nettie alone. "But if he comes to or even starts to, holler for me and get yourself out of that cell."

"Okay. Now go." Nettie shooed Sara away. "And I only hope you're right about him being the Gentleman Caller," she muttered, turning back toward their guest and studying his face.

Without the cap hiding his features, he seemed more coolly handsome and less dangerous than he had before. A tiny frown nestled between his brows, but otherwise all trace of anger was gone. The lips that had curved sometimes seductively, sometimes sardonically were now soft and neutral.

Ernie had described him as "normally-looking." Nettie thought his face deserved a more creative description than that. His features were refined, projecting intelligence even though his eyes were closed. Eyes open, his sheer physical presence had been unnerving.

She shivered, or maybe it was more of a tingle. He had stared at her, this man. Stared the way she hadn't been stared at in a long, long time.

"Who are you?" she whispered. And what was he doing in Kalamoose? Because something told her this situation was not as straightforward as Sara believed it to be.

When he'd fallen face-first onto the cot, she and Sara had

turned him right side up and straightened him out. Now, if Nettie wanted to, she could reach into the front pocket of his jeans to look for the identification he had either lost, as he claimed, or refused to produce.

Quickly, she glanced toward the storeroom. She could hear Sara rummaging around and swearing, looking for the first-aid kit she probably hadn't seen in months.

Beginning with one hand in front of her mouth, Nettie reached out tentatively with the other, patting the right front pocket of his jeans. She detected the outline of a set of keys. Nothing else. She could have stopped there. She should have stopped there. But something told her to press on, some hunch that he might be carrying I.D.

Gaining a bit more courage, she stretched across the man's body to reach his left side. The tip of her tongue came out to rest at the corner of her mouth as she investigated the pocket below his waistband. She felt something here…something sort of square, but not solid enough to be the wallet. Probably the wad of cash. His jacket had pockets, too. She moved there next.

Nothing on the right. Reaching over to the left side, she hunted around the area of his ribcage, trying to determine whether his jacket had an interior pocket.

As she patted him gently, feeling for a telltale corner or edge, he gave an unexpected jerk. Nettie's hand froze. Looking left, she glanced at his face.

His eyes were open and trained her way. "I'm ticklish," he announced, sounding as bleary as he looked. "Are you?"

Nettie's mouth dropped open. Bent over the cot, she was mere inches above him. "How…how long have you been awake?"

"I'm not sure I'm awake now." He frowned, scanning what he could see of her, beginning at her hairline and ending in the vicinity of her bosom, where her sweater opened to reveal a scoop-necked T-shirt. Gaze lingering, he drawled, "Did I miss any good stuff?"

Nettie whipped her hand from his chest, then felt like kicking herself for betraying her nervousness. Forcing herself to move more slowly, she straightened. "No," she answered as calmly as she could. "Most of the good stuff happened before you passed out."

The Gentleman Caller grunted. With effort, he raised himself to a sitting position, then seemed to remember something and grimaced. "Where's Belle Star?"

His tone conveyed such ominous foreboding, Nettie had to smile. "She's getting the first-aid kit."

"Awww." He groaned and lowered his voice. "You wouldn't let her touch a wounded man, would you?"

This time Nettie checked her answering grin to defend her flesh and blood. "Sara's only trying to do her job. She said you resisted arrest. And," she added, watching him closely, "you fit the description of the Gentleman Caller."

"I look like the Gentleman Caller," he repeated in a murmur, obviously bemused. He seemed to roll the information around in his brain a while, then raised his brows in perfect horror. "You mean that red-headed hellion arrests people she wants to date?" He was wide awake now. "Forget about it—"

"No, of course not!" Nettie interrupted. "What a ridiculous idea."

Relief flooded his face before his expression turned wry. "Yeah, I don't know what I was thinking. After all, everything's been so normal up until now."

Nettie conceded the point. Her concern mounted. As a thief, he could, of course, be an excellent actor, but she was increasingly inclined to believe that they had all made a terrible mistake.

Chase studied the woman before him. She nibbled at her full bottom lip, appearing worried, but no longer frightened of him.

With his hands bound behind his back, he pushed himself off the cot. The dull ache in his temples turned into a pulsing throb. His arms were beginning to feel sore, too. He wondered what time it was, how long he'd been out, but before he could ask, he caught the scent of the woman's hair. Flowers...no...clover. She smelled like the clover fields he'd passed on his way into town.

For more reasons than Chase cared to count, he had no business thinking what he was thinking in regard to this woman. If nothing else, the timing was absurd. Still, he couldn't help but notice that if they stood a few inches closer, the top of her head would tuck very neatly beneath his chin. A good fit...

For the first time, he felt almost grateful for the cuffs around his wrists. If his hands had been free, he might have brushed one of those wild black curls off of her cheek, might have tested her reaction.

His gaze moved where his hand could not. "You aren't afraid of me anymore," he stated softly, with male satisfaction.

Nettie's mouth opened and closed in protest. "I was never afraid of you. I'm just cautious."

Chase grinned. "Where you and I are concerned, angel, caution seems like a good rule of thumb." Leaning forward enough to be heard if he whispered, he couldn't help adding, "Then again, the next time we meet we won't be standing in a jail cell...and my hands won't be behind my back."

Nettie stared up at him, her mouth dry, her palms moist and the sound of the ocean at high tide roaring in her ears. Sara rushed in, saving her from a response, and Nettie had never been so glad for—or so irked by—her sister's timing.

Clutching the first-aid kit, Sara breathed, "Okay, I found it. Now what—" She stopped, realizing the Gentleman Caller was on his feet and that he and Nettie were standing only inches apart.

For a second, no one said anything, then Nettie, feeling as if she'd been caught with her hand in a till, pointed to the suspect. "He's awake."

"I see that." Sara's lips pulled back from her teeth, but it didn't look like she was smiling. "What is going on?" she asked her sister.

The Gentleman Caller answered, nodding toward Nettie. "She was tickling me." A slow smile curved his lips. "I liked it."

Sara stared at her sister.

"I was not!" Nettie denied, swiveling toward the man. "I was not tickling you! I was...conducting a frisk."

He coughed discreetly. "I don't mean to be rude, miss, but I've been searched before and from experience I can confirm that what you did was not at all frisk-like. Now if you feel you could improve, I'd be happy to let you practice." His eyes danced with pure devilish humor.

Nettie did something then that shocked her sister, surprised the man watching her, but most of all shocked herself: She giggled. As the absurdity of this whole situation struck her with increasing clarity, she clapped a hand over her mouth and laughed until her stomach ached and tears rolled down her cheeks. The harder she tried to stop, the more hysterical she felt.

"You should have seen…the look on your face…" Pointing at the Gentleman Caller, she struggled to speak intelligibly through gasps of laughter, "…when the lamp hit your head!"

Somehow it didn't seem to matter any more that this situation was almost as embarrassing as it was ridiculous, or that she usually embarrassed faster than flies found honey. Where pain typically resided, Nettie felt a long-forgotten giddiness, and she caught a glimpse of enjoyment and curiosity on the man's handsome face before tears blurred her eyes again.

"Nettie, what is the matter with you?"

Nettie shook her head. "I'm sorry, Sara, but you should have seen your face, too…when he passed out." She doubled up as the laughter made her stomach cramp. "You looked like you thought he was dead, and you saw your fifty thousand dollars flying right out the window!"

"I didn't think he was dead," Sara snapped, "but he'd be a lot less trouble if he were. And I'd still get my reward."

"Not if he's not the Gentleman Caller, you wouldn't," Nettie countered. "You'd just have a really good-looking dead guy." She dissolved into another round of giggles.

"Thank you." The guy in question grinned. "I think."

As Nettie continued to entertain them with her unusual response, the door to the jail opened and closed. Boot heels scuffed across the hardwood floor, halting at the cell. The three people inside turned toward the newcomer. Sara stiffened immediately. Nettie regained some control over herself, but slowly. "Hello, Nick," she said, grinning.

Nick Brady leaned against the iron post of the cell door, thumbs hooked casually in the belt loops of his denim jeans. Dense brows angled over dark eyes as he noted the hands cuffed behind the stranger's back.

Ignoring Sara completely, he shifted his gaze back to Nettie and nodded. "Good to see you enjoying yourself." Eyes narrowed, he stalked past Sara to stand face-to-face with her prisoner.

The two men were of similar height and build, with Nick perhaps a shade taller and stockier. What they shared was an aura of strength, masculine, arrogant and unequivocal. Nick noted again the suspect's bound arms and a small smear of blood in the upper right corner of the younger man's forehead. This time he turned toward Sara with a glare that was so frankly disapproving, Nettie saw her audacious, defiant sister actually blush.

Turning back to the other man, Nick nodded. "Chase," he greeted, "I see you've met the Owens sisters."

# Chapter Three

Slouched at the kitchen table while Nettie chopped carrots at the sink, Sara ripped the head off a gingerbread man, her sixth casualty in an hour. "It's eleven-thirty," she growled, stuffing her mouth full of cookie. "Why are you doing that now?"

"I told you." Briefly, Nettie suspended the knife. *"Chopping...relaxes...me."* She brought the cleaver down, halving a carrot with a swift, ruthless *thwack*.

Food crimes were on the rise in the Owenses' kitchen tonight.

Nick's arrival at the jail had cleared up a few questions, most pertinently the identity of Sara's prisoner. On his way home from a buying trip, Nick had stopped in at Good Eats, heard from Ernie about the evening's activities and headed directly for the jail, where he informed the women that they had in their clutches—bloodied, verbally abused, handcuffed and nearly shot—Chase Reynolds, special reporter for a top cable news program and Nick's houseguest for the next two weeks.

Well, who knew?

Nettie whacked another carrot. Bad enough she'd nearly shot a man who'd once won a William Jay award for excellence in on-camera reporting; she'd also frisked one of *People* magazine's "Fifty Most Beautiful People." It didn't seem funny anymore.

"We should have recognized him," she muttered, not for the first time. "This is what comes from discontinuing cable. Although how you could arrest a man when you don't even have a composite sketch to ID him is really beyond—"

"I told you." Sara slapped her cookie onto the table. "I *had* it. I just couldn't *find* it. And as far as I'm concerned, he was just another suspect. I was following protocol."

Nettie paused in her chopping to lean one hand on the counter, the other on her hip. "When you were insulting him or when you were punting him into the cell?"

"That's it!" Sara shoved the glass of milk away from her, scraping her chair back from the table. "I don't have to listen to this." She stabbed a thumb at her own chest. "I had a reasonable suspicion."

"Really. What tipped the scales for you, Sherlock, the fact that he's a fast eater?"

Sara gaped at her sister. "What is the matter with you tonight? You've been sniping at me since we got home." She waved a hand. "I don't see what you're so upset about, anyway. He's not going to sue *you*."

"I'm sorry." Nettie put a hand over her eyes and shook her head. "It's just all so…humiliating! But don't worry, he won't sue. We're not important enough for him to sue." She resumed rapid dicing. "By the time he leaves here we'll be just another cocktail party anecdote. Something to entertain Barbara Walters with while he's stirring martinis: 'Did I ever tell you about the time I was held captive by two women in Kalamoose? One olive or two?'"

"Well if that's all we have to worry about, big deal. Who cares what he says to Barbara Walters as long as he doesn't cause trouble around here?"

*I do.* "What's someone like Chase Reynolds doing in Kalamoose, anyway?" Nettie tried to sound offhand, but her true interest felt almost raw in its intensity. "How do you suppose he met Nick?"

"I don't know, and I don't care," Sara replied unsatisfactorily. She took a last swallow of milk. "I'm going to bed. I've got a lot to do tomorrow." Crossing to the swinging door that led to the dining room, she paused. "Listen, about you grabbing that rifle tonight—"

Nettie groaned. "Don't remind me. I swear I will never again touch one of your guns, just please, *please* do not talk about it!"

"No, no, I wasn't going to... I mean I'm not upset. I—" Never one to speak easily about her feelings, Sara scratched her neck and shifted uneasily. "I just wanted to say, you know...thank you." She shrugged. "I know you were trying to protect me, and... I think you put the fear of God into him when you knocked off that shot." A smile nudged her freckled cheeks. "Put it into me." Hesitating a moment longer, she nodded toward the severed carrots. "Bet those would make a good cake." Wishing her sister a good-night, she left the kitchen and headed upstairs.

Nettie pressed her palms to her cheeks. She stood like that a moment, breathing, trying not to think at all. Then she dragged a plastic container out from one of the bottom cabinets and put the carrots in the refrigerator.

Twenty minutes later she was upstairs, a pink terry robe wrapped around her just-showered body, her mind still as active as a kitten with a ball of string. Forget sleep.

Tiptoeing past Sara's room, Nettie headed for a small attic work studio. Stepping inside, she closed the door softly behind her.

The room smelled pleasingly of canvas and paint and of the oil-based pastels she arranged by hue in old soup tins and plastic cups. This was her private aerie, the sanctum to which she escaped each day. When she flicked the light on, a soft yellow glow illuminated her easel and drawing board and a corner desk, where she wrote the children's stories that were winning a loyal and ever-growing audience. A bookshelf she'd hand-painted housed copies of her There I Go Again books, a series of illustrated tales featuring a little boy named Barnaby, whose incredible adventures took place at night while his parents were sleeping. Barnaby trotted the globe, engaging in acts of daring or heroism or simply having outlandish good fun and then returning home to a bed shaped like a racecar and to parents he trusted to keep him safe.

Crossing to the bookcase, Nettie ran her fingers across the

spines of several books, then touched the top of a small pewter frame. Her body stiffened as she awaited the customary catch in her throat.

Inside the flower-stamped border was a five-by-seven color snapshot of a man and woman barely out of their teens. The girl sported a purple maternity top with a big golden happy face over her protruding belly and the young man wore a smile that gave validity to the description "a mile wide."

She and Brian. Back in the days when they'd expected only good things to happen.

Nettie held the picture with both hands. Sweet longing filled her chest even as her stomach muscles clenched with a pain so bitter she thought she could taste it. They'd been so trusting—two children bringing a baby into the world.

Anger snaked up from her belly like a weed threatening to choke her. Falling in love and having a baby were acts of faith that should have been rewarded.

And they had been, she supposed, for a time. The photograph was evidence. Also on the bookshelf, propped on a small display easel, was a likeness of her son's face, sculpted from clay then cast into plaster. One of Brian's art projects. Smooth and perfect in illusionary 3-D, it seemed capable of coming to life. Brian had intended to sculpt their son's face every three years, beginning with age two and a half. This was the only sculpture Nettie had. She kept it on the shelf even though it was fragile, even though there was only one. And she was grateful that she had it. Although there were times when touching it—tracing the nose and the chin and the brow—served only to increase her loneliness.

Every day for three years she had tried to remember…and tried not to. What good, she sometimes wondered, were memories when the heart couldn't touch hair or skin, the heart couldn't hold hands with Brian or press kisses against Tucker's soft, soft cheek?

And she wanted that. God, there were times when she didn't think she could live another minute without it—one more chance to touch.

Returning her focus to the picture of herself and her husband, she flattened her fingers against the cold glass protecting the photo as tears began to run, salty and hot, over her lips. She'd been living in limbo, and she knew it. Couldn't go forward, couldn't back up. A quick, watery laugh escaped her lips. Brian would have hated that for her.

She had begun to hate it herself.

She closed her eyes and a man's smile—not Brian's—came into view. A smile so recent she could still see it without effort: Wry and searching, flirtatious and bold. And then, as if Chase Reynolds were there in the room, she felt again the deep-down tingle, the chord of anticipation his smile had struck.

Opening her eyes, she noticed that her hand was starting to shake. Holding the picture frame tightly against her stomach, Nettie turned toward her desk. Her legs felt so heavy and wooden she had to command them to move. When she reached her desk, she opened a bottom drawer.

The pain in her stomach rose to her throat and like the anger, it squeezed. She bit her lip as she placed the photo gently inside the drawer.

"Oh, God."

For an instant she thought she might stop breathing, honestly felt as if she'd pushed a red button that could destroy the whole world. She waited, feeling the pounding in her chest, the tightness of grief.

It was then, with a clarity that seemed brittle, that she understood more completely the awful price of choosing to go on.

Standing, she sent a brief, silent apology to heaven. She'd been a girl when she'd married, barely a woman when she'd lost everything she loved most. With all that had passed since then, she'd earned her womanhood. Chase Reynolds was the first man who made her want to explore it.

She didn't expect to have what she'd had before—the hopes, the dreams of a future. The innocence. Not with him or any other man. She didn't even want that. With a new relationship, one that was obviously impermanent from the start, she wouldn't have a whole thunderstorm to deal with. Just a little bit of lightning to say she was still alive.

Looking down at the drawer, Nettie drew a breath that felt like needles pricking her lungs. Then she made herself whisper what had to be the most difficult word in the whole English language. "Goodbye."

\* \* \*

It was 10:30 a.m. when Nettie guided the Owenses' old wood-paneled Jeep Wagoneer up the long drive that led to Nick's farm. Patches of wild mustard splotched the bright emerald grass leading to the house. A gentle breeze snatched the echo of clover from fields across the road, scenting the air with a clean spicy freshness. As moderate as the temperature was outside the car, however, inside the vehicle it felt like high noon.

Perspiration bathed Nettie's forehead and upper lip. Her palms were sweating, her back felt clammy and her stomach whirred like a washing machine stuck on "spin."

She hadn't driven alone in years, not since she'd started having anxiety attacks in the car. The first time she had a panic attack while driving, she'd thought that surely she would lose control of the vehicle. For no reason at all, it had seemed, she had begun to feel hot and clammy, then nauseous, weak and scared. Her arms had started to shake, her vision had blurred and her heart had pounded and raced and skipped beats. The more she had fought the sensations, the worse they had become. By the time she'd reached home, she had been exhausted and utterly confused about what had just happened to her. When she had another attack two weeks later, she went to see her doctor. "Post-traumatic stress," he had called it. It felt like impending death.

Eventually Nettie had stopped driving unless there was someone in the car with her, hoping to avoid the sudden attacks. She knew more now about anxiety attacks, what they were and what they weren't, but she hadn't yet overcome her fear of driving alone. Unfortunately Nick's farm was not within walking distance. If Nettie wanted to see Chase Reynolds again—without Sara in attendance—she had to get behind the wheel all by herself and drive. She'd spent half the morning convincing herself she could do it. She'd spent the other half getting ready.

For a jolt of confidence, she had chosen to wear a gauzy dress that Lilah had sent her from a chi-chi boutique in Los Angeles, but now the thin material glommed to her back in a decidedly less than chi-chi way.

Plus, a glance in the rearview mirror showed that her makeup was running south. "Very seductive," she muttered, scrounging in her purse for a tissue to blot her damp forehead and cheeks.

At least focusing on her appearance allowed her anxiety to abate somewhat and by the time she pulled up to Nick's house, her body felt more pliable again.

For a minute she sat, taking in the realization that she'd done it—she'd driven!

The remaining jitteriness in her limbs began to turn into a feeling of excitement. "Oh, my gosh," Nettie whispered. To someone else it would have been a small thing, not an accomplishment at all. But she understood the importance of what she had just done—and the reason she had done it. Chase Reynolds was obviously a powerful prescription.

Peering through the windshield for signs of life, Nettie squared her shoulders and opened the car door. Her sandaled feet had barely touched the hard gravel when she heard the wet snuffle of an equine snort. Assuming Nick was out for a ride on King, she felt herself relax a bit more.

Nick was an old friend who knew about her anxiety attacks. Picturing his surprise when he saw her emerge from behind the driver's seat, Nettie allowed herself a taste of victory.

"Good morning." She smiled broadly as she turned. "I bet you didn't expect to see me here all by myself, but I— Oh." Her smile turned to stark surprise when she saw Chase Reynolds astride King.

Nettie stared at him. He stared back.

He'd shaved since last night. There was no mistaking his identity now. He looked exactly like his picture in *People* magazine—masculine, intelligent, hazardous to a woman's peace.

They each waited for the other person to speak.

Bringing his right leg over the saddle, Chase dropped to the ground. He was hatless, his eyes masked only by an unreadable expression.

"You were saying?"

Nettie blinked. Heat sizzled steadily through her body, and suddenly her brain seemed too full. She was saying…

Chase raised a brow. He walked forward, bringing the horse with him. "You bet I didn't expect to see you here all by yourself, but you…" he prompted.

Nettie licked her dry lips and mustered a smile. "Um, I thought you were Nick."

Black eyes narrowed. Tilting his head, he considered the admission. "You're not here to see me?"

"You? No." Caught off guard, Nettie squeaked the denial. "I..." She shook her head. "No."

"Hmm." He frowned, musing. "That's funny. Because actually, I *was* expecting you."

Nettie stared at him. Embarrassment crept up her neck as she imagined those night-dark eyes reading her thoughts. Okay, so she *had* arrived here this morning hoping to flirt with him, or rather, hoping he'd flirt with her. But even before anxiety, she had never been the kind of woman who could admit to such a thing.

"Actually, Mr. Reynolds, I didn't know you'd still be here."

He scratched his neck, obviously unmoved by the denial.

"If I had known," Nettie insisted, a distinct chill in her voice, "I certainly wouldn't have shown up unannounced."

He brushed at a fly that buzzed past.

"Right, I am here unannounced," she conceded. "But not to see you."

"I just thought you might want to apologize."

"Apologize?"

"It's the usual practice after you've nearly shot an innocent man, Ms. Owens." He shrugged. "Maybe that's a city custom."

He stood calmly, looking down at her.

It was his straight-faced irony that eventually penetrated her attempt to remain cool. A smile tugged at her mouth, urged her cheeks, and she relented, nodding. "You're right. I should have come here to apologize. How's your head?"

Chase rubbed the spot where the lamp had smacked him. "Not bad. Although my barber once told me I had a perfectly shaped head, so I never had to worry about going bald. I guess that's shot."

She laughed outright at that. "I really am sorry."

The breeze pulled a lock of her hair across her face. It caught between her lips, and she brushed it away. Chase watched her steadily, his gaze focused on her mouth.

Nettie felt her gaze drop to his mouth, too. It was closed, lips firm. When she looked back up, into his eyes, she felt her heart thump with adrenaline. They were like two animals on the prairie—circling, watching, testing. She waited as long as she could for him to make the next move, but the anticipation made her feel like a balloon ready to pop. Feeling her heart beat faster, she gathered her courage.

"Can I make it up to you?" she asked, her voice sounding as if she'd swallowed too much prairie dust. "How about dinner while you're here? As amends for all you've suffered. Nick's not much of a cook, but I'm pretty fair, so you could consider yourself safe. Not much chance of food poisoning or of offending the chef by having to rush out for a burger or anything." She smiled.

The wind whipped up again. This time he reached for the hair that blew in front of her face, pushing it back with a touch as subtle as a whisper. His knuckles brushed her cheek and even that slight touch sent a shiver through her. "I bet there isn't a burger joint within twenty miles of here," he said.

"That's true," she agreed, too breathlessly. "There's only Ernie's."

"Ernie's?"

"The diner."

"Ah." He nodded. "Pass."

Nettie wondered if he knew that a little groove appeared between his brows when he was thinking. Or that the laugh line on the right side of his mouth was deeper than the one on his left. His smile seemed to begin mostly on the right....

She was still lost in her study when Chase said quietly, "Well, Miss Nettie Owens, I thank you very much for your offer. Dinner isn't necessary, though. And you have nothing to make amends for."

Was he letting her know he wanted dinner to be her choice and not her obligation, Nettie wondered? The possibility made her feel flattered and satisfied, and some of the lightness of the morning seemed to enter her own spirit.

"Oh, sure, you say that now," she replied, engaging in some teasing of her own. "But one day I'll turn on the TV and there'll you'll be, telling Mike Wallace all about last night. I'll come out looking like the bad guy, and I can't have that. I'll have you know I won Miss Congeniality twelve years ago at the Kalamoose Founder's Day Fair." Her tone suggested he ought to be mightily impressed.

Chase smiled, the humor deepening in his eyes, and Nettie's courage took flight. "So now you'll have to come over, if only to preserve my reputation." She smiled more freely. "I'll make stew and soda bread. My mother's family was Irish. I have a great recipe—"

"I can't." The refusal was swift and decisive.

Chase's expression grew taut. Softness and humor vanished like mist, and his voice became a gravel-paved monotone. "I'm not going to be here very long, two weeks at the most. It's going to be a busy time. Thanks anyway. Is there anything you'd like me to tell Nick?"

*Nick.*

"He's not here. But I can give him a message."

*Oh, that Nick.*

Nettie frowned, trying to think. Chase's mood, his entire being, had altered so rapidly, she couldn't quite grasp what had just happened, other than the fact that she'd been rejected. Thoroughly. Utterly.

Swallowing hard, she decided that getting out of here with even a smidgeon of dignity was now her first order of business.

"Nick," she said, forcing her mind to work. "Yes, please do tell him…" *What?* She gave a small shake of her head. Chase Reynolds had a life filled with adventure and amazing people. *Come over…I'll make stew?* What had she been thinking?!

"Please tell Nick," she continued, "that I came by to pick up the eggs." The lie emerged in a voice too strained to sound wholly genuine. "He usually brings some to the house each week." That much was true. "He's been so busy lately, though, I thought I'd save him the trouble."

She should have let it go at that and left, but with no hint to suggest Chase believed her, Nettie felt the compulsive urge to try harder. "He always has extra. Eggs. Nick does. His chickens are such good liars—layers!" *Oh, my God.* Chase Reynolds gave no indication that he noticed the slip, but Nettie began to speak double-time to cover it up. "I use the extra to make cakes and muffins…" She pointed again. "There's a nursing home on Fifth and C Street. They love sweets. Of course, there is the cholesterol issue, but when you're pushing eighty, who's counting, right?" Smiling broadly, as if this were an actual conversation rather than one person's rambling attempt to sound convincing, she closed with a brisk nod. "Well, I can see you're not an egg man. So, I'll just come back another

time. Oh! If you think about it, you can tell Nick I plan to
make that stew sometime this week. He loves Irish stew.'' She
nodded again. ''Well, so long.''

Taking a step toward the car, relief almost outweighed disappointment until she realized that now she was going to have
to drive back, her efforts fruitless, feeling more alone than she
had when she set out this morning.

Nick's absurdly long driveway loomed ahead of her like a
broad jump. The nausea that had blessedly subsided rolled inside her again now and she knew she couldn't face another
anxiety attack, not yet.

''If you don't mind,'' she said hoarsely, reluctantly glancing
around, ''I think I'll—'' Chase was already heading toward the
barn with King, oblivious to her dilemma.

''—sit on the porch and wait for Nick,'' she finished, speaking aloud to Chase's departing back. She watched him go, resentment beginning to edge out embarrassment.

Maybe she was no longer the calmest person in three
counties, but at least she was polite and consistent. Chase
Reynolds had just made Dr. Jekyll and Mr. Hyde seem pre-
dictable. Had she *completely* misread him last night? Her exhalation turned into a dismal sigh. She was so out of practice
with this whole man-woman thing. Come to think of it, she
hadn't had a first date since high school.

Trudging up the porch steps, she seated herself with a thunk
on the blue-painted wood.

This was worse, far worse even than high school, when the
boy you had a crush on ignored you and you spent your lunch
hour in the girls' room crying into a wad of toilet paper. Pulling
her legs toward her chest, Nettie lowered her forehead to her
knees.

There was never a girls' room around when you needed one.

Chase paused outside the barn, his conscience and his ego
taking turns pummeling him.

If the lovely Nettie had come to see him, then he probably
ought to be shot for the way he'd treated her. If, on the other
hand, she'd merely come to pick up eggs from Nick— Muscles

bunched in Chase's jaw. He didn't like that possibility one little bit.

Whipping the reins over King's ears, Chase made the horse prance nervously and had to pause a moment to settle him down.

He doubted there was another woman in North America right now capable of making him rethink his moratorium on women, but something about this Midwest country girl got under his skin. *Everything* about this Midwest country girl was getting under his skin.

Chase shook his head. He'd had relationships with models, news reporters, a foreign head of state once. Sophisticated, fascinating women about whom he had never lost his objectivity. Maintaining emotional distance was one of his innate gifts.

That gift warned him clearly now: A hometown girl who hung curtains in a jail was not someone to add to his little black book.

His yearning in response to the simple offer *Come over...I'll make stew* had scared him, made him feel like he was standing in a minefield. Domesticity was not detectable in the Reynolds family's DNA pattern. As a rule, he only dated women who shared the same biological aberration.

That left Miss Nettie Owens clean out of the running. Which brought him back to the source of his present agitation: He'd had no business flirting with her. And *absolutely* no business wanting to hear her say she'd come to see him rather than Nick.

Shaking his head in disgust over his lack of mental discipline, Chase led King toward his stall. "I suppose I should have unsaddled you outside," he told the large gelding, trying not to listen for the sound of Nettie's station wagon pulling away, "but we can handle the cramped quarters."

Soon now he would have the results of the DNA tests he'd taken before he'd left New York. Maybe then he'd be the pilot of his own mind again. It was the damned living in limbo that bothered him the most.

Holding the reins in his right hand, Chase reached with his left for the door to the stall. A flash of movement caught his eye. Before he could investigate, King was rearing, pawing the air with his front hooves and neighing in distress. The horse nicked Chase's forearm on his descent, then reared again.

"Whoa! Hang on there." Confounded by the horse's behavior, Chase tugged the reins. "Settle down!" King was not re-assured by a stranger pulling on his bit and became more ag-itated.

Chase stood too close, crowding the large animal, and this time when King dropped to all fours, the big animal caught Chase's shoulder with enough force to off-balance them both. Falling into the stall, Chase let go of the reins and the horse took off like a shot.

Outside, Nettie saw King emerge from the barn in a near panic. She stood as the horse headed for the barley field, changed his mind and turned sharply toward the house.

She was down the porch steps in a flash. In years gone by she'd ridden King with great relish. She knew the horse well, and once she caught sight of Chester, Nick's cat, sitting calmly outside the barn door, cleaning his paws, she had a pretty good idea of what had spooked the sensitive gelding.

King snorted and stamped the ground as Nettie approached. "Shh-shh," she soothed. "Shh, you're all right." Carefully, she reached for King's bridle. "Did that big old cat scare you again? Hmm?" Stroking the bridge of his nose, she guided him gently as he calmed, so that he was facing the barn again as the cat strolled leisurely toward the side of the house. She con-tinued her ministrations as Chase reached them.

"I don't know what happened in there." Without preamble, he described the scene in the barn. "I was trying to get him into the stall, and he took off."

Nettie sent a sidelong glance to the man at her side. Bits of straw stuck to his crisp jeans and shirt. A larger piece of hay nestled in his mahogany hair. Rumpled and bemused, he seemed more approachable than he had earlier. Nettie felt her pulse increase—with interest, not nerves—but she pasted a cool expression on her face. "Mmm," she murmured, "maybe he didn't like your attitude, Mr. Reynolds."

Dark brows spiked in surprise. Nettie held his gaze. Slowly, a reluctant smile edged Chase's mouth. "You think that was it?"

Hesitating a moment, Nettie shrugged. "No. Actually," she nodded toward Chester, "there's your culprit."

Following her gaze, Chase squinted, then brought his hands to his hips and craned his neck forward. "A cat?"

"Mm-hmm. King and Chester have a long and complicated history."

"Is that so?" Chase massaged his sore shoulder, eyeing King with displeasure. "So the cat was in the barn." He shook his head. "You're not going to tell me a big animal like that is afraid of a stupid little cat?"

"Chester isn't stupid." Nettie countered. "And King is perfectly comfortable around an average barn cat. He's only afraid of Chester."

"What the devil for?" When Chase raised his voice, King danced unhappily again. Nettie cooed to him as if to a child before she explained.

"Chester is wily. He jumped on King's back years ago when they were both young and scared the heck out of him. Once he got that reaction, he dedicated himself to tormenting King every chance he got. Call it little-man syndrome. He's not allowed in the barn anymore. Usually Nick keeps Chester in the house when King is out."

"I let the cat out this morning," Chase confessed. "He was meowing."

"Ah." She smiled at his sheepishness. "Well, no real harm done. King just had a good fright, didn't you, boy?" Nettie pressed the length of her palm against King's forehead. He pushed back, nuzzling into her.

Chase stood to the side, watching her soothe the horse. She communicated with the big animal, no doubt about it, by look, by touch. "You're good with him."

Lightly, she ran her knuckles along the soft area of King's nose, ducking her head so that she was almost forehead to forehead with the horse. When finally she turned her head to glance shyly at Chase, he felt his stomach muscles clench. "This is something I know a bit about," she said.

Chase felt bewitched. "Horses?" he murmured.

Nettie meant fear, but didn't say so. Patting King's neck, she said, "I think he's calm enough to unsaddle now. I bet he'd enjoy a good rubdown, too, wouldn't you, fella?"

With one hand on the bridle and one holding the reins, she walked King to a post outside the barn. Chase followed, admiring the grace of her movements, noting and enjoying the quick glances she directed his way as she looped the reins around the wood.

With her hand on King's neck, she spoke to Chase, but it took him a moment to register the soft request: water. She wanted a bucket of water, a currycomb and a brush.

"Can you find all that in the barn?"

Chase nodded. He wouldn't be able to find his own head with two hands and a flashlight if he didn't stop staring at her.

He answered gruffly, "Right," then turned and strode into the barn.

Looking for a currycomb seemed like an innocuous activity, but then the fresh bedding in the stalls reminded him of all the Westerns he'd seen in which the hero and heroine eventually wound up lying in straw....

Picturing Nettie with straw in her long curly hair wasn't much of a mental leap.

Clenching his jaw, Chase concentrated on collecting the grooming supplies, but the image of her hands, gentle and feminine, and her amazing innocence as she awkwardly asked him to dinner refused to leave his mind.

He'd had a damned hard time not questioning Nick about her last night, trying hard to convince himself there was nothing he needed to know.

With a bucket of water in one hand, brush and currycomb in the other, he walked into the sunlight, frowning when he saw that Nettie had unbuckled the cinch and was attempting to drag the heavy saddle from King's back. The Western-style gear was cumbersome and though she didn't appear weak, unsaddling the tall horse was obviously an effort.

Immediately, he wanted to take over and wondered if she would care about the political incorrectness of his response. There were women in his circle who would throttle him for interfering.

While he hesitated, King shifted sideways toward Nettie. She murmured to him, balanced herself and repositioned her grip on the saddle. Chase heard her count, "One, two, three," then watched her heave the saddle up and off the animal's back just as Chester the Devil Cat strolled lazily—and deliberately— within view of the horse.

"I'll be damned—" Chase began in amazement, then forgot

about the cat as King fussed and bumped into Nettie, throwing her off balance. She began to teeter. Trying to calm King and save herself at the same time proved to be too much, and she stumbled, emitting a little yelp as she started to fall backward.

The yelp did it.

Chase dropped the bucket, tossed the grooming tools and was behind Nettie in a flash. She was slight enough that his arms circled her with ease as he reached for the saddle she clutched to her belly. Sandwiching her between himself and the saddle with a triumphant "Gotcha!" he felt her slender shoulders, the curve of her derriere and finally the back of her head as she stumbled against him. He'd have to be a mannequin not to react to the feel of her.

He hung onto the saddle more easily than he did his sanity while she steadied herself. Her sandaled feet danced around his borrowed cowboy boots, and the scent of flowers wafted up from her hair so that he barely registered pain when she ground her heel on his instep.

Chest to back, they breathed together. He felt her body expand and contract, felt his own breathing quicken in time with hers. His biceps bunched as he carried the weight of the saddle, but what he really noticed was the softness of her arms against the hardness of his. This was not an effective way to avoid thinking about her. Chase stayed very still, hoping she wouldn't notice that body parts other than his biceps had gone rather...solid. His mouth twisted wryly. He was reacting like a high-schooler with runaway hormones.

When she was balanced on her own two feet again, she pulled away slightly, tilted her head up and around and said, so softly that he had to read her lips to make out the words, "Thank you."

Chase nodded. And gritted his teeth. *Those lips.* Soft, lush, ripe. Cupid had drawn them to drive a man crazy.

*Neutral,* he reminded himself. *Think of Switzerland.*

Tensely, he waited for her to turn around again or to slip out from beneath his arms...something. But she stayed put, eyes so wide and so beautiful that he wanted to capture them on film.

He failed to come up with a single neutral thought that would stick as his gaze locked with hers, as the delicate, perfect parting of her lips made her look as if she were on the verge of saying something.

If his expression conveyed anything at all, she must be able to guess what he wanted. And yet she didn't turn away.

Directly under his gaze, her breasts rose and fell, and he thought—in fact, he could have sworn—he heard her sigh.

*Switzerland. Capital city, Bern. Swiss...banks. Swiss...chocolate. Swiss...*

"Ah, to hell with it—"

Forced between his teeth, the words hovered between them for a moment. Then Chase answered the mild surprise on Nettie's face by claiming that glorious mouth with his own.

# Chapter Four

He meant it to last a moment; but her lips were soft and tasted like cherries, so he lingered a moment longer and then—

Chase stifled the groan that wanted to rise from his belly. Her lips parted—just a bit—but the temptation to press his mouth more firmly against hers became irresistible.

Holding the saddle in his hands was an exercise in frustration. He craved the freedom to turn her around, thread his fingers through her thick, curly hair and let his other hand roam where he knew it shouldn't.

Guilt made his muscles tighten. He had no business kissing her like this. She was trapped between the saddle and his chest. He hadn't asked if he could kiss her and he didn't want it to go any further…. He didn't.

Exerting more effort than it usually took to finish his last set of curls at the gym, Chase tensed his jaw, stopped kissing and lifted his head. Then he stared down at the beautiful woman before him.

Her eyes remained closed a while. When her lids fluttered, she looked up and Chase found himself staring into two huge blue pools of soft dreamy surprise.

He almost growled.

He didn't want innocence in a woman. Never had. Where there was innocence there was also expectation. The only expectations he ever wanted to live up to were his own.

"I need to put the saddle down." His voice was a disgustingly weak croak.

Nettie blinked at him dazedly, then nodded. "Yes." Smiling a little shyly—which, dammit, made him want to kiss her again—she glanced around, finally deciding to slip down under his arms.

Chase silently nodded his thanks. Walking past her, he slung the saddle over the tie-out and turned back. She looked uncertain, but full of anticipation and utterly beautiful. She looked—

As though she wanted to be kissed again.

Grimly, Chase shook his head. *Don't even think about it.* He walked toward her. Time to say good-bye.

Nettie watched Chase Reynolds with a curious blend of excitement and objectivity.

Brian had been handsome, but in a boyish way. Until a minute ago, he had been the only man she'd ever kissed.

Kissing Chase Reynolds was different. He kissed the way he looked: sleek and dangerous, vital and strong. Her lips were still tingling. There had been a moment there when she'd been sure he was going to kiss her again, and the sheer excitement of expecting it had been exhilarating.

*Good grief, Annette Louise, you've barely stepped into the starting gate and already you want to race down the track!*

"Slow down," she murmured under her breath, not even aware she'd spoken until Chase responded by holding up a hand.

"I'm sorry." His voice was low, gravelly and somber. "That was a mistake."

It took a moment to realize he was responding to her. "No!" she said. "I wasn't talking about the kiss. I meant… It was?"

Chase grimaced, looking like he wanted to kick himself. "Not a *mistake.* That wasn't the right…"

"Word. No. No, it didn't feel like a mistake." She blushed. *Pay attention. The man is telling you he's sorry he kissed you.*

"Maybe it was a bit precipitous." No way was she going to let him think he was the only one regretting this.

"Precipitous?" Ironic humor poked at the corner of his mouth. "Good word." He walked toward her, stopping when there was less than a foot between them. Even that short space seemed to be filled with something. An electric charge. A magnetic pull.

"There are rules about kisses," Chase said, his smile fading. His eyes grew dark and sober.

"Rules?"

"Don't kiss before the first date."

His closeness made it hard for Nettie to take a deep breath. "I suppose that's a good policy," she agreed, sounding, she thought, as if she'd just run a mile. "Is that it?"

He shook his head. "No. Rule number two: Never kiss a small-town girl if you know you're not planning to stay."

Nettie's lips thinned. To a man like Chase, *small-town* no doubt implied a certain naiveté, a husband-hungry woman who expected to hear the word *forever* every time she was kissed. Nettie's eyes narrowed. Well, you got the wrong girl. *Forever* was no longer a part of her vocabulary.

It occurred to her suddenly that she was sick and tired of other people's opinions. Fed up with following rules, about dating or anything else. She'd followed rules all her life, either other people's or the ones she'd made up for herself, the ones that were supposed to keep everyone safe and calm and happy. A lot of good that had done her.

What if, just this once, she did what she wanted and not what she thought she *ought* to do?

"I'm not a woman who follows rules," she said. The lie tasted so good on her lips she followed it immediately with another. "Never have been. Never will be." In a decidedly un-Nettie-like move, she traced an instructive index finger slowly up the middle of his chest from breast to collarbone. "But if I were, I would remind you about rule number three: Always consult the woman in question before making executive decisions."

Chase exhaled heavily. "Are you real?" he asked.

"If you're asking whether I mean what I say, there's only one way to find out."

For a moment there was only silence. Neither of them so much as twitched.

Nettie could have sworn Chase moved first, but when she thought about it later she couldn't be absolutely certain. In the long run, who cared? In an instant they were moving together, grabbing shoulders, tracing hands across backs, melding lips and clinging with an abandon that electrified her down to her toes.

She lost all track of time and her surroundings. They both seemed to. When tires crunched along the driveway, neither reacted. They didn't hear the sound of a truck parking in the driveway or of a door opening and closing. They weren't aware of a thing except each other, until Nick coughed loudly behind them. Even then, it took a moment to respond.

Chase reacted first, squeezing Nettie's arm before he broke off the kiss and lifted his head.

He cleared his throat. "Company," he murmured, holding and shielding her from Nick's view until she collected herself.

Nettie tuned into her surroundings slowly. She felt like she was quite literally melting, as if she were being filled right that very moment with drippy, delicious golden sunshine and couldn't be troubled to move or think or worry about a thing.

She moistened her lips. And smiled. "Hello, Nick." She giggled. Her voice sounded like she'd spent too much time on a hot beach.

Nick didn't seem to appreciate the perfection of the moment. He divided his scowl between Nettie and Chase, finally demanding tightly of the other man, "What's going on?"

Chase stiffened beside her. He let go of Nettie's arm and faced his host squarely. Tall, broad and appearing remarkably adversarial for two people who were supposed to be friends, the men held each other's gazes while Nick waited for an answer and Chase stubbornly refused to give one.

Finally, Nick broke the stare and turned toward Nettie. "Where's Sara?"

"Sara?" Nettie shrugged. "In town, I suppose."

Nick glanced toward the Wagoneer parked in front of his house. "How did you get out here?"

Since he was looking at the answer, there should have been no need for the question. But Nick was aware that Nettie hadn't driven anywhere all by herself for some time.

Their parents had been good friends. Nick had acted as a protective big brother through the years, and as appreciative as Nettie was for his steady presence in their lives, she did not want him blabbing about her fears in front of Chase.

Hurriedly stepping in front of Chase, she said, "I drove, of course," then gave Nick a don't-say-*anything* look. He didn't seem to get it.

"By yourself?"

"Well, of course!" Trying once more to communicate by expression alone, she winked and puckered her lips to mouth *shh.* "I came to pick up the eggs."

"The eggs?"

"Yes." She winked again, longer. "I know you usually bring *the eggs* over to our place, but I wanted to save you the bother since you've been so busy lately. Besides, you know how *I love to drive.*" She smiled over her shoulder at Chase. "I'm always out somewhere." She waved a hand. "Flying here, flying there."

Nick's brows shot up briefly. He glanced between the two of them without exercising any subtlety whatsoever before his expression filled with understanding.

Wishing she could kick Nick hard in the shins, Nettie said, "I'll get the eggs now."

She started toward the car, intending to get one of the boxes she'd thrown in the car to support her excuse for coming over. Nick's voice stopped her. "Nettie?"

She turned.

"I don't have chickens."

An awful heat crept up her neck. She focused on Nick, not even daring to glance Chase's way. She could have sworn...

Nick shook his head.

The heat moved into her face. "Well. My goodness, where did the chickens go?" Silently, she pleaded for Nick to help her out.

He scowled. Scratching his sideburns where they met his beard, he looked extremely uncomfortable as he improvised, "They…ran away."

Nettie affected dismayed surprise. "Again?"

Both men stared at her. Chase shook his head in utter disbelief, then laughed at his friend. "What kind of chickens run away from home?"

"The kind that don't want to get eaten!" Nick growled, glaring to say he didn't intend to discuss it any further. He looked at Nettie. "Did you come over for anything—" His quick glance at Chase told her he knew exactly why she'd braved the drive over today. "—besides eggs?"

"No." She prayed fervently that she wouldn't blush again. "That was all." Nettie nodded toward the horse still waiting to be attended to. "King needs to be rubbed down. And the cat is around here somewhere. I've got to get home." She began backing toward the car. "Nice seeing you again, Chase." He appeared a little off-kilter, which under the circumstances was probably a good way to leave him.

Hoping Nick wouldn't blow her cover once she left, Nettie nodded to her old friend. "Bye, Nick. Sorry to hear about your chickens." She turned and hustled to the car. Smiling as she started the vehicle, she turned it around and waved to the two men who watched her head down the driveway as if she didn't have a care in the world.

She was halfway down the road that led home before she had to pull over to the shoulder to catch her shaky breath.

In a single morning she, the self-confessed Miss Goody Two-Shoes of Kalamoose County, had turned into a liar, a flirt and—

She expelled a long noisy breath. "I'm a hussy."

She hadn't just made a date to get together for drinks or coffee; she hadn't climbed back in the saddle, as it were, by agreeing to go on a blind date. Nope. One minute she'd decided to reenter the dating scene and the next she'd locked lips with Chase Reynolds, the sexiest man on the planet.

When she decided to change, she *really* changed.

A smile, genuine this time, stretched across Nettie's lips. The sexiest man on the planet hadn't been exactly reluctant to kiss her, either. What would have happened, she wondered, if Nick hadn't shown up? How did you talk to a man you barely knew after kissing him like that?

Throwing the car into drive, she eased back onto the empty road. Sunlight relaxed her like a warm bath as it streamed through the window. The hot rays weren't nearly as toasty, though, as the memory of Chase's incredibly male, hungry lips.

Imagining the scene that might have ensued if Nick hadn't shown up kept Nettie occupied all the way home.

It wasn't yet noon when Nettie pulled the Wagoneer to the back of her house. A familiar patrol car was parked out front, and the door to the mud porch was wide open. Sara must have returned home for lunch.

Nettie had only reached the porch steps when Sara sailed through the open door. "You gave me the fright of my life, hang it all! I came home and you and Jezebel were both gone. Who's with you?" Craning her neck, she tried to look over Nettie's head toward the Wagoneer.

"No one is with me," Nettie said with enviable calm and poise. "I decided to go for a little drive. Alone." She edged past her sister into the house. The surprise and confusion on Sara's normally confident face was almost worth the panic Nettie had suffered when she'd first got into the car.

"You went alone?" Sara dogged her heels into the house. "All alone? How? I thought you couldn't drive since—" Sara stopped short of saying "the accident."

Nettie kept moving as she decided how to answer. She went to the refrigerator and pulled out cold chicken, mayonnaise and a tomato, crossed to the bread bin and took out two large potato rolls. As she reached for plates, she spoke quietly. "I couldn't. Or I *thought* I couldn't." She shrugged. "Now I can." Without looking in her sister's direction, Nettie could feel Sara watching her closely.

"Just like that?"

"Yes." Unwrapping the chicken, she amended, "Sort of. I've been listening to some audio tapes Lilah sent me."

"You mean those New Age voodoo hypnotist tapes?"

"They're not voodoo! They're part of a very practical, very common-sense program to heal agoraphobia. It was designed by a therapist. And I think it's helping."

Sara snorted grudgingly. "If they're so common-sense, I wonder how Lilah found them? Boy, leave it to her to handle a problem long-distance."

Nettie scrunched the foil into a tight ball. "When you say *problem,* just what *problem* are you talking about? Me? I certainly hope not, because I am not your problem or Lilah's!"

"I didn't say you were. Don't be so touchy. I just didn't expect to come home and find you gone, that's all."

"Well, expect it more often, because I may not be here a lot in the future." Yanking a knife from a wooden block on the counter, Nettie carved several pieces of chicken for sandwiches. "I drove all the way to Nick's place today, and I liked it."

Halfway into the act of snatching a piece of chicken, Sara paused. "Nick's place? Why would you go—?" Her mouth opened to form an O, or in this case, an Oh, no. "You went there to see him, didn't you?"

Nettie skirted around her uniformed sister on her way to the pantry. "You want lettuce on your sandwich? I'm going to put cranberry sauce on mine."

Sara attempted to block Nettie's path. "If there's something going on between the two of you, I think I should know."

"Really. Why?" Looping around Sara, she grabbed a can of cranberry sauce and looped around Sara again.

"This is a small town. People are going to talk."

Nettie bristled. "So what?" Deciding she was very hungry, Nettie piled chicken on the rolls. "It'll give them something to do between 'Golden Girls' reruns."

"This family has had enough gossip about it with Lilah dating anything that didn't walk on all fours!"

"Oh, stop exaggerating."

"I'm not exaggerating." Sara thumped her hand on the kitchen counter. "Hang it all! Are his intentions serious?"

"Sara, for heaven's sake, you sound like Uncle Harm." Beginning to see some humor in the situation, Nettie laughed. "No one has any intentions right now, serious or otherwise." She tossed the tomato once in the air before setting it on a plate. "All we did was kiss."

Wickedly enjoying the absolute shock on Sara's face, Nettie cut thick slices of tomato, laying them precisely atop the chicken as if sandwich assembly was the only thing on her mind right now. She couldn't decide which was more red—Sara's cheeks or the tomato.

"You kissed him." The tight line of her Sara's lips were pinched and disapproving.

"That's right."

"Was it the first time?"

Nettie paused in the act of spreading mayonnaise across the cut top halves of the rolls. "That is so none of your business. It's my life."

Sara obviously wanted to say more, but didn't know how. She opened and closed her mouth uselessly a couple of times. "Fine!" She strode to the door. "Do whatever you want!"

"Where are you going? Don't you want lunch?"

"I lost my appetite," Sara grumbled. "I'll eat at Ernie's."

"If you're going to eat at Ernie's, you haven't lost your appetite."

Swinging around, Sara aimed her thumb at her chest. "It's my appetite. I know when I've lost it."

Scooping the chicken off Sara's roll, Nettie transferred it to her own. "Fine."

Staring at her naked roll as if Nettie had just committed the ultimate act of betrayal, Sara nodded ominously. "Fine!" She marched out to the squad car.

As Sara drove off, Nettie slapped cranberry sauce on top of the mayonnaise and smooshed the huge sandwich together. "Fine back!"

Quashing guilt, she carried her plate to the living room. Aside from the fact that she'd just participated in the single most inane conversation she'd ever had, she thought she'd made her point fairly well: Things were going to be changing around the Owens household; *she* was changing.

Chewing with more force than necessary, she considered the choices that had brought her to this point.

For as long as she could remember, she'd been the family peacemaker, a veritable bottomless pit of nurturing and reliability.

"Couldn't get more boring than that as a teenager." She'd struck a bargain with God at an early age: She'd follow all the rules and He would keep everyone happy and safe forever and ever, amen.

She'd kept her part of the bargain.

It was high time that she considered the cost of such diligent obedience. She was twenty-five and if she thought about it, she wasn't sure she'd ever really asked herself what she wanted or what she liked. She rented the movies her family enjoyed. She cooked the food she knew other people preferred.

Frowning heavily, Nettie pulled the chicken out of her sandwich until all she had left was tomato, cranberry sauce and mayo on a fluffy white roll. She took a large, ferocious bite. *Yes.* A smile of satisfaction curved her lips. Limited nutritional value, but exactly what she wanted.

By being so *good* for so long, she'd given everyone else a chance to test their wings while her own had grown cramped from disuse. All right. It was time to find out what she wanted, what she liked… And with luck it would be more exciting than a tomato-and-cranberry-sauce sandwich.

Putting her feet on the coffee table, Nettie chewed and thought. She liked country music. And painting. She enjoyed an ice-cold beer on a hot summer day, but she didn't want to turn that into a hobby. She wiggled her foot. What else? What else did she like—

Kisses. Chase Reynolds' kisses.

Yep, if pure enjoyment were the goal, those kisses would go a long, long way.

"Goes without saying. But you can't run around kissing people for kicks." She set her sandwich on the plate.

*Not people,* a voice inside her responded, *just Chase.*

"That's not a hobby."

*It could be.*

"Please. Embrace reality. The man was featured in *People* magazine. He's probably kissed Madonna."

*So? He kissed you. He liked it.*

Her foot stopped wriggling. "Well, that's still not a hobby," she mumbled, setting her plate on the coffee table. "I need something I can do on a regular basis, like knitting."

*Good choice. Why kiss a hunk when you can purl a scarf?*

That settled it. Nettie plunked her elbows on her knees and rested her chin on her upturned palms. She was going to see Chase again. And not only because he made the ground shake when he kissed her. Not only because his hands made her feel warm through and through for the first time in years.

Not because she forgot the past and stopped wondering about the future when she looked into his eyes.

No, those weren't the reasons she was going to see him again. She was going to see Chase Reynolds again because if she didn't, she would spend the next ten years knitting scarves and wondering what could have come after the kisses.

## Chapter Five

Nick's coffee tasted like mud with caffeine. It tasted angry, Chase mused, evidently reflecting the mood of the man who'd made it.

Sprawled in a tan suede easy chair, Nick was, at present, glaring at his houseguest.

Taking another sip, just to be social, Chase met the blatant disapproval in his friend's eyes and decided, *the heck with polite.* Setting his mug on the coffee table, he sat back and volleyed the glare.

With a pointed glance at the mug, Nick growled, "What's wrong?"

Chase felt his shoulders square as if he were preparing to fight, not chat. "It's a little strong, don't you think?"

"I like it strong."

As casually as he could, Chase shrugged.

Nick was on his feet in an instant. "What's that supposed to mean?"

"You need to get out more." Chase crossed an ankle over his knee. "Because if this is really about coffee, I'm scared for you, buddy."

Nick glowered a bit longer, then sat back down, elbows on knees, hands clasped.

Chase studied his former college roommate and suddenly knew what was coming. "This is about her—your friend—isn't it?"

"'Her?' 'My friend?'" Nick offered a disgusted snort. "You don't even know her name."

"Of course I know her name!"

"What is it?"

"Nettie!" Angry himself now, Chase swore. Some strong emotion bubbled beneath the anger. Disappointment? Frustration? His gaze narrowed as he demanded of Nick, "Why didn't you tell me yesterday that she was off limits?" *And why was she kissing me?*

"You've been in town one day and you spent part of that in a jail cell." Nick ran a hand over black wavy hair that was as thick as it had been in college. "I forgot what a fast mover you are."

"'Fast mover?'" Uncrossing his legs, Chase leaned forward, too. Fast mover. He despised that term. It implied instability, insincerity and a shallowness that was chronic—

Nick arched a coal-black brow.

"In college I might have—"

A corner of Nick's mouth joined the brow.

To work off some of his mounting irritation, Chase stood and crossed the wood floors of the old farmhouse. The view from the living-room windows was too peaceful; it irritated him further. "You're telling me to stay away from her?"

Nick nodded slowly, watching Chase carefully as he said, "You don't know her, so I'm going to tell you flat out— A relationship with you is not what she needs." He waited only long enough for Chase to narrow his eyes before he added, "Think about what you're doing here. You're hiding out from the press while you wait for a paternity test. If it's negative, you're out of here and off to where next? Wherever the next big story is, right?" Nick persisted. "Do you know what you're going to do if the boy turns out to be your son?"

Just hearing the words aloud made Chase's heart pound. Even his throat tightened. What did he know about being a father? Zilch. Less than zilch.

Nick paced to the fireplace. He reached for a carved wooden box, withdrew a piece of cigarette paper and a large pinch of tobacco and began rolling a cigarette.

Chase grimaced. "Haven't you given those up, yet? They'll kill you."

"I used to think the same thing about your career. I read that you were shot in the thigh last year while you were trying to run down a big drug story in Brazil."

"It was just a graze. I was back on the job in two days."

Nick nodded. "I read that, too. So what's the boy's name?"

Inhaling and exhaling deeply, Chase made a quarter turn toward the window. "Colin."

"And he's six, right?"

"Seven."

"How long had you known his mother? You never really said."

No, Chase thought, and he didn't want to say. He didn't want to think about this situation at all, not until he was forced to. Every time his mind moved in that direction, he felt a completely unsettling guilt, and he had nothing to feel guilty about. He hadn't even known about Colin until two weeks ago. Chase ran both hands over his head, from his forehead to his nape. "I met Julia in England."

"The supermodel, right? I read about the two of you. I was in line at the grocery at the time."

"Yeah." Chase acknowledged the gibe. "We were together four months, a record for me, as you've pointed out. And a record for Julia, too. We parted very happily. I had a job in the Middle East, and she went to France, where she fell head over heels for a Paris baker who wanted to be a performance artist. Using bread dough."

"Eclectic."

"Uh-huh. I spoke with her once, twice—who even remembers now? She could have contacted me anytime, though. Through the station, if nothing else."

"Does it bother you that she didn't?"

Chase rounded on his friend, fierce outrage in his golden-brown eyes. "If he's my son? Of course it 'bothers' me! What in hell kind of question—" He stopped, realizing the implication was completely fair. He hadn't planned to have a child. He hadn't called Nick, ecstatic over the possibility when the lawyers had phoned. He'd called looking for a place to hide out while he prayed his life would stay exactly as it was.

Nick licked the edge of the paper to seal his cigarette. "You and I are bachelors through and through."

"What are you talking about? You were married."

"According to Deborah, I was a bachelor then, too. She put up with me for three years. It hurt her pretty badly." Reaching for an old-fashioned silver lighter, he touched a flame to the end of his cigarette and snapped the lid. "Nettie's like Deborah. Home and family are everything to her. She doesn't move in your world. She couldn't."

Recalling Nettie's admonition about making decisions for women, Chase began to smile. "You sure about that?"

Nick exhaled a long stream of smoke. "I'm sure." His expression turned grim. "I understand what I saw. I know she was kissing you back. You're a celebrity, pal, and she grew up in a small town. You're glamorous."

Chase winced at the word. "Give her some credit."

"I am. She's a rare person, good through and through. I don't want her to be hurt. Not when I can see it coming and stop it."

Chase got the point. He was an old friend and a welcome guest as long as he played by the rules. It hovered on the tip of his tongue to point out that *People* magazine considered him a pretty good catch. Right up there with Sean Puffy Combs. Irony curved his lips. The qualities that made him successful in his career ruled him out as family material. He knew that, but it had never bothered him before.

It didn't bother him now.

Nick waited for an agreement. Chase let him wait a little longer while he turned the tables instead. "What are you doing these days, relationship-wise?"

"There's a woman in Minot I see every now and then. Nice lady, but she doesn't have a candle in the window for me, if you know what I mean. She's fine if I'm there and fine if I'm not. That's the only kind of woman you and I should have anything to with. The kind we can't hurt."

It was exactly what Chase had always said. It was the way he'd lived all of his adult life. But it ticked him off royally to hear it today.

In the absence of a verbal response, Nick persisted. "Nettie can be hurt."

"All right, I get the picture."

"She *is* the candle-in-the-window type."

"Got it." Chase was beginning to sound snappish.

"And you are *not* the candle-in-the-window type."

"All right, I said. I get it!" He stalked toward the entryway to the hall, intending to find some solace in the upstairs guest bedroom Nick had given him. "I hope this woman in Minot doesn't mind reruns," he said on a parting shot. "Because you are the most repetitive sonova—"

Nick pointed with the cigarette. "That temper of yours is another reason you ought to stay away from—"

*"I said no problem!"* Chase stormed out of the room and up the stairs.

Nick spoke quietly after him, but the sound carried. "Good. I'm glad we're in agreement."

Cloudless, the night sky looked like a billowing swatch of black velvet. Like a magic carpet, Nettie thought as she lay in the queen-size bed tucked beneath a double window in her second-story bedroom. She'd placed the bed under the window in lieu of a headboard so she could watch the stars glimmer and change on clear nights like this. In winter, before the harshest storms came, she scooched the bed over. Lightning and thunder were not as friendly as black velvet and stars.

The full moon was high and amazingly bright tonight. Wondering what time it was she lifted her head to look at the digital clock on her dresser. Only a little after midnight. Oh, brother. One more sleepless night, and her eyes would be as swollen as the moon. She'd spent the past two nights tossing and turning as she thought about Chase. Or as she tried not to think about him.

She hadn't seen him since the day she'd driven to Nick's, and that was three days ago. Despite her conviction that she *would* see him again, she had to admit she'd expected him to come to her this time. Or that they'd run into each other in town. There was only one tiny grocery in Kalamoose. If he intended to buy food in town, surely she would see him there. Working on that assumption, in three days she'd bought two heads of lettuce she hadn't needed, way too many canned goods and enough peanut butter to last half a year.

Sighing, Nettie flopped onto her side and pulled the quilt over her bare shoulder. The beloved wedding-ring quilt covering her bed had been in her family for three generations. In years gone by, it had made her feel cozy and happy simply to look at it and think about tradition—the tradition of handing down heirlooms, the tradition of marriage.

"That's your problem," she muttered, burrowing more deeply into her soft pillow. "You want to live a Courtney Love life, but you've got a Donna Reed brain. Women who live for the moment have silk sheets." She rolled onto her stomach. "And if you want to see Chase again, you're going to have to hang out where he hangs out." From her stomach, she moved to her other side and then her back. "I wonder where he's hanging out in Kalamoose?" By now the town should have been buzzing with news about his presence. Celebrities were rare in Kalamoose, but so far she hadn't heard a word.

A sharp tap made her open her eyes. When she heard it again, she sat up abruptly and looked around. "What—"

*Ting!*

Something hit her window. Nettie turned, leaning on her pillows to look out the window and down to the ground. Sara always left the porch light glowing because it deterred criminals (not that they were inundated with them way out here) and because as the sheriff she felt she was on-call twenty-four seven. The front porch was around the corner, but the light spilled over to softly illuminate the side of the house on which Nettie's bedroom was located.

She squinted. There was a man down there. And he was throwing something at her window.

Quickly she sat up, all but pressing her nose against the glass as she tried to see who was out there.

The man ran a hand over his head, searched the ground, picked something up and *ping!*

Nettie jerked back as another stone hit the window. With the man's face upturned, she recognized Chase.

Scuttling off the bed, she raced to the bedroom door, but realized an instant after she flung it open that her nightgown was sheer wispy nylon, hardly adequate covering for running out of the house in the middle of the night, so she hurried to the closet, searched madly for a robe and wrestled herself into it as she ran down the stairs.

"Don't leave, don't leave," she chanted, forcing herself to slow down as she reached the front door. Sara slept like a rock, but Nettie didn't want to take any chances. Opening and closing the door carefully, she trotted barefoot down the porch steps and around the side of the house.

Chase was there, winding up to pitch another stone at her window. She smiled. Her heart skipped and a shiver that had nothing to do with the chill night air skittered along her arms. Suddenly she felt as young, as light and carefree as she had at sixteen.

Silently, she crept up behind Chase and whispered, "Are you sure that's her window?"

With his arm raised to throw the stone, he turned so quickly he almost lost his balance.

His deep-brown hair was ruffled, and Nettie thought he must have run his hands through it several times tonight. His expression conveyed first surprise, then chagrin and finally sheepishness.

"Caught throwing stones at the girl's window." She shook her head and grinned. "That misdemeanor carries quite a fine in Kalamoose."

It wouldn't have shocked her a bit to discover that her blood had turned to golden honey; she felt so sweet and warm as his face relaxed and his left eyebrow hitched with the same humor that curled his masculine lips. His eyes said clearly that seeing her made him very, very happy.

Chase cocked his head. "I committed the crime, I'll do the time."

Amusement sparkled in Nettie's eyes and made dimples appear in her cheeks. The sight pleased Chase more than scooping the collapse of a foreign syndicate. He didn't want her to be awed or to find him "glamorous," as Nick suggested. He wanted their interaction to be clean and unbiased, just one man and one woman, on a prairie in the middle of North Dakota.

Tousled from bed, Nettie's wild black curls fell softly around her cheeks and past her shoulders. Gently, carefully, he reached out to release a section of her hair from beneath the collar of her silky robe. Her huge eyes blinked heavily, as if she were sleepy, or hypnotized.

Chase had been feted and flattered so often, he barely noticed it anymore. He'd seen so many exquisite women, he tended to take beauty for granted. Yet standing in front of this woman made him feel like a sixteen-year-old misfit who'd been granted a date with the homecoming queen.

He was in deep, deep trouble.

"I've been warned to stay away from you, Ms. Owens." His intention was to keep this light and amusing, but he didn't feel light or amused.

Her surprise was evident. "By who?"

"Nick. He thinks I'll hurt you." Again he had the urge to touch her hair. This time he resisted. The effort further tightened his tone. "He's probably right. I'm not…" Chase sighed, unsure of how to proceed. He didn't like being unsure.

"You're not 'serious.'" She finished his sentence with a startling matter-of-factness. "You're not staying in Kalamoose." The blue eyes rolled. "Duh." She used her fingers to tick off the next couple of facts. "You're not looking for anything permanent, and I'm a small-town girl who's not going anywhere—" About to continue in the same vein, she stopped and shifted gears. "What did Nick say about me?"

"He respects you. Admires you. He says you're good through and through. And that you're a home-and-hearth type." All complimentary stuff as far as Chase was concerned, but it made Nettie's teeth clench. She muttered something he didn't catch. "Beg your pardon?"

"Donna Reed," she growled. "He's making me sound like the mother in a nineteen-fifties sitcom."

"And that's not you?"

Her eyes narrowed, and she answered grimly. "No. On all counts."

He found himself wanting to believe her, because it would be easier. But Nick had also said, "Home and family were everything to her." *Were.* What did that mean? She'd had a family and now didn't? Chase had assumed Nick was talking about the loss of her parents.

"How did you know which bedroom was mine?" Nettie

asked, before Chase could pursue his line of thought. "Sara could be standing here right now."

He winced. "Not a chance. She'd have shot me from the window."

The smile returned to her face. Chase really didn't want to answer the question. The truth, the *whole* truth, was that he'd scoped the house out earlier this evening, which made him sound like either a high-school freshman or a total pervert. He settled for a partial truth.

"One bedroom has lace curtains, one has shutters and one has a hand-lettered sign that says This House Patrolled by N.D.P.D. stuck in the window. I took my best shot."

She laughed. "I'm glad."

"You're not angry? It's past midnight."

Nettie shook her head. Her eyes never left his. "I'm not angry."

The words emanated from some newborn place inside her. She felt herself grow calmer and more sure of herself by the minute. "I was warned away from you, too."

Chase frowned. "Nick gets around."

"He hasn't said anything to me. I warned myself." It was the truth, and amazingly she didn't feel a bit embarrassed saying it. "I told myself you've had relationships with some of the most beautiful women in the world. With exciting women. 'What could he possibly see in you?' I said."

"How did you answer that?"

"I didn't. You did. You threw stones at my window."

Nettie took a breath at the same time that she took a step forward. It made her appear both bold and nervous. Chase didn't want to wait another second. Desire coursed through his veins; he had wanted women in the past, of course. Wanted them physically, wanted them *now*. This was different, though he didn't know quite how, except that in the past his desire had seemed like a wind—swift and strong and fleeting. What he felt now was an uncontrolled burn, a fire that gained strength as it moved.

"You are so damn lovely." His hoarse whisper cloaked them like the night. "You should see what I see." The eyes of the women he typically dated would have smiled with satisfaction if he'd said the same words to them. Nettie's eyes widened happily, hungrily. Chase thought his self-control had never been so tested. "You should listen to Nick," he told her, his voice more a growl now than a whisper. "Or *I* should listen."

Because he didn't think he could stand not touching her a moment longer—yet didn't want to hold her in a passionate way—he grasped her upper arms and promised himself his hands would not wander.

"I travel all over the world," he told her. "I'm never in one place very long. I haven't slept in my apartment more than three nights in a row for the past five years. And I am lousy at relationships. Lousy. I can tell you who's who in the Middle East political scene, but if you want a shoulder to cry on or a comforting voice in the middle of the night, or someone who'll remember your birthday—"

Nettie's hands came up to hold his face, as firmly as he had taken her arms. "You talk way too much." She stepped closer, unmindful of the fingers that tightened unconsciously around her. As she raised her face, she felt energy, like a buzz, at the contact. When she touched her lips to his, a shudder of barely exerted control ran through him, and Nettie felt a surge of delicious power.

Last time, he'd controlled the kiss, and, dazed, she'd simply hung on for the ride. This time when their lips met, Nettie took control of the vehicle and wasn't about to let go for anything!

Still holding his face, she began the kiss softly, an explorer in uncharted country. One…two…three gentle touches, each lasting a bit longer than the one before. After the third kiss, she lingered, allowing herself to be excruciatingly aware—of his skin, of the infinitesimal beard he would have to shave tomorrow morning, of the aftershave she'd noticed that first night and which she decided she really loved. What she wanted, truly wanted, was to move along the outline of his lips to the corner of his mouth and then down, teasing that little nook between his lower lip and chin.

So she did it. She did exactly what she wanted, exactly the way she wanted and for at least forty seconds she paid no attention to the fact that she was standing in her side yard in the middle of the night, wearing only a thin, plain gown and robe, with a man *People* magazine had called "beautiful."

When she kissed his chin, Chase kissed her nose. Nettie had the blissful urge to snuggle into him like a cat. She lifted her

face and again pressed her lips to his, this time allowing them
to part slightly. It was a hesitant move, and Chase stayed absolutely still, letting her set the pace. She looked up. His eyes
were shadowed by the silky night, but she could tell that they
were open and watching her. In one electrified instant she felt
everything...everything...the whisper of his breath, the thud of
her own heart, cold grass beneath her bare feet and his warm,
warm hands resting on her upper arms.

"What are you doing to me, Nettie Owens?" Chase's whispered question held a smile. His hands began to move down her
arms, pulling her closer, settling on the curve of her lower back.

Nettie released his face reluctantly. Suddenly she felt self-
conscious. Winding her arms around his neck seemed too intimate, somehow, a sensibility that smacked of the ridiculous in
light of the kisses they were sharing. Still, he was fully clothed
and she was pressed against him in a silk robe—no bra. Her
bare feet, taking tiny steps toward him for balance, bumped into
his leather boots, and that, too, seemed achingly intimate.

So what to do with her hands? She settled for lowering them,
resting her palms on his shoulders.

Chase was still looking down into her face. "What now, Nettie?"

Good question. *What now?* He wasn't staying. A relationship
would go nowhere, and she appreciated his honesty in saying
so. She didn't even know how long he planned to stay. But he
felt so warm and sturdy, holding her this way, closely but lightly,
too, giving her the freedom to make a choice.

As for wanting a man who would provide a shoulder for her
to cry on, tears were not what she was interested in. She'd cried
enough already.

"October twenty-third," she said.

Bemused, Chase edged his head back a bit. "What's that?"

"My birthday. Think you can remember it?"

Chase's smile carried through the shadows. "I think so."

Unconsciously, Nettie sighed. Looking him square in the eye,
she said, "Good enough."

Clearly he had no idea what she was talking about at first.
Then understanding dawned. A gratifying look of wonder lit his
face, punctuated swiftly by a frown. "Are you telling me you
want a relationship given everything I've said?"

Was she? Nettie nodded.

Chase's arms stiffened around her. "Say it, Nettie. Out loud. I need to hear it, because when I look at you, I see babies and Christmas trees and dinners at home before the PTA meeting—"

*"No."* Swift and adamant, the denial left no room for doubt. His simple description was all she needed to hear to know that her decision was made. "Look again," she said. "I don't want..." Knowing she would choke up if she told him what she didn't want, she focused instead on what she did. "How long will you be in town?"

Chase grimaced. "Two weeks, maybe three. But I—"

She interrupted him. "Fine. A few weeks." Wrapped in his arms, feeling vulnerable but surprisingly strong, she raised a brow. "You'll miss my birthday, but we could celebrate early. Or not." She took a breath. "Do you want a girlfriend while you're here?"

"A girlfriend?"

She stood taller. He was smiling at her, gently and with a tinge of amusement. If he wanted to hear her say something sophisticated, like *lover,* she didn't think she could do it. There was only so much daring she could handle in one night. If he asked her what she meant by *girlfriend,* she wondered whether she could define her picture of the next two weeks in his company, for him and for herself, out loud.

He released her, bringing his hands up to her neck and cupping her jaw in his palms. Before she could speak, he rubbed a thumb lightly across her lips. "I'd like you to be my girlfriend. I would like it very much."

He didn't add, "while I'm here." He didn't need to. An agreement had been struck, an agreement that was rife with implications.

Nothing innocent about it, Nettie thought. And nothing ordinary. For a woman who played by the rules, she was bending quite a few of them tonight.

She'd had only one lover in her life. She had no complaints about her sex life with her late husband, but once she'd unearthed a copy of *The Women's Guide to Sexual Satisfaction* while cleaning out Lilah's old room and had laughed herself silly. Either half the things in that book were physically impossible or she and Brian had been as daring as Ozzie and Harriet.

Chase was an experienced man. No doubt he'd had experienced lovers.

When he brought one hand up to smooth the hair back from her temple, his fingers tangled in her long curls. He smiled and suddenly it was just the two of them. No other people, no pasts, no future beyond the next two weeks. Even the night seemed to fall away. The only thing Nettie saw was Chase's head lowering. All she felt was a bubbly, tingling anticipation as suddenly his mouth was less than a whisper away. "Nettie—"

A door clicked, a screen slammed, and whatever he had been about to say was lost to the sound of Sara's heel-heavy steps marching onto the porch.

"Nettie! Are you out here?"

Nettie jumped. Caught by surprise, she let out a little squeal. Grabbing fistfuls of Chase's sweater, she began pushing him toward the side of the house. "Shh."

Automatically, Chase held her more protectively, cupping the back of her head.

"Nettie?"

"It's my sister," she hissed.

"I know." He whispered back.

"If she sees us, this is going to be the longest two weeks of our lives. She thinks you're a playboy."

"Last night she thought I was a bank robber." His breath was warm in her ear. "We won't be able to hide from her for two weeks."

"I know. But for right now…" Nettie figured that if she sounded like she was pleading…well, she was. She didn't want to have to fight with Sara or to explain herself over and over. She didn't want to talk about Chase. Not now. Maybe not ever. "Please, you've got to go. I'll call you at Nick's tomorrow."

First Chase shook his head. Then he grinned. "I have a feeling this boyfriend gig isn't going to be as easy as it sounds." Repeating her promise as a command, he said, "Call me tomorrow," then kissed her temple at the corner of her eyebrow.

They heard Sara's footsteps, a bit softer now, heading in their direction. With a quick glance back toward the porch, Chase gave Nettie a brief salute and trotted around the corner of the house. When he was cleanly out of the light, Nettie heard him pick up speed and jog across the lawn.

"Wha— Who is that? Hey!" Sara rushed down the porch steps and along the side of the house.

"Sara!"

"Nettie?" The lanky redhead stopped and searched the shadows for her sister. Dressed in a pair of plaid pajama bottoms and an I Love Fargo T-shirt, her feet stuffed into leather-soled moccasins and her hair plaited into a single sleep-mussed braid, Sara looked as cranky as she sounded. "What the heck is going on out here? Who is that?" She pointed demandingly toward the road.

Nettie made a great show of peering into the yard, which at this time of night didn't look like anything more than a great black void. "Who's who?"

"That person!" Sara stabbed the air.

"Person?" Nettie blinked, managing a stunning show of bemusement for someone not used to lying. "What person?"

"The one who is running through your yard!" Sara's head swung dizzyingly from Nettie to the yard and back again— twice—as she obviously wrestled with an impulse to run after whoever was out there; the only thing stopping her was the fact that she wouldn't be able to see more than three feet in front of her. "What is going on out here?"

"Person?" Nettie murmured. "Person. Ohh, you mean the dog."

"Dog?"

"Yes." Nettie yawned. "A really big dog. Nice, though. I'm going back to bed."

"Ho-o-old it!" Sara's lips folded together to form a tight, firm line. She inhaled to a slow count of three and exhaled noisily, a sign that she was trying to control herself, which usually meant the big explosion was right around the corner. "What are you trying to hide?"

"Hide? Sara—" Nettie sighed. "Okay, I might as well tell you. You're bound to find out, anyway."

"That's right."

"I am hiding something from you."

"I knew it."

"But only because I don't want you to get upset."

Immediately Sara became upset. "I'm not going to get upset. Why would I even care? Why does everybody think—"

"Sara, you don't even know what it is yet."

Shoving at the heavy red waves that were slipping out of her braid, Sara crossed her arms. "Fine. Let's have it."

Nettie pulled her robe more closely around her and tightened the sash. "Well. I've been kind of lonely lately, you know. You've been working extra-long hours since your deputy moved to Minot, and I'm here a lot by myself, and…I adopted a dog."

Sara stared. "Dog."

"Yes. Well, not adopted, officially. It probably belongs to someone up the road. But it comes around, and I…pet it. Talk to it. Feed it leftovers. He loves salmon patties. Isn't that funny?"

"You expect me to believe you were feeding a dog at midnight?"

"I know. He likes to eat at the oddest times. I didn't tell you, because…this dog looks just like poor old Skipper, and I know how upset you were when Skipper died."

"I was ten when Skipper died. I'm over it."

"Good for you!" Nettie yawned again. A great, noisy, stretched-arm yawn. "Oh, boy, I'm pooped. I'm going to bed." She walked past Sara and up the porch steps. "'Night."

Sara stood with her arms crossed. She didn't say a word, just let Nettie walk past her and into the house. As the screen door clanked shut, Nettie expelled a pent-up breath. Lying was not something that came easily to her. On the other hand…

She giggled. She was doing lots of things tonight that didn't usually come easily to her. A delicious jittery excitement tingled through her. She'd almost been caught kissing Chase Reynolds by the side of her house at midnight. Sounded like a country-and-western song.

Heading up the stairs to her bedroom, she realized that sleep was the last thing on her mind. Why go unconscious when there was so much to think about, so many wonderful sensations to relive while they were still fresh?

Two weeks. She had two weeks to make new wonderful sensations that she would remember long after he was gone and this lovely interlude had ended. A tiny dullness threatened to encroach upon her mood. Resolutely she shook her head. She had made a decision, struck a bargain, in a sense. Whatever happened over the next two weeks, she would accept the inevitable finality of her parting from Chase. Two weeks and no regrets.

*Call me tomorrow...*

Nettie returned to her bedroom, closed the door softly and climbed under the covers once more. The sheets were cold and she had to mush the quilt around her to retain some warmth. She would have fourteen exhilarating days to look back on when nights got cold in the future.

And, she had tonight to wonder what "temporary girlfriend" would mean for an experienced man like Chase and a daredevil woman like herself.

# Chapter Six

Sara moved around the house like an angry bear the next morning. Plagued by a spate of post-fib guilt, Nettie cut into her own work schedule to prepare waffles for breakfast, but Sara declined, grumbling that she was watching her weight. Standing over the sink, she crunched her way through a bowl of shredded wheat, which she detested, then left the house without saying good-bye.

Wishing she really did have a dog to stuff full of leftovers, Nettie dumped the waffles and wrapped the sausage up for later. Darn it! Sara never watched her weight, and she never turned down pecan waffles. She never turned down food, period. Her gusto for life was all-encompassing.

That's all I'm doing now, Nettie thought, feeling gusto. She simply wanted to do it without an audience.

Heading upstairs to her studio, where work on her sixth There I Go Again! book awaited her, Nettie decided to put everything—Sara and the future and even Chase—out of her mind until later.

"Later" came midmorning.

Working on a particularly fun section of a watercolor painting that depicted her little-boy hero, Barnaby, wandering through a Moroccan bazaar, Nettie was vaguely aware of noise downstairs. Thinking it must be Sara coming home for lunch and perhaps a truce, Nettie continued to work as she waited for her sister to let herself in. A series of firm thuds on the front door convinced her to put down her brush. She wiped her hands on the rag she kept looped through her jeans. Tugging at the blue, paint-smeared man's shirt she wore over her T-shirt and jeans, she headed downstairs, but even as she reached the front door, she was thinking "Sara" or "delivery person," not—

"Chase!"

Dressed in pale blue jeans and a blue shirt—as she was, but minus the paint—Chase stood on the front porch, facing out toward the road, apparently thinking about leaving. He turned when he heard his name.

A smile so naturally sexy it should have been outlawed lit his face. "I saw your wagon, but thought you might be out on another run." That intriguing almost-dimple on his left cheek deepened. "I know I said I'd call first, but I realized I didn't have your number."

"Actually, I was supposed to call you."

"That's right." Chase snapped his fingers. "I forgot."

Nettie leaned against the edge of the front door, but left the screen closed. "That is a big fat lie."

Affecting deep dismay, he placed a hand over his heart. "Journalists do not lie. We interpret facts."

"The fact is you're lying."

Chase moved in so close, his nose almost touched the screen that separated them. "The fact is I didn't want to wait. And I'm usually very good at waiting." The glibness, the teasing was gone. "Were you going to call?"

Thudding happily, Nettie's heart responded before she did. A fall breeze streamed gently through the screen door, the sun shone and a beautiful man stood on her porch. All in all, not a bad morning.

She took a moment to appreciate "the facts": His hair looked like a sea of coffee-hued waves. His even white teeth were perfect. Ditto the muscular shoulders that tapered to a lean waist and truly excellent hips. Shallow physical attributes aside, however, Chase Reynolds also had an exciting life and a wonderful future.

*And all that perfection wants me!*

She grinned. To deny the pleasure of this moment would be to look a cosmic gift horse in the mouth.

"Well, I thought about calling, but then—" shoulder and hip against the door, she swayed with it slightly "—I remembered what my sister Lilah said about making men wait."

Chase grimaced. "I'm not sure I want to hear this," he murmured. "What did Lilah say?"

"She said, 'Men who wait seldom hesitate.'"

"What does that mean?"

"I have no idea. But Lilah's always had a healthy social life."

"Mmm." Chase turned away to walk toward the porch steps.

Amazed by the disappointment that socked her square in the chest, Nettie opened her mouth to call out to him, to tell him she'd only been teasing and that Lilah had said that back in high school and who took high-school dating advice seriously, anyway? but then Chase plunked himself down on the top step of the porch.

She opened the screen. "What are you doing?"

Picking up a small twig lying next to him, he tossed it lazily into the yard. He checked his watch, stretched his legs out and leaned back on his elbows. "I'm waiting." Arching his neck, he looked up at her. "Any idea how long this will take?"

Nettie ran over and swatted him with her rag. "Brat!"

Smiling broadly, Chase raised an arm to fend her off. "Hey, I'm not complaining. It's just that it's almost lunch time and I may get hungry." Grabbing one end of the cloth, he held on and tugged, pulling so that her only choice was to let go or bend down.

Nettie bent.

Inches away, he said quietly, "I'm sorry for coming over without calling. Have lunch with me anyway."

She usually worked right through lunch. She usually ate a sandwich that wound up having watercolor fingerprints on the bread. She usually adhered to a firm work schedule, and she'd already deviated from it this week when she drove out to Nick's. She was under deadline....

"There's nowhere to go in Kalamoose where we wouldn't be

seen.'' Whispering just seemed right when you were literally face-to-face.

''We'll have to come out of the closet or go someplace farther away.'' The tension remained taut on the towel they both held.

''Farther away,'' Nettie chose.

''Done.'' He tugged the rag, levering up at the same time to plant a swift, firm kiss on her lips. Jumping smoothly to his feet, Chase raised the towel between them. ''This is wet.'' Water-based paint stained his palm lightly.

''I was working when you knocked.'' She examined his hand and giggled. ''It looks like a henna tattoo.''

''Mmm. Very exotic. You a painter?''

''An illustrator. Come in the house. I'll show you where the bathroom is so you can wash off while I change.''

''Okay. What do you illustrate?''

Chase followed her into the old farmhouse. Nettie had grown up here. It had been her home on and off for most of her life, and it offered a simple comfort she loved. The house provided a good indication of the kind of life she led: simple, perhaps even provincial when viewed through the eyes of a man who'd traveled in style all over the world.

In the living room, Nettie turned to gauge Chase's reaction to braided rugs, rough-hewn floors and an overabundance of checks.

He appeared to be holding up pretty well under the ''Country Living'' assault. His gaze roamed from the fireplace mantel, wreathed in dried flowers and branches and topped by family photos, to the old sofa covered with throw pillows, including the needlepoint cushion Nettie's mother had made which read God Bless Our Happy Home.

Returning his smiling gaze to Nettie, he took a stab at his own question. ''You illustrate the *Saturday Evening Post*.''

She thwacked him again with the towel. ''I suppose you're a chrome and leather man.''

''Depends on whether we're talking about furniture or ladies' lingerie.'' Laughing when Nettie went speechless, Chase addressed her with utter sincerity. ''I like your house. I like the way it's decorated. It looks like you.''

''Oh.'' She mock-winced. ''Comfortable?''

''Welcoming.'' He indulged himself by delving his fingers

into the black-as-night waves she'd clipped up in some kind of loose twist behind her head. "A sight to come home to," he said, having had no idea until that moment that he'd been thinking any such thing. "Like open arms."

Once the words were out of his mouth, Chase realized that he absolutely meant them. Still, it was the wrong thing to say, truthful or not.

"That's nice," she responded simply, smiling but obviously not reading anything deeply personal into the comment. Chase should have been happy for small favors. Instead, he wanted to kick his sorry butt. This was exactly what Nick had been talking about. Chase's future resembled a jigsaw puzzle with too many pieces. He and Nettie had already agreed—wisely, maturely— that their relationship would be…non-permanent. The line between "for now" and "forever" should not be blurred—not in her mind. Not in his own.

He dropped his hand, but didn't have to recover verbally, because Nettie had apparently moved on already in her own mind. "There's a downstairs bathroom in the hall by the staircase." She walked him over to it. "It used to be a closet. These old farms typically had lots of bedroom additions, all built around one poor, overworked bathroom. My father put this one in after I was born. I think he anticipated a loss of good humor if he had to share one bathroom with a bunch of women."

"A man with vision. I like him."

Nettie inclined her head. "You would have, I think. Politics and current events fascinated him."

"Nick mentioned your parents passed away when you were very young."

Nettie nodded. "Uncle Harm, my father's brother, pretty much raised Sara and Lilah and me."

"Uncle Harm was a bachelor?"

"Yep." Nettie moved up a few stairs and leaned on the banister. "Except for us. He blessed my father's foresight on the bathroom facilities every time Lilah had a date." She grinned. "Actually, we all did."

Chase, too, leaned an arm on the banister. "And you? What were you like on date nights?"

"Like any other girl, I guess."

Chase shook his head. "No, I don't think so. Teenagers are notoriously narcissistic."

"Were you?"

"Of course." He grinned shamelessly. "Still am. Not you, though."

Nettie inclined her head. "You sound awfully sure."

"I am. I'm a reporter, remember? Good at interpreting the facts."

"You don't have all the facts."

"No. So tell me more."

For some reason Chase couldn't fathom at the moment, the mood had changed. Pushing away from the banister, Nettie tried to maintain her smile. She tried too hard. "I think that's enough family history before lunch."

She was too eager to stop talking. Chase wasn't sure whether the reporter in him demanded to know more or whether the man did. In any case, he persisted. "You were raised by a bachelor uncle. You had one sister who was obviously a tomboy and another who grew up, I'm guessing, a little more interested in boys than homemaking. But the jail windows are all curtained and this place is a paean to family life." He nodded to the photographs, contemporary and old, that decorated the wall behind her. "Somebody worked hard to make that happen. My bet is on you."

"The curtains in the jail only mean I'm no Martha Stewart. I'm sure she'd recommend something more appropriate. Maybe a *Shawshank Redemption* theme."

Chase laughed. "Or *Papillon.*" He reached over the banister to tug on the lapel of her shirt. "I like the blue curtains. Nice little ruffle on the bottom. Very cheery."

"Sara's regulars seem to like it."

"Her regulars?"

"Lefty Bruener, Otto Callendar and Violet Jenks."

Chase shook his head. "This I have to hear."

"Lefty shoplifts from Otto's market every Tuesday like clockwork. Otto gets furious and chases Lefty down the block, throwing old produce at him, which causes a public nuisance. Otto insists on pressing charges against Lefty, and the other shopkeepers want to press charges against Otto because he has terrible aim and usually winds up lobbing moldy cantaloupes at the hair salon. Sara finally figured out that arresting both of them right away keeps everyone happy.''

"This goes on every Tuesday?"

"Haven't missed one in years."

"And Violet?"

Nettie leaned her forearms on the banister again. Her smile softened, becoming once more the winsome curve of lips Chase found so irresistible. "Violet is seventy-eight, almost ten years older than Otto, but she's been in love with him for as long as anyone can remember."

Chase held up a hand. "Don't tell me. I want to guess. Miss Violet attacks Lefty in defense of her true love."

Nettie grinned. "Don't be silly. Violet wouldn't hurt a fly."

"What does she do?"

"Spits in front of the jail."

Chase took a beat to process this information. "And Sara arrests her for that?"

"Violet spits repeatedly."

"Because…"

"Because she thinks it's a crime. She wants to get arrested. That way she can stay up all night in the next cell, reading love poems out loud."

"Otto likes to be serenaded with love poems?"

"Hates it. But Otto is German and Violet makes the best *mandelbreidt* cookies in town. Otto says they taste just like his mother's. Lefty likes them, too. So for Christmas a few years back, Lefty bought a pair of very discreet earplugs for Otto and another pair for himself. Now they can sit in their cell eating cookies all night while Violet reads next door."

Chase rested his forehead against the banister. His shoulders shook with laughter.

"Hey, don't laugh at us," Nettie protested. "We small-town folk take our romance seriously."

That sobered Chase up right away. Strolling around the banister he took the first stair. She was standing on the third. Paint stains streaked her shirt, reminding him that she was an artist and that he didn't know nearly enough about her yet.

Burning with curiosity now, he moved up to the second stair. "Do you have an Otto?" he asked quietly.

Nettie's hand trailed farther up the banister as he advanced. "What—" she cleared her throat "—what do you mean?"

Standing on the adjoining steps, they were almost eye-to-eye. "You're a beautiful woman. Is there somebody out there who would be willing to get arrested just to be close to Nettie Owens?" His hunger to know amazed him. Was there a man out there somewhere who wanted this woman completely, who would fight to win her and sacrifice anything to keep her? Chase had always believed that degree of emotion was reserved for books and movies. God knew he'd never noted any evidence of it in the real world. As far as he could tell, people fought for land, for power; they fought to stay alive.

But to risk everything for the privilege of loving someone who may or may not always love you in return?

At another time he would have written Violet off as a silly old woman. Yet at the moment, all Chase could dredge up was a kind of grudging admiration for the old gal.

He looked at Nettie closely. She hadn't answered him. Perhaps he hadn't asked the right question.

Moving forward on the deep step, Chase said, "Would you risk everything for love?"

Even as the words left his mouth, his heart began to pound and he decided to tape his tongue to the roof of his mouth till he got sane again. Nobody—nobody—risked everything for love. People looked out for themselves first whether they thought so or not. And there was nothing wrong with that.

What a damn dumb question he'd just asked.

But the really, really damn dumb thing was how much he wanted to hear her answer "yes."

Nettie felt so immobile suddenly, she couldn't even swallow. How could she answer Chase honestly? If she said, "Yes," she would only invite more questions: Who? When? What happened?

She didn't want to talk about the two great loves of her life, her late husband and her son. Time with Chase hung suspended—no past to mourn or regret, no future to fear.

A person always risked everything for love, whether they knew it or not, because the chance always existed that you might outlive or out-love the person who held your heart and hopes. Nettie stiffened against the feelings that rose like a reflex. She would never love like that again. Not ever.

"No," she said hoarsely, with Chase's mouth hovering mere inches from hers. She could see every fleck of bright gold in his eyes. Stubbornly she infused her tone with strength and finality. "No, I wouldn't risk everything for love."

She saw his eyes blink in what appeared to be surprise. A sudden pang of sadness for the trusting girl she'd been filled her, but only briefly; she shoved the feeling right down again. That girl was gone, and the woman who'd taken her place meant what she'd said.

It wasn't the answer Chase expected.

He'd intended to kiss her, had been aching to kiss her from the moment she'd answered the door. Her response should make everything easier. She wanted what he did—an absence of strings. And he, who had mastered the art of transient attraction, ought to feel mighty pleased.

He leaned forward, about an inch. He *was* mighty pleased. It would take only an inch or two more to show her *how* pleased.

Open and watchful, her eyes remained steady as she awaited his kiss. Chase gave her a small, sexy smile. The moment his lips curved, he realized with a jolt that the pre-kiss smile was a standard part of his repertoire. His brows swooped into a frown.

Until this moment he hadn't consciously recognized that he had a repertoire.

Swallowing a weird lump in his throat, he pulled back. His throat was dry. In fact, he felt like he was coming down with something.

"We ought to get going." He sounded hoarse. "I mean, if we're going to have lunch someplace else. It'll take time to drive." The frown turned into a scowl. He sounded like a damned kid.

Nettie nodded, appearing no happier than Chase felt, but she recovered, quickly and deliberately. "Good idea. I'm starving. I'll get cleaned up and meet you back down here in ten minutes."

Mutely, Chase nodded.

Nettie backed up the stairs. "Help yourself to a drink in the kitchen, and there's candy in the jar on the coffee table if you can't wait for lunch." She tossed him a smile, then turned to continue up the stairs and out of sight.

For some reason, Chase began to perspire. He shook his head, wishing he could shake out the cobwebs that had collected there recently. He'd been under too much stress. He was starting to question himself, to lose his intrinsic confidence. He was a knife with a dull edge, that's what he was.

Words began to flash in his mind. Unwelcome words.

Two weeks and no strings. *No strings…no strings…*

A dull throb started in his temples. He shook his head again. Oh, yeah, he was definitely coming down with something.

*No, I wouldn't risk everything for love….*

The dull throb intensified.

"What difference does it make?" he growled to the empty room, "I wouldn't risk everything, either."

# Chapter Seven

Glory Bea's Café was located ten-point-eight miles due east from Nettie's house. Not too far, but Nettie was a sweaty, shaky, dizzy mess before they'd gone halfway.

For some reason, Chase had turned silent and glowering—at least that's how it looked from the passenger seat.

Clutching her purse with one hand, the door handle with the other so she'd have something solid to hang onto, Nettie tried to relax by focusing on the road ahead. Unfortunately, it seemed to be spinning.

Wondering what *Cosmopolitan* magazine would say about projectile vomiting in her date's Porsche, Nettie gave up on the idea of relaxing and attempted simply to *endure* the drive to Glory Bea's. Shutting her eyes against the traitorously undulating highway, she tried to recapture that ain't-life-grand delight she'd experienced while flirting with Chase on her front porch.

No dice.

In the time it had taken her to run upstairs and change clothes, Chase had changed, too—into a different man. The Chase who had welcomed her return with a low whistle was smooth and polished, with the demeanor of a man who dated often. Too often. Nettie felt awkward, uncertain and, well, cheated, as if suddenly she were going to lunch with Chase's plastic soap-opera twin.

Risking vertigo, she opened her left eye and glanced at him. Ray Ban sunglasses hid his eyes, and the remaining three-quarters of his face wasn't giving away any secrets, either. She was seated just a little over a foot away from him and yet she felt as if she were in the car alone.

Alone. She hated feeling alone.

Her nausea increased. She wanted to be breezy, sophisticated. She wanted to laugh and flirt and pretend she didn't have a care in the world.

Chase hit a pothole. Nettie slammed her one open eye shut. Oh, lordy! What if she became really and truly ill, right here, right now? What if she had the panic attack to top all panic attacks and couldn't hide it from Chase? That would be entirely too much reality to interject into a relationship that had a shelf life of two weeks, tops. A relationship like theirs was meant to be fun, casual and distinctly un-serious. She squeezed the door handle harder.

"Are you all right?"

The question pierced her fog of distress. Wanting desperately to appear calm and poised, Nettie turned toward him and forced a wide smile. "Just fine." Unfortunately, she forgot to open her eyes, which somewhat marred the effect she was after.

Gradually, she became aware of the car slowing as Chase pulled to the shoulder of the road and shifted to Park. She felt him turn in the bucket seat.

"Are your eyes closed for a reason?"

"Yes. I'm resting."

"Ah. Would you mind not resting for a moment?"

"No." She shook her head. "I don't mind." Gingerly, she let her lids flutter open, testing for spinning scenery. Thankfully, the world beyond the automobile appeared to be fairly stable for the moment, so she turned to look at Chase. He'd pushed his sunglasses on top of his head and was studying her with one of the expressions she had come to know and appreciate: intent, curious and sincere. It was a sexier look than any hey-baby grin he could have manufactured.

"What's wrong, Nettie?"

"Wrong?" *Remember, think fun. Think casual. Think "fling."*

"Nothing's wrong." She attempted a laugh that unfortunately made her sound like a demented canary.

The mouth that had so fascinated her the night before lifted slightly. He nodded toward the passenger-side door. "Can you let go of that handle?"

Nettie looked down, surprised to see that she was still squeezing the door handle to within an inch of its life. When she tried to let go, her frozen fingers refused to unfurl.

"They're stuck," she murmured.

"Mmm. So it seems." Gently, Chase reached for her other hand, the one grasping her purse, and eased first one finger, then another from around the leather straps. Transferring the purse from Nettie's lap to the floorboards, he palmed her hand with both of his, massaging slowly. "What's going on?"

*Oh, dear.* She glanced away, searching empty space for a reasonable answer.

With a crooked finger, Chase nudged her chin, insisting that she look at him again. He leaned across the center console, his gaze dark and penetrating. "I've been told I'm a pretty exciting guy. But I can't recall making a woman hyperventilate in the first ten minutes of a date before. Tell me what's happening here."

When her shoulders stiffened around her ears, Nettie tried consciously—and futilely—to relax. *Oh, what's the use,* she conceded silently. *Tell him.* Bluffing wasn't working, and if she became any more tense from the effort it would start to look as if rigor mortis had set in.

Frustration and resistance mingled with surrender. She had wanted the next two weeks to be her Camelot, with Chase starring as Sir Lancelot, the one passionate, wild indiscretion in her otherwise painfully cautious existence. But there were no panic attacks in Camelot, no pasts to overcome or wounds to heal. That didn't happen until after the wild indiscretion.

Defeated, Nettie sighed. This would be, she was sure, her only date with Chase. He had signed up for a two-week fling, not a double dose of reality.

Even if *he* wanted to try again, she wasn't sure *she* could live through it.

"I'm having an anxiety attack," she confessed as her gaze drifted away from his. "I get them from time to time."

A little understatement. When she'd first started having the attacks after Brian and Tucker died, "from time to time" had sometimes meant around the clock. She couldn't count the nights she'd awakened with the dreaded symptoms already in full swing, her heart pounding, her body sweating and her mind so convinced something awful was about to happen that she had wanted to run screaming from the house.

She felt Chase studying her before he responded. "It embarrasses you?"

Her gaze snapped back to his. "Yes, it embarrasses me. Of course it does." Letting go of the door handle, she gestured expansively. "I'm in an air-conditioned Porsche having a hot flash. And I'm only twenty-five."

"What do you usually do when you have an anxiety attack?"

"Usually?" Her lips quirked. "I panic more." Chase smiled and brushed her cheek with his finger. The touch felt infinitely soothing. "Lately I've been listening to self-help tapes."

"And what do they suggest?"

Nettie rolled her eyes. "You don't want to talk about this."

Chase raised a brow. "How do you know? Maybe *I* need the help. I'm a little anxious myself."

"You are." Nettie scoffed. "You don't strike me as someone who panics over nothing."

"Nothing?" His knuckle ran lightly down her cheek, following the curve to her full lower lip. "Why wouldn't I be anxious? I'm on a date with a beautiful woman." He spoke softly, hypnotically. "My mind is racing. Does she like me? Will I say something I shouldn't? What if I move too fast?" He smiled. "Or not fast enough? What if I don't want this date to end, and she can't wait to go home?"

He shook his head slightly, his voice dropping to a murmur. "It's like being sixteen again."

Mesmerized by this man who had spoken her thoughts, Nettie nodded. "Yes."

His thumb grazed her lower lip. "What would your program suggest in a nerve-wracking moment like this?"

She swallowed as the pad of his thumb circled around to her upper lip, tracing its shape. There were no other moments like this. "It suggests accepting the feelings, the, uh, body sensations and then, um... What are you doing?" Her lips were moving beneath his fingers. It was the most incredibly sensual sensation.

"You have a beautiful mouth," he said. "Like an angel's. After you accept the feelings what does your program tell you to do?"

Bemused by his effortless hop from personal to prosaic, Nettie smiled. *And they say men can't multitask.* "Then you float."

"Hmm. Float?" He arched a brow. Leaving her lips, his fingers trailed lightly down the side of her neck.

"Float." Nettie tried to concentrate. "Distract yourself, get involved in something else." When his knuckles dipped into the curve of her collarbone, she thought she might do something embarrassing, like moan in broad daylight. Before lunch, even.

"Then?"

"Then you, um, let time pass." How curious. Until now she'd had no idea her collarbone was an erogenous zone.

"Let time pass," Chase repeated, adding, "Surrender."

Nettie's eyelids drifted all the way closed. "Surrender?"

"Be willing to lose control." He drew closer, and she wondered how he did that with his fingers—touched so lightly, yet left a trail of sensation that said, *I was here.* "Are you willing to lose control, Nettie?"

With her eyes still closed, she felt him brush so close that his mouth almost, but not quite, met hers. She smelled his skin, warm and clean and spicy, as he passed by her neck to rest his ear against the uppermost part of her chest. Nettie's heart pounded against her breastbone. She shivered.

"Strong," he said, staying where he was for another moment. "Your heartbeat is quick and strong." Lifting his head, he followed the same path up her neck, past her chin to her lips. This time he stayed right there, a hair's breadth away, as he reached for her right hand to place it over his heart. "Mine is the same. Quick, strong—because of you. There's nothing wrong with that, Nettie. Is there?"

*Lord, no.* Willing herself to open her eyes, she looked directly into his. He was going to kiss her, and, no, there didn't seem to be a thing wrong with that.

\* \* \*

Chase closed the passenger-side door to his Porsche and watched Nettie skip lightly up the porch steps to her front door.

"Thanks for lunch. I've never—" She turned as she spoke, laughing when she saw him still standing by the car. "What are you doing down there?"

"Admiring the view."

Her gaze flicked over his head to the green fields beyond her property. "You're facing the wrong way."

Slowly, he shook his head, his mouth curving into a grin. "Nope." Pushing away from the car, he made quick work of the porch steps and stood in front of her, looking down.

He simply didn't tire of looking at her, he thought, not even when he tried.

After he'd kissed her in the car, he'd asked her if she felt distracted enough to forget about the anxiety. "What anxiety?" she'd murmured on a sigh so breathy and sexy he'd kissed her again. In a cherry-red, scoop-necked T-shirt and blue jeans, she was sexier, more feminine and classier than any woman with whom he'd ever been involved.

Smiling at him smiling at her, Nettie said, "I was going to say thank-you for lunch. I've never eaten french fries dunked in a chocolate shake before."

"No?" Seeing that she had her house keys in her hand and aware that in her effort to keep their relationship under wraps she might not want him to linger, Chase placed a palm on the screen door high above Nettie's head. Classic male-takes-control pose. He hadn't tried it since high school; he hadn't needed to since high school. "So, what's your verdict?"

Nettie glanced at his hand, back at his face, appeared to know exactly what he was doing and didn't seem to mind. "Not bad. A little messy, but somehow they tasted…right…like that."

"I told you. Once you try them that way, you never go back." He'd fed them to her himself. Picking out the longest, skinniest fries on his plate, he'd dipped them leisurely into the frosty drink, held them up and dared her to taste. He had absolutely loved watching the ice cream drip onto her chin, watching her giggle and lick it off and then watching her eyes widen with surprise when she realized he hadn't been kidding, that the odd combo really did taste good. Most of all, though, he had loved the way her crystal-blue gaze had held his while he'd dropped the fries into her mouth.

Chase shifted on the porch. She engendered the damnedest combination of affection and lust he'd ever felt.

"I had a great time, too," he said quietly. His free hand went to his hip as an idea came to mind and he considered whether to pursue it. Before he progressed to a conscious decision, the words poured out. "Listen, Nick offered to let me use a little cabin or, I don't know, a hut or something on his property while I'm here."

Nettie giggled. "It's not a 'hut.' It's the Enchanted Cottage."

"Come again?"

"Haven't you seen that movie?" Still sheltered by his raised arm, she leaned against the screen door and chatted as if she didn't have a care in the world or a single thought of shooing him away before they were seen. "*The Enchanted Cottage* is a lovely romance. Lilah and I must have watched it twenty times when we were teenagers. There's a little house on Nick's place that's only been used off and on for years, so we'd sneak in and camp out there sometimes with our girlfriends. We'd tell ourselves we were in the enchanted cottage from the movie."

She looked impish and winsome as she spoke. Chase felt her carving a permanent smile on his memory. "You'd sneak in, huh? Breaking and entering."

"Don't tell Sara."

He raised his free hand in a Boy Scout salute. "Your shady past is safe with me. For now. So what would you do there?"

"Ooh, fun things. Talk about boys and eat graham crackers with canned frosting."

Chase laughed. "Pretty wild." He lowered his head toward hers. "Let's get down to the nitty gritty. Did you ever take a boy there?"

Nettie squinted an eye as if she couldn't quite remember and was trying to see back into the past. "I think Lilah may have. Trespassing with girlfriends was about as daring as I was willing to get. At the time."

"I can't give you the thrill of trespassing, but I could use your input."

"About?"

"Nick offered me the use of your cottage, because he thought

I might want a little privacy while I'm here. I think he might want me out of his hair, too.''

A dimple appeared in Nettie's cheek. "The farmhouse is too small for two big strapping individualists like you?"

Actually, what Nick had said was, *If the boy turns out to be yours, and you want to get to know him without anyone else in the way, I've got a little place…*

Chase shook his head. He still wasn't ready to talk about this. Several times during lunch, he'd tried to direct the conversation to a more personal level. Each time, she'd turned the tables on him, deflecting his questions. He'd discovered that she wrote and illustrated kids' storybooks for a living and that her favorite Christmas gift had been a set of forty colored pencils when she was eight, but that was it. She hadn't allowed the conversation to get any more personal, except to make it clear that she was a career girl.

A career girl who accepted the fact that he was a career man. The rules had already been set. A few weeks. No strings.

"I thought a little privacy might not be a half-bad idea," he said and then scowled. That had sounded better in his head than it did out loud. Aloud it sounded like he was making a play for her. Like he'd been thinking about it, planning for it. *Which,* he reminded himself, *you are.*

"What I meant was—"

"I think privacy is a good idea."

Chase sucked in a breath. At another time, with another woman, he would have anticipated that response. He'd feel pleased. He'd begin to envision the rendezvous, but in a relaxed, even lazy way. He might not think about it again at all until the moment was at hand, except perhaps to pick up a bottle of champagne.

So why, now, was his heart hammering and his brow starting to perspire?

When he realized he was starting to sweat all over, Chase dropped his hand and shook his head. This was the damnedest thing.

"What?" Nettie asked, tilting her head.

"What…what?" *Ah, you are an articulate son-of-a-gun,* Chase applauded himself. *You've been a journalist for how long?*

"You were shaking your head," Nettie answered him.

"Right." He wiped his palm on his jeans as discreetly as he could, then swiped the perspiration from his upper lip.

Where was his will? He was a fighter by nature. He possessed a strong mind. If he wanted to be casual, then, dammit, he ought to be able to *make* himself be casual.

"I know you've got a work schedule," he began.

She nodded. "But I'm due for a vacation."

Chase swallowed. That's it. He was a goner. "I'm picking you up tomorrow at nine. Nick's driving into Minot. He'll be gone until early afternoon. I make great French toast, so be hungry."

Nettie groaned. "You dare say that while I'm still digesting a Giant Dakota Burger, fries and a chocolate shake? After those calories, we women tend to stick to salad and grapefruit for the next couple of meals."

The confusion and ambivalence Chase had been feeling dried up in a flash. He bent over her. "Not *my* woman."

With a quick, hard kiss, he was back at his car, leaving Nettie open-mouthed, dewy-eyed and slightly off-balance as she stared after him.

"Nine o'clock." He winked. "I hope you like lots of syrup."

# Chapter Eight

Nettie awoke at quarter past six the next morning. She had also awakened at three-thirty, four-ten and five-eighteen.

Plunging her feet into the soft, cushioned slippers at her bedside, she moved by feel to the chintz-covered chair where she'd tossed her robe the night before. There was something private and, yes, romantic about the early-morning darkness—lavender sky, pale hint of a moon and birds beginning to arise and sing. She didn't want to lose the mood by turning on a light.

Slipping the robe around her, she tiptoed to the bathroom, trying not to waken Sara, then made her way downstairs to the kitchen. Might as well start the caffeine drip. Not that I'm the least bit tired, she thought. Nope. Not at all. She let her fingers dance lightly along the banister.

Singing a little something from the Dixie Chicks as she scooped Otto's finest French Roast—five twenty-nine a pound; buy one, get one free—into a paper filter, she wondered what Chase was doing right now.

"Probably sleeping." She grinned, knowing she hadn't been this anxious to start a day in longer than she could remember.

Dropping the coffee scoop into the can, Nettie snapped the

filter unit into place and hit the start button on the coffee machine. Searching a cupboard for corn flakes, since breakfast with Chase was still a good three hours away, she marveled at her own appetite. Excitement did that to her, she guessed—woke up all her senses, taste included. She'd felt like this last night, too. Craving music, she'd turned on the radio and blared country and rock. She'd gone back to work and painted with bold strokes and splashes of the most brilliant colors she'd ever used. Later in the evening she'd lit an aromatherapy candle, climbed into a foamy tub and shaved her legs for today, slathering them with moisturizer and then putting on the softest cotton leggings she owned. The feeling of whisper-soft material on smooth skin had been sensuous. And everything she did, every single thing all night long had made her think of Chase.

Grabbing a handful of corn flakes straight from the box, she searched the fridge for bacon.

The coffee had brewed fragrantly and the fry pan was sizzling when Sara ambled into the kitchen around seven.

"Oh, good, you're up!" Nettie sang cheerfully, adding several hot, crisp slices of bacon to the mound already draining on a paper towel. "Now we can up the music." She danced over to a portable radio tucked into a built-in shelf and raised the volume on Billy Ocean. Then she danced her way back to the stove.

Barefoot and squinting from an apparent lack of rest, Sara stomped to the radio and turned it down. "I'm gonna to puke if I have to listen to that this early in the morning."

Shrugging, Nettie hummed "Get Outta My Dreams and into My Car" as she fried bacon.

Sara dragged a mug down from a shelf and slammed the cupboard door. "What's the matter with you? You're acting like Martha Stewart on speed."

Nettie laughed. "I'm happy. It's a beautiful morning. Have you looked outside yet?" Sara grunted, poured herself some coffee and trudged to the table. "Well, it's going to be a glorious day. I hope you're hungry."

"Not really."

Nettie stopped what she was doing and turned toward her sister. "Sara, are you sick?"

"No." The three heaping teaspoons of sugar she dumped into

her coffee more or less proved the point. Slumping over the mug, she stirred.

Nettie brought the first plate of bacon to the table. "Here then. Help me out. I can't possibly eat all this myself. I'm having breakfast at nine."

Sara's head whipped up. "Why are you cooking now if you're having breakfast— Who are you having breakfast with?"

Disapproval edged Sara's tone. Nettie turned to pull juice from the fridge, biting her tongue before she let her own irritation show. Like Nettie, Sara was most comfortable when she had a set of immutable rules to follow. Losing their parents so suddenly had made life seem unpredictable and chaotic for the Owens sisters. Lilah had coped by embracing chaos and unpredictability as a way of life. Sara had divided the world into good and bad and literally tried to jail anything that upset her. Nettie had become very, very, very, very, very, very good in the hope that bad things did not happen to *very* good people.

She shook her head, musing. *Maybe we should all be more like Lilah.* Never one to linger over relationships or sorrows, Lilah had once insisted that life was like toothpaste and everyone had a choice: You could give the tube a squish, here a little, there a little, or start at one end and squeeze out every last drop. Either way, the tube was going to get tossed.

Maybe that was the right idea. Enjoy life and, as much as anyone can, keep it simple. Sara, however, would never agree. She considered Lilah wild and unforgivably irresponsible.

"What is happening at nine?" Sara demanded, again with a tone that foreshadowed the litany of cautions to come.

*It's my life,* Nettie reminded herself and then answered, "I'm having breakfast with a friend." As Sara's lips formed the word *who,* Nettie stated, "I'm not discussing this. My social calendar is not open for examination. Or debate," she added when Sara geared up for exactly that. "Now," Nettie said, tempering her own urge to argue, "do you care for juice?" She raised the carton.

"No, I do not care for juice!" Grabbing her coffee cup and a handful of bacon, Sara marched to the door, but couldn't resist turning around to add, "You know what kind of trouble you could get into? No man who sneaks around is interested in a woman's good name."

Nettie laughed out loud. "I certainly hope not."

Sara stared at her sister in growing dismay, but she said nothing else before pushing through the door and heading back to her bedroom.

Nettie stared at the wood panel, listening to the stomp of Sara's footsteps and determinedly resisting the urge to make peace at whatever cost.

She busied herself awhile, cleaning up and trying not to think, but her mood was less buoyant than before and she had a hard time ignoring the guilt that stabbed at her. All Sara wanted was order in the court.

By eight-thirty, Nettie was more concerned for herself than she was for her sister. Sara wasn't talking, she wasn't eating and she sure wasn't leaving. The door to her bedroom was still closed. She hadn't emerged to shower yet, and Chase was due to arrive in half an hour.

Dressed and ready to go herself, Nettie stared at Sara's door and made a decision: She would head over to the farm on her own, right now, before Chase left.

Running downstairs to use the phone in the kitchen, Nettie remembered how easily Chase had handled her panic yesterday in the car. He'd simply accepted her as she was and effectively distracted her very, very effectively.

Today she would have to distract herself. A twinge of nerves made her legs feel jittery and weak.

*Surrender.* The word drifted through her mind in a man's voice and with it came a warm, buttery feeling of relief. Surrender. If she chose, she could surrender to the feelings in her body, to the excitement and the nervousness and to the risk inherent in being alive.

With a long, deep breath, Nettie reached for the phone to tell Chase she'd see him in a few minutes. Punching in the number, she felt a genuine smile spread across her face. *This girl's going to squeeze some toothpaste.*


"Where did you learn to cook?" Nettie asked as she and Chase trekked over to the cottage after breakfast.

Wearing a white V-neck T-shirt, denim pedal pushers and lace-up espadrilles, she walked along the grass that bordered

Nick's barley fields. Chase strolled by her side. Breakfast had been wonderful. Thick-sliced French toast dripping with warm maple syrup, sausages that tasted of apple and sage and perfect coffee. Chase had seated her at the kitchen table with a mimosa and hadn't let her lift a finger. She sneaked a glance in his direction. Obviously he hadn't spent all his time chasing stories along the Sudan.

Hoping she sounded casual even as she admitted to herself that she was dying to know, she nudged again, "Fess up. Who taught you to cook? Mother, sister or girlfriend?"

"Who said I could cook? You just tasted a full half of my repertoire."

He'd neatly skirted the answer, but Nettie had no idea how to probe further without being obvious, so she asked instead, "What's the other half?"

"Chocolate chip cookies."

"From scratch?"

"My own recipe."

"Are they really good?"

He twirled a long twig from the fields between his teeth. "People have killed for less."

"You don't say. I make a pretty mean cookie myself. What's your secret?"

A dark brow arched as he glanced her way. "If I told you, it wouldn't be a secret."

Nettie laughed. The day was sunny; the conversation was sunny. If hearts could grin, she figured hers was.

"Come on," she wheedled happily. "I won't blab to *People* magazine, if that's what you're worried about. In fact, if anyone ever asks me what one of the Fifty Most Beautiful Bachelors likes to do in his spare time, I give you my word never to mention how natural you looked in your sweet little apron, holding a fry pan."

Clamping his teeth around the twig, Chase scowled. "I wasn't wearing an apron."

"Makes a better story, though, doesn't it?" Laughing, she skipped ahead of him, then turned to walk backwards a few paces while he stood still, glowering. Until now, Nettie had had no idea that teasing someone could be this much fun. "Ah, I know what's bothering you," she sang out. "You're afraid *Peo-*

*ple*'s female audience will find out that you're beautiful *and* you bake chocolate chip cookies and you'll be hounded by single women. Hungry single women. You know, I think you're actually very shy.''

Disposing of the twig, Chase gave her a wide, unarguably sexy grin. ''Why, Nettie,'' he said, his voice a silky smooth purr, ''I had no idea you think I'm beautiful.''

This time Nettie stopped walking as he strolled on. ''I didn't say that,'' she claimed while he strutted like a peacock with its tail feathers spread.

Chase wriggled the twig with his tongue. ''Did too.''

''I was referring to the article.''

He shook his head. ''I don't think so.''

Catching up with him, Nettie fell into step without glancing his way. ''Well, think again.'' Under her breath, but loudly enough for him to hear, she muttered, ''Egomaniac.''

Chase didn't even blink. He simply stretched a leg in front of hers, deliberately tripping her. As she shrieked and started to fall, he pivoted neatly, placing himself in front of her and grasping both her arms. Then in one smooth move, he dropped onto his back, bringing her harmlessly down on top of her.

The sheer surprise left Nettie panting. Chase's hands were warm and firm around her upper arms. ''Admit it,'' he commanded in a low sexy growl. Before she had time to catch her breath, he rolled them over, placing his palms on the ground and hovering over her. ''Admit you want me badly.''

Bracketed by his arms, Nettie shook her head. He was teasing, but the energy that sizzled between them was no joke. ''I admit I want your cookie recipe,'' she breathed, refusing to give in. Playing the game.

Chase grinned appreciatively. He lowered his head. ''Ve haf vays of making you speak.'' Closer and closer he moved until he was nuzzling her cheek with his nose and lips.

A strong shiver raced through her body, followed by a dozen tiny, delicious shivers. She tried to mask the intensity of her reaction, but when his tongue came out to tickle the corner of her mouth, Nettie thought she would go berserk if she had to stay silent and still.

''You taste like maple syrup,'' Chase whispered.

Someone moaned. *Probably me,* Nettie thought, then couldn't have formed a coherent sentence to save her sanity as he used his lips to nibble the spot he'd just licked.

Chase was in control. He was sure of it. Until her fingers delved mindlessly into his hair. Until she arched beneath him with total abandon. Until she moaned.

She was part siren, part playmate. What started out as a game to urge her to say she wanted him had turned into a trap he'd set for himself. He wanted her. Now.

Nettie raised her right knee and his thigh slid between hers. There was no way she could mistake his desire, yet she gave no hint of wanting to pull back.

This is no place to make love, Chase thought even as his mouth covered hers completely. Her lips parted, and he sank into the kiss like a drowning man. On the other hand, it might be the perfect place. Earth below, sunup above. There was another groan, this time issuing from him.

Chase's hand caressed and explored as it roamed from her breast to her waist. Nettie strained against him. He curved a palm around her hip. She began to wriggle, which just about drove him crazy. If she kept moving like that, he'd have them both out of their clothes before their hearts took the next beat.

He clamped a hand on her hip. She strained against him and her hands left his hair, moving to his shoulders, first pulling then pushing until she reached for the hand holding her hip and tried to throw it off.

With a Herculean effort, Chase broke the kiss and raised his head. "Sweetheart," he groaned, his voice hoarse. "I want to give us what we both want, believe me, but I—"

"Off," she gasped.

Chase frowned. *Off?*

"Get. Off." This time she pushed the words through gritted teeth. There was no mistaking her intention as she brought the heels of her hands to his shoulders and shoved as hard as she could. *"Now!"*

Chase leaped up. Nettie followed. Before Chase's ever-widening eyes, she grabbed her T-shirt and all but ripped it from the waistband of her pants.

"Fire ants!" she cried.

"What?"

''Fire ants.'' Wriggling like a trapped lizard, Nettie indicated, ''In my shirt.''

She began a mad dance, hopping up and down and flapping the hem of the shirt as she tried desperately to rid herself of the biting insects.

Chase watched with a kind of fascination and some notion that he ought to help, but damned if he knew how. He was a guy. A guy would just—

''Take off your shirt,'' he shouted above her yelps. She didn't hear him. Chase strode over and grasped her wrists. When he had her attention, he directed again, ''Take your shirt off.''

If he was afraid she wouldn't comply, he was in for a surprise. Nettie flung the shirt over her head and onto the ground faster than lightening. Unmindful, at least initially, of the fact that she stood in her bra, she rubbed her skin with her hands, reaching around to her upper back.

''Are they all gone?'' she asked, twisting and turning.

Chase was not unmindful of the fact that she stood in her bra. Not for a second. He clasped her shoulders, turned her around and held her steady while he brushed the last little clingers off her skin. Perfect silken skin. His touch should have been purely clinical under the circumstances, but to claim that it was would have been pure fiction.

The back she presented to him was a work of art, the shoulders broad for a woman, but the bone structure refined and graceful. Her ribcage tapered to a waist he wanted to span with his hands. Gently, almost tentatively, he splayed his fingers across her back. Like a kid, he thought. Like a kid who's breaking the rule ''look, but don't touch.''

''Are they gone?'' Nettie repeated the question over her shoulder.

Attempting language, Chase managed only a grunt at first. He cleared his throat. ''Yes.'' His hand, he noticed, stayed right where it was.

Slowly, Nettie faced him. His palm skimmed her waist as she turned, and goose bumps rose on her flesh. He felt them. So did she.

Every sense Chase possessed sang at this new sight of her. She wore a gossamer bra of pale blue lace and satin that cupped her round breasts, emphasizing their fullness. He made no attempt to mask the direction of his gaze, deliberately touching her with it, feeling unabashed pleasure when she visibly responded, her nipples growing and tightening beneath his eyes. She was all gentle female flesh, shapely but lush, no evidence of a personal trainer who'd carved curves into angles. Most of the women he knew were aggressively lean. Nettie's definitively female body was, Chase realized, the perfect expression of her personality.

Two-weeks-and-no-strings could go to Hades. It wasn't going to work. *It wasn't,* and he wanted to hear her admit it more than he wanted to deny the truth to himself.

Conveniently disregarding the fact that his hand was still on her waist, Chase swore to himself that he wouldn't touch her again until they'd had a chance to talk. Because…

…he watched her eyes darken to an impossible shade of blue as she raised her hands to his chest.…

…because they needed to talk before…before…

His thoughts scattered as he noted the quickening of her breath. Unerringly, her fingers found the third button of his shirt and unfastened it.

Okay. All right. He needed to stop her because they had to talk. The rules of the game had changed and she needed to know that before she went one step further.

She undid the next button.

*Nettie.* Her name made it into his mind, but not out of his mouth.

As the buttons popped free, she explored his chest with interest and tenderness, the likes of which he'd never before experienced. When she brushed his nipple with her fingertips— whether intentionally or inadvertently he couldn't quite tell— Chase actually growled.

The effort to maintain control under the circumstances was inhumane. And, anyway, he didn't want to. New plan: Touch now; talk later.

Good plan.

The instant Chase cupped her breast with his palm, a host of new feelings and thoughts rushed through him, including a sense of triumph. *Mine. This woman is mine.* The whole two-week thing was a stupid safety net. In the midst of a flight this high, a safety net was only extra baggage.

Nettie's eyes closed, and she swayed toward him, palms pressed flat against his chest. Chase slid his hands around her back, pulling her close. Abandoning any notion of holding back, he kissed her so there would be no mistake: He was asking to have her, body and soul.

Like whispers of smoke, Nettie's arms wound around his neck. She raised onto her toes, straining closer, returning his kiss with a gusto and sweetness that made him ache.

Just as Chase decided it was time to get off this field and into a house, the relative privacy they had was shattered by the sound of hooves pounding the earth as a horse and rider bore down on them.

Thankfully this time they heard Nick before they saw him, which gave Chase time to yank off his own shirt and toss it around Nettie. Acting almost reflexively, she managed to shove her arms through the sleeves, but was still fumbling with the buttons when Nick reined in.

The three of them stood awkwardly, Chase naked now from the waist up and Nettie clothed in his shirt.

Chase eyed the buttons she'd stuck in the wrong holes and felt a rush of pure affection. *Mine,* he thought again and this time a smile of happiness started in his chest and rose to his lips. It died when he looked at Nick's sober face.

"What?" Chase glared, communicating via expression that he would welcome another big-daddy lecture about as much as he welcomed a case of head lice. He reached for Nettie's elbow in a show of protectiveness and support that was altogether deliberate.

Nick, who had mastered the art of the inscrutable expression, merely nodded a greeting. "Sorry to interrupt. I saw Nettie's car when I got home and thought you might have headed this way."

Nettie said nothing, but Chase noted the tiny frown between her brows and the distracted look in her eyes. He couldn't tell if she was beginning to regret what had taken place, if she was embarrassed, or if it was simply the interruption that bothered her. In any case, he wanted to get rid of Nick and talk to her alone ASAP.

He turned his attention back to Nick, but before he could speak, Nick held out a large flat envelope. "I picked this up while I was in town. Thought you should have it right away."

Chase easily identified the envelope. Express Mail. Without dismounting or riding closer, Nick forced Chase to step away from Nettie in order to accept the envelope, a symbolic move if ever Chase had seen one. Nick, too, understood what was in the envelope.

Intending to snap the flat package out of Nick's grasp, Chase was startled to witness his own hand shake. Inside that thick envelope was the answer to the question *Am I a father?* His lawyer had offered to intercept the results of the DNA tests and then phone, which now seemed like an excellent idea. Unfortunately Chase, being Chase, had wanted full control. He'd insisted the results be mailed directly.

Cursing his shaking hand, he looked at Nettie, who was paying more attention now. His trembling increased.

He grabbed the envelope with a tersely muttered, "Thanks." Feeling like a jackass, standing there with his shirt off, holding an Express Mail envelope he had no intention of opening while Nick leaned on the pommel of his saddle and Nettie stared at him, waiting.

As far as Chase could see, there were no really good options available. He did not want to open that envelope in front of Nettie. With his forehead and palms starting to sweat, he turned to her. "Maybe we'd…"

He paused as she tilted her head in question. Wearing his shirt, her kissed lips full and red as summer cherries, she looked at him with absolute trust and interest in whatever he had to tell her.

Chase felt sick to his stomach.

All along he'd known what he wanted to find in that envelope: Proof that someone else had fathered Julia's child.

"We'd better get back to the house," he said, his voice a pathetic croak.

Nettie simply looked at him, beautiful and surprised and confused.

Accurately estimating Chase's predicament and the discomfort both his friends were feeling, Nick dismounted. "King's been nursing a fetlock." He gave the big horse a solid pat. "Think I'll give him a break. Mind if I walk along with you?" He addressed Nettie, whose questioning eyes fastened on Chase. Cursing himself, wanting to kick his sorry butt for the first conscious act of cowardice he could remember, Chase shrugged and immediately looked away.

With Nettie by his side, Nick headed toward the farmhouse. Carrying the envelope and a million colliding thoughts, Chase brought up the rear by himself.

# Chapter Nine

"So what kind of kiss was it?"

Nettie dug a paint scraper into the side of the house with both hands while she clamped a cordless phone between her shoulder and chin. Phoning her sister Lilah for a little commiseration and some solid dating advice had seemed like a good idea twenty minutes ago. Did people actually describe kisses out loud? Help. Dating was going to be the end of her.

Evidently hesitant, she asked, "What do you mean, 'what kind'?"

Lilah shifted the receiver of her own phone as she slapped a bottle of nail polish several times against her palm. "Soft?" she prompted. "Wet, dry? Long or short? I need details."

A yellow paint chip went flying. "Lilah, I don't know! I wasn't taking notes."

"You don't want to kiss and tell, you mean." Nettie heard the grin in the other woman's voice. "I still can't believe my little sister got up close and personal with a bona fide celebrity."

"I'm not your little sister. I'm a grown woman."

"You'll always be my little sister, silly," Lilah agreed easily.

"Besides, when it comes to flirtation, darling, you really are a youngster. If I'm Methuselah, you're practically neonatal."

"Thanks a lot."

"We have to embrace our strengths. So, let me get this straight," she said. "You kiss like there's no tomorrow, then Nick rides up with the mystery mail. End of date?"

"End of date, end of story unless you help me. When we got back to the farmhouse, Chase was so ruffled he couldn't get away fast enough."

Lilah hmmed on the other end of the line. "How did he excuse himself?"

"He said he had business to take care of."

"Maybe he's a workaholic. Although the pictures I've seen of him suggest he plays as hard as he works."

Already Nettie was experiencing that swallowed-a-cannon-ball sensation in the pit of her stomach. "What kind of pictures?"

"He was splashed all over the pages of *Premiere* magazine during the Cannes Film Festival last year. Charlize Theron couldn't keep her hands off him."

"Charlize Theron. The actress who looks like a twenty-year-old blond Elizabeth Taylor?"

"Only better. Yep."

Nettie glanced down. She'd changed into jeans, a thin red sweater that was starting to pill and red Keds. The epitome of Kalamoose haute couture. "Was Charlize wearing deck shoes?"

"Beg your pardon?"

"Nothing. Cannes is in France, right?"

"Yes." Lilah sounded wistful. "On the beach. Wall-to-wall superstars. Parties all night long. Fabulous entertainment. Heaven." In the backround a refrigerator door opened and closed. "How long can you keep egg salad?"

"A few days, max."

"Rats."

Nettie rested her forehead on a paint-scraped shingle. "Do you have to cross bodies of water by air or ship to get to Cannes?" she muttered sickly.

"Of course." Lilah laughed, then sobered. "Oh, Net, are you worried about having to travel with him? Are those anxiety tapes helping at all? They say they can help you overcome any phobia, even flying.''

''I'm not worried about having to travel with him,'' Nettie sighed. ''Our relationship isn't going to last that long.''

''Yes, it will. Any man would be crazy not to hang on to you.''

''Your sisterly devotion is duly noted, but I mean we've already agreed on a two-week fling. And before you rake him over the verbal coals,'' Nettie said as Lilah inhaled loudly, preparing to do exactly that, ''I'm not interested in anything permanent. Or even remotely stable.'' There was silence and then another inhalation, which Nettie again cut off at the pass. ''I mean it. I know what I want.''

''Okay. What?''

This time Nettie paused, but briefly. ''More. More of the feeling I get when he kisses me.''

''That good?''

''Yes.'' Relief wooshed through her, relief and glorious freedom. Oh, it felt wonderful to say it out loud. ''I want this for myself, Lilah. For two weeks I want to live without a past or a future. I want to forget everything but how good I feel when I'm with him. You know what I mean?''

''Yeah,'' Lilah responded quietly. ''Yes, I do. Is that what he wants, too?''

''I think so.'' With a fingernail, Nettie picked at the chipping paint.

''Or, I thought so. He turned off so quickly today, now I'm not sure. Maybe I'm a terrible kisser.'' The prospect was so depressing, she lowered her head and groaned.

''Don't be silly,'' Lilah rebuked. ''You are not.''

''How do you know? Have you ever met anyone my age with less experience, sexually speaking?''

''That's part of your charm.''

''Part of the novelty, you mean. Novelty wears off. Suppose I kiss like a fish?''

''Will you stop it! And if Chase Reynolds is interested in you because you're a novelty to him, then he can go to—''

''He's a novelty to me, too, Lilah,'' Nettie interrupted with rigorous honesty.

"If you think you're in this for sex and nothing else, you're lying to yourself, Net. I know you better than that."

"Not this time. I told you."

"Yeah, 'Seize the day,' *Carpe Diem.* I understand the principle. I live in Hollywood. We seize the second out here. But that's not who you are. And I don't care what you say," she insisted when Nettie tried to rebut. "Your heart is in everything you do. I don't want you to get hurt."

Concern traversed the miles. Nettie walked the tightrope between gratitude and frustration. "Think about who you are talking to for a minute. 'Try not to get hurt' is my mantra. I feel like a turtle with its head hermetically sealed in the shell." The strength and confidence of a decision firmly made infused her body. She stood straight, spoke straight. "I'm going to do this, Lilah, so don't go all 'Sara' on me. I need advice! What would you do if you were in the middle of a great date with your fantasy man and he suddenly decided he had some pressing e-mail he had to take care of?"

"I'd put on my highest heels, my shortest dress and a lot of very red lipstick. Then I'd find him and make him forget he even had a computer."

"Wow." Nettie took a moment to admire the spirit of her sister's approach. "But my highest shoes are a pair of Dr. Scholls and my shortest dress ends an inch above my knees."

"That's bad. In your case, I'd try to find out what was in that envelope or at least where it came from. See if that's what dimmed the man's lights. Then I'd do some serious shopping. I mean, really—Dr. Scholls?"

If she'd had a pen, Nettie would have taken notes. "How can I investigate the envelope? The postal service gets so prickly about dispensing that kind of information."

"Pry it out of Nick. He must know or he wouldn't have made a special trip to give it to Chase."

"Right!" Nettie frowned. "How do I do that?"

"Are you kidding?" Lilah sounded more like Lilah now— blithe, carefree. "You can wrap Nick around your little finger if you give it half a shot. There's always a way to get what you want, baby doll, remember that. Sara drives him nuts and he thinks I'm decadent, but he's always had loads of respect for you."

Nettie smiled. "Now I'm going to ruin it by asking him to snitch on his friend?"

"You're in the market for a new image."

"True. Thanks." Nettie heard Lilah open and close a cupboard door.

"Can peanut butter go bad?" she asked.

"Does it smell like old axle grease?"

There was the sound of a lid being unscrewed. "Rats!" The peanut butter jar rebounded against the inside of a trash can. "I'm starving. All I've had today was ginger tea and a stale tortilla."

"Lilah, don't you ever have any food in the house that won't cause botulism?"

"I'm an actress. I'm not supposed to have food in my apartment, only Slim Fast. I'm gonna go now. Are you okay?"

"Yes, fine. Thanks for the advice. And for listening."

"No problem, but Net...?"

"Yeah?"

Lilah hesitated. "Don't throw the baby out with the bathwater, right? Who you are is damned fine. I admire you. Everyone admires you."

"Okay. Thanks. I won't. Go eat." Lilah hung up and Nettie let the phone and the paint scraper drop to her side.

Admired. She was admired. A Pyrrhic victory if there was no fun or relaxation or lust in her life. Lust *for* her life.

Checking her watch, Nettie realized it was only a quarter past one. Plenty of time to mix a batch of brownies—Nick's favorite—and a pitcher of frosty lemonade. Then she'd phone him and ask if he could please take a look at the kitchen faucet, which was going to start leaking as soon as she loosened the elbow joint. It was sneaky, it was manipulative—not one bit admirable—and it might work. If she could weasel enough information about Chase from Nick, it was possible that she could make sense of why her fling had begun to flop. Then, if she knew Chase's withdrawal was nothing personal, she could embark on an exhaustive application of all her seductive skills. Which, given what she knew, wouldn't take long.

Acting before she could talk herself out of the vague plan she had only barely talked herself into, Nettie raised the phone, punched the Talk button and phoned Nick.

* * *

"How are the brownies?"

"Just the way I like them." Nettie hovered near the kitchen sink she had deliberately sabotaged so Nick would come over to fix it. He leaned against the counter, a fat fudge brownie in one hand, tall, cold drink in the other.

"And the lemonade?"

He winked his approval. "Icy cold."

"Good." Baring her teeth she offered a facsimile of a smile. Why wouldn't Nick sit down? He was making her nervous, standing there as if his sole intention was to eat his brownie quickly and then go. Nettie felt pressed to acquire her information *now*, before he left. How did investigative reporters stand the pressure?

She'd thought of and discarded a dozen different ways to ask Nick about Chase. She wanted to appear casual, sure of herself. Nick, she sensed, was being deliberately obtuse. He hadn't even mentioned finding her in his field wearing Chase's mis-buttoned shirt. She'd known Nick long enough to know he was thinking a lot more than he was saying.

Draining his glass, Nick set it on the yellow-tiled counter. "Thanks. Let me know if you have any more trouble with that sink. I'm around if you need me."

He started toward the door and Nettie watched her chance to pry walking right out of the kitchen with him.

"Wait! I do need you! I need to, uh…"

Nick turned. Nettie wondered what she could run off and break in the bathroom while he waited here, then quickly snapped herself back to sanity. *Be direct.*

Nick's brow rose. "Something you want?"

"Yes." She stiffened her spine and met Nick's gaze full-on. "What was in that envelope you brought Chase?"

*Whoa!* Nettie felt as surprised as Nick looked. He recovered fairly quickly to plaster a bland smile on his face. "How would I know?"

"You knew it was important." In for a penny, in for a pound. She waved a hand. "Oh, look, Nick, I know it's none of my business, but I don't care. We were getting along very well before you rode up. Then you handed him that envelope and he couldn't leave fast enough. I want to be sure it was the contents of the envelope and not me that turned him off.''

Nettie took a deep breath. *Whoa with a bullet!* Folding her arms, she dared Nick to deny her the information she sought.

His poker face faltered as he wrestled with and finally reached a decision. Re-entering the kitchen, he set the covered pan of brownies on the table and pulled out a chair. ''Let's sit down.''

Finally! Releasing the breath she'd been holding, Nettie moved eagerly to the table. Nick took the chair opposite her. His obvious discomfort as he searched for a way to begin aroused her guilt, but not enough to call a halt.

''I can't tell you what was in the envelope. Not definitely. In part that's because Chase hasn't told me and partly because it's his information to keep or to share. I can tell you a few things, though. Things I think you should know.''

Nick's gravity gave Nettie the impression they were both going to need something stiffer than lemonade.

''Do you know who Chase's parents are?'' he asked.

Surprised, Nettie shrugged. ''His father is a newscaster, isn't he?''

Nick shook his head. ''Not 'a newscaster.' Lloyd Williams is the Walter Cronkite of cable. He owns most of his station.''

''Chase's last name is Reynolds.''

''It's his mother's maiden name. Lana Reynolds, the heiress to Reynolds Worldwide Shipping and the Sojourners Cruise Line.''

Nettie had never heard of Lana Reynolds, but she'd seen zillions of ads for the cruise line. ''Oh, Good Lord.'' She gulped. ''I can't date him. It was bad enough when I thought he was just your everyday average celebrity.''

That elicited a brief smile from Nick. ''Not quite. Chase was raised with the proverbial silver spoon. Lloyd groomed him from the cradle to take over the anchor desk. And Chase made it easy to believe it would happen. He has the looks, the voice, and the intelligence. Everything he needs to make Lloyd's dream come true.''

''Isn't that what Chase wants, too?''

Nick emitted a gruff snort that passed for a laugh. ''Not by a long shot.'' He shifted in his seat as if he found it uncomfortable. This was, Nettie realized, the segment of the conversation about which Nick felt guilty. "You can't understand Chase without understanding his background. His mother and father divorced when he was young, still in grammar school, I think. His mother hit the society trail, which left Chase to be raised by a series of housekeepers."

Nettie couldn't conceal her shock or disapproval. "She walked out on a little boy?"

Nick's lips twisted sourly. "She managed a visit every other Christmas or so."

"And his father?"

"Lloyd wasn't well endowed with parenting skills, either. He believes in three things: hard work, power and power. He expected a lot from Chase."

The tug on Nettie's heart was swift and strong. Lilah's words came back to her and Nettie struggled to remember that she'd made a deal with herself: Keep your heart out of this. As far as her heart was concerned, it was winter and she was hibernating.

Focus, she told herself. Find out about the envelope. That's all you need to know.

"Chase is very successful," she said. "His father has to be pleased with all he's accomplished." Her nose wrinkled. How pat did that sound?

Nick didn't seem to notice that she'd turned into the mother on "Leave It To Beaver." He shook his head. "I don't think Lloyd has ever given Chase the thumbs-up. In college, Chase said he wanted to be an 'in-the-mud, get-the-story journalist,' that he wanted to report the news, not become it."

Nettie gritted her teeth. She was caught, like a fish who'd seen the hook, but couldn't resist the bait. "What happened?"

"The more Chase pulled, the harder Lloyd pushed. Chase was offered jobs no struggling young journalist could possibly refuse. He thought he was getting them solely on his own merit—that's why he took his mother's name—and he didn't find out until later that Lloyd was pulling strings. Lloyd directed the spotlight on Chase every way he could and when an anchor position came up, he expected Chase to sit right down and say, 'Thank you.'"

"Chase didn't?"

Nick shook his head. "And Lloyd barely spoke to him for the next two years. Nothing Chase did was good enough."

Two years. Holidays flashed immediately to mind. Nettie

couldn't imagine being without one's family by choice, or because you were trying to punish someone. She'd never, ever been alone for the holidays, and a part of her didn't even want to ask, "What about the rest of his family?"

Nick's shrug was eloquent. "He has a half sister who travels—he rarely sees her. His mother he sees once every couple of years when he arranges to be in the same city she's in. Chase tells it all with a lot of humor, but it's part of who he's become, Nettie."

"Why are you telling me this?"

Nick clasped his hands atop the kitchen table. "Chase gets a lot of attention, but he's a private man. I don't enjoy betraying his confidence, but if you're dead set on a relationship with him…" The low slash of Nick's brow told her how he still felt about that. "You need to know that he doesn't stay in one place because he doesn't *want* attachments. If he ever did decide to settle down—" after a brief struggle with guilt, Nick spoke with firm conviction "—I don't think he'd be good at it."

This was the point, Nettie knew, at which she was supposed to remind the world once again that she was *not* in the market for settling down. But that's not what came to mind. What came to mind was how blasted unfair it was for other people to take what they knew about you—a bunch of cheap facts—and then pigeonhole you for the rest of your life. What came to mind was that, despite everything she'd told herself, Nick was wrong about Chase.

"Chase is honest and caring, and he's kind." The words spilled out with equal measures of confidence and indignation. "If he decides that putting down roots is what he wants, then I say he'll be great at it!"

Pushing away from the table, she stood. She realized she hadn't achieved her objective this afternoon, but at the moment, she couldn't quite recover the reason she'd thought the envelope and its contents were so bloody important. She would see Chase again, regardless.

She had to.

Nettie's legs wobbled as she excused herself to use the bathroom. She wanted to splash some cold water on her face and collect her thoughts. Attempting to appear far more poised than she felt, she straightened her spine and moved toward the swinging door between the kitchen and living rooms. She walked swiftly and pushed firmly, startled by a loud thud and sharp cry on the other side of the door.

Nettie poked her head through the door. "Sara!"

Behind her, Nick scraped his chair across the linoleum and repeated her exclamation.

Sara walked sheepishly through the door, a hand over her eye. "What were you doing?"

Sara looked at her sister through her good eye and shrugged.

"She was listening at the door. Weren't you?" Nick growled. "When did you sneak in here? With that kind of stealth, you'd make a better criminal than sheriff."

Sara rallied under Nick's censure. "I didn't have to sneak. This is my house."

"No, you didn't have to sneak," Nick agreed, "but you did." He stalked forward. "What are you up to?"

Sara's expression spoke volumes as she glanced between Nettie and Nick. "Seems to me there's been a lot of sneaking going on around here." She stabbed a finger between the two of them. "You've been seeing that reporter guy and everybody—" she glared at Nick "—knew about it but me. How do you think that makes me feel? I thought…" She faltered.

Nettie put her hands on her hips. The skin around Sara's injured eye was starting to bruise, but she refused to let herself feel guilty or try to fix it. For once, she was putting her own life first. "You thought what?" she demanded.

Sara's cheeks turned red. She had trouble, suddenly, meeting Nettie's gaze and couldn't look at Nick at all. Her hands went to the back of her uniform, where she fiddled with her belt. "I thought…uh…" Unable to defend her eavesdropping, she returned to the offensive, where she was clearly more comfortable. "You've been so secretive lately, I didn't know what to think. And now that I know you've got yourself stuck on the pretty boy, I see I was right to be concerned." Her freckled nose lifted an inch. "For once I agree with Nick."

"How reassuring," Nick murmured. "I may rescind my warning."

"I don't want warnings," Nettie interjected before Sara could strike back. "And I'm not interested in an opinion—from either of you." Splitting her gaze between the people she'd known all her life, Nettie said, "I know you think you're trying to help. But people change. Their desires change, their beliefs change. All you know about me is what you *think* you know about me. You have no idea what I really want."

A car pulled up in front of the house. Nick and Sara were too busy staring at Nettie to react to the sound or to the open and slam of the car door, but she crossed immediately to the window above the kitchen sink. Already, she recognized the sound of that engine, and her body reacted before her mind. Chase. Through the open window, she saw him head toward the front door. "Stay there! I'll be right out," Nettie called through the kitchen window.

Momentarily startled, Chase stopped, located her and then nodded. He looked different. Slightly uncertain. Less perfect, more human. Her heart responded instantly. She sent him a reassuring smile because she thought he needed it, and almost immediately his features relaxed. She didn't even bother with her purse or to offer a word to the two people who watched her in silence.

I'm choosing, she thought, facing them once, briefly. I'm choosing me. I'm choosing Chase. Over you, over your opinions of what's good for me. Damn the torpedoes, and if you don't like it, lump it!

As tremulous, as thrilled as if she were sitting at the top peak of a roller coaster, Nettie flew out the back door and around the front of the house, where Chase stood waiting.

"Let's go for a drive," she said, as breathless as a teenage girl about to sneak off with a forbidden love.

Bemused but agreeable, Chase moved without a word to open the passenger-side door.

Nettie glanced at the kitchen window. Sara and Nick stood side by side, peering through the glass like two old biddies. Following an impulse stronger than reason, Nettie reared back, gave Chase a swift, solid kiss somewhere between his mouth and his cheek and got into the car.

Now there were three people staring at her in varying degrees of surprise.

# Chapter Ten

Clover fields waved before Chase like a verdant carpet, more brilliantly green than he would have supposed before arriving in North Dakota. Studded with wild mustard, the landscape looked like a impressionist painting, composed of an infinitude of tiny green and yellow strokes.

Chase inhaled deeply, having to remind himself that mere days ago he had envisioned the area as dry, if not barren then certainly brown and unappealing.

Days ago. He shook his head. How had so many things changed in such a brief span of time?

A few yards behind him, Nettie stood beneath a squat tree. They had spoken little on the drive here. He had something to tell her—two things—and his reluctance to begin amazed him.

Swiping at the perspiration that popped out along his upper lip, Chase endeavored to convince himself it was the heat and not his thoughts that elicited the moisture. The erratic pumping of his heart, however, told a different story.

Through experience, he had come to believe he could usually get what he wanted. He believed in the bulldogged pursuit of a goal, but also in matching a goal to one's capabilities. Now he had the unfamiliar feeling he was in over his head.

Moving toward Nettie, he watched the corners of her mouth turn up. With her back against the tree, she stared at the vista behind him.

"Lovely, isn't it?" she said. "Chicago was so big and fascinating. I was never bored there, but it's the kind of place that happens to you. Know what I mean? All you have to do is stand still and there are a million things to see or do. North Dakota is much, much subtler. You have to look with a more patient eye, interact with her, seek her beauty. Then she can be a wonderful place."

Chase nodded, swallowed and tried to breathe through the tension gathering in his chest. "You lived in Chicago?"

"For a few years. I went to college there."

"College," he murmured. "Not so long ago for you."

She rolled her eyes. "Seems like forever."

Chase smiled. He'd never asked her age, but guessed her to be in her mid-twenties. "Yeah, you're ancient. What did you get your degree in?"

"I don't have one." She shrugged, smiled as if to say *no big deal,* but she seemed awkward suddenly, her cheeks turning pink. "I didn't graduate. You know how kids are."

"Mm." *Not really,* he thought, but because he saw her discomfort, he didn't pursue it. Career had always meant everything to him and college had been a stepping-stone. It had never occurred to him to let anything get in his way. At least, not for long. Personal goals were another matter, however, largely because he'd never had any. Until now.

More perspiration beaded along his upper back and chest. He gestured toward the shaded spot where she stood. "Let's sit down. Do you mind?"

Nettie shook her head and settled herself on a carpet of grass a short distance from the gnarled roots of the tree. Chase hesitated a moment, trying to decide if he wanted to sit beside her or face her head-on.

Irritated by the immediate surge of sick tension that threatened to destroy his stomach lining before the day was through, he sat opposite her. *Head-on. Head-on and get to the point.*

Nettie toyed with the grass. Her long hair was loose, spilling casually over her shoulders as she plucked a green blade and looked up at him. The light breeze and the shade from the tree cooled some of the heat inside Chase, eliciting a brief gratitude as he forced himself to begin.

His reputed silver tongue felt more like brass.

"I have no idea how to start," he admitted, trying candor on for size.

Nettie exhaled. "Sounds ominous already."

"I hope not. I hope…" Dragging a hand over his cheeks and jaw, Chase shook his head. *Oh, man.* He looked at her, telling himself he would replace the trepidation he saw with something better. *He hoped.*

"About this morning… I acted like an idiot, and I'm sorry."

She frowned. "When?"

"When?"

"Yes. Do you mean when we kissed or when you left?" Clearly embarrassed by her own question, she nonetheless held her ground. "Because if you're talking about the kiss," she shook her head, lips thinning to a firm line while her eyes filled with fire, "don't you dare. I thought it was wonderful!" Her mouth rounded to a surprised *O* as a thought struck. "You didn't think it was wonderful?" Pressing fingertips to her forehead, she cringed. "I knew it! I kiss like a fish!"

"What?"

She tossed the blade of grass and flapped her hand in a gesture of surrender. "I know. I'm just…not that… Ohhh! I wanted to appear sophisticated, so I haven't said anything, but the truth is I'm not very experienced. Sexually speaking."

Chase endeavored to appear far more surprised than he felt, and a whole lot less pleased. "I never would have guessed."

She started to say something else, but stopped, shifting gears. "Really?"

He nodded. "Where does the fish come in?"

"Well." She raised both hands this time, letting them slap against her jeans-clad thighs. "I've never kissed me, so I'm only guessing, but if you're sorry—"

"Hold on, I'm not sorry we kissed. I'm not sorry about anything we did. It was great. I'm only sorry I ran out on you."

"You're not? You are? It was?"

"Hell, no! And, yes. Of course. Nettie," he reached for her

hand, but told himself he'd never get through this if he was actually touching her, so he pulled back to rake his fingers through his hair. "Kissing you was one of the sweetest experiences of my life. Don't make a face," he laughed when her smile fell on the word *sweet*. Matter-of-factly he told her, "I've been pretty short on sweet experiences. Nobody," he leaned forward to caress her with his eyes, which felt far safer than any other manner of touch, "but *nobody* would ever accuse you of kissing like a fish."

She leaned forward, too, her smile nearly killing him with its innocence and its pleasure. "I'm glad."

"Nettie." He cleared his throat, determined to stay on course. "I'm usually a man of my word, but this time I'm going to break it. When we agreed to a fling..." Feeling his jaw tighten even as he said the word, Chase slowly shook his head. "That was a bad idea."

Nettie's brows dipped. He could see her swallow. "Was it?"

Chase began to smile. "Oh, yeah. Very bad. I think we should renegotiate."

He loved the way surprise entered her expression, the way it evolved slowly but surely to expectation. "Will I need a lawyer?" she asked.

"Nah." Grinning now, so entranced by her reaction that the cannonball of tension in his chest began to melt, Chase said, "We can work it out ourselves, keep it simple. Keep it," he took a breath, watching her closely, "open-ended. What do you think?"

It was the only time he'd said anything remotely like that to a woman. The words had barely hit the air before his heart began to carom like a pinball against his ribs. Quickly, silently, ferociously he fought every doubt that clawed at him. Not a one of them had to do with her, anyway. They were all about him.

Her expression became a dance of emotion, and the one he sought was the last to come: pleasure. Unfortunately fear followed swiftly behind.

Okay, he could handle that. He was scared, too.

Nettie's insides tingled like a blanket filled with static electricity. She had not anticipated this moment. How could she? He was supposed to be leaving. She hadn't even imagined his wanting to be with her beyond his stay here.

*Liar.* She'd started imagining it when Nick was telling her who Chase was.

*Liar, liar.* She'd been imagining it since he'd thrown the first stone at her window. Fantasies had flown in and out of her mind since she'd stood barefoot and blissful with him on her side lawn. Simple fantasies...

Like dancing in the city—she wasn't even sure which city— but somewhere that glittered, somewhere the night was as bright as the day.

And Chase laughing with her as they rode bikes down to Ernie's for the last of the summer's chokecherry pie.

And then she'd imagined the two of them ensconced in the oldest cliché in the book: lying on a rug before a crackling fire, with winter howling outside.... They hadn't even been in Kala- moose in that scenario. She'd pictured a penthouse overlooking sparkling lights.

It was ridiculous. She couldn't do those things, hadn't been to the city in years and never danced anymore.

Then again, before Chase had come to town, she hadn't driven a car in years, either. She hadn't stood up for herself so thor- oughly or spent hours laughing, not thinking about anything se- rious at all.

Before Chase had come to town, she'd been asleep. Now the prince who had kissed her awake didn't want the fairytale to end. Not yet, anyway.

Suddenly Nettie had no desire to deny the sheer gladness that bubbled inside her.

"Are you planning to stay in town, then?" she asked Chase, amazed when she caught herself thinking, *If he says he has to leave and wants me to meet him somewhere, I will. I don't know how, yet, but I'll do it!*

She braced herself, almost exhilarated, as she waited for him to say, *I'm flying to Bora Bora in the morning. The envelope I received held instructions regarding my next assignment. Ever been to Bora Bora?*

Instead he arched a brow. "You haven't answered my ques- tion yet."

Shamelessly relishing the power he'd just handed her, Nettie affected a frown. "Hmm. Well, if you need an answer now, let me think..."

Glorious male pride sparked a flash of protest in Chase's eyes. Impulsively, she sprang to her knees and flung out her arms, catching him round the neck. "Yes. The answer is yes!" She grinned, basking in the surprise and the relief she saw in his answering smile.

Chase clasped her upper arms and pressed her into the grass. "Tease," he growled, letting the rebuke linger as he took the kiss she offered.

He kissed her in a kind of lover's Morse code: long-short-short-very long, each kiss a comment. She could drive him mad with a look, and he loved it. His lips told her so.

With her eyes closed she smiled like a cat full of cream, and Chase knew, he knew in that moment, that he wanted to tell her everything. Here, at last, was a woman he felt he *could* tell. Not just about Colin—his *son*—but about how damn humiliatingly terrified he had been when he'd opened that envelope.

For almost three weeks he hadn't known how he would feel or what he would do if the paternity tests proved he had a seven-year-old son. He'd thought that, quite possibly, he might want to run. Not from the financial responsibility, certainly, but from the emotional commitment. What did he know about emotional commitment? He wasn't sure he could define the term, except to say it was the opposite of everything he knew.

Gently, with a touch he hadn't realized he possessed, he traced an invisible *I* over Nettie's face, across her forehead, down the bridge of her nose and along her lips. Her skin was milky and translucent, but between her brows he saw two small worry lines. She was gentle. She was strong. She was authentic. There didn't seem to be a harsh or critical bone in her body. To her and only to her, could he imagine confessing the truth he hated admitting even to himself: He was thirty-four years old, and he didn't think he'd ever loved anyone.

At the farmhouse he had sat on the edge of his bed in Nick's guest room, the door locked, and he'd stared hard at the sheet of paper stating definitively that there was a child in the world with Chase's blood coursing through his veins. Amazingly, Chase hadn't wanted to run—thank God—but he hadn't felt anything a human being might term love, either. He'd felt clammy and cold and so inadequate it had made him nauseous. Then he'd thought of Nettie and without trying, his muscles had relaxed. Her smile had filled his mind and suddenly his body had warmed.

He'd sat there alone, his thoughts disordered, and finally it had come to him that he was shaking not because he wanted to run away from something, but because he wanted to move toward it.

He had a son. And, for the first time, a woman in his life he would rather spend his time talking to than trying to charm.

Moving so that his shadow fell across Nettie's face, he plucked a blade of tall grass and traced the path his fingers had taken. The feathery touch tickled, and she opened her eyes.

"Keep them closed," he whispered, moving the blade of grass tenderly over her skin. "I have something else to tell you. I should have told you before, but I was…" Sighing, he settled onto his elbow. "I've been pretty confused, Nettie Owens, and I don't like being confused."

To Nettie, the last line sounded more like a growl than a spoken statement. She suspected this conversation ought to be pursued with eyes open, but decided this was one of those Men-Are-from-Mars moments and let him have his way.

Keeping her eyes closed and her tone neutral, she asked, "What's confusing you?"

After a brief pause, through which she remained carefully still, he responded, "The difference between what I want and what I thought I wanted. Ever been there?"

Nettie laughed. "Been there? I own property on that block."

Even with her eyes closed, she could feel his smile and the slow wag of his head. "I'm a new resident. Career hasn't been my top priority, Nettie, it's been my only priority. The whole idea of kids, the white picket fence route—that left me pretty cold." The blade of grass had stopped its patterning. "I have a sister who's been married three times, and she just turned thirty. She's on a world cruise right now with Husband Number Three's money. I never did meet the guy. I think his name is Chuck."

Resting his arm along his side, Chase let his gaze drift to the tree as he continued.

"I haven't done much better in terms of relationships. The only difference is I haven't tried as hard. I figured I'd concentrate on what I was good at and told myself there was a certain honor in sparing the world another screwed-up family. But as it turns out..."

Here, he thought, comes the hard part. Feelings he had no idea how to define poured into his voice when he said, "As it turns out, I'm going to get a crack at raising a family, after all."

Nerves suffused his voice, but once the words were out, relief flowed through him, clearing a path for new reactions. Suddenly he felt glad, incomprehensibly, shockingly glad. Blowing out a long-pent-up breath, he flopped onto his back. Maybe the sun and blue sky were harbingers: Everything was going to be all right.

"I have a son," he murmured, realizing Nettie would forever be the first person to whom he'd spoken the words. "I have a son. He's seven. His name is Colin. And I've never met him." Placing an arm over his eyes, he decided to let the sun burn away his guilt. From this point on he would begin to make things right. "I knew his mother years ago in London. We were together a few months and then went our separate ways. Apparently Julia died several months ago. She was in the States, living in Florida. After she died, Colin got shuffled off to some friend of hers, and...it's a long, long story. I didn't know anything about Colin until last month, and I didn't know he was really mine until this morning."

"The envelope."

"Yeah. Proof positive. Although, I think I knew when I got the call. It's weird, but I think I sensed the connection the moment I heard his name. That sounds crazy."

"No. No it doesn't."

Amazed, Chase found himself laughing. "My God, Nettie, I have a son! And I want..." He choked, wondering if every "new parent" had to deal with this ocean of undulating emotions. "I want so damn much to make up for the time we've missed."

Dropping his arm, he arose, expectant and grateful to be with someone who would understand his burgeoning excitement, someone who had "family" stamped all over her. With pride out of the way, he wouldn't mind a few pointers—about what holidays were supposed to look like, for example. Man, he had a lot to learn!

Nettie was already sitting up, looking almost as stunned as he felt.

He shook his head. "I'm sorry I sprang this on you." After another brief struggle with his ego, he admitted, "I thought I could ignore the whole thing until it went away. I don't have much to be proud of in this situation. Not yet."

Raw energy coursed through his system. Feeling he had to move, Chase stood and walked to the tree. "You could put everything I know about being a father in a thimble and it wouldn't be half full. But I'm going to do this." He thumped the rough bark with the heel of his hand. "I'm going to be the best damn—" he actually had to take a breath before he could say the word in reference to himself "—*dad* that kid will ever need!"

His vehemence was utterly male—masking self-doubt, filled with determination and trepidation in near-equal measures. Sitting on her knees, Nettie thought no man had ever looked so beautiful, so powerful or brave or scared. Except...

Tears gathered without warning behind her eyes.

Brian. Yes, except for Brian on the day she gave birth to their son. He'd held the tiny body and though doctors and nurses had bustled around them, Brian had seen only his child. Nettie had thought then it was like watching Columbus discover America. O, brave new world. Where nothing would ever be the same again.

She closed her eyes. Another man. Another child. Another bright, uncertain future. *Ah, Chase. Forgive me, forgive me for what I'm going to do.* Through willpower alone, her eyes were dry when she opened them.

Chase stood beneath the tree, knowing he'd gotten carried away, but his adrenaline was pumping. He'd stacked his reputation on maintaining equilibrium in the midst of chaos. Now his legs were so wobbly, he wondered briefly if they could actually buckle.

"You were the first person I wanted to tell, you know." He released a shaky laugh that sounded as though it came from someone else's mouth. "I think that means something. Don't you?" He smiled, waiting for Nettie's sweet smile in return.

Waiting. And then hoping.

She twined her fingers, gripping her hands in a tight ball on her lap. "I am glad for you, Chase. I am...so glad. Glad you told me, too. And I think you'll be a wonderful father."

Sounding reserved, she offered him...platitudes.

You caught her off-guard, he reminded himself. You're misreading her. You've had time to get used to it. She's probably wondering why you didn't tell her right away. Women like to be told.

Pushing away from the tree, he stepped forward. "I should have brought this up earlier. I wish—"

"No." Nettie shook her head—vehemently, or so it seemed to him. "No, it's not that. I—I could be handling this better."

His muscles tensed. "Handling it?" He shook his head. "Just say it. Whatever it is."

Only by the tiniest flicker of eyelashes did she betray her nerves.

"I've enjoyed every moment we've spent together," she told him, and he sensed immediately that those words were going to be his consolation prize. "But this is all so sudden, and... Under the circumstances, I really can't... I don't think we should..." Annoyed with her hesitation, she paused, cranked her composure up a notch and unloaded the rest of the pistol straight from the hip. "The truth is, I don't want to see you anymore."

# *Chapter Eleven*

Sara sat at her desk in the Kalamoose jail, tapping a pen rapidly against a stained blotter while Nettie balanced herself on a cot in one of the cells, measuring for curtains.

*New curtains, for crying out dang loud!* Just what they needed, more girly stuff to make a perfectly good jail look like a sorority house. As if the old ruffles weren't torture enough.

Tossing the pen, Sara pulled a couple sticks of Juicy Fruit from the desk drawer, blew to remove excess dust, then unwrapped and crammed them both into her mouth. In four days, Nettie had scraped the paint off the entire lower half of their house, slip-covered Sara's favorite TV chair and arranged the contents of the snack cabinet in alphabetical order, which meant Sara had to dig for the Pop Tarts, but the dried apples were right up front. Nothing was safe.

"Come on, let's go," she said, rising from the chair. "It's almost seven, and my stomach's going to cave in if I don't put something in it soon."

Nettie turned from the window. The same cheerful smile she'd worn for days—as if her cheek muscles had frozen solid—wreathed her face. "I didn't realize the time," she chirped, hopping down from the bed. "I've got an Irish stew in the Crock Pot. I made chicken Oscar, too. We can pop that into the oven, if you'd rather. Or I can freeze it for another time. Oh, and there's soda bread, but I could whip up a batch of biscuits if you—"

*"No!"* Burying a choice swear word beneath her breath, Sara pleaded, "Don't whip anything." Heading for the door, she grabbed her hat, smashing it onto her head. All she wanted for dinner was a triple-decker peanut butter and jelly with a handful of the potato chips that were shelved somewhere between Oreos and Raisinettes. "Let's just go."

Since Nettie had walked to the jail, after Sara locked up, they both got into the squad car, neither of them speaking on the short drive home. Staring out the window with her arms and legs crossed, Nettie knew she had morphed into Heloise and was driving Sara half mad, but she couldn't stop herself. She didn't want to stop herself. Each desperate act of domesticity enabled her to cease thinking and to feel in control, at least for a while.

When they reached the house, she jumped out of the car and ran up the porch steps to busy herself with dinner preparations. With any luck she'd be tired enough to turn in before the last smear of grease was sponged off the last plate.

As soon as she opened the door, she realized something was odd. Lights were on all over the house, yet she didn't remember turning on any lamps before she left. There was also a definite aroma of flowers in the air.

Nettie crossed the threshold, about to comment to Sara, when she noticed several things at once: a shawl tossed over the living-room lounger, chunky-heeled sandals kicked off carelessly at the base of the stairs near a leather carryall, and a huge candle with three wicks, lighted and sitting on the coffee table.

Her gaze rose to the top of the stairs and her mouth opened in astonishment. "Lilah!"

Wearing powder-pink leggings and a soft V-neck sweater that looked as if it had been woven from cotton candy, the second-born of the three Owens girls was the picture of nonchalant glamour. Her golden hair curled halfway down her elegant back. Perfect makeup highlighted a gorgeous smile and brilliant blue eyes that sparkled with life.

"Nettie-Belle!" Skipping down the stairs with the grace of a dancer, the enthusiasm of a puppy, Lilah wrapped her arms around her sister, squeezing until Nettie thought she might see stars from lack of oxygen. "Mmm, you feel good. Let me look at you." Lilah pulled back and sighed. "Beautiful as ever. Come back to Los Angeles with me, baby, I'll make you a star."

"Yeah, that's what we need in this family, more dramatics." Sara's grumble provided a perfect and oh-so-typical foil for Lilah's effusiveness.

"Hello, Eeyore." Turning her attention to her older sib, Lilah put her hands on her hips. "Look who's complaining about dramatics. I haven't seen you for a year and you're still wearing the same costume."

"It's a uniform."

"Mmm." Lilah tilted her head. "Needs a scarf or something." Before Sara could respond, Lilah grabbed her in a bear hug, rocking excessively and planting a smacking, lipstick-staining kiss on Sara's cosmetics-free cheek.

"Oh, for crying out loud." Wriggling free, Sara wiped her face.

Over Lilah's contagious laughter, Nettie realized Sara had shown no surprise at all. "Did you know about this?"

"I'm your birthday present," Lilah answered in her sister's stead. "You know how Sara feels about shopping."

Nettie's eyes widened. Her birthday was still several weeks away. And Lilah's infrequent visits were often rushed. "You don't have to head right back then?"

The blonde shook her head. "I'm taking a long vacation." She tossed an arm around Nettie's shoulders and grabbed Sara in a near chokehold. "Come on. I brought food, Irish Cream and presents."

"Lilah! This is…scandalous!" Laughing delightedly, Nettie held up a scrap of royal purple material that was, she assumed, a thong. "What am I supposed to do with it?"

"Wear it, of course."

Sara grabbed a vanilla wafer and dragged it through a pot of peanut butter melted with the butterscotch morsels Lilah had pulled from her overnight bag. The unusual combination was a classic Owens sleepover snack, something the girls' mother used to make.

"You expect her to wear that thing out of the house?" Sara said with her mouth full.

"Under the proper attire, yes." Lilah swirled her Bailey's Irish Cream over ice.

"Well," Sara picked up a huge strawberry, dunked it in the sweet fondue, tipped back her head and took a bite, "why wear the thing at all then? Looks uncomfortable."

"Sara, if you have to ask what for, you've been alone way too long." Lilah grinned.

They'd been eating, chatting and opening gifts for the past hour. Lilah had brought Sara an autographed copy of the screenplay for *The Quick and the Dead* and a box of designer chocolates from a ritzy store on Rodeo Drive. She'd given Nettie perfume, the thong and a matching bra.

"I know better than to call a shoestring underwear," Sara claimed, flipping through the front pages of the script.

"Men love them."

"Huh," Sara grunted. "They don't have to wear 'em. Try chasing a bank robber in one of those things. You'd hang yourself."

Lilah's bright laughter filled the room. "And speaking of chasing men," she said, mischief darkening her eyes, "How's Nick?"

Sara turned as red as the strawberry she'd just popped into her mouth. "How should I know?" she sputtered, leaping to her feet so quickly, she nearly overturned the coffee table. "I'm going to bed. I have to get up early for work tomorrow. And don't leave that candle burning, when you go upstairs. It wouldn't surprise me if you burned the house down with your candles and your...thongs, and..." Tossing her strawberry stem onto the fruit plate, Sara stalked off.

Lilah took another sip of her drink and murmured, "Still carrying a torch, I see. And not doing a thing about it."

"How did you know?" Nettie asked when Sara was safely up the stairs and out of earshot. She slapped a hand to her forehead. She herself had just started suspecting, but she'd been too immersed on her own life to pursue the thought. "I can't believe I was so blind. How long have you known?"

"She's been ga-ga over Nick since high school, but she makes a second career out of pretending she couldn't care less." Lilah shook her head. "She's so tough about some things, but when it comes to any man who's not on the FBI's Ten-Most-Wanted list, she's a big 'fraidy cat."

"Sara?" Nettie shook her head. "I know she hasn't dated much, but I never think of Sara as being afraid of anything."

Lilah sighed. "Sweetie, when it comes to the opposite sex, we're all afraid of something. Or someone." Curling her long legs beneath her, she settled more cozily into the plaid chair that had always been her personal favorite. "So how about you?" She arched an impeccably groomed brow. "How's your fling coming along?"

Nettie's heart had to squeeze out the next beat, but she managed to shove her cheeks back into smile mode. "Oh, that," she tossed off as lightly as she could. "I'm afraid my fling is *finito.*" Rising, she began to gather the used napkins and plates. "You were right. I'm not fling material."

"What happened? Did he say no to a longer commitment?" Sisterly loyalty put palpable anger in Lilah's tone.

Nettie shook her head, mopping smears of peanut butter dip off the oak table.

"Why don't you leave that stuff and sit and talk to me," Lilah suggested. "Sara says you've been doing your Martha Stewart impersonation again."

Nettie stopped wiping and looked up. "Is that why you came?"

"She's concerned. I'm concerned, too. Sara wasn't sure how to help you, so she called."

Lilah shrugged with her customary casual grace. This time it irritated Nettie to no end. "You were both worried when I was planning to have an affair. Now you're worried that I'm not? Seems a little ironic, wouldn't you say?"

"We just want you to be happy, Net."

Nettie gave an uncharacteristically cynical huff of laughter. "Yeah. As long as my happiness doesn't interfere with Sara's feeding schedule or your next audition."

It was a shocking, completely uncharacteristic thing for Nettie to say, and they both knew what she was referring to. Lilah's face went pale beneath her makeup.

"We were scared, Nettie. We thought you wanted…to be alone. We didn't know what to do."

"Well, that made three of us."

After Brian and Tucker had died, Nettie had been helpless to take care of anyone's emotions, even her own. It was understandable, but frightening to the two women who had relied on her most of their lives. Even through her own despair, Nettie had seen her sisters' discomfort and though she had felt like a marionette lying limp and disjointed on the ground, she'd somehow managed to scrape herself together and hold her body upright long enough to tell her sisters to go home, get on with their lives…she'd be fine. Like a marionette, she'd been hanging on by a thread.

Guilty but relieved, they had left, and at the time Nettie had felt grateful that she could still "be there" for her family. Make everything feel normal and safe for them, just as she always had. Except that by then she'd understood there was no such thing as "safe."

Well, this time she was fresh out of illusions. The dream of experiencing a happiness with Chase that couldn't be snatched away was only that—a dream.

Facing Lilah with an uncompromising stare, Nettie said, "He has a son. Seven years old." That was it, all she had to say, really. Tucker would have been six.

Lilah so clearly wanted to respond, wanted to tell her *So what? Go for it,* but she didn't dare.

"Who will be there this time, Lilah, if everything falls apart?" Nettie drove her point home. "Sara? You? Will you stick around and pick up the pieces? Because—" Her voice started to break. Relentlessly, she pressed on. "I wouldn't survive it another time. I don't think I'd want to."

"But maybe it won't fall apart this time, Net. You've had your share—"

"You think that's how the world works? You still think it's *fair?* Tragedy isn't dealt out like a deck of cards—everyone gets five and then you go around in a circle and tell the dealer what you want. No one cares what you want! Nobody's checking to make sure you only get what you can handle." Nettie slashed a hand through the air. "That is such a crock! Mother and Daddy were thirty-four when they died and they had three children. And everyone else on that plane had people who loved them and needed them. You want to talk about fair? Brian was twenty-three. *Twenty-three.''* She didn't even say Tucker's name; she couldn't. ''Maybe the truth is some people get more than their share because they're jinxed. Maybe I'm doing Chase a big favor—''

Nettie began to shake. As if she were standing with her feet in ice, the shivering started from the legs up, until her entire body quivered without control.

All she'd wanted was a little bit of joy to remind her she was still alive. What she'd got instead were reminders she didn't want of a life she'd never have again.

Leaving everything—plates, napkins, Lilah—right where they were, Nettie turned to run up the stairs. If a life lived in avoidance meant she was only half alive, fine. It was also half the pain.

It had taken seven years for Chase to discover he was a father, mere hours to travel to Florida to meet his son for the first time, a couple of minutes to note all the physical resemblances between them and about two seconds to realize he was in over his head. Way over.

Twisting the top off a bottle of cold beer, he slumped into a chair at the kitchen table. Given an aisle seat on the plane ride back to North Dakota, Colin had preferred to gaze silently out the window, rather than converse with his father. Chase wondered if they should have spent a few days at Disneyworld, or if he should have brought a gift, something to break the ice. Hell, he hadn't thought to take along a single thing a kid might want to eat or play with or wear.

On the ride from the airport to Nick's, Chase told his son about Nick's horse, received an encouraging but brief flicker of interest and then…zilch.

Now Colin was upstairs, preferring to unpack on his own while Chase remained downstairs, nursing a cold beer and a gutful of self-doubt rather than the walloping sock in the chest of fatherly love he'd expected to feel.

Chase took a long pull from the bottle of Budweiser. Yeah, this father gig was a real piece of cake.

Elbows on the table, he dropped his forehead onto his palms. He wanted to talk to someone. But not just any someone.

*Nettie.*

She was the first person who came to mind. And the second. Furious with himself, Chase shook his head. She'd bailed. Only moments after those robin's egg eyes had said, yes, her mouth had uttered no to any possibility of a relationship. Because he had a kid.

Chase put a hand on his breast pocket, remembered he'd foolishly given up smoking and rose to pace to the window.

He knew firsthand what it was like to be an unwanted kid. Nothing…no one…would make his son feel that way.

Forget her, Chase ordered himself. Forget her, it's done. He must have had too much adrenaline in his system, anyway, to imagine that he was ready for a relationship with a woman *and* a child. One at a time would be more than enough.

Returning to the table, he grabbed the beer and opened the refrigerator. Nick was out of town for a few days, which meant he and Colin were on their own for meals. Unfortunately, Chase didn't cook. He had no reason to; he was never at home. Peering at the shelves, he searched for something that looked like kid food.

Catsup, bratwurst, more beer, butter. There was a loaf of bread and a box of cereal on top of the fridge. Bratwurst on bread with catsup? Slamming the refrigerator door, he hung his head. He was in serious trouble.

Leaving his beer on the sink, he headed upstairs, heart thumping as if *he* were the kid. When he reached the guest room, he halted at the door. Colin stood at the window, staring out. His small sloping shoulders appeared to hold the weight of the world. Chase felt his anger rise at anyone—everyone, himself included—who had contributed to that sadness.

The simple act of drawing his own child's attention filled Chase once again with an aggravating self-doubt. He didn't know how to address his own kid—how pathetic was that? It was on the tip of his tongue to say, *son,* but that seemed wrong, as if he hadn't earned the right.

Resigning himself to indecision, high blood pressure and ulcers for the remainder of his natural life, Chase cleared his throat and smiled when Colin turned. ''Listen I'm getting hungry, and

I thought, uh…" *Come on, this is easy. It's only food.* "My favorite dinner is a cheeseburger, french fries and a vanilla shake. How about you?"

Huge brown eyes gazed warily beneath a mop of straight coffee-hued hair. "I like chocolate." No smile and only a halting enthusiasm, but Chase was encouraged.

"Ever been to a real old-fashioned diner?" Confused, Colin shrugged. Okay, no frame of reference for a diner. "Come on." Chase gestured to the door. "Have you ever had a milkshake served in a tall silver cup? No?" Feigning disbelief, Chase followed his son down the hall. "Aw, man, are you in for a surprise.…"

Given its status as "the only restaurant for twenty miles," Ernie's did a fairly brisk business in the early evenings, particularly when the weather was good. Chase ushered his son into a dining room that was crowded, relatively speaking, and filled with the aromas of grilled meat, homemade gravy and pie that smelled freshly baked.

Obeying a sign that read Take a Menu, Take a Seat and Wait Yer Turn, Chase chose a booth near a window, watched his son crawl across the vinyl seat and then slid in opposite him.

Ernie arrived almost immediately with a pot of coffee, pouring before Chase could accept or decline.

"Welcome back!" Ernie displayed overly large dentures in a sincere greeting as he sloshed hot liquid into a brown ceramic mug. "Thought you might carry a few hard feelings after you got yourself arrested the first time you was here, but I can see you're a man with a sense of humor." He slapped Chase heartily on the back.

Chase lurched forward, amazed by the wizened old codger's strength. "Yeah." He reached for the creamer. "I love a joke."

"Glad to hear it. And who's this good-lookin' fella?"

Colin stared at Ernie with more interest than he'd shown in anything so far. It was understandable. Ernie resembled an elf come to life. Smiling, Chase made the introduction exactly as it first came into his head. "This is Colin, my son. He just got into town."

"Happy to meet you, Colin." Ernie stuck out a knobby hand, which Colin accepted and manfully shook. "This your first visit to North Dakota?"

Colin nodded.

"Well, that's fine. There may not be much to do, but we got plenty to see. Say, did your dad tell you he spent the night in the same jail that once housed the great Toothless Shoeless Pistol Pete and Dead Eye Dunnigan the night before they was both hanged for bank robbery? Same thing your dad was arrested for."

Colin's eyes bugged wide. He stared at his father with new interest. Chase winced. Turning to Colin, he said firmly, so there would be no misunderstanding, "I didn't rob anything. It was a mistake. The sheriff mistook me for somebody else."

Colin's interest didn't dim a bit. "You were in jail?"

Chase shifted uncomfortably, earning another whack from the old man. "Now, don't be embarrassed, son. Plenty a folks has been falsely accused. Important thing is no one was shot." Ernie went into another fit of cackling. Obviously at least some of the story had made the rounds in town. Interestingly, Ernie didn't seem to be distressed by the part he'd played.

"I was never really 'in jail,'" Chase insisted. "The sheriff took me to jail, but I was never officially booked for any crime."

"I want to be a policeman." Colin announced.

"You oughtta meet our sheriff, then," Ernie said. "She knew she wanted to be sheriff from the time she was your age."

"The sheriff is a girl?" Colin seemed doubtful.

"Yep." Ernie looked proud. "She's our very own Calamity Jane. I bet she'd give you a tour of our jail."

"Really?" Powered by enthusiasm, Colin's feet smacked the legs of the table. "When can I go? When are the tours?" He hopped out of the booth.

"Okay, Colin, sit down. We're going to have dinner—"

"Sheriff's right over there." Ernie pointed to a booth across the dining room. "Why don't you ask her?"

"Oh, boy!" The seven-year-old took off like a shot.

Ernie chuckled. "Kids." He shook his head. "They got so much dang energy."

Chase twisted around, sliding to the edge of the bench-style seat.

"Don't worry." Ernie hastened to reassure him. "He's not bothering anyone. We're all friends here."

But Chase was worried. His body stiffened as his gaze settled

on the three women in a booth across the restaurant. Digging
into a huge slice of pie à la mode that was placed on the table
between them, the women were laughing, wielding their forks
like swords as they battled for control of the dessert.

When Colin skidded to a halt at their table, they glanced up.
Chase spared only a glance for the redheaded sheriff, who was,
as usual, dressed in uniform, and for the unfamiliar blonde who
smiled at his son.

Now that he was at their table, Colin seemed to suffer another
attack of reserve, twisting his small hands behind his back as he
addressed himself to the local law. Chase had no idea what was
spoken between Sara and his son, but he realized Colin must
have identified him as "father," when, almost as a unit, the
women turned to look in his direction.

Nettie's gaze locked with his and she looked, he thought,
exactly the way he felt—as if he'd suffered a punch to his sternum.

Briefly, he considered staying right where he was and waiting
for Colin to return to the table. In fact, he might have—thereby
letting both himself and Nettie off the hook—except for one
thing: Before she'd noticed him, Nettie had been having a perfectly good time. The relationship she'd killed wasn't even cold
in the grave, and she'd managed to put it behind her. And that
irked him. Big time.

Sliding out of the booth, Chase begged a cursory pardon as
he brushed past Ernie.

From her place in the corner of the booth, Nettie watched his
approach. Shifting her gaze between father and child, she felt
the few bites of pie she had taken turn to cannonballs inside her
churning stomach.

This was Chase's son, the boy she hadn't wanted to meet. He
stood, nervous yet fascinated, gazing at Sara. Tall for his age,
sturdy and obviously hale beneath a too-sober countenance,
Colin bore a striking resemblance to his father, though his hair
was a shade darker and impossibly thick, sitting atop his head
like a thatched roof. His mother must have had a devil of a time
running a comb through it.

Feeling herself smile, Nettie abruptly reined in her thoughts.
That was exactly the kind of thing she didn't want to think.

When Chase reached their table, he put a protective hand on

Colin's shoulder. His expression stony, he looked at Nettie but remained silent, almost daring her to speak first.

Nettie had no idea what to say. From her peripheral vision, she noted Lilah turning her head, assessing the situation. When no one ventured a word, Lilah took the bull by the horns, thrusting out a hand.

Chase reacted in slow motion, pulling his attention off Nettie and putting it on the vivacious blonde.

"You must be this charming young man's father." Taking the hand Chase proffered, she flashed him a dazzling grin. "I'm Lilah Owens. And your name is?" To Nettie's amazement, Lilah tilted her head, actually batting her long, mascara-laden lashes.

*Flirting?* She was flirting with him? In disbelief, Nettie watched Chase respond with a smile that said he was duly charmed. "My name is Chase, Ms. Owens."

"Lilah," she corrected.

"Lilah," Chase agreed, keeping her hand. "I'd know you anywhere. From the photo on the mantel in your family's home," he clarified when she arched a brow in question.

"Such an old, old photo," she laughed.

"But so clearly indicative of the great beauty to come."

"I may hurl." Sara could have been referring to the quantity of pie she continued to consume, but Nettie knew better and for once she shared the sentiment.

Lilah continued as if Sara hadn't spoken. "Ah, you've been to our house?" Gracefully withdrawing her hand, she glanced around the table and then back at Chase. "You must know my sisters then." Her surprise was a shade too enthusiastic to be genuine.

Chase's eyes met Nettie's. She longed to kick Lilah beneath the table. What kind of game was her sister playing? Sitting in the corner of the booth, Nettie felt her anger rise. Now Chase was going to think she hadn't cared enough about their relationship to tell her own sister about it! On the other hand, she corrected herself sternly, it made no difference. She certainly didn't want him to think she was carrying a torch for him. Did she? No! Of course not.

Afraid she looked as fidgety and uncomfortable as she felt, Nettie tried to use the pie as a focal point to gather her racing thoughts, but Sara kept hacking away at it with her fork. And

Lilah kept staring at Chase in that *irritating* way. And Chase…
Already he'd removed his gaze from Nettie and returned it to
her blonder, sexier sibling. Irrationally she felt more piqued.
What kind of inconstant jilted would-be lover was he, anyway?

With a lazy smile, he confirmed for Lilah, "I've had the pleasure of getting to know both your sisters. My stay in North
Dakota will always be highlighted by the memory of your family's…unusually warm welcome."

Nettie's eyes narrowed. Unusually warm? Either he was referring to being handcuffed and nearly shot or…to being prop-
ositioned by a country widow within a week of his rolling into
town. Either way, it didn't sound like a compliment.

"Excuse me," she said, finding her voice at last and determined to nullify his insinuation that they had somehow embarrassed themselves, "but the fact is, we greet everyone like that."

His brow rose. "That must be a boon to North Dakota tourism."

Nettie lifted her chin and tightened her jaw to keep from grimacing. *Damn. Damn!*

Chase squeezed his son's shoulder. "Come on, Colin. I'm
sure these ladies want to get back to their dessert, and we've
got some great burgers waiting for us."

Colin craned his neck to look up. "But we haven't ordered
yet."

"Right." Chase laughed. "That's right. So let's do that.
Ladies." Studiously avoiding Nettie, he nodded.

"But I want to see the jail," Colin resisted his father's tug.
"Will you show me your jail?" he asked Sara. "I want to be a
policeman."

Judging by the expressions on their faces, Sara and Chase
were in a dead heat for Least Enthusiastic About the Idea. On
the other hand, Nettie watched the eager face of the child and
wanted to kick both adults for allowing their personal grievances
to stand in the way of a simple request. The child had lost his
mother. He'd been shuttled to a new place with a father he barely
knew. A tour of local points of interest wasn't much to ask.

"We can see about that later, Colin," Chase said, trying to
move the boy along.

"Come by anytime and take a look around." Stated with
resolve, Nettie's offer surprised everyone. Beneath their stares,

she addressed herself to Colin. "If Sara's not too busy, I bet she'll even let you stand inside a cell." She smiled and received a tentative smile in return.

Sara looked as disgruntled as a mule and Chase regarded Nettie with a wary mix of curiosity and reproach. Nettie stared back at them both. True, she'd taken into her own hand matters that weren't hers, but in this isolated instance she wasn't sorry. It was simply meant to quench a child's thirst for adventure.

After an abrupt nod, Chase led his son back to their booth. Pretending a renewed interest in dessert, Nettie picked up her fork and stuck it into the sliver of pie still remaining. She felt her sisters' stares like lasers blazing through her skin.

"I thought you were through with that guy," Sara said, her disapproval blatant. "Now he's going to show up at the jail—him and his kid—and that'll be nothing but trouble. If you ask me— Ow!" She jerked in her seat. Reaching below the table to rub her shin, Sara glared at Lilah, who had obviously kicked her. "You nearly broke my leg."

Lilah smiled unapologetically. "Oops. Sorry," she said, utterly insincere. "My foot slipped. Ow!" Lilah's gorgeous features scrunched into a furious scowl as her own leg took a blow. "Revenge is childish," she growled at Sara. "Or hadn't you heard?"

"That one was from me." Nettie forked a bite of sweet dark berries and flaky crust into her mouth and chewed calmly. She swallowed, nudged Lilah with her elbow this time and said, "Scoot out."

"I'd love to, but my shin bone has been fractured. What was that for, anyway?"

Moving with enviable calm, Nettie gathered her sweater and purse. "Lilah Owens, you are still the most outrageous flirt in Kalamoose County."

At first Lilah appeared ready to launch into an automatic protest. Then she changed her mind and shrugged. "So? He's good looking, he's single—he's a celebrity, so he's probably rich—if you don't want him, why should we let him go to waste?"

"Listen to you!" Sara leaned far over the table before Nettie could respond and sneered at Lilah. "Not let him go to waste. As if he's got an expiration date! Men are just so much hamburger to you. Like that time you kissed Nick at your sweet sixteen party."

Lilah rolled her eyes. "You're still harping on that?"

"'Sweet sixteen and never been missed,'" Sara taunted, "'Every guy she saw, she kissed!'"

"All right, kiddies," Nettie said equably. "Time to go home and clean up your rooms now." Again she nudged Lilah. "Slide out."

Lilah remained stubbornly right where she was. "Not until you tell me whether Chase Reynolds—" she lowered her voice "—is up for grabs or off limits. Fish or cut bait, little sister. What's it going to be?"

Nettie saw it then—the challenge and appraisal in her sister's eyes. Lilah was testing her. Pushing her to make a choice. And Nettie, who had believed her choice was already made, understood that in the game of romance minds were made up, changed, and made up again, sometimes over and over. *Choose again,* Lilah was telling her.

"Let's just say I don't want my sister to cast her line." Refusing to say more than that, Nettie stared at Lilah levelly until the other woman gave up and slid out of the booth. Keeping her back straight, her eyes focused straight ahead of her—and away from Chase's table—she made her way to the front of the restaurant.

# *Chapter Twelve*

Four days later, Nettie thought that perhaps she'd seen the last of Chase. He hadn't brought Colin to the jail. The only reason she knew they were still in town was that Etta Schlag, who owned the bakery, had rattled on for ten minutes this morning about how handsome Chase was and that he and his son had eaten three of her Bavarian cream donuts yesterday—three, she hoped to tell you, and she made them extra large—plus, they'd each had a cup of hot chocolate, besides. Then Chase—"that sweetheart"—had told her that if she ever decided to move to New York, he'd set her up in a donut shop and they'd be bigger someday than Krispy Kreme. Whatever, Etta said, that was.

Nettie had taken her loaf of German sourdough rye and walked home.

She'd tried hard to concentrate on her work, spending most of the morning illustrating a scene from her latest book, but by early afternoon she'd been too restless to sit still. Lilah had gone into Minot for the day, so Nettie walked back into town. Now she was hanging the curtains she'd made for the jail...and trying not to admit to herself that standing in the cell where she'd first met Chase was far more satisfying than staying home, pretending she wasn't thinking about him.

Sara had gone out on a call fifteen minutes ago, answering a summons from the janitor at the local elementary school. That left Nettie once more alone with her thoughts.

By now she had to confess—to herself only—that she'd been living a four-day-long fantasy about seeing Chase again. The fact that she hadn't seen him left her feeling utterly disappointed.

Yeah, right, she thought, bunching a panel of curtains along their rod. "Flat-out rejected" was more like it. And that was so dumb! She had chosen not to continue their relationship. Reason still told her she'd made the right decision, the one with the least potential for excruciating pain in the long run, but there seemed to be a gap the size of the Grand Canyon between what her reason told her and what desire demanded.

Desire... She desired to see him again. To feel her skin tingle and her heart skip from the look in his eyes. And from trying to judge when, where and how he was going to kiss her. There were certain sensations of danger, she was beginning to realize, that felt mighty good.

Shoving the curtain rod into a bracket, Nettie hopped down from the cot. Emotions were the most illogical things. She was better off without them.

Looking around, she wondered what else she could dust, mop or redecorate to within an inch of its life, but before she could determine her next victim, Sara stormed through the door, grumbling something about ''...stray dogs and kittens...''

"Come on," Sara said, holding open the solid wood door. "You're under arrest, so don't give me any resistance or back talk."

Nettie watched with interest as a little boy, his shoulders straight and his eyes huge with curiosity, marched through the door, the most willing prisoner she had ever seen.

Nettie lifted a brow in inquiry.

"He was wandering around Wilbur Elementary," Sara explained. "Hank found him drawing on the chalkboard in a schoolroom that was supposed to be locked. Breaking and entering is a crime, so I arrested him." Colin's thin shoulders were manfully squared. He stared straight ahead, chin up, countenance solemn but oddly dignified, as if he was telling them, *I committed the crime; I'll do the time.*

"The school is almost two miles from Nick's place. Was, uh, your prisoner by himself?" Nettie asked.

"Yep. Rode his bike. Nice shiny new bike. It's in the back of the squad car now. Impounded."

While Kalamoose was by no means the crime capital of North Dakota, Nettie didn't like the idea of a seven-year-old riding his bike two miles in one direction in an area that was unfamiliar to him. "Does your father know where you are?" she asked, receiving a noncommittal shrug in return.

"He says Chase told him he could go wherever he wanted. I called Nick's place. No one's there."

That made no sense to Nettie. She knew she was overly cautious, but to tell a child he could go wherever he desired and then leave so there wasn't an adult at home while he rode off to explore? If that was Chase's idea of parenting, it left a lot to be desired. Every child needed an anchor. She looked at the little boy.

Colin maintained the posture of Repentant Convict until he noticed Sara's police radio. Then he broke into a gallop. "Wow! Does this thing really work?"

"Of course it works!" Following him, Sara grabbed him by the collar of his shirt and hauled him several steps back. Colin didn't seem to mind a bit. "Don't touch it, though. I use it for official police business only. It's not a toy. In fact, nothing in here is a toy." Placing her hands on her hips, just above her gun belt, she added, "I expect you to remember that."

Colin nodded. "I will." He turned around. "Can I look in the cells?"

Sara rolled her eyes, as if the effort to show him around kept her from something hugely important. "Yeah, I guess. You're going to make it quick, though, because I'm putting you under house arrest with my sister in charge."

"What?"

"What's that mean?"

Nettie and Colin spoke at the same time, Colin mildly curious but with most of his attention on the configuration of the cells. Nettie, on the other hand, felt every nerve-ending buzz to life.

"Explain that," she said to Sara while Colin crawled beneath one of the cots, looking for a trap door or other means of escape.

"His father isn't home." Sara tossed her hat like a Frisbee, cleanly hitting a peg of the coat rack. "Nick's not there, either, and I don't have time to baby-sit till they get back. Besides, a jail isn't day care." She lowered her voice, crossing toward her desk. "I've got guns here, too many things I don't want him messing with. I figure you can take him to our place until his wayward parent decides to show up. Anyway, that way if he gets hungry or thirsty, you'll know what to do with him. Little kid rode his bike almost two miles. He's got to be hungry, and I don't know anything about feeding kids."

"Right." Nettie's tone was droll. She refrained from pointing out that Sara fed her inner child several times a day. Looking at Colin as he crawled around on the hardwood floor, she felt her pulse increase. She was about to take responsibility for a little boy again. And sooner rather than later, she was going to see Chase.


"I like these waaayyy better than the ones he got us." Colin sat at the kitchen table, swinging his legs while he ate homemade oatmeal cookies and sipped from a tall glass of milk.

"'He' meaning your father?" Nettie stood with her back against the counter. Colin had seemed shy on the walk home, but a quick tour of Nettie's studio and a handful of cookies had relaxed him considerably.

"He can't cook. He made spaghetti last night and it tasted like barf."

It was stated so matter-of-factly, Nettie burst into laughter. "It wasn't that bad, was it?"

Colin bobbed his head. "Yeah. The noodles were weird."

"Weird?"

Mouth full, he rocked and kicked the rungs of the chair, filled with boyish energy. "Kinda like Goop."

"Goop?" Nettie was familiar with the strangely gelatinous toy, though she'd never had the pleasure of tasting it. "That's not good."

Colin shook his head vigorously. "And he burned the oatmeal. And then he put jam on it 'cause we ran out of sugar!"

Affording his onlooker the courtesy of first swallowing his cookie, Colin mimed throwing up.

"Mmm. This does sound serious." She felt vaguely sorry for Chase. He was probably making a lot of peanut butter and jelly sandwiches to stand in for ruined meals. It certainly explained his gratitude for Etta's Bavarian creams.

"Can I have another cookie?"

Noting his still scissoring feet, Nettie took pity on Chase and vetoed the notion of more sugar. "How about a sandwich?" she suggested. "Have you ever had a roast beef club?"

While she built the sandwich, Colin studied the two books she'd autographed for him. The stories and illustrations were sophisticated enough to hold his attention and he studied them intently, seeming engrossed by the element of magic.

Nettie found herself smiling as she glanced at him, smiling as she sliced cheese and stuck a knife into the mayonnaise jar. All the daily, innocuous acts she seldom gave a second thought to suddenly infused her with a quiet happiness that felt almost…holy. If this had been Tucker, if she'd been making sandwiches for her own son these three mislaid, lonely years, would such commonplace moments have begun to slip by virtually unnoticed?

She'd never know. So for now, each swipe of mayonnaise over wheat bread and each crisp turn of the page as Colin read her book was something that stood out like a little gift.

How, she wondered, trying not to be judgmental and failing miserably, could Chase be so bored with fatherhood already that he'd encourage this child to simply wander off on his own? Besides, a day like this, when the weather hung between summer and fall and the lazy breeze coaxed a person into the sun, a perfect day like this was simply meant to be spent with someone you loved. Chase had told her that commitment and constancy were not his strong suits. Apparently, he'd told the truth.

Nettie sliced the sandwich into triangles, using more force than necessary, but she was angry. Not for her own sake. No, that'd be a waste of cortisol. She and Chase were past history. But for his son's sake—yes. On behalf of that little boy, Chase Reynolds was going to have to learn to commit.

She was hunting through the snack cabinet, in search of Sara's stash of barbecued potato chips, when a car pulled too quickly up to the house. The driver cut the engine and Nettie realized she easily recognized the sound of Chase's car.

Moving as if her heart wasn't racing a mile-a-minute, Nettie set the sandwich and chips in front of Colin, then went to open the door the senior Reynolds was already pounding on. Not just knocking, actually pounding.

He looked as though someone had stuffed him into a washing machine and left him too long on the spin cycle. His hair was disheveled as if he'd plowed his hands through it dozens of times, and in fact he did so now as he entered the house. His eyes were at once tired and sharply alert, like a man standing watch.

"Is he here?" Eschewing preliminaries, Chase marched into the house and looked around. "There was a message on Nick's machine, from Sara."

"He's here," Nettie said. "He's eating lunch in the kitchen. He's fine."

Her last statement was clearly the most important to Chase. Again, his restless fingers raked his hair, but this time he released a long sigh of relief, as well. "Sara said she found him at the elementary school. I've been driving all over! Where the hell is the elementary school?"

"A couple of miles from Nick's."

Chase's reaction was almost identical to Nettie's. "Two miles? He's only seven! He rode his bike two miles?" Obviously intending to relieve some of his agitation in a lecture, Chase started toward the kitchen.

Nettie stopped him with a hand on his forearm. "Let's sit down," she suggested, gesturing to the couch.

Chase sank to the sofa, elbows on his knees and forehead resting against his clasped hands.

"Were you home when he left the house?" she asked quietly, and Chase nodded. "You didn't even know he was leaving, did you?"

"No." He raised his head, pressing his lips against his knuckles. Guilt seemed to emanate from his very pores, and Nettie felt a surge of protectiveness. She was beginning to get a clearer picture of what had transpired this afternoon.

He turned to look at her, his eyes puffy and tired. Several days of hands-on fatherhood had taken a toll. "I blew it. I was working, writing an article." He wagged his head. "I'm trying to figure out how to have a kid and a career at the same time. I can't keep traveling. I mean, he's got to go to school in one place, right?" Frustration and uncertainty coiled his muscles. "I'm no damn good at this! Some people shouldn't be parents. I've always known that. What kind of a father doesn't know where his son is?"

Nettie sighed, immensely sorry for having judged him. Real life so seldom played out like the picture in your head. Chase thought he knew what fatherhood was supposed to look like and figured he was coming up short.

Studying him she felt a surge of compassion—for him and for herself as well. There was such a gap between who we thought we *should* be and who we feared we actually were. And the truth, Nettie was beginning to realize, wasn't either of those false notions. The truth was somewhere in the middle. Like most people, Chase was neither as perfect as he'd hoped nor as puny as he feared. Maybe that's what happiness is, she thought, watching him silently wrestle with his "shoulds." It's making peace with that gap in the middle.

Sensing the coil of energy that was about to make Chase stand up and start pacing, Nettie placed a hand on his. She meant the touch to be a comfort, but a zing that felt like static electricity sizzled beneath her palm.

Unsure of whether Chase felt it, too, she tried to speak calmly. "Tell me what happened."

Searching her face, Chase nodded. "Colin was restless. I was busy, trying to concentrate, and it wasn't going well. So I told him to play in his room while I finished and when he said it was boring in his room, I said then play outside. I bought him a bike a couple of days ago, but I never figured..." Lips thinned, he shook his head, far angrier with himself than his son. "All of a sudden, the article started kicking in for me. I don't think I looked up for the next hour. I wasn't even thinking about him. It was like I completely forgot—" Chase smacked a fist into his palm.

"That is so normal. Yes," Nettie insisted when he shook his head. "Getting frustrated, telling him to play outside, even becoming lost in your work and losing track of the time—and certainly not being able to anticipate a child's next move—it's all normal, Chase. You are not a bad parent.'' Then more quietly she said, ''He wasn't running away from you, you know. He wasn't leaving *you*.''

The hungry expression on Chase's face told her how much he craved that very affirmation. A faint smile of gratitude curved his lips, but he shook his head. ''Thanks. I appreciate the thought. Really. And I hope this doesn't sound rude or condescending, but I think this is one of those things you can't quite understand until you've been there.'' He gave a brief laugh. ''I certainly didn't. Being a parent...'' He wiped a hand down his face. ''I've never felt this responsible for anything or anyone else in my life. I can't even describe how it feels.''

It was the perfect opportunity to tell him everything. They had more of a kinship than he had any idea of.

The moment came. The moment went. With another small smile at her Chase stood.

''I'd better get in there,'' he said. ''I'll be picking him up in Fargo if we leave him alone too long.''

Raising her brows in appreciation of the humor, Nettie stood and followed him into the kitchen. The ping-pong match between tell and don't tell hadn't lasted long, but residual tension curled in her stomach.

Still working on the sandwich and chips, Colin was again immersed in one of Nettie's books. He didn't even glance up when his father walked in.

''I've been looking for you,'' Chase opened the conversation with a well-restrained neutral tone, but only by a hair. ''I thought you were right outside the house, playing. That's where I expected you to be when I told you to play outside.'' He paused. ''When I realized you weren't there and that your bike was gone, and I wasn't sure how long...''

Trying to be calm and rational was obviously too tall an order. Colin still hadn't looked up, but Chase knelt by his son's chair. In one swift movement, he gathered Colin in a hug as fierce as it was unexpected.

''Don't do that again! Don't ever leave like that without telling me, okay?'' All the emotions Chase said he couldn't describe filled his voice as he held onto a child who was truly a small version of him. ''You scared the cra— You scared me,'' Chase breathed. ''I thought something might have happened to you.''

It was clearly their first hug; the moment seemed awkward and new.

Colin sat stiffly at first, but the break in his father's voice weakened his childish resolve not to care what Chase thought. Held against a man's chest, tears sprang to his eyes and muffled his response. "Okay."

They remained there awhile and then released each other, Chase surreptitiously wiping his eyes before he pointed to the plate with Colin's half-eaten snack. "That's a good-looking sandwich," he commented, trying to normalize the moment. "Are you enjoying it?"

Colin nodded. "She makes good cookies, too." He picked up one half of the sandwich and took an enthusiastic bite.

"Cookies, too," Chase murmured. He turned to Nettie. "Thanks. It seems cooking is not one of my inherent skills. I tried spaghetti last night. Canned sauce—how hard can that be?" He wagged his head. "It tasted like…"

"Goop?" Nettie suggested when he had trouble finding an apt description. She lowered her voice as if slipping him the answer to a pop quiz. "You overcooked the pasta. Also, a little oil in the pot helps keep the noodles from sticking together."

Chase sent Colin a glare that was clearly playful. "Blabber-mouth." The little boy grinned. "We wind up eating a lot of baloney. I may be stunting his growth."

"He seems tall for his age. You've probably got a couple of inches to play with." Nettie traded a smile with Chase and time hung, stealing her breath.

It was Chase who broke the moment. "We'd better get out of your hair. Thanks for everything." To his son, he instructed, "I'm sure Nettie has to get back to work. Tell her thank you for keeping you from starvation one more day and let's get going."

"But I still gotta eat," Colin protested, swinging his legs and pointing to the remaining half of his roast beef, turkey and cheese.

"Grab it. You can eat in the car."

"Sure you can." Fighting a wave of disappointment that they were leaving, Nettie wrapped Colin's sandwich in a napkin. "There," she said, handing it back to him, "that ought to keep the guts from leaking all over your father's Porsche. Nothing

sloppier than stacked sandwiches in sleek, shiny vehicles.''
Colin giggled while Nettie segued from disappointment to a
buzzing sense of urgency. Would she see them again? When did
Chase plan to leave North Dakota? How inappropriate, stupid
or out-and-out unwelcome would an invitation to dinner be?

Before she had time to find out, Colin used his free hand to
awkwardly scoop up the books he'd been perusing.

"Can I take these to look at some more?" he asked Nettie.

"Sure. Absolutely. I want you to keep them. They're yours."

His eyes grew round with pleasure. "Thanks!" Colin breathed
with the kind of excitement she might have expected him to
reserve for a Harry Potter item. He swung around to look at his
father, awkwardly juggling the large books and his sandwich.
"She wrote these!" he trumpeted, sharing his awe. "And she
drew the pictures. By herself. I can draw by myself. But not as
good as this yet."

Relieving his son of the books, Chase examined them carefully before looking up at Nettie. He wore a somber, largely
unreadable expression. "Not only an artist," he said. "A children's book author." He read from the inside back flap.
"'Gifted author and illustrator Annette Ecklund…'" Arching a
brow, he questioned, "Pen name?"

His eyes narrowed and Nettie saw a hint of censure, heard a
note of betrayal in his otherwise painstakingly even voice.

"Kind of," she answered quietly, holding his gaze, knowing
the time for hiding in the shadows—professionally or personally—was coming to an end. "I use it as a pseudonym now.
Annette Ecklund was my married name."

# Chapter Thirteen

Chase lowered the book he'd been reading to his lap and rubbed his eyes. He couldn't remember the last time he'd read a kid's book, or two, in one night. In one sitting. Three times each.

Behind his broad-backed chair, a standing lamp cast an amber glow in Nick's den. A grandfather clock logged the time, its heavy pendulum clicking with slow, even precision. Chase wanted to get up, open the glass door and rip the pendulum from its housing. He didn't need a reminder of the time. This night was crawling by like an arthritic turtle.

Not that the reading material on his lap wasn't entertaining. On the contrary. Annette *Ecklund's* illustrated stories easily held an adult's attention. And she certainly knew how to tickle a child's imagination.

She certainly knew children.

Flipping the top book over, Chase opened the back cover and looked again at the studio portrait above her bio. She was beautiful, as always, but thinner in the photo, with a smile that appeared less spontaneous than it did in person.

*Who are you?* He demanded of the photo for the umpteenth

time that evening, but it remained stubbornly mum. Like the woman.

He could no longer believe she'd rejected him because she didn't like kids. That excuse had been shot full of holes. And clearly there had been a time when she had wanted commitment in a relationship.

Closing the back cover, Chase laid both books on the table beside his chair and reached for the cognac he'd poured earlier. There was only a little left and he downed it in a gulp, welcoming the fire that burned a path down the back of his throat and into his stomach. Whom had Nettie Owens married? What man had inspired a commitment from her? And what had happened to end that commitment?

Chase's craving to know more—a lot more—about Nettie's marriage had been driving him crazy all evening. After leaving her today, he'd spent the rest of the afternoon trying once again to get acquainted with his son. They had, in fact, had a better time of it, with chatter flowing more easily than it had before. They'd gone marketing at a large grocery two towns over, and Chase had dropped any pretense that he knew what he was doing when it came to the feeding of a seven-year-old boy.

Interestingly, with his defenses lowered, he and Colin had become partners in the search for "bachelor food." Together they had decided that the cooking of chicken was a mystery but that steak was worth a shot. Potatoes were easier than rice, and when Chase saw the vast assortment of frozen spuds, he almost wept, choosing cheese and bacon-stuffed potatoes for himself and letting Colin dump bags of tater tots, french fries and hash browns into their basket. By the time he handed his plastic over to the cashier, he knew he was going to buy the biggest freezer he could find when they moved to his apartment in New York.

That is, if New York was where they wound up. At the moment, he wasn't a hundred percent sure. About anything.

In the past he had taken pains not to base his career choices on anybody's interests but his own. Part of him—sometimes a big part—longed to continue in that vein. It was easy.

But it wasn't the best thing for his son.

Checking the grandfather clock, Chase saw that it was almost 11:00 p.m. Colin had been in bed for two hours. Already, Chase understood that enforcing bedtime was as much an opportunity to exert a little parental power as it was a way to make sure that Colin got his rest. Unfortunately for Chase, the hours between 9:00 p.m. and 1:00 a.m., when he typically retired, stretched like miles of inhospitable desert.

Half sighing, half growling, he rose with his empty glass, deciding not to pour another. Prowling to the kitchen, working on the premise that a light snack might make him sleepy, he grabbed a box of the frozen toaster pastries Colin had suggested as a breakfast option—and which Chase had forgotten to freeze…oops. Well, they'd heat faster this way, he comforted himself, pulling two from the box.

Nick's ancient toaster took forever to spit anything out. Reaching into a bag of cream-filled wafer cookies that tasted like two pieces of cardboard stuck together with vanilla grout, Chase munched while he waited for his pastries, and then realized what he was doing. He was going to wind up in a diet group, learning how to make cottage cheese dip if he didn't work out what to do with his nights—soon.

Figuring at least one of the pastries had to be warm enough to eat, he reached into the toaster. He plucked gingerly, expecting the toaster to be reasonably warm, but apparently it worked faster and better than he'd originally assumed, and he burned his fingers.

"Ow!" Pulling back and shaking his stinging hand, Chase stuck the two fingers in his mouth to cool them off. Anger made him more determined. He reached in again.

"Ha, gotcha!" he crowed, extracting the rectangular Danish just as the doorbell rang. Startled, he whirled around, dropped his snack on the floor and swore.

Who would be ringing Nick's doorbell at this time of night? Taking an automatic step toward the living room before the late-night caller could awaken Colin, Chase brought his foot down directly on top of the fallen Danish. His bare foot. Hot raspberry filling squooshed out.

"Ow! Sonova—"

Hopping around, he swiped at the burning goo. A soft but insistent knock sounded at the door, and a split second later the toaster spit out the other pastry. Chase swore all the way around.

Walking as much as he could on the side of his abused foot, he limped to the door and yanked it open, eager to vent an anger

that had started long before he burned himself. He would begin
by giving a piece of his mind to the person who dared to ring
a doorbell at 11:00 p.m. out here in the middle of nowhereville,
where decent people had gone to bed by now!

Hand poised to knock, Nettie offered a tentative smile across
the threshold.

She looked as if she was arriving for afternoon tea, dressed
in the same low-necked lavender sundress she'd worn the day
they had first kissed. Fresh as a daisy—that's how she looked,
and it ticked him off royally, considering that she was one of
the big reasons he hadn't slept in several days...the main reason
he was angry...the reason he'd decided to scarf toaster pastries
at 11:00 p.m...the reason he'd stepped on hot raspberry goo.

She widened her smile in greeting.

Chase scowled harder.

He was so damn glad to see her. Too glad. He wanted to grab
her hand, pull her into the house, sit her down and talk to her
about everything. Absolutely everything.

Controlling himself, he leaned—lazily—against the doorjamb.
"It's late."

Undaunted by his rude excuse for a welcome, she nodded.
"It is."

Chase waited, refusing to give an inch, refusing to feel guilty
as her pretty fingers twined together.

"Are you stopping by for eggs?" he baited, sounding like a
snarly, sarcastic old coot. It took her only a moment to pick up
on the reference.

"No." She shook her head and then sighed. "Although I was
about to tell you that I was in the neighborhood, saw your lights
on and thought, 'well, might as well stop by.'" Nettie's straw-
berry-glossed lips inched into a sheepish smile that was bound
to make mincemeat of his self-control.

"But that wouldn't be the truth?"

"Only the part about seeing your lights on. I wouldn't have
knocked otherwise."

"Hm." The truth was he wanted her to knock anyway. He
wanted her to knock if it was 3:00 a.m. and there wasn't another
soul awake or a single light burning for twenty miles. He wanted
to tell her that if this were his home she wouldn't have to knock
at all. "So—"

"Well—"

They spoke at the same time. Chase tipped his head to her. "You first." If she was here for any reason other than to throw herself into his arms and demand passionate lovemaking, he'd save himself a lot of frustration by letting her speak before his hopes or his imagination got the best of him.

Lowering her head, Nettie performed a quick mental recap of why the heck she was here. What had compelled her to put on a dress and makeup and to squirt mousse in her hair when normally she'd be in her jammies by now, preparing to watch "The Late Show"?

This afternoon she'd told herself it simply wasn't right to stand by, doing nothing while a man tried as hard as Chase to be a good father. It was heartless, yes, a veritable sin not to lend a hand. But she could have wandered by tomorrow morning, say sometime after sunup, to drop off a meat loaf or offer advice about children's Tylenol versus Bayer.

Right, so that question again: Why was she here on Nick's doorstep, with Nick out of town, wearing a dress and makeup and a pair of Lilah's high-heeled sandals at 11:00 p.m., staring at a man who was obviously still furious with her because she hadn't had the guts to tell him the truth in the first place?

*I'm here because I don't want him to be hurt and furious. I'm here because of the love and protectiveness and fear on his face when he hugged his son. I'm here because if he leaves and I never see him again except on cable news, I want him to know... I want him to know—*

Still with her head lowered, Nettie closed her eyes, took a deep breath, opened them again and said, "I want you to know, I..." Something caught her eye. "I want... What's on your foot?"

"You want what's on my foot."

"I...no. What *is* on your foot? Is that blood?" She peered down, squinting in the dimly lit entry. "Oh, my goodness, it is. You're bleeding!"

Pushing him back, she crossed the threshold, half bent to look down.

"I'm not bleeding."

"Yes. Look!" She pointed. "You must have stepped on

something. Did you break a glass? Here, come sit down. We have to take care of it.''

She propelled him backward into the living room, and Chase found her sincere concern so welcome he decided to wait just a minute before telling her the ''blood'' was raspberry jam.

He plopped backward onto the couch, tracking, he was sure, raspberry goo all over Nick's carpet. But it was worth it. He'd call a carpet cleaner tomorrow, but right now it was worth any expense or extra effort to feel the first gentle touch of her fingers on his bare skin. Even if it was only his foot.

As she probed softly, Chase let his eyes drift closed for a moment. Just a moment. Did she have any idea how good it felt to be touched like this…ministered to…cared about? Did she know the simplest touch from her could make him feel weaker than a newborn colt…and more powerful than a tiger on the hunt?

He stifled a groan as Nettie lifted his foot, holding the heel and ankle with one hand while she explored in tentative dabs. There was a considerable pause. ''This is unusually sticky,'' she said finally, referring to the red stains.

Reluctantly, Chase opened his eyes. She was a glorious picture, her long hair spilling over her beautiful bosom as she knelt on the floor by the sofa—holding his non-bleeding foot.

''It's not blood,'' he said.

She sat back. ''What is it?''

''Raspberry…stuff. I think. I mean, I think it's raspberry. I haven't tasted it yet.''

''You haven't tasted it. Yet. I see,'' she murmured, pondering his foot a moment. ''Is this anything like drinking champagne out of a woman's slipper?''

Chase grinned. He couldn't help it. He couldn't stay angry and he couldn't remain aloof, not when every cell in his body was trying to convince him he was sixteen again.

Leaning forward, he said, ''This is nothing like drinking champagne from a woman's slipper.'' Rearing back a bit, he regretfully eased his ankle out of her hand to rest it on his opposite knee. ''What a mess. I'd better get cleaned up.''

He started to rise, but Nettie touched his knee. ''Why don't you sit tight for a minute? I'll get something so you can wipe this off before you walk on it.''

On behalf of Nick's carpet, Chase accepted her offer. She disappeared briefly, returning quickly with a damp kitchen towel.

"Here we go," she said. He expected her to hand him the towel, but instead she knelt again and began to wipe off the stains as if the action were the most natural thing in the world, almost nonphysical.

It certainly didn't feel nonphysical, though, not to Chase. After her first automatic swipe, Nettie, too, seemed aware that no physical contact between them could be classified as platonic. Her swabs slowed to a crawl, which only made them more potent and torturous for Chase. He clamped a hand on her wrist.

She gazed up at him, eyes wide and unfocused. They were both breathing harder than a little cleanup could account for.

Chase swore he could feel her pulse beat beneath his fingers. He felt his own pulse throbbing in his temple and the side of his neck and wondered if she could see it. Playing it cool no longer seemed an option.

"Why are you here?" His tone sounded as ragged as the question was blunt.

This time Nettie didn't even think to prevaricate. "I was afraid I might never see you again." She wagged her head slowly, gaze linked with his. "I don't want that."

Chase firmed his grip on her wrist. With his other hand, he reached for her upper arm and pulled her onto the couch beside him. A hairbreadth of time passed while they looked at each other, but even that hairbreadth seemed like an eternity.

Chase let go of her wrist and they came together like spark and fuel.

Nettie felt the heat inside her, deep inside. Where there hadn't been an ember for years, now a conflagration roared to life. In the past, lovemaking, or merely the anticipation of it, had made her tremble, left her giddy and pleasantly weak. Not now. Chase kissed her, opening her mouth with his, no preliminaries, no tentative probe to inquire if she was willing. He knew. She knew. And the certainty of it filled her with strength.

As his arms curved around her and one of his hands cupped the back of her head, she wound her own arms around his neck, plowing fingers into the thick hair at his crown. Molten lava flowed through the center of her body, a long lusty river of it, when his tongue entered her mouth. She met it with her own and they dueled. Nettie surprised herself and Chase: In the sweet, cunning dance of desire, she didn't want to follow; she wanted to lead. Just like he did.

Her fingers tightened in his hair, holding him as she pulled back, deliberately depriving him of the mouth he wanted to control. She took his lower lip between her teeth and bit, tugging as she held his head still.

Chase groaned, and Nettie felt a surge of delight in her own power. Her control, though, however sweet, was short-lived. Chase wanted it back, and when he took it his groan turned into a growl.

He shook his head like a lion, loosing her grip. Getting off the couch, he reached for her, lifting her in one fluid motion. Nettie circled his neck with her arms, eyes on his face as he carried her into the downstairs guestroom and laid her on the bed.

He'd waited too long for this, waited all his adult life to feel this hunger, to feel a need that was more than just sexual but a damn sight stronger than "sweet."

Bracing himself with one hand beside her head, he smoothed a palm up over her stomach to her breasts. The thin material of her dress moved with his touch. Her eyes glowed as she watched him.

When he reached her breastbone, Chase paused then slid his hand to the right, cupping one full gorgeous globe. She shuddered. Her eyes half closed, she released a sound that started as a sigh and ended in a moan that seemed to rise up from her toes. A desire to possess, to brand and to keep roared through his veins. He searched Nettie's face, gauging her willingness, assessing her hunger, needing to know it it matched his own.

Methodically, wanting her to feel the anticipation as he did, Chase unlooped the small buttons down the front of her dress, pushing the material away until he revealed her bra. Purple. He smiled, but quickly forgot about the hue as he realized the iridescent material was sheer enough to afford him his first access to a bosom he'd only been able to admire until now.

Brushing his thumb across her nipple, he felt it spring eagerly to life. His groin tightened. Urged by her sharp intake of breath and his own need, he bent lower to put his mouth where his hand had just roamed. Biting gently, using his tongue, too, he captured her nipple with his teeth and s-l-o-w-l-y, exquisitely tugged.

Nettie's hands dove into his hair. She arched, writhing beneath him, lifting a leg in a mindless motion that made their thighs brush. The soft bare skin on the inside of her thigh brushed his rough jeans, and she moaned. Chase reached down to hold her leg where it was, halting all motion, because in another second he was going to reach between their bodies to touch her far more personally and that, he felt sure, would be the beginning of the rest of the night.

Rising up, barely able to resist the cry of complaint in the back of her throat, he divested himself of his shirt with quick jagged motions, never taking his eyes from her. If she wanted to stop, this would be the time. The last time. He tossed his shirt to the floor and looked at her in question.

Lips parted, eyes open, Nettie sat up beneath him. She scooted back a bit, giving herself more room to move and Chase felt a flare of crushing disappointment until he saw her hands go to the front of her dress. She unfastened the remaining buttons, watching him all the while, and slipped the dress slowly off her shoulders. Reaching around, she unhooked her bra, and Chase wondered if she could see his heart as it threatened to pound through the wall of his chest.

"Are you—" *Sure,* he started to ask, but she took his face between her hands and answered before he completed the question.

"Does it look like I'm sure?"

## *Chapter Fourteen*

With her palms cupping his face, Nettie leaned back, drawing Chase down with her. She tried to lie still while he kissed her again, to mark and remember every sensation of his hands skimming her torso, eliciting a quiver she knew he could feel.

When his knuckles grazed her belly and his fingers slipped beneath the band of the scanty purple thong, a shudder wracked her. His touch was gentle yet bold and absolutely unabashed. With each stroke, he possessed her, shaking her free of the control she had struggled to maintain for so long. Nettie felt herself open, body and heart, for the first time in forever.

Chase pulled away from her mouth, moving lower to kiss her neck, her breasts, while his fingers explored deeper. He had reached the limit of his own restraint. She could tell by the increased intensity of his touch, by the way his muscles bunched and strained beneath her hands as she moved them along his back.

Moving purposefully, he rolled her flimsy undergarment away then lifted off her to shed his own clothing. When he sank down again, he joined their bodies, and the act was as welcome and gratifying as a summer rain. Tears built behind Nettie's eyes as pressure mounted inside her body. She gripped the arms that bracketed her, clutched Chase's back. Her breath came in pants then gasps that matched and mingled with his. She was standing on the edge of a cliff with a voice urging, "jump."

Her entire body surged upward as Chase's bore down. He growled her name—twice—as he arched over her, burying his face in her neck. The words were almost unintelligible, primal. He stoked the tension in her body, propelling her on until Nettie cried out with the pleasure of release and the incomparable satisfaction of feeling Chase above her, relinquishing his control, too, as he followed her over the edge.

For Nettie, the lingering moments after making love with Chase felt new and exhilarating and awkward and uncertain. She wished she could read his mind. And was grateful that she couldn't.

Reaching for the sheet they'd eventually crawled under, Nettie tucked it around her body and started to rise. Though Chase said Colin was a sound sleeper, she wasn't altogether reassured.

"I'd better go," she said.

Chase looked at her with calm eyes. Grabbing her wrist he pulled her back on to the bed and propped himself on one elbow. "You don't have to go."

"Yes, I—"

"No." Prying her hands from the sheet, he twined his fingers with hers and rested their clasped hands above her head. "I want you to have breakfast with me—with us—tomorrow morning. I want to watch the sun rise over those barley fields with you." There was something almost endearingly serious in his expression. "If you have regrets about tonight, tell me."

Extracting one of her hands from the love knot Chase had created, Nettie smoothed her thumb over the vertical line between his brows. "No regrets," she said, and her voice was strong.

No regrets. She'd made love to only one other man in her life, her husband, and that was after they'd married. She believed unequivocally that she never would marry again, but Lilah had been right when she'd insisted sex could never be casual for Nettie. This night with Chase, even if it never happened again, would be imprinted on her mind and heart the way the feel of his hands would be imprinted on her skin.

"I'll stay." She traced a tiny scar at the corner of his right eye. She hadn't noticed it before. There would be so many things to discover in a relationship that promised tomorrow…and tomorrow…. A pang of sadness tried to encroach on the quiet, sweet moment. Nettie pushed it away. "So what are you making for breakfast?"

Chase grinned. "Toaster pastries."

He gave her a long, lazy kiss. The fact that she was staying filled him with satisfaction. No, more than that—pleasure. The middle of the night was fast approaching, and she would be here. The sun would edge up from the eastern horizon. She'd be here. His son would come downstairs for breakfast, and the three of them would sit at the table together.

It was right. Chase's kiss increased in intensity. If he could transfer his conviction to her via a kiss, he would do it. If by making love to her from now till morning he could convince her they deserved a chance at forever, he wouldn't have let her get dressed in the first place.

Forever. Chase could hardly believe he was thinking about a future with one woman, the same woman, day after day, night after night. Lifting his head, he looked at Nettie while she stood with her eyes happily closed, smiling a little, swaying toward him. A big goofy grin claimed his face. Oh, yeah, he was thinking about it. A few days ago, she'd shut the door on any possibility of a relationship between them. Now it was a whole new ballgame. He had no idea how it would all play out, but that wasn't the point. The point was they deserved this chance.

"Colin won't be up until seven tomorrow. Really," he said when she regarded him doubtfully. "You can set your watch by him. We can sneak out of bed, watch the sun come up and have breakfast on the table before his eyes are all the way open."

"Okay," Nettie agreed, "but try not to make too much noise. I'd hate to have to explain what I'm doing here."

"I don't think I'm the one we have to worry about when it comes to decibels. You are—how should I put it?—surprisingly vocal."

"I—" Nettie frowned, then her eyes grew wide. "What do you mean? You mean during…? I am not!"

Chase laughed. "I'm not complaining." He growled in her ear. "I love it."

Goose bumps raced along her neck and arms. She wriggled in his embrace. "Just the same, I'm not…noisy."

He gave her an Eskimo kiss, the first he could recall ever bestowing. "Noisiest woman I've ever met."

Cheeks flushed beet red, she tried to scowl at him. "Am not."

Chase loved the way she did that—managed to look both virginally innocent and gorgeously wanton at the same time.

"Are too."

"Not."

Bending low, he grinned. "Let's find out."

The next morning Chase felt something so unfamiliar that at first he wasn't one hundred percent certain what it was.

Standing at the stove, wrapped in a ridiculous striped apron Nettie had tied around his waist, he listened to his son chatter about the books she had given him and about a movie called *Shrek* that he'd seen four times. Chase pushed bacon around an iron skillet with the spatula Nettie had placed in his hand and realized that what he felt was happiness. Pure and simple. He felt plainly, cleanly, deliriously happy.

"I hear a lot of talk over there, but I don't hear any offers of, 'hey, I'll set the table,' or 'let me pour the juice.'" He glanced over his shoulder to see Nettie confer with Colin.

"That must be a hint," she said dryly as she scraped back her chair.

"I can set the table. I know how." Colin scrambled down from his seat to gather an excessive number of utensils from the cutlery drawer.

Nettie pulled a carton of juice from the fridge and brought glasses and plates down from a shelf.

Chase grinned to himself. He couldn't care less if anyone helped this morning or if he stumbled through breakfast preparations himself, start to finish. He just wanted to be in on the conversation. Man, what a lovesick bufflehead he had turned out to be!

"What are you grinning about?" Nettie sidled up, peering into the skillet.

"Me? Nothin'." Chase bumped her shoulder discreetly with his. "You get along pretty well with my kid." He lowered his voice, working hard not to turn around and plant a kiss on the tip of her nose.

"Great kid," she said simply, snapping off a bit of bacon from the pile she had shown him how to drain on paper towels. Chase shook his head. Apparently bacon had to "drain." Who knew?

"This is going to be a mighty fine breakfast," he boasted, feeling, he decided, mighty proud of himself, too. The bacon looked good. The juice and waffles were no problem. This was the first meal he hadn't ruined.

Nettie pressed the lever on the toaster and followed Colin around the table, setting down plates. "Toaster waffles, toaster pastries," she said. "I detect a culinary theme."

Chase agreed without apology. "You got that right. And if some enterprising manufacturer comes up with the perfect toaster cheeseburger, I'll be stocking up on those, too."

Nettie laughed. "Remind me to give you a few easy cooking lessons sometime in the near future. Nick's freezer isn't that large."

Chase wanted to cheer at the prospect. More time together fit in perfectly with his plans.

Colin liked the idea, too, but on a different basis. "Can you teach him to make spaghetti," he asked with a child's guileless clarity, "the right way?"

Nettie's eyes sparkled at Chase. "Yeah, I think he could handle that."

"How about garlic bread?" Chase added. "The perfect Caesar dressing and..." He pondered. "Zabaglione for dessert?" The more time he spent with her, the better.

Nettie's eyes widened as she listened to his menu. "You want to learn to make zabaglione? You? The toaster pastry king?"

"Yeah, Miss Smarty." He looked at Colin. "I think a well-rounded menu is important."

"What's zab...ra...?" Colin searched for the word.

"Zabaglione," Nettie supplied. "It's sort of an Italian pudding. You won't like it."

"I like pudding!" Colin insisted. He added extra forks to each place setting until he'd used all the utensils. "Can we have zab...zabra...that pudding stuff tonight?"

"It's not the kind of pudding you're used to." Nettie poured three glasses of juice, plus a glass of milk for Colin.

"We have to eat something, though," Chase reasoned, removing the last pieces of bacon from the skillet and bringing the plate to the table. He slid an arm around Nettie's waist as he moved behind her. Lingering there, he drew her gently against him, pleased when she relaxed. Reveling in the clean fresh scent of her and the softness of her hair, he nuzzled the pillow of curls, trying not to be too obvious about it. "I like this home-cooking stuff. How about teaching me to make an Italian dinner tonight? Plus chocolate pudding for Colin?"

While Colin waxed on about his love of chocolate pudding, Chase whispered into Nettie's ear, "I know it's a lot of work— probably the last thing you'd like to do with your afternoon— but I promise to make it worth your while. And tomorrow I'll find a baby-sitter so you and I can go into Minot for dinner. Maybe some dancing?"

Warm and soft, Chase's breath made Nettie tingle. His suggestion made her shiver. He was planning their tomorrow as if they were an average couple. She looked at Colin, at the table they had set, at the food. It all looked so normal; it all felt so right.

When she failed to respond verbally, Chase leaned around to look in her face. "Are you free tomorrow?" he asked, sounding less certain now.

Nettie smiled. She liked that, too.

"No, I'm not free," she murmured, exercising a feminine coyness she'd never really tested before. Turning in Chase's arms, she leaned forward till their noses were almost touching and added, "If I'm spending half the evening in the kitchen teaching you how to cook, it's going to cost you."

They were only halfway through breakfast when the phone rang.

Colin had insisted that he could not eat a waffle unless every "ditch" was filled with syrup, and his father seemed mystified by the universal stickiness that ensued. No part of breakfast, the table itself or Colin, it seemed, was currently maple syrup free.

The phone rang a second time.

"Telephone!" Colin announced loudly, clearly convinced he was the only one in the room who possessed ears. "Someone's gotta get it."

"Yeah, you stay where you are and eat." Chase pointed to his son's plate. "And don't touch anything except the food on your plate and your own fork until I get back."

Nettie grinned. Chase was definitely getting a crash course in parenthood. Breakfast lesson number one: The time it takes a child to make a mess of his meal is only a fraction of the time it will take him to eat it.

Sipping her juice, Nettie kept an eye on Colin while Chase picked up the kitchen extension. Colin asked her if there were lizards in North Dakota, then proceeded to tell her he knew how to make a good "lizard house" and asked if she had any shoeboxes he could "borrow."

Dividing her attention between answering the seven-year-old's questions and urging him to eat some of his waffle before his father got off the phone, Nettie was vaguely aware that Chase had taken advantage of the long phone cord to pull the receiver through the kitchen door and into the hallway as he spoke.

When he returned to the table some time later, Nettie saw that his mood had changed considerably. She kept up the dialogue with Colin, but Chase seemed unwilling or unable to reenter the conversation. After several long minutes, Nettie rose, ushered Colin into the bathroom to get him started on the process of cleaning up and then rejoined Chase.

"What's wrong?" she asked without preamble, approaching him in concern. Having shuttled Colin's plate to the sink, Chase now leaned heavily on the counter, looking very much as though he was in pain.

He glanced around.

"In the bathroom, cleaning up," Nettie said, responding in unconscious shorthand to the question in Chase's eyes. "There was syrup on his clothes, so I told him to change. It should take awhile." Without giving it any thought, she placed a comforting hand on his back. "What's going on?"

Chase shook his head, keeping his palms braced on the sink

as if he required the support to remain upright. "That was my lawyer on the phone." His voice was low and unsteady. "When I went to Florida to get Colin, there were no other known relatives. Now—" He stopped, turning to scan the kitchen, needing to make sure once again that Colin was not within earshot. "Julia's parents have been located."

"Julia was Colin's mother?"

Chase nodded. "Her parents live in England. Julia was estranged from them. Her choice, apparently, not theirs. They say she wrote them a letter a couple months before she was killed, indicating that she wanted to reconcile and…" Chase shook his head, obviously shell-shocked by the pieces of information he'd been given. "They want Colin. They want custody."

Chase faced her. He looked like a man who'd been sucker punched—disoriented, hurt and angry all at once.

Nettie felt a rush of blood to her head. "But how can they ask such a thing? Don't they know he's with you?"

Chase emitted a harsh laugh. "The news left them unimpressed. Given the fact that I didn't even know about Colin for the first seven years of his life, they have grave doubts their grandson's well-being will be served under my care."

Clearly parroting his lawyer, Chase's words filled Nettie with indignation. How unfair! How…*how dare they?* They hadn't even seen Chase with Colin; they didn't know how much he loved his son already.

A fierce desire to protect this man, this come-lately father who didn't know enough to take the syrup bottle off the table after it had been poured, who'd had no idea how to fry bacon, and who was often clearly uncertain how to talk to his son…but who so desperately wanted to try…rose inside Nettie with the strength of a thousand armed troops.

"Where have *they* been?" she demanded. "How well do they know Colin? Have they ever met him?"

"I don't know."

"Well, then they can't possibly have all the power here. I can't imagine they'd even get to court."

"I don't know," Chase repeated. "My lawyer wants me to call him back as soon as possible."

They heard Colin running from his room upstairs. Nettie saw additional concern cross Chase's face and hastened to reassure him. "I'll take him with me. Lilah's at home. Between the two of us, we'll keep him occupied until you can get there." Moving in close, she rubbed his chest and shoulder.

Capturing her hand, Chase pressed a kiss into the palm. His eyes communicated his gratitude.

When Colin clattered into the kitchen, Nettie gave Chase a moment to compose himself. She forced a bright smile that relaxed into something more genuine when she saw Colin's Don't Sweat the Small Stuff...And I'm Small Stuff T-shirt. "Hey, kiddo. How'd you like to come over to my place and help me draw a picture for my next book?"

Colin proved to be a bit more careful with paint than he was with a syrup bottle, but not much. Nettie hoped his T-shirt was not new, given that yellow ochre, jade and crimson decorated its surface in a variety of blops, smudges and stripes.

Leaving the paint-happy boy ensconced in her studio, Nettie went downstairs, where Lilah waited for her in the living room. Lounging in the wingback chair, bare pedicured feet propped on the coffee table, the inherently glamorous blonde held a tall glass of lemonade in her hand. There was another waiting on the end table for Nettie.

"Thanks." Nettie grabbed the icy tumbler and plopped onto the couch. "I must be out of shape. Keeping up with a seven-year-old has me worn out already and it's barely noon." She pressed the glass against her cheek.

"Is that what wore you out?" Lilah wriggled her toes. "And here I thought lack of sleep was the culprit." Innuendo curled her lips as she sipped her lemonade.

"Yeah, you're funny," Nettie applauded dryly. "Did Sara say anything when I wasn't here this morning?"

"She doesn't know. I closed your bedroom door as soon as I realized you were gone." Lilah wagged a shaming finger. "Then I told her you had a headache and had decided to sleep in."

Expelling a sigh of relief, Nettie toasted her sister in thanks. "I don't feel like dodging the Sara Owens third degree today."

"I don't blame you. She used to grill me if I came home five minutes after curfew when we were in high school. And she's only two years older! Drove me crazy." Lilah shook her head. "So, Nettie-Belle, tell me one thing— What are his intentions?" Slyly, she grinned. "'Cause I know where you were and who you were with."

Setting her lemonade on the side table, Nettie covered her face with her hands, pounded her feet on the floor as if she were running in place and squealed. "Oh, Lilah! It was so, so...not me!" She lowered her hands and met her sister's affectionate smile. "I think I seduced him," she whispered.

Lilah hooted with laughter. Nettie giggled, too. "We made breakfast together this morning and it wasn't awkward at all. It was..."

"What?"

*Right.* It...just...felt....right. But she didn't want to say that. No, didn't even want to think it. It was too much, too soon, too scary. Adages popped into mind.

What goes up must come down....

Every back has a front....

The bigger they are, the harder they fall....

The more right something feels, the more wrong it can go.... Okay, so that last one was hers, but the point remained the same: Keep your expectations simple. Keep plans to a minimum. So, instead of saying this morning had felt "right" or "wonderful" or, heaven forbid, "perfect," Nettie murmured, "Nice. Yeah, it was nice." An understatement, to be sure.

"And now you have Colin here." Lilah watched her sister with loving eyes. "How does that feel, Nettie-Belle?"

"Not as hard as I thought it would be." The truth came as more of a surprise to Nettie than to her sister. "I thought I'd be sad, that it would be too painful to have a child here. Or that I'd feel guilty, like I was somehow betraying..." She took a breath. "Tucker. And Brian." Smiling through a pang of sadness that hit her dully in the center of her chest, she shook her head. "Silly."

"No," Lilah said softly. "Not at all. So, tell me. Why did you bring Colin here by yourself? Where's Chase?"

Briefly, Nettie explained what she knew about the phone call and Chase's need to converse with his lawyer without Colin around to overhear.

Lilah pursed her lips. "So he might find himself in the middle of a custody battle?"

"I don't know." Frowning, Nettie shook her head. "I can't imagine it going that far. When you watch Chase and Colin together, it's so easy to see they're building a relationship. Who would stand in the way of that?"

"Plenty of people, Nettie-Belle. Plenty of people." Lilah's expression flowed from interest to concern. "Oh, sweetie, you know I want you to get out into the world and live again. But I thought you'd go for the pleasure and shelve the pain for awhile."

"I am." When Lilah looked doubtful, Nettie persisted, "Truly. First of all, Chase is not going to lose that child. I know it. But he does have to deal with this, see his lawyer, rearrange his life to include a little boy." She smoothed her palms over the jeans she'd donned upon arriving home. "Any time now he's going to knock on that door and tell me he's booked their flight home to New York." With an admirably level gaze, she maintained, "I'm ready for that. I was ready for it before he got the phone call this morning. That's why I was able to stay with him last night."

"I don't know if I like the sound of that. I wonder if *he'd* like the sound of that."

Amazingly, Nettie found she was able to laugh and that fact encouraged her. She was going to be okay when Chase said good-bye. She really was. "He's going to like the sound of that just fine. Believe me. He's got more than enough on his plate as it is. He doesn't need a woman clinging to his arm."

"Mm."

Lilah looked like she had more to say, but Colin chose that moment to holler from upstairs. "Nettie!" He clambered down the staircase, skidding to a breathless stop when he saw her in the living room.

There was even more paint on him now.

"What is it?" She rose immediately.

"Um, you know that thing you put the picture on? That folding thing?"

"The easel? Yes."

"Well, um, it sorta fell over, sorta."

"It did?" Relieved there was no real emergency, she asked, "What happened to the canvas?"

"Is that the picture?"

Nettie nodded.

Colin looked worried. "It landed on the ground."

While Lilah covered a smile, Nettie had a moment of gratitude for watercolors.

"Okay. Let's go upstairs and see if we can salvage the picture."

As it turned out, repairing the painting didn't take as much effort as cleaning Colin up for the second time that day. While Nettie tossed his T-shirt into the washing machine, Lilah took a phone call from Chase. He asked her to pass along the message that he had travel arrangements to make but would be over shortly.

Given the message, Nettie found her body responding almost before her mind. With a fluttering heart she realized, *This is it. This is goodbye.*

*He's going to tell me they have to leave for New York immediately. Before we make spaghetti. They'll start their life together as a family, and I...*

Swallowing heavily, she told herself to buck up. This was simple. She would begin again, too. That's what people did every day, anyway, wasn't it? Especially after losing someone. You woke up, you made the choice to begin again. Every day.

On a deep breath, Nettie looked at Colin as he gobbled more of her homemade cookies and peppered her with questions like, "How come when you put the green in the red it turns brown?"

It had been a fun morning. And that, Nettie told herself, was enough.

Chase arrived while Colin's T-shirt was still tumbling in the dryer. Appearing weary but calm, he greeted Nettie by drawing her into his arms for a long hug. Pulling back, he turned the embrace into a soul-satisfying kiss.

"I needed that," he growled low in her ear. His warm breath sent showers of goose bumps racing down her neck and arms.

He told Lilah he was making travel plans, Nettie reminded herself as soon as she could form a coherent thought.

"Colin's with Lilah," she said. Pull out of his arms now...atta girl...turn away...keep talking... "They're in the backyard, collecting earth in buckets.'' She began edging toward the kitchen. ''Want some coffee? I just a made a pot.''

''Sure.'' He followed her. ''Dare I ask what they're planning to do with this 'earth'?''

''Lilah told him she thought they could make a million dollars by making North Dakota mud packs for rich women in Beverly Hills.''

''I see. So my son shows a precocious entrepreneurial spirit?''

''Mm, mostly I think he liked the idea of digging in dirt.''

''Ah.'' Chase watched her while she poured the coffee, set out milk and sugar and pulled cookies from a ceramic jar in the shape of a merry pig. When she handed him the plate of snacks, he grinned, first at it and then at her.

''What?'' Her forehead creased. ''Is something wrong?''

''No, no. I was just trying to remember the last time a woman handed me a plate of cookies.''

''And?''

''And I can't remember.''

Nettie made a face. ''Wonderful. In an ocean of exotic memories, someday you'll look back and think of me as Betty Crocker.''

''You bet,'' he agreed. Plucking a cookie from the plate, he took a bite, gave her a wink and let his gaze wander slowly down her body. ''Covered in chocolate, frilly little apron, naked underneath…''

Nettie snapped a dishtowel in his direction, but his reply pleased her enormously. ''Shame on you! C'mon, let's go into the living room. I want to know what your lawyer said.'' *Very good!* Her inner coach commended her efforts to remember what was about to transpire here. *Stay on track… simply ignore that nasty woosh of longing to rip his clothes off…or yours.…*

Steeling herself to appear poised, sophisticated and serene throughout his account of the call even—no, especially—when he got to the part about heading back to New York, Nettie perched on the edge of the couch and waited for him to begin.

Chase leaned back against the cushions, took a sip of the very strong coffee and sat a moment, simply collecting his thoughts. ''What a day.'' Setting his mug on the table, he opened an arm in Nettie's direction. ''Hey, come here.'' He tilted his head and motioned for her to snuggle against him.

*Danger…danger… Do not go there.* She stared hungrily at the side of his torso and the warm, perfectly shaped alcove of his underarm.

*We-e-e-ll, would it hurt, really, to scoot in for just a moment? There's no harm,* she reasoned, *in being comfortable while he says goodbye.*

She scooched over on the sofa, but remained committed—absolutely—to holding her body in a rigid, unyielding line so there would be no mistake about what was going on here: She might be getting physically close, but she was distancing herself emotionally.

Chase folded his arm around her. He brought his other arm up to gather her into what might have been interpreted—by somebody else—as a circle of love and protection.

"There," he murmured, his muscles softening as he sighed manfully. "I've been wanting to do this all day."

"Me—" Catching herself in the nick of time, Nettie mumbled, "Um, so what did your lawyer say?"

Chase released another sigh, this one rough and weary. "He said things I'd like to forget about until Colin is eighteen. Unfortunately burying my head in the sand is not an option if I want to keep my son."

"And you do."

He reared back to look at her. "I like the way you say that. Like it's a given. My lawyer put it somewhat differently. He said, 'Be sure that raising this boy is what you want, because if this goes to court, you're in for the fight of your life.'"

"But why? I still can't fathom how Colin's grandparents can threaten your custody."

"Because of me. Because of things I've done. And said." He settled back against the couch again, and Nettie felt the resonance of his voice as she leaned against his chest. He spoke slowly, carefully. "I've never felt any particular pride in the way I've lived my life up to now. But I can't say I've had any discomfort with it, either. I guess I've lived like your classic bachelor. The only rules I followed were mine."

"Well, you were a bachelor. You are."

Chase gave a wry grunt. "Maybe I should rephrase it more accurately. I lived like a bachelor who's been on the cover of

*Star* magazine. There are plenty of opportunities for socializing when you're regarded as a celebrity.''

"I know." Toying with the hairs on the back of his wrist, Nettie confessed, "I got on the Internet one night and looked you up. You've dated *way* too many models." She gave a couple of hairs a firm tweak. "Weren't you afraid of becoming a cliché?''

She posed the question facetiously, but Chase groaned. "Yes," he said emphatically. "Hell yes, I've dated way too many women, period." He tightened his hold on her. "Are you losing respect for me?''

"Mm, gettin' there." She rubbed the hairs she'd pulled. Then more seriously she added, "If the women were willing, who can fault you?" Nettie was thinking of herself, no question. To a rag magazine like *Star* she supposed she'd be considered just another one of Chase Reynolds's women. The thought poked a finger of jealousy right in her sternum. Jealousy and possessiveness. She didn't even want to explore that and was relieved when Chase claimed her attention.

"A court can fault me," he answered her question and Nettie heard the frown in his voice. "Grandparents can fault me. Social services—''

"Now wait a minute. Aren't you being overly harsh? You didn't even suspect you were a father until a few weeks ago."

There was a pause. "Before you let me off the hook, there's more you need to know. I never wanted kids, Nettie." Rather than shifting to see her better, Chase stayed where he was and Nettie understood it was easier for him to get this out without looking at her. "That's an understatement. Any lawyer with the competence of Daffy Duck will be able to wallpaper the courthouse with evidence of my position on commitment. And for awhile there, I was pretty vocal about being opposed to fatherhood.''

"All right, I understand your concern. Maybe I can even understand Colin's grandparents' concern—because they don't know you. But judges are mandated to be impartial. A couple of gossipy articles from your past can't mean that much."

"Maybe not," he agreed. "But one really stupid comment I made a few weeks ago could do us in."

Chase sounded sick with remorse. This time Nettie wriggled

out of his arms to face him. He looked at her, but his eyes held a faraway, unhappy expression. She waited.

Scraping a hand through his hair, he shook his head, then swore beneath his breath, damning himself.

"Julia's boyfriend in Florida was the first person to contact me about Colin. When he told me Julia had a son who was seven and that I was the father, I said—" Chase closed his eyes, wincing at the memory. "I said, 'Bullshit. The kid isn't mine.'"

When he reopened his eyes, he looked like a condemned man so filled with guilt he would refuse his own pardon. Nettie's heart reached out to him. Whatever had made him reject the idea of fatherhood so vehemently, clearly a lot had changed in a few weeks. "Are you afraid Julia's boyfriend will be a witness for her parents?"

"Their lawyer has already spoken to him. I don't think he cares one way or the other who gets custody as long as it's not him. But if he's subpoenaed, it won't be good for us."

"You and Colin have so much to handle right now. Becoming a family is challenging enough without all this hanging over you."

"I just don't want Colin to suffer because his father shot off his stupid mouth." Restless, Chase stood and paced the room. "I came to North Dakota to elude the press as long as I could, but my lawyer tells me the story broke in England today, and it's bound to hit a few papers in the states. That means photographers and pictures of Colin." He swore again, but more mildly. "It's weird, all these feelings I've never had before. I just want to protect him, Nettie. I want to make life…*everything*…better for him, not worse."

The impulse to rush to Chase, to hold and reassure him was so strong Nettie almost gave in. Exerting all her willpower, she stayed where she was. "Lilah said you mentioned something about travel plans. I imagine you'll be leaving…" Traitorously, her voice wobbled. "Leaving soon," she said. To prove she was fine, perfectly fine, with whatever he had to do, she added, "It makes sense. School will be starting in a little while. You'll have to register Colin, and I'm sure you want to be near your lawyer. And your family. We haven't even talked about your family and how they feel about Colin. They must be so excited. When…" Her hands were clutched so tightly on her lap, she feared she might cut off the circulation to her wrists. "When do you leave?"

Standing at the fireplace, Chase looked at her quizzically. "I'm not leaving. I made travel plans for my lawyer, Nelson, to come out. Besides, Colin's grandparents want to meet him, and I'd rather have that happen here than in New York. For the time being, we're staying put. We're staying in North Dakota."

## Chapter Fifteen

The relief was dizzying.

Why bother to deny it, Nettie thought as the tension she hadn't even realized she was carrying began to drain from her neck and shoulders. The news that Chase was staying—even temporarily—acted on her like a good antihistamine: all at once she could breathe again.

Outwardly, she strove to present a calm and serene front while she considered the best response. "Gee, that's nice," "Anything I can do to help?" and "North Dakota's glad to have you" all exemplified the poise she wanted to possess.

Shouting "Thank You, God…Thank You, God…Thank You, God!" while throwing her arms around Chase's neck would be more genuine.

In the end, she compromised, walking to him as calmly as she could and circling his waist in a gentle hug while the giddy smile inside her bubbled to the surface. "I'm glad."

Tension drained from him, too, as he hugged her back, resting his cheek on the top of her head.

In the kitchen, the back door opened and closed. Sneakered feet raced noisily across linoleum and over the hardwood, skidding to a stop in the living room. More languidly, feet shod in sandals clicked across the floor.

Lilah halted next to Colin and, like him, stared at the scene in front of the fireplace. "If this were Christmas, I'd turn you into a postcard."

Her wry comment pulled the couple slightly apart. Still with their arms around each other's waists, they glanced over. Nettie was flushed and happy.

"Told you," Colin said in a stage whisper to his new partner in dirt digging. "They kept huggin' like that while I was trying to eat breakfast."

Lilah nodded. "Speaking as a professional actor, I can tell you this doesn't look a bit like 'good-bye.'"

Chase's lawyer, Nelson Dale, was booked on a flight from New York to Minot for the following week. In the meantime Chase accepted Nick's offer to move into the two-bedroom cottage that sat on its own patch of fallow land about a half mile from the barley fields. Nick's father had built the stone-and-stucco bungalow for his second wife—Nick's beloved stepmother, Bea—who had moved to North Dakota from the countryside of England. It was the house Nettie had told him about.

"The enchanted cottage," Chase muttered darkly as he and Nettie stood outside, assessing the work they needed to do. Warned by Nick that the place had been neglected for years, Chase had requested Nettie's expertise in returning it to a state of hominess, but he hadn't expected quite so much disrepair.

"Looks more like the house on haunted hill," he grumbled, hands resting on his hips as he wondered if renting a place in town might be a better option. His lawyer had stressed the importance of presenting a picture of home and hearth.

Chase shook his head. If this place had a hearth, he seriously doubted their ability to locate it. Weeds and a tangled vine that should have been eulogized a long time ago shrouded the exterior of the cottage. A thick crust of dirt covered the windowpanes. Chase could imagine the condition of the interior...but wasn't sure he wanted to.

"If I'd known it looked like this, I never would have asked you to help," he told Nettie, who was already attempting to peer through the grime encasing the window. Some hot date he'd turned out to be.

Swinging around from her preliminary fact-finding mission, she faced him with shining eyes.

Dazed, he surmised. Probably in shock. Wants to tell me to stuff it, but isn't quite certain how. "Nick's description of the place leaves a lot to be desired."

Nettie nodded in agreement. "I don't think he ever appreciated it the way we girls did." She made a sweeping gesture with her hand. "Isn't it wonderful?"

Chase simply stood there, wondering if he heard her correctly. "'Scuse me?"

She stepped off the porch to examine the perimeter. "When Bea was alive she kept an English garden. No one knew how she could nurture so many gorgeous flowers with our harsh weather. The ladies at church suspected she imported dirt from England!" Rubbing her palms with enthusiasm, she urged, "Let's go in."

"You want to see the inside?" he asked incredulously. "After lunch? If the mess is bigger inside than out, I, for one, am in danger of tossing my cookies."

"Don't be silly," Nettie laughed. "This is a great challenge! Wait'll you see the fireplace, you'll love it. This sweet old girl deserves to be returned to her former glory."

Chase withheld comment on her definition of "glory" and produced the key Nick kept on a hook in his kitchen. "I bet he hasn't tried this key in years," he said as he made his first attempt at wriggling it into the lock.

"Probably not. Nick never came here much, anyway. It was Bea's haven. She shared it with the women in town and with us girls. We had the best sleepovers here. I loved it."

"Sleepovers," Chase mused. Good idea. He glanced at the eager woman beside him. If she promised to sleep over he'd work from sunup to sunup making the cottage presentable.

Would he have chosen to remain in North Dakota if not for Nettie? Doubtful. Very doubtful.

His lawyer had advised him to transform his image. A white-carpeted, chrome-and-leather-trimmed apartment in Manhattan with neighbors whose names he doubted he'd ever known, did not seem like a route to that goal. At this point, Chase had no idea where he and Colin would wind up permanently, though he knew he could have chosen someplace less rural for their temporary abode. Connecticut, for instance, or upstate New York. But then they would have been alone.

He looked again at Nettie and found himself thinking the word *home*.

Why fight it? A smile pushed his cheeks into grinning-fool mode as he opened the rough-hewn door and watched her rush inside, as thrilled with the dark, dust-laden interior as if he'd just opened the door to Buckingham Palace.

Chase filled his lungs with the stale, musty air and echoed her sigh. Yep, he'd toil from sunup to sunup. While visions of sleep-overs danced in his head....

Three days later, the "enchanted cottage" was...

"Cute," Chase observed, kicking back on the living-room sofa, whose overstuffed cushions and garden floral upholstery managed to seem stylish twenty years after their purchase.

"Cute?" Nettie echoed indignantly. Arranging knickknacks on the mantel, shifting their positions to satisfy herself, she grumbled, "Three days of slave labor and the best he can do is 'cute.'"

Chase gladly took the bait, hoisting his tired bones from the couch to come up behind her, and Nettie squealed when he grabbed her around the waist, tipping her back into a dramatic dip.

"Slave labor," Chase chided. "Is that what you call yester-day?"

"Yesterday?"

"Whisking the mattress in the master bedroom?"

Nettie's eyes darkened. He referred, of course, to what had taken place after the mattress whisking...when they were sup-posed to have been putting linens on the bed and wound up in it, instead. Her lips parted unconsciously as she remembered the moment, and he almost carried her into the bedroom for an instant replay. Although, he assured himself, feeling his body respond faithfully, it wouldn't be so "instant."

"How," Nettie asked insouciantly, "does the, um, 'mattress whisking' negate my allegation of slave labor?"

"You were richly rewarded," Chase growled low in her ear.

Slowly, deliberately she wagged her head. "*You* were richly rewarded."

"Sassy." He grinned, taking advantage of her position to rain kisses down her neck. "Sassy and sooo right...."

Some time later, they resurfaced to begin dinner preparations in the newly cleaned brick and copper kitchen. Chase suggested that dinner out would be a fitting reward for all their hard work, but Nettie insisted on christening the cottage with a simple home-cooked meal around the carved oak dining table. She'd barely won the argument before the doorbell rang.

Lilah, with Colin in tow, stood on the porch, a huge picnic basket in her hands. "There's more in the car," she tossed over her shoulder at Chase as she breezed by. "Place looks spiffy," she added on her way to the kitchen.

"Yeah. Spiffy." Colin trotted happily after his babysitter, lugging a small Igloo ice chest. He wore, Chase noticed, a brand-new pair of sunglasses—like Lilah—and had mousse in his hair.

Lilah had been a great help the past few days, sometimes pitching in to set the house aright, sometimes baby-sitting Colin when it was clear the child needed a break from housecleaning. So if she had his son looking like a pint-sized Hollywood producer, oh well. What was the harm?

Agreeably, Chase went to the car, the same huge clunker Nettie drove, and hefted a box filled with covered baking dishes from the open tailgate. "Whoa! What the heck..."

How much food had she brought? He wondered, taking several steps backward under its weight.

"Unless you're psychic," he said to Lilah upon entering the kitchen, "something tells me this is not an impromptu home-cooked meal." He set the box on the small center island, pulled out a large slow cooker and lifted the lid to inhale the savory aroma of barbecued beef. "You can cook," he complimented.

"An Owens trait." She shrugged to suggest it was really no big deal.

"What about Sara? Can she cook, too?" Somehow, he couldn't fathom it.

"No. But I can buy." As if on cue, the sheriff of Kalamoose strolled into the kitchen with a stack of pink boxes.

"Ooh, baby! What kind did you get?" Lilah hurried over to peek inside.

"I dunno. Whatever Ernie had. It's all good."

"Hi, Sara! I've been practicing my quick draw." Colin raced toward the uniformed woman. Miming a holster and pistol, he "drew" three times in quick succession.

Chase glanced at Nettie, who was smiling at his son and her sisters while she unpacked their dinner. "Did you bring the drinks? Oh, good!" From the picnic basket, she withdrew four bottles, two of champagne and two of sparkling cider.

Chase felt a warm glow deep in his chest as realization dawned. Nettie had set up a kind of housewarming. Stowing the drinks in the refrigerator for the time being, she turned with a satisfied look in his direction. The cottage could have fallen down at that point, and he wouldn't have been able to look away.

"Did you do potato and pasta salad?" Sara asked, while she dangled her handcuffs in front of Colin.

"Yes." Lilah answered with her head in a pie box. "Peach! Oh, Ernie, you doll, you!"

"How about baked beans?"

"Of course."

"Hey, Sara, can I handcuff myself to the doorknob?"

"Sure, squirt. I'll come unlock you in a minute."

Conversation eddied around them. Chase and Nettie continued to stare at each other. "Thank you," he mouthed.

"You're welcome." Her smile broadened—just for him—and Chase knew in that moment he could have said much more than "Thank you." And meant it.


Four days later, Nelson Dale arrived to brief Chase on what was now officially his custody case, and Chase began to understand for the first time in his life what "family" felt like.

It wasn't silence, polite or contentious, while silverware clinked on bone china and classical music underscored an abundance of good taste.

It wasn't white carpets, empty apartments, travel that seemed never-ending.

And it wasn't muscling through every challenge in life totally on one's own because to ask for help might be perceived as weak by the people who were supposed to love you.

No.

"Family" was laughter, raucous and tolerant, when your son chose dinnertime to practice his new skill—voluntary belching.

Family was braided rugs that hid dirt, homes with too many people and not enough privacy, and towns where everyone knew your name and too much of your business.

Most of all, he realized that family was, indeed, not asking for help...because by the time you got around to it, help had already arrived.

The news that Colin's grandparents had already decided to pursue custody hit everyone like a thunderbolt. Nelson Dale felt terrible bearing the bad tidings. He closeted himself with Chase for several hours at the cottage while Nettie took Colin for the day.

"You seem...I don't know...content here," Nelson commented, looking comfortable in a leather wingback. "Present circumstances aside."

The two men were holed up in the "library," a small room lined with recessed bookshelves and appointed in rich leather and dark wood. Nelson, a small, wiry fellow with glasses and a hairline more recessed than the bookshelves, eyed his client and friend over the rim of his coffee mug. "If I didn't know better, I could almost believe you planned to stay."

"In Kalamoose?" Distracted, Chase brushed the notion aside without giving it any consideration. "What would I do here?"

"Mmm. That is a point, of course. But still, it's too bad."

"What? Why?" Chase gave Nelson more of his attention. He'd known Nelson since college, had retained him as a lawyer for the past eight years and in all that time, whether they met in a business or social setting, Chase had never seen his friend relax. Not that Chase had ever really noticed before, but clearly the man was wired for city living. Even today, where no one knew him and his only client was wearing jeans, Nelson wore a suit and tie, gold cufflinks and a pocket watch. A pocket watch, for crying out loud. "Since when have you appreciated rural life?"

"Since you became the defendant in a custody suit. When the court assigns a social worker to your case, you could be treated to a drop-in visit." He scanned the room behind his glasses. "This place makes a persuasive presentation. As does your friend."

"Nettie?" Nelson nodded and Chase frowned. He didn't like hearing his "friend" or his home—even if it was only his borrowed, temporary home—described like something from a movie set. He didn't like feeling compelled to orchestrate his life; he just wanted to live it. Most of all, he detested and resented like hell the hovering sense of fear that he could lose his son.

"I'm not a custody attorney," Nelson said, concern puckering his brow.

"You've told me."

"Yes, but you don't seem to be listening. Soon—very soon—you will have to engage an attorney who specializes. In the meantime," he raced on when Chase opened his mouth to swear (he'd been doing a lot of that this morning), "I'm going to advise you the way I believe a custody attorney would. You have somehow placed yourself in the midst of a lifestyle that bears no resemblance whatsoever to the life you formerly led. In your present situation this is a very good thing. It could, however, also be construed as a ploy to appease the courts. Nothing more than a well-constructed fiction. Needless to say, that would not be good."

"Yes, it is needless to say," Chase growled—rudely, given the fact that Nelson had come here to help. He pinched the bridge of his nose. "So what's your point?"

"Your past—distant and more recent—does not speak well of your commitment to fatherhood. Your lifestyle does not recommend itself to the nurturing of a small child, nor do these facts compel one to believe that you will be deeply committed to retain your current level of domesticity."

"What the bloody hell is your point, Nelson?"

Reaching over to a pad of paper on the small table between them, Nelson scribbled "discuss temper management." Chase sighed.

Setting the pencil down, Nelson looked his client calmly in the eye. "My point is I can think of one thing that might solve all your problems."

Chase waited a beat while Nelson sipped his coffee, a small

smile playing about his lips and a mischievous glint in his sharp eyes. "Do you want me to guess?" Chase asked, nerves stretching his patience about as thin as it could get.

"Fatherhood is still new to you. I imagine the sheen hasn't worn off yet. We haven't discussed it, but you could agree to share custody with Julia's parents. For that matter, you've always spent a good portion of the year overseas. With sufficient visitation—"

*That did it!* Chase bolted from his chair.

Calmly setting his cup on the table, Nelson showed his palms in a gesture of surrender. Sadly, he shook his head. "Everyone blames the messenger. All right." Getting serious, he leaned forward. "How badly do you want full custody? To what lengths are you willing to go?"

"Any lengths." The answer was swift, adamant, and Chase's tone stated clearly that this was not a topic up for debate.

Nelson nodded. "There is a very effective cure for the problems plaguing this case." Again he paused, as if his client was supposed to supply the answer himself.

Chase hissed through gritted teeth. "I'm waiting."

"Yes, you are. And you know what they say about he who hesitates? Always a bridesmaid, never... No, that's not it." Nelson tapped a thin finger against his lips. "What is that...? What is it they say...?" He shrugged in defeat. "Ah, well." Folding his thin, lawyerly hands neatly over his flat stomach, his myopic eyes never blinked. "Get married."

Nettie drank flavored iced tea from a bottle, taking a brief pause from the amusing domestic anecdote she'd been sharing. Chase was hovering around the kitchen, listening to her, but obviously distracted and tense, a product, no doubt, of his current circumstance and of spending the past two days in a small enclosed area with a lawyer.

Hoping to relax him, she continued her account of the past two days at her house, where she and her sisters had babysat Colin while Chase tried to figure out how not to lose him.

The irony of Chase's situation in relation to her own was not lost on Nettie. It was an uneasy balancing act she played. On the one hand, nothing seemed more important than helping

Chase keep Colin. She wanted to devote herself to the cause, do anything she could to help him through the desert of uncertainty, share with him that she understood, as well as anyone and better than most.

On the other hand, the closer she got to father and son and the more she imagined the unthinkable—that Colin could be whisked away to England—the more nervous and frightened she became, for Chase and for herself. She doubted she would see Colin again, ever, if he went to live with his grandparents. England, after all, might as well be on another planet as far as she was concerned.

She hadn't thought much about anxiety for the past few weeks. She was still using the program Lilah had gotten for her and was able to drive all over Kalamoose and even into the two cities flanking her hometown. After three years of being afraid of life—and even more afraid of the fear—getting back in a car, driving and actually enjoying herself felt like an accomplishment of heroic proportions. "Excitement" was replacing "fear." But flying across a continent and an ocean? That was another matter entirely. Imagining Colin on a plane ride that long made her as jittery as a jumping bean. Picturing him in another country with people she didn't know and had no reason to trust, wondering if he was happy and well and never truly knowing…

That was something she couldn't think about at all. So the balancing act was to accept her desire to help, while reminding herself that caring about Colin and Chase was a temporary occupation. A goodbye was coming; it was just a matter of time. The only uncertainty lay in the details.

Reaching into a grocery bag, she continued her story, finding solace and distraction in the chatter. "So this afternoon Colin told Lilah he wants to be an actor, like her, when he grows up. But before you panic, a half hour later he told Sara he wants to be a police officer. Now here's the absolutely adorable part. He looks at me and obviously doesn't want to hurt my feelings, either, so he says—" Nettie laughed at the memory "—he says, 'I'm going to write books and draw the pictures, too. Probably on the weekends.' With that kind of schedule, your son will need a personal secretary by the time he's eight!" Grinning, she set a bag of red peppers on the sink.

"Yeah." Chase stared absently at her growing pile of spaghetti sauce ingredients.

"He has a caring heart, that boy of yours."

"Yeah. He does." Restless, Chase hopped off the tall stool he'd just sat on. "Listen, this all looks great," he indicated the food, "but why don't we go out tonight, just the two of us?" He reached for the tomatoes, intending to store them in the refrigerator.

Nettie slapped his hands. "Drop the veggies, pal. You're not wriggling out of a cooking lesson tonight." Grabbing his cheeks like a respectable Italian mama, she said, "You gonna make-a such a beautiful sauce. The best you ever had." Planting a quick hard kiss on his lips, she patted his cheek and turned back to the ingredients. "All right." She rubbed her palms together. "Let's get started."

Without allowing him time to protest again, Nettie put him to work peeling garlic and onions, explaining the difference between a chop and a mince, a fry and a gentle sauté. Chase tried to concentrate...sort of...but he knew darn well that he was just avoiding the real task tonight.

*Task.*

He shook his head. Asking a woman to marry you and be your wife and the mother to your child should not be a "task."

Darn it, he ought to go back to covering wars and dodging land mines for cable news; it was a helluva lot less stressful than trying to maneuver in all these relationships.

Tears sprang to Chase's eyes as he macerated an onion with a large rectangular knife. *Terrific.* Nervous as a cat at a rottweiler convention and now crying to boot. Since that seemed like a pretty lame time to ask a woman to marry him, Chase procrastinated awhile longer.

He'd had the most interesting reaction to Nelson's suggestion of marriage as a solution to his present predicament: Immediate dismissal followed swiftly and incongruently by grateful concurrence.

The thought of Nettie and Colin and him together as a family filled Chase with satisfaction, even pride, as if family were some mind-blowing new concept he'd come up with all on his own. *Forever* had always scared the filling out of him. What seemed frightening now was that she might say no.

"The timing couldn't be worse," he grumbled, hacking into the second onion.

"What?" Nettie turned from the sink, where she was peeling the tomatoes.

"Huh? Oh." Surprised that he'd spoken aloud, Chase lifted his arm to wipe his tearing eyes on his sleeve. "Timing on onions and…garlic. Do you sauté the garlic a long time and then add the onions or…not?"

Cleaning her hands on a dishrag, Nettie approached Chase with a smile and a paper towel to wipe his flowing eyes. "I should have sliced a piece of potato for you to hold in your mouth. Keeps you from crying."

"You're kidding." She shook her head, and he asked, "Why aren't you crying?"

Nettie shrugged. "Onions never make me cry. Only movies about old people and animals who have to find their way home."

He smiled. Even a coarse paper towel felt soft with her gentle ministrations.

How could he ask Nettie to marry him? Proposals were supposed to be romantic or lighthearted or tender. Not practical. And the fact was, Chase's need was as great as his desire. A woman like Nettie deserved more than a "practical" proposal.

Nettie started to turn away, back to the cooking, but Chase caught her wrist. When she glanced back in question, he said, "We need to talk." Immediately, his heart rate accelerated. "But not here," he added quickly, cowardly. "Not…"

"Not what?"

"Not…in the kitchen…with all these tomatoes."

Her finely arched brows rose higher. Chase cursed himself. There was an engagement ring burning a hole in his pocket. He'd driven into Minot yesterday and picked it out, barely an hour after he'd told Nelson to mind his own business.

"Let's go out," he tried again. "We'll clean all this stuff up and make the spaghetti tomorrow. I'll spend a few hours with Colin now and you can go home and—" his hand stirred the air "—take a bubble bath or whatever you do, and I'll pick you up for a late dinner. Lobster. And champagne."

"In Kalamoose?" Nettie laughed. "Something tells me Ernie's fresh out of seafood."

"We'll drive to Minot. How about it?"

"We can't. We have to make dinner here because—"

"No. No 'have to's.' Not today." He reached for her hands, realized his were covered in onion and garlic and went to rinse them under the sink. Man, the stench.… "How do you get this smell off?"

"Yeah, garlic does tend to linger. We can rub them with lemon, but the best way, really, is to soak your hands in vanilla."

Chase scowled. "Okay, never mind." He grabbed a dish-towel, dried off and decided not to wait to ask her to marry him.

Colin's grandparents made their first appearance next week; if Chase waited until then to ask her, he would never be able to convince her that his proposal was anything more than an attempt to secure his future with his son.

But if he asked now, if he could somehow find the right words so she understood that this was what he wanted even though it was too soon and they hadn't had enough time to themselves and he had no idea how to be a husband, well then perhaps together, over time, they could build a future. One that was rich and worthwhile. One that would last.

Chase began to perspire.

A kitchen seemed like an asinine place to propose, but something prodded him. Now or never.

Taking Nettie's hands in his, he walked her over to the high stool by the center work island. "Here. Sit."

Bemusedly but without argument, Nettie did as he asked and Chase felt some minor encouragement.

Now, if he knelt down as in a proper proposal…

He'd be making his pitch to her kneecap. Chase grimaced. Maybe the stool wasn't a good idea.

"Stand up," he redirected. Nettie tilted her head, looking at him as if he'd lost his mind. "All right, never mind. You sit. I'll stand." Taking a moment to assess their positions before he asked his question, he nodded to himself. "Okay, this is good. This works."

Perspiration gathered with ever-increasing momentum along his brow and above his upper lip.

Letting go of one of her hands, he touched the ring in his pocket for reassurance. His throat felt dry as dust. Attempting to clear it once, he tried to swallow, then hacked again more forcefully.

"Do you want something to drink?"

"Do you have champagne?"

"No." She looked confused. "I thought maybe water for your—" she touched the base of her neck "—congestion or whatever...."

Congestion. He sighed. Score one for suave. "No," he said. "I'm fine."

Nettie sat atop the stool, one hand held rather tightly in Chase's and wondered what was going on. She had seen Chase tense, had witnessed his fear and glimpsed his anger. But this was different. This afternoon he was discombobulated.

"Are you especially worried about Colin?" she asked gently. "Did Nelson say something that upset you?"

"You mean something more than usual? No. Well." He nodded. "Yeah, of course. Nelson's mission in life is to say something that upsets me."

"Tell me."

Breathing heavily, Chase swiped the perspiration from his upper lip. Man-o-mighty, his heart was backfiring like a '78 Chevy. He couldn't believe people actually enjoyed this. If Nettie said no, he would just stay single the rest of his life.

"So?" Nettie softly encouraged him.

"Right." Hoarse, he cleared his throat again. "Right. So... Nelson and I were discussing my life, and he pointed out that I've never been the most stable sort when it comes to, well, my life. What he meant was I'm always traveling, can't remember the neighbors' names. In five years I haven't been home long enough to finish a quart of milk."

*Great. Good strategy, genius, begin with the low points.* "Of course, Nelson knew me in college, so his perspective may be a little—"

"You went to college together? I didn't realize that."

"—warped...what? Yeah. Yeah, and he thinks—"

"Has he been your lawyer since he passed the bar exam?"

"Huh? Yeah."

Nettie beamed. "I'd say that shows stability right there."

Chase thought about it. "Right. That's right! Well, he thinks I should get stable in other areas, too. And I said, 'Which other areas, for example?' And he said, 'For example, women. Most of your relationships haven't outlived the average housefly.' So after I punched him—'' Chase laughed heartily ''—I said, 'What do you suggest, Nelson?' And he said, 'Turn over a new leaf. Get married.''' Chase paused, lips peeled in an unnatural smile.

What an idiot! He expected her to say yes to *that?* Mentally Chase kicked himself. How could a man who had been all over the world, who had previously been hailed as the king of self-assurance, turn into such an incontrovertible doofus?

Nettie Owens was either the best thing that had ever happened to him or she'd be the end of him before he hit forty.

He needed to begin again. Dropping the smile, he asked, ''Can you forget everything I just said?''

''No.'' Nettie studied Chase with an unblinking frown. ''No, I don't think so.'' Perhaps, she mused, she felt as calm as she did because he was so obviously keyed up. She didn't feel any of the emotions she might have expected to feel under the circumstances. Or under what she thought were the circumstances. ''Are you proposing to me?''

''No!'' Chase grimaced. ''I mean, yes, but not like that.'' He blew out a long, forceful stream of air. ''You ever feel like you were trying to order filet mignon and you wound up with hash?''

Nettie smiled. He *was* proposing. Her heart thumped strongly but steadily in her chest. ''Hmm. I suppose I have.'' There was something both sweet and endearing about his utter lack of confidence.

He let go of her hand finally, and Nettie flattened it on her jeans. Her nails were clipped short, serviceable for work and for sticking her hands in a bowlful of bread dough. She wasn't a decorative person.

''I'm not the filet mignon type,'' she admitted aloud. ''I like hash.''

## Chapter Sixteen

Chase looked up from his scowling contemplation of the linoleum, and the hope that suffused his face was a sight to behold. Nettie felt her first flutter of nerves.

"Lilah and I were talking last night about you and Colin. She said pretty much the same thing Nelson did."

Chase winced, but some humor returned to his countenance. "What? That I'm a relationship-shy workaholic?"

"No." Nettie tilted her head. "I think she said 'commitment phobic.'" Chase gawped. "Just kidding."

Inching a hand out to fiddle with a bunch of parsley, Nettie said, "Lilah watches reruns of 'The Practice' and 'LA Law' in case she ever has to play an attorney, so she gets most of her ideas from TV, but she thinks that if Colin's grandparents thought you were getting married, they'd have to back off."

The parsley leaves began to wilt as she toyed with them. She couldn't believe she was saying this to him. She couldn't believe she was this relatively calm.

Last night, her conversation with Lilah had seemed like nothing more than the result of an overactive imagination and too much cable TV. But with Chase bringing up the topic of marriage and clearly feeling so clumsy and awkward it seemed merciful to admit that she and Lilah had talked about it, too.

"Lilah thinks you and I ought to pretend to be engaged for a while until they can see for themselves that Colin belongs with you. Once they're reassured and they go back to England, the engagement could just naturally break up." Letting go of the greens, she laughed a little. "See? You and Lilah had the same idea. Not that Lilah's ideas are exactly *mainstream.*"

Nettie released a breath that felt a bit shaky. Was she accepting his proposal? Defining terms of the agreement? Or simply reassuring him? She braved a look at Chase's face. He was frowning.

"Let me get this straight," he said. "We pretend to be engaged for an indefinite period of time."

"Yes—*if* we decide to actually do it…if it seems like getting engaged is really a good idea, then yes. I imagine the time period will be indefinite. But closed-ended. No one will be able to fault you if the breakup is timed properly. Lilah says timing is everything."

"It sure is," Chase muttered. He looked decidedly less than pleased as he muttered, "A fake engagement."

"Temporary engagement," Nettie corrected. "Lilah says that when you're playing a role, you want to believe in it as much as possible. So anytime you discuss it, even if you're only rehearsing, you should talk about it as if you believe it's true."

There was a long, heavy pause. "You'd agree to something like this?"

Nettie breathed in. *Now* she was nervous. Very. Her mind began to race. What would she be agreeing to? A temporary engagement for the sole purpose of preserving the relationship between a father and son. Put like that, it sounded rather altruistic. Of course, for a few weeks…or what, a month at the most?…she'd be pretending that she had a commitment to the man and child who made her days hum with life and purpose again. Put like that, it sounded altogether dangerous.

Feeling her arms and legs quiver, Nettie reminded herself there was a built-in safety net in the knowledge that the relationship was not meant to last. The stated end gave her a sense of control. Her main intention was to keep Chase and Colin together; stealing a few more moments of joy would be her reward for a job well done.

A woosh of adrenaline sent her heart skittering, but she told herself to embrace the sensation; after all, she was about to do something that would make anyone's heart palpitate.

Surprised by the strength in her tone, Nettie said, "Yes. Yes, I'd agree to a temporary engagement."

Slowly, Chase nodded.

It was a strange way to accept a proposal, he thought. But then, it had been a strange way to extend one.

She'd misunderstood him entirely. Heat filled his chest. Dammit, he hadn't been talking about temporary. Now he felt like an ass. A frustrated and angry ass.

But he could get this right. If he could report the news with bullets whizzing a hundred feet behind him, he could propose in a way that made his intentions clear: No one could predict the future, but when it came to marriage and family, he intended to give "open-ended" a run for the money.

"Listen, about tonight—"

The doorbell rang. Bullet number one. *Whizzzzz.*

"One of us should answer that," Nettie said when he stood like an animal caught in a mud hole.

Reluctantly Chase stomped to the door, prepared to quickly dispatch whoever it was. A moment later, however, he was stalking back into the kitchen, carrying yet another grocery bag, this one from a specialty store in Minot. Trailing behind him was a happily chirping Lilah.

"...so I bought two pitiful-looking avocados that cost an arm and a leg—this is why I moved to California—and the parmesan cheese, but I couldn't find the exact red wine she asked for. Oh, Nettie-Belle, you're already cooking!" Lilah strolled to the sink, where Nettie had resumed peeling and seeding tomatoes, hoping the activity would calm her down. "Anything I can do?"

Nettie hesitated, shooting a glance in Chase's direction. "Actually, I think we're going to handle this on our own."

"Oh, right, it's a cooking lesson." She winked at Chase. "Real men make pasta?" Grabbing a jar of cured black olives, she unscrewed the lid, plucked out an olive and popped it into her mouth. "Mmm, salt."

"I need those for the sauce," Nettie said.

"Okay, I'll go home and eat potato chips. What time do you want us here, by the way?"

"Umm...." Guiltily, Nettie cast another glance at Chase.

"We're cooking for company?" he grumbled without a shred of hospitality.

"I thought it would be more fun." She shrugged, half apologetic, half persuasive. Chase could have sworn he heard another bullet whiz by. "It's Nick's homecoming."

"Nick's coming?"

"And Sara, of course." Lilah reached into the jar for a few more olives. "And that cute little lawyer of yours. Nelson."

*Whiz.*

Nettie confiscated the olive jar. "Colin is with Sara right now, I assume."

"Yep. I told Chase when I came in. Colin didn't want to go shopping, so he's hanging out with *la sheriffe*. Probably learning how to spit and shoot. You don't mind, do you?" she asked Chase.

"Mind? I'm beyond minding," he said, "about anything."

He and Nettie shared a long look.

"Am I interrupting something?" Lilah eyed them both speculatively. "I suddenly feel like the fifth wheel on a bobsled."

Nettie made a face. "Bobsleds don't have wheels."

"Exactly."

"You're not interrupting anything."

Chase crossed his arms. "Yes, she is."

Someone knocked on the door to the mud porch. Chase closed his eyes. *Whiz.*

"Come in!" he shouted, crossing to the women, grabbing the olive jar and carrying it back to the other side of the kitchen to dig into it. Nick opened the door.

"Hey," he smiled, newly returned from Chicago, where he had participated in a panel lecture about twenty-first-century agricultural techniques and the environment. "This place looks great. I ought to feel ashamed for letting it sit so long."

Chewing an olive, Chase nodded an acknowledgement, the best he felt like doing at the moment. No one else seemed inclined to speak, either.

Nick glanced around. "Something wrong?"

Nettie shook her head and smiled. "No."

Lilah overlapped her, shrugging. "Seems like it."

Chase overrode them both. "Yes! Dammit, I was in the middle of proposing."

"Proposing?" This time Lilah and Nick spoke in surround-sound.

They glanced back and forth between Nettie and Chase.

The protracted silence while Nettie wondered how much to say proved to be too hard for Lilah to handle. "Well, what did you say?" she demanded, bouncing up and down like a kid.

"I said yes," Nettie answered and was rewarded immediately with a squeal and a huge bear hug from her sister.

On the other side of the work island, Nick approached Chase with an outstretched hand. "Congratulations." He sounded almost as pleased as Lilah. "Good choice."

Trying to settle her bouncing sister, Nettie whispered, "It's temporary, remember. It's what we talked about last night."

Lilah pulled away. She glanced at Chase. "Right. I know. But it's still a cause for celebration."

Nick stepped forward. "What did you say? Temporary?"

Chase felt a ferocious scowl cover his brow. He was a split second away from kicking the two interlopers out of the house, barring the door to dinner guests and then kissing the word *temporary* right out of Nettie's vocabulary. In fact...

He opened his mouth, intending to do just that, when Lilah began explaining to Nick, "They're doing it for Colin. The grandparents are showing up next week."

"I know. Chase told me." Nick looked at his friend. "So you're going to put on a show for these people?"

"And for the court, if it comes to that," Lilah answered.

"I'm afraid you're going to be sucked into this, too, Nick," Nettie warned him. "I think it's really important that we all act as natural as possible."

"That's right. We have to act as if this engagement is the real thing. So that means absolute commitment to the situation." Lilah purloined the wedge of Parmesan cheese, withdrew a sharp knife from a wooden block on the counter and began cutting. "You know, I don't think we should tell Sara that your engagement is only temporary. She has a lousy poker face. No acting technique whatsoever." She bit into the cheese. "Yuck. Too dry." She swallowed, then clutched her throat.

Nettie poured a glass of the blush wine she intended to serve with the hors d'oeuvres and handed it to her gagging sister. "I hate to make Sara feel like she's been duped, but I agree with you. One stray comment and this whole thing could backfire. You know what I really hate, though?" She poured another glass and handed it to Nick.

Chase saw his private afternoon turning into a damned cocktail party. He had to intervene now and get this train back on the right track. "Listen, everyone—"

"I hate lying to Colin. I don't want to hurt him."

"Yeah." Lilah sipped her wine and nodded. "But maybe now is not the time to think about the end of your engagement."

*Damn straight.* Chase nodded.

"Right." Nick frowned in Chase's direction. "That's putting the cart before the horse. Seems to me you ought to concentrate on what you're starting before you try to figure out how to end it."

*Well, you don't have to tell me!* Chase felt a very male need to hit something. "All right, look, everybody—"

"Hey, open up! We're carrying stuff!" The call came from the back door.

"Sara!" Nettie said, appearing rattled.

"It's okay, stay calm. No one's doing anything wrong here." Nick reassured in an even tone that absolutely infuriated Chase. *Duh,* they weren't doing anything wrong!

He gritted his teeth until his jaw hurt. This was a miserable situation, but it was *his* miserable situation, and he had totally lost control of it.

"Don't tell her to stay calm," he growled, stalking over to stand nose-to-nose with Nick.

"Why not?"

Chase put his hands on his hips. "Be…cause."

A thoroughly obnoxious grin curled up Nick's face. "I just meant she shouldn't worry. We'll handle Sara." He indicated himself and Lilah.

"Wrong." Chase stabbed a finger at Nick's chest. "There is nothing to handle. My *fiancée* and I have everything under control." He glared around the room. "This is an engagement, not espionage. Got it?" This time he let his gaze linger on Nettie.

"Got it," she murmured.

Lilah leaned over to her sister. "He must be a Method actor."

Ignoring that, Chase strode to the door, giving instructions over his shoulder. "Colin is obviously with her, so I want to keep this as low-key as possible for the time being. We don't even have to mention it tonight. Not until we have the details worked out."

He'd shout news of their engagement from the rooftops if he thought Nettie was committed to a permanent union, or a decent stab at one, anyway. How the heck had a simple marriage proposal turned into a bad scene from a B movie?

Chase felt a rise in blood pressure and knew this was not the time to settle anything. He'd talk to Nettie later when the peanut gallery had disbanded. She'd realize she had misunderstood him, he'd show her the ring, and the whole situation would be straightened out. In the meantime...

With a hand on the doorknob, he turned to the expectant group. "We're all in agreement here, right? Low-key. Underplay."

Nods all around. Nettie spoke up. "Absolutely."

"Hey, c'mon! Hurry up, already! I've got two half-gallons of ice cream you'll be able to drink through a straw if you don't—"

Chase opened the door to his son and, he hoped, future sister-in-law. She wrinkled her face in disgust. "'Bout damn time." She glanced at Colin, who stood beside her, weighed down by a smaller grocery bag. "Oh, sorry, kid. Remember what I told you about bad language."

Colin nodded as he walked past Chase into the kitchen. "Toilet mouths wind up with their sorry butts in a sling."

"Right."

"Sara!" Nettie shook her head.

"What?" Sara dumped her bag on the counter with the rest of the food and then reached down for Colin's.

"You spent too much time with Uncle Harm, that's what," Lilah said in disgust.

Bemused by the comment, Sara shrugged. She pulled a container of mocha-almond-fudge ice cream out of the sack, followed by a carton of a flavor called fresh summer peach. "So what's the big celebration tonight? We already had a housewarming."

Nettie took the ice cream to the freezer. "Nick wasn't here, though."

Looking up, Sara noticed her old nemesis across the room and curled a lip ungraciously. "Thought I saw your truck. Back from the big city, huh?"

"That's right. And looking forward to heading out again as soon as I find a good excuse."

"Is that what we're celebrating?"

Lilah poured a couple more glasses of blush wine. "Of course not. We're celebrating Nettie and Chase."

"Li…" Nettie cautioned, nodding pointedly at Colin.

Chase cleared his throat.

Sara glanced between the two of them. "What about Nettie and Chase?"

Unable, apparently, to contain her enthusiasm—or to recall a conversation that took place only two minutes ago—Lilah faced her sister and bounced up and down on her high-heeled sandals. "Chase proposed to Nettie. They're getting married!" She squealed like a debutante with a new Nordstrom's card.

Nettie opened her mouth in a disbelieving *O*.

Sara's eyes bugged wide at the news. Lilah grabbed her arm and shook it. "Isn't that great?"

Sara nodded. "Yeah." Slowly a wide smile spread across her face. "Yeah, it is." She didn't bounce like Lilah, but when the other woman embraced her, Sara hugged back. "So when did this happen?"

"Just before you got here." Nick strolled over to pick up a glass of wine. "I think it calls for a toast."

"Nick!" Nettie gave him a pleading look. He and Lilah had promised to help, not dig a hole for Nettie and Chase to jump into!

"Oh, right," Nick said, remembering Colin, who was all eyes and ears. "We'd better get juice for you."

Distressed, Nettie turned to Chase. He shrugged, but his eyes narrowed in assessment. No two people could be this lame. Lilah and Nick were clearly working their own agenda. With little effort, they had just turned a "phony" engagement into the real thing.

He smiled.

Colin wore a huge grin as Nick poured him a tumbler of

cranapple and then clinked glasses with him before raising his goblet in a toast.

"To Nettie and Chase." Then, including Colin, Nick added, "And family."

"To family," Lilah and Sara repeated.

Moving forward, slipping a hand around his fiancée's waist, Chase accepted the wine Lilah poured for him. Nettie appeared absolutely stupefied. He looked around at the others as they beamed, truly happy and blithely ignoring his orders to keep the "temporary" engagement under wraps. And Colin was in the middle of it all, a bit dazed, but clearly enjoying the hoopla.

Nothing today had gone according to Chase's plan. On the other hand, what was that saying? All roads lead to Rome.

Yes, indeed, he thought, raising his glass. "To family."

"So where are you planning to have the wedding?" Sara asked. "Because, you might not have thought about it, but the jail's available."

Lilah choked on her wine. "The jail! Are you joking?"

"No. Hey, it happens to be a good idea. It's where they met. They could have a theme wedding."

"Ohhh." Lilah snapped her fingers. "Of course. I read about theme weddings all the time in *Martha Stewart Living*. Nettie can wear something from the Vera Wang penitentiary collection."

Sara scowled. "Sarcasm is a sign of weakness."

Swirling the wine in her glass, Lilah rolled her eyes. "Whatever."

"Well, I still say—"

When the phone rang, Chase kissed Nettie's temple. "Good luck," he murmured, hating to let go of her. At the first opportunity, he would take her aside, just the two of them, to talk.

"Hello." Grabbing the phone in the kitchen, he had to stick a finger in his ear to hear above the noisy argument behind him. "Nelson! What's up, man? Are you coming to dinner tonight, too? What? I can't hear you? Who's coming over? Who— Wait a minute." Covering the mouthpiece of the phone, Chase called out, "I'm not dressing like Wild Bill Hickok, Sara. Can you guys keep it down for a minute? Nelson's on the line, and I can't hear."

Lilah and Sara continued the theme-wedding debate, but at lower decibels.

"Okay, Nelson, shoot." Chase listened as his attorney filled him in on the status of the custody case. His stomach began to churn and sweat tickled his upper lip. "I thought you were going to make sure we had some advance notice." He paused. "Yeah, well, I'm not talking about two weeks. Anything over two hours would be fine." His sarcasm was unmistakable. "Yes, I understand spontaneity is the point, but you're *my* lawyer. Aren't you supposed to fight for my rights? I know you're not that kind of lawyer, will you stop saying that!"

The talking in the kitchen ceased. All heads turned toward Chase. Breaking away from the others, Nettie came to stand by his side. Without knowing what had him so riled, she put a hand on his shoulder. Her touch was surprisingly strong, affirming; it communicated support not suppression, but Chase found himself relaxing almost against his own will.

"Sorry," he said, to the people watching him and into the phone. "I think I need a blood-pressure pill."

"You have high blood pressure?" Nettie murmured, sounding concerned.

"Only when I'm talking to Nelson." He offered a quick re-assuring smile to Colin and shot a pleading look at Nick.

Taking his hint, the three adults started talking to Colin at the same time.

Chase pulled Nettie into his arms, amazed by the immediate comfort of having her so near. "All right," he said into the phone. "Tell her we'll expect her around seven."

With his arms resting casually on the small of her back and his chin settled on the top of her head, he murmured for Nettie's ears only, "We're having company for dessert."

Dinner was not quite as festive as Nettie had planned. The mood in the little cottage changed considerably when Chase announced that a social worker would be arriving later in the evening to "evaluate" him. Everyone but Colin understood the significance of the meeting. Chase and now Nettie, too, would be scrutinized. All the adults at the table seemed to share their nerves and apprehension. Only Colin, in fact, ate with gusto, somehow managing to maintain a running monologue about dead outlaws between noisy slurps of spaghetti.

Nelson arrived late, between the salad and pasta courses, and he, too, appeared distracted by concern, so as soon as the last noodle had been twirled, Sara took Colin outside to ride the tractor lawnmower, leaving the others to speak freely.

"We all need to be on the same page," Nelson said, eyeing them over his steepled fingers. "Being engaged is a good thing, a very good thing. But the timing is suspect. I think it's important to point out tonight that you two—" he nodded to Nettie and Chase "—began to have strong feelings for each other prior to finding out about Colin."

"I can vouch for that," Nick said. "I've known Chase for fifteen years, and I saw him falling for Nettie the first night they met."

Chase looked surprised. And sheepish. He literally squirmed in his chair.

"And Nettie called me a couple of weeks ago absolutely besotted." Lilah grinned. "I haven't heard her like that since…" she faltered. "In a long time."

"I—" Nettie started to protest, but Lilah had, after all, only spoken the truth. Still, she shot her sister a quelling glare.

Chase cocked a brow. "Come on. I'll confess if you confess."

Nettie felt four sets of eyes upon her. Her blood heated. Without a chance to speak with Chase alone since his proposal, she felt like a ship being tossed at sea. Nelson wanted them to be "on the same page?" She wasn't sure they were reading the same book!

Addressing herself to Chase only, she said, "I take the fifth. For now."

Nick and Lilah grinned. Chase gave her a look that promised he'd weasel a confession from her later.

Nelson shook his head. "No good. The social worker's name is Georgiana Rees, and Ms. Rees is going to want to hear that this love affair, of which she has not been apprised, was rock solid before there was even the hint of a custody battle. In fact it will send your attorney into paroxysms of joy to learn that you two have been meeting on the sly for a considerable time, say months or even years. Not that I'm advising you to lie, but if Chase visited Nick over the years…"

Chase shook his head.

"...or perhaps Nettie has traveled to New York..." Nettie gestured in the negative. "Or overseas..."

"No. Sorry."

Nelson tapped an index finger against his lips and looked at his client. "When did you propose?"

"This afternoon. You know that."

"What I am aware of is that you *announced* your engagement today. I imagine you proposed..." he waved a hand "...a week ago?"

Chase glanced at Nettie. She took a breath and nodded. After all, if the purpose of the engagement was to protect Colin, what difference did it make *when* they got engaged?

Though his distaste for lying couldn't have been more clear, Chase agreed. He rubbed his eyes, clasped his hands on top of the dining-room table and looked at Nelson. "Why don't you tell us about our engagement."

"How come I hafta wear a tie?"

Standing in front of his father, Colin tugged on his too-tight collar and made faces into the mirror. Chase attempted to put a part in his son's impossibly thick hair, but the comb barely made an impression.

"Because we're having a guest. It's a gesture of politeness."

"We already had guests. We didn't hafta wear ties for them."

Chase smiled. Tempting logic. His own tie felt like a noose. "This guest is different," he said, smoothing a hand over Colin's hair. He'd had hair like this, too, at Colin's age, hair that stuck out all over even with the shortest cut. It had driven his ultra-conservative parents crazy.

"Why's this guest different?"

Chase hadn't told Colin about the custody dispute. He hoped he never had to tell him. The last thing he wanted to give his son was more instability.

Speaking quietly, while Colin continued to experiment with the myriad shapes a mouth could make, Chase explained, "Nettie and her family are our friends, so we don't have to be formal with them. But Ms. Rees is sort of a...business acquaintance. She's coming over to help us."

"How?" Colin stuck out his tongue and tried to see if he could curl it up at the edges.

"She's going to make sure I'm taking good care of you. She'll probably ask you some questions. You okay with that?"

Colin's tongue retracted quickly, like a lizard's. He stared solemnly at Chase's reflection in the mirror. "You take good care of me."

Simple words, but Chase had to consciously remind himself to speak. "Think so?"

Colin nodded. "How come you keep holding my head?"

Chase looked down. His palm still capped Colin's thick hair. Hmm.

Because it feels good, Chase thought to himself. It feels right to be your parent, to touch and protect you. And because I don't ever want to stop holding and protecting you...my son. Suddenly Chase remembered all the ways in which he'd tried to measure up when he was a kid—the parent-approved clothes, tamed hair, impeccable manners, the achievements. His achievements had been his defining characteristic.

"What do you want to wear to meet Ms. Rees?" he asked.

Colin mulled it over. "My 'N Sync T-shirt...no, maybe my purple sweater?" The purple V-neck pullover was a new purchase, not a bad choice at all.

"Go put it on."

"No tie?"

"No tie." Chase felt like he'd actually scored a major parental success when Colin whooped and began digging through a dresser drawer. "One more thing," he said. Colin looked over, and Chase put his hand once more on Colin's head. This time he mussed up his son's hair. "That's better."

Colin looked in the mirror and grinned up at his dad.

With hugs for good luck, Sara, Lilah, Nick and finally Nelson left the cottage, intending to wait at Nick's place till the coast was clear. Nettie knew she should talk to Chase alone before the social worker arrived. Trying to calm herself had been an uphill battle all afternoon. The knot in her stomach felt like the boulder in *Raiders of the Lost Ark*.

Prepping for their interview, Nettie slicked on lipstick, although "slick" was a misnomer. She dabbed her lips with the tube whenever her quaking hand got close enough to make contact.

Lowering the lipstick, she rested her palms on the bathroom sink and took a deep breath. She'd been extra jittery for days, which seemed pretty normal under the circumstances, but she knew there was something more tweaking her emotions. It was hard to concentrate on anything lately. She felt sad and clingy, and several times this week she'd wanted to cry for no obvious reason.

Nettie examined her eyes in the mirror. Red and puffy. Maybe she was coming down with something or it was time for her period or...

*Oh.*

"It's August fourteenth." The awareness hit her like a moving freight train. Tucker's birthday was on the sixteenth.

"How could I have forgotten?" She thumped the heel of her hand on the porcelain sink. What kind of mother simply forgot? What kind of mother didn't even think about her child's birthday until she was practically right up on it?

Each year Nettie picked out a gift, something small, something Tuck would have liked at the age he would have been. Should have been. All at once the memory of putting the photo of herself and Brian into the desk drawer came rushing back.

"It's our baby's birthday," she whispered, wishing that somehow, somewhere Brian could hear her. Closing her eyes, she tried to picture a heaven in which her husband and son would be together on Tuck's birthday, eating Tuck's favorite cake and remembering how birthdays used to be. And maybe thinking of her for a few minutes and feeling how much she loved them.

Opening her eyes again, she wondered what Brian would think of her current situation. Pretending to be engaged for the sake of a child. Infatuated with the father. Living a temporary fantasy.

"You always said I overcomplicated things." She smiled, but an uncomfortable heaviness grew in the pit of her stomach.

She tried to put a name to the feeling. It wasn't guilt. Brian would never begrudge her the chance to be happy. He'd been an uncomplicated man, incapable of severe judgment or blame. She might think the dance of hello and goodbye had the most intricate steps, but he would have said the pattern was simple: just listen to the music and don't fight the beat.

The doorbell rang. Nettie jumped, sending the tube of lipstick clattering into the sink. She checked her watch. Seven on the dot. The boulder in her tummy transformed into a hundred fluttering butterflies. Ms. Georgiana Rees, MSW, had arrived.

Plump and no-nonsense, with a striking resemblance to Julia Child, Georgiana Rees shook hands with Chase, nodded brusquely to Nettie and boomed down at Colin, "Hello, young man. Show me your room."

Perfectly amenable to the request, Colin displayed his books and several toys while Nettie and Chase watched anxiously from the doorway. Bored with a Buzz Lightyear doll that had seen better days, Colin announced, "I got better stuff at our other place. We didn't bring it all over here, yet."

"Your other place?"

"Yep." Colin tossed Buzz onto the bed. "We used to live at Nick's."

"Ah. Do you like your room?" Ms. Rees queried, looking at a framed print of a very British foxhunt. Not exactly Disney memorabilia.

But Colin nodded. "My dad's getting me a bed shaped like a car."

*Dad.* The three adults in the room all noted the name. Only Chase, though, feared his legs would no longer support him.

*Dad.*

Feeling her fiancé's body tremble beside her, Nettie looked up. She saw the tears in his eyes and remembered the first time Tuck had called her Mommy. Shakespeare, bless him, was dead wrong on that "rose by any other name" issue.

With one word, a seven-year-old boy had just given a grown man his place in the world. Forevermore.

## Chapter Seventeen

"My what a yummy, yummy fudge sauce." Ms. Rees— Georgiana—licked the back of her spoon, wiped a drip of chocolate from the rim of her dessert glass and sucked her finger. She made a loud smacking sound. "Is it purchased?"

"Ah, no. I made it." Try as she might, Nettie could not reconcile the stolid Ms. Rees with a word like *yummy*. Georgiana had spent an hour with them and had done little more than chat thus far. Nettie's nerves were tight as piano wire, and Chase appeared to be ready to jump out of his skin. Lilah had called to ask how things were going and even she sounded nervous and tense. Only Colin and Georgiana were able to concentrate on their ice-cream sundaes.

Ensconsed on the couch, the formidable woman made one more swipe around her dessert glass while Colin, seated on the floor with his sundae in front of him on the coffee table, found a more interesting pursuit in lifting his spoon to create a mini waterfall of melted peach ice cream.

Nettie and Chase sat on side-by-side chairs facing the social worker.

"Well," Georgiana said, dropping her spoon into the glass

with a clatter and clapping her knees. "Let's get down to business." From her large handbag, she dug out a yellow legal pad and a pen. Balancing a pair of old-fashioned bifocals low on the bridge of her nose, she scribbled with strong stokes and made a bold slash beneath whatever she had written. She glanced up at them, smiling.

"I was surprised to hear you two were engaged. Rather sudden, was it?" Her voice was energetic, her gaze uncompromising.

Chase felt his hackles rise. *Calm and cooperative,* he reminded himself, realizing he'd gain little by suggesting she mind her own damn business. First, though…

"Colin, would you take your dish and Ms. Rees's into the kitchen, please?"

"I'm not done."

With a pointed glance at the melted sundae, Chase nodded. "Yeah, you are. Put the dishes on the sink and then run out back and rewind the hose for me. You can water Nettie's flowers first, if you want."

Because there was nothing Colin liked better than to spray the world with a garden hose, he was on his feet in an instant. "I know how to water them. Nettie showed me." As carefully as he could given his haste to go outside, he transported the dishes to the kitchen.

Georgiana scribbled furiously.

Chase waited until the back door opened and closed. Then he said, "I've known Nettie three weeks. I've never been married or engaged before and never wanted to be. Whatever you've heard about my reputation where relationships are concerned is probably true, and I don't know if I would have been smart enough to notice the diamond in my path if we'd met even a few months ago." He looked at Nettie and his harsh gaze softened considerably. "I like to think I would have." Turning back to the attentive social worker, he said, "I do know this— Whether or not Colin had turned out to be mine, I would have pursued my relationship with Nettie. With or without a custody hearing, I would have proposed."

Georgiana raised a brow dyed I-Love-Lucy red. "What about you?" she questioned Nettie. "Would you have accepted? With or without a custody hearing?"

Chase knew he couldn't hang on the answer, not in any obvious way.

Nettie appeared startled. Whether by Chase's declaration or Georgiana's question wasn't clear, but it took her a moment to regroup. "Yes. Absolutely. With or without."

Another note went down on the legal pad. Georgiana, however, was not smiling. Chase reached over to take Nettie's hand and give it an encouraging squeeze.

"Your career is quite demanding as I understand it," the social worker said to him. "How do you plan to address the demands of parenthood and a job that requires extended periods of travel to other countries?"

"I haven't had time yet to work out the details, but there will be changes, of course."

"Are you quite confident you can mother a seven-year-old boy?" Abruptly, Georgiana transferred her focus back to Nettie. "It certainly seems possible, given Mr. Reynold's career choice—current career choice," she amended when Chase started to speak, "that you will be called upon to be a so-called single parent at times. Tell me how you feel about that responsibility. In your own words," she added sternly as again Chase attempted to interrupt.

Nettie pulled her hand away from Chase. She had not expected questions to be addressed to her, specifically. And questions about motherhood...

Clearing her throat, she answered, "I take motherhood very seriously. I understand the responsibilities."

"How old are you?"

*At least a hundred.* "Twenty-five."

"Do you have nieces or nephews?"

"No."

"Would you like children of your own someday?"

Nettie's tongue grew instantly thick. Her head felt fuzzy. "I— That...isn't necessary. Right now I'm concentrating on Colin."

Strategically, it was the wrong answer. She could see that in Georgiana Rees's face. Nettie felt Chase's gaze upon her, but refused to meet it.

"What, in your opinion," the other woman pursued, "are the qualities that make a good mother?"

A horrid, prickling heat bubbled in Nettie's veins. She couldn't think. Dumbly, she stared.

"Have you given it much consideration yet?"

An awful urge to scream filled her throat. *Every day. All day.* And whatever else she came up with, Nettie always returned to the conviction that whatever the qualities were, she didn't possess them. If she did, her three-year-old child would not have died without his mother there to help or to hold him. But those were the nighttime thoughts. The two-in-the-morning-when-you're-all-alone-and-can't-push-them-away-anymore  thoughts. Useless, useless thoughts that yielded neither to reason nor to compassion.

Was that what Georgiana Rees wanted to know? If Chase suspected how dark Nettie's musings were when it came to motherhood or marriage, if he had any inkling of the fears that robbed her of her usefulness, he wouldn't have asked her to be his fiancée, even as a ruse.

"Are you all right?" The man she had optimistically offered to help sat forward in his chair.

She had to speak. If she continued to sit dumbly like this, she might cost him the custody of his son singlehandedly.

"I— Yes. No," Nettie confessed, "I'm not feeling very well."

Chase left his chair in an instant. "I'll help you to the bedroom. You can lie down."

"No." Unsteadily, Nettie rose. "Actually, I'd like to go home." Belatedly, she realized she had no car here. She'd have to walk to Nick's, where Sara and Lilah were waiting, and surely it would appear odd to Georgiana to see Nettie walk away from a cottage in the middle of a lonely field while her fiancé stayed behind.

Alternatively, she could call Nick's and have one of her sisters come get her, but that option required more explanation. She began to feel trapped, which often led quickly to feelings of claustrophobia, which led to panic and the horrid, indefinable dread that accompanied an attack. She wanted to run. She wanted to run now and she wanted to run far.

Chase frowned at her, but with more concern than anger or disapproval. "I'd like you to stay," he said in a low voice, as if she were the only other person in the room. "But if you definitely need to leave, I'll take you."

He was concerned about her. Let down by the woman he had counted on to help, his first concern was still for her.

Deep breaths, Nettie reminded herself. You are not a coward. It's just anxiety. You can bear the discomfort until Georgiana Rees leaves. Then you'll run.

With her head spinning and her stomach gyrating in the opposite direction, she tried to stand straight and give the illusion, at least, of control. "No, that's all right. I'll stay." But she wouldn't answer any more questions. "Why don't I make us some coffee?"

That's it, she breathed, distract yourself. When in doubt, play Donna Reed.

Through sheer will, she sent a smile, albeit a brittle one, in Ms. Rees's direction. The woman eyed her like a hawk. In fact, Nettie thought, I'd rather be eyed by a hawk. A hawk would not be in the position to destroy Chase's happiness. A hawk would not tease the past out of Nettie in slow, tortuous nibbles. When hawks went for their pray, they were swift and unequivocal. No pretense.

She took two steps, but her legs felt like tubes of jelly. Breathe. You can relax your body and walk at the same time. She knew it was the truth, but lacked faith that a body reacting as strongly as hers was right now could actually make it all the way to the kitchen. What if Georgiana saw her stumble or start to shake? What if anxiety this extreme really could make a person go absolutely bonkers, and she fell apart in front of the social worker and Chase and even, heaven forbid, Colin?

The dread intensified. She was telling herself all the wrong things. Too many "what if" statements poured more adrenaline into her already sensitive system and within seconds she was afraid she wouldn't be able to walk at all. Without thinking, she grabbed the back of the chair for support.

Chase reacted immediately. Her fiancé had no way of knowing, of course, that there was nothing physically wrong with her, that her body was reacting to a truckload of blame that turned into anxiety. So without another word, he swept her into his arms. There was no pretense in the action; his focus was Nettie.

He was concerned. Even though she was supposed to be helping him, he was concerned.

Brushing aside her protest, Chase murmured to her soothingly as he strode to the bedroom. Guilty and ashamed, she looked into his face, but all she saw was love.

If a heart could swell and break at the same time, hers did.

Gently he laid her on the bed. Gently took her hand and asked if there was anything he could bring her.

"Go back to Georgiana," Nettie told him, taking his hand for a moment. He relaxed at her touch. She could feel it. "I'm fine. I just want to rest awhile." Rest and try not to think, an impossible task.

Chase nodded. "I'll get rid of Georgiana as soon as I can."

It was on the tip of Nettie's tongue to promise she'd turn in a better acting job next time, but it wouldn't be true. She couldn't sit calmly with Georgiana and tell glib lies about motherhood.

Sadly, worried about Chase and Colin and deeply concerned about the part she could play in separating them, Nettie withdrew her hand. "Don't rush her out. Please. Not for me."

Bending forward, he kissed the tip of her nose. "I think we've all had enough for one evening."

When Chase left the room, closing the door behind him, Nettie felt a tiredness so profound, she thought she could sleep for days. She couldn't let herself rest, though. She had to figure out a way to extricate herself from any more of Georigiana's cross-examinations without endangering Chase's case.

A splatter of water hit the exterior wall of the bedroom. Nettie scooted off the bed and went to the window. Pushing aside the curtain, she saw Colin holding the garden hose and turning in circles, spraying everything he could and wrapping himself in a coil of rubber. Give a little boy a chore, and he turned it into an adventure.

She smiled. How could Chase ever let you go?

The thought came unbidden and with it, a tide of emotion that swelled too quickly for her to stem. She had to make sure Colin and Chase stayed together. She *had* to. She could tolerate goodbye…she *would* tolerate goodbye as long as she knew that Chase didn't have to. She had to be able to picture him with his son after they left North Dakota. She could stand being alone again if she knew that Chase wasn't.

"He deserves that," she said, gazing out the window. "He's a good man." She thought of that first night in the jail. And their first kiss when she'd helped him unsaddle King. She remembered how nervous and happy and vulnerable he'd seemed when he told her he had a son.

"Please don't let him be hurt," Nettie whispered to the God she hadn't spoken to much the past few years. She wasn't sure she believed, anymore, in prayers being answered or in a Power that protected... In heaven above. It had hurt to believe almost more than it hurt not to.

She watched Colin. Wound in the hose, he began to struggle with it as if fighting some enemy force. In his imagination, he would always win. But he lived in a world that often changed the rules of the game just when you finally thought you knew how to play.

"Don't get hurt," she whispered. "Don't get hurt." She put a hand on the window, overwhelmed by an urge to call him inside.

He wasn't hers to coddle, and that was a good thing because her fears had made her overly protective. Still, for this brief span of time, there was something she could do.

Quickly, before she wasted any more time, Nettie ran from the bedroom. She smoothed her skirt as she returned to where Georgiana and Chase were still convened, Chase talking and Georgiana still scribbling.

They looked up as she entered. "I'm sorry I rushed out like that," she apologized breathlessly to Georgiana, anxiety unnoticed as she concentrated on winning the other woman over. "A little too much pasta, I think." Smiling as if her illness were already a thing of the past, she patted her belly.

"You certainly look better." Georgiana considered her.

"I am." Nettie ignored Chase's concern as she moved to stand by his chair. "I thought about my answer to your last question, and I'm afraid I may have given the wrong impression."

Georgiana raised a brow, and Nettie knew that nothing but utter sincerity would move the other woman. "I have no immediate desire to have more children," she admitted, and the honesty bolstered her, "precisely because nothing is more sacred to me than motherhood. I know it's the most challenging, most important occupation a woman can undertake. In becoming Colin's mother," she hesitated only briefly, "my focus would be on Colin. He lost his mother. I lost mine, too, when I was still a child. It's inappropriate to discuss more children right now. The one we've got deserves our full attention."

From the corner of her eye, she caught Chase's upturned gaze, though she couldn't see his expression. Georgiana appeared pleased by Nettie's words, but Nettie wasn't through yet. "I also think it's inappropriate to threaten a man with a custody suit when you haven't even met him. Julia's parents are more than welcome to visit—they should visit—but not in a spirit of judgment. Chase and Colin are a brand-new family. They need support, not threats. And they don't need to be put under a microscope. If a few magazine articles are bothering everyone, I can tell you right now that Chase's womanizing days are over. He adores his son. If he didn't…I couldn't adore him."

The words were out. There for everyone to hear, and to remember. Well, it was the truth. Nettie lifted her chin. She'd said what she needed to, and she was glad. Glad and, frankly, proud of herself.

She waited for Georgiana's response. The woman regarded her steadily and with some surprise. Finally she made her copious scribbles.

Nettie glanced at Chase, but met only the top of his head as he watched Georgiana write.

Stabbing a period on the end of a sentence, Georgiana stuffed the yellow legal pad into her oversized handbag and stood. "Thank you. You've both given me a great deal to think about." Chase stood as well. "I'm not supposed to say anything one way or the other regarding a custody case, Mr. Reynolds. However, I'm going to break that rule, because," she shrugged, "because I feel like it. I believe that you are sincere in your intent to be a good father. Your son's grandparents, the Foster-Smiths, are equally sincere in their concern and in their desire to insure the well-being of their grandson. This case will go to court if there's a T left uncrossed."

"And you've found a T?" Chase asked.

Georgiana frowned, musing. "I'm not sure." She included

Nettie, too, in her gaze. "Your willingness to marry for Colin's sake—and I do think that's what's going on here—is admirable. But how much it secures his future happiness, I don't know. And whether it'll persuade the Foster-Smiths to drop the case, I rather doubt. There's still the issue of your moving about so much, who will be at home with this child, where will his home be, etcetera. You have your work cut out for you." She smiled the brusque no-nonsense smile that seemed typical of her.

Chase shook her hand. "I appreciate your candor."

"And wish you could tell me to take a flying leap!" Georgiana's laugh boomed heartily. "Unfortunately, you'll probably be seeing me again." She extended her hand to Nettie for a firm shake and then walked out to her car with Chase.

When he returned, Georgiana's car was already kicking dust down the dirt path. Chase headed for the kitchen. "You want wine?"

"No." Nettie followed him. From the refrigerator, he pulled a bottle of the cabernet that they'd opened at dinner and poured what was left of it into a goblet. "Is Colin still watering?"

"He's winding the hose." Chase took a swallow of wine. "I told him he could play outside until it's dark."

He wasn't looking at her. Like his responses, his movements were spare.

"You're really worried now, aren't you?"

"Shouldn't I be?"

"I think Georgiana likes you. Respects you." Nettie approached the center island, where he stood. "I know it didn't go as well as we'd hoped, but as she said, you'll be seeing her again."

"You think that will help?"

"Don't you?"

"Who knows?" He took another long swallow of wine and set the glass on the counter. A self-mocking curve shaped his lips. "I tend to think I'm pretty clever. I usually get what I want. But this time…" He shook his head. From his contemplation of the Italian tiles, he looked up. His expression was sober, his gaze as focused as a laser. "Why, Nettie?"

She shook her head, unsure of what he was asking.

"When Georgiana wondered if you wanted children of your

own—it occurs to me that was a yes or no question. But it wasn't that simple for you.''

''I explained when I came back into the room—''

Chase shook his head, his narrowed eyes and uncompromising countenance as effective an interruption as if he had spoken. ''Not good enough. You knew what was at stake the first time. Even if you'd said no—cleanly—it might have seemed like a normal response.'' He crossed halfway toward her. ''It was your hesitation, your confusion that made her doubt us.''

''I realize that.'' Frustrated, Nettie spread her hands. ''I made a mistake. I also fixed it.''

''Why?''

''What do you mean? Chase, I know you're worried and upset, and, yes, you have a right to be. I didn't play my part the way I should have. But I did try to correct it, and if you ask me, I did a pretty good job.''

''Played your part,'' he muttered, jaw hardening. He nodded. ''Yes, a 'good *job*' is exactly how I'd put it.''

Nettie put her clenched hands on her hips. ''Why are you dissecting my words? Chase, you're nitpicking, and it's not fair. I did my best. She caught me off guard.''

''We're all caught off guard.'' Continuing around the center island, he closed the gap between them. ''It occurs to me that we've talked plenty about my inability to commit.'' His voice was soft, deceptively so. ''But what about yours? Why do words like *temporary* and *brief* keep coming up, Nettie?''

Calm demeanor or no, Nettie sensed the anger and frustration within him. Surprisingly, it chased away her guilt, leaving *her* frustrated and angry in turn. There was an implied judgment in this cross-examination, and she didn't like it. He had no idea how much courage it had taken to help him with this custody case to begin with.

''We never discussed permanent,'' she reminded him. ''Right from the start we said there would be an end to this.''

''*You* said—''

''No.'' She shook her head emphatically. ''If you recall, you warned me that you weren't a stick-around kind of guy.''

''And you said that was all right with you.''

''It is.''

''Why?'' Holding her shoulders, seemingly unaware that he

was even doing so, Chase searched her face. "Why is it all right for a man to walk in and out of your life? It's obvious that family means everything to you. I've read your books. I've watched you with Colin. You love kids. You were born to have a family of your own. Colin loves—"

"Stop. Will you please stop!" She tossed up her hands and shook her head. "No, look, you've been "committed" all of what, two weeks? All of a sudden you think that makes you the world authority on family dynamics? Or on what other people need?" Nettie watched her verbal attack fall on Chase like a series of blows, but she felt desperate, desperate to stop him before he finished his sentence, and desperate to end this conversation before he somehow convinced her he was right. It wasn't only her heart at stake, it was her sanity. "I will not let you make me feel guilty for turning out to be exactly who I said I was. I told you I don't want a long-term relationship. I told you I can't give it."

"I don't believe you."

"You don't know me!"

"Then tell me." Chase's grasp tightened on her shoulders. "Dammit! Tell me why I can make you laugh, and I can make you smile. And I can make your eyes flash when we make love, but I can't make you want forever."

A volcano was ready to erupt in Nettie's chest. "Is that what's bothering you? You can't understand how a woman can say no now that you've decided to play family man?" She shook her head. "Well, maybe the idea of family is all novel and appealing to you, but I have been there, and I've done that, and I don't ever, ever, *ever* want to do it again!"

Stunned momentarily, Chase shook his head as if to clear it. "What do you mean, you—"

"No!" Nettie twisted away from him. Eyes filling with tears she refused to let fall, she held his gaze. "You were fun…we were fun together. But that's all. Leave it at that." Her voice fell to a whisper as harsh as a desert wind. "I wanted to help you with Colin. Don't try to turn this into anything else. Please. I can't…I don't love you."

The moment, the very instant the words fell from her lips, Nettie realized the lie she had just told. Like a bolt of lightning, truth shot through her chest—hot and sharp and unmistakable:

She loved Chase Reynolds, she loved his son. Once more life was offering her the chance to need two people fully and completely, with so much of her heart that to lose them would be to lose the part of her that pumped blood, the part that enabled her to breathe.

She hoped God would forgive her for returning the gift, but it didn't fit. Not anymore. There simply wasn't enough of her heart left to break off another piece.

Chase watched her for a long, silent moment. He dug in his pocket, pulled out a small silver box and set it on the counter beside them. "I don't love you, either." He opened the box. Nestled inside the silver cardboard was another box, this one velvet black. "I didn't buy this for you." Without ever taking his eyes off her, he flipped up the lid. A round diamond set in platinum almost as white as the stone and flanked by two trillion-cut sapphires sparkled at Nettie as if it were trying to speak. "I haven't felt like a kid at Christmas every time I imagined you opening this box, and I'm not *angry as hell* right now that something—or someone—in your past means more to you than I ever could." A smile so grim and utterly devoid of humor that it was chilling twisted Chase's lips. "There. We're even now. We've both lied."

Leaving the ring where it was, tucked in a box rather than on the finger for which it had originally been intended, Chase walked from the room, the air of finality as clear as the diamond he had purchased for his intended.

## *Chapter Eighteen*

Two days later, Chase was in New York, involved in what promised to be all-day meetings. Both he and the director of his TV station hoped the caucuses would result in a new career direction, one that would keep him at the station and in the states, or more accurately, in one state—New York. Chase hoped, also, to locate a more kid-friendly apartment. Lilah had agreed to watch Colin while he was away.

Aware of the turbulent and apparently permanent parting between her sister and Chase, Lilah had mercifully chosen to stay at the cottage rather than bring the little boy to the house, but on the afternoon of the second day, she got a call from her agent, alerting her to a plum movie audition back in Los Angeles.

"I booked a plane ticket for the day after next," she told Nettie in a rapid spate of enthusiasm. "I need a manicure and a pedicure before I leave, because there won't be time after I get home. And where am I going to find a decent hairdresser around here who can take me on short notice? I have got to do something about this." She pointed to the top of her head, the bright light in Nettie's second-floor studio illuminating traitorous ash-brown roots that had to be eliminated.

Drying a paintbrush on a rag, Nettie tried to dredge up some empathy for her sister's plight. "Are you going to leave before Chase gets back?"

"Not if he flies in tomorrow night, like he said he would. But if he's delayed…" She shrugged. "Look, I know you're uncomfortable with this, but Colin really enjoys himself over here, and I can't miss this audition, Nettie. I've had a little dry spell, lately. I need the work."

"I know. I don't mind watching him." But Chase had asked Lilah, not her. He was still furious with her. And he had good reason.

It was dead-on accurate to say that fear was the devil that made her want to end their relationship. But Nettie figured that was her business and her right. What depressed her was that she'd promised to help him with his custody case, and she'd blown it. Fear again. It had made her drop the ball after she'd given her word to help.

"Look," Lilah said, misinterpreting the troubled look on her sister's face. "Let's just deal with today…and my dark roots. I'll be home in a few hours, and I'm sure Chase'll be back before I have to fly out of here, so you won't even have to see him if that's what you want. Although I still—"

"It's what he wants, too, Lilah." Chase had made it clear that even the engagement of convenience was over. Georgiana had not been overly impressed by it, anyway.

"—think that you're nuts." Lilah spoke over her sister's comment and then narrowed her eyes. "Fine, so you're both nuts. A perfect match." Scooping her oversized purse up off the floor where she'd dropped it, she flung the bag over her shoulder. "Did Nadine Ritchie ever open a beauty salon in Anamoose, like she kept saying she would?"

"Yes. It's on Main Street. You can't miss it."

"Good. I hope she's not still p.o.'d about my going to the junior prom with Denny Kelter."

"She is."

Lilah rolled her eyes. "Still a twit, but she knows hair. As long as she doesn't deliberately dye me purple I should be okay." She blew Nettie a quick kiss. "I'll see you in a while. I brought Colin's bike over. He wanted to ride it. I told him he could go as far as the Seaforths' place and back." Heading down the upstairs hallway, she spoke while walking backwards. "I think he's hoping you'll read him one of your stories later." She smiled. "He thinks they're about him, you know." Fluttering her fingers, she headed down the stairs.

Lilah disappeared and Nettie sighed. *Nice parting shot, sis.*

Dropping the brush into a can of other clean brushes, she looked at the lone picture left on her bookshelf. Tucker grinned back at her. Wiping her hands and tossing the rag onto her desk, she moved to stand before the photo, running a fingertip along the pewter frame.

"Happy birthday, my big little boy." Softly she tapped the train engineer's hat they'd given Tuck for his birthday. Even at three he'd been thrilled with the striped cap that looked just like the one in his favorite storybook. Along with the hat, Nettie had found a beautiful miniature train, the first of what she had expected to be a growing collection for her locomotive-loving son. Tucker had played with the toy every day, rarely allowing it out of his sight and showing it to anyone who had the patience to affect an interest. He'd had it with him in the car that awful ice-laden day.

Nettie replaced the photo. Next to it on the shelf was the plaster mask of Tucker.

As carefully as if she were handling Limoges, Nettie picked up the heavy mask. Brian had crafted it to look like Tucker was smiling. "Number one in a series," he'd promised as she'd withdrawn the mask from a gift box he'd wrapped for her birthday. She'd loved it then; she loved it now. Gently, she turned the mask over. Tucker Ecklund, Brian had written into the plaster. Thirty Months.

For just a moment, she held the mask close to her heart. It was her most precious keepsake, the only *thing* she could say she truly treasured, a memento of a life measured in months. On the emptiest of afternoons, she could glance at the mask and the expression Brian had captured so well and be instantly transported to the giggle-laced days and cuddle-filled nights of Tuck's babyhood. Just that quickly Nettie could recall all the dear pedestrian dreams she had held for her family. She had never wanted the moon, only a growing collection of sweetly average tomorrows.

Setting the mask back on its stand, Nettie wished briefly that

she could resume painting. Working on Tucker's birthday had
become a habit, a way to keep from feeling or thinking too
much. But Colin was outside, riding his bike, and Lilah was
puttering down the driveway in their ancient car, which meant
it was time for Nettie to take over.

The first couple of hours' baby-sitting went pretty well, Nettie
thought. Colin rode his bike into town while she followed on
foot. The sky had gone unseasonably overcast, but the weather
was still hot, so they stopped for a cool drink and a snack at the
bakery. On the way home, they watched Ina Petty's schnauzer
piddle on Lois Johnson's pink plastic flamingo and fed bits of
Colin's doughnut to two flickertail squirrels that grabbed the
food and chased each other up an American elm.

When they returned to the house, Colin asked if they could
go to Nettie's studio to pick out a book to read.

"I like your books," he said as he stomped up the stairs ahead
of her.

"Thanks, buddy." She laughed at the huge, roundhouse-style
steps he took, clearly playing out some mini-adventure in his
mind.

"You choose," she said, leading him to the bookshelf while
she went to collect the paint-splotched rags she had used that
morning. "My last book was set on a deserted island. Kind of
like 'Gilligan's Island.' My sisters and I watched that show all
the time when we were kids. We used to make up skits and take
turns playing all the characters. Have you ever seen that show?
I think they still play it on classic TV."

Nettie turned to see Colin standing on tiptoe, reaching for the
life mask of Tucker, a look of pure fascination on his face.

"Oh, Colin, don't!" In a knee-jerk reaction, she rushed to
him. "Don't play with that, honey!" She stayed his hand. "It's
not a toy."

Colin stepped back in confusion. "What is it?"

"It's called a life mask."

Interest lit Colin's eyes. "A mask? Like the kind you wear
on Halloween?"

"No, not like that." Mentally fatigued, Nettie wondered if
suggesting a nap would land like a lead balloon. Sighing, she
searched for an impersonal explanation. "This isn't the kind of

mask you play with. It's a keepsake. Something you put up just to look at. Like collecting baseball cards.''

''You can play with baseball cards.''

''Right. Well, there are some things you keep, but don't play with.''

''Why?''

''Because some things would break too easily if you played with them.''

He looked at the mask. ''Is it expensive?''

''No. But it's very special to me.'' Hoping he was ready for a change in topic, she pulled three books off the shelf, two of hers and one by an author from South Dakota, someone whose work was particularly imaginative. With any luck, Colin's interest would be engaged, and she could take a little breather. Beneath fatigue, Nettie felt a mounting restlessness.

''Here,'' she said, handing Colin the books. ''Let's go downstairs and read.''

He wriggled close to her on the couch, asking first that she read to him and then choosing to read aloud on his own. Constant motion made his thin body feel warm; the skin on his arms was child-soft, as it would be for a few more years. Focusing on the printed words as Colin read, Nettie couldn't help but notice how good it felt to sit like this at the end of a long day.

Abruptly, in the middle of a page, Colin interrupted himself to announce, ''My dad says we're moving to New York soon.''

''R...really.'' So Chase had decided definitely then? Colin's legs fidgeted a little against Nettie's. ''You'll like New York, I'm sure,'' she said, forcing an enthusiasm she didn't feel. ''Have you ever been there?''

''No. They got the Statue...the Statue...'' Colin frowned. ''A statue of a really big lady.''

''The Statue of Liberty.'' Nettie smiled. ''You'll like seeing that, I bet.''

Colin shrugged. ''I like it here,'' he said in voice that was small and hopeful. ''How come we can't stay here?''

Taking a deep breath, praying for words that would soothe a child who had said too many goodbyes in his life already, Nettie put an arm around his shoulders. ''Your dad needs to live in the city, because that's where his job is. He wants to take care of you really, really well, and to do that he has to work.''

"He could work here. He could be a sheriff, like Sara," Colin obviously thought he'd hit on the perfect solution, "Or... somethin'...like Nick. Then we wouldn't have to move! I like coming here. You smell good and Sara knows how to shoot guns and Lilah says she's goin' to be in a movie someday, and I can go see it for free. And I like helpin' you paint books 'n' plant the flowers. If I go, who'll water the flowers?"

Oh, Colin, Colin, she thought, don't do this. Not now, not today. I don't want to cry until after you've gone.

Taking the book from which he'd been reading, Nettie set it on her own lap and focused on the pictures, turning pages slowly, calming her breathing before she replied. "I'll water them." But she knew that from now on visiting the cottage would elicit a host of memories that could do little more than add to the longing in her soul.

"You can ride in cars that are underground in New York," he said, brightening a bit before remembering, "Sara said she'd teach me to slingshoot."

Tough as Sara was, or pretended to be, Nettie knew her sister had fallen for Colin hook, line and sinker. She even referred to him now as "Little Deputy."

"Maybe there'll be time before you go."

Colin shrugged. Silently, he sat for a moment, looking at his knees.

Nettie's eyes blurred. Images of a dozen future events in Colin's life tried to crowd her mind. And she was there in every vision...she and Chase.

"I love being with you, too," she said, even as she tried to press the yearning aside. Concentrate on the reality. Concentrate on the reality and try to minimize the pain. "But New York is such an exciting place. After you've been there awhile, you'll know so many people and you'll have so much to do, why, I bet you won't have time to think about us much at all!" Cheerful words. Empty words. True for him, probably, over time, but a bald lie for her.

She would think about Colin every day and when she did, she would picture Chase. She would remember what the first stirrings of desire had felt like, how her body had awakened again under his gaze and his touch, and how, despite her best efforts, love had awakened again, too.

Nettie realized that in the off-guard moments when she remembered and pictured him and felt him, she would feel her loneliness afresh, but it would be a pain she could handle. The knowledge that Chase and Colin were alive and well somewhere would help her handle it. And someday…maybe soon…Chase would marry and have more babies and then Nettie would stop thinking about him altogether…well, mostly. There would be no more use of dreaming once he moved on. The only pain she'd have to deal with then would be the one she'd already grown used to: emptiness.

The top of Colin's head invited her to press a soft kiss in his bountiful hair. She kept the touch light and doubted he'd even felt it.

"Looks like it's getting kind of rainy out," she murmured, searching for a diversion. "Want to make cookies with me?" Leaning in, she indulged herself by holding him close in a hug. "When Lilah comes back, we'll have a snack ready for her. She'll probably be hungry after gallivanting around all afternoon."

"What's gavel…gavlan…"

"Gallivanting. It means running around."

Colin nodded. "I'm always hungry after gavlanting."

"Let's do it then," Nettie said, imbuing her voice with enthusiasm. "What kind of cookies?"

He thought about it a moment. "Chocolate chip. 'Cause she's a girl and girls don't get as hungry as boys, but even if you're not hungry, you can eat chocolate chip cookies!"

Nettie laughed. "I believe you're right." Relinquishing her hold on him, she handed Colin the books they'd been reading. "Here. You take those back upstairs, and I'll get all the ingredients out for the cookies."

"Okay." He scooted off the couch.

Outside, the gray sky had begun to sprinkle warm summer rain and echoing in the distance came a muted rumble of thunder. Listening to the storm, Nettie moved to the kitchen to concentrate on the blessedly mundane task of baking.

Butter and eggs from the fridge… Flour and baking soda and brown sugar from the cupboard… She'd stashed a bag of chocolate chips in here somewhere, so Sara couldn't find and empty

them into the Cocoa Puffs box, but where...? Ah! Perfect. A
whole bag....

Setting out a mixing bowl and cookie sheet, Nettie pulled a
stepladder up to the counter so Colin could reach. It had surprised her somewhat over the past couple of weeks to discover
how much Colin enjoyed helping her in the kitchen.

Then again, hot gooey baked goods and spoons and bowls to
lick out were persuasive rewards!

Tucker, too, she mused, had loved still-warm cookies and the
doughnuts she had made from scratch. His favorite sweet,
though, oddly enough, had been cheesecake. He had grinned and
cooed over every bite, from his very first. Would he have enjoyed baking with his mom, Nettie wondered? What would he
have looked like at age seven, powdered in flour as she taught
him to measure ingredients? Nettie's lips curled at the image,
but the corresponding pang in her heart made her pull herself
up short. Thoughts like that were not helpful to her, not now
when she had to remain positive and concentrate on the task at
hand.

Turning the radio on, she focused on song lyrics and baking
items. She whistled and she hummed, but while she tried to use
her head to remain upbeat, her spirit began to feel weighty, a
little more and a little more with each passing moment. The time
of evening when she took a few minutes to privately commem-
orate her son's birthday was rapidly approaching, and her body
seemed to feel it.

With everything laid out on the counter and the oven pre-
heating, Nettie began to wonder what was keeping Colin.

"Colin, where are you, bud?" she called from the door to the
kitchen. "Hey, Colin!"

When there was no answer, she trudged upstairs to see what
he was up to. Her body felt heavy and lethargic, too, so maybe
she was down with something. As she reached the landing, Nettie noticed dark clouds gathering in the distance and wondered
how much longer Lilah would be. The early evening was shifting rapidly from cozy to gloomy.

"Colin?" she called again as she rounded the door to her
studio. "Are you in here? I've got everything ready down— Oh,
Colin!"

Abruptly, Nettie came to a halt. She stood frozen in the doorway, surveying with awful apprehension the scene before her.

Sitting on his knees, Colin examined the sculpture of Nettie's son. He held a piece of it in each hand, two large chunks. Smaller broken chips lay scattered on the floor around him.

"What have you done?" Nettie's voice rasped. Her limbs felt like stone.

"I wanted to put it on." Colin looked up at her, contrite but unaware of the full import of his actions. "You said it was a mask, but it's waay heavier than masks are s'posed to be."

Nettie felt pressure build inside her.

"I told you not to play with it! Weren't you listening to me?" She knelt in front of him. "I told you it wasn't a toy. It wasn't meant for you!" She heard the sharpness of the words, saw the uncertainty and concern come over Colin's face, but she felt such grief she couldn't stop herself.

"I could fix it prob'ly." Awkwardly, Colin tried to fit the two mask pieces together, like a puzzle. Another tiny chip dropped to the ground.

"No!" Nettie pulled the mask from his hands. "Leave it, just…"

All the breath seemed to go out of her. Sitting on her knees on the hardwood floor, she realized her hands were shaking as she looked at the broken plaster, sick with the feeling that she had somehow been careless or thoughtless. If she'd put it somewhere else, somewhere higher or hidden…

"My dad could get you another, I bet," Colin offered, his confidence returning. "He knows where to get lots of stuff. I'm gonna ask him and then—"

"No!" Nettie raised her eyes to the robust little boy, brimming with childish conviction that what was broken could surely be repaired again. "There are things you can't fix once you break them. That's why you listen to people when they tell you, Colin." She shook her head, unaware of the tears that welled in her eyes. "You…you have to listen!"

Colin stood a moment, uncertainty filling his small body. He had no idea what to do. Clearly he was frightened by Nettie's strong response. Not knowing how to express it, however, his fear turned quickly to anger. "It was just a dumb ugly old mask, anyway," he shot back at her, lower lip trembling, eyes blazing with wounded pride. "You couldn't even wear it!" Before Nettie could say a word or do anything, he tore out of the room.

Nettie wanted to call after him, later she thought she might even have tried, without quite realizing it. She couldn't have made much of a sound, though; tears choked her throat and blurred her vision. Her arms and legs felt boneless. Pain gripped her stomach and for an indeterminate amount of time, she could do no more than sit where she was, caved in on herself, trying desperately not to give in to the pain. If she cried for her baby and Brian, if she ached for the mistakes she had made and could never recall, and for the awful, endless…void…she might never stop.

Taking breaths, she waited until she felt solid again and could stand. Then she got up, still holding the two pieces of plaster. They didn't resemble anything, anymore. Feeling numb, Nettie set what was left of the mask on the shelf.

Just do what's next, she directed herself.

Colin was downstairs, upset and confused. He'd made a mistake, and she'd answered it with another. It was up to her to iron out the clash before Lilah came home. Colin would be gone from her life altogether before she knew it; she couldn't let him leave with anger creating distance between them.

The thought put an uncomfortable urgency in her step. There were so many things in this world you could neither control nor count on, but you could make sure that people knew you loved them before you said goodbye.

Outside, distant thunder had begun its slow, grumbling roll across the evening sky. It had started to rain, too, she noted with vague surprise, though inside the house the air was humid and still.

Nettie expected Colin to be in the living room, sitting in front of the television—his favorite evening spot when no other activities had been mandated—and she took a breath as she hit the base of the stairs, hoping for the right words.

She'd taken only one step into the foyer when she realized there was no sound coming from the TV. The living room was empty. Ditto the dining room and kitchen.

"Colin?" Grimacing in the too-warm kitchen, she glanced at the butter softening to a near melt on the counter and turned the stove down for the time being. "Colin!"

Nettie checked the bathroom, the downstairs coat closet and then ran back up to the bedrooms. Was he hiding? "Colin, I know you're upset, but wherever you are, you need to come out now, so we can talk." Again she investigated all the closets…and under the beds. He was nowhere. Standing with her hands on her hips in the middle of Sara's bedroom, she raised her eyes to the ceiling as thunder rolled closer. "Bike," Nettie murmured. "His bike's outside."

She sped down the stairs a second time, heading this time for the mud porch. They'd leaned his bike against the porch steps. *Be there…be there.*

An impressive crack sounded overhead as Nettie opened the door. Lightning flashed and then sizzled, and the thunder rolled again. He couldn't have ridden anywhere in this; he wouldn't have—

No bike.

"Oh…" Nettie indulged in a cussword that would have done Sara proud. Unmindful of the pouring rain, she ran outside, sandals crunching on the wet gravel driveway. She scanned the distance in all directions, but saw no one, and she shivered suddenly, though not from cold. The rain was warm, the air thick and musky. Summer storms, with their deceptive temperatures and dramatic electrical displays could be the most brutal. Without the bitter cold, there seemed to be less to fear, but lightning and dry summer fields were a combustible duo.

Turning toward the house with the intention of getting her car keys, Nettie realized halfway up the porch steps that Lilah was driving Jezebel.

"All right, think. *Think.*" She thumped her forehead with a loose fist. "Sara!"

Racing up the remainder of the steps, she grabbed the phone and hit Sara's number on the speed dial. The sheriff was out on a call. Swearing again, but determined not to waste precious minutes hesitating, Nettie simply took the next logical action— she changed from sandals to sneakers. If she had to go after Colin on foot, she would. Her shorts and T-shirt would be rain-soaked in minutes, but she had no time to deal with that. She grabbed the thin jacket Colin had brought with him and then, in shoes with no socks, dived back into the storm.

Like a good catastrophist, Nettie's mind treated her to a rapid series of visuals involving flash floods, lightning-struck trees that cracked in two or exploded into flame, metal bike frames as potential lightning conductors—

*"Stop it!"* she hissed out loud. "Think of Colin. And safety and blankets and warm beds and hot cocoa." She pursued the positive with all the relentless determination of Sister Maria in *The Sound of Music.* A mere instant before she began warbling about raindrops on roses and whiskers on kittens, Nettie had a flash of memory that propelled her jogging feet toward the garage.

Nearly a year ago, Sara had bought a truck from Ernie, an ancient, rust-pocked Ford, which she had stowed in the garage and was gamely trying to restore on her days off. She'd paid a hundred dollars and promised that she'd drive the truck in the annual Pioneer Days Parade with a sign that read Good Eats at Ernie's, but most people thought Ernie'd got the better part of the bargain. Privately, Nettie had considered the heap a waste of good garage space, but right now she felt like kissing Ernie and Sara and maybe even the truck.

Raising the garage door, she searched a rack of hooks for the correct key. Once she had it, she opened a door whose aching hinges made so much noise it seemed possible the panel might fall off altogether. Nonetheless, she climbed into the driver's seat, worked the key into the ignition, and started to pray.

At her sister's request, Nettie had started the truck a couple of times and run through the gears while Sara had stuck her head under the raised hood and listened to the engine. Now as she turned the key, Nettie chanted, "Please work—oh, please work—oh, please work—oh, please work…"

To her undying gratitude, the engine turned over with phlegmy compliance. As the vehicle wheezed its way to life, Nettie wrapped her fingers around the floor-mounted stick shift and stepped on the clutch. Jezebel had similar manual controls, but they handled more smoothly, and that wasn't saying much. Her first attempt to move the vehicle resulted in a giant lurch backwards, a neck-snapping halt as the truck stalled, and the threat of tears—her own—as she tried once more to re-start it.

This time, Nettie managed to back all the way out of the garage and to turn toward the road.

Rain obscured her vision and a sudden wind whistled against

the windows. For once, however, Mother Nature's muscle-flexing served to anger Nettie more than frighten her.

"Work with me," she growled, hunkering over the steering wheel as she searched for something resembling wiper controls. "Howl all you want, but I will bring Colin home safe and sound!"

When she reached the end of the driveway, Nettie realized she had a decision to make: Which direction had Colin taken? Would he have headed back to Nick's or into town? Over to the grammar and middle school? He liked the playground there....

*Relax and it'll come to you.* As if someone were standing inside her head, the words arrived to calm her racing mind. Nick's. It made the most sense that Colin would have pedaled home.

With sweaty palms, a racing heart and a glance at the thundering heavens, Nettie guided the truck onto the road and hoped that she was right.

## Chapter Nineteen

Thunder rocked the earth as Nettie arrived at the farm. In the cab of an old truck with no luxuries to insulate it, she experienced every shuddering ka-boom as if she were standing in an orchestra pit next to the kettledrum.

"Please be here, please be here," she prayed as she opened the driver's-side door, ducked her head and raced to the porch. Lightning struck the earth with angry velocity, as if someone were hurling javelins from the sky. Each wicked flash turned the dark gray sky into blinding daylight.

No lights were visible from the front of the cottage nor was Colin's bike anywhere in sight. Nettie pounded on the door, anyway, shouting his name as loudly as she could, but the time and effort were wasted. She'd guessed wrong.

Diving into the shelter of the pickup, she shoved the vehicle into reverse, grinding the gears as she pointed herself toward the road again. It was slow going. Hitting every bump and dip on the unpaved path, she had plenty of time to consider where she ought to search next. If Colin had headed straight into town when he left the house, he would have found shelter by now. He might have headed for the jail, and even if Sara was out on a call, he'd be safe from the storm. If, on the other hand, he'd headed away from the house, in the direction of the school, there would be no relief from the elements at all. The elementary school was closed for summer. The best Colin would be able to do was huddle in a doorway. Unable to bear the mental picture of him alone and unprotected, Nettie turned in the direction of the school when she reached the road. Each rotation of the tires took her farther from town—and from the people she relied on for the strength and resilience she no longer believed she possessed.

As she drove, she had to fight not to feel disoriented by the amazing constancy of the lightning and thunder. Was Colin frightened by electrical storms? she wondered. They had many in Florida. Having lived in North Dakota for most of her life, Nettie was certainly no stranger to storms, but she couldn't remember ever having driven in one this aggressive.

*Brian had.*

The unbidden thought arrived with all the jagged sharpness of the lightning. Why was it that time washed crispness from good memories, leaving them as muted as if they wore veils, but did little to blunt the edges of less pleasant recollections? Nettie remembered so clearly Brian's insistence on traveling to his parents' house that bleak Christmas three years ago, despite the weather report of unfavorable driving conditions.

*Unfavorable doesn't mean impossible,* he had argued.

*Very unfavorable,* she'd argued back. They'd been living in Chicago then, two struggling young art students with a new baby. Brian's parents lived thirty miles outside the city. In the Midwest, harsh winter weather could make thirty miles feel like a cross-country trip. Tucker had been sniffling, Nettie insisted, and shouldn't be out in the cold. Why couldn't they wait until the weekend? There were still four days to go before Christmas....

But Brian had been stubborn that day, calling her a worrywart. The harder she'd fought, the more insistent he had become.

In the end, she had flatly refused to go; he had refused to stay. It was Christmas and his parents wanted to see the baby, and Tucker was excited about going. Rigid with disapproval, Nettie had watched Brian bundle Tuck into his car seat and drive off while the rain turned steadily into snow. *If I stay here,* she'd thought, he won't be gone long. He'll reach the first freeway exit, and then he'll turn back....

But she had guessed wrong, then, too, and Brian and Tucker had been alone in the car when it hit a patch of black ice. She hadn't been there to warn Brian or to tell him she loved him. She hadn't been there to hold her baby.

Gripping the steering wheel too tightly, Nettie told herself to stop—stop remembering, stop thinking, stop everything but what she was doing right this moment. Her racing mind, however, refused to quiet, and she wished with all her might that she had a cell phone so she could call Sara or Lilah, who might know what to do, who might make the *right* decision for this situation. It began to occur to her that she hadn't driven this far by herself—or in a storm at all—for three years. Her hands began to shake.

"I should have gone by the house again after I left Nick's to see if Lilah came home. It wouldn't have taken that long." Hindsight was a curse. "Damn. Damn, damn, damn!"

She was so busy shaking and chiding, that she almost missed it—a boy's new Schwinn mountain bike sticking up from a gully, half in and half out, on the side of the road.

She slammed her feet on the brake and clutch, grateful beyond words when the truck stopped without stalling. In the horizon a grouping of clouds had turned almost black. Nettie spared it only the barest glance before hurtling out of the cab once again. Her heart was in her throat as she approached the gully, and she began calling Colin's name before she hit the shoulder of the road. No answer came; no answer could. Colin lay at the bottom of the ditch, stomach down, his head turned to the side, facing her, one arm beneath his head, like a pillow.

Panic threatened, but not as the feverish, blinding desire to flee Nettie had grown used to. This panic was cold; it froze her heart and her blood. It froze time.

As if she were watching from somewhere outside herself, Nettie felt a vague surprise that she was able to keep moving. Half running, half sliding down the side of the ditch, she dropped to her knees beside Colin's inert body. He looked so tiny lying there alone in a rough, gravel-lined ditch; by contrast Mother Nature's rough howling seemed almost petty and mean.

Struggling under the dark sky and the consecutive, too-bright flashes of light, Nettie checked for injuries. He was breathing evenly, thank God. There were no visible signs of bleeding, external or internal, and his skin was warm.

"Colin," she said firmly, brushing hair from his forehead and bending close to him. "Colin, wake up, buddy. Come on, sweetheart, talk to me."

Nothing.

A rush of emotions squeezed her chest. Anger, frustration and fear made her tremble; determination made her refuse to kowtow to the distress. She couldn't crumble and she couldn't cave in to worry or indecision. She was all Colin had.

Taking his hand, she began to rub it, smoothing her fingers firmly between his knuckles, over his wrist and up his forearm, willing energy into his small body. "I'm sorry that I yelled. Or that I made you feel you weren't as important to me as that mask. Because you are. I think you're wonderful—funny and brave and smart. Your father loves you as much as any man has ever loved a little boy, so you have to be okay Colin. You have to be okay."

As she continued the massage, Nettie looked around, gauging their distance from the road and the steepness of the sides of the gully. She was going to have to carry Colin to the truck, and she knew she would have to take special care with his other arm, which looked as if it might be broken or dislocated.

"I've got to lift you now, buddy," she said as she rose to a crouch. "I'll be as careful as I can." Moving around him, she searched for an angle where she would have better leverage.

She was about to slide an arm under Colin's legs when the first pellets of hail struck the earth. Within seconds, knots of ice were being spit from the sky like hardballs in a batting cage. As the ice hit the truck, it sounded like a machine gun peppering metal.

Colin stirred and whined. "Owww. Stop it!" The sound of a child's complaint had never sounded so dear to Nettie's ears.

"Colin! That's it, wake up, honey. I'm here!"

He turned toward the sound of her voice, but hail struck his face. Immediately, Nettie braced herself over him, forming a protective tent with her own body. Wind propelled the ice with such force that she felt as if she were being struck in the back with fists. She didn't care. All that mattered was that Colin was awake, and he was all right.

He began a litany of mumbled woes, about his aching arm and that he couldn't breathe with her on top of him and that the "rain" was cold. Nettie answered in soothing murmurs, thrilled simply that he was coherent, not even bothering for now to think beyond getting him to the truck as soon as this ice show was over. Then, as abruptly as it had begun, the hailstorm stopped.

There was a moment's blessed, refreshing silence. Relief relaxed and filled Nettie's lungs. But the relief was as brief as it was earnest. She glanced up to a thick sky the mucky black-green shade of a stagnant pond. A second later, she heard it: the sound of a waterfall where no waterfall could possibly be. There wasn't even time to think the word before she heard the roar and saw the furious, spinning funnel.

*Oh, my God.* "Tornado," she breathed.

It was heading right toward them.


The emergency room of the small Queen of Angels Hospital in Detale, North Dakota, teemed with the kind of activity it rarely saw, save during flu season. Behind the check-in desk, the air hummed with barked instructions and other commotion; in the waiting room, complaints about the wait carried over murmured conversation and competed with the nightly news coming from a television set mounted high on the wall.

In sharp contrast to the bustling at ground level, all was relatively quiet on the second floor, where the patient rooms were located and where one heard mostly the soft sounds of a hospital at night. In fact, for the past hour, the only noise in the O-shaped corridor had been the rhythmic squish-squeak of rubber-soled shoes. Then the elevator doors opened and out hurried a different pair of feet with a decidedly different agenda. Pounding over the floor, unmindful of the Careful When Wet sign, these feet raced a man to the nurses' station, where he hung over the desk and with neither "Hello" nor "How are you?" gave his name and then demanded to know which room his son was in.

Chase was moving again before the room number was completely out of the young nurse's mouth. He didn't stop running until he pushed open the door to room 2012. A pale blue curtain divided the room into halves. In the bed closest to the door, a little boy lay beneath a thin acrylic blanket, his small body seeming to disappear into the large mattress. A bulky cast covered his right arm.

Colin appeared tired but animated as he regaled Lilah with an account of the tornado that "almost got us." She nodded calmly as if she'd heard this information once or twice already this evening.

When Colin saw his father, his face creased in a wide smile. "Dad!"

Chase moved to the bed immediately. He placed his palm lovingly on the top of his son's head, but realized quickly that the limited contact was not nearly enough. Lowering the safety rail, he sat on the bed and carefully took his son into his arms.

"I was in a tornado, Dad!" Colin's voice was muffled against Chase's shirtsleeve.

"I know that." Grateful that his head was lowered, Chase felt tears fill his eyes. He'd been on the plane already, heading back to North Dakota a day early, when the pilot's voice had announced that a tornado had hit central North Dakota. Chase had listened to the news with interest, but detachment, too. For some reason it had not once occurred to him that the people he loved might be affected. He was used to reporting the news, not being touched by it.

"What were you doing out in a tornado, huh?" Chase pulled back just enough to examine his son, to study his face and count his fingers, the mental tallies one might make with a newborn. "You scared me."

Chase had called home immediately upon disembarking the plane, but there'd been no answer. He'd phoned Nettie's house next and spoke to Lilah as she was heading out the door on her way to the hospital. Nettie and Colin had been caught in the tornado. They were at a small hospital in a town called Detale. That was all Lilah knew.

Chase hadn't just been scared at that point, he'd been more frightened than ever before in his life. He turned toward Lilah now and with his eyes asked the question: *Nettie?*

"I wasn't scared at first because I didn't know it was a tornado," Colin said, speaking before Lilah had a chance to respond. "But then Nettie said it was, and she said stay down in the ditch and don't be frightened 'cause she was takin' care of me, and then the wind got so loud I couldn't hear anything, and she laid down right on top of me and squeezed way too tight, but I wasn't mad or anything. And then the wind stopped and she started to laugh and I told her I had to go to the bathroom really bad so she let me go next to the road where cars could've seen and everything, and then we drove here.''

As a nightly news special report, it would have been shy a few pertinent details and overgenerous regarding a couple of others, but Chase figured he caught the gist. Most importantly, Colin said Nettie had started laughing, which had to mean she was okay, right?

Once more he looked at Lilah. ''Where is—''

''All right, everybody.'' Knocking and bumbling her way through the door—using shoulder, elbow, and forearm—Nettie hopped into the room. ''Who wants to be the first to sign my—'' Her eyes widened when she saw Chase. ''You're here.''

''You got crutches! That's cool!'' Colin said as his father rose from the bed. The little boy looked at Nettie with interest, but his energy was obviously flagging.

Moving swiftly to the door, Chase assessed the rest of her quickly, and he frowned deeply as he noticed the tangled hair, small scrapes on her uninjured leg and a cut on her cheek. Dirt streaked her white top.

He wanted to hold her, kiss her, stare at her until he was positive there was no damage other than the obvious and until his heart had stopped pounding.

''That's quite a load you're hauling around,'' Lilah spoke from behind them. ''Here, take my chair.''

Immediately Chase moved away from the door. Of course she'd want to sit down! She needed rest, she needed care.... ''Why are they letting you walk around? Shouldn't you be in a wheelchair?''

''A wheelchair? No, I— Chase! What are you doing?''

As carefully as he could, he scooped her into his arms.

''My crutches!''

''Drop them.''

''I've got them.'' With a smirk, Lilah relieved Nettie of the unwieldy burden. ''Nice service,'' she said as he delivered Nettie with infinite care into the chair. Dramatically, she sighed. "Now why can't I find a man who will treat me like porcelain?"

"Actually," Nettie said quietly, never taking her gaze off Chase, "porcelain is one of the strongest ceramic compounds."

Tenderly he raised a hand and touched her cheek, careful to avoid the abrasion. "My son tells me you were pretty heroic." He shook his head. "I should have been here."

"Well, you didn't know there was going to be a tornado."

"Doesn't matter." Chase frowned. He looked back at Colin. "This is where my family is." Returning his attention to the woman who had protected his son with her own body, he gazed at her as if he'd like to memorize every line, every detail. "When I think of what could have happened, and I wasn't here—"

Nettie touched a hand to his lips, stopping the words. He looked at her in question then gave a brief nod. She was right; this wasn't the right place.

"Colin's going to stay overnight. Did they tell you?" she asked quietly, while Lilah stood near the bed, talking to the rapidly tiring seven-year-old.

"No. I arrived only a minute or two before you came in." Worry, a once-unfamiliar sensation for Chase, crept into his stomach and chest for the umpteenth time since he'd become a dad. "Is everything—"

"He seems to be fine," she hastened to reassure him. "But he was out cold when I found him. He'd fallen off his bike into a ditch. Since Kalamoose is a full hour from here, the doctor thinks it'd be a good idea if he stayed overnight."

Chase expelled a noisy breath. His stomach was starting to roll as if he were on the high seas. Resignedly, he wagged his head. Who knew that the simple act of loving would require Dramamine? "What about you?" he demanded of the brave, gorgeous woman before him. He touched the cast. "Is this a bad break? I don't even know how it happened."

Nettie made a face. "I slipped on my way into the hospital," she muttered.

"Hey, kids," Lilah called softly. "I think the patient could use a little shut-eye. Maybe you two should take the conversation outside for awhile?"

"Nnooo," Colin mumbled plaintively from the bed, though his eyes were already closed. "I'm not sleepy. Ice cream..."

Chase smiled at Nettie, rose and moved to his son's bed. He bent to give Colin a kiss filled with gratitude. Every time he thought about how close he'd come to never knowing his son, it took the breath right out of him. "Rest," he said quietly, stroking Colin's hair. "Tomorrow we'll have a party. Hot dogs and potato chips and so many flavors of ice cream, Baskin-Robbins will be jealous." Before Chase had even finished his sentence, Colin was snoring softly.

Lilah grinned.

"How are *you?*" he asked, touching her elbow.

"Absolutely fine. My hairdo got rained on," she patted the bouncy, blonder-than-before waves, "but I never even saw the funnel. Anyway, I'm heading back to California soon, where the only natural disasters are earthquakes and running out of Kava Kava." She nudged his arm. "Why don't you take my sister to the cafeteria for a cup of their gruesome decaf and a little hospital food? She hasn't had dinner yet."

"What about you?" Nettie said. "Have you eaten?"

"I have a diet bar and a candy bar in my purse. If you two will get going, I can eat the candy bar and pretend I did it by mistake. Here," she handed Nettie the crutches then whispered in her ear, "Interesting newsflash on porcelain—being the strongest compound and all." She winked. "Good luck."

Nettie smiled then waved off all help as she maneuvered herself up. It was tricky going, but she did it. Chase held the door while she preceded him into the hallway. He hovered near her elbow. From the corner of her eye, she saw him reach for her several times as she tottered, but each time he stopped himself, and slowly but surely they made their way to the elevator and down to the first floor. Silently, they disembarked the elevator. The wall directly in front of them had an arrow pointing left for the cafeteria, but when Chase turned that way, Nettie stopped him.

"Not yet," she said. "I want to go someplace else first."

Chased raised a quizzical brow, but followed her without comment. He seemed immersed in thought and spoke little as she led him to a small chapel tucked into a corner of the first floor.

The walls were painted the cool new blue of a morning sky. Pictures of angels and saints hung at various points and though clearly this was a Catholic chapel, a petite statue of the Virgin Mary shared space at the front of the room with a simple cross and the Star of David. Peace and comfort filled the room as if they were entities.

"I like it here," Nettie said, speaking in a respectful hush even though she and Chase were the chapel's only visitors. "I spent a lot of time here when Uncle Harm was sick. I'd sit in that front pew," she nodded, "and I wouldn't think of anything. I wouldn't even pray, really. I'd just be here and feel the stillness."

When she paused, Chase put a hand on her back. "Do you want to sit down?"

Instead of answering, Nettie executed a skipping quarter turn to face him. There was so much to say, and she swallowed hard, unsure of how to begin. The last time they were together, she'd told him she did not love him and never could. On top of her bureau at home, the engagement ring he'd bought for her sat, still in its box, waiting to be returned. Oh, she'd made a series of wrong turns on the road to this moment. And looking at Chase now, Nettie wondered if he'd even want to hear what she had to say.

Fidgeting, she tottered on her crutches. Immediately, Chase put a hand beneath her elbow to steady her. "Come on, let's sit down. I'm afraid you're going to tip over." Carefully he helped her to a pew.

"Thanks," she said as he took her crutches and propped them against the pew in front.

"I haven't thanked you yet. I'm not even sure how." He gazed at her, sober eyes reflecting the depth of his gratitude. "Protecting Colin during that tornado was incredibly brave."

"Brave?" She shook her head. "Oh, no. I don't think I was brave," she admitted, undoubtedly the easiest confession she would attempt this afternoon. "When I first went out in the storm, I was petrified." She shivered again, merely thinking about it. "By the time I realized we were in a tornado, I wasn't thinking at all."

He smiled. "That's what the great heroes say, you know. That at some point they stop thinking and act on instinct."

Great heroes? Nettie grimaced. "I'm not a hero, Chase." She braced herself to deliver the first critical truth of the day. "In fact, it was my fault Colin was in the storm to begin with. I yelled at him because he broke something that was...well, it was special to me. I completely overreacted, though. I wasn't being fair, and I hurt his feelings."

"What did he break?"

She took a breath. "A plaster casting. It was a likeness of my son."

Chase's expression told her she'd blindsided him completely. His brow darkened with so many emotions Nettie couldn't hope to read them all. "Your son?"

Feeling somehow as if she were standing on the edge of a precipice, about to jump, she nodded. "Today is Tucker's birthday. He would have been six."

"Would have been?" The question was raw and reluctant.

"My son died three years ago in a car accident with my husband."

The words emerged more evenly than Nettie would have believed possible. But as she watched Chase quickly attempt to school his features, she saw not only the pain he felt on her behalf but also the pain of not being given this information sooner.

"I don't talk about it often, Chase. Not to anyone."

Beside her on the cushioned pew, Chase clasped his hands behind his neck and shook his head. Two floors above the softly lit chapel, his son lay recovering from an accident already being viewed as a terrific adventure. He looked at Nettie again, dusty and injured from her attempts to help his child, and he wanted to take her in his arms. He wanted to squeeze her way too tightly to remind himself that she was real and that she was fine and that everyone was safe.

When he felt the touch of her fingers, soft and warm, on his hand, he was shocked to feel longing burn behind his eyes. Nettie was watching him with an expression that was earnest and seeking.

"I want to talk about it with you," she said, "if you want to listen."

He nodded, and she began in a voice sometimes halting, sometimes flowing like an undammed stream, to tell the story of the losses she had known, beginning with her parents, ending with her child.

"For the longest time I thought the accident was my fault. If I'd been there in the car, there might have been something I could do. Or if I hadn't fought with Brian before they left..." Briefly she closed her eyes then reopened them and looked directly at Chase. "It sounds so ridiculous when I say it out loud, but I truly believed I should always be able to keep the people I loved safe."

"It doesn't sound ridiculous to me, Nettie. Not anymore." Chase did pull her into his arms then, burying his lips in the dark curls still matted from their wrestle with the wind. "My God, when I think of you alone in that storm with Colin—"

"But we weren't alone." She pulled back to look at him, hoping that what she had to say would somehow make sense to a man who was inherently brave. "I have been terrified of this life. I've been frightened of anything I couldn't control or predict, and my fear became like an armor. I put it on every morning, and all day and all night I let it steer me away from anything I thought could possibly hurt me or someone I loved." She reached around to take one of his hands, looking down at it, smoothing the strong fingers. "Life is small when you live it in fear. There isn't room for anything wild or unpredictable. And that's what love is."

With his free hand, Chase wove through the hair at her nape. "I came back early from New York," he confessed, "because nothing made sense there without you. I got on that plane today promising myself I wouldn't push you. But I'd already decided we'd wait—Colin and I. We'd wait just as long as it took for you to realize you wanted us, too."

When tears came to Nettie's eyes, Chase gently swept them away. "I've never been as scared in my life as I was when I heard you were in that tornado," he muttered fiercely. "Every time I picture the two of you..." Again he pulled her close, enveloping her. "I understand that you're frightened. You have every right to be. But I swear I'll always protect you, Nettie. You and Colin. On my life, I'll protect you."

With her cheek nestled against his chest, Nettie shook her head. "You can't, you know," she said softly and without regret. "No one can protect anyone all the time. But I love that you want to."

Stubbornly, Chase insisted, "I never should have left in the first place. If I hadn't, you wouldn't have been alone. I would have been there today."

"But you were." Nettie arched back to look at him. "You see, that's the whole point. Oh, Chase, no one can make a tornado stop. You can't guarantee we'll always be safe. But you were with us. I felt you, as truly as if you were in that ditch, like a great warm coat had settled over my shoulders. And suddenly I was strong. Holding Colin in my arms and loving him, *feeling* you love me—that seemed more real than anything else in the world." She blinked up at him, this man who had come to rescue her from a life drained by caution. "I don't want to be safe, anymore, Chase. I just want to love you."

Chase stared at the woman in front of him a long time before dropping his arms. Lightly, giving her room to move also, he cupped her face and brought his lips to hers. The kiss they shared began slowly and with relief, like a homecoming, but soon it built to something breathless and risky and wild, ripe with all the danger of desire and all the glorious exuberant promise.

When they pulled away, they were both grinning dazedly.

"I love you."

"I love you."

The avows overlapped each other.

Nettie's brows rose. "No fair," she complained. "I wanted to say it first."

Chase laughed. "You can say it first next time. In fact…" Taking her left hand, he brought it to his lips. "How about if we spend the rest of our lives taking turns?"

"The rest of our lives?" Nettie managed a watery grin. "See, there you go again," she said in a choked whisper. "I wanted to say it first."

For a moment, they simply looked at each other. Then Nettie launched herself at the man she loved and kissed him with every corner of her heart.

High on the morning-blue walls of the hospital chapel, painted angels looked down benevolently as a young woman chose life and love again and a man staked his claim to forever. Anyone watching would have sworn the angels danced for joy.

\* \* \* \* \*

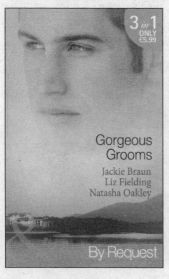
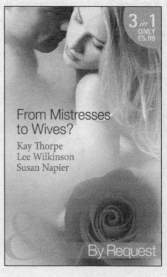

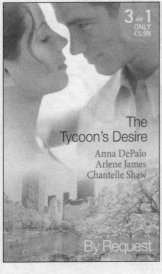

# INTRODUCED BY BESTSELLING AUTHOR KATIE FFORDE

Four fabulous new writers

**Lynn Raye Harris**
*Kept for the Sheikh's Pleasure*

**Nikki Logan**
Seven-Day Love Story

**Molly Evans**
*Her No.1 Doctor*

**Ann Lethbridge**
*The Governess and the Earl*

We know you're going to love them!

## Available 20th August 2010

# All the magic you'll need this Christmas…

When **Daniel** is left with his brother's kids, only one person can help. But it'll take more than mistletoe before **Stella** helps him…

**Patrick** hadn't advertised for a housekeeper. But when **Hayley** appears, she's the gift he didn't even realise he needed.

**Alfie** and his little sister know a lot about the magic of Christmas – and they're about to teach the grown-ups a much-needed lesson!

## Available 1st October 2010

# Spend Christmas with NORA ROBERTS

Daniel MacGregor is the clan patriarch. He's powerful, rich – and determined to see his three career-minded granddaughters married. So he chooses three unsuspecting men he considers worthy and sets his plans in motion!

As Christmas approaches, will his independent granddaughters escape his schemes? Or can the magic of the season melt their hearts – and allow Daniel's plans to succeed?

## Available 1st October 2010

www.millsandboon.co.uk

# *Mystery, magic and... marriage*

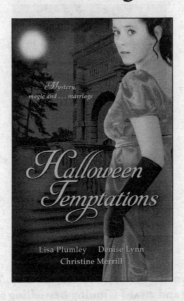

Sorcery and seduction…
A dark and spooky night…
Trick, treat…or a Halloween temptation?

### *Things are not quite as they seem on All Hallows' Eve…*

## Available 1st October 2010

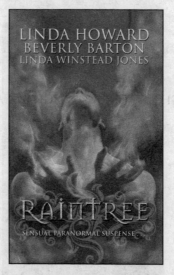

# THE *Balfour* LEGACY

### EIGHT SISTERS, EIGHT SCANDALS

**VOLUME 5 – OCTOBER 2010**

*Zoe's Lesson*
by Kate Hewitt

**VOLUME 6 – NOVEMBER 2010**

*Annie's Secret*
by Carole Mortimer

**VOLUME 7 – DECEMBER 2010**

*Bella's Disgrace*
by Sarah Morgan

**VOLUME 8 – JANUARY 2011**

*Olivia's Awakening*
by Margaret Way

8 VOLUMES IN ALL TO COLLECT!